A Caribbean Mystery

A Pocket Full of Rye

The Mirror Crack'd From
Side to Side

They Do It With Mirrors

———————————

Agatha Christie

Diamond Books
An Imprint of HarperCollins*Publishers*,
77–85 Fulham Palace Road,
Hammersmith, London W6 8JB

This Diamond Books Omnibus Edition first published 1993
9 8 7 6 5 4 3 2 1

Published in the UK by Grange Books
An Imprint of Grange Books plc
The Grange, Grange Yard, London SE1 3AG

A Caribbean Mystery © Agatha Christie Ltd 1964
A Pocket Full of Rye © Agatha Christie Mallowan 1953
The Mirror Crack'd From Side to Side © Agatha Christie Ltd 1962
They Do It With Mirrors © Agatha Christie 1952

ISBN 1 85627 423 3 (UK)
ISBN Diamond Books 0 261 66148 5 (international edition)

Typeset by Hewer Text Composition Services, Edinburgh
Printed in Great Britain by Mackays of Chatham Ltd

Contents

A Caribbean Mystery   5

A Pocket Full of Rye   155

The Mirror Crack'd From
Side to Side   319

They Do It With Mirrors   507

BOOKS BY AGATHA CHRISTIE

The ABC Murders
The Adventure of the
  Christmas Pudding
After the Funeral
And Then There Were None
Appointment with Death
At Bertram's Hotel
The Big Four
The Body in the Library
By the Pricking of My Thumbs
Cards on the Table
A Carribbean Mystery
Cat Among the Pigeons
The Clocks
Crooked House
Curtain: Poirot's Last Case
Dead Man's Folly
Death Comes as the End
Death in the Clouds
Death on the Nile
Destination Unknown
Dumb Witness
Elephants Can Remember
Endless Night
Evil Under the Sun
Five Little Pigs
4.50 from Paddington
Hallowe'en Party
Hercule Poirot's Christmas
Hickory Dickory Dock
The Hollow
The Hound of Death
The Labours of Hercules
The Listerdale Mystery
Lord Edgware Dies
The Man in the Brown Suit
The Mirror Crack'd from Side
  to Side
Miss Marple's Final Cases
The Moving Finger
Mrs McGinty's Dead
The Murder at the Vicarage
Murder in Mesopotamia
Murder in the Mews
A Murder is Announced
Murder is Easy
The Murder of Roger Ackroyd
Murder on the Links
Murder on the Orient Express

The Mysterious Affair at Styles
The Mysterious Mr Quin
The Mystery of the Blue Train
Nemesis
N or M?
One, Two, Buckle My Shoe
Ordeal by Innocence
The Pale Horse
Parker Pyne Investigates
Partners in Crime
Passenger to Frankfurt
Peril at End House
A Pocket Full of Rye
Poirot Investigates
Poirot's Early Cases
Postern of Fate
Problem at Pollensa Bay
Sad Cypress
The Secret Adversary
The Secret of Chimneys
The Seven Dials Mystery
The Sittaford Mystery
Sleeping Murder
Sparkling Cyanide
Taken at the Flood
They Came to Baghdad
They Do It With Mirrors
Third Girl
The Thirteen Problems
Three-Act Tragedy
Towards Zero
Why Didn't They Ask Evans

Novels under the Nom de Plume of
'Mary Westmacott'
Absent in the Spring
The Burden
A Daughter's A Daughter
Giant's Bread
The Rose and the Tew Tree
Unfinished Portrait

Books under the name of
Agatha Christie Mallowan
Come Tell me How You Live
Star Over Bethlehem

Autobiography
Agatha Christie: An Autobiography

A Caribbean Mystery

To my old friend
John Cruickshank Rose
with happy memories of
my visit to the West Indies

Contents

1. Major Palgrave tells a Story   9
2. Miss Marple makes Comparisons   16
3. A Death in the Hotel   23
4. Miss Marple seeks Medical Attention   27
5. Miss Marple makes a Decision   30
6. In the Small Hours   34
7. Morning on the Beach   38
8. A Talk with Esther Walters   46
9. Miss Prescott and Others   51
10. A Decision in Jamestown   58
11. Evening at the Golden Palm   60
12. Old Sins Cast Long Shadows   67
13. Exit Victoria Johnson   71
14. Inquiry   74
15. Inquiry continued   79
16. Miss Marple seeks Assistance   86
17. Mr Rafiel takes Charge   96
18. Without Benefit of Clergy   106
19. Uses of a Shoe   114
20. Night Alarm   118
21. Jackson on Cosmetics   125
22. A Man in her Life?   131
23. The Last Day   136
24. Nemesis   141
25. Miss Marple uses her Imagination   146
     Epilogue   152

CHAPTER ONE

Major Palgrave tells a Story

'Take all this business about Kenya,' said Major Palgrave.

'Lots of chaps gabbing away who know nothing about the place! Now *I* spent fourteen years of my life there. Some of the best years of my life, too – '

Old Miss Marple inclined her head.

It was a gentle gesture of courtesy. Whilst Major Palgrave proceeded with the somewhat uninteresting recollections of a lifetime, Miss Marple peacefully pursued her own thoughts. It was a routine with which she was well acquainted. The locale varied. In the past, it had been predominantly India. Majors, Colonels, Lieutenant-Generals – and a familiar series of words: *Simla. Bearers. Tigers. Chota Hazri – Tiffin. Khitmagars*, and so on. With Major Palgrave the terms were slightly different. *Safari. Kikuyu. Elephants. Swahili.* But the pattern was essentially the same. An elderly man who needed a listener so that he could, in memory, relive days in which he had been happy. Days when his back had been straight, his eyesight keen, his hearing acute. Some of these talkers had been handsome soldierly old boys, some again had been regrettably unattractive; and Major Palgrave, purple of face, with a glass eye, and the general appearance of a stuffed frog, belonged in the latter category.

Miss Marple had bestowed on all of them the same gentle charity. She had sat attentively, inclining her head from time to time in gentle agreement, thinking her own thoughts and enjoying what there was to enjoy: in this case the deep blue of a Caribbean Sea.

So kind of dear Raymond, – she was thinking gratefully, so really and truly kind . . . Why he should take so much trouble about his old aunt, she really did not know. Conscience, perhaps; family feeling? Or possibly he was truly fond of her . . .

She thought, on the whole, that he *was* fond of her – he always had been – in a slightly exasperated and contemptuous way! Always trying to bring her up to date. Sending her books to read. Modern novels. So difficult – all about such unpleasant people, doing such very odd things and not, apparently, even enjoying them. 'Sex' as a word had not been mentioned in Miss Marple's young days; but there had been plenty of it – not talked about so much – but enjoyed far more than nowadays, or so it seemed to her. Though usually labelled Sin, she couldn't help feeling that that was preferable to what it seemed to be nowadays – a kind of Duty.

Her glance strayed for a moment to the book on her lap lying open at page twenty-three which was as far as she had got (and indeed as far as she felt like getting!).

'"Do you mean that you've had no sexual experience at ALL?" demanded the young man incredulously. "At *nineteen*? But you *must*. It's vital."

'The girl hung her head unhappily, her straight greasy hair fell forward over her face.

'"I know," she muttered, "I know."

'He looked at her, stained old jersey, the bare feet, the dirty toe nails, the smell of rancid fat . . . He wondered why he found her so maddeningly attractive.'

Miss Marple wondered too! And really! To have sex experience urged on you exactly as though it was an iron tonic! Poor young things . . .

'My dear Aunt Jane, why must you bury your head in the sand like a very delightful ostrich? All bound up in this idyllic rural life of yours. REAL LIFE – that's what matters.'

Thus Raymond – and his Aunt Jane had looked properly abashed – and said 'Yes,' she was afraid she *was* rather old-fashioned.

Though really rural life was far from idyllic. People like Raymond were so ignorant. In the course of her duties in a country parish, Jane Marple had acquired quite a comprehensive knowledge of the facts of rural life. She had no urge to *talk* about them, far less to *write* about them – but she knew them. Plenty of sex, natural and unnatural. Rape, incest, perversion of all kinds. (Some kinds, indeed, that even the clever young men from Oxford who wrote books didn't seem to have heard about.)

Miss Marple came back to the Caribbean and took up the thread of what Major Palgrave was saying . . .

'A very unusual experience,' she said encouragingly. '*Most* interesting.'

'I could tell you a lot more. Some of the things, of course, not fit for a lady's ears – '

10

With the ease of long practice, Miss Marple dropped her eyelids in a fluttery fashion, and Major Palgrave continued his bowdlerized version of tribal customs whilst Miss Marple resumed her thoughts of her affectionate nephew.

Raymond West was a very successful novelist and made a large income, and he conscientiously and kindly did all he could to alleviate the life of his elderly aunt. The preceding winter she had had a bad go of pneumonia, and medical opinion had advised sunshine. In lordly fashion Raymond had suggested a trip to the West Indies. Miss Marple had demurred – at the expense, the distance, the difficulties of travel, and at abandoning her house in St Mary Mead. Raymond had dealt with everything. A friend who was writing a book wanted a quiet place in the country. 'He'll look after the house all right. He's very house proud. He's a queer. I mean – '

He had paused, slightly embarrassed – but surely even dear old Aunt Jane must have heard of queers.

He went on to deal with the next points. Travel was nothing nowadays. She would go by air – another friend, Diana Horrocks, was going out to Trinidad and would see Aunt Jane was all right as far as there, and at St Honoré she would stay at the Golden Palm Hotel which was run by the Sandersons. Nicest couple in the world. They'd see she was all right. He'd write to them straight away.

As it happened the Sandersons had returned to England. But their successors, the Kendals, had been very nice and friendly and had assured Raymond that he need have no qualms about his aunt. There was a very good doctor on the island in case of emergency and they themselves would keep an eye on her and see to her comfort.

They had been as good as their word, too. Molly Kendal was an ingenuous blonde of twenty odd, always apparently in good spirits. She had greeted the old lady warmly and did everything to make her comfortable. Tim Kendal, her husband, lean, dark and in his thirties, had also been kindness itself.

So there she was, thought Miss Marple, far from the rigours of the English climate, with a nice bungalow of her own, with friendly smiling West Indian girls to wait on her, Tim Kendal to meet her in the dining-room and crack a joke as he advised her about the day's menu, and an easy path from her bungalow to the sea front and the bathing beach where she could sit in a comfortable basket chair and watch the bathing. There were even a few elderly guests for company. Old Mr Rafiel, Dr Graham, Canon Prescott and his sister, and her present cavalier Major Palgrave.

What more could an elderly lady want?

It is deeply to be regretted, and Miss Marple felt guilty even admitting it to herself, but she was not as satisfied as she ought to be.

Lovely and warm, yes – and *so* good for her rheumatism – and beautiful scenery, though perhaps – a trifle monotonous? So *many* palm trees. Everything the same every day – never anything *happening*. Not like St Mary Mead where something was always happening. Her nephew had once compared life in St Mary Mead to scum on a pond, and she had indignantly pointed out that smeared on a slide under the microscope there would be plenty of life to be observed. Yes, indeed, in St Mary Mead, there was always something going on. Incident after incident flashed through Miss Marple's mind, the mistake in old Mrs Linnett's cough mixture – that very odd behaviour of young Polegate – the time when Georgy Wood's mother had come down to see him – (but *was* she his mother –?) the real cause of the quarrel between Joe Arden and his wife. So many interesting human problems – giving rise to endless pleasurable hours of speculation. If only there were something here that she could – well – get her teeth into.

With a start she realized that Major Palgrave had abandoned Kenya for the North West Frontier and was relating his experiences as a subaltern. Unfortunately he was asking her with great earnestness: 'Now don't you agree?'

Long practice had made Miss Marple quite an adept at dealing with that one.

'I don't really feel that I've got sufficient experience to judge. I'm afraid I've led rather a sheltered life.'

'And so you should, dear lady, so you should,' cried Major Palgrave gallantly.

'You've had such a very varied life,' went on Miss Marple, determined to make amends for her former pleasurable inattention.

'Not bad,' said Major Palgrave, complacently. 'Not bad at all.' He looked round him appreciatively. 'Lovely place, this.'

'Yes, indeed,' said Miss Marple and was then unable to stop herself going on: 'Does anything ever happen here, I wonder?'

Major Palgrave stared.

'Oh rather. Plenty of scandals – eh what? Why, I could tell you – '

But it wasn't really scandals Miss Marple wanted. Nothing to get your teeth into in scandals nowadays. Just men and women changing

12

partners, and calling attention to it, instead of trying decently to hush it up and be properly ashamed of themselves.

'There was even a murder here a couple of years ago. Man called Harry Western. Made a big splash in the papers. Dare say you remember it.'

Miss Marple nodded without enthusiasm. It had not been her kind of murder. It had made a big splash mainly because everyone concerned had been very rich. It had seemed likely enough that Harry Western had shot the Count de Ferrari, his wife's lover, and equally likely that his well-arranged alibi had been bought and paid for. Everyone seemed to have been drunk, and there was a fine scattering of dope addicts. Not really interesting people, thought Miss Marple – although no doubt very spectacular and attractive to *look* at. But definitely not *her* cup of tea.

'And if you ask me, that wasn't the only murder about that time.' He nodded and winked. 'I had my suspicions – oh! – well – '

Miss Marple dropped her ball of wool, and the Major stooped and picked it up for her.

'Talking of murder,' he went on. 'I once came across a very curious case – not exactly personally.'

Miss Marple smiled encouragingly.

'Lot of chaps talking at the club one day, you know, and a chap began telling a story. Medical man he was. One of his cases. Young fellow came and knocked him up in the middle of the night. His wife had hanged herself. They hadn't got a telephone, so after the chap had cut her down and done what he could, he'd got out his car and hared off looking for a doctor. Well, she wasn't dead but pretty far gone. Anyway, she pulled through. Young fellow seemed devoted to her. Cried like a child. He'd noticed that she'd been odd for some time, fits of depression and all that. Well, that was that. Everything seemed all right. But actually, about a month later, the wife took an overdose of sleeping stuff and passed out. Sad case.'

Major Palgrave paused, and nodded his head several times. Since there was obviously more to come Miss Marple waited.

'And that's that, you might say. Nothing there. Neurotic woman, nothing out of the usual. But about a year later, this medical chap was swapping yarns with a fellow medico, and the other chap told him about a woman who'd tried to drown herself, husband got her out, got a doctor, they pulled her round – and then a few weeks later she gassed herself.

'Well, a bit of a coincidence – eh? Same sort of story. My chap

13

said – "I had a case rather like that. Name of Jones (or whatever the name was) – What was your man's name?" "Can't remember. Robinson I think. Certainly not Jones."

'Well, the chaps looked at each other and said it was pretty odd. And then my chap pulled out a snapshot. He showed it to the second chap. "That's the fellow," he said – "I'd gone along the next day to check up on the particulars, and I noticed a magnificent species of hibiscus just by the front door, a variety I'd never seen before in this country. My camera was in the car and I took a photo. Just as I snapped the shutter the husband came out of the front door so I got him as well. Don't think he realized it. I asked him about the hibiscus but he couldn't tell me its name.' Second medico looked at the snap. He said: 'It's a bit out of focus – But I could swear – at any rate I'm almost sure – *it's the same man.*'

'Don't know if they followed it up. But if so they didn't get anywhere. Expect Mr Jones or Robinson covered his tracks too well. But queer story, isn't it? Wouldn't think things like that could happen.'

'Oh, yes, I would,' said Miss Marple placidly. 'Practically every day.'

'Oh, come, come. That's a bit fantastic.'

'If a man gets a formula that works – he won't stop. He'll go on.'

'Brides in the bath – eh?'

'That kind of thing, yes.'

'Doctor let me have that snap just as a curiosity – '

Major Palgrave began fumbling through an overstuffed wallet murmuring to himself: 'Lots of things in here – don't know why I keep all these things . . .'

Miss Marple thought she did know. They were part of the Major's stock-in-trade. They illustrated his repertoire of stories. The story he had just told, or so she suspected, had not been originally like that – it had been worked up a good deal in repeated telling.

The Major was still shuffling and muttering – 'Forgotten all about *that* business. Good-looking woman *she* was, you'd never suspect – now *where* – Ah – that takes my mind back – what tusks! I must show you – '

He stopped – sorted out a small photographic print and peered down at it.

'Like to see the picture of a murderer?'

He was about to pass it to her when his movement was suddenly arrested. Looking more like a stuffed frog than ever, Major Palgrave appeared to be staring fixedly over her right shoulder – from whence came the sound of approaching footsteps and voices.

'Well, I'm damned – I mean – ' He stuffed everything back into his wallet and crammed it into his pocket.

His face went an even deeper shade of purplish red – He exclaimed in a loud, artificial voice:

'As I was saying – I'd like to have shown you those elephant tusks – Biggest elephant I've ever shot – Ah, hallo!' His voice took on a somewhat spurious hearty note.

'Look who's here! The great quartette – Flora and Fauna – What luck have you had today – Eh?'

The approaching footsteps resolved themselves into four of the hotel guests whom Miss Marple already knew by sight. They consisted of two married couples and though Miss Marple was not as yet acquainted with their surnames, she knew that the big man with the upstanding bush of thick grey hair was addressed as 'Greg', that the golden blonde woman, his wife, was known as Lucky – and that the other married couple, the dark lean man and the handsome but rather weather-beaten woman, were Edward and Evelyn. They were botanists, she understood, and also interested in birds.

'No luck at all,' said Greg – 'At least no luck in getting what we were after.'

'Don't know if you know Miss Marple? Colonel and Mrs Hillingdon and Greg and Lucky Dyson.'

They greeted her pleasantly and Lucky said loudly that she'd die if she didn't have a drink at once or sooner.

Greg hailed Tim Kendal who was sitting a little way away with his wife poring over account books.

'Hi, Tim. Get us some drinks.' He addressed the others. 'Planters Punch?'

They agreed.

'Same for you, Miss Marple?'

Miss Marple said Thank you, but she would prefer fresh lime.

'Fresh lime it is,' said Tim Kendal 'and five Planters Punches.'

'Join us, Tim?'

'Wish I could. But I've got to fix up these accounts. Can't leave Molly to cope with everything. Steel band tonight, by the way.'

'Good,' cried Lucky. 'Damn it,' she winced, 'I'm all over thorns. Ouch! Edward deliberately rammed me into a thorn bush!'

'Lovely pink flowers,' said Hillingdon.

'And lovely long thorns. Sadistic brute, aren't you, Edward?'

'Not like me,' said Greg, grinning. 'Full of the milk of human kindness.'

Evelyn Hillingdon sat down by Miss Marple and started talking to her in an easy pleasant way.

Miss Marple put her knitting down on her lap. Slowly and with some difficulty, owing to rheumatism in the neck, she turned her head over her right shoulder to look behind her. At some little distance there was the large bungalow occupied by the rich Mr Rafiel. But it showed no sign of life.

She replied suitably to Evelyn's remarks (really, how kind people were to her!) but her eyes scanned thoughtfully the faces of the two men.

Edward Hillingdon looked a nice man. Quiet but with a lot of charm . . . And Greg – big, boisterous, happy-looking. He and Lucky were Canadian or American, she thought.

She looked at Major Palgrave, still acting a *bonhomie* a little larger than life.

Interesting . . .

CHAPTER TWO

Miss Marple makes Comparisons

It was very gay that evening at the Golden Palm Hotel.

Seated at her little corner table, Miss Marple looked round her in an interested fashion. The dining-room was a large room open on three sides to the soft warm scented air of the West Indies. There were small table lamps, all softly coloured. Most of the women were in evening dress: light cotton prints out of which bronzed shoulders and arms emerged. Miss Marple herself had been urged by her nephew's wife, Joan, in the sweetest way possible, to accept 'a small cheque'.

'Because, Aunt Jane, it will be rather hot out there, and I don't expect you have any very thin clothes.'

Jane Marple had thanked her and had accepted the cheque. She

16

came of the age when it was natural for the old to support and finance the young, but also for the middle-aged to look after the old. She could not, however, force herself to buy anything very *thin*! At her age she seldom felt more than pleasantly warm even in the hottest weather, and the temperature of St Honoré was not really what is referred to as 'tropical heat'. This evening she was attired in the best traditions of the provincial gentlewoman of England – grey lace.

Not that she was the only elderly person present. There were representatives of all ages in the room. There were elderly tycoons with young third or fourth wives. There were middle-aged couples from the North of England. There was a gay family from Caracas complete with children. The various countries of South America were well represented, all chattering loudly in Spanish or Portuguese. There was a solid English background of two clergymen, one doctor and one retired judge. There was even a family of Chinese. The dining-room service was mainly done by women, tall black girls of proud carriage, dressed in crisp white; but there was an experienced Italian head waiter in charge, and a French wine waiter, and there was the attentive eye of Tim Kendal watching over everything, pausing here and there to have a social word with people at their tables. His wife seconded him ably. She was a good-looking girl. Her hair was a natural golden blonde and she had a wide generous mouth that laughed easily. It was very seldom that Molly Kendal was out of temper. Her staff worked for her enthusiastically, and she adapted her manner carefully to suit her different guests. With the elderly men she laughed and flirted; she congratulated the younger women on their clothes.

'Oh, what a smashing dress you've got on tonight, Mrs Dyson. I'm so jealous I could tear it off your back.' But she looked very well in her own dress, or so Miss Marple thought: a white sheath, with a pale green embroidered silk shawl thrown over her shoulders. Lucky was fingering the shawl. 'Lovely colour! I'd like one like it.' 'You can get them at the shop here,' Molly told her and passed on. She did not pause by Miss Marple's table. Elderly ladies she usually left to her husband. 'The old dears like a man much better,' she used to say.

Tim Kendal came and bent over Miss Marple.

'Nothing special you want, is there?' he asked. 'Because you've only got to tell me – and I could get it specially cooked for you. Hotel food, and semi-tropical at that, isn't quite what you're used to at home, I expect?'

17

Miss Marple smiled and said that that was one of the pleasures of coming abroad.

'That's all right, then. But if there *is* anything – '

'Such as?'

'Well – ' Tim Kendal looked a little doubtful – 'Bread and butter pudding?' he hazarded.

Miss Marple smiled and said that she thought she could do without bread and butter pudding very nicely for the present.

She picked up her spoon and began to eat her passion fruit sundae with cheerful appreciation.

Then the steel band began to play. The steel bands were one of the main attractions of the islands. Truth to tell, Miss Marple could have done very well without them. She considered that they made a hideous noise, unnecessarily loud. The pleasure that everyone else took in them was undeniable, however, and Miss Marple, in the true spirit of her youth, decided that as they had to be, she must manage somehow to learn to like them. She could hardly request Tim Kendal to conjure up from somewhere the muted strains of the 'Blue Danube'. (So graceful – waltzing.) Most peculiar, the way people danced nowadays. Flinging themselves about, seeming quite *contorted*. Oh well, young people must enjoy – Her thoughts were arrested. Because, now she came to think of it, very few of these people *were* young. Dancing, lights, the music of a band (even a steel band), all that surely was for *youth*. But where was youth? Studying, she supposed, at universities, or doing a job – with a fortnight's holiday a year. A place like this was too far away and too expensive. This gay and carefree life was all for the thirties and the forties – and the old men who were trying to live up (or down) to their young wives. It seemed, somehow, a *pity*.

Miss Marple sighed for youth. There was Mrs Kendal, of course. She wasn't more than twenty-two or three, probably, and she seemed to be enjoying herself – but even so, it was a *job* she was doing.

At a table nearby Canon Prescott and his sister were sitting. They motioned to Miss Marple to join them for coffee and she did so. Miss Prescott was a thin severe-looking woman, the Canon was a round, rubicund man, breathing geniality.

Coffee was brought, and chairs were pushed a little way away from the tables. Miss Prescott opened a work bag and took out some frankly hideous table mats that she was hemming. She told Miss Marple all about the day's events. They had visited a new

Girls' School in the morning. After an afternoon's rest, they had walked through a cane plantation to have tea at a *pension* where some friends of theirs were staying.

Since the Prescotts had been at the Golden Palm longer than Miss Marple, they were able to enlighten her as to some of her fellow guests.

That very old man, Mr Rafiel. He came every year. Fantastically rich! Owned an enormous chain of supermarkets in the North of England. The young woman with him was his secretary, Esther Walters – a widow. (Quite all *right*, of course. Nothing improper. After all, he was nearly eighty!)

Miss Marple accepted the propriety of the relationship with an understanding nod and the Canon remarked:

'A very nice young woman; her mother, I understand, is a widow and lives in Chichester.'

'Mr Rafiel has a valet with him, too. Or rather a kind of Nurse Attendant – he's a qualified masseur, I believe. Jackson, his name is. Poor Mr Rafiel is practically paralysed. So sad – with all that money, too.'

'A generous and cheerful giver,' said Canon Prescott approvingly.

People were regrouping themselves round about, some going farther from the steel band, others crowding up to it. Major Palgrave had joined the Hillingdon-Dyson quartette.

'Now those people – ' said Miss Prescott, lowering her voice quite unnecessarily since the steel band easily drowned it.

'Yes, I was going to ask you about them.'

'They were here last year. They spend three months every year in the West Indies, going round the different islands. The tall thin man is Colonel Hillingdon and the dark woman is his wife – they are botanists. The other two, Mr and Mrs Gregory Dyson – they're American. He writes on butterflies, I believe. And all of them are interested in birds.'

'So nice for people to have open-air hobbies,' said Canon Prescott genially.

'I don't think they'd like to hear you call it hobbies, Jeremy,' said his sister. 'They have articles printed in the *National Geographic* and in the *Royal Horticultural Journal*. They take themselves very seriously.'

A loud outburst of laughter came from the table they had been observing. It was loud enough to overcome the steel band. Gregory Dyson was leaning back in his chair and thumping the table, his wife

19

was protesting, and Major Palgrave emptied his glass and seemed to be applauding.

They hardly qualified for the moment as people who took themselves seriously.

'Major Palgrave should not drink so much,' said Miss Prescott acidly. 'He has blood pressure.'

A fresh supply of Planters Punches was brought to the table.

'It's so nice to get people sorted out,' said Miss Marple. 'When I met them this afternoon I wasn't sure which was married to which.'

There was a slight pause. Miss Prescott coughed a small dry cough, and said – 'Well, as to that – '

'Joan,' said the Canon in an admonitory voice. 'Perhaps it would be wise to say no more.'

'Really, Jeremy, I wasn't going to say *anything*. Only that last year, for some reason or other – I really don't know *why* – we got the idea that Mrs Dyson was Mrs Hillingdon until someone told us she wasn't.'

'It's odd how one gets impressions, isn't it?' said Miss Marple innocently. Her eyes met Miss Prescott's for a moment. A flash of womanly understanding passed between them.

A more sensitive man than Canon Prescott might have felt that he was *de trop*.

Another signal passed between the women. It said as clearly as if the words had been spoken: '*Some other time . . .*'

'Mr Dyson calls his wife "Lucky". Is that her real name or a nickname?' asked Miss Marple.

'It can hardly be her real name, I should think.'

'I happened to ask him,' said the Canon. 'He said he called her Lucky because she was his good-luck piece. If he lost her, he said, he'd lose his luck. Very nicely put, I thought.'

'He's very fond of joking,' said Miss Prescott.

The Canon looked at his sister doubtfully.

The steel band outdid itself with a wild burst of cacophony and a troupe of dancers came racing on to the floor.

Miss Marple and the others turned their chairs to watch. Miss Marple enjoyed the dancing better than the music; she liked the shuffling feet and the rhythmic sway of the bodies. It seemed, she thought, very *real*. It had a kind of power of understatement.

Tonight, for the first time, she began to feel slightly at home in her new environment . . . Up to now, she had missed what she usually found so easy, points of resemblance in the people she met, to various people known to her personally. She had, possibly, been dazzled by the gay clothes and the exotic colouring; but soon, she felt, she would be able to make some interesting comparisons.

Molly Kendal, for instance, was like that nice girl whose name she couldn't remember, but who was a conductress on the Market Basing bus. Helped you in, and never rang the bus on until she was sure you'd sat down safely. Tim Kendal was just a little like the head waiter at the Royal George in Medchester. Self-confident, and yet, at the same time, worried. (He had had an ulcer, she remembered.) As for Major Palgrave, he was undistinguishable from General Leroy, Captain Flemming, Admiral Wicklow and Commander Richardson. She went on to someone more interesting. Greg for instance? Greg was difficult because he was American. A dash of Sir George Trollope, perhaps, always so full of jokes at the Civil Defence meetings – or perhaps Mr Murdoch the butcher. Mr Murdoch had had rather a bad reputation, but some people said it was just gossip, and that Mr Murdoch himself liked to encourage the rumours! 'Lucky' now? Well, that was easy – Marleen at the Three Crowns. Evelyn Hillingdon? She couldn't fit Evelyn in precisely. In appearance she fitted many roles – tall thin weather-beaten Englishwomen were plentiful. Lady Caroline Wolfe, Peter Wolfe's first wife, who had committed suicide? Or there was Leslie James – that quiet woman who seldom showed what she felt and who had sold up her house and left without ever telling anyone she was going. Colonel Hillingdon? No immediate clue there. She'd have to get to know him a little first. One of those quiet men with good manners. You never knew what they were thinking about. Sometimes they surprised you. Major Harper, she remembered, had quietly cut his throat one day. Nobody had ever known why. Miss Marple thought that she did know – but she'd never been quite sure . . .

Her eyes strayed to Mr Rafiel's table. The principal thing known about Mr Rafiel was that he was incredibly rich, he came every year to the West Indies, he was semi-paralysed and looked like a wrinkled old bird of prey. His clothes hung loosely on his shrunken form. He might have been seventy or eighty, or even ninety. His eyes were shrewd and he was frequently rude, but people seldom took offence, partly because he was so rich, and partly because of his overwhelming personality which hypnotized you into feeling that somehow, Mr Rafiel had the right to be rude if he wanted to.

With him sat his secretary, Mrs Walters. She had corn-coloured

21

hair, and a pleasant face. Mr Rafiel was frequently very rude to her, but she never seemed to notice it – She was not so much subservient, as oblivious. She behaved like a well-trained hospital nurse. Possibly, thought Miss Marple, she had been a hospital nurse.

A young man, tall and good-looking, in a white jacket, came to stand by Mr Rafiel's chair. The old man looked up at him, nodded, then motioned him to a chair. The young man sat down as bidden. 'Mr Jackson, I presume,' said Miss Marple to herself – 'His valet-attendant.'

She studied Mr Jackson with some attention.

II

In the bar, Molly Kendal stretched her back, and slipped off her high-heeled shoes. Tim came in from the terrace to join her. They had the bar to themselves for the moment.

'Tired, darling?' he asked.

'Just a bit. I seem to be feeling my feet tonight.'

'Not too much for you, is it? All this? I know it's hard work.' He looked at her anxiously.

She laughed. 'Oh, Tim, don't be ridiculous. I love it here. It's gorgeous. The kind of dream I've always had, come true.'

'Yes, it would be all right – if one was just a guest. But running the show – that's work.'

'Well, you can't have anything for nothing, can you?' said Molly Kendal reasonably.

Tim Kendal frowned.

'You think it's going all right? A success? We're making a go of it?'

'Of course we are.'

'You don't think people are saying. "It's not the same as when the Sandersons were here".'

'Of course *someone* will be saying that – they always do! But only some old stick-in-the-mud. I'm sure that we're far better at the job than they were. We're more glamorous. You charm the old pussies and manage to look as though you'd like to make love to the desperate forties and fifties, and I ogle the old gentlemen and make them feel sexy dogs – or play the sweet little daughter the sentimental ones would love to have had. Oh, we've got it all taped splendidly.'

22

Tim's frown vanished.

'As long as *you* think so. I get scared. We've risked everything on making a job of this. I chucked my job – '

'And quite right to do so,' Molly put in quickly. 'It was soul-destroying.'

He laughed and kissed the tip of her nose.

'I tell you we've got it taped,' she repeated. 'Why do you always worry?'

'Made that way, I suppose. I'm always thinking – suppose something should go wrong.'

'What sort of thing – '

'Oh, I don't know. Somebody might get drowned.'

'Not they. It's one of the safest of all the beaches. And we've got that hulking Swede always on guard.'

'I'm a fool,' said Tim Kendal. He hesitated – and then said, 'You – haven't had any more of those dreams, have you?'

'That was shellfish,' said Molly, and laughed.

CHAPTER THREE

A Death in the Hotel

Miss Marple had her breakfast brought to her in bed as usual. Tea, a boiled egg, and a slice of paw-paw.

The fruit on the island, thought Miss Marple, was rather disappointing. It seemed always to be paw-paw. If she could have a nice apple now – but apples seemed to be unknown.

Now that she had been here a week, Miss Marple had cured herself of the impulse to ask what the weather was like. The weather was always the same – fine. No interesting variations.

'The many-splendoured weather of an English day' she murmured to herself and wondered if it was a quotation, or whether she had made it up.

There were, of course, hurricanes, or so she understood. But hurricanes were not weather in Miss Marple's sense of the word. They were more in the nature of an Act of God. There was rain, short violent rainfall that lasted five minutes and stopped abruptly. Everything and everyone was wringing wet, but in another five minutes they were dry again.

The black West Indian girl smiled and said Good Morning as she placed the tray on Miss Marple's knees. Such lovely white teeth and so happy and smiling. Nice natures, all these girls, and a pity they were so averse to getting married. It worried Canon Prescott a good deal. Plenty of christenings, he said, trying to console himself, but no weddings.

Miss Marple ate her breakfast and decided how she would spend her day. It didn't really take much deciding. She would get up at her leisure, moving slowly because it was rather hot and her fingers weren't as nimble as they used to be. Then she would rest for ten minutes or so, and she would take her knitting and walk slowly along towards the hotel and decide where she would settle herself. On the terrace overlooking the sea? Or should she go on to the bathing beach to watch the bathers and the children? Usually it was the latter. In the afternoon, after her rest, she might take a drive. It really didn't matter very much.

Today would be a day like any other day, she said to herself.

Only, of course, it wasn't.

Miss Marple carried out her programme as planned and was slowly making her way along the path towards the hotel when she met Molly Kendal. For once that sunny young woman was not smiling. Her air of distress was so unlike her that Miss Marple said immediately:

'My dear, is anything wrong?'

Molly nodded. She hesitated and then said: 'Well, you'll have to know – everyone will have to know. It's Major Palgrave. He's dead.'

'Dead?'

'Yes. He died in the night.'

'Oh, dear, I *am* sorry.'

'Yes, it's horrid having a death here. It makes everyone depressed. Of course – he *was* quite old.'

'He seemed quite well and cheerful yesterday,' said Miss Marple, slightly resenting this calm assumption that everyone of advanced years was liable to die at any minute.

'He seemed quite healthy,' she added.

'He had high blood pressure,' said Molly.

'But surely there are things one takes nowadays – some kind of pill. Science is so wonderful.'

24

'Oh yes, but perhaps he forgot to take his pills, or took too many of them. Like insulin, you know.'

Miss Marple did not think that diabetes and high blood pressure were at all the same kind of thing. She asked:

'What does the doctor say?'

'Oh, Dr Graham, who's practically retired now, and lives in the hotel, took a look at him, and the local people came officially, of course, to give a death certificate, but it all seems quite straight-forward. This kind of thing is quite liable to happen when you have high blood pressure, especially if you overdo the alcohol, and Major Palgrave was really very naughty that way. Last night, for instance.'

'Yes, I noticed,' said Miss Marple.

'He probably forgot to take his pills. It is bad luck for the old boy – but people can't live for ever, can they? But it's terribly worrying for me and Tim, I mean. People might suggest it was something in the food.'

'But surely the symptoms of food poisoning and of blood pressure are *quite* different?'

'Yes. But people do *say* things so easily. And if people decided the food was bad – and left – or told their friends – '

'I really don't think you need worry,' said Miss Marple kindly. 'As you say, an elderly man like Major Palgrave – he must have been over seventy – is quite liable to die. To most people it will seem quite an ordinary occurrence – sad, but not out of the way at all.'

'If only,' said Molly unhappily, 'it hadn't been so *sudden*.'

Yes, it had been very sudden, Miss Marple thought as she walked slowly on. There he had been last night, laughing and talking in the best of spirits with the Hillingdons and the Dysons.

The Hillingdons and the Dysons . . . Miss Marple walked more slowly still . . . Finally she stopped abruptly. Instead of going to the bathing beach she settled herself in a shady corner of the terrace. She took out her knitting and the needles clicked rapidly as though they were trying to match the speed of her thoughts. *She didn't like it – no she didn't like it. It came so pat.*

She went over the occurrences of yesterday in her mind.

Major Palgrave and his stories . . .

That was all as usual and one didn't need to listen very closely . . . Perhaps, though, it would have been better if she had.

Kenya – he had talked about Kenya and then India – the North West Frontier – and then – for some reason they had

25

got on to murder – And even *then* she hadn't really been listening . . .

Some famous case that had taken place out here – that had been in the newspapers –

It was after that – when he picked up her ball of wool – that he had begun telling her about a snapshot – *A snapshot of a murderer* – that is what he had said.

Miss Marple closed her eyes and tried to remember just exactly how that story had gone.

It had been rather a confused story – told to the Major in his club – or in somebody else's club – told him by a doctor – who had heard it from another doctor – and one doctor had taken a snapshot of someone coming through a front door – someone who was a murderer –

Yes, that was it – the various details were coming back to her now –

And he had offered to show her that snapshot – He had got out his wallet and begun hunting through its contents – talking all the time . . .

And then still talking, he had looked up – had looked – not at her – but at something behind her – behind her right shoulder to be accurate. And he had stopped talking, his face had gone purple – and he had started stuffing back everything into his wallet with slightly shaky hands and had begun talking in a loud unnatural voice about elephant tusks!

A moment or two later the Hillingdons and the Dysons had joined them . . .

It was then that she had turned her head over her right shoulder to look . . . But there had been nothing and nobody to see. To her left, some distance away, in the direction of the hotel, there had been Tim Kendal and his wife; and beyond them a family group of Venezuelans. But Major Palgrave had not been looking in that direction . . .

Miss Marple meditated until lunch time.

After lunch she did not go for a drive.

Instead she sent a message to say that she was not feeling very well and to ask if Dr Graham would be kind enough to come and see her.

CHAPTER FOUR

Miss Marple seeks Medical Attention

Dr Graham was a kindly elderly man of about sixty-five. He had practised in the West Indies for many years, but was now semi-retired, and left most of his work to his West Indian partners. He greeted Miss Marple pleasantly and asked her what the trouble was. Fortunately at Miss Marple's age, there was always some ailment that could be discussed with slight exaggerations on the patient's part. Miss Marple hesitated between 'her shoulder' and 'her knee', but finally decided upon the knee. Miss Marple's knee, as she would have put it to herself, was always with her.

Dr Graham was exceedingly kindly but he refrained from putting into words the fact that at her time of life such troubles were only to be expected. He prescribed for her one of the brands of useful little pills that form the basis of a doctor's prescriptions. Since he knew by experience that many elderly people could be lonely when they first came to St Honoré, he remained for a while gently chatting.

'A very nice man,' thought Miss Marple to herself, 'and I really feel rather ashamed of having to tell him lies. But I don't quite see what else I can do.'

Miss Marple had been brought up to have a proper regard for truth and was indeed by nature a very truthful person. But on certain occasions, when she considered it her duty so to do, she could tell lies with a really astonishing verisimilitude.

She cleared her throat, uttered an apologetic little cough, and said, in an old ladyish and slightly twittering manner:

'There is something, Dr Graham, I would like to ask you. I don't really like mentioning it – but I don't quite see what else I am to do – although of course it's *quite* unimportant really. But you see, it's important to *me*. And I hope you will understand and not think what I am asking is tiresome or – or unpardonable in any way.'

To this opening Dr Graham replied kindly: 'Something is worrying you? Do let me help.'

'It's connected with Major Palgrave. *So* sad about his dying. It was quite a shock when I heard it this morning.'

'Yes,' said Dr Graham, 'it was very sudden, I'm afraid. He seemed in such good spirits yesterday.' He spoke kindly, but conventionally. To him, clearly, Major Palgrave's death was nothing out of the way. Miss Marple wondered whether she was really making something out of nothing. Was this suspicious habit of mind growing on her? Perhaps she could no longer trust her own judgment. Not that it was judgment really, only suspicion. Anyway she was in for it now! She must go ahead.

'We were sitting talking together yesterday afternoon,' she said. 'He was telling me about his very varied and interesting life. So many strange parts of the globe.'

'Yes indeed,' said Dr Graham, who had been bored many times by the Major's reminiscences.

'And then he spoke of his family, boyhood rather, and I told him a little about my own nephews and nieces and he listened very sympathetically. And I showed him a snapshot I had with me of one of my nephews. Such a dear boy – at least not exactly a boy now, but always a boy to *me* if you understand.'

'Quite so,' said Dr Graham, wondering how long it would be before the old lady was going to come to the point.

'I had handed it to him and he was examining it when quite suddenly those people – those very nice people – who collect wild flowers and butterflies, Colonel and Mrs Hillingdon I think the name is – '

'Oh yes? The Hillingdons and the Dysons.'

'Yes, that's right. They came suddenly along laughing and talking. They sat down and ordered drinks and we all talked together. Very pleasant it was. But without thinking, Major Palgrave must have put back my snapshot into his wallet and returned it to his pocket. I wasn't paying very much attention at the time but I remembered afterward and I said to myself – "I mustn't forget to ask the Major to give me back my picture of Denzil." I *did* think of it last night while the dancing and the band was going on, but I didn't like to interrupt him just then, because they were having such a merry party together and I thought "I will remember to ask him for it in the morning." Only this morning – ' Miss Marple paused – out of breath.

'Yes, yes,' said Dr Graham, 'I quite understand. And you – well, naturally you want the snapshot back. Is that it?'

Miss Marple nodded her head in eager agreement.

'Yes. That's it. You see, it is the only one I have got and I haven't got the negative. And I would hate to lose that snapshot, because poor Denzil died some five or six years ago and he was my favourite nephew. This is the only picture I have to remind me of him. I wondered – I hoped – it is rather tiresome of me to ask – whether you could possibly manage to get hold of it for me? I don't really know who else to ask, you see. I don't know who'll attend to all his belongings and things like that. It is all so difficult. They would think it such a nuisance of me. You see, they don't understand. Nobody could quite understand what this snapshot means to me.'

'Of course, of course,' said Dr Graham. 'I quite understand. A most natural feeling on your part. Actually, I am meeting the local authorities shortly – the funeral is tomorrow – and someone will be coming from the Administrator's office to look over his papers and effects before communicating with the next of kin – all that sort of thing – If you could describe this snapshot.'

'It was just the front of a house,' said Miss Marple. 'And someone – Denzil, I mean – was just coming out of the front door. As I say it was taken by one of my other nephews who is very keen on flower shows – and he was photographing a hibiscus, I think, or one of those beautiful – something like antipasto – lilies. Denzil just happened to come out of the front door at that time. It wasn't a very good photograph of him – just a trifle blurred – But I liked it and have always kept it.'

'Well,' said Dr Graham, 'that seems clear enough. I think we'll have no difficulty in getting back your picture for you, Miss Marple.'

He rose from his chair. Miss Marple smiled up at him.

'You are very kind, Dr Graham, very kind *indeed*. You do understand, don't you?'

'Of course I do, of course I do,' said Dr Graham, shaking her warmly by the hand. 'Now don't you worry. Exercise that knee every day gently but not too much, and I'll send you round these tablets. Take one three times a day.'

CHAPTER FIVE

Miss Marple makes a Decision

The funeral service was said over the body of the late Major Palgrave on the following day. Miss Marple attended in company with Miss Prescott. The Canon read the service – after that life went on as usual.

Major Palgrave's death was already only an incident, a slightly unpleasant incident, but one that was soon forgotten. Life here was sunshine, sea, and social pleasures. A grim visitor had interrupted these activities, casting a momentary shadow, but the shadow was now gone. After all, nobody had known the deceased very well. He had been rather a garrulous elderly man of the club-bore type, always telling you personal reminiscences that you had no particular desire to hear. He had had little to anchor himself to any particular part of the world. His wife had died many years ago. He had had a lonely life and a lonely death. But it had been the kind of loneliness that spends itself in living amongst people, and in passing the time that way not unpleasantly. Major Palgrave might have been a lonely man, he had also been quite a cheerful one. He had enjoyed himself in his own particular way. And now he was dead, buried, and nobody cared very much, and in another week's time nobody would even remember him or spare him a passing thought.

The only person who could possibly be said to miss him was Miss Marple. Not indeed out of any personal affection, but he represented a kind of life that she knew. As one grew older, so she reflected to herself, one got more and more into the habit of listening; listening possibly without any great interest, but there had been between her and the Major the gentle give and take of two old people. It had had a cheerful, human quality. She did not actually mourn Major Palgrave but she missed him.

On the afternoon of the funeral, as she was sitting knitting in her favourite spot, Dr Graham came and joined her. She put her needles down and greeted him. He said at once, rather apologetically:

'I am afraid I have rather disappointing news, Miss Marple.'

'Indeed? About my – '

'Yes. We haven't found that precious snapshot of yours. I'm afraid that will be a disappointment to you.'

'Yes. Yes it is. But of course it does not *really* matter. It was a sentimentality. I do realize that now. It wasn't in Major Palgrave's wallet?'

'No. Nor anywhere else among his things. There were a few letters and newspaper clippings and odds and ends, and a few old photographs, but no sign of a snapshot such as you mentioned.'

'Oh dear,' said Miss Marple. 'Well, it can't be helped . . . Thank you very much, Dr Graham, for the trouble you've taken.'

'Oh it was no trouble, indeed. But I know quite well from my own experience how much family trifles mean to one, especially as one is getting older.'

The old lady was really taking it very well, he thought. Major Palgrave, he presumed, had probably come across the snapshot when taking something out of his wallet, and not even realizing how it had come there, had torn it up as something of no importance. But of course it was of great importance to this old lady. Still, she seemed quite cheerful and philosophical about it.

Internally, however, Miss Marple was far from being either cheerful or philosophical. She wanted a little time in which to think things out, but she was also determined to use her present opportunities to the fullest effect.

She engaged Dr Graham in conversation with an eagerness which she did not attempt to conceal. That kindly man, putting down her flow of talk to the natural loneliness of an old lady, exerted himself to divert her mind from the loss of the snapshot, by conversing easily and pleasantly about life in St Honoré, and the various interesting places perhaps Miss Marple might like to visit. He hardly knew himself how the conversation drifted back to Major Palgrave's decease.

'It seems so sad,' said Miss Marple. 'To think of anyone dying like this away from home. Though I gather, from what he himself told me, that he had no immediate family. It seems he lived by himself in London.'

'He travelled a fair amount, I believe,' said Dr Graham. 'At any rate in the winters. He didn't care for our English winters. Can't say I blame him.'

'No, indeed,' said Miss Marple. 'And perhaps he had some special reason like a weakness of the lungs or something which made it necessary for him to winter abroad?'

'Oh no, I don't think so.'

'He had high blood pressure, I believe. So sad nowadays. One hears so much of it.'

'He spoke about it to you, did he?'

'Oh no. No, *he* never mentioned it. It was somebody else who told me.'

'Ah, really.'

'I suppose,' went on Miss Marple, 'that death was to be expected under those circumstances.'

'Not necessarily,' said Dr Graham. 'There are methods of controlling blood pressure nowadays.'

'His death *seemed* very sudden – but I suppose *you* weren't surprised.'

'Well I wasn't particularly surprised in a man of that age. But I certainly didn't expect it. Frankly, he always seemed to me in very good form, but I hadn't ever attended him professionally. I'd never taken his blood pressure or anything like that.'

'Does one know – I mean, does a doctor know – when a man has high blood pressure just by looking at him?' Miss Marple inquired with a kind of dewy innocence.

'Not just by looking,' said the doctor, smiling. 'One has to do a bit of testing.'

'Oh I see. That dreadful thing when you put a rubber band round somebody's arm and blow it up – I dislike it *so* much. But my doctor said that my blood pressure was really very good for my age.'

'Well that's good hearing,' said Dr Graham.

'Of course, the Major *was* rather fond of Planters Punch,' said Miss Marple thoughtfully.

'Yes. Not the best thing with blood pressure – alcohol.'

'One takes tablets, doesn't one, or so I have heard?'

'Yes. There are several on the market. There was a bottle of one of them in his room – Serenite.'

'How wonderful science is nowadays,' said Miss Marple. 'Doctors can do so much, can't they?'

'We all have one great competitor,' said Dr Graham. 'Nature, you know. And some of the good old-fashioned home remedies come back from time to time.'

'Like putting cobwebs on a cut?' said Miss Marple. 'We always used to do that when I was a child.'

'Very sensible,' said Dr Graham.

'And a linseed poultice on the chest and rubbing in camphorated oil for a bad cough.'

'I see you know it all!' said Dr Graham laughing. He got up. 'How's the knee? Not been too troublesome?'

'No, it seems much, much better.'

'Well, we won't say whether that's Nature or my pills,' said Dr Graham. 'Sorry I couldn't have been of more help to you.'

'But you have been most kind – I am really ashamed of taking up your time – Did you say that there were no photographs in the Major's wallet?'

'Oh yes – a very old one of the Major himself as quite a young man on a polo pony – and one of a dead tiger – He was standing with his foot on it. Snaps of that sort – memories of his younger days – But I looked very carefully, I assure you, and the one you describe of your nephew was definitely not there – '

'Oh I'm sure you looked carefully – I didn't mean that – I was just interested – We all tend to keep such very odd things – '

'Treasures from the past,' said the doctor smiling.

He said goodbye and departed.

Miss Marple remained looking thoughtfully at the palm trees and the sea. She did not pick up her knitting again for some minutes. She had a fact now. She had to think about that fact and what it meant. The snapshot that the Major had brought out of his wallet and replaced so hurriedly was *not there after he died*. It was not the sort of thing the Major would throw away. He had replaced it in his wallet and it ought to have been in his wallet after his death. Money might have been stolen, but no one would want to steal a snapshot. Unless, that is, they had a special reason for so doing . . .

Miss Marple's face was grave. She had to take a decision. Was she, or was she not, going to allow Major Palgrave to remain quietly in his grave? Might it not be better to do just that? She quoted under her breath. 'Duncan is dead. After Life's fitful fever he sleeps well!' Nothing could hurt Major Palgrave now. He had gone where danger could not touch him. Was it just a coincidence that he should have died on that particular night? Or was it just possibly *not* a coincidence? Doctors accepted the deaths of elderly men so easily. Especially since in his room there had been a bottle of the tablets that people with high blood pressure had to take every day of their lives. But if someone had taken the snapshot from the Major's wallet, that same person could have put that bottle of tablets

33

in the Major's room. She herself never remembered *seeing* the Major take tablets; he had never spoken about his blood pressure to her. The only thing he had ever said about his health was the admission – 'Not as young as I was.' He had been occasionally a little short of breath, a trifle asthmatic, nothing else. But someone had mentioned that Major Palgrave had high blood pressure – Molly? Miss Prescott? She couldn't remember.

Miss Marple sighed, then admonished herself in words, though she did not speak those words aloud.

'Now, Jane, what are you suggesting or thinking? Are you, perhaps, just making the whole thing up? Have you *really* got anything to build on?'

She went over, step by step, as nearly as she could, the conversation between herself and the Major on the subject of murder and murderers.

'Oh dear,' said Miss Marple. 'Even if – really, I *don't* see how I *can* do anything about it – '

But she knew that she meant to try.

CHAPTER SIX

In the Small Hours

Miss Marple woke early. Like many old people she slept lightly and had periods of wakefulness which she used for the planning of some action or actions to be carried out on the next or following days. Usually, of course, these were of a wholly private or domestic nature, of little interest to anybody but herself. But this morning Miss Marple lay thinking soberly and constructively of murder, and what, if her suspicions were correct, she could do about it. It wasn't going to be easy. She had one weapon and one weapon only, and that was conversation.

Old ladies were given to a good deal of rambling conversation. People were bored by this, but certainly did not suspect them of ulterior motives. It would not be a case of asking direct questions. (Indeed, she would have found it difficult to know what questions to ask!) It would be a question of finding out a little more about certain people. She reviewed these certain people in her mind.

She could find out, possibly, a little more about Major Palgrave, but would that really help her? She doubted if it would. If Major Palgrave had been killed it was not because of secrets in his life or to inherit his money or for revenge upon him. In fact, although he was the victim, it was one of those rare cases where a greater knowledge of the victim does not help you or lead you in any way to his murderer. The point, it seemed to her, and the sole point, was that Major Palgrave talked too much!

She had learnt one rather interesting fact from Dr Graham. He had had in his wallet various photographs: one of himself in company with a polo pony, one of a dead tiger, also one or two other shots of the same nature. Now why did Major Palgrave carry these about with him? Obviously, thought Miss Marple, with long experience of old admirals, brigadier-generals and mere majors behind her, because he had certain stories which he enjoyed telling to people. Starting off with 'Curious thing happened once when I was out tiger shooting in India . . .' Or a reminiscence of himself and a polo pony. Therefore this story about a suspected murderer would in due course be illustrated by the production of the snapshot from his wallet.

He had been following that pattern in his conversation with her. The subject of murder having come up, and to focus interest on his story, he had done what he no doubt usually did, produced his snapshot and said something in the nature of 'Wouldn't think this chap was a murderer, would you?'

The point was that it had been a *habit* of his. This murderer story was one of his regular repertoire. If any reference to murder came up, then away went the Major, full steam ahead.

In that case, reflected Miss Marple, he might *already* have told his story to someone else here. Or to more than one person – If that were so, then she herself might learn from that person what the further details of the story had been, possibly what the person in the snapshot had looked like.

She nodded her head in satisfaction – That would be a beginning.

And, of course, there were the people she called in her mind the 'Four Suspects'. Though really, since Major Palgrave had been talking about a *man* – there were only two. Colonel Hillingdon or Mr Dyson, very unlikely-looking murderers, but then murderers so often *were* unlikely. Could there have been anyone else? She had

35

seen no one when she turned her head to look. There was the bungalow of course. Mr Rafiel's bungalow. Could somebody have come out of the bungalow and gone in again before she had had time to turn her head? If so, it could only have been the valet-attendant. What was his name? Oh yes, Jackson. Could it have been *Jackson* who had come out of the door? That would have been the same pose as the photograph. *A man coming out of a door*. Recognition might have struck suddenly. Up till then, Major Palgrave would not have looked at Arthur Jackson, valet-attendant, with any interest. His roving and curious eye was essentially a snobbish eye – Arthur Jackson was not a *pukka sahib* – Major Palgrave would not have glanced at him twice.

Until, perhaps, he had had the snapshot in his hand, and had looked over Miss Marple's right shoulder and had seen a man coming out of a door . . .?

Miss Marple turned over on her pillow – Programme for tomorrow – or rather for today – Further investigation of the Hillingdons, the Dysons and Arthur Jackson, valet-attendant.

II

Dr Graham also woke early. Usually he turned over and went to sleep again. But today he was uneasy and sleep failed to come. This anxiety that made it so difficult to go to sleep again was a thing he had not suffered from for a long time. What was causing this anxiety? Really, he couldn't make it out. He lay there thinking it over. Something to do with – something to do with – yes, Major Palgrave. Major Palgrave's death? He didn't see, though, what there could be to make him uneasy there. Was it something that that twittery old lady had said? Bad luck for her about her snapshot. She'd taken it very well. But now what was it she had said, what chance word of hers had it been, that had given him this funny feeling of uneasiness? After all, there was nothing *odd* about the Major's death. Nothing at all. At least he supposed there was nothing at all.

It was quite clear that in the Major's state of health – a faint check came in his thought process. Did he really know much *about* Major Palgrave's state of health? Everybody *said* that he'd suffered from high blood pressure. But he himself had never had any conversation with the Major about it. But then he'd never had much conversation

36

with Major Palgrave anyway. Palgrave was an old bore and he avoided old bores. Why on earth should he have this idea that perhaps everything *mightn't* be all right? Was it that old woman? But after all she hadn't *said* anything. Anyway, it was none of his business. The local authorities were quite satisfied. There had been that bottle of Serenite tablets, and the old boy had apparently talked to people about his blood pressure quite freely.

Dr Graham turned over in bed and soon went to sleep again.

III

Outside the hotel grounds, in one of a row of shanty cabins beside a creek, the girl Victoria Johnson rolled over and sat up in bed. The St Honoré girl was a magnificent creature with a torso of black marble such as a sculptor would have enjoyed. She ran her fingers through her dark, tightly curling hair. With her foot she nudged her sleeping companion in the ribs.

'Wake up, man.'

The man grunted and turned.

'What you want? It's not morning.'

'Wake up, man. I want to talk to you.'

The man sat up, stretched, showed a wide mouth and beautiful teeth.

'What's worrying you, woman?'

'That Major man who died. Something I don't like. Something wrong about it.'

'Ah, what d'you want to worry about that? He was old. He died.'

'Listen, man. It's them pills. Them pills the doctor asked me about.'

'Well, what about them? He took too many maybe.'

'No. It's not that. Listen.' She leant towards him, talking vehemently. He yawned and lay down again.

'There's nothing in that. What're you talking about?'

'All the same, I'll speak to Mrs Kendal about it in the morning. I think there's something wrong there somewhere.'

'Shouldn't bother,' said the man who, without benefit of ceremony, she considered as her present husband. 'Don't let's look for trouble,' he said and rolled over on his side yawning.

CHAPTER SEVEN

Morning on the Beach

It was mid-morning on the beach below the hotel.

Evelyn Hillingdon came out of the water and dropped on the warm golden sand. She took off her bathing cap and shook her dark head vigorously. The beach was not a very big one. People tended to congregate there in the mornings and about 11.30 there was always something of a social reunion. To Evelyn's left in one of the exotic-looking modern basket chairs lay Señora de Caspearo, a handsome woman from Venezuela. Next to her was old Mr Rafiel who was by now the doyen of the Golden Palm Hotel and held the sway that only an elderly invalid of great wealth could attain. Esther Walters was in attendance on him. She usually had her shorthand notebook and pencil with her in case Mr Rafiel should suddenly think of urgent business cables which must be got off at once. Mr Rafiel in beach attire was incredibly desiccated, his bones draped with festoons of dry skin. Though looking like a man on the point of death, he had looked exactly the same for at least the last eight years – or so it was said in the islands. Sharp blue eyes peered out of his wrinkled cheeks, and his principal pleasure in life was denying robustly anything that anyone else said.

Miss Marple was also present. As usual she sat and knitted and listened to what went on, and very occasionally joined in the conversation. When she did so, everyone was surprised because they had usually forgotten that she was there! Evelyn Hillingdon looked at her indulgently, and thought that she was a nice old pussy.

Señora de Caspearo rubbed some more oil on her long beautiful legs and hummed to herself. She was not a woman who spoke much. She looked discontentedly at the flask of sun oil.

'This is not so good as Frangipanio,' she said, sadly. 'One cannot get it here. A pity.' Her eyelids drooped again.

'Are you going in for your dip now, Mr Rafiel?' asked Esther Walters.

'I'll go in when I'm ready,' said Mr Rafiel, snappishly.

'It's half past eleven,' said Mrs Walters.

'What of it?' said Mr Rafiel. 'Think I'm the kind of man to be tied by the clock? Do this at the hour, do this at twenty minutes past, do that at twenty to – bah!'

Mrs Walters had been in attendance on Mr Rafiel long enough to have adopted her own formula for dealing with him. She knew that he liked a good space of time in which to recover from the exertion of bathing and she had therefore reminded him of the time, allowing a good ten minutes for him to rebut her suggestion and then be able to adopt it without seeming to do so.

'I don't like these espadrilles,' said Mr Rafiel raising a foot and looking at it. 'I told that fool Jackson so. The man never pays attention to a word I say.'

'I'll fetch you some others, shall I, Mr Rafiel?'

'No, you won't, you'll sit here and keep quiet. I hate people rushing about like clucking hens.'

Evelyn shifted slightly in the warm sand, stretching out her arms.

Miss Marple, intent on her knitting – or so it seemed – stretched out a foot, then hastily she apologized.

'I'm so sorry, so very sorry, Mrs Hillingdon. I'm afraid I kicked you.'

'Oh, it's quite all right,' said Evelyn. 'This beach gets rather crowded.'

'Oh, please don't move. Please. I'll move my chair a little back so that I won't do it again.'

As Miss Marple resettled herself, she went on talking in a childish and garrulous manner.

'It still seems so wonderful to be *here*! I've never been to the West Indies before, you know. I thought it was the kind of place I never should come to and here I am. All by the kindness of my dear nephew. I suppose you know this part of the world very well, don't you, Mrs Hillingdon?'

'I have been in this island once or twice before and of course in most of the others.'

'Oh yes. Butterflies isn't it, and wild flowers? You and your – your friends – or are they relations?'

'Friends. Nothing more.'

'And I suppose you go about together a great deal because of your interests being the same?'

39

'Yes. We've travelled together for some years now.'

'I suppose you must have had some rather exciting adventures sometimes?'

'I don't think so,' said Evelyn. Her voice was unaccentuated, slightly bored. 'Adventures always seem to happen to other people.' She yawned.

'No dangerous encounters with snakes or with wild animals or with natives gone berserk?'

('What a fool I sound,' thought Miss Marple.)

'Nothing worse than insect bites,' Evelyn assured her.

'Poor Major Palgrave, you know, was bitten by a snake once,' said Miss Marple, making a purely fictitious statement.

'Was he?'

'Did he never tell you about it?'

'Perhaps. I don't remember.'

'I suppose you knew him quite well, didn't you?'

'Major Palgrave? No, hardly at all.'

'He always had so many interesting stories to tell.'

'Ghastly old bore,' said Mr Rafiel. 'Silly fool, too. He needn't have died if he'd looked after himself properly.'

'Oh come now, Mr Rafiel,' said Mrs Walters.

'I know what I'm talking about. If you look after your health properly you're all right anywhere. Look at me. The doctors gave *me* up years ago. All right, I said, I've got my own rules of health and I shall keep to them. And here I am.'

He looked round proudly.

It did indeed seem rather a mistake that he should be there.

'Poor Major Palgrave had high blood pressure,' said Mrs Walters.

'Nonsense,' said Mr Rafiel.

'Oh, but he did,' said Evelyn Hillingdon. She spoke with sudden, unexpected authority.

'Who says so?' said Mr Rafiel. 'Did he tell you so?'

'Somebody said so.'

'He looked very red in the face,' Miss Marple contributed.

'Can't go by that,' said Mr Rafiel. 'And anyway he *didn't* have high blood pressure because he told me so.'

'What do you mean, he told you so?' said Mrs Walters. 'I mean, you can't exactly tell people you *haven't* got a thing.'

'Yes you can. I said to him once when he was downing all those Planters Punches, and eating too much, I said, "You ought to watch your diet and your drink. You've got to think of your blood pressure at your age." And he said he'd nothing to look out for in that line, that his blood pressure was very good for his age.'

'But he took some stuff for it, I believe,' said Miss Marple, entering the conversation once more. 'Some stuff called – oh, something like – was it Serenite?'

'If you ask me,' said Evelyn Hillingdon, 'I don't think he ever liked to admit that there could be anything the matter with him or that he could be ill. I think he was one of those people who are afraid of illness and therefore deny there's ever anything wrong with them.'

It was a long speech for her. Miss Marple looked thoughtfully down at the top of her dark head.

'The trouble is,' said Mr Rafiel dictatorially 'everybody's too fond of knowing other people's ailments. They think everybody over fifty is going to die of hypertension or coronary thrombosis or one of those things – poppy-cock! If a man says there's nothing much wrong with him I don't suppose there is. A man ought to know about his own health. What's the time? Quarter to twelve? I ought to have had my dip long ago. Why can't you remind me about these things, Esther?'

Mrs Walters made no protest. She rose to her feet and with some deftness assisted Mr Rafiel to his. Together they went down the beach, she supporting him carefully. Together they stepped into the sea.

Señora de Caspearo opened her eyes and murmured: 'How ugly are old men! Oh how they are ugly! They should all be put to death at forty, or perhaps thirty-five would be better. Yes?'

Edward Hillingdon and Gregory Dyson came crunching down the beach.

'What's the water like, Evelyn?'

'Just the same as always.'

'Never much variation, is there? Where's Lucky?'

'I don't know,' said Evelyn.

Again Miss Marple looked down thoughtfully at the dark head.

'Well, now I give my imitation of a whale,' said Gregory. He threw off his gaily patterned Bermuda shirt and tore down the beach, flinging himself, puffing and panting, into the sea, doing a fast crawl. Edward Hillingdon sat down on the beach by his wife. Presently he asked, 'Coming in again?'

She smiled – put on her cap – and they went down the beach together in a much less spectacular manner.

Señora de Caspearo opened her eyes again.

'I think at first those two they are on their honeymoon, he is so charming to her, but I hear they have been married eight – nine years. It is incredible, is it not?'

'I wonder where Mrs Dyson is?' said Miss Marple.

'That Lucky? She is with some man.'

'You – you think so?'

'It is certain,' said Señora de Caspearo. 'She is that type. But she is not so young any longer – Her husband – already his eyes go elsewhere – He makes passes – here, there, all the time. I know.'

'Yes,' said Miss Marple. 'I expect you would know.'

Señora de Caspearo shot a surprised glance at her. It was clearly not what she had expected from that quarter.

Miss Marple, however, was looking at the waves with an air of gentle innocence.

II

'May I speak to you, ma'am, Mrs Kendal?'

'Yes, of course,' said Molly. She was sitting at her desk in the office.

Victoria Johnson, tall and buoyant in her crisp white uniform, came in farther and shut the door behind her with a somewhat mysterious air.

'I like to tell you something, please, Mrs Kendal.'

'Yes, what is it? Is anything wrong?'

'I don't know that. Not for sure. It's the old gentleman who died. The Major gentleman. He die in his sleep.'

'Yes, yes. What about it?'

'There was a bottle of pills in his room. Doctor, he asked me about them.'

'Yes?'

'The doctor said – 'Let me see what he has here on the bathroom shelf,' and he looked, you see. He see there was tooth powder and indigestion pills and aspirin and cascara pills, and then these pills in a bottle called Serenite.'

'Yes,' repeated Molly yet again.

'And the doctor looked at them. He seemed quite satisfied, and nodded his head. But I get to thinking afterwards. Those pills weren't there before. I've not seen them in his bathroom before. The others, yes. The tooth powder and the aspirin and the aftershave lotion and all the rest. But those pills, those Serenite pills, I never noticed them before.'

'So you think – ' Molly looked puzzled.

'I don't know what to think,' said Victoria. 'I just think it's not right, so I think I better tell you about it. Perhaps you tell doctor? Perhaps it means something. Perhaps *someone* put those pills there so he take them and he died.'

'Oh, I don't think that's likely at all,' said Molly.

Victoria shook her dark head. 'You never know. People do bad things.'

Molly glanced out of the window. The place looked like an earthly paradise. With its sunshine, its sea, its coral reef, its music, its dancing, it seemed a Garden of Eden. But even in the Garden of Eden, there had been a shadow – the shadow of the Serpent – *Bad things* – how hateful to hear those words.

'I'll make inquiries, Victoria,' she said sharply. 'Don't worry. And above all don't go starting a lot of silly rumours.'

Tim Kendal came in, just as Victoria was, somewhat unwillingly, leaving.

'Anything wrong, Molly?'

She hesitated – but Victoria might go to him – She told him what the girl had said.

'I don't see what all this rigmarole – what *were* these pills anyway?'

'Well, I don't really know, Tim. Dr Robertson when he came said they – were something to do with blood pressure, I think.'

'Well, that would be all right, wouldn't it? I mean, he *had* high blood pressure, and he *would* be taking things for it, wouldn't he? People do. I've seen them, lots of times.'

'Yes,' Molly hesitated, 'but Victoria seemed to think that he might have taken one of these pills and it would have killed him.'

'Oh darling, that is a bit *too* melodramatic! You mean that somebody might have changed his blood pressure pills for something else, and that they poisoned him?'

'It does sound absurd,' said Molly apologetically, 'when you say it like that. But that seemed to be what Victoria thought!'

'Silly girl! We *could* go and ask Dr Graham about it, I suppose he'd know. But really it's such nonsense that it's not worth bothering him.'

'That's what I think.'

43

'What on earth made the girl think anybody would have changed the pills? You mean, put different pills into the same bottle?'

'I didn't quite gather,' said Molly, looking rather helpless. 'Victoria seemed to think that was the first time that Serenite bottle had been there.'

'Oh but that's nonsense,' said Tim Kendal. 'He had to take those pills all the time to keep his blood pressure down.' And he went off cheerfully to consult with Fernando the *maître d'hôtel*.

But Molly could not dismiss the matter so lightly. After the stress of lunch was over she said to her husband:

'Tim – I've been thinking – If Victoria is going around talking about this perhaps we ought just to ask someone about it?'

'My dear girl! Robertson and all the rest of them came and looked at everything and asked all the questions they wanted at the time.'

'Yes, but you know how they work themselves up, these girls – '

'Oh, all right! I'll tell you what – we'll go and ask Graham – he'll know.'

Dr Graham was sitting on his loggia with a book. The young couple came in and Molly plunged into her recital. It was a little incoherent and Tim took over.

'Sounds rather idiotic,' he said apologetically, 'but as far as I can make out, this girl has got it into her head that someone put some poison tablets in the – what's the name of the stuff – Sera – something bottle.'

'But why should she get this idea into her head?' asked Dr Graham. 'Did she see anything or hear anything or – I mean, why should she think so?'

'I don't know,' said Tim rather helplessly. 'Was it a different bottle? Was that it, Molly?'

'No,' said Molly. 'I think what she said was that there was a bottle there labelled – Seven – Seren – '

'Serenite,' said the doctor. 'That's quite right. A well-known preparation. He'd been taking it regularly.'

'Victoria said she'd never seen it in his room before.'

'Never seen it in his room before?' said Graham sharply. 'What does she mean by that?'

'Well, that's what she *said*. She said there were all sorts of things on the bathroom shelf. You know, tooth powder, aspirin and aftershave and – oh – she rattled them off gaily. I suppose she's always cleaning them and so she knows them all off by heart. But this one – the Serenite – she hadn't seen it there until the day after he died.'

'That's very odd,' said Dr Graham, rather sharply. 'Is she sure?'

The unusual sharpness of his tone made both of the Kendals look up at him. They had not expected Dr Graham to take up quite this attitude.

'She sounded sure,' said Molly slowly.

'Perhaps she just wanted to be sensational,' suggested Tim.

'I think perhaps,' said Dr Graham, 'I'd better have a few words with the girl myself.'

Victoria displayed a distinct pleasure at being allowed to tell her story.

'I don't want to get in no trouble,' she said. '*I* didn't put that bottle there and I don't know who did.'

'But you think it *was* put there?' asked Graham.

'Well, you see, Doctor, it *must* have been put there if it wasn't there before.'

'Major Palgrave could have kept it in a drawer – or a dispatch-case, something like that.'

Victoria shook her head shrewdly.

'Wouldn't do that if he was taking it all the time, would he?'

'No,' said Graham reluctantly. 'No, it was stuff he would have to take several times a day. You never saw him taking it or anything of that kind?'

'He didn't have it there before. I just thought – word got round as that stuff had something to do with his death, poisoned his blood or something, and I thought maybe he had an enemy put it there so as to kill him.'

'Nonsense, my girl,' said the doctor robustly. 'Sheer nonsense'

Victoria looked shaken.

'You say as this stuff was medicine, good medicine?' she asked doubtfully.

'Good medicine, and what is more, *necessary* medicine,' said Dr Graham. 'So you needn't worry, Victoria. I can assure you there was nothing wrong with that medicine. It was the proper thing for a man to take who had his complaint.'

'Surely you've taken a load off my mind,' said Victoria. She showed white teeth at him in a cheerful smile.

But the load was not taken off Dr Graham's mind. That uneasiness of his that had been so nebulous was now becoming tangible.

CHAPTER EIGHT

A Talk with Esther Walters

'This place isn't what it used to be,' said Mr Rafiel, irritably, as he observed Miss Marple approaching the spot where he and his secretary were sitting. 'Can't move a step without some old hen getting under your feet. What do old ladies want to come to the West Indies for?'

'Where do you suggest they should go?' asked Esther Walters.

'To Cheltenham,' said Mr Rafiel promptly. 'Or Bournemouth,' he offered, 'or Torquay or Llandrindod Wells. Plenty of choice. They like it there – they're quite happy.'

'They can't often afford to come to the West Indies, I suppose,' said Esther. 'It isn't everyone who is as lucky as you are.'

'That's right,' said Mr Rafiel. 'Rub it in. Here am I, a mass of aches and pains and disjoints. You grudge me any alleviation! And you don't do any work – Why haven't you typed out those letters yet?'

'I haven't had time.'

'Well, get on with it, can't you? I bring you out here to do a bit of work, not to sit about sunning yourself and showing off your figure.'

Some people would have considered Mr Rafiel's remarks quite insupportable but Esther Walters had worked for him for some years and she knew well enough that Mr Rafiel's bark was a great deal worse than his bite. He was a man who suffered almost continual pain, and making disagreeable remarks was one of his ways of letting off steam. No matter what he said she remained quite imperturbable.

'Such a lovely evening, isn't it?' said Miss Marple, pausing beside them.

'Why not?' said Mr Rafiel. 'That's what we're here for, isn't it?'

Miss Marple gave a tinkly little laugh.

'You're so severe – of course the weather *is* a very English subject

46

of conversation – one forgets – Oh dear – this is the wrong coloured wool.' She deposited her knitting bag on the garden table and trotted towards her own bungalow.

'Jackson!' yelled Mr Rafiel.

Jackson appeared.

'Take me back inside,' said Mr Rafiel. 'I'll have my massage now before that chattering hen comes back. Not that massage does me a bit of good,' he added. Having said which, he allowed himself to be deftly helped to his feet and went off with the masseur beside him into his bungalow.

Esther Walters looked after them and then turned her head as Miss Marple came back with a ball of wool to sit down near her.

'I hope I'm not disturbing you?' said Miss Marple.

'Of course not,' said Esther Walters, 'I've got to go off and do some typing in a minute, but I'm going to enjoy another ten minutes of the sunset first.'

Miss Marple sat down and in a gentle voice began to talk. As she talked, she summed up Esther Walters. Not at all glamorous, but could be attractive-looking if she tried. Miss Marple wondered why she didn't try. It could be, of course, because Mr Rafiel would not have liked it, but Miss Marple didn't think Mr Rafiel would really mind in the least. He was so completely taken up with himself that so long as he was not personally neglected, his secretary might have got herself up like a houri in Paradise without his objecting. Besides, he usually went to bed early and in the evening hours of steel bands and dancing, Esther Walters might easily have – Miss Marple paused to select a word in her mind, at the same time conversing cheerfully about her visit to Jamestown – Ah yes, *blossomed*. Esther Walters might have blossomed in the evening hours.

She led the conversation gently in the direction of Jackson.

On the subject of Jackson Esther Walters was rather vague.

'He's very competent,' she said. 'A fully trained masseur.'

'I suppose he's been with Mr Rafiel a long time?'

'Oh no – about nine months, I think – '

'Is he married?' Miss Marple hazarded.

'Married? I don't think so,' said Esther slightly surprised. 'He's never mentioned it if so –

'No,' she added. 'Definitely *not* married, I should say.' And she showed amusement.

Miss Marple interpreted that by adding to it in her own mind the

47

following sentence – 'At any rate he doesn't behave as though he were married.'

But then, how many married men there were who behaved as though they weren't married! Miss Marple could think of a dozen examples!

'He's quite good-looking,' she said thoughtfully.

'Yes – I suppose he is,' said Esther without interest.

Miss Marple considered her thoughtfully. Uninterested in men? The kind of woman, perhaps, who was only interested in one man – A widow, they had said.

She asked – 'Have you worked for Mr Rafiel long?'

'Four or five years. After my husband died, I had to take a job again. I've got a daughter at school and my husband left me very badly off.'

'Mr Rafiel must be a difficult man to work for?' Miss Marple hazarded.

'Not really, when you get to know him. He flies into rages and is very contradictory. I think the real trouble is he gets tired of people. He's had five different valet-attendants in two years. He likes having someone new to bully. But he and I have always got on very well.'

'Mr Jackson seems a very obliging young man?'

'He's very tactful and resourceful,' said Esther. 'Of course, he's sometimes a little – ' She broke off.

Miss Marple considered. 'Rather a difficult position sometimes?' she suggested.

'Well, yes. Neither one thing nor the other. However – ' she smiled – 'I think he manages to have quite a good time.'

Miss Marple considered this also. It didn't help her much. She continued her twittering conversation and soon she was hearing a good deal about that nature-loving quartet, the Dysons and the Hillingdons.

'The Hillingdons have been here for the last three or four years at least,' said Esther, 'but Gregory Dyson has been here much longer than that. He knows the West Indies very well. He came here, originally, I believe, with his first wife. She was delicate and had to go abroad in the winters, or go somewhere warm, at any rate.'

'And she died? Or was it divorce?'

'No. She died. Out here, I believe. I don't mean this particular island but one of the West Indies islands. There was some sort of trouble, I believe, some kind of scandal or other. He never talks

48

about her. Somebody else told me about it. They didn't, I gather, get on very well together.'

'And then he married this wife. "Lucky".' Miss Marple said the word with faint dissatisfaction as if to say 'Really, a most incredible name!'

'I believe she was a relation of his first wife.'

'Have they known the Hillingdons a great many years?'

'Oh, I think only since the Hillingdons came out here. Three or four years, not more.'

'The Hillingdons seem very pleasant,' said Miss Marple. 'Quiet, of course.'

'Yes. They're both quiet.'

'Everyone says they're very devoted to each other,' said Miss Marple. The tone of her voice was quite non-committal but Esther Walters looked at her sharply.

'But you don't think they are?' she said.

'You don't really think so yourself, do you, my dear?'

'Well, I've wondered sometimes . . .'

'Quiet men, like Colonel Hillingdon,' said Miss Marple, 'are often attracted to flamboyant types.' And she added, after a significant pause, 'Lucky – such a curious name. Do you think Mr Dyson has any idea of – of what might be going on?'

'Old scandal-monger,' thought Esther Walters. 'Really, these old women!'

She said rather coldly, 'I've no idea.'

Miss Marple shifted to another subject. 'It's very sad about poor Major Palgrave isn't it?' she said.

Esther Walters agreed, though in a somewhat perfunctory fashion.

'The people I'm really sorry for are the Kendals,' she said.

'Yes, I suppose it is really rather unfortunate when something of that kind happens in a hotel.'

'People come here, you see, to enjoy themselves, don't they?' said Esther. 'To forget about illnesses and deaths and income tax and frozen pipes and all the rest of it. They don't like – ' she went on, with a sudden flash of an entirely different manner – 'any reminders of mortality.'

Miss Marple laid down her knitting. 'Now that is very well put, my dear,' she said, 'very well put indeed. Yes, it is as you say.'

'And you see they're quite a young couple,' went on Esther Walters. 'They only just took over from the Sandersons six months ago and they're terribly worried about whether they're going to succeed or not, because they haven't had much experience.'

'And you think this might be really disadvantageous to them?'

'Well, no, I don't, frankly,' said Esther Walters. 'I don't think people remember anything for more than a day or two, not in this atmosphere of "we've-all-come-out-here-to-enjoy-ourselves-let's-get-on-with-it." I think a death just gives them a jolt for about twenty-four hours or so and then they don't think of it again once the funeral is over. Not unless they're reminded of it, that is. I've told Molly so, but of course she is a worrier.'

'Mrs Kendal is a worrier? She always seems so carefree.'

'I think a lot of that is put on,' said Esther slowly. 'Actually, I think she's one of those anxious sort of people who can't help worrying all the time that things *may* go wrong.'

'I should have thought *he* worried more than she did.'

'No, I don't think so. I think she's the worrier and he worries because she worries if you know what I mean.'

'That is interesting,' said Miss Marple.

'I think Molly wants desperately to try and appear very gay and to be enjoying herself. She works at it very hard but the effort exhausts her. Then she has these odd fits of depression. She's not – well, not really well-balanced.'

'Poor child,' said Miss Marple. 'There certainly are people like that, and very often outsiders don't suspect it.'

'No, they put on such a good show, don't they? However,' Esther added, 'I don't think Molly has really anything to worry about in this case. I mean, people are dying of coronary thrombosis or cerebral hæmorrhage or things of that kind all the time nowadays. Far more than they used to, as far as I can see. It's only food poisoning or typhoid or something like that, that makes people get het up.'

'Major Palgrave never mentioned to *me* that he had high blood pressure,' said Miss Marple. 'Did he to you?'

'He said so to somebody – I don't know who – it may have been to Mr Rafiel. I know Mr Rafiel says just the opposite – but then he's like that! Certainly Jackson mentioned it to me once. He said the Major ought to be more careful over the alcohol he took.'

'I see,' said Miss Marple, thoughtfully. She went on: 'I expect you found him rather a boring old man? He told a lot of stories and I expect repeated himself a good deal.'

'That's the worst of it,' said Esther. 'You do hear the same story again and again unless you can manage to be quick enough to fend it off.'

'Of course *I* didn't mind so much,' said Miss Marple, 'because I'm used to that sort of thing. If I get stories told to me rather often, I don't really mind hearing them again because I've usually forgotten them.'

'There is that,' said Esther and laughed cheerfully.

'There was one story he was very fond of telling,' said Miss Marple, 'about a murder. I expect he told you that, didn't he?'

Esther Walters opened her handbag and started searching through it. She drew out her lipstick saying, 'I thought I'd lost it.' Then she asked, 'I beg your pardon, what did you say?'

'I asked if Major Palgrave told you his favourite murder story?'

'I believe he did, now I come to think of it. Something about someone who gassed themselves, wasn't it? Only really it was the *wife* who gassed him. I mean she'd given him a sedative of some kind and then stuck his head in the gas oven. Was that it?'

'I don't think that was exactly it,' said Miss Marple. She looked at Esther Walters thoughtfully.

'He told such a lot of stories,' said Esther Walters, apologetically, 'and as I said, one didn't always listen.'

'He had a snapshot,' said Miss Marple, 'that he used to show people.'

'I believe he did . . . I can't remember what it was now. Did he show it to you?'

'No,' said Miss Marple. 'He didn't show it to me. We were interrupted – '

CHAPTER NINE

Miss Prescott and Others

'The story *I* heard,' began Miss Prescott, lowering her voice, and looking carefully around.

Miss Marple drew her chair a little closer. It had been some time before she had been able to get together with Miss Prescott for a heart-to-heart chat. This was owing to the fact that clergymen are very strong family men so that Miss Prescott was nearly always accompanied by her brother, and there was no doubt that Miss Marple and Miss Prescott found it less easy to take their back hair down in a good gossip when the jovial Canon was of their company.

'It seems,' said Miss Prescott, 'though of course I don't want to talk any scandal and I really know *nothing* about it – '

'Oh, I *quite* understand,' said Miss Marple.

'It seems there was some scandal when his first wife was still alive! Apparently this woman, Lucky – such a name! – who I think was a cousin of his first wife, came out here and joined them and I think did some work with him on flowers or butterflies or whatever it was. And people talked a lot because they got on so well together – if you know what I mean.'

'People do *notice* things so much, don't they?' said Miss Marple.

'And then of course, when his wife died rather suddenly – '

'She died here, on this island?'

'No. No, I think they were in Martinique or Tobago at the time.'

'I see.'

'But I gathered from some other people who were there at the time, and who came on here and talked about things, that the doctor wasn't very satisfied.'

'Indeed,' said Miss Marple, with interest.

'It was only *gossip*,' of course, 'but – well, Mr Dyson certainly married again *very quickly*.' She lowered her voice again. 'Only a *month* I believe.'

'Only a month,' said Miss Marple.

The two women looked at each other. 'It seemed – unfeeling,' said Miss Prescott.

'Yes,' said Miss Marple. 'It certainly did.' She added delicately, 'Was there – any money?'

'I don't really know. He makes his little joke – perhaps you've heard him – about his wife being his "lucky piece" – '

'Yes, I've heard him,' said Miss Marple.

'And some people think that means that he was lucky to marry a rich wife. Though, of course,' said Miss Prescott with the air of one being entirely fair, 'she's very good-looking too, if you care for that type. And I think myself that it was the *first* wife who had the money.'

'Are the Hillingdons well off?'

'Well, I think they're *well off*. I don't mean fabulously rich, I just mean well off. They have two boys at public school and a very nice place in England, I believe, and they travel most of the winter.'

The Canon appearing at this moment to suggest a brisk walk, Miss Prescott rose to join her brother. Miss Marple remained sitting there.

A few minutes later Gregory Dyson passed her striding along towards the hotel. He waved a cheerful hand as he passed.

'Penny for your thoughts,' he called out.

Miss Marple smiled gently, wondering how he would have reacted if she had replied:

'I was wondering if you were a murderer.'

It really seemed most probable that he was. It all fitted in so nicely – This story about the death of the first Mrs Dyson – Major Palgrave had certainly been talking about a wife killer – with special reference to the 'Brides in the bath Case'.

Yes – it fitted – the only objection was that it fitted almost too well. But Miss Marple reproved herself for this thought – who was she to demand Murders Made to Measure?

A voice made her jump – a somewhat raucous one.

'Seen Greg any place, Miss – cr – '

Lucky, Miss Marple thought, was not in a good temper.

'He passed by just now – going towards the hotel.'

'I'll bet!' Lucky uttered an irritated ejaculation and hurried on.

'Forty, if she's a day, and looks it this morning,' thought Miss Marple.

Pity invaded her – pity for the Luckys of the world – who were so vulnerable to Time –

At the sound of a noise behind her, she turned her chair round – Mr Rafiel, supported by Jackson, was making his morning appearance and coming out of his bungalow –

Jackson settled his employer in his wheelchair and fussed round him. Mr Rafiel waved his attendant away impatiently and Jackson went off in the direction of the hotel.

Miss Marple lost no time – Mr Rafiel was never left alone for long – Probably Esther Walters would come and join him. Miss Marple wanted a word alone with Mr Rafiel and now, she thought, was her chance. She would have to be quick about what she wanted to say. There could be no leading up to things. Mr Rafiel was not a man who cared for the idle twittering conversation of old ladies. He would probably retreat again into his bungalow, definitely regarding himself the victim of persecution. Miss Marple decided to plump for downrightness.

She made her way to where he was sitting, drew up a chair, sat down, and said:

'I want to ask you something, Mr Rafiel.'

'All right, all right,' said Mr Rafiel, 'let's have it. What do you want – a subscription, I suppose? Missions in Africa or repairing a church, something of that kind?'

'Yes,' said Miss Marple. 'I am interested in several objects of that nature, and I shall be delighted if you will give me a subscription for them. But that wasn't actually what I was going to ask you. What I was going to ask you was if Major Palgrave ever told you a story about a murder.'

'Oho,' said Mr Rafiel. 'So he told it to you too, did he? And I suppose you fell for it, hook, line and sinker.'

'I didn't really know what to think,' said Miss Marple. 'What exactly did he tell you?'

'He prattled on,' said Mr Rafiel, 'about a lovely creature, Lucrezia Borgia reincarnated. Beautiful, young, golden-haired, everything.'

'Oh,' said Miss Marple slightly taken aback, 'and who did she murder?'

'Her husband, of course,' said Mr Rafiel, 'who do you think?'

'Poison?'

'No, I think she gave him a sleeping draught and then stuck him in a gas oven. Resourceful female. Then she said it was suicide. She got off quite lightly. Diminished responsibility or something. That's what it's called nowadays if you're a good-looking woman, or some miserable young hooligan whose mother's been too fond of him. Bah!'

'Did the Major show you a snapshot?'

'What – a snapshot of the woman? No. Why should he?'

'Oh – ' said Miss Marple.

She sat there, rather taken aback. Apparently Major Palgrave spent his life telling people not only about tigers he had shot and elephants he had hunted but also about murderers he had met. Perhaps he had a whole repertoire of murder stories. One had to face it – She was startled by Mr Rafiel suddenly giving a roar of 'Jackson!' There was no response.

'Shall I find him for you?' said Miss Marple rising.

'You won't find him. Tom-catting somewhere, that's what he

does. No good, that fellow. Bad character. But he suits me all right.'

'I'll go and look for him,' said Miss Marple.

Miss Marple found Jackson sitting on the far side of the hotel terrace having a drink with Tim Kendal.

'Mr Rafiel is asking for you,' she said.

Jackson made an expressive grimace, drained his glass, and rose to his feet.

'Here we go again,' he said. 'No peace for the wicked – Two telephone calls and a special diet order – I thought that might give me a quarter of an hour's alibi – Apparently not! Thank you, Miss Marple. Thanks for the drink, Mr Kendal.'

He strode away.

'I feel sorry for that chap,' said Tim. 'I have to stand him a drink now and then, just to cheer him up – Can I offer you something, Miss Marple – How about fresh lime? I know you're fond of that.'

'Not just now, thank you – I suppose looking after someone like Mr Rafiel must always be rather exacting. Invalids are frequently difficult – '

'I didn't mean only that – It's very well paid and you expect to put up with a good deal of crotchetiness – old Rafiel's not really a bad sort. I mean more that – ' he hesitated.

Miss Marple looked inquiring.

'Well – how shall I put it – it's difficult for him socially. People are so damned snobbish – there's no one here of his class. He's better than a servant – and below the average visitor – or they think he is. Rather like the Victorian governess. Even the secretary woman, Mrs Walters – feels she's a cut above him. Makes things difficult.' Tim paused, then said with feeling: 'It's really awful the amount of social problems there are in a place like this.'

Dr Graham passed them – he had a book in his hand. He went and sat at a table overlooking the sea.

'Dr Graham looks rather worried,' remarked Miss Marple.

'Oh! We're all worried.'

'You too? Because of Major Palgrave's death?'

'I've left off worrying about that. People seem to have forgotten it – taken it in their stride. No – it's my wife Molly – Do you know anything about dreams?'

'Dreams?' Miss Marple was surprised.

'Yes – bad dreams – nightmares, I suppose. Oh, we all get that sort of thing sometimes. But Molly – she seems to have them nearly all the time. They frighten her. Is there anything one can do about them? Take for them? She's got some sleeping pills, but she says they make it worse – she struggles to wake up and can't.'

'What are the dreams about?'

'Oh, something or someone chasing her – Or watching her and spying on her – she can't shake off the feeling even when she's awake.'

'Surely a doctor – '

'She's got a thing against doctors. Won't hear of it – Oh well – I dare say it will all pass off – But we were so happy. It was all such fun – And now, just lately – Perhaps old Palgrave's death upset her. She seems like a different person since . . .'

He got up.

'Must get on with the daily chores – are you sure you won't have that fresh lime?'

Miss Marple shook her head.

She sat there, thinking. Her face was grave and anxious.

She glanced over at Dr Graham.

Presently she came to a decision.

She rose and went across to his table.

'I have got to apologize to you, Dr Graham,' she said.

'Indeed?' The doctor looked at her in kindly surprise. He pulled forward a chair and she sat down.

'I am afraid I have done the most disgraceful thing,' said Miss Marple. 'I told you, Dr Graham, a deliberate lie.'

She looked at him apprehensively.

Dr Graham did not look at all shattered, but he did look a little surprised.

'Really?' he said. 'Ah well, you mustn't let that worry you too much.'

What had the dear old thing been telling lies about, he wondered; her age? Though as far as he could remember she hadn't mentioned her age. 'Well, let's hear about it,' he said, since she clearly wished to confess.

'You remember my speaking to you about a snapshot of my nephew, one that I showed to Major Palgrave, and that he didn't give back to me?'

'Yes, yes, of course I remember. Sorry we couldn't find it for you.'

'There wasn't any such thing,' said Miss Marple, in a small frightened voice.

'I beg your pardon?'

'There wasn't any such thing. I made up that story, I'm afraid.'

'You made it up?' Dr Graham looked slightly annoyed. 'Why?'

Miss Marple told him. She told him quite clearly, without twittering. She told him about Major Palgrave's murder story and how he'd been about to show her this particular snapshot and his sudden confusion and then she went on to her own anxiety and to her final decision to try somehow to obtain a view of it.

'And really, I couldn't see any way of doing so without telling you something that was quite untrue,' she said, 'I do hope you will forgive me.'

'You thought that what he had been about to show you was a picture of a murderer?'

'That's what he said it was,' said Miss Marple. 'At least he said it was given him by this acquaintance who had told him the story about a man who was a murderer.'

'Yes, yes. And – excuse me – you believed him?'

'I don't know if I really believed him or not at the time,' said Miss Marple. 'But then, you see, the next day he died.'

'Yes,' said Dr Graham, struck suddenly by the clarity of that one sentence. *The next day he died* . . .

'And the snapshot had disappeared.'

Dr Graham looked at her. He didn't know quite what to say.

'Excuse me, Miss Marple,' he said at last, 'but is what you're telling me now – is it really true this time?'

'I don't wonder your doubting me,' said Miss Marple. 'I should, in your place. Yes, it is true what I am telling you now, but I quite realize that you have only my word for it. Still, even if you don't believe me, I thought I ought to tell you.'

'Why?'

'I realized that you ought to have the fullest information possible – in case – '

'In case what?'

'In case you decided to take any steps about it.'

CHAPTER TEN

A Decision in Jamestown

Dr Graham was in Jamestown, in the Administrator's office, sitting at a table opposite his friend Daventry, a grave young man of thirty-five.

'You sounded rather mysterious on the phone, Graham,' said Daventry. 'Anything special the matter?'

'I don't know,' said Dr Graham, 'but I'm worried.'

Daventry looked at the other's face, then he nodded as drinks were brought in. He spoke lightly of a fishing expedition he had made lately. Then when the servant had gone away, he sat back in his chair and looked at the other man.

'Now then,' he said, 'let's have it.'

Dr Graham recounted the facts that had worried him. Daventry gave a slow long whistle.

'I see. You think maybe there's something funny about old Palgrave's death? You're no longer sure that it was just natural causes? Who certified the death? Robertson, I suppose. He didn't have any doubts, did he?'

'No, but I think he may have been influenced in giving the certificate by the fact of the Serenite tablets in the bathroom. He asked me if Palgrave had mentioned that he suffered from hypertension, and I said No, I'd never had any medical conversation with him myself, but apparently he had talked about it to other people in the hotel. The whole thing – the bottle of tablets, and what Palgrave had said to people – it all fitted in – no earthly reason to suspect anything else. It was a perfectly natural inference to make – but I think now it may not have been correct. If it had been my business to give the certificate, I'd have given it without a second thought. The appearances are quite consistent with his having died from that cause. I'd never have thought about it since if it hadn't been for the odd disappearance of that snapshot . . .'

'But look here, Graham,' said Daventry, 'if you will allow me

58

to say so, aren't you relying a little too much on a rather fanciful story told you by an elderly lady? You know what these elderly ladies are like. They magnify some small detail and work the whole thing up.'

'Yes, I know,' said Dr Graham, unhappily. 'I know that. I've said to myself that it may be so, that it probably *is* so. But I can't quite convince myself. She was so very clear and detailed in her statement.'

'The whole thing seems wildly improbable to me,' said Daventry. 'Some old lady tells a story about a snapshot that ought not to be there – no I'm getting mixed myself – I mean the other way about don't I? – but the only thing you've really got to go on is that a chambermaid says that a bottle of pills which the authorities had relied on for evidence, wasn't in the Major's room the day before his death. But there are a hundred explanations for that. He might always have carried those pills about in his pocket.'

'It's possible, I suppose, yes.'

'Or the chambermaid may have made a mistake and she simply hadn't noticed them before – '

'That's possible, too.'

'Well, then.'

Graham said slowly:

'The girl was very positive.'

'Well, the St Honoré people are very excitable. You know. Emotional. Work themselves up easily. Are you thinking that she knows – a little more than she has said?'

'I think it might be so,' said Dr Graham slowly.

'You'd better try and get it out of her, if so. We don't want to make an unnecessary fuss – unless we've something definite to go on. If he didn't die of blood pressure, what do you think it was?'

'There are too many things it might be nowadays,' said Dr Graham.

'You mean things that don't leave recognizable traces?'

'Not everyone,' said Dr Graham dryly, 'is so considerate as to use arsenic.'

'Now let's get things quite clear – what's the suggestion? That a bottle of pills was substituted for the real ones? And that Major Palgrave was poisoned in that way?'

'No – it's not like that. That's what the girl – Victoria Something thinks – But she's got it all wrong – If it was decided to get rid of the Major – quickly – he would have been given something – most

59

likely in a drink of some kind. Then to make it appear a natural death, a bottle of the tablets prescribed to relieve blood pressure was put in his room. And the rumour was put about that he suffered from high blood pressure.'

'Who put the rumour about?'

'I've tried to find out – with no success – It's been too cleverly done. A says "I *think* B told me" – B, asked, says "No, I didn't say so but I do remember C mentioning it one day." C says "Several people talked about it – one of them, I think, was A." And there we are, back again.'

'Someone was clever?'

'Yes. As soon as the death was discovered, everybody seemed to be talking about the Major's high blood pressure and repeating round what other people had said.'

'Wouldn't it have been simpler just to poison him and let it go at that?'

'No. That might have meant an inquiry – possibly an autopsy – This way, a doctor would accept the death and give a certificate – as he did.'

'What do you want me to do? Go to the CID? Suggest they dig the chap up? It'd make a lot of stink – '

'It could be kept quite quiet.'

'Could it? In St Honoré? Think again! The grapevine would be on to it before it had happened. All the same,' Daventry sighed – 'I suppose we'll have to do something. But if you ask me, it's all a mare's nest!'

'I devoutly hope it is,' said Dr Graham.

CHAPTER ELEVEN

Evening at the Golden Palm

Molly rearranged a few of the table decorations in the dining-room, removed an extra knife, straightened a fork, reset a glass or two, stood back to look at the effect and then walked out on to the terrace outside. There was no one about just at present and she strolled to the far corner and stood by the balustrade. Soon another evening would begin. Chattering, talking, drinking, all so gay and carefree, the sort of life she had longed for and, up to a few days ago, had enjoyed so much. Now even Tim seemed anxious and worried. Natural, perhaps, that he should worry a little. It was important that this venture of theirs should turn out all right. After all, he had sunk all he had in it.

But that, thought Molly, is not *really* what's worrying him. It's *me*. But I don't see, said Molly to herself, why he should worry about *me*. Because he did worry about her. That she was quite sure of. The questions he put, the quick nervous glance he shot at her from time to time. 'But why?' thought Molly. 'I've been very careful.' She summed up things in her mind. She didn't understand it really herself. She couldn't remember when it had begun. She wasn't even very sure what it was. She'd begun to be frightened of people. She didn't know why. What could they do to her? What should they want to do to her?

She nodded her head, then started violently as a hand touched her arm. She spun round to find Gregory Dyson, slightly taken aback, looking apologetic.

'Ever so sorry. Did I startle you, little girl?'

Molly hated being called 'little girl'. She said quickly and brightly: 'I didn't hear you coming, Mr Dyson, so it made me jump.'

'Mr Dyson? We're very formal tonight. Aren't we all one great happy family here? Ed and me and Lucky and Evelyn and you and Tim and Esther Walters and old Rafiel. All the lot of us one happy family.'

'He's had plenty to drink already,' thought Molly. She smiled at him pleasantly.

'Oh! I come over the heavy hostess sometimes,' she said, lightly. 'Tim and I think it's more polite not to be too handy with Christian names.'

'Aw! we don't want any of that stuffed-shirt business. Now then, Molly my lovely, have a drink with me.'

'Ask me later,' said Molly. 'I have a few things to get on with.'

'Now don't run away.' His arm fastened round her arm. 'You're a lovely girl, Molly. I hope Tim appreciates his good luck.'

'Oh, I see to it that he does,' said Molly cheerfully.

'I could go for you, you know, in a big way.' He leered at her – 'though I wouldn't let my wife hear me say so.'

'Did you have a good trip this afternoon?'

'I suppose so. Between you and me I get a bit fed up sometimes. You can get tired of the birds and butterflies. What say you and I go for a little picnic on our own one day?'

'We'll have to see about that,' said Molly gaily. 'I'll be looking forward to it.'

With a light laugh she escaped, and went back into the bar.

'Hallo, Molly,' said Tim, 'you seem in a hurry. Who's that you've been with out there?'

He peered out.

'Gregory Dyson.'

'What does he want?'

'Wanted to make a pass at me,' said Molly.

'Blast him,' said Tim.

'Don't worry,' said Molly, 'I can do all the blasting necessary.'

Tim started to answer her, caught sight of Fernando and went over to him shouting out some directions. Molly slipped away through the kitchen door and down the steps to the beach.

Gregory Dyson swore under his breath. Then he walked slowly back in the direction of his bungalow. He had nearly got there when a voice spoke to him from the shadow of one of the bushes. He turned his head, startled. In the gathering dusk he thought for a moment that it was a ghostly figure that stood there. Then he laughed. It had looked like a faceless apparition but that was because, though the dress was white, the face was black.

Victoria stepped out of the bushes on to the path.

'Mr Dyson, please?'

'Yes. What is it?'

Ashamed of being startled, he spoke with a touch of impatience.

'I brought you this, sir.' She held out her hand. In it was a bottle of tablets. 'This belongs to you, doesn't it? Yes?'

'Oh, my bottle of Serenite tablets. Yes, of course. Where did you find it?'

'I found it where it had been put. In the gentleman's room.'

'What do you mean – in the gentleman's room?'

'The gentleman who is dead,' she added gravely. 'I do not think he sleeps very well in his grave.'

'Why the devil not?' asked Dyson.

Victoria stood looking at him.

'I still don't know what you're talking about. You mean you found this bottle of tablets in Major Palgrave's bungalow?'

'That's right, yes. After the doctor and the Jamestown people go away, they give me all the things in his bathroom to throw away. The toothpaste and the lotions, and all the other things – including this.'

'Well, why didn't you throw it away?'

'Because these are yours. You missed them. You remember, you asked about them?'

'Yes – well – yes, I did. I – I thought I'd just mislaid them.'

'No, you did not mislay them. They were taken from your bungalow and put in Major Palgrave's bungalow.'

'How do you know?' He spoke roughly.

'I know. I saw.' She smiled at him in a sudden flash of white teeth. 'Someone put them in the dead gentleman's room. Now I give them back to you.'

'Here – wait. What do you mean? What – who did you see?'

She hurried away, back into the darkness of the bushes. Greg made as to move after her and then stopped. He stood stroking his chin.

'What's the matter, Greg? Seen a ghost?' asked Mrs Dyson, as she came along the path from their bungalow.

'Thought I had for a minute or two.'

'Who was that you were talking to?'

'The coloured girl who does our place. Victoria, her name is, isn't it?'

'What did she want? Making a pass at you?'

'Don't be stupid, Lucky. That girl's got some idiotic idea into her head.'

'Idea about what?'

'You remember I couldn't find my Serenite the other day?'

'You said you couldn't.'

'What do you mean "I said I couldn't"?'

'Oh, for heck's sake, have you got to take me up on everything?'

'I'm sorry,' said Greg. 'Everybody goes about being so damn' mysterious.' He held out his hand with the bottle in it. 'That girl brought them back to me.'

'Had she pinched them?'

'No. She – found them somewhere I think.'

'Well, what of it? What's the mystery about?'

'Oh, nothing,' said Greg. 'She just riled me, that's all.'

'Look here, Greg, what is this stuff all about? Come along and have a drink before dinner.'

II

Molly had gone down to the beach. She pulled out one of the old basket chairs, one of the more rickety ones that were seldom used. She sat in it for a while looking at the sea, then suddenly she dropped her head in her hands and burst into tears. She sat there sobbing unrestrainedly for some time. Then she heard a rustle close by her and glanced up sharply to see Mrs Hillingdon looking down at her.

'Hallo, Evelyn, I didn't hear you. I – I'm sorry.'

'What's the matter, child?' said Evelyn. 'Something gone wrong?' She pulled another chair forward and sat down. 'Tell me.'

'There's nothing wrong,' said Molly. 'Nothing at all.'

'Of course there is. You wouldn't sit and cry here for nothing. Can't you tell me? Is it – some trouble between you and Tim?'

'Oh *no*.'

'I'm glad of that. You always look so happy together.'

'Not more than you do,' said Molly. 'Tim and I always think how wonderful it is that you and Edward should seem so happy together after being married so many years.'

'Oh, that,' said Evelyn. Her voice was sharp as she spoke but Molly hardly noticed.

'People bicker so,' she said, 'and have such rows. Even if they're quite fond of each other they still seem to have rows and not to mind a bit whether they have them in public or not.'

'Some people like living that way,' said Evelyn. 'It doesn't really mean anything.'

'Well, I think it's horrid,' said Molly.

'So do I, really,' said Evelyn.

'But to see you and Edward – '

'Oh it's no good, Molly. I can't let you go on thinking things of that kind. Edward and I – ' she paused. 'If you want to know the truth, we've hardly said a word to each other in private for the last three years.'

'What!' Molly stared at her, appalled. 'I – I can't believe it.'

'Oh, we both put up quite a good show,' said Evelyn. 'We're neither of us the kind that like having rows in public. And anyway there's nothing really to have a row about.'

'But what went wrong?' asked Molly.

'Just the usual.'

'What do you mean by the usual? Another – '

'Yes, another woman in the case, and I don't suppose it will be difficult for you to guess who the woman is.'

'Do you mean Mrs Dyson – Lucky?'

Evelyn nodded.

'I know they always flirt together a lot,' said Molly, 'but I thought that was just . . .'

'Just high spirits?' said Evelyn. 'Nothing behind it?'

'But why – ' Molly paused and tried again. 'But didn't you – oh I mean, well I suppose I oughtn't to ask.'

'Ask anything you like,' said Evelyn. 'I'm tired of never saying a word, tired of being a well-bred happy wife. Edward just lost his head completely about Lucky. He was stupid enough to come and tell me about it. It made him feel better I suppose. Truthful. Honourable. All that sort of stuff. It didn't occur to him to think that it wouldn't make *me* feel better.'

'Did he want to leave you?'

Evelyn shook her head. 'We've got two children, you know,' she said. 'Children whom we're both very fond of. They're at school in England. We didn't want to break up the home. And then of course, Lucky didn't want a divorce either. Greg's a very rich man. His first wife left a lot of money. So we agreed to live and let live – Edward and Lucky in happy immorality, Greg in blissful ignorance, and Edward and I just good friends.' She spoke with scalding bitterness.

'How – how can you bear it?'

'One gets used to anything. But sometimes – '

'Yes?' said Molly.

'Sometimes I'd like to kill that woman.'

The passion behind her voice startled Molly.

'Don't let's talk any more about me,' said Evelyn. 'Let's talk about you. I want to know what's the matter.'

Molly was silent for some moments and then she said, 'It's only – it's only that I think there's something wrong about me.'

'Wrong? What do you mean?'

Molly shook her head unhappily. 'I'm frightened,' she said. 'I'm terribly frightened.'

'Frightened of what?'

'Everything,' said Molly. 'It's – growing on me. Voices in the bushes, footsteps – or things that people say. As though someone were watching me all the time, spying on me. Somebody hates me. That's what I keep feeling. Somebody hates me.'

'My dear child.' Evelyn was shocked and startled. 'How long has this been going on?'

'I don't know. It came – it started by degrees. And there have been other things too.'

'What sort of things?'

'There are times,' said Molly slowly, 'that I can't account for, that I can't remember.'

'Do you mean you have blackouts – that sort of thing?'

'I suppose so. I mean sometimes it's – oh, say it's five o'clock – and I can't remember anything since about half past one or two.'

'Oh my dear, but that's just that you've been asleep. Had a doze.'

'No,' said Molly, 'it's not like that at all. Because you see, at the end of the time it's not as though I'd just dozed off. I'm in a different *place*. Sometimes I'm wearing different clothes and sometimes I seem to have been doing things – even saying things to people, talked to someone, and not remembering that I've done so.'

Evelyn looked shocked. 'But Molly, my dear, if this is so, then you ought to see a doctor.'

'I won't see a doctor! I don't want to. I wouldn't go *near* a doctor.'

Evelyn looked sharply down into her face, then she took the girl's hand in hers.

'You may be frightening yourself for nothing, Molly. You know there are all kinds of nervous disorders that aren't really serious at all. A doctor would soon reassure you.'

'He mightn't. He might say that there was something really wrong with me.'

'Why should there be anything wrong with you?'

'Because – ' Molly spoke and then was silent '– no reason, I suppose,' she said.

'Couldn't your family – haven't you any family, any mother or sisters or someone who could come out here?'

'I don't get on with my mother. I never have. I've got sisters. They're married but I suppose – I suppose they could come if I wanted them. But I don't want them. I don't want anyone – anyone except Tim.'

'Does Tim know about this? Have you told him?'

'Not really,' said Molly. 'But he's anxious about me and he watches me. It's as though he were trying to – to help me or to shield me. But if he does that it means I want shielding, doesn't it?'

66

'I think a lot of it may be imagination but I still think you ought to see a doctor.'

'Old Dr Graham? He wouldn't be any good.'

'There are other doctors on the island.'

'It's all right, really,' said Molly. 'I just – mustn't think of it. I expect, as you say, it's all imagination. Good gracious, it's getting frightfully late. I ought to be on duty now in the dining-room. I – I must go back.'

She looked sharply and almost offensively at Evelyn Hillingdon, and then hurried off. Evelyn stared after her.

CHAPTER TWELVE

Old Sins Cast Long Shadows

'I think as I am on to something, man.'

'What's that you say, Victoria?'

'I think I'm on to something. It may mean money. Big money.'

'Now look, girl, you be careful, you'll not tangle yourself up in something. Maybe I'd better tackle what it is.'

Victoria laughed, a deep rich chuckle.

'You wait and see,' she said. 'I know how to play this hand. It's money, man, it's big money. Something I see, and something I guess. I think I guess right.'

And again the soft rich chuckle rolled out on the night.

II

'Evelyn . . .'

'Yes?'

Evelyn Hillingdon spoke mechanically, without interest. She did not look at her husband.

'Evelyn, would you mind if we chucked all this and went home to England?'

She had been combing her short dark hair. Now her hands came down from her head sharply. She turned towards him.

'You mean – but we've only just come. We've not been out here in the islands for more than three weeks.'

'I know. But – would you mind?'

Her eyes searched him incredulously.

'You really want to go back to England? Back home?'

'Yes.'

'Leaving – Lucky?'

He winced.

'You've known all the time, I suppose, that – that it was going on?'

'Pretty well. Yes.'

'You've never said anything.'

'Why should I? We had the whole thing out years ago. Neither of us wanted to make a break. So we agreed to go our separate ways – but keep up the show in public.' Then she added before he could speak, 'But why are you so set on going back to England *now*?'

'Because I'm at breaking point. I can't stick it any longer, Evelyn. I can't.' The quiet Edward Hillingdon was transformed. His hands shook, he swallowed, his calm unemotional face seemed distorted by pain.

'For God's sake, Edward, what's the *matter*?'

'Nothing's the matter except that I want to get out of here – '

'You fell wildly in love with Lucky. And now you've got over it. Is that what you're telling me?'

'Yes. I don't suppose you'll ever feel the same.'

'Oh let's not go into that now! I want to understand what's upsetting you so much, Edward.'

'I'm not particularly upset.'

'But you are. Why?'

'Isn't it obvious?'

'No, it isn't,' said Evelyn. 'Let's put it in plain concrete terms. You've had an affair with a woman. That happens often enough. And now it's over. Or isn't it over? Perhaps it isn't over on *her* side. Is that it? Does Greg know about it? I've often wondered.'

'I don't know,' said Edward. 'He's never said anything. He always seems friendly enough.'

'Men can be extraordinarily obtuse,' said Evelyn thoughtfully. 'Or else – Perhaps Greg has got an outside interest of his own!'

'He's made passes at you, hasn't he?' said Edward. 'Answer me – I know he has – '

'Oh yes,' said Evelyn, carelessly, 'but he makes passes at everyone. That's just Greg. It doesn't ever really mean much, I imagine. It's just part of the Greg he-man act.'

'Do you care for him, Evelyn? I'd rather know the truth.'

'Greg? I'm quite fond of him – he amuses me. He's a good friend.'

'And that's all? I wish I could believe you.'

'I can't really see how it can possibly matter to you,' said Evelyn dryly.

'I suppose I deserve that.'

Evelyn walked to the window, looked out across the veranda and came back again.

'I wish you would tell me what's *really* upsetting you, Edward.'

'I've told you.'

'I wonder.'

'You can't understand, I suppose, how extraordinary a temporary madness of this kind can seem to you after you've got over it.'

'I can try, I suppose. But what's worrying me now is that Lucky seems to have got some kind of stranglehold upon you. She's not just a discarded mistress. She's a tigress with claws. You *must* tell me the truth, Edward. It's the only way if you want me to stand by you.'

Edward said in a low voice: 'If I don't get away from her soon – I shall kill her.'

'Kill Lucky? Why?'

'Because of what she made me do . . .'

'What did she make you do?'

'I helped her to commit a murder – '

The words were out – There was silence – Evelyn stared at him.

'Do you know what you are saying?'

'Yes. I didn't know I was doing it. There were things she asked me to get for her – at the chemist's. I didn't know – I hadn't the least idea what she wanted them for – She got me to copy out a prescription she had . . .'

'When was this?'

'Four years ago. When we were in Martinique. When – when Greg's wife – '

'You mean Greg's first wife – Gail? You mean Lucky poisoned her?'

'Yes – and I helped her. When I realized – '

Evelyn interrupted him.

'When you realized what had happened, Lucky pointed out to you that *you* had written out the prescription, that *you* had got the drugs, that you and she were in it together? Is that right?'

'Yes. She said she had done it out of pity – that Gail was suffering – that she had begged Lucky to get something that would end it all.'

'A mercy killing! I see. And you believed *that*?'

Edward Hillingdon was silent a moment – then he said:

'No – I didn't really – not deep down – I accepted it because I *wanted* to believe it – because I was infatuated with Lucky.'

'And afterwards – when she married Greg – did you still believe it?'

'I'd made myself believe it by then.'

'And Greg – how much did he know about it all?'

'Nothing at all.'

'That I find hard to believe!'

Edward Hillingdon broke out –

'Evelyn, I've *got* to get free of it all! That woman taunts me still with what I did. She knows I don't care for her any longer. Care for her? – I've come to hate her – But she makes me feel I'm tied to her – by the thing we did together – '

Evelyn walked up and down the room – then she stopped and faced him.

'The entire trouble with you, Edward, is that you are ridiculously sensitive – and also incredibly suggestible. That devil of a woman has got you just where she wants you by playing on your sense of guilt – And I'll tell you this in plain Bible terms, the guilt that weighs on you is the guilt of adultery – not murder – you were guilt-stricken about your affair with Lucky – and then she made a cat's-paw of you for her murder scheme, and managed to make you feel you shared her guilt. You *don't*.'

'Evelyn' . . . He stepped towards her –

She stepped back a minute – and looked at him searchingly.

'Is this all true, Edward – *Is* it? Or are you making it up?'

'Evelyn! Why on earth should I do such a thing?'

'I don't know,' said Evelyn Hillingdon slowly – 'It's just perhaps – because I find it hard to trust – anybody. And because – Oh! I don't know – I've got, I suppose, so that I don't know the truth when I hear it.'

'Let's chuck all this – Go back home to England.'

'Yes – We will – But not now.'

'Why not?'

'We must carry on as usual – just for the present. It's important. Do you understand, Edward? Don't let Lucky have an inkling of what we're up to – '

CHAPTER THIRTEEN

Exit Victoria Johnson

The evening was drawing to a close. The steel band was at last relaxing its efforts. Tim stood by the dining-room looking over the terrace. He extinguished a few lights on tables that had been vacated.

A voice spoke behind him. 'Tim, can I speak to you a moment?'

Tim Kendal started.

'Hallo, Evelyn, is there anything I can do for you?'

Evelyn looked round.

'Come to this table here, and let's sit down a minute.'

She led the way to a table at the extreme end of the terrace. There were no other people near them.

'Tim, you must forgive me talking to you, but I'm worried about Molly.'

His face changed at once.

'What about Molly?' he said stiffly.

'I don't think she's awfully well. She seems upset.'

'Things do seem to upset her rather easily just lately.'

'She ought to see a doctor, I think.'

'Yes, I know, but she doesn't want to. She'd hate it.'

'Why?'

'Eh? What d'you mean?'

'I said why? Why should she hate seeing a doctor?'

'Well,' said Tim rather vaguely, 'people do sometimes, you know. It's – well, it sort of makes them feel frightened about themselves.'

'You're worried about her yourself, aren't you, Tim?'

'Yes. Yes, I am rather.'

'Isn't there anyone of her family who could come out here to be with her?'

'No. That'd make things worse, far worse.'

'What *is* the trouble – with her family, I mean?'

'Oh, just one of those things. I suppose she's just highly strung and – she didn't get on with them – particularly her mother. She never has. They're – they're rather an odd family in some ways and she cut loose from them. Good thing she did, I think.'

Evelyn said hesitantly – 'She seems to have had blackouts, from what she told me, and to be frightened of people. Almost like persecution mania.'

'Don't say that,' said Tim angrily. 'Persecution mania! People always say that about people. Just because she – well – maybe she's a bit nervy. Coming out here to the West Indies. All the dark faces. You know, people are rather queer, sometimes, about the West Indies and coloured people.'

'Surely not girls like Molly?'

'Oh, how does one know the things people are frightened of? There are people who can't be in the room with cats. And other people who faint if a caterpillar drops on them.'

'I hate suggesting it – but don't you think perhaps she ought to see a – well, a psychiatrist?'

'*No!*' said Tim explosively. 'I won't have people like that monkeying about with her. I don't believe in them. They make people worse. If her mother had left psychiatrists alone . . .'

'So there *was* trouble of that kind in her family – was there? I mean a history of – ' she chose the word carefully – 'instability.'

'I don't want to talk about it – I took her away from it all and she was all right, quite all right. She has just got into a nervous state . . . But these things aren't hereditary. Everybody knows that nowadays. It's an exploded idea. Molly's perfectly sane. It's just that – oh! I believe it was that wretched old Palgrave dying that started it all off.'

'I see,' said Evelyn thoughtfully. 'But there was nothing really to worry anyone in Major Palgrave's death, was there?'

'No, of course there wasn't. But it's a kind of shock when somebody dies suddenly.'

He looked so desperate and defeated that Evelyn's heart smote her. She put her hand on his arm.

'Well, I hope you know what you're doing, Tim, but if I could help in any way – I mean if I could go with Molly to New York – I could fly with her there or Miami or somewhere where she could get really first-class medical advice.'

'It's very good of you, Evelyn, but Molly's all right. She's getting over it, anyway.'

Evelyn shook her head in doubt. She turned away slowly and looked along the line of the terrace. Most people had gone by now to their bungalows. Evelyn was walking towards her table to see if she'd left anything behind there, when she heard Tim give an exclamation. She looked up sharply. He was staring towards the steps at the end of the terrace and she followed his gaze. Then she too caught her breath.

Molly was coming up the steps from the beach. She was breathless with deep, sobbing breaths, her body swayed to and fro as she came, in a curious directionless run. Tim cried:

'*Molly*! What's the matter?'

He ran towards her and Evelyn followed him. Molly was at the top of the steps now and she stood there, both hands behind her back. She said in sobbing breaths:

'I found her . . . She's there in the bushes . . . There in the bushes . . . And look at my hands – look at my *hands*.' She held them out and Evelyn caught her breath as she saw the queer dark stains. They looked dark in the subdued lighting but she knew well enough that their real colour was red.

'What's happened, Molly?' cried Tim.

'Down there,' said Molly. She swayed on her feet. 'In the bushes . . .'

Tim hesitated, looked at Evelyn, then shoved Molly a little towards Evelyn and ran down the steps. Evelyn put her arm round the girl.

'Come. Sit down, Molly. Here. You'd better have something to drink.'

Molly collapsed in a chair and leaned forward on the table, her forehead on her crossed arm. Evelyn did not question her any more. She thought it better to leave her time to recover.

'It'll be all right, you know,' said Evelyn gently. 'It'll be all right.'

'I don't know,' said Molly. 'I don't know what happened. I don't know anything. I can't remember. I – ' she raised her head suddenly. 'What's the matter with me? What's the *matter* with me?'

'It's all right, child. It's all right.'

Tim was coming slowly up the steps. His face was ghastly. Evelyn looked up at him, raising her eyebrows in a query.

'It's one of our girls,' he said. 'What's-her-name – Victoria. Somebody's put a knife in her.'

CHAPTER FOURTEEN

Inquiry

Molly lay on her bed. Dr Graham and Dr Robertson, the West Indian police doctor, stood on one side – Tim on the other. Robertson had his hand on Molly's pulse – He nodded to the man at the foot of the bed, a slender dark man in police uniform, Inspector Weston of the St Honoré Police Force.

'A bare statement – no more,' the doctor said.

The other nodded.

'Now, Mrs Kendal – just tell us how you came to find this girl.'

For a moment or two it was as though the figure on the bed had not heard. Then she spoke in a faint, faraway voice.

'In the bushes – white . . .'

'You saw something white – and you looked to see what it was? Is that it?'

'Yes – white – lying there – I tried – tried to lift – she it – blood – blood all over my hands.'

She began to tremble.

Dr Graham shook his head at them. Robertson whispered – 'She can't stand much more.'

'What were you doing on the beach path, Mrs Kendal?'

'Warm – nice – by the sea – '

'You knew who the girl was?'

'Victoria – nice – nice girl – laughs – she used to laugh – oh! and now she won't – She won't ever laugh again. I'll never forget it – I'll never forget it – ' Her voice rose hysterically.

'Molly – don't.' It was Tim.

'Quiet – Quiet –,' Dr Robertson spoke with a soothing authority

– 'Just relax – relax – Now just a small prick – ' He withdrew the hypodermic.

'She'll be in no fit condition to be questioned for at least twenty-four hours,' he said – 'I'll let you know when.'

II

The big handsome negro looked from one to the other of the men sitting at the table.

'Ah declare to God,' he said. 'That's all Ah know. Ah don't know nothing but what Ah've told you.'

The perspiration stood out on his forehead. Daventry sighed. The man presiding at the table, Inspector Weston of the St Honoré CID, made a gesture of dismissal. Big Jim Ellis shuffled out of the room.

'It's not all he knows, of course,' Weston said. He had the soft Island voice. 'But it's all we shall learn from him.'

'You think he's in the clear himself?' asked Daventry.

'Yes. They seem to have been on good terms together.'

'They weren't married?'

A faint smile appeared on Lieutenant Weston's lips. 'No,' he said, 'they weren't married. We don't have so many marriages on the Island. They christen the children, though. He's had two children by Victoria.'

'Do you think he was in it, whatever it was, with her?'

'Probably not. I think he'd have been nervous of anything of that kind. And I'd say, too, that what she did know wasn't very much.'

'But enough for blackmail?'

'I don't know that I'd even call it that. I doubt if the girl would even understand that word. Payment for being discreet isn't thought of as blackmail. You see, some of the people who stay here are the rich playboy lot and their morals won't bear much investigation.' His voice was slightly scathing.

'We get all kinds, I agree,' said Daventry. 'A woman, maybe, doesn't want it known that she's sleeping around, so she gives a present to the girl who waits on her. It's tacitly understood that the payment's for discretion.'

'Exactly.'

'But this,' objected Daventry, 'wasn't anything of *that* kind. It was murder.'

'I should doubt, though, if the girl knew it was serious. She saw something, some puzzling incident, something to do presumably with this bottle of pills. It belonged to Mr Dyson, I understand. We'd better see him next.'

Gregory came in with his usual hearty air.

'Here I am,' he said, 'what can I do to help? Too bad about this girl. She was a nice girl. We both liked her. I suppose it was some sort of quarrel or other with a man, but she seemed quite happy and no signs of being in trouble about anything. I was kidding her only last night.'

'I believe you take a preparation, Mr Dyson, called Serenite?'

'Quite right. Little pink tablets.'

'You have them on prescription from a physician?'

'Yes. I can show it to you if you like. Suffer a bit from high blood pressure, like so many people do nowadays.'

'Very few people seem to be aware of that fact.'

'Well, I don't go talking about it. I – well, I've always been well and hearty and I never like people who talk about their ailments all the time.'

'How many of the pills do you take?'

'Two, three times a day.'

'Do you have a fairly large stock with you?'

'Yes. I've got about half a dozen bottles. But they're locked up, you know, in a suitcase. I only keep out one, the one that's in current use.'

'And you missed this bottle a short time ago, so I hear?'

'Quite right.'

'And you asked this girl, Victoria Johnson, whether she'd seen it?'

'Yes, I did.'

'And what did she say?'

'She said the last time she'd seen it was on the shelf in our bathroom. She said she'd looked around.'

'And after that?'

'She came and returned the bottle to me some time later. She said was this the bottle that was missing?'

'And you said?'

'I said "that's it, all right, where did you find it?" and she said it was in old Major Palgrave's room. I said "how on earth did it get there?"'

'And what did she answer to that?'

'She said she didn't know, but – ' he hesitated.

'Yes, Mr Dyson?'

'Well, she gave me the feeling that she did know a little more than she was saying, but I didn't pay much attention. After all, it wasn't very important. As I say, I've got other bottles of the pills with me. I thought perhaps I'd left it around in the restaurant or somewhere and old Palgrave picked it up for some reason. Perhaps he put it in his pocket meaning to return it to me, then forgot.'

'And that's all you know about it, Mr Dyson?'

'That's all I know. Sorry to be so unhelpful. Is it important? Why?'

Weston shrugged his shoulders. 'As things are, anything may be important.'

'I don't see where pills come in. I thought you'd want to know about what my movements were when this wretched girl was stabbed. I've written them all down as carefully as I can.'

Weston looked at him thoughtfully.

'Indeed? That was very helpful of you, Mr Dyson.'

'Save everybody trouble, I thought,' said Greg. He shoved a piece of paper across the table.

Weston studied it and Daventry drew his chair a little closer and looked over his shoulder.

'That seems very clear,' said Weston, after a moment or two. 'You and your wife were together changing for dinner in your bungalow until ten minutes to nine. You then went along to the terrace where you had drinks with Señora de Caspearo. At quarter past nine Colonel and Mrs Hillingdon joined you and you went in to dine. As far as you can remember, you went off to bed at about half past eleven.'

'Of course,' said Greg. 'I don't know what time the girl was actually killed –?'

There was a faint semblance of a question in the words. Lieutenant Weston, however, did not appear to notice it.

'Mrs Kendal found her, I understand? Must have been a very nasty shock for her.'

'Yes. Dr Robertson had to give her a sedative.'

'This was quite late, wasn't it, when most people had trundled off to bed?'

'Yes.'

'Had she been dead long? When Mrs Kendal found her, I mean?'

'We're not quite certain of the exact time yet,' said Weston smoothly.

'Poor little Molly. It must have been a nasty shock for her. Matter of fact, I didn't notice *her* about last night. Thought she might have had a headache or something and was lying down.'

'When was the last time you *did* see Mrs Kendal?'

'Oh, quite early, before I went to change. She was playing about with some of the table decorations and things. Rearranging the knives.'

'I see.'

'She was quite cheerful then,' said Greg. 'Kidding and all that. She's a great girl. We're all very fond of her. Tim's a lucky fellow.'

'Well, thank you, Mr Dyson. You can't remember anything more than you've told us about what the girl Victoria said when she returned the tablets?'

'No . . . It was just as I say. Asked me were these the tablets I'd been asking for. Said she'd found them in old Palgrave's room.'

'She'd no idea who put them there?'

'Don't think so – can't remember, really.'

'Thank you, Mr Dyson.'

Gregory went out.

'Very thoughtful of him,' said Weston, gently tapping the paper with his fingernail, 'to be so anxious to want us to know for sure exactly where he was last night.'

'A little over-anxious do you think?' asked Daventry.

'That's very difficult to tell. There are people, you know, who are naturally nervous about their own safety, about being mixed up with anything. It isn't necessarily because they have any guilty knowledge. On the other hand it might be just that.'

'What about opportunity? Nobody's really got much of an alibi, what with the band and the dancing and the coming and going. People are getting up, leaving their tables, coming back. Women go to powder their noses. Men take a stroll. Dyson could have slipped away. Anybody could have slipped away. But he does seem rather anxious to prove that *he* didn't.' He looked thoughtfully down at the paper. 'So Mrs Kendal was rearranging knives on the table,' he said. 'I rather wonder if he dragged that in on purpose.'

'Did it sound like it to you?'

The other considered. 'I think it's possible.'

Outside the room where the two men were sitting, a noise had arisen. A high voice was demanding admittance shrilly.

'I've got something to tell. I've got something to tell. You take me in to where the gentlemen are. You take me in to where the policeman is.'

A uniformed policeman pushed open the door.

'It's one of the cooks here,' he said, 'very anxious to see you. Says he's got something you ought to know.'

A frightened dark man in a cook's cap pushed past him and came into the room. It was one of the minor cooks. A Cuban, not a native of St Honoré.

'I tell you something. I tell you,' he said. 'She come through my kitchen, she did, and she had a knife with her. A knife, I tell you. She had a knife in her hand. She come through my kitchen and out the door. Out into the garden. I saw her.'

'Now calm down,' said Daventry, 'calm down. Who are you talking about?'

'I tell you who I'm talking about. I'm talking about the boss's wife. Mrs Kendal. I'm talking about her. She have a knife in her hand and she go out into the dark. Before dinner that was – and *she didn't come back.*'

CHAPTER FIFTEEN

Inquiry continued

'Can we have a word with you, Mr Kendal?'

'Of course.' Tim looked up from his desk. He pushed some papers aside and indicated chairs. His face was drawn and miserable. 'How are you getting on? Got any forwarder? There seems to be a doom in this place. People are wanting to leave, you know, asking about air passages. Just when it seemed everything was being a success. Oh lord, you don't know what it means, this place, to me and to Molly. We staked everything on it.'

'It's very hard on you, I know,' said Inspector Weston. 'Don't think that we don't sympathize.'

'If it all could be cleared up quickly,' said Tim. 'This wretched girl Victoria – Oh! I oughtn't to talk about her like that. She was quite a good sort, Victoria was. But – but there must be some quite simple reason, some – kind of intrigue, or love affair she had. Perhaps her husband – '

'Jim Ellis wasn't her husband, and they seemed a settled sort of couple.'

'If it could only be cleared up *quickly*,' said Tim again. 'I'm sorry. You wanted to talk to me about something, ask me something.'

'Yes. It was about last night. According to medical evidence Victoria was killed some time between 10.30 pm and midnight. Alibis under the circumstances that prevail here are not very easy to prove. People are moving about, dancing, walking away from the terrace, coming back. It's all very difficult.'

'I suppose so. But does that mean that you definitely consider Victoria was killed by one of the guests here?'

'Well, we have to examine that possibility, Mr Kendal. What I want to ask you particularly about, is a statement made by one of your cooks.'

'Oh? Which one? What does he say?'

'He's a Cuban, I understand.'

'We've got two Cubans and a Puerto Rican.'

'This man Enrico states that your wife passed through the kitchen on her way from the dining-room, and went out into the garden and that she was carrying a knife.'

Tim stared at him.

'Molly, carrying a knife? Well, why shouldn't she? I mean – why – you don't think – what are you trying to suggest?'

'I am talking of the time before people had come into the dining-room. It would be, I suppose, some time about 8.30. You yourself were in the dining-room talking to the head waiter, Fernando, I believe.'

'Yes.' Tim cast his mind back. 'Yes, I remember.'

'And your wife came in from the terrace?'

'Yes, she did,' Tim agreed. 'She always went out to look over the tables. Sometimes the boys set things wrong, forgot some of the cutlery, things like that. Very likely that's what it was. She may have been rearranging cutlery or something. She might have had a spare knife or a spoon, something like that in her hand.'

'And she came from the terrace into the dining-room. Did she speak to you?'

80

'Yes, we had a word or two together.'

'What did she say? Can you remember?'

'I think I asked her who she'd been talking to. I heard her voice out there.'

'And who did she say she'd been talking to?'

'Gregory Dyson.'

'Ah. Yes. That is what *he* said.'

Tim went on, 'He'd been making a pass at her, I understand. He was a bit given to that kind of thing. It annoyed me and I said "Blast him" and Molly laughed and said she could do all the blasting that needed to be done. Molly's a very clever girl that way. It's not always an easy position, you know. You can't offend guests, and so an attractive girl like Molly has to pass things off with a laugh and a shrug. Gregory Dyson finds it difficult to keep his hands off any good-looking woman.'

'Had there been an altercation between them?'

'No, I don't think so. I think, as I say, she just laughed it off as usual.'

'You can't say definitely whether she had a knife in her hand or not?'

'I can't remember – I'm almost sure she didn't – in fact quite sure she didn't.'

'But you said just now . . .'

'Look here, what I meant was that if she was in the dining-room or in the kitchen it's quite likely she might have picked up a knife or had one in her hand. Matter of fact I can remember quite well, she came in from the dining-room and she had *nothing* in her hand. Nothing at all. That's definite.'

'I see,' said Weston.

Tim looked at him uneasily.

'What on earth is this you're getting at? What did that damn' fool Enrico – Manuel – whoever it was – say?'

'He said your wife came out into the kitchen, that she looked upset, that she had a knife in her hand.'

'He's just dramatizing.'

'Did you have any further conversation with your wife during dinner or after?'

'No, I don't think I did really. Matter of fact I was rather busy.'

'Was your wife there in the dining-room during the meal?'

'I – oh – yes, we always move about among the guests and things like that. See how things are going on.'

'Did you speak to her at all?'

'No, I don't think I did . . . We're usually fairly busy. We don't always notice what the other one's doing and we certainly haven't got time to talk to each other.'

'Actually you don't remember speaking to her until she came up the steps three hours later, after finding the body?'

'It was an awful shock for her. It upset her terribly.'

'I know. A very unpleasant experience. How did she come to be walking along the beach path?'

'After the stress of dinner being served, she often does go for a turn. You know, get away from the guests for a minute or two, get a breather.'

'When she came back, I understand you were talking to Mrs Hillingdon.'

'Yes. Practically everyone else had gone to bed.'

'What was the subject of your conversation with Mrs Hillingdon?'

'Nothing particular. Why? What's she been saying?'

'So far she hasn't said anything. We haven't asked her.'

'We were just talking of this and that. Molly, and hotel running, and one thing and another.'

'And then – your wife came up the steps of the terrace and told you what had happened?'

'Yes.'

'There was blood on her hands?'

'Of course there was! She'd been over the girl, tried to lift her, couldn't understand what had happened, what was the matter with her. Of course there was blood on her hands! Look here, what the hell are you suggesting? You *are* suggesting something?'

'Please calm down,' said Daventry. 'It's all a great strain on you I know, Tim, but we have to get the facts clear. I understand your wife hasn't been feeling very well lately?'

'Nonsense – she's all right. Major Palgrave's death upset her a bit. Naturally. She's a sensitive girl.'

'We shall have to ask her a few questions as soon as she's fit enough,' said Weston.

'Well, you can't now. The doctor gave her a sedative and said she wasn't to be disturbed. I won't have her upset and brow-beaten, d'you hear?'

'We're not going to do any brow-beating,' said Weston. 'We've just got to get the facts clear. We won't disturb her at present, but as soon as the doctor allows us, we'll have to see her.' His voice was gentle – inflexible.

Tim looked at him, opened his mouth, but said nothing.

II

Evelyn Hillingdon, calm and composed as usual, sat down in the chair indicated. She considered the few questions asked her, taking her time over it. Her dark, intelligent eyes looked at Weston thoughtfully.

'Yes,' she said, 'I was talking to Mr Kendal on the terrace when his wife came up the steps and told us about the murder.'

'Your husband wasn't there?'

'No, he had gone to bed.'

'Had you any special reason for your conversation with Mr Kendal?'

Evelyn raised her finely pencilled eyebrows – It was a definite rebuke.

She said coldly:

'What a very odd question. No – there was nothing special about our conversation.'

'Did you discuss the matter of his wife's health?'

Again Evelyn took her time.

'I really can't remember,' she said at last.

'Are you sure of that?'

'Sure that I can't remember? What a curious way of putting it – one talks about so many things at different times.'

'Mrs Kendal has not been in good health lately, I understand.'

'She looked quite all right – a little tired perhaps. Of course running a place like this means a lot of worries, and she is quite inexperienced. Naturally, she gets flustered now and then.'

'Flustered.' Weston repeated the word. 'That was the way you would describe it?'

'It's an old-fashioned word, perhaps, but just as good as the modern jargon we use for everything – A "virus infection" for a bilious attack – an "anxiety neurosis" for the minor bothers of daily life – '

Her smile made Weston feel slightly ridiculous. He thought to himself that Evelyn Hillingdon was a clever woman. He looked at

83

Daventry whose face remained unmoved and wondered what he thought.

'Thank you, Mrs Hillingdon,' said Weston.

III

'We don't want to worry you, Mrs Kendal, but we have to have your account of just how you came to find this girl. Dr Graham says you are sufficiently recovered to talk about it now.'

'Oh yes,' said Molly, 'I'm really quite all right again.' She gave them a small nervous smile. 'It was just the shock – It *was* rather awful, you know.'

'Yes, indeed it must have been – I understand you went for a walk after dinner.'

'Yes – I often do.'

Her eyes shifted, Daventry noticed, and the fingers of her hands twined and untwined about each other.

'What time would that have been, Mrs Kendal?' asked Weston.

'Well, I don't really know – we don't go much by the time.'

'The steel band was still playing?'

'Yes – at least – I think so – I can't really remember.'

'And you walked – which way?'

'Oh, along the beach path.'

'To the left or the right?'

'Oh! First one way – and then the other – I – I – really didn't notice.'

'Why didn't you notice, Mrs Kendal?'

She frowned.

'I suppose I was – well – thinking of things.'

'Thinking of anything particular?'

'No – No – Nothing particular – Just things that had to be done – seen to – in the hotel.' Again that nervous twining and untwining of fingers. 'And then – I noticed something white – in a clump of hibiscus bushes – and I wondered what it was. I stopped and – and pulled – ' She swallowed convulsively – 'And it was her – Victoria – all huddled up – and I tried to raise her head up and I got – blood – on my hands.'

She looked at them and repeated wonderingly as though recalling something impossible:

'Blood – on my hands.'

84

'Yes – Yes – A very dreadful experience. There is no need for you to tell us more about that part of it – How long had you been walking, do you think, when you found her – '

'I don't know – I have no idea.'

'An hour? Half an hour? Or more than an hour – '

'I don't know,' Molly repeated.

Daventry asked in a quiet everyday voice:

'Did you take a knife with you on your – walk?'

'A knife?' Molly sounded surprised. 'Why should I take a knife?'

'I only ask because one of the kitchen staff mentioned that you had a knife in your hand when you went out of the kitchen into the garden.'

Molly frowned.

'But I didn't go out of the kitchen – oh you mean earlier – before dinner – I – I don't *think* so – '

'You had been rearranging the cutlery on the tables, perhaps.'

'I have to, sometimes. They lay things wrong – not enough knives – or too many. The wrong number of forks and spoons – that sort of thing.'

'So you may have gone out of the kitchen that evening carrying a knife in your hand?'

'I don't think I did – I'm sure I didn't – ' She added – 'Tim was there – he would know. Ask him.'

'Did you like this girl – Victoria – was she good at her work?' asked Weston.

'Yes – she was a very nice girl.'

'You had no dispute with her?'

'Dispute? No.'

'She had never threatened you – in any way?'

'Threatened me? What do you mean?'

'It doesn't matter – You have no idea of who could have killed her? No idea at all?'

'None.' She spoke positively.

'Well, thank you, Mrs Kendal.' He smiled. 'It wasn't so terrible, was it?'

'That's all?'

'That's all for now.'

'Daventry got up, opened the door for her, and watched her go out.

'Tim would know,' he quoted as he returned to his chair. 'And Tim says definitely that she *didn't* have a knife.'

85

Weston said gravely:

'I think that that is what any husband would feel called upon to say.'

'A table knife seems a very poor type of knife to use for murder.'

'But it was a *steak* knife, Mr Daventry. Steaks were on the menu that evening. Steak knives are kept sharp.'

'I really can't bring myself to believe that that girl we've just been talking to is a red-handed murderess, Weston.'

'It is not necessary to believe it yet. It could be that Mrs Kendal went out into the garden before dinner, clasping a knife she had taken off one of the tables because it was superfluous – she might not even have noticed she was holding it, and she could have put it down somewhere – or dropped it – It could have been found and used by someone else – I, too, think her an unlikely murderess.'

'All the same,' said Daventry thoughtfully, 'I'm pretty sure she is not telling all she knows. Her vagueness over time is odd – where was she – what was she doing out there? Nobody, so far, seems to have noticed her in the dining-room that evening.'

'The husband was about as usual – but not the wife – '

'You think she went to meet someone – Victoria Johnson?'

'Perhaps – or perhaps she saw whoever it was who did go to meet Victoria.'

'You're thinking of Gregory Dyson?'

'We know he was talking to Victoria earlier – He may have arranged to meet her again later – everyone moved around freely on the terrace, remember – dancing, drinking – in and out of the bar.'

'No alibi like a steel band,' said Daventry wryly.

CHAPTER SIXTEEN

Miss Marple seeks Assistance

If anybody had been there to observe the gentle-looking elderly lady who stood meditatively on the loggia outside her bungalow, they would have thought she had nothing more on her mind than deliberation on how to arrange her time that day – An expedition, perhaps, to Castle Cliff – a visit to Jamestown – a nice drive and lunch at Pelican Point – or just a quiet morning on the beach –

But the gentle old lady was deliberating quite other matters – she was in militant mood.

'*Something has got to be done*,' said Miss Marple to herself.

Moreover, she was convinced that there was no time to be lost – There was urgency.

But who was there that she could convince of that fact? Given time, she thought she could find out the truth by herself.

She had found out a good deal. But not enough – not nearly enough. And time was short.

She realized, bitterly, that here on this Paradise of an island, she had none of her usual allies.

She thought regretfully of her friends in England – Sir Henry Clithering – always willing to listen indulgently – his godson Dermot, who in spite of his increased status at Scotland Yard was still ready to believe that when Miss Marple voiced an opinion there was usually something behind it.

But would that soft-voiced native police officer pay any attention to an old lady's urgency? Dr Graham? But Dr Graham was not what she needed – too gentle and hesitant, certainly not a man of quick decisions and rapid actions.

Miss Marple, feeling rather like a humble deputy of the Almighty, almost cried aloud her need in Biblical phrasing.

Who will go for me?

Whom shall I send?

The sound that reached her ears a moment later was not instantly recognized by her as an answer to prayer – far from it – At the back of her mind it registered only as a man possibly calling his dog.

'Hi!'

Miss Marple, lost in perplexity, paid no attention.

'Hi!' The volume thus increased, Miss Marple looked vaguely round.

'HI!' called Mr Rafiel impatiently. He added – 'You there – '

Miss Marple had not at first realized that Mr Rafiel's 'Hi You' was addressed to her. It was not a method that anyone had ever used before to summon her. It was certainly not a gentlemanly mode of address. Miss Marple did not resent it, because people seldom did resent Mr Rafiel's somewhat arbitrary method of doing things. He was a law unto himself and people accepted him as such. Miss Marple looked across the intervening space between her bungalow and his. Mr Rafiel was sitting outside on his loggia and he beckoned her.

'You were calling me?' she asked.

'Of course I was calling you,' said Mr Rafiel. 'Who did you think I was calling – a cat? Come over here.'

Miss Marple looked round for her handbag, picked it up, and crossed the intervening space.

'I can't come to you unless someone helps me,' explained Mr Rafiel, 'so you've got to come to me.'

'Oh yes,' said Miss Marple, 'I quite understand *that*.'

Mr Rafiel pointed to an adjacent chair. 'Sit down,' he said, 'I want to talk to you. Something damned odd is going on in this island.'

'Yes, indeed,' agreed Miss Marple, taking the chair as indicated. By sheer habit she drew her knitting out of her bag.

'Don't start knitting again,' said Mr Rafiel, 'I can't stand it. I hate women knitting. It irritates me.'

Miss Marple returned her knitting to her bag. She did this with no undue air of meekness, rather with the air of one who makes allowances for a fractious patient.

'There's a lot of chit-chat going on,' said Mr Rafiel, 'and I bet you're in the forefront of it. You and the parson and his sister.'

'It is, perhaps, only natural that there should be chit-chat,' said Miss Marple with spirit, 'given the circumstances.'

'This Island girl gets herself knifed. Found in the bushes. *Might* be ordinary enough. That chap she was living with might have got jealous of another man – or he'd got himself another girl and she got jealous and they had a row. Sex in the tropics. That sort of stuff. What do you say?'

'No,' said Miss Marple, shaking her head.

'The authorities don't think so, either.'

'They would say more to you,' pointed out Miss Marple, 'than they would say to me.'

'All the same, I bet you know more about it than I do. You've listened to the tittle-tattle.'

'Certainly I have,' said Miss Marple.

'Nothing much else to do, have you, except listen to tittle-tattle?'

'It is often informative and useful.'

'D'you know,' said Mr Rafiel, studying her attentively. 'I made

88

a mistake about you. I don't often make mistakes about people. There's a lot more to you than I thought there was. All these rumours about Major Palgrave and the stories he told. You think he was bumped off, don't you?'

'I very much fear so,' said Miss Marple.

'Well, he was,' said Mr Rafiel.

Miss Marple drew a deep breath. 'That is definite, is it?' she asked.

'Yes, it's definite enough. I had it from Daventry. I'm not breaking a confidence because the facts of the autopsy will have to come out. You told Graham something, he went to Daventry, Daventry went to the Administrator, the CID were informed, and between them they agreed that things looked fishy, so they dug up old Palgrave and had a look.'

'And they found?' Miss Marple paused interrogatively.

'They found he'd had a lethal dose of something that only a doctor could pronounce properly. As far as I remember it sounds vaguely like di-flor, hexagonalethylcarbenzol. That's not the right name. But that's roughly what it *sounds* like. The police doctor put it that way so that nobody should know, I suppose, what it really *was*. The stuff's probably got some quite simple nice easy name like Evipan or Veronal or Easton's Syrup or something of that kind. This is its official name to baffle laymen with. Anyway, a sizeable dose of it, I gather, would produce death, and the signs would be much the same as those of high blood pressure aggravated by over-indulgence in alcohol on a gay evening. In fact, it all looked perfectly natural and nobody questioned it for a moment. Just said "poor old chap" and buried him quick. Now they wonder if he ever had high blood pressure at all. Did he ever say he had to you?'

'No.'

'Exactly! And yet everyone seems to have taken it as a fact.'

'Apparently he told people he had.'

'It's like seeing ghosts,' said Mr Rafiel. 'You never meet the chap who's seen the ghost himself. It's always the second cousin of his aunt, or a friend, or a friend of a friend. But leave that for a moment. They thought he had blood pressure, because there was a bottle of tablets controlling blood pressure found in his room but – and now we're coming to the point – I gather that this girl who was killed went about saying that that bottle was put there by somebody else, and that *actually* it belonged to that fellow Greg.'

'Mr Dyson *has* got blood pressure. His wife mentioned it,' said Miss Marple.

'So it was put in Palgrave's room to suggest that he suffered from blood pressure and to make his death seem natural.'

'Exactly,' said Miss Marple. 'And the story was put about, very cleverly, that he had frequently mentioned to people that he had high blood pressure. But you know, it's very easy to put about a story. Very easy. I've seen a lot of it in my time.'

'I bet you have,' said Mr Rafiel.

'It only needs a murmur here and there,' said Miss Marple. 'You don't say it of your own knowledge, you just say that Mrs B. told you that Colonel C. told her. It's always at second hand or third hand or fourth hand and it's very difficult to find out who was the original whisperer. Oh yes, it can be done. And the people you say it to go on and repeat it to others as if they know it of their own knowledge.'

'Somebody's been clever,' said Mr Rafiel thoughtfully.

'Yes,' said Miss Marple, 'I think somebody's been quite clever.'

'This girl saw something, or knew something and tried blackmail, I suppose,' said Mr Rafiel.

'She mayn't have thought of it as blackmail,' said Miss Marple. 'In these large hotels, there are often things the maids know that some people would rather not have repeated. And so they hand out a larger tip or a little present of money. The girl possibly didn't realize at first the importance of what she knew.'

'Still, she got a knife in her back all right,' said Mr Rafiel brutally.

'Yes. Evidently someone couldn't afford to let her talk.'

'Well? Let's hear what you think about it all.'

Miss Marple looked at him thoughtfully.

'Why should you think I know any more than you do, Mr Rafiel?'

'Probably you don't,' said Mr Rafiel, 'but I'm interested to hear your ideas about what you do know.'

'But why?'

'There's not very much to do out here,' said Mr Rafiel, 'except make money.'

Miss Marple looked slightly surprised.

'Make money? Out here?'

'You can send out half a dozen cables in code every day if you like,' said Mr Rafiel. 'That's how I amuse myself.'

'Take-over bids?' Miss Marple asked doubtfully, in the tone of one who speaks a foreign language.

'That kind of thing,' agreed Mr Rafiel. 'Pitting your wits against other people's wits. The trouble is it doesn't occupy enough time, so I've got interested in this business. It's aroused my curiosity. Palgrave spent a good deal of his time talking to you. Nobody else would be bothered with him, I expect. What did he say?'

'He told me a good many stories,' said Miss Marple.

'I know he did. Damn' boring, most of them. And you hadn't only got to hear them once. If you got anywhere within range you heard them three or four times over.'

'I know,' said Miss Marple. 'I'm afraid that does happen when gentlemen get older.'

Mr Rafiel looked at her very sharply.

'I don't tell stories,' he said. 'Go on. It started with one of Palgrave's stories, did it?'

'He said he knew a murderer,' said Miss Marple. 'There's nothing really special about that,' she added in her gentle voice, 'because I suppose it happens to nearly everybody.'

'I don't follow you,' said Mr Rafiel.

'I don't mean specifically,' said Miss Marple, 'but surely, Mr Rafiel, if you cast over in your mind your recollections of various events in your life, hasn't there nearly always been an occasion when somebody has made some careless reference such as "Oh yes I knew the So-and-So's quite well – he died very suddenly and they always say his wife did him in, but I daresay that's just gossip." You've heard people say something like that, haven't you?'

'Well, I suppose so – yes, something of the kind. But not – well, not seriously.'

'Exactly,' said Miss Marple, 'but Major Palgrave was a very serious man. I think he enjoyed telling this story. He said he had a snapshot of the murderer. He was going to show it to me but – actually – he didn't.'

'Why?'

'Because he saw something,' said Miss Marple. 'Saw someone, I suspect. His face got very red and he shoved back the snapshot into his wallet and began talking on another subject.'

'Who did he see?'

'I've thought about that a good deal,' said Miss Marple. 'I was sitting outside my bungalow, and he was sitting nearly opposite me and – whatever he saw, he saw over my right shoulder.'

'Someone coming along the path then from behind you on the right, the path from the creek and the car park – '

'Yes.'

'*Was* anyone coming along the path?'

'Mr and Mrs Dyson and Colonel and Mrs Hillingdon.'

'Anybody else?'

'Not that I can find out. Of course, your bungalow would also be in his line of vision . . .'

'Ah. Then we include – shall we say – Esther Walters and my chap, Jackson. Is that right? Either of them, I suppose, *might* have come out of the bungalow and gone back inside again without your seeing them.'

'They might have,' said Miss Marple, 'I didn't turn my head at once.'

'The Dysons, the Hillingdons, Esther, Jackson. One of them's a murderer. Or, of course, myself,' he added; obviously as an afterthought.

Miss Marple smiled faintly.

'And he spoke of the murderer as a *man*?'

'Yes.'

'Right. That cuts out Evelyn Hillingdon, Lucky and Esther Walters. So your murderer, allowing that all this far-fetched nonsense is true, your murderer is Dyson, Hillingdon or my smooth-tongued Jackson.'

'Or yourself,' said Miss Marple.

Mr Rafiel ignored this last point.

'Don't say things to irritate me,' he said. 'I'll tell you the first thing that strikes me, and which you don't seem to have thought of. *If* it's one of those three, why the devil didn't old Palgrave recognize him before? Dash it all, they've all been sitting round looking at each other for the last two weeks. That doesn't seem to make sense.'

'I think it could,' said Miss Marple.

'Well, tell me how.'

'You see, in Major Palgrave's story he hadn't seen this man *himself* at any time. It was a story told to him by a doctor. The doctor gave him the snapshot as a curiosity. Major Palgrave may have looked at the snapshot fairly closely at the time but after that he'd just stack it away in his wallet and keep it as a souvenir. Occasionally, perhaps, he'd take it out and show it to someone he was telling the story to. And another thing, Mr Rafiel, we don't know how long ago this happened. He didn't give me any indication of that when he was telling the story. I mean this may have been a story he's been telling to people for *years*. Five years

92

– ten years – longer still perhaps. Some of his tiger stories go back about twenty years.'

'They would!' said Mr Rafiel.

'So I don't suppose for a moment that Major Palgrave would recognize the face in the snapshot if he came across the man casually. What I think happened, what I'm almost sure *must* have happened, is that as he told his story he fumbled for the snapshot, took it out, looked down at it studying the face and then looked up to see *the same face*, or one with a strong resemblance, coming towards him from a distance of about ten or twelve feet away.'

'Yes,' said Mr Rafiel consideringly, 'yes, that's possible.'

'He was taken aback,' said Miss Marple, 'and he shoved it back in his wallet and began to talk loudly about something else.'

'He couldn't have been sure,' said Mr Rafiel, shrewdly.

'No,' said Miss Marple, 'he couldn't have been sure. But of course afterwards he would have studied the snapshot very carefully and would have looked at the man and tried to make up his mind whether it was just a likeness or whether it could actually be the same person.'

Mr Rafiel reflected a moment or two, then he shook his head.

'There's something wrong here. The motive's inadequate. Absolutely inadequate. He was speaking to you loudly, was he?'

'Yes,' said Miss Marple, 'quite loudly. He always did.'

'True enough. Yes, he did shout. So whoever was approaching would hear what he said?'

'I should imagine you could hear it for quite a good radius round.'

Mr Rafiel shook his head again. He said, 'It's fantastic, too fantastic. Anybody would laugh at such a story. Here's an old booby telling a story about another story somebody told him, and showing a snapshot, and all of it centring round a murder which had taken place years ago! Or at any rate, a year or two. How on earth can *that* worry the man in question? No evidence, just a bit of hearsay, a story at third hand. He could even admit a likeness, he could say: "Yes, I *do* look rather like that fellow, don't I! Ha, ha!" Nobody's going to take old Palgrave's identification seriously. Don't tell me so, because I won't believe it. No, the chap, if it *was* the chap, had nothing to fear – nothing whatever. It's the kind of accusation he can just laugh off. Why on earth should he proceed to murder old Palgrave? It's absolutely unnecessary. You must see that.'

'Oh I do see that,' said Miss Marple. 'I couldn't agree with you more. That's what makes me uneasy. So very uneasy that I really couldn't sleep last night.'

Mr Rafiel stared at her. 'Let's hear what's on your mind,' he said quietly.

'I may be entirely wrong,' said Miss Marple hesitantly.

'Probably you are,' said Mr Rafiel with his usual lack of courtesy, 'but at any rate let's hear what you've thought up in the small hours.'

'There could be a very powerful motive if – '

'If what?'

'If there was going to be – quite soon – *another murder*.'

Mr Rafiel stared at her. He tried to pull himself up a little in his chair.

'Let's get this clear,' he said.

'I am so bad at explaining.' Miss Marple spoke rapidly and rather incoherently. A pink flush rose to her cheeks. 'Supposing there was a murder planned. If you remember, the story Major Palgrave told me concerned a man whose wife died under suspicious circumstances. Then, after a certain lapse of time, there was another murder under exactly the same circumstances. A man of a different name had a wife who died in much the same way and the doctor who was telling it recognized him as the same man, although he'd changed his name. Well, it does look, doesn't it, as though this murderer might be the kind of murderer who made a habit of the thing?'

'You mean like Smith, Brides in the Bath, that kind of thing. Yes.'

'As far as I can make out,' said Miss Marple, 'and from what I have heard and read, a man who does a wicked thing like this and gets away with it the first time, is, alas, *encouraged*. He thinks it's easy, he thinks he's clever. And so he repeats it. And in the end, as you say, like Smith and the Brides in the Bath, it becomes a *habit*. Each time in a different place and each time the man changes his name. But the crimes themselves are all very much alike. So it seems to me, although I may be quite wrong – '

'But you don't think you are wrong, do you?' Mr Rafiel put in shrewdly.

Miss Marple went on without answering. '– that if that *were* so and if this – this person had got things all lined up for a murder out here, for getting rid of *another* wife, say, and if this is crime

94

three or four, well then, the Major's story *would* matter because the murderer couldn't afford to have any similarity pointed out. If you remember, that was exactly the way Smith got caught. The circumstances of a crime attracted the attention of somebody who compared it with a newspaper clipping of some other case. So you do see, don't you, that if this wicked person has got a crime planned, arranged, and shortly about to take place, he couldn't afford to let Major Palgrave go about telling this story and showing that snapshot.'

She stopped and looked appealingly at Mr Rafiel.

'So you see he had to do something very quickly, as quickly as possible.'

Mr Rafiel spoke. 'In fact, that very same night, eh?'

'Yes,' said Miss Marple.

'Quick work,' said Mr Rafiel, 'but it could be done. Put the tablets in old Palgrave's room, spread the blood pressure rumour about and add a little of our fourteen-syllable drug to a Planters Punch. Is that it?'

'Yes – But that's all over – we needn't worry about it. It's the *future*. It's now. With Major Palgrave out of the way and the snapshot destroyed, *this man will go on with his murder as planned*.'

Mr Rafiel whistled.

'You've got it all worked out, haven't you?'

Miss Marple nodded. She said in a most unaccustomed voice, firm and almost dictarorial, 'And we've got to stop it. *You've* got to stop it, Mr Rafiel.'

'Me?' said Mr Rafiel, astonished, 'why me?'

'Because you're rich and important,' said Miss Marple, simply. 'People will take notice of what you say or suggest. They wouldn't listen to me for a moment. They would say that I was an old lady imagining things.'

'They might at that,' said Mr Rafiel. 'More fools if they did. I must say, though, that nobody would think you had any brains in your head to hear your usual line of talk. Actually, you've got a logical mind. Very few women have.' He shifted himself uncomfortably in his chair. 'Where the hell's Esther or Jackson?' he said. 'I need resettling. No, it's no good your doing it. You're not strong enough. I don't know what they mean, leaving me alone like this.'

'I'll go and find them.'

'No, you won't. You'll stay here – and thrash this out. Which of them is it? The egregious Greg? The quiet Edward Hillingdon or my fellow Jackson? It's got to be one of the three, hasn't it?'

CHAPTER SEVENTEEN

Mr Rafiel takes Charge

'I don't know,' said Miss Marple.

'What do you mean? What have we been talking about for the last twenty minutes?'

'It has occurred to me that I may have been wrong.'

Mr Rafiel stared at her.

'Scatty after all!' he said disgustedly. 'And you sounded so sure of yourself.'

'Oh, I am sure – about the *murder*. It's the *murderer* I'm not sure about. You see I've found out that Major Palgrave had more than one murder story – you told me yourself he'd told you one about a kind of Lucrezia Borgia – '

'So he did – at that. But that was quite a different kind of story.'

'I know. And Mrs Walters said he had one about someone being gassed in a gas oven – '

'But the story he told you – '

Miss Marple allowed herself to interrupt – a thing that did not often happen to Mr Rafiel.

She spoke with desperate earnestness and only moderate incoherence.

'Don't you see – it's so difficult to be *sure*. The whole point is that – so often – one doesn't *listen*. Ask Mrs Walters – she said the same thing – you listen to begin with – and then your attention flags – your mind wanders – and suddenly you find you've missed a bit. I just wonder if possibly there may have been a gap – a very small one – between the story he was telling me – about a *man* – and the moment when he was getting out his wallet and saying – "Like to see a picture of a murderer."'

'But you thought it was a picture of the man he had been talking about?'

'I thought so – yes. It never occurred to me that it mightn't have been. But now – how can I be *sure*?'

Mr Rafiel looked at her very thoughtfully . . .

'The trouble with you is,' he said, 'that you're too conscientious. Great mistake – Make up your mind and don't shilly shally. You didn't shilly shally to begin with. If you ask me, in all this chit-chat you've been having with the parson's sister and the rest of them, you've got hold of something that's unsettled you.'

'Perhaps you're right.'

'Well, cut it out for the moment. Let's go ahead with what you had to begin with. Because, nine times out of ten, one's original judgments are right – or so I've found. We've got three suspects. Let's take 'em out and have a good look at them. Any preference?'

'I really haven't,' said Miss Marple, 'all three of them seem so very unlikely.'

'We'll take Greg first,' said Mr Rafiel. 'Can't stand the fellow. Doesn't make him a murderer, though. Still, there *are* one or two points against him. Those blood pressure tablets belonged to him. Nice and handy to make use of.'

'That would be a little obvious, wouldn't it?' Miss Marple objected.

'I don't know that it would,' said Mr Rafiel. 'After all, the main thing was to do something *quickly*, and he'd got the tablets. Hadn't much time to go looking round for tablets that somebody else might have. Let's say it's Greg. All right. *If* he wanted to put his dear wife Lucky out of the way – (Good job, too, I'd say. In fact I'm in sympathy with him.) I can't actually see his motive. From all accounts he's rich. Inherited money from his first wife who had pots of it. He qualifies on that as a possible wife murderer all right. But that's over and done with. He got away with it. But Lucky was his first wife's poor relation. No money there, so if he wants to put *her* out of the way it must be in order to marry somebody else. Any gossip going around about that?'

Miss Marple shook her head.

'Not that I have heard. He – er – has a very gallant manner with *all* the ladies.'

'Well, that's a nice, old-fashioned way of putting it,' said Mr Rafiel. 'All right, he's a stoat. He makes passes. Not enough! We want more than that. Let's go on to Edward Hillingdon. Now there's a dark horse, if ever there was one.'

'He is not, I think, a happy man,' offered Miss Marple.

Mr Rafiel looked at her thoughtfully.

'Do you think a murderer ought to be a happy man?'

Miss Marple coughed.

'Well, they usually have been in my experience.'

'I don't suppose your experience has gone very far,' said Mr Rafiel.

In this assumption, as Miss Marple could have told him, he was wrong. But she forbore to contest his statement. Gentlemen, she knew, did not like to be put right in their facts.

'I rather fancy Hillingdon myself,' said Mr Rafiel. 'I've an idea that there is something a bit odd going on between him and his wife. You noticed it at all?'

'Oh yes,' said Miss Marple, 'I have noticed it. Their behaviour is perfect in public, of course, but that one would expect.'

'You probably know more about those sort of people than I would,' said Mr Rafiel. 'Very well, then, everything is in perfectly good taste but it's a probability that, in a gentlemanly way, Edward Hillingdon is contemplating doing away with Evelyn Hillingdon. Do you agree?'

'If so,' said Miss Marple, 'there must be another woman.'

Miss Marple shook her head in a dissatisfied manner.

'I can't help feeling – I really can't – that it's not all quite as simple as that.'

'Well, who shall we consider next – Jackson? We leave me out of it.'

Miss Marple smiled for the first time.

'And why do we leave you out of it, Mr Rafiel?'

'Because if you want to discuss the possibilities of my being a murderer you'd have to do it with somebody else. Waste of time talking about it to me. And anyway, I ask you, am I cut out for the part? Helpless, hauled out of bed like a dummy, dressed, wheeled about in a chair, shuffled along for a walk. What earthly chance have *I* of going and murdering anyone?'

'Probably as good a chance as anyone else,' said Miss Marple vigorously.

'And how do you make that out?'

'Well, you would agree yourself, I think, that you have brains?'

'Of course I've got brains,' declared Mr Rafiel. 'A good deal more than anybody else in this community, I'd say.'

'And having brains,' went on Miss Marple, 'would enable you to overcome the physical difficulties of being a murderer.'

98

'It would take some doing!'

'Yes,' said Miss Marple, 'it would take some doing. But then, I think, Mr Rafiel, you would enjoy that.'

Mr Rafiel stared at her for a long time and then he suddenly laughed.

'You've got a nerve!' he said. 'Not quite the gentle fluffy old lady you look, are you? So you really think I'm a murderer?'

'No,' said Miss Marple, 'I do not.'

'And why?'

'Well, really, I think just *because* you have got brains. Having brains, you can get most things you want without having recourse to murder. Murder is stupid.'

'And anyway who the devil should I want to murder?'

'That would be a very interesting question,' said Miss Marple. 'I have not yet had the pleasure of sufficient conversation with you to evolve a theory as to that.'

Mr Rafiel's smile broadened.

'Conversations with you might be dangerous,' he said.

'Conversations are always dangerous, if you have something to hide,' said Miss Marple.

'You may be right. Let's get on to Jackson. What do you think of Jackson?'

'It is difficult for me to say. I have not had the opportunity really of *any* conversation with him.'

'So you've no views on the subject?'

'He reminds me a little,' said Miss Marple reflectively, 'of a young man in the Town Clerk's office near where I live, Jonas Parry.'

'And?' Mr Rafiel asked and paused.

'He was not,' said Miss Marple, 'very satisfactory.'

'Jackson's not wholly satisfactory either. He suits me all right. He's first class at his job, and he doesn't mind being sworn at. He knows he's damn' well paid and so he puts up with things. I wouldn't employ him in a position of trust, but I don't have to trust him. Maybe his past is blameless, maybe it isn't. His references were all right but I discern – shall I say – a note of reserve. Fortunately, I'm not a man who has any guilty secrets, so I'm not a subject for blackmail.'

'No secrets?' said Miss Marple, thoughtfully. 'Surely, Mr Rafiel, you have business secrets?'

'Not where Jackson can get at them. No. Jackson is a smooth article, one might say, but I really don't see him as a murderer. I'd say that wasn't his line at all.'

99

He paused a minute and then said suddenly, 'Do you know, if one stands back and takes a good look at all this fantastic business, Major Palgrave and his ridiculous stories and all the rest of it, the *emphasis* is entirely wrong. *I'm* the person who ought to be murdered.'

Miss Marple looked at him in some surprise.

'Proper type casting,' explained Mr Rafiel. 'Who's the victim in murder stories? Elderly men with lots of money.'

'And lots of people with a good reason for wishing him out of the way, so as to get that money,' said Miss Marple. 'Is that true also?'

'Well – ' Mr Rafiel considered. 'I can count up to five or six men in London who wouldn't burst into tears if they read my obituary in *The Times*. But they wouldn't go so far as to do anything to bring about my demise. After all, why should they? I'm expected to die any day. In fact the bug – blighters are astonished that I've lasted so long. The doctors are surprised too.'

'You have, of course, a great will to live,' said Miss Marple.

'You think that's odd, I suppose,' said Mr Rafiel.

Miss Marple shook her head.

'Oh no,' she said, 'I think it's quite natural. Life is more worth living, more full of interest when you are likely to lose it. It shouldn't be, perhaps, but it is. When you're young and strong and healthy, and life stretches ahead of you, living isn't really important at all. It's young people who commit suicide easily, out of despair from love, sometimes from sheer anxiety and worry. But old people know how valuable life is and how interesting.'

'Hah!' said Mr Rafiel, snorting. 'Listen to a couple of old crocks.'

'Well, what I said is true, isn't it?' demanded Miss Marple.

'Oh, yes,' said Mr Rafiel, 'it's true enough. But don't you think I'm right when I say that I ought to be cast as the victim?'

'It depends on who has reason to gain by your death,' said Miss Marple.

'Nobody, really,' said Mr Rafiel. 'Apart, as I've said, from my competitors in the business world who, as I have also said, can count comfortably on my being out of it before very long. I'm not such a fool as to leave a lot of money divided up among my relations. Precious little they'd get of it after the Government had taken practically the lot. Oh, no, I've attended to all that years ago. Settlements, trusts and all the rest of it.'

'Jackson, for instance, wouldn't profit by your death?'

'He wouldn't get a penny,' said Mr Rafiel cheerfully. 'I pay him double the salary that he'd get from anyone else. That's because he has to put up with my bad temper; and he knows quite well that he will be the loser when I die.'

'And Mrs Walters?'

'The same goes for Esther. She's a good girl. First-class secretary, intelligent, good-tempered, understands my ways, doesn't turn a hair if I fly off the handle, couldn't care less if I insult her. Behaves like a nice nursery governess in charge of an outrageous and obstreperous child. She irritates me a bit sometimes, but who doesn't? There's nothing outstanding about her. She's rather a commonplace young woman in many ways, but I couldn't have anyone who suited me better. She's had a lot of trouble in her life. Married a man who wasn't much good. I'd say she never had much judgment when it came to men. Some women haven't. They fall for anyone who tells them a hard-luck story. Always convinced that all the man needs is proper female understanding. That, once married to her, he'll pull up his socks and make a go of life! But of course that type of man never does. Anyway, fortunately her unsatisfactory husband died; drank too much at a party one night and stepped in front of a bus. Esther had a daughter to support and she went back to her secretarial job. She's been with me five years. I made it quite clear to her from the start that she need have no expectations from me in the event of my death. I paid her from the start a very large salary, and that salary I've augmented by as much as a quarter as much again each year. However decent and honest people are, one should never trust *anybody* – that's why I told Esther quite clearly that she'd nothing to hope for from my death. Every year I live she'll get a bigger salary. If she puts most of that aside every year – and that's what I think she has done – she'll be quite a well-to-do woman by the time I kick the bucket. I've made myself responsible for her daughter's schooling and I've put a sum in trust for the daughter which she'll get when she comes of age. So Mrs Esther Walters is very comfortably placed. My death, let me tell you, would mean a serious financial loss to her.' He looked very hard at Miss Marple. 'She fully realizes all that. She's very sensible, Esther is.'

'Do she and Jackson get on?' asked Miss Marple.

Mr Rafiel shot a quick glance at her.

'Noticed something, have you?' he said. 'Yes, I think Jackson's done a bit of tom-catting around, with an eye in her direction, especially lately. He's a good-looking chap, of course, but he hasn't cut any ice in that direction. For one thing, there's class distinction. She's just a cut above him. Not very much. If she was *really* a cut above him it wouldn't matter, but the lower middle class – they're very particular. Her mother was a school teacher and her father a bank clerk. No, she won't make a fool of herself about Jackson. Dare say he's after her little nest egg, but he won't get it.'

'Hush – she's coming now!' said Miss Marple.

They both looked at Esther Walters as she came along the hotel path towards them.

'She's quite a good-looking girl, you know,' said Mr Rafiel, 'but not an atom of glamour. I don't know why, she's quite nicely turned out.'

Miss Marple sighed, a sigh that any woman will give however old at what might be considered wasted opportunities. What was lacking in Esther had been called by so many names during Miss Marple's span of existence. 'Not really attractive to me.' 'No SA.' 'Lacks Come-hither in her eye.' Fair hair, good complexion, hazel eyes, quite a good figure, pleasant smile, but lacking that something that makes a man's head turn when he passes a woman in the street.

'She ought to get married again,' said Miss Marple, lowering her voice.

'Of course she ought. She'd make a man a good wife.'

Esther Walters joined them and Mr Rafiel said, in a slightly artificial voice:

'So there you are at last! What's been keeping you?'

'Everyone seemed to be sending cables this morning,' said Esther. 'What with that, and people trying to check out – '

'Trying to check out, are they? A result of this murder business?'

'I suppose so. Poor Tim Kendal is worried to death.'

'And well he might be. Bad luck for that young couple, I must say.'

'I know. I gather it was rather a big undertaking for them to take on this place. They've been worried about making a success of it. They were doing very well, too.'

'They were doing a good job,' agreed Mr Rafiel. 'He's very capable and a damned hard worker. She's a very nice girl – attractive too. They've both worked like blacks, though that's an odd term to use out here, for blacks don't work themselves to death at all, so far as I can see. Was looking at a fellow shinning up a coconut tree to get his breakfast, then he goes to sleep for the rest of the day. Nice life.'

102

He added, 'We've been discussing the murder here.'

Esther Walters looked slightly startled. She turned her head towards Miss Marple.

'I've been wrong about her,' said Mr Rafiel, with characteristic frankness. 'Never been much of a one for the old pussies. All knitting wool and tittle-tattle. But this one's got something. Eyes and ears, and she uses them.'

Esther Walters looked apologetically at Miss Marple, but Miss Marple did not appear to take offence.

'That's really meant to be a compliment, you know,' Esther explained.

'I quite realize that,' said Miss Marple. 'I realize, too, that Mr Rafiel is privileged, or thinks he is.'

'What do you mean – privileged?' asked Mr Rafiel.

'To be rude if you want to be rude,' said Miss Marple.

'Have I been rude?' said Mr Rafiel, surprised. 'I'm sorry if I've offended you.'

'You haven't offended me,' said Miss Marple, 'I make allowances.'

'Now, don't be nasty. Esther, get a chair and bring it here. Maybe you can help.'

Esther walked a few steps to the balcony of the bungalow and brought over a light basket chair.

'We'll go on with our consultation,' said Mr Rafiel. 'We started with old Palgrave, deceased, and his eternal stories.'

'Oh, dear,' sighed Esther. 'I'm afraid I used to escape from him whenever I could.'

'Miss Marple was more patient,' said Mr Rafiel. 'Tell me, Esther, did he ever tell you a story about a murderer?'

'Oh yes,' said Esther. 'Several times.'

'What was it exactly? Let's have *your* recollection.'

'Well – ' Esther paused to think. 'The trouble is,' she said apologetically, 'I didn't really listen very closely. You see, it was rather like that terrible story about the lion in Rhodesia which used to go on and on. One did get rather in the habit of not listening.'

'Well, tell us what you *do* remember.'

'I think it arose out of some murder case that had been in the papers. Major Palgrave said that he'd had an experience not every person had had. He'd actually met a murderer face to face.'

'Met?' Mr Rafiel exclaimed. 'Did he actually use the word "Met"?'

Esther looked confused.

'I think so.' She was doubtful. 'Or he may have said, "I can point you out a murderer."'

'Well, which was it? There's a difference.'

'I can't really be sure . . . I *think* he said he'd show me a picture of someone.'

'That's better.'

'And then he talked a lot about Lucrezia Borgia.'

'Never mind Lucrezia Borgia. We know all about her.'

'He talked about poisoners and that Lucrezia was very beautiful and had red hair. He said there were probably far more women poisoners going about the world than anyone knew.'

'That I fear is *quite* likely,' said Miss Marple.

'And he talked about poison being a woman's weapon.'

'Seems to have been wandering from the point a bit,' said Mr Rafiel.

'Well, of course, he always did wander from the point in his stories. And then one used to stop listening and just say "Yes" and "Really?" And "You don't say so".'

'What about this picture he was going to show you?'

'I don't remember. It may have been something he'd seen in the paper – '

'He didn't actually show you a snapshot?'

'A snapshot? No.' She shook her head. 'I'm quite sure of that. He did say that she was a good-looking woman, and you'd never think she was a murderer to look at her.'

'She?'

'There you are,' exclaimed Miss Marple. 'It makes it all so confusing.'

'He was talking about a woman?' Mr Rafiel asked.

'Oh, yes.'

'The snapshot was a snapshot of a woman?'

'Yes.'

'It can't have been!'

'But it was,' Esther persisted. 'He said "She's here in this island. I'll point her out to you, and then I'll tell you the whole story."'

Mr Rafiel swore. In saying what he thought of the late Major Palgrave he did not mince his words.

'The probabilities are,' he finished, 'that not a word of anything he said was true!'

'One does begin to wonder,' Miss Marple murmured.

'So there we are,' said Mr Rafiel. 'The old booby started telling you hunting tales. Pig sticking, tiger shooting, elephant hunting, narrow escapes from lions. One or two of them might have been fact. Several of them were fiction, and others had happened to somebody else! Then he gets on to the subject of murder and he tells one murder story to cap another murder story. And what's more he tells them all as if they'd happened to *him*. Ten to one most of them were a hash-up of what he'd read in the paper, or seen on TV.'

He turned accusingly on Esther. 'You admit that you weren't listening closely. Perhaps you misunderstood what he was saying.'

'I'm certain he was talking about a woman,' said Esther obstinately, 'because of course I wondered who it was.'

'Who do you think it was?' asked Miss Marple.

Esther flushed and looked slightly embarrassed.

'Oh, I didn't really – I mean, I wouldn't like to – '

Miss Marple did not insist. The presence of Mr Rafiel, she thought, was inimical to her finding out exactly what suppositions Esther Walters had made. That could only be cosily brought out in a tête-à-tête between two women. And there was, of course, the possibility that Esther Walters was lying. Naturally, Miss Marple did not suggest this aloud. She registered it as a possibility but she was not inclined to believe in it. For one thing she did not think that Esther Walters was a liar (though one never knew) and for another, she could see no point in such a lie.

'But *you* say,' Mr Rafiel was now turning upon Miss Marple, '*you* say that he told you this yarn about a murderer and that he then said he had a picture of him which he was going to show you.'

'I thought so, yes.'

'You thought so? You were sure enough to begin with!'

Miss Marple retorted with spirit.

'It is never easy to repeat a conversation and be entirely accurate in what the other party to it has said. One is always inclined to jump at what you think they *meant*. Then, afterwards, you put actual words into their mouths. Major Palgrave told me this story, yes. He told me that the man who told it to him, this doctor, had shown him a snapshot of the murderer; but if I am to be quite honest I must admit that what he actually said to me was "Would you like to see a snapshot of a murderer?" and naturally I assumed that it was the same snapshot he had been talking about. That it was the snapshot of that particular murderer. But I have to admit that it is possible – only remotely possible, but still possible – that by an association of ideas in his mind he leaped from the snapshot he had been shown in the past, to a snapshot he had taken recently of someone here who he was convinced was a murderer.'

'Women!' snorted Mr Rafiel in exasperation. 'You're all the same, the whole blinking lot of you! Can't be accurate. You're never exactly *sure* of what a thing was. And now,' he added irritably, 'where does *that* leave us?' He snorted. 'Evelyn Hillingdon, or Greg's wife, Lucky? The whole thing is a mess.'

There was a slight apologetic cough. Arthur Jackson was standing at Mr Rafiel's elbow. He had come so noiselessly that nobody had noticed him.

'Time for your massage, sir,' he said.

Mr Rafiel displayed immediate temper.

'What do you mean by sneaking up on me in that way and making me jump? I never heard you.'

'Very sorry, sir.'

'I don't think I'll have any massage today. It never does me a damn' bit of good.'

'Oh, come sir, you mustn't say that.' Jackson was full of professional cheerfulness. 'You'd soon notice if you left it off.'

He wheeled the chair deftly round.

Miss Marple rose to her feet, smiled at Esther and went down to the beach.

CHAPTER EIGHTEEN

Without Benefit of Clergy

The beach was rather empty this morning. Greg was splashing in the water in his usual noisy style, Lucky was lying on her face on the beach with a sun-tanned back well oiled and her blonde hair splayed over her shoulders. The Hillingdons were not there. Señora de Caspearo, with an assorted bag of gentlemen in attendance, was lying face upwards and talking deep-throated, happy Spanish. Some French and Italian children were playing at the water's edge and laughing. Canon and Miss Prescott were sitting in beach chairs observing the scene. The Canon had his hat tilted forward over his eyes and seemed half asleep. There was a convenient chair next to Miss Prescott and Miss Marple made for it and sat down.

'Oh dear,' she said with a deep sigh.

'I know,' said Miss Prescott.

It was their joint tribute to violent death.

'That poor girl,' said Miss Marple.

'Very sad,' said the Canon. 'Most deplorable.'

'For a moment or two,' said Miss Prescott, 'we really thought of leaving, Jeremy and I. But then we decided against it. It would not really be fair, I felt, on the Kendals. After all, it's not *their* fault – It might have happened anywhere.'

'In the midst of life we are in death,' said the Canon solemnly.

'It's very important, you know,' said Miss Prescott, 'that they should make a go of this place. They have sunk all their capital in it.'

'A very sweet girl,' said Miss Marple, 'but not looking at all well lately.'

'Very nervy,' agreed Miss Prescott. 'Of course her family – ' she shook her head.

'I really think, Joan,' said the Canon in mild reproof, 'that there are some things – '

'Everybody knows about it,' said Miss Prescott. 'Her family live in our part of the world. A great-aunt – most peculiar – and one of her uncles took off all his clothes in one of the tube stations. Green Park, I believe it was.'

'Joan, that is a thing that should *not* be repeated.'

'Very sad,' said Miss Marple, shaking her head, 'though I believe not an uncommon form of madness. I know when we were working for the Armenian relief, a most respectable elderly clergyman was afflicted the same way. They telephoned his wife and she came along at once and took him home in a cab, wrapped in a blanket.'

'Of course, Molly's immediate family's all right,' said Miss Prescott. 'She never got on very well with her mother, but then so few girls seem to get on with their mothers nowadays.'

'Such a pity,' said Miss Marple, shaking her head, 'because really a young girl needs her mother's knowledge of the world and experience.'

'Exactly,' said Miss Prescott with emphasis. 'Molly, you know, took up with some man – *quite* unsuitable, I understand.'

'It so often happens,' said Miss Marple.

'Her family disapproved, naturally. *She* didn't tell them about it. They heard about it from a complete outsider. Of course her mother said she must bring him along so that they met him properly. This, I understand, the girl refused to do. She said it was humiliating to him. Most insulting to be made to come and meet her family and be looked over. Just as though you were a horse, she said.'

Miss Marple sighed. 'One does need so much *tact* when dealing with the young,' she murmured.

'Anyway there it was! They forbade her to see him.'

'But you can't *do* that nowadays,' said Miss Marple. 'Girls have jobs and they meet people whether anyone forbids them or not.'

'But then, very fortunately,' went on Miss Prescott, 'she met Tim Kendal, and the other man sort of faded out of the picture. I can't *tell* you how relieved the family was.'

'I hope they didn't show it too plainly,' said Miss Marple. 'That so often puts girls off from forming suitable attachments.'

'Yes, indeed.'

'One remembers oneself – ' murmured Miss Marple, her mind going back to the past. A young man she had met at a croquet party. He had seemed so nice – rather gay, almost *Bohemian* in his views. And then he had been unexpectedly warmly welcomed by her father. He had been suitable, eligible; he had been asked freely to the house more than once, and Miss Marple had found that, after all, he was *dull*. Very dull.

The Canon seemed safely comatose and Miss Marple advanced tentatively to the subject she was anxious to pursue.

'Of course you know so much about this place,' she murmured. 'You have been here several years running, have you not?'

'Well, last year and two years before that. We like St Honoré very much. Always such nice people here. Not the flashy, ultra-rich set.'

'So I suppose you know the Hillingdons and the Dysons well?'

'Yes, fairly well.'

Miss Marple coughed and lowered her voice slightly.

'Major Palgrave told me such an interesting story,' she said.

'He had a great repertoire of stories, hadn't he? Of course he had travelled very widely. Africa, India, even China I believe.'

'Yes indeed,' said Miss Marple. 'But I didn't mean one of *those* stories. This was a story concerned with – well, with one of the people I have just mentioned.'

'Oh!' said Miss Prescott. Her voice held meaning.

'Yes. Now I wonder – ' Miss Marple allowed her eyes to travel gently round the beach to where Lucky lay sunning her back. 'Very beautifully tanned, isn't she,' remarked Miss Marple. 'And her hair. Most attractive. Practically the same colour as Molly Kendal's, isn't it?'

'The only difference,' said Miss Prescott, 'is that Molly's is natural and Lucky's comes out of a bottle!'

'Really, Joan,' the Canon protested, unexpectedly awake again. 'Don't you think that is *rather* an uncharitable thing to say?'

'It's not uncharitable,' said Miss Prescott, acidly. 'Merely a *fact*.'

'It looks very nice to *me*,' said the Canon.

'Of course. That's why she does it. But I assure you, my dear Jeremy, it wouldn't deceive any *woman* for a moment. Would it?' She appealed to Miss Marple.

'Well, I'm afraid ' said Miss Marple, 'of course I haven't the experience that you have – but I'm afraid – yes I should say definitely *not natural*. The appearance at the roots every fifth or sixth day – ' She looked at Miss Prescott and they both nodded with quiet female assurance.

The Canon appeared to be dropping off again.

'Major Palgrave told me a really extraordinary story,' murmured Miss Marple, 'about – well I couldn't quite make out. I am a little deaf sometimes. He appeared to be saying or hinting – ' she paused.

'I know what you mean. There was a great deal of talk at the time – '

'You mean at the time that – '

'When the first Mrs Dyson died. Her death was quite unexpected. In fact, everybody thought she was a *malade imaginaire* – a hypochondriac. So when she had the attack and died so unexpectedly, well, of course, people did talk.'

'There wasn't – any – trouble at the time?'

'The doctor was puzzled. He was quite a young man and he hadn't had much experience. He was what I call one of those antibiotics-for-all men. You know, the kind that doesn't bother to look at the patient much, or worry what's the matter with him. They just give them some kind of pill out of a bottle and if they don't get better, then they try a different pill. Yes, I believe he *was* puzzled, but it seemed she had had gastric trouble before. At least her husband said so, and there seemed no reason for believing anything was *wrong*.'

'But you yourself think – '

'Well, I always try to keep an open mind, but one does wonder, you know. And what with various things people said – '

'Joan!' The Canon sat up. He looked belligerent. 'I don't like – I really don't like to hear this kind of ill-natured gossip being repeated. We've always set our faces against that kind of thing. See no evil, hear no evil, speak no evil – and what is more, *think* no evil! That should be the motto of every Christian man and woman.'

The two women sat in silence. They were rebuked, and in deference to their training they deferred to the criticism of a man. But inwardly they were frustrated, irritated and quite unrepentant. Miss Prescott threw a frank glance of irritation towards her brother. Miss Marple took out her knitting and looked at it. Fortunately for them Chance was on their side.

'*Mon père*,' said a small shrill voice. It was one of the French children who had been playing at the water's edge. She had come up unnoticed, and was standing by Canon Prescott's chair.

'*Mon père*,' she fluted.

'Eh? Yes, my dear? *Oui, qu'est-ce qu'il y a, ma petite*?'

The child explained. There had been a dispute about who should have the water-wings next and also other matters of seaside etiquette. Canon Prescott was extremely fond of children, especially small girls. He was always delighted to be summoned to act as arbiter in their disputes. He rose willingly now and accompanied the child to the water's edge. Miss Marple and Miss Prescott breathed deep sighs and turned avidly towards each other.

'Jeremy, of course rightly, is very against ill-natured gossip,' said Miss Prescott, 'but one cannot really ignore what people are saying. And there was, as I say, a great deal of talk at the time.'

'Yes?' Miss Marple's tone urged her forward.

'This young woman, you see, Miss Greatorex I think her name was then, I can't remember now, was a kind of cousin and she looked after Mrs Dyson. Gave her all her medicines and things like that.' There was a short, meaningless pause. 'And of course there had, I understand' – Miss Prescott's voice was lowered – 'been goings-on between Mr Dyson and Miss Greatorex. A lot of people had noticed them. I mean things like that are quickly observed in a place like this. Then there was some curious story about some stuff that Edward Hillingdon got for her at a chemist.'

'Oh, Edward Hillingdon came into it?'

'Oh yes, he was very much attracted. People noticed it. And Lucky

– Miss Greatorex – played them off against each other. Gregory Dyson and Edward Hillingdon. One has to face it, she has always been an attractive woman.'

'Though not as young as she was,' Miss Marple replied.

'Exactly. But she was always very well turned out and made up. Of course not so flamboyant when she was just the poor relation. She always *seemed* very devoted to the invalid. But, well, you see how it was.'

'What was this story about the chemist – how did that get known?'

'Well, it wasn't in Jamestown, I think it was when they were in Martinique. The French, I believe, are more lax than we are in the matter of drugs – This chemist talked to someone, and the story got around – Well, you know how these things happen.'

Miss Marple did. None better.

'He said something about Colonel Hillingdon asking for something and not seeming to know what it was he was asking for. Consulting a piece of paper, you know, on which it was written down. Anyway, as I say, there was *talk*.'

'But I don't see quite why Colonel Hillingdon – ' Miss Marple frowned in perplexity.

'I suppose he was just being used as a *cat's-paw*. Anyway, Gregory Dyson married again in an almost indecently short time. Barely a month later, I understand.'

They looked at each other.

'But there was no *real* suspicion?' Miss Marple asked.

'Oh no, it was just – well, *talk*. Of course there may have been absolutely nothing in it.'

'Major Palgrave thought there was.'

'Did he say so to you?'

'I wasn't really listening very closely,' confessed Miss Marple. 'I just wondered if – er – well, if he'd said the same thing to you?'

'He did point her out to me one day,' said Miss Prescott.

'Really? He actually pointed her out?'

'Yes. As a matter of fact, I thought at first it was Mrs Hillingdon he was pointing out. He wheezed and chuckled a bit and said "Look at that woman over there. In my opinion that's a woman who's done murder and got away with it." I was very shocked, of course. I said, "Surely you're joking, Major Palgrave," and he said "Yes, yes, dear lady, let's call it joking." The Dysons and the Hillingdons were sitting at a table quite near to us, and I was afraid they'd overhear. He

111

chuckled and said "Wouldn't care to go to a drinks party and have a certain person mix me a cocktail. Too much like supper with the Borgias.'"

'How *very* interesting,' said Miss Marple. 'Did he mention – a – a photograph?'

'I don't remember . . . Was it some newspaper cutting?'

Miss Marple, about to speak, shut her lips. The sun was momentarily obscured by a shadow. Evelyn Hillingdon paused beside them.

'Good morning,' she said.

'I was wondering where you were,' said Miss Prescott, looking up brightly.

'I've been to Jamestown, shopping.'

'Oh, I see.'

Miss Prescott looked round vaguely and Evelyn Hillingdon said:

'Oh, I didn't take Edward with me. Men hate shopping.'

'Did you find anything of interest?'

'It wasn't that sort of shopping. I just had to go to the chemist.'

With a smile and a slight nod she went on down the beach.

'Such nice people, the Hillingdons,' said Miss Prescott, 'though she's not really very easy to know, is she? I mean, she's always very pleasant and all that, but one never seems to get to know her any better.'

Miss Marple agreed thoughtfully.

'One never knows what she is thinking,' said Miss Prescott.

'Perhaps that is just as well,' said Miss Marple.

'I beg your pardon?'

'Oh nothing really, only that I've always had the feeling that perhaps her thoughts might be rather disconcerting.'

'Oh,' said Miss Prescott, looking puzzled. 'I see what you mean.' She went on with a slight change of subject. 'I believe they have a very charming place in Hampshire, and a boy – or is it two boys – who have just gone – or one of them – to Winchester.'

'Do you know Hampshire well?'

'No. Hardly at all. I believe their house is somewhere near Alton.'

'I see.' Miss Marple paused and then said, 'And where do the Dysons live?'

'California,' said Miss Prescott. 'When they are at home, that is. They are great travellers.'

'One really knows so little about the people one meets when

112

one is travelling,' said Miss Marple. 'I mean – how shall I put it – one only knows, doesn't one, what they choose to tell you about themselves. For instance, you don't *really* know that the Dysons live in California.'

Miss Prescott looked startled.

'I'm sure Mr Dyson mentioned it.'

'Yes. Yes, exactly. That's what I mean. And the same thing perhaps with the Hillingdons. I mean when you say that they live in Hampshire, you're really repeating what *they* told *you*, aren't you?'

Miss Prescott looked slightly alarmed. 'Do you mean that they don't live in Hampshire?' she asked.

'No, no, not for one moment,' said Miss Marple, quickly apologetic. 'I was only using them as an instance as to what one knows or doesn't know about people.' She added, '*I* have told you that I live at St Mary Mead, which is a place, no doubt, of which you have never heard. But you don't, if I may say so, know it of your *own* knowledge, do you?'

Miss Prescott forbore from saying that she really couldn't care less *where* Miss Marple lived. It was somewhere in the country and in the south of England and that is all she knew. 'Oh, I do see what you mean,' she agreed hastily, 'and I know that one can't possibly be too careful when one is abroad.'

'I didn't exactly mean *that*,' said Miss Marple.

There were some odd thoughts going through Miss Marple's mind. Did she really know, she was asking herself, that Canon Prescott and Miss Prescott were really Canon Prescott and Miss Prescott? They said so. There was no evidence to contradict them. It would really be easy, would it not, to put on a dog-collar, to wear the appropriate clothes, to make the appropriate conversation. If there was a motive . . .

Miss Marple was fairly knowledgeable about the clergy in her part of the world, but the Prescotts came from the north. Durham, wasn't it? She had no doubt they were the Prescotts, but still, it came back to the same thing – one believed what people said to one.

Perhaps one ought to be on one's guard against that. Perhaps . . . She shook her head thoughtfully.

CHAPTER NINETEEN

Uses of a Shoe

Canon Prescott came back from the water's edge slightly short of breath (playing with children is always exhausting).

Presently he and his sister went back to the hotel, finding the beach a little too hot.

'But,' said Señora de Caspearo scornfully as they walked away – 'how can a beach be too hot? It is nonsense that – And look what she wears – her arms and her neck are all covered up. Perhaps it is as well, that. Her skin it is hideous, like a plucked chicken!'

Miss Marple drew a deep breath. Now or never was the time for conversation with Señora de Caspearo. Unfortunately she did not know what to say. There seemed to be no common ground on which they could meet.

'You have children, Señora?' she inquired.

'I have three angels,' said Señora de Caspearo, kissing her fingertips.

Miss Marple was rather uncertain as to whether this meant that Señora de Caspearo's offspring were in Heaven or whether it merely referred to their characters.

One of the gentlemen in attendance made a remark in Spanish and Señora de Caspearo flung back her head appreciatively and laughed loudly and melodiously.

'You understand what he said?' she inquired of Miss Marple.

'I'm afraid not,' said Miss Marple apologetically.

'It is just as well. He is a wicked man.'

A rapid and spirited interchange of Spanish badinage followed.

'It is infamous – infamous,' said Señora de Caspearo, reverting to English with sudden gravity, 'that the police do not let us go from this island. I storm, I scream, I stamp my foot – but all they say is No – No. You know how it will end – we shall all be killed.'

Her bodyguard attempted to reassure her.

'But yes – I tell you it is unlucky here. I knew it from the first – That

114

old Major, the ugly one – he had the Evil Eye – you remember? His eyes they crossed – It is bad, that! I make the Sign of the Horns every time when he looks my way.' She made it in illustration. 'Though since he is cross-eyed I am not always sure when he does look my way – '

'He had a glass eye,' said Miss Marple in an explanatory voice. 'An accident, I understand, when he was quite young. It was not his fault.'

'I tell you he brought bad luck – I say it is the Evil Eye he had.'

Her hand shot out again in the well-known Latin gesture – the first finger and the little finger sticking out, the two middle ones doubled in. 'Anyway,' she said cheerfully, 'he is dead – I do not have to look at him any more. I do not like to look at things that are ugly.'

It was, Miss Marple thought, a somewhat cruel epitaph on Major Palgrave.

Farther down the beach Gregory Dyson had come out of the sea. Lucky had turned herself over on the sand. Evelyn Hillingdon was looking at Lucky, and her expression, for some reason, made Miss Marple shiver.

'Surely I can't be cold – in this hot sun,' she thought.

What was the old phrase – '*A goose walking over your grave* – '

She got up and went slowly back to her bungalow.

On the way she passed Mr Rafiel and Esther Walters coming down the beach. Mr Rafiel winked at her. Miss Marple did not wink back. She looked disapproving.

She went into her bungalow and lay down on her bed. She felt old and tired and worried.

She was quite certain that there was no time to be lost – no time – to – be lost . . . It was getting late . . . The sun was going to set – the sun – one must always look at the sun through smoked glass – Where was that piece of smoked glass that someone had given her? . . .

No, she wouldn't need it after all. A shadow had come over the sun blotting it out. A shadow. Evelyn Hillingdon's shadow – No, not Evelyn Hillingdon – The Shadow (what were the words?) the *Shadow of the Valley of Death*. That was it. She must – what was it? Make the Sign of the Horns – to avert the Evil Eye – Major Palgrave's Evil Eye.

Her eyelids flickered open – she had been asleep. But there *was* a shadow – someone peering in at her window.

115

The shadow moved away – and Miss Marple saw who it was – It was Jackson.

'Impertinence – peering in like that,' she thought – and added parenthetically 'Just like Jonas Parry.'

The comparison reflected no credit on Jackson.

Then she wondered *why* Jackson had been peering into her bedroom. To see if she was there? Or to note that she was there, but was asleep.

She got up, went into the bathroom and peered cautiously through the window.

Arthur Jackson was standing by the door of the bungalow next door. Mr Rafiel's bungalow. She saw him give a rapid glance round and then slip quickly inside. Interesting, thought Miss Marple. Why did he have to look round in that furtive manner? Nothing in the world could have been more natural than his going into Mr Rafiel's bungalow since he himself had a room at the back of it. He was always going in and out of it on some errand or other. So why that quick, guilty glance round? 'Only one reason,' said Miss Marple answering her own question, 'he wanted to be sure that nobody was observing him enter at this particular moment because of something he was going to do in there.'

Everybody, of course, was on the beach at this moment except those who had gone for expeditions. In about twenty minutes or so, Jackson himself would arrive on the beach in the course of his duties to aid Mr Rafiel to take his sea dip. If he wanted to do anything in the bungalow unobserved, now was a very good time. He had satisfied himself that Miss Marple was asleep on her bed, he had satisfied himself that there was nobody near at hand to observe his movements. Well, she must do her best to do exactly that.

Sitting down on her bed, Miss Marple removed her neat sandal shoes and replaced them with a pair of plimsolls. Then she shook her head, removed the plimsolls, burrowed in her suitcase and took out a pair of shoes the heel of one of which she had recently caught on a hook by the door. It was now in a slightly precarious state and Miss Marple adroitly rendered it even more precarious by attention with a nail file. Then she emerged with due precaution from her door walking in stockinged feet. With all the care of a Big Game Hunter approaching up-wind of a herd of antelope, Miss Marple gently circumnavigated Mr Rafiel's bungalow. Cautiously she manoeuvred her way around the corner of the house. She put on one of the shoes she was carrying, gave a final wrench to the heel of the

116

other, sank gently to her knees and lay prone under the window. If Jackson heard anything, if he came to the window to look out, an old lady would have had a fall owing to the heel coming off her shoe. But evidently Jackson had heard nothing.

Very, very gently Miss Marple raised her head. The windows of the bungalow were low. Shielding herself slightly with a festoon of creeper she peered inside . . .

Jackson was on his knees before a suitcase. The lid of the suitcase was up and Miss Marple could see that it was a specially fitted affair containing compartments filled with various kinds of papers. Jackson was looking through the papers, occasionally drawing documents out of long envelopes. Miss Marple did not remain at her observation post for long. All she wanted was to know what Jackson was doing. She knew now. Jackson was snooping. Whether he was looking for something in particular, or whether he was just indulging his natural instincts, she had no means of judging. But it confirmed her in her belief that Arthur Jackson and Jonas Parry had strong affinities in other things than facial resemblance.

Her problem was now to withdraw. Very carefully she dropped down again and crept along the flower-bed until she was clear of the window. She returned to her bungalow and carefully put away the shoe and the heel that she had detached from it. She looked at them with affection. A good device which she could use on another day if necessary. She resumed her own sandal shoes, and went thoughtfully down to the beach again.

Choosing a moment when Esther Walters was in the water, Miss Marple moved into the chair Esther had vacated.

Greg and Lucky were laughing and talking with Señora de Caspearo and making a good deal of noise.

Miss Marple spoke very quietly, almost under her breath, without looking at Mr Rafiel.

'Do you know that Jackson snoops?'

'Doesn't surprise me,' said Mr Rafiel. 'Caught him at it, did you?'

'I managed to observe him through a window. He had one of your suitcases open and was looking through your papers.'

'Must have managed to get hold of a key to it. Resourceful fellow. He'll be disappointed though. Nothing he gets hold of in that way will do him a mite of good.'

'He's coming down now,' said Miss Marple, glancing up towards the hotel.

'Time for that idiotic sea dip of mine.'

He spoke again – very quietly.

'As for you – don't be too enterprising. We don't want to be attending *your* funeral next. Remember your age, and be careful. There's somebody about who isn't too scrupulous, remember.'

CHAPTER TWENTY

Night Alarm

Evening came – The lights came up on the terrace – People dined and talked and laughed, albeit less loudly and merrily than they had a day or two ago – The steel band played.

But the dancing ended early. People yawned – went off to bed – The lights went out – There was darkness and stillness – The Golden Palm Tree slept . . .

'Evelyn. Evelyn!' The whisper came sharp and urgent.

Evelyn Hillingdon stirred and turned on her pillow.

'*Evelyn*. Please wake up.'

Evelyn Hillingdon sat up abruptly. Tim Kendal was standing in the doorway. She stared at him in surprise.

'Evelyn, *please*, could you come? It's – Molly. She's ill. I don't know what's the matter with her. I think she must have taken something.'

Evelyn was quick, decisive.

'All right, Tim. I'll come. You go back to her. I'll be with you in a moment.'

Tim Kendal disappeared. Evelyn slipped out of bed, threw on a dressing-gown and looked across at the other bed. Her husband, it seemed, had not been awakened. He lay there, his head turned away, breathing quietly. Evelyn hesitated for a moment, then decided not to disturb him. She went out of the door and walked rapidly to the main building and beyond it to the Kendals' bungalow. She caught up with Tim in the doorway.

Molly lay in bed. Her eyes were closed and her breathing was clearly not natural. Evelyn bent over her, rolled up an eyelid, felt her pulse and then looked at the bedside table. There was a glass there which had been used. Beside it was an empty phial of tablets. She picked it up.

'They were her sleeping pills,' said Tim, 'but that bottle was half full yesterday or the day before. I think she must have taken the lot.'

'Go and get Dr Graham,' said Evelyn, 'and on the way knock them up and tell them to make strong coffee. Strong as possible. Hurry.'

Tim dashed off. Just outside the doorway he collided with Edward Hillingdon.

'Oh, sorry, Edward.'

'What's happening here?' demanded Hillingdon. 'What's going on?'

'It's Molly. Evelyn's with her. I must get hold of the doctor. I suppose I ought to have gone to him first but I – I wasn't sure and I thought Evelyn would know. Molly would have hated it if I'd fetched a doctor when it wasn't necessary.'

He went off, running. Edward Hillingdon looked after him for a moment and then he walked into the bedroom.

'What's happening?' he said. 'Is it serious?'

'Oh, there you are, Edward. I wondered if you'd woken up. This silly child has been taking things.'

'Is it bad?'

'One can't tell without knowing how much she's taken. I shouldn't think it was too bad if we get going in time. I've sent for coffee. If we can get some of that down her – '

'But why should she do such a thing? You don't think – ' He stopped.

'What don't I think?' said Evelyn.

'You don't think it's because of the inquiry – the police – all that?'

'It's possible, of course. That sort of thing could be very alarming to a nervous type.'

'Molly never used to seem a nervous type.'

'One can't really tell,' said Evelyn. 'It's the most unlikely people sometimes who lose their nerve.'

'Yes, I remember . . .' Again he stopped.

'The truth is,' said Evelyn, 'that one doesn't really know anything about anybody.' She added, 'Not even the people who are nearest to you . . .'

'Isn't that going a little too far, Evelyn – exaggerating too much?'

'I don't think is. When you think of people, it is in the image you have made of them for yourself.'

'I know you,' said Edward Hillingdon quietly.

'You think you do.'

'No. I'm sure.' He added, 'And you're sure of me.'

Evelyn looked at him then turned back to the bed. She took Molly by the shoulders and shook her.

'We ought to be doing something, but I suppose it's better to wait until Dr Graham comes – Oh, I think I hear them.'

II

'She'll do now.' Dr Graham stepped back, wiped his forehead with a handkerchief and breathed a sigh of relief.

'You think she'll be all right, sir?' Tim demanded anxiously.

'Yes, yes. We got to her in good time. Anyway, she probably didn't take enough to kill her. A couple of days and she'll be as right as rain but she'll have a rather nasty day or two first.' He picked up the empty bottle. 'Who gave her these things anyway?'

'A doctor in New York. She wasn't sleeping well.'

'Well, well. I know all we medicos hand these things out freely nowadays. Nobody tells young women who can't sleep to count sheep, or get up and eat a biscuit, or write a couple of letters and then go back to bed. Instant remedies, that's what people demand nowadays. Sometimes I think it's a pity we give them to them. You've got to learn to put up with things in life. All very well to stuff a comforter into a baby's mouth to stop it crying. Can't go on doing that all a person's life.' He gave a small chuckle. 'I bet you, if you asked Miss Marple what she does if she can't sleep, she'd tell you she counted sheep going under a gate.' He turned back to the bed where Molly was stirring. Her eyes were open now. She looked at them without interest or recognition. Dr Graham took her hand.

'Well, well, my dear, and what have you been doing to yourself?'

She blinked but did not reply.

'Why did you do it, Molly, why? Tell me why?' Tim took her other hand.

Still her eyes did not move. If they rested on anyone it was on Evelyn Hillingdon. There might have been even a faint question in them but it was hard to tell. Evelyn spoke as though there had been the question.

'Tim came and fetched me,' she said.

Her eyes went to Tim, then shifted to Dr Graham.

'You're going to be all right now,' said Dr Graham, 'but don't do it again.'

'She didn't mean to do it,' said Tim quietly. 'I'm sure she didn't mean to do it. She just wanted a good night's rest. Perhaps the pills didn't work at first and so she took more of them. Is that it, Molly?'

Her head moved very faintly in a negative motion.

'You mean – you took them on purpose?' said Tim.

Molly spoke then. 'Yes,' she said.

'But why, Molly, why?'

The eyelids faltered 'Afraid ' The word was just heard.

'Afraid? Of what?'

But her eyelids closed down.

'Better let her be,' said Dr Graham. Tim spoke impetuously.

'Afraid of what? The police? Because they've been hounding you, asking you questions? I don't wonder. Anyone might feel frightened. But it's just their way, that's all. Nobody thinks for one moment – ' he broke off.

Dr Graham made him a decisive gesture.

'I want to go to sleep,' said Molly.

'The best thing for you,' said Dr Graham.

He moved to the door and the others followed him.

'She'll sleep all right,' said Graham.

'Is there anything I ought to do?' asked Tim. He had the usual, slightly apprehensive attitude of a man in illness.

'I'll stay if you like,' said Evelyn kindly.

'Oh no. No, that's quite all right,' said Tim.

Evelyn went back towards the bed. 'Shall I stay with you, Molly?'

Molly's eyes opened again. She said, 'No,' and then after a pause, 'just Tim.'

Tim came back and sat down by the bed.

'I'm here, Molly,' he said and took her hand. 'Just go to sleep. I won't leave you.'

She sighed faintly and her eyes closed.

121

The doctor paused outside the bungalow and the Hillingdons stood with him.

'You're sure there's nothing more I can do?' asked Evelyn.

'I don't think so, thank you, Mrs Hillingdon. She'll be better with her husband now. But possibly tomorrow – after all, he's got this hotel to run – I think someone should be with her.'

'D'you think she might – try again?' asked Hillingdon.

Graham rubbed his forehead irritably.

'One never knows in these cases. Actually, it's most unlikely. As you've seen for yourselves, the restorative treatment is extremely unpleasant. But of course one can never be absolutely certain. She may have more of this stuff hidden away somewhere.'

'I should never have thought of suicide in connection with a girl like Molly,' said Hillingdon.

Graham said dryly, 'It's not the people who are always talking of killing themselves, threatening to do so, who do it. They dramatize themselves that way and let off steam.'

'Molly always seemed such a happy girl. I think perhaps' – Evelyn hesitated – 'I ought to tell you, Dr Graham.' She told him then about her interview with Molly on the beach the night that Victoria had been killed. Graham's face was very grave when she had finished.

'I'm glad you've told me, Mrs Hillingdon. There are very definite indications there of some kind of deep-rooted trouble. Yes. I'll have a word with her husband in the morning.'

III

'I want to talk to you seriously, Kendal, about your wife.'

They were sitting in Tim's office. Evelyn Hillingdon had taken his place by Molly's bedside and Lucky had promised to come and, as she expressed it, 'spell her' later. Miss Marple had also offered her services. Poor Tim was torn between his hotel commitments and his wife's condition.

'I can't understand it,' said Tim, 'I can't understand Molly any longer. She's changed. Changed out of all seeming.'

'I understand she's been having bad dreams?'

'Yes. Yes, she complained about them a good deal.'

'For how long?'

'Oh, I don't know. About – oh I suppose a month – perhaps

122

longer. She – we – thought they were just – well, nightmares, you know.'

'Yes, yes, I quite understand. But what's a much more serious sign is the fact that she seems to have felt afraid of someone. Did she complain about that to you?'

'Well, yes. She said once or twice that – oh, people were following her.'

'Ah! Spying on her?'

'Yes, she did use that term once. She said they were her enemies and they'd followed her here.'

'Did she have enemies, Mr Kendal? – '

'No. Of course she didn't.'

'No incident in England, anything you know about before you were married?'

'Oh no, nothing of that kind. She didn't get on with her family very well, that was all. Her mother was rather an eccentric woman, difficult to live with perhaps, but . . .'

'Any signs of mental instability in her family?'

Tim opened his mouth impulsively, then shut it again. He pushed a fountain pen about on the desk in front of him.

The doctor said:

'I must stress the fact that it would be better to tell me, Tim, if that is the case.'

'Well, yes, I believe so. Nothing serious, but I believe there was an aunt or something who was a bit batty. But that's nothing. I mean – well you get that in almost any family.'

'Oh yes, yes, that's quite true. I'm not trying to alarm you about that, but it just might show a tendency to – well, to break down or imagine things if any stress arose.'

'I don't really know very much,' said Tim. 'After all, people don't pour out all their family histories to you, do they?'

'No, no. Quite so. She had no former friend – she was not engaged to anyone, anyone who might have threatened her or made jealous threats? That sort of thing?'

'I don't know. I don't think so. Molly *was* engaged to some other man before I came along. Her parents were very against it, I understand, and I think she really stuck to the chap more out of opposition and defiance than anything else.' He gave a sudden half-grin. 'You know what it is when you're young. If people cut up a fuss it makes you much keener on whoever it is.'

Dr Graham smiled too. 'Ah yes, one often sees that. One should never take exception to one's children's objectionable friends. Usually they grow out of them naturally. This man, whoever he was, didn't make threats of any kind against Molly?'

'No, I'm sure he didn't. She would have told me. She said herself she just had a silly adolescent craze on him, mainly because he had such a bad reputation.'

'Yes, yes. Well, that doesn't sound serious. Now there's another thing. Apparently your wife has had what she describes as blackouts. Brief passages of time during which she can't account for her actions. Did you know about that, Tim?'

'No,' said Tim slowly. 'No. I didn't. She never told me. I did notice, you know, now you mention it, that she seemed rather vague sometimes and . . .' He paused, thinking. 'Yes, that explains it. I couldn't understand how she seemed to have forgotten the simplest things, or sometimes not to seem to know what time of day it was. I just thought she was absent-minded, I suppose.'

'What it amounts to, Tim, is just this. I advise you most strongly to take your wife to see a good specialist.'

Tim flushed angrily.

'You mean a mental specialist, I suppose?'

'Now, now, don't be upset by labels. A neurologist, a psychologist, someone who specializes in what the layman calls nervous breakdowns. There's a good man in Kingston. Or there's New York of course. There is something that is causing these nervous terrors of your wife's. Something perhaps for which she hardly knows the reason herself. Get advice about her, Tim. Get advice as soon as possible.'

He clapped his hand on the young man's shoulder and got up.

'There's no immediate worry. Your wife has good friends and we'll all be keeping an eye on her.'

'She won't – you don't think she'll try it again?'

'I think it most unlikely,' said Dr Graham.

'You can't be sure,' said Tim.

'One can never be sure,' said Dr Graham, 'that's one of the first things you learn in my profession.' Again he laid a hand on Tim's shoulder. 'Don't worry too much.'

'That's easy to say,' said Tim as the doctor went out of the door. 'Don't worry, indeed! What does he think I'm made of?'

CHAPTER TWENTY-ONE

Jackson on Cosmetics

'You're sure you don't mind, Miss Marple?' said Evelyn Hillingdon.

'No, indeed, my dear,' said Miss Marple. 'I'm only too delighted to be of use in any way. At my age, you know, one feels very useless in the world. Especially when I am in a place like this, just enjoying myself. No duties of any kind. No, I'll be delighted to sit with Molly. You go along on your expedition. Pelican Point, wasn't it?'

'Yes,' said Evelyn. 'Both Edward and I love it. I never get tired of seeing the birds diving down, catching up the fish. Tim's with Molly now. But he's got things to do and he doesn't seem to like her being left alone.'

'He's quite right,' said Miss Marple. 'I wouldn't in his place. One never knows, does one? When anyone has attempted anything of that kind – Well, go along, my dear.'

Evelyn went off to join a little group that was waiting for her. Her husband, the Dysons and three or four other people. Miss Marple checked her knitting requirements, saw that she had all she wanted with her, and walked over towards the Kendals' bungalow.

As she came up on to the loggia she heard Tim's voice through the half-open french window.

'If you'd only tell me *why* you did it, Molly. What made you? Was it anything I did? There must be some reason. If you'd only tell me.'

Miss Marple paused. There was a little pause inside before Molly spoke. Her voice was flat and tired.

'I don't know, Tim, I really don't know. I suppose – something came over me.'

Miss Marple tapped on the window and walked in.

'Oh, there you are, Miss Marple. It is very good of you.'

'Not at all,' said Miss Marple. 'I'm delighted to be of any help. Shall I sit here in this chair? You're looking much better, Molly. I'm so glad.'

'I'm all right,' said Molly. 'Quite all right. Just – oh, just sleepy.'

'I shan't talk,' said Miss Marple. 'You just lie quiet and rest. I'll get on with my knitting.'

Tim Kendal threw her a grateful glance and went out. Miss Marple established herself in her chair.

Molly was lying on her left side. She had a half-stupefied, exhausted look. She said in a voice that was almost a whisper:

'It's very kind of you, Miss Marple. I – I think I'll go to sleep.'

She half turned away on her pillows and closed her eyes. Her breathing grew more regular though it was still far from normal. Long experience of nursing made Miss Marple almost automatically straighten the sheet and tuck it under the mattress on her side of the bed. As she did so her hand encountered something hard and rectangular under the mattress. Rather surprised she took hold of this and pulled it out. It was a book. Miss Marple threw a quick glance at the girl in the bed, but she lay there utterly quiescent. She was evidently asleep. Miss Marple opened the book. It was, she saw, a current work on nervous diseases. It came open naturally at a certain place which gave a description of the onset of persecution mania and various other manifestations of schizophrenia and allied complaints.

It was not a highly technical book, but one that could be easily understood by a layman. Miss Marple's face grew very grave as she read. After a minute or two she closed the book and stayed thinking. Then she bent forward and with care replaced the book where she had found it, under the mattress.

She shook her head in some perplexity. Noiselessly she rose from her chair. She walked the few steps towards the window, then turned her head sharply over her shoulder. Molly's eyes were open but even as Miss Marple turned the eyes shut again. For a minute or two Miss Marple was not quite certain whether she might not have imagined that quick, sharp glance. Was Molly then only pretending to be asleep? That might be natural enough. She might feel that Miss Marple would start talking to her if she showed herself awake. Yes, that could be all it was.

Was she reading into that glance of Molly's a kind of slyness that was somehow innately disagreeable? One doesn't know, Miss Marple thought to herself, one really doesn't know.

She decided that she would try to manage a little talk with Dr Graham as soon as it could be managed. She came back to her chair by the bed. She decided after about five minutes or so that Molly was really asleep. No one could have lain so still, could have breathed so evenly. Miss Marple got up again. She was wearing her plimsolls today. Not perhaps very elegant, but admirably suited to this climate and comfortable and roomy for the feet.

She moved gently round the bedroom, pausing at both of the windows, which gave out in two different directions.

The hotel grounds seemed quiet and deserted. Miss Marple came back and was standing a little uncertainly before regaining her seat, when she thought she heard a faint sound outside. Like the scrape of a shoe on the loggia? She hesitated a moment then she went to the window, pushed it a little farther open, stepped out and turned her head back into the room as she spoke.

'I shall be gone only a very short time, dear,' she said, 'just back to my bungalow, to see where I could possibly have put that pattern. I was so sure I had brought it with me. You'll be quite all right till I come back, won't you?' Then turning her head back, she nodded to herself. 'Asleep, poor child. A good thing.'

She went quietly along the loggia, down the steps and turned sharp right to the path there. Passing along between the screen of some hibiscus bushes an observer might have been curious to see that Miss Marple veered sharply on to the flower-bed, passed round to the back of the bungalow and entered it again through the second door there. This led directly into a small room that Tim sometimes used as an unofficial office and from that into the sitting-room.

Here there were wide curtains semi-drawn to keep the room cool. Miss Marple slipped behind one of them. Then she waited. From the window here she had a good view of anyone who approached Molly's bedroom. It was some few minutes, four or five, before she saw anything.

The neat figure of Jackson in his white uniform went up the steps of the loggia. He paused for a minute at the balcony there, and then appeared to be giving a tiny discreet tap on the door of the window that was ajar. There was no response that Miss Marple could hear. Jackson looked around him, a quick furtive glance, then he slipped inside the open doors. Miss Marple moved to the door which led into the adjoining bathroom. Miss Marple's eyebrows rose in slight surprise. She reflected a minute or two, then walked out into the passageway and into the bathroom by the other door.

Jackson spun round from examining the shelf over the wash-basin. He looked taken aback, which was not surprising.

'Oh,' he said, 'I – I didn't . . .'

'Mr Jackson,' said Miss Marple, in great surprise.

'I thought you'd be here somewhere,' said Jackson.

'Did you want anything?' inquired Miss Marple.

'Actually,' said Jackson, 'I was just looking at Mrs Kendal's brand of face cream.'

Miss Marple appreciated the fact that as Jackson was standing with a jar of face cream in his hand he had been adroit in mentioning the fact at once.

'Nice smell,' he said, wrinkling up his nose. 'Fairly good stuff, as these preparations go. The cheaper brands don't suit every skin. Bring it out in a rash as likely as not. The same thing with face powders sometimes.'

'You seem to be very knowledgeable on the subject,' said Miss Marple.

'Worked in the pharmaceutical line for a bit,' said Jackson. 'One learns to know a good deal about cosmetics there. Put stuff in a fancy jar, package it expensively, and it's astonishing what you could rook women for.'

'Is that what you –?' Miss Marple broke off deliberately.

'Well no, I didn't come in here to talk about cosmetics,' Jackson agreed.

'You've not had much time to think up a lie,' thought Miss Marple to herself. 'Let's see what you'll come out with.'

'Matter of fact,' said Jackson, 'Mrs Walters lent her lipstick to Mrs Kendal the other day. I came in to get it back for her. I tapped on the window and then I saw Mrs Kendal was fast asleep, so I thought it would be quite all right if I just walked across into the bathroom and looked for it.'

'I see,' said Miss Marple. 'And did you find it?'

Jackson shook his head. 'Probably in one of her handbags,' he said lightly. 'I won't bother. Mrs Walters didn't make a point of it. She only just mentioned it casually.' He went on, surveying the toilet preparations: 'Doesn't have very much, does she? Ah well, doesn't need it at her age. Good natural skin.'

'You must look at women with quite a different eye from ordinary men,' said Miss Marple, smiling pleasantly.

'Yes. I suppose various jobs do alter one's angle.'

'You know a good deal about drugs?'

'Oh yes. Good working acquaintance with them. If you ask me, there are too many of them about nowadays. Too many tranquillizers and pep pills and miracle drugs and all the rest of it. All right if they're given on prescription, but there are too many of them you can get without prescription. Some of them can be dangerous.'

'I suppose so,' said Miss Marple. 'Yes, I suppose so.'

'They have a great effect, you know, on behaviour. A lot of this teenage hysteria you get from time to time. It's not natural causes. The kids've been taking things. Oh, there's nothing new about it. It's been known for ages. Out in the East – not that I've ever been there – all sorts of funny things used to happen. You'd be surprised at some of the things women gave their husbands. In India, for example, in the bad old days, a young wife who married an old husband. Didn't want to get rid of him, I suppose, because she'd have been burnt on the funeral pyre, or if she wasn't burnt she'd have been treated as an outcast by the family. No catch to have been a widow in India in those days. But she could keep an elderly husband under drugs, make him semi-imbecile, give him hallucinations, drive him more or less off his head.' He shook his head. 'Yes, lot of dirty work.'

He went on: 'And witches, you know. There's a lot of interesting things known now about witches. Why did they always confess, why did they admit so readily that they *were* witches, that they had flown on broomsticks to the Witches' Sabbath?'

'Torture,' said Miss Marple.

'Not always,' said Jackson. 'Oh yes, torture accounted for a lot of it, but they came out with some of those confessions almost before torture was mentioned. They didn't so much confess as boast about it. Well, they rubbed themselves with ointment, you know. Anointing they used to call it. Some of the preparations, belladonna, atropine, all that sort of thing; if you rub them on the skin they give you hallucinations of levitation, of flying through the air. They thought it all was genuine, poor devils. And look at the Assassins – medieval people, out in Syria, the Lebanon, somewhere like that. They fed them Indian hemp, gave them hallucinations of Paradise and houris, and endless time. They were told that that was what would happen to them after death, but to attain it they had to go and do a ritual killing. Oh, I'm not putting it in fancy language, but that's what it came to.'

'What it came to,' said Miss Marple, 'is in essence the fact that people are highly credulous.'

'Well yes, I suppose you could put it like that.'

'They believe what they are told,' said Miss Marple. 'Yes indeed, we're all inclined to do that,' she added. Then she said sharply, 'Who told you these stories about India, about the doping of husbands with datura,' and she added sharply, before he could answer, 'Was it Major Palgrave?'

Jackson looked slightly surprised. 'Well – yes, as a matter of fact, it was. He told me a lot of stories like that. Of course most of it must have been before his time, but he seemed to know all about it.'

'Major Palgrave was under the impression that he knew a lot about everything,' said Miss Marple. 'He was often inaccurate in what he told people.' She shook her head thoughtfully. 'Major Palgrave,' she said, 'has a lot to answer for.'

There was a slight sound from the adjoining bedroom. Miss Marple turned her head sharply. She went quickly out of the bathroom into the bedroom. Lucky Dyson was standing just inside the window.

'I – oh! I didn't think you were here, Miss Marple.'

'I just stepped into the bathroom for a moment,' said Miss Marple, with dignity and a faint air of Victorian reserve.

In the bathroom, Jackson grinned broadly. Victorian modesty always amused him.

'I just wondered if you'd like me to sit with Molly for a bit,' said Lucky. She looked over towards the bed. 'She's asleep, isn't she?'

'I think so,' said Miss Marple. 'But it's really quite all right. You go and amuse yourself, my dear. I thought you'd gone on that expedition?'

'I was going,' said Lucky, 'but I had such a filthy headache that at the last moment I cried off. So I thought I might as well make myself useful.'

'That was very nice of you,' said Miss Marple. She reseated herself by the bed and resumed her knitting, 'but I'm *quite* happy here.'

Lucky hesitated for a moment or two and then turned away and went out. Miss Marple waited a moment then tiptoed back into the bathroom, but Jackson had departed, no doubt through the other door. Miss Marple picked up the jar of face cream he had been holding, and slipped it into her pocket.

CHAPTER TWENTY-TWO

A Man in her Life?

Getting a little chat in a natural manner with Dr Graham was not so easy as Miss Marple had hoped. She was particularly anxious not to approach him directly since she did not want to lend undue importance to the questions that she was going to ask him.

Tim was back, looking after Molly, and Miss Marple had arranged that she should relieve him there during the time that dinner was served and he was needed in the dining-room. He had assured her that Mrs Dyson was quite willing to take that on, or even Mrs Hillingdon, but Miss Marple said firmly that they were both young women who liked enjoying themselves and that she herself preferred a light meal early and so that would suit everybody. Tim once again thanked her warmly. Hovering rather uncertainly round the hotel and on the pathway which connected with various bungalows, among them Dr Graham's, Miss Marple tried to plan what she was going to do next.

She had a lot of confused and contradictory ideas in her head and if there was one thing that Miss Marple did not like, it was to have confused and contradictory ideas. This whole business had started out clearly enough. Major Palgrave with his regrettable capacity for telling stories, his indiscretion that had obviously been overheard and the corollary, his death within twenty-four hours. Nothing difficult about *that*, thought Miss Marple.

But afterwards, she was forced to admit, there was nothing *but* difficulty. Everything pointed in too many different directions at once. Once admit that you didn't believe a word that anybody had said to you, that nobody could be trusted, and that many of the persons with whom she had conversed here had regrettable resemblances to certain persons at St Mary Mead, and where did that lead you?

Her mind was increasingly focused on the victim. Someone was going to be killed and she had the increasing feeling that she ought to know quite well who that someone was. There had been *something*. Something she had heard? Noticed? Seen?

Something someone had told her that had a bearing on the case. Joan Prescott? Joan Prescott had said a lot of things about a lot of people. Scandal? Gossip? What exactly *had* Joan Prescott said?

Gregory Dyson, Lucky – Miss Marple's mind hovered over Lucky. Lucky, she was convinced with a certainty born of her natural suspicions, had been actively concerned in the death of Gregory Dyson's first wife. Everything pointed to it. Could it be that the predestined victim over whom she was worrying was Gregory Dyson? That Lucky intended to try her luck again with another husband, and for that reason wanted not only freedom but the handsome inheritance that she would get as Gregory Dyson's widow?

'But really,' said Miss Marple to herself, 'this is all pure conjecture. I'm being stupid. I know I'm being stupid. The truth must be quite plain, if one could just clear away the litter. Too much litter, that's what's the matter.'

'Talking to yourself?' said Mr Rafiel.

Miss Marple jumped. She had not noticed his approach. Esther Walters was supporting him and he was coming slowly down from his bungalow to the terrace.

'I really didn't notice you, Mr Rafiel.'

'Your lips were moving. What's become of all this urgency of yours?'

'It's still urgent,' said Miss Marple, 'only I can't just see what must be perfectly plain –'

'I'm glad it's as simple as that – Well, if you want any help, count on me.'

He turned his head as Jackson approached them along the path.

'So there you are, Jackson. Where the devil have you been? Never about when I want you.'

'Sorry, Mr Rafiel.'

Dexterously he slipped his shoulder under Mr Rafiel's. 'Down to the terrace, sir?'

'You can take me to the bar,' said Mr Rafiel. 'All right, Esther, you can go now and change into your evening togs. Meet me on the terrace in half an hour.'

He and Jackson went off together. Mrs Walters dropped into the chair by Miss Marple. She rubbed her arm gently.

'He *seems* a very light weight,' she observed, 'but at the moment my arm feels quite numb. I haven't seen you this afternoon at all, Miss Marple.'

'No, I've been sitting with Molly Kendal,' Miss Marple explained. 'She seems really very much better.'

'If you ask me there was never very much wrong with her,' said Esther Walters.

Miss Marple raised her eyebrows. Esther Walters's tone had been decidedly dry.

'You mean – you think her suicide attempt . . .'

'I don't think there *was* any suicide attempt,' said Esther Walters. 'I don't believe for a moment she took a real overdose and I think Dr Graham knows that perfectly well.'

'Now you interest me very much,' said Miss Marple. 'I wonder why you say that?'

'Because I'm almost certain that it's the case. Oh, it's a thing that happens very often. It's a way, I suppose, of calling attention to oneself,' went on Esther Walters.

'"You'll be sorry when I'm dead"?' quoted Miss Marple.

'That sort of thing,' agreed Esther Walters, 'though I don't think that was the motive in this particular instance. That's the sort of thing you feel like when your husband's playing you up and you're terribly fond of him.'

'You don't think Molly Kendal is fond of her husband?'

'Well,' said Esther Walters, 'do you?'

Miss Marple considered. 'I have,' she said, 'more or less assumed it.' She paused a moment before adding, 'perhaps wrongly.'

Esther was smiling her rather wry smile.

'I've heard a little about her, you know. About the whole business.'

'From Miss Prescott?'

'Oh,' said Esther, 'from one or two people. There's a man in the case. Someone she was keen on. Her people were dead against him.'

'Yes,' said Miss Marple, 'I did hear that.'

'And then she married Tim. Perhaps she was fond of him in a way. But the other man didn't give up. I've wondered once or twice if he didn't actually follow her out here.'

'Indeed. But – who?'

'I've no idea who,' said Esther, 'and I should imagine that they've been very careful.'

'You think she cares for this other man?'

133

Esther shrugged her shoulders. 'I dare say he's a bad lot,' she said, 'but that's very often the kind who knows how to get under a woman's skin and stay there.'

'You never heard what kind of a man – what he did – anything like that?'

Esther shook her head. 'No. People hazard guesses, but you can't go by that type of thing. He may have been a married man. That may have been why her people disliked it, or he may have been a real bad lot. Perhaps he drank. Perhaps he tangled with the law – I don't know. But she cares for him still. That I know positively.'

'You've seen something, heard something?' Miss Marple hazarded.

'I know what I'm talking about,' said Esther. Her voice was harsh and unfriendly.

'These murders – ' began Miss Marple.

'Can't you forget murders?' said Esther. 'You've got Mr Rafiel now all tangled up in them. Can't you just – let them be? You'll never find out any more, I'm sure of that.'

Miss Marple looked at her.

'You think you know, don't you?' she said.

'I think I do, yes. I'm fairly sure.'

'Then oughtn't you to tell what you know – do something about it?'

'Why should I? What good would it do? I couldn't prove anything. What would happen anyway? People get let off nowadays so easily. They call it diminished responsibility and things like that. A few years in prison and you're out again, as right as rain.'

'Supposing, because you don't tell what you know, somebody else gets killed – another victim?'

Esther shook her head with confidence. 'That won't happen,' she said.

'You can't be sure of it.'

'I am sure. And in any case I don't see who – ' She frowned. 'Anyway,' she added, almost inconsequently, 'perhaps it *is* – diminished responsibility. Perhaps you can't help it – not if you are really mentally unbalanced. Oh, I don't know. By far the best thing would be if she went off with whoever it is, then we could all forget about things.'

She glanced at her watch, gave an exclamation of dismay and got up.

'I must go and change.'

Miss Marple sat looking after her. Pronouns, she thought, were always puzzling and women like Esther Walters were particularly prone to strew them about haphazard. Was Esther Walters for some reason convinced that a *woman* had been responsible for the deaths of Major Palgrave and Victoria? It sounded like it. Miss Marple considered.

'Ah, Miss Marple, sitting here all alone – and not even knitting?'

It was Dr Graham for whom she had sought so long and so unsuccessfully. And here he was prepared of his own accord to sit down for a few minutes' chat. He wouldn't stay long, Miss Marple thought, because he too was bent on changing for dinner, and he usually dined fairly early. She explained that she had been sitting by Molly Kendal's bedside that afternoon.

'One can hardly believe she has made such a good recovery so quickly,' she said.

'Oh well,' said Dr Graham, 'it's not very surprising. She didn't take a very heavy overdose, you know.'

'Oh, I understood she'd taken quite a half-bottle full of tablets.'

Dr Graham was smiling indulgently.

'No,' he said, 'I don't think she took that amount. I dare say she meant to take them, then probably at the last moment she threw half of them away. People, even when they think they want to commit suicide, often don't *really* want to do it. They manage not to take a full overdose. It's not always deliberate deceit, it's just the subconscious looking after itself.'

'Or, I suppose it might be deliberate. I mean, wanting it to appear that . . .' Miss Marple paused.

'It's possible,' said Dr Graham.

'If she and Tim had had a row, for instance?'

'They don't have rows, you know. They seem very fond of each other. Still, I suppose it can always happen once. No, I don't think there's very much wrong with her now. She could really get up and go about as usual. Still, it's safer to keep her where she is for a day or two – '

He got up, nodded cheerfully and went off towards the hotel. Miss Marple sat where she was a little while longer.

Various thoughts passed through her mind – The book under Molly's mattress – The way Molly had feigned sleep –

Things Joan Prescott and, later, Esther Walters, had said . . .

135

And then she went back to the beginning of it all – to Major Palgrave –

Something struggled in her mind. Something about Major Palgrave –

Something that if she could only remember –

CHAPTER TWENTY-THREE

The Last Day

'*And the evening and the morning were the last day,*' said Miss Marple to herself.

Then, slightly confused, she sat upright again in her chair. She had dozed off, an incredible thing to do because the steel band was playing and anyone who could doze off during the steel band – Well, it showed, thought Miss Marple, that she was getting used to this place! What was it she had been saying? Some quotation that she'd got wrong. Last day? *First* day. That's what it ought to be. This wasn't the first day. Presumably it wasn't the last day either.

She sat upright again. The fact was that she was extremely tired. All this anxiety, this feeling of having been shamefully inadequate in some way . . . She remembered unpleasantly once more that queer sly look that Molly had given her from under her half-closed eyelids. What had been going on in that girl's head? How different, thought Miss Marple, everything had seemed at first. Tim Kendal and Molly, such a natural happy young couple. The Hillingdons so pleasant, so well-bred, such what is called 'nice' people. The gay hearty extrovert, Greg Dyson, and the gay strident Lucky, talking nineteen to the dozen, pleased with herself and the world . . . A quartet of people getting on so well together. Canon Prescott, that genial kindly man. Joan Prescott, an acid streak in her, but a very nice woman, and nice women had to have their gossipy distractions. They have to know what is going on, to know when two and two make four, and when it is possible to stretch them to five! There was no harm in such women. Their tongues wagged but they were kind if you were in misfortune. Mr Rafiel, a personality, a man of character, a man that you would never by any chance

136

forget. But Miss Marple thought she knew something else about Mr Rafiel.

The doctors had often given him up, so he had said, but this time, she thought, they had been more certain in their pronouncements. Mr Rafiel knew that his days were numbered.

Knowing this with certainty, was there any action he might have been likely to take?

Miss Marple considered the question.

It might, she thought, be important.

What was it exactly he had said, his voice a little too loud, a little too sure? Miss Marple was very skilful in tones of voice. She had done so much listening in her life.

Mr Rafiel had been telling her something that wasn't true.

Miss Marple looked round her. The night air, the soft fragrance of flowers, the tables with their little lights, the women with their pretty dresses, Evelyn in a dark indigo and white print, Lucky in a white sheath, her golden hair shining. Everybody seemed gay and full of life tonight. Even Tim Kendal was smiling. He passed her table and said:

'Can't thank you enough for all you've done. Molly's practically herself again. The doc says she can get up tomorrow.'

Miss Marple smiled at him and said that that was good hearing. She found it, however, quite an effort to smile. Decidedly, she was tired . . .

She got up and walked slowly back to her bungalow. She would have liked to go on thinking, puzzling, trying to remember, trying to assemble various facts and words and glances. But she wasn't able to do it. The tired mind rebelled. It said 'Sleep! You've got to go to sleep!'

Miss Marple undressed, got into bed, read a few verses of the Thomas à Kempis which she kept by her bed, then she turned out the light. In the darkness she sent up a prayer. One couldn't do everything oneself. One had to have help. 'Nothing will happen tonight,' she murmured hopefully.

II

Miss Marple woke suddenly and sat up in bed. Her heart was beating. She switched on the light and looked at the little clock by her bedside.

137

Two am. Two am and outside activity of some kind was going on. She got up, put on her dressing-gown and slippers, and a woollen scarf round her head and went out to reconnoitre. There were people moving about with torches. Among them she saw Canon Prescott and went to him.

'What's happening?'

'Oh, Miss Marple? It's Mrs Kendal. Her husband woke up, found she'd slipped out of bed and gone out. We're looking for her.'

He hurried on. Miss Marple walked more slowly after him. Where had Molly gone? Why? Had she planned this deliberately, planned to slip away as soon as the guard on her was relaxed, and while her husband was deep in sleep? Miss Marple thought it was probable. But why? What was the reason? Was there, as Esther Walters had so strongly hinted, some other man? If so, who could that man be? Or was there some more sinister reason?

Miss Marple walked on, looking around her, peering under bushes. Then suddenly she heard a faint call:

'Here . . . This way . . .'

The cry had come from some little distance beyond the hotel grounds. It must be, thought Miss Marple, near the creek of water that ran down to the sea. She went in that direction as briskly as she could.

There were not really so many searchers as it had seemed to her at first. Most people must still be asleep in their bungalows. She saw a place on the creek bank where there were people standing. Someone pushed past her, almost knocking her down, running in that direction. It was Tim Kendal. A minute or two later she heard his voice cry out:

'Molly! My God, Molly!'

It was a minute or two before Miss Marple was able to join the little group. It consisted of one of the Cuban waiters, Evelyn Hillingdon, and two of the native girls. They had parted to let Tim through. Miss Marple arrived as he was bending over to look.

'Molly . . .' He slowly dropped on to his knees. Miss Marple saw the girl's body clearly, lying there in the creek, her face below the level of the water, her golden hair spread over the pale green embroidered shawl that covered her shoulders. With the leaves and rushes of the creek, it seemed almost like a scene from *Hamlet* with Molly as the dead Ophelia . . .

As Tim stretched out a hand to touch her, the quiet, common-sense Miss Marple took charge and spoke sharply and authoritatively.

'Don't move her, Mr Kendal,' she said. 'She mustn't be moved.'
Tim turned a dazed face up to her.
'But – I must – it's Molly. I must . . .'
Evelyn Hillingdon touched his shoulder.
'She's dead, Tim. I didn't move her, but I did feel her pulse.'
'Dead?' said Tim unbelievingly. 'Dead? You mean she's – *drowned* herself?'
'I'm afraid so. It looks like it.'
'But *why*?' A great cry burst from the young man. '*Why*? She was so happy this morning. Talking about what we'd do tomorrow. Why should this terrible death wish come over her again? Why should she steal away as she did – rush out into the night, come down here and drown herself? What despair did she have – what misery – why couldn't she *tell* me anything?'
'I don't know, my dear,' said Evelyn gently. 'I don't know.'
Miss Marple said:
'Somebody had better get Dr Graham. And someone will have to telephone the police.'
'The police?' Tim uttered a bitter laugh. 'What good will they be?'
'The police have to be notified in a case of suicide,' said Miss Marple.
Tim rose slowly to his feet.
'I'll get Graham,' he said heavily. 'Perhaps – even now – he could – do something.'
He stumbled away in the direction of the hotel.
Evelyn Hillingdon and Miss Marple stood side by side looking down at the dead girl.
Evelyn shook her head. 'It's too late. She's quite cold. She must have been dead at least an hour – perhaps more. What a tragedy it all is. Those two always seemed so happy. I suppose she was always unbalanced.'
'No,' said Miss Marple. 'I don't think she was unbalanced.'
Evelyn looked at her curiously. 'What do you mean?'
The moon had been behind a cloud, but now it came out into the open. It shone with a luminous silvery brightness on Molly's outspread hair . . .
Miss Marple gave a sudden ejaculation. She bent down, peering, then stretched out her hand and touched the golden head. She spoke to Evelyn Hillingdon, and her voice sounded quite different.
'I think,' she said, 'that we had better make sure.'

139

Evelyn Hillingdon stared at her in astonishment.

'But you yourself told Tim we mustn't touch anything?'

'I know. But the moon wasn't out. I hadn't seen – '

Her finger pointed. Then, very gently, she touched the blonde hair and parted it so that the roots were exposed . . .

Evelyn gave a sharp ejaculation.

'*Lucky*!'

And then after a moment she repeated:

'Not Molly . . . Lucky.'

Miss Marple nodded. 'Their hair was of much the same colour – but hers, of course, was dark at the roots because it was dyed.'

'But she's wearing Molly's shawl?'

'She admired it. I heard her say she was going to get one like it. Evidently she did.'

'So that's why we were – deceived . . .'

Evelyn broke off as she met Miss Marple's eyes watching her.

'Someone,' said Miss Marple, 'will have to tell her husband.'

There was a moment's pause, then Evelyn said:

'All right. I'll do it.'

She turned and walked away through the palm trees.

Miss Marple remained for a moment motionless, then she turned her head very slightly, and said:

'Yes, Colonel Hillingdon?'

Edward Hillingdon came from the trees behind her to stand by her side.

'You knew I was there?'

'You cast a shadow,' said Miss Marple.

They stood a moment in silence.

He said, more as though he were speaking to himself:

'So, in the end, she played her luck too far . . .'

'You are, I think, glad that she is dead?'

'And that shocks you? Well, I will not deny it. I am glad she is dead.'

'Death is often a solution to problems.'

Edward Hillingdon turned his head slowly. Miss Marple met his eyes calmly and steadfastly.

'If you think – ' he took a sharp step towards her.

There was a sudden menace in his tone.

Miss Marple said quietly:

'Your wife will be back with Mr Dyson in a moment. Or Mr Kendal will be here with Dr Graham.'

140

Edward Hillingdon relaxed. He turned back to look down at the dead woman.

Miss Marple slipped away quietly. Presently her pace quickened.

Just before reaching her own bungalow, she paused. It was here that she had sat that day talking to Major Palgrave. It was here that he had fumbled in his wallet looking for the snapshot of a murderer . . .

She remembered how he had looked up, and how his face had gone purple and red . . . 'So ugly,' as Señora de Caspearo had said. 'He has the Evil Eye.'

The Evil Eye . . . Eye . . . Eye . . .

CHAPTER TWENTY-FOUR

Nemesis

Whatever the alarms and excursions of the night, Mr Rafiel had not heard them.

He was fast asleep in bed, a faint thin snore coming from his nostrils, when he was taken by the shoulders and shaken violently.

'Eh – what – what the devil's this?'

'It's me,' said Miss Marple, for once ungrammatical, 'though I should put it a little more strongly than that. The Greeks, I believe, had a word for it. Nemesis, if I am not wrong.'

Mr Rafiel raised himself on his pillows as far as he could. He stared at her. Miss Marple, standing there in the moonlight, her head encased in a fluffy scarf of pale pink wool, looked as unlike a figure of Nemesis as it was possible to imagine.

'So you're Nemesis, are you?' said Mr Rafiel after a momentary pause.

'I hope to be – with your help.'

'Do you mind telling me quite plainly what you're talking about like this in the middle of the night.'

'I think we may have to act quickly. Very quickly. I have been foolish. Extremely foolish. I ought to have known from the very beginning what all this was about. It was so simple.'

'What was simple, and what are you talking about?'

'You slept through a good deal,' said Miss Marple. 'A body was found. We thought at first it was the body of Molly Kendal. It wasn't, it was Lucky Dyson. Drowned in the creek.'

'Lucky, eh?' said Mr Rafiel. 'And drowned? In the creek. Did she drown herself or did somebody drown her?'

'Somebody drowned her,' said Miss Marple.

'I see. At least I think I see. That's what you mean by saying it's so simple, is it? Greg Dyson was always the first possibility, and he's the right one. Is that it? Is that what you're thinking? And what you're afraid of is that he may get away with it.'

Miss Marple took a deep breath.

'Mr Rafiel, will you trust me? We have got to stop a murder being committed.'

'I thought you said it *had* been committed.'

'That murder was committed in error. Another murder may be committed any moment now. There's no time to lose. We must prevent it happening. We must go at once.'

'It's all very well to talk like that,' said Mr Rafiel. '*We*, you say? What do you think *I* can do about it? I can't even walk without help. How can you and I set about preventing a murder? You're about a hundred and I'm a broken-up old crock.'

'I was thinking of Jackson,' said Miss Marple. 'Jackson will do what you tell him, won't he?'

'He will indeed,' said Mr Rafiel, 'especially if I add that I'll make it worth his while. Is that what you want?'

'Yes. Tell him to come with me and tell him to obey any orders I give him.'

Mr Rafiel looked at her for about six seconds. Then he said:

'Done. I expect I'm taking the biggest risk of my life. Well, it won't be the first one.' He raised his voice. 'Jackson.' At the same time he picked up the electric bell that lay beside his hand and pressed the button.

Hardly thirty seconds passed before Jackson appeared through the connecting door to the adjoining room.

'You called and rang, sir? Anything wrong?' He broke off, staring at Miss Marple.

'Now Jackson, do as I tell you. You will go with this lady, Miss Marple. You'll go where she takes you and you'll do exactly as she says. You'll obey every order she gives you. Is that understood?'

'I – '

'*Is that understood*?'

'Yes, sir.'

'And for doing that,' said Mr Rafiel, 'you won't be the loser. I'll make it worth your while.'

'Thank you, sir.'

'Come along, Mr Jackson,' said Miss Marple. She spoke over her shoulder to Mr Rafiel. 'We'll tell Mrs Walters to come to you on your way. Get her to get you out of bed and bring you along.'

'Bring me along where?'

'To the Kendals' bungalow,' said Miss Marple. 'I think Molly will be coming back there.'

II

Molly came up the path from the sea. Her eyes stared fixedly ahead of her. Occasionally, under her breath, she gave a little whimper . . .

She went up the steps of the loggia, paused a moment, then pushed open the window and walked into the bedroom. The lights were on, but the room itself was empty. Molly went across to the bed and sat down. She sat for some minutes, now and again passing her hand over her forehead and frowning.

Then, after a quick surreptitious glance round, she slipped her hand under the mattress and brought out the book that was hidden there. She bent over it, turning the pages to find what she wanted.

Then she raised her head as a sound of running footsteps came from outside. With a quick guilty movement she pushed the book behind her back.

Tim Kendal, panting and out of breath, came in, and uttered a great sigh of relief at the sight of her.

'Thank God. Where have you been, Molly? I've been searching everywhere for you.'

'I went to the creek.'

'You went – ' he stopped.

'Yes. I went to the creek. But I couldn't wait there. I couldn't. There was someone in the water – and she was dead.'

'You mean – Do you know I thought it was *you*. I've only just found out it was Lucky.'

'I didn't kill her. Really, Tim, I didn't kill her. I'm sure I didn't. I mean – I'd remember if I did, wouldn't I?'

Tim sank slowly down on the end of the bed.

'You didn't – Are you sure that –? No. No, of course you didn't!' He fairly shouted the words. 'Don't start thinking like that, Molly. Lucky drowned herself. Of course she drowned herself. Hillingdon was through with her. She went and lay down with her face in the water – '

'Lucky wouldn't do that. She'd never do that. But *I* didn't kill her. I swear I didn't.'

'Darling, of course you didn't!' He put his arms round her but she pulled herself away.

'I hate this place. It ought to be all sunlight. It seemed to be all sunlight. But it isn't. Instead there's a shadow a big black shadow . . . And I'm in it – and I can't get out – '

Her voice had risen to a shout.

'Hush, Molly. For God's sake, hush!' He went into the bathroom, came back with a glass.

'Look. Drink this. It'll steady you.'

'I – I can't drink anything. My teeth are chattering so.'

'Yes you can, darling. Sit down. Here, on the bed.' He put his arm round her. He approached the glass to her lips. 'There you are now. Drink it.'

A voice spoke from the window.

'Jackson,' said Miss Marple clearly. 'Go over. Take that glass from him and hold it tightly. Be careful. He's strong and he may be pretty desperate.'

There were certain points about Jackson. He was a man with a great love for money, and money had been promised him by his employer, that employer being a man of stature and authority. He was also a man of extreme muscular development heightened by his training. His not to reason why, his but to do.

Swift as a flash he had crossed the room. His hand went over the glass that Tim was holding to Molly's lips, his other arm had fastened round Tim. A quick flick of the wrist and he had the glass. Tim turned on him wildly, but Jackson held him firmly.

'What the devil – let go of me. Let go of me. Have you gone mad? What are you doing?'

Tim struggled violently.

'Hold him, Jackson,' said Miss Marple.

'What's going on? What's the matter here?'

Supported by Esther Walters, Mr Rafiel came through the window.

'You ask what's the matter?' shouted Tim. 'Your man's gone mad, stark, staring mad, that's what's the matter. Tell him to let go of me.'

'No,' said Miss Marple.

Mr Rafiel turned to her.

'Speak up, Nemesis,' he said. 'We've got to have chapter and verse of some kind.'

'I've been stupid and a fool,' said Miss Marple, 'but I'm not being a fool now. When the contents of that glass that he was trying to make his wife drink have been analysed, I'll wager – yes, I'll wager my immortal soul that you'll find it's got a lethal dose of narcotic in it. It's the same pattern, you see, the same pattern as in Major Palgrave's story. A wife in a depressed state, and she tries to do away with herself, husband saves her in time. Then the second time she succeeds. Yes, it's the right pattern. Major Palgrave told me the story and he took out a snapshot and then he looked up and saw – '

'Over your right shoulder – ' continued Mr Rafiel.

'No,' said Miss Marple, shaking her head. '*He didn't see anything over my right shoulder*.'

'What are you talking about? You told me . . .'

'I told you wrong. I was completely wrong. I was stupid beyond belief. Major Palgrave *appeared* to me to be looking over my right shoulder, glaring, in fact, at something – But he couldn't have *seen* anything, because he was looking through his left eye and his left eye was his glass eye.'

'I remember – he *had* a glass eye,' said Mr Rafiel. 'I'd forgotten – or I took it for granted. You mean he couldn't see anything?'

'Of course he could *see*,' said Miss Marple. 'He could *see* all right, but he could only see with one eye. The eye he *could* see with was his *right* eye. And so, you see, he must have been looking at something or someone not to the right of me but to the *left* of me.'

'Was there anyone on the left of you?'

'Yes,' said Miss Marple. 'Tim Kendal and his wife were sitting not far off. Sitting at a table just by a big hibiscus bush. They were doing accounts there. So you see the Major looked up. His glass left eye was glaring over my shoulder, but what he *saw* with his other eye was a man sitting by a hibiscus bush and the face was the same, only rather older, as the face in the snapshot. Also by a hibiscus bush. Tim Kendal had heard the story the Major had been telling and he saw that the Major had recognized him. So, of course, he had

to kill him. Later, he had to kill the girl, Victoria, because she'd
seen him putting a bottle of tablets in the Major's room. She didn't
think anything of it at first because of course it was quite natural on
various occasions for Tim Kendal to go into the guests' bungalows.
He might have just been returning something to it that had been
left on a restaurant table. But she thought about it and then she
asked him questions and so he had to get rid of her. But this is
the real murder, the murder he's been planning all along. He's a
wife-killer, you see.'

'What damned nonsense, what – ' Tim Kendal shouted.

There was a sudden cry, a wild angry cry. Esther Walters detached
herself from Mr Rafiel, almost flinging him down, and rushed across
the room. She pulled vainly at Jackson.

'Let go of him – let go of him. It's not true. Not a word of it's
true. Tim – Tim darling, it's not true. You could never kill anyone,
I know you couldn't. I know you wouldn't. It's that horrible girl you
married. She's been telling lies about you. They're not true. None
of them are true. I believe in you. I love you and trust in you. I'll
never believe a word anyone says. I'll – '

Then Tim Kendal lost control of himself.

'For God's sake, you damned bitch,' he said, 'shut up, can't you?
D'you want to get me hanged? Shut up, I tell you. Shut that big,
ugly mouth of yours.'

'Poor silly creature,' said Mr Rafiel softly. 'So that's what's been
going on, is it?'

CHAPTER TWENTY-FIVE

Miss Marple uses her Imagination

'So that's what had been going on?' said Mr Rafiel.

He and Miss Marple were sitting together in a confidential manner.

'She'd been having an affair with Tim Kendal, had she?'

'Hardly an affair, I imagine,' said Miss Marple, primly. 'It was, I
think, a romantic attachment with the prospect of marriage in the
future.'

'What – after his wife was dead?'

'I don't think poor Esther Walters knew that Molly was going to die,' said Miss Marple. 'I just think she believed the story Tim Kendal told her about Molly having been in love with another man, and the man having followed her here, and I think she counted on Tim's getting a divorce. I think it was all quite proper and respectable. But she was very much in love with him.'

'Well, that's easily understood. He was an attractive chap. But what made *him* go for her – d'you know that too?'

'*You* know, don't you?' said Miss Marple.

'I dare say I've got a pretty fair idea, but I don't know how you should know about it. As far as that goes, I don't see how Tim Kendal could know about it.'

'Well, I really think I could explain all that with a little imagination, though it would be simpler if you told me.'

'I'm not going to tell you,' said Mr Rafiel. 'You tell me, since you're being so clever.'

'Well, it seems to me possible,' said Miss Marple, 'that as I have already hinted to you, your man Jackson was in the habit of taking a good snoop through your various papers from time to time.'

'Perfectly possible,' said Mr Rafiel, 'but I shouldn't have said there was anything there that could do him much good. I took care of that.'

'I imagine,' said Miss Marple, 'he read your will.'

'Oh I see. Yes, yes, I did have a copy of my will along.'

'You told me,' said Miss Marple, 'you told me – (as Humpty Dumpty said – very loud and clear) that you had *not* left anything to Esther Walters in your will. You had impressed that fact upon her, and also upon Jackson. It was true in Jackson's case, I should imagine. You have not left *him* anything, but you *had* left Esther Walters money, though you weren't going to let her have any inkling of the fact. Isn't that right?'

'Yes, it's quite right, but I don't know how *you* knew.'

'Well, it's the way you insisted on the point,' said Miss Marple. 'I have a certain experience of the way people tell lies.'

'I give in,' said Mr Rafiel. 'All right. I left Esther £50,000. It would come as a nice surprise to her when I died. I suppose that, knowing this, Tim Kendal decided to exterminate his present wife with a nice dose of something or other and marry £50,000 and Esther Walters. Possibly to dispose of her also in good time. But how did *he* know she was going to have £50,000?'

'Jackson told him, of course,' said Miss Marple. 'They were very friendly, those two. Tim Kendal was nice to Jackson and, quite, I should imagine, without ulterior motive. But amongst the bits of gossip that Jackson let slip I think Jackson told him that unbeknownst to herself, Esther Walters was going to inherit a fat lot of money, and he may have said that he himself hoped to induce Esther Walters to marry him though he hadn't had much success so far in taking her fancy. Yes, I think that's how it happened.'

'The things you imagine always seem perfectly plausible,' said Mr Rafiel.

'But I was stupid,' said Miss Marple, 'very stupid. Everything fitted in really, you see. Tim Kendal was a very clever man as well as being a very wicked one. He was particularly good at putting about rumours. Half the things I've been told here came from him originally, I imagine. There were stories going around about Molly wanting to marry an undesirable young man, but I rather fancy that the undesirable young man was actually Tim Kendal himself, though that wasn't the name he was using then. Her people had heard something, perhaps that his background was fishy. So he put on a high indignation act, refused to be taken by Molly to be 'shown off' to her people and then he brewed up a little scheme with her which they both thought great fun. She pretended to sulk and pine for him. Then a Mr Tim Kendal turned up, primed with the names of various old friends of Molly's people, and they welcomed him with open arms as being the sort of young man who would put the former delinquent one out of Molly's head. I am afraid Molly and he must have laughed over it a good deal. Anyway, he married her, and with her money he bought out the people who ran this place and they came out here. I should imagine that he ran through her money at a pretty fair rate. Then he came across Esther Walters and he saw a nice prospect of more money.'

'Why didn't he bump me off?' said Mr Rafiel.

Miss Marple coughed.

'I expect he wanted to be fairly sure of Mrs Walters first. Besides – I mean . . .' She stopped, a little confused.

'Besides, he realized he wouldn't have to wait long,' said Mr Rafiel, 'and it would clearly be better for me to die a natural death. Being so rich. Deaths of millionaires are scrutinized rather carefully, aren't they, unlike mere wives?'

'Yes, you're quite right. Such a lot of lies as he told,' said Miss Marple. 'Look at the lies he got Molly herself to believe – putting that book on mental disorders in her way. Giving her drugs which would give her dreams and hallucinations. You know, your Jackson was rather clever over that. I think he recognized certain of Molly's symptoms as being the result of drugs. And he came into the bungalow that day to potter about a bit in the bathroom. That face cream he examined. He might have got some idea from the old tales of witches rubbing themselves with ointments that had belladonna in them. Belladonna in face cream could have produced just that result. Molly would have blackouts. Times she couldn't account for, dreams of flying through the air. No wonder she got frightened about herself. She had all the signs of mental illness, Jackson was on the right track. Maybe he got the idea from Major Palgrave's stories about the use of datura by Indian women on their husbands.'

'Major Palgrave!' said Mr Rafiel. 'Really, that man!'

'He brought about his own murder,' said Miss Marple, 'and that poor girl Victoria's murder, and he nearly brought about Molly's murder. But he recognized a murderer all right.'

'What made you suddenly remember about his glass eye?' asked Mr Rafiel curiously.

'Something that Señora de Caspearo said. She talked some nonsense about his being ugly, and having the Evil Eye; and I said it was only a glass eye, and he couldn't help that, poor man, and she said his eyes looked different ways, they were cross-eyes – which, of course, they were. And she said it brought bad luck. I knew – I *knew* that I had heard something that day that was important. Last night, just after Lucky's death, it came to me what it was! And then I realized there was no time to waste . . .'

'How did Tim Kendal come to kill the wrong woman?'

'Sheer chance. I think his plan was this: Having convinced everybody – and that included Molly herself – that she was mentally unbalanced, and after giving her a sizeable dose of the drug he was using, he told her that between them they were going to clear up all these murder puzzles. But she had got to help him. After everyone was asleep, they would go separately and meet at an agreed spot by the creek.

'He said he had a very good idea who the murderer was, and they would trap him. Molly went off obediently – but she was confused and stupefied with the drug she had been given, and it slowed her up. Tim arrived there first and saw what he thought was Molly. Golden hair and pale green shawl. He came up behind her, put his hand over her mouth, and forced her down into the water and held her there.'

'Nice fellow! But wouldn't it have been easier just to give her an overdose of narcotic?'

'Much easier, of course. But that *might* have given rise to suspicion. All narcotics and sedatives have been very carefully removed from Molly's reach, remember. And if she *had* got hold of a fresh supply, who more likely to have supplied it than her husband? But if, in a fit of despair, she went out and drowned herself whilst her innocent husband slept, the whole thing would be a romantic tragedy, and no one would be likely to suggest that she had been drowned deliberately. Besides,' added Miss Marple, 'murderers always find it difficult to keep things simple. They can't keep themselves from elaborating.'

'You seem convinced you know all there is to be known about murderers! So you believe Tim didn't know he had killed the wrong woman?'

Miss Marple shook her head.

'He didn't even look at her face, just hurried off as quickly as he could, let an hour elapse, then started to organize a search for her, playing the part of a distracted husband.'

'But what the devil was Lucky doing hanging about the creek in the middle of the night?'

Miss Marple gave an embarrassed little cough.

'It is possible, I think, that she was – er – waiting to meet someone.'

'Edward Hillingdon?'

'Oh *no*,' said Miss Marple. 'That's all over, I wondered whether – just possibly – she might have been waiting for Jackson.'

'Waiting for *Jackson*?'

'I've noticed her – look at him once or twice,' murmured Miss Marple, averting her eyes.

Mr Rafiel whistled.

'My Tom Cat Jackson! I wouldn't put it past him! Tim must have had a shock later when he found he'd killed the wrong woman.'

'Yes, indeed. He must have felt quite desperate. Here was Molly alive and wandering about. And the story he'd circulated so carefully about her mental condition wouldn't stand up for a moment once she got into the hands of competent mental specialists. And once she told her damning story of his having asked her to meet him at the creek, where would Tim Kendal be? He'd only one hope – to finish off Molly as quickly as possible. Then there was a very good chance that everyone would believe that Molly, in a fit of mania,

150

had drowned Lucky, and had then, horrified by what she had done, taken her own life.'

'And it was then,' said Mr Rafiel, 'that you decided to play Nemesis, eh?'

He leaned back suddenly and roared with laughter. 'It's a damned good joke,' he said. 'If you knew what you looked like that night with that fluffy pink wool all round your head, standing there and saying you were Nemesis! I'll never forget it!'

EPILOGUE

The time had come and Miss Marple was waiting at the airport for her plane. Quite a lot of people had come to see her off. The Hillingdons had left already. Gregory Dyson had flown to one of the other islands and the rumour had come that he was devoting himself to an Argentinian widow. Señora de Caspearo had returned to South America.

Molly had come to see Miss Marple off. She was pale and thin but she had weathered the shock of her discovery bravely and with the help of one of Mr Rafiel's nominees whom he had wired for to England, she was carrying on with the running of the hotel.

'Do you good to be busy,' Mr Rafiel observed. 'Keep you from thinking. Got a good thing here.'

'You don't think the murders – '

'People love murders when they're all cleared up,' Mr Rafiel had assured her. 'You carry on, girl, and keep your heart up. Don't distrust all men because you've met one bad lot.'

'You sound like Miss Marple,' Molly had said, 'she's always telling me Mr Right will come along one day.'

Mr Rafiel grinned at this sentiment. So Molly was there and the two Prescotts and Mr Rafiel, of course, and Esther – an Esther who looked older and sadder and to whom Mr Rafiel was quite often unexpectedly kind. Jackson also was very much to the fore pretending to be looking after Miss Marple's baggage. He was all smiles these days and let it be known that he had come into money.

There was a hum in the sky. The plane was arriving. Things were somewhat informal here. There was no 'taking your place by Channel 8' or Channel 9. You just walked out from the little flower-covered pavilion on to the tarmac.

'Goodbye, darling Miss Marple.' Molly kissed her.

'Goodbye. Do try and come and visit us.' Miss Prescott shook her warmly by the hand.

'It has been a great pleasure to know you,' said the Canon. ' second my sister's invitation most warmly.'

'All the best, Madam,' said Jackson, 'and remember any time you want any massage free, just you send me a line and we'll make an appointment.'

Only Esther Walters turned slightly away when the time came for goodbyes. Miss Marple did not force one upon her. Mr Rafiel came last. He took her hand.

'*Ave Caesar, nos morituri te salutamus*,' he said.

'I'm afraid,' said Miss Marple, 'I don't know very much Latin.'

'But you understand that?'

'Yes.' She said no more. She knew quite well what he was telling her.

'It has been a great pleasure to know you,' she said.

Then she walked across the tarmac and got into the plane.

A Pocket Full of Rye

For Bruce Ingram
Who liked and published my
first short stories

CHAPTER ONE

It was Miss Somers's turn to make the tea. Miss Somers was the newest and the most inefficient of the typists. She was no longer young and had a mild worried face like a sheep. The kettle was not quite boiling when Miss Somers poured the water on to the tea, but poor Miss Somers was never quite sure when a kettle *was* boiling. It was one of the many worries that afflicted her in life.

She poured out the tea and took the cups round with a couple of limp, sweet biscuits in each saucer.

Miss Griffith, the efficient head typist, a grey-haired martinet who had been with Consolidated Investments Trust for sixteen years, said sharply: 'Water not boiling *again*, Somers!' and Miss Somers's worried meek face went pink and she said, 'Oh dear, I *did* think it was boiling *this* time.'

Miss Griffith thought to herself: 'She'll last for another month, perhaps, just while we're so busy . . . But really! The mess the silly idiot made of that letter to Eastern Developments – a perfectly straightforward job, and always so stupid over the tea. If it weren't so difficult to get hold of any intelligent typists – and the biscuit tin lid wasn't shut tightly last time, either. *Really* – '

Like so many of Miss Griffith's indignant inner communings the sentence went unfinished.

At that moment Miss Grosvenor sailed in to make Mr Fortescue's sacred tea. Mr Fortescue had different tea, and different china and special biscuits. Only the kettle and the water from the cloakroom tap were the same. But on this occasion, being Mr Fortescue's tea, the water boiled. Miss Grosvenor saw to that.

Miss Grosvenor was an incredibly glamorous blonde. She wore an expensively cut little black suit and her shapely legs were encased in the very best and most expensive black-market nylons.

She sailed back through the typists' room without deigning to give anyone a word or a glance. The typists might have been so many blackbeetles. Miss Grosvenor was Mr Fortescue's own

159

special personal secretary; unkind rumour always hinted that she was something more, but actually this was not true. Mr Fortescue had recently married a second wife, both glamorous and expensive, and fully capable of absorbing all his attention. Miss Grosvenor was to Mr Fortescue just a necessary part of the office décor – which was all very luxurious and very expensive.

Miss Grosvenor sailed back with the tray held out in front of her like a ritual offering. Through the inner office and through the waiting-room, where the more important clients were allowed to sit, and through her own ante-room, and finally with a light tap on the door she entered the holy of holies, Mr Fortescue's office.

It was a large room with a gleaming expanse of parquet floor on which were dotted expensive oriental rugs. It was delicately panelled in pale wood and there were some enormous stuffed chairs upholstered in pale buff leather. Behind a colossal sycamore desk, the centre and focus of the room, sat Mr Fortescue himself.

Mr Fortescue was less impressive than he should have been to match the room, but he did his best. He was a large flabby man with a gleaming bald head. It was his affectation to wear loosely cut country tweeds in his city office. He was frowning down at some papers on his desk when Miss Grosvenor glided up to him in her swanlike manner. Placing the tray on the desk at his elbow, she murmured in a low impersonal voice, 'Your tea, Mr Fortescue,' and withdrew.

Mr Fortescue's contribution to the ritual was a grunt.

Seated at her own desk again Miss Grosvenor proceeded with the business in hand. She made two telephone calls, corrected some letters that were lying there typed ready for Mr Fortescue to sign and took one incoming call.

'Ay'm afraid it's impossible just now,' she said in haughty accents. 'Mr Fortescue is in conference.'

As she laid down the receiver she glanced at the clock. It was ten minutes past eleven.

It was just then that an unusual sound penetrated through the almost sound-proof door of Mr Fortescue's office. Muffled, it was yet fully recognizable, a strangled agonized cry. At the same moment the buzzer on Miss Grosvenor's desk sounded in a long-drawn frenzied summons. Miss Grosvenor, startled for a moment into complete immobility, rose uncertainly to her feet. Confronted by the unexpected, her poise was shaken. However, she moved towards Mr Fortescue's door in her usual statuesque fashion, tapped and entered.

160

What she saw upset her poise still further. Her employer behind his desk seemed contorted with agony. His convulsive movements were alarming to watch.

Miss Grosvenor said, 'Oh dear, Mr Fortescue, are you ill?' and was immediately conscious of the idiocy of the question. There was no doubt but that Mr Fortescue was very seriously ill. Even as she came up to him, his body was convulsed in a painful spasmodic movement.

Words came out in jerky gasps.

'Tea – what the hell – you put in the tea – get help – quick get a doctor – '

Miss Grosvenor fled from the room. She was no longer the supercilious blonde secretary – she was a thoroughly frightened woman who had lost her head.

She came running into the typists' office crying out:

'Mr Fortescue's having a fit – he's dying – we must get a doctor – he looks awful – I'm sure he's dying.'

Reactions were immediate and varied a good deal.

Miss Bell, the youngest typist, said, 'If it's epilepsy we ought to put a cork in his mouth. Who's got a cork?'

Nobody had a cork.

Miss Somers said, 'At his age it's probably apoplexy.'

Miss Griffith said, 'We must get a doctor – *at once*.'

But she was hampered in her usual efficiency because in all her sixteen years of service it had never been necessary to call a doctor to the city office. There was her own doctor but that was at Streatham Hill. Where was there a doctor near here?

Nobody knew. Miss Bell seized a telephone directory and began looking up Doctors under D. But it was not a classified directory and doctors were not automatically listed like taxi ranks. Someone suggested a hospital – but which hospital? 'It has to be the right hospital,' Miss Somers insisted, 'or else they won't come. Because of the National Health, I mean. It's got to be in the area.'

Someone suggested 999 but Miss Griffith was shocked at that and said it would mean the police and that would never do. For citizens of a country which enjoyed the benefits of Medical Service for all, a group of quite reasonably intelligent women showed incredible ignorance of correct procedure. Miss Bell started looking up Ambulances under A. Miss Griffith said, 'There's his own doctor – he must *have* a doctor.' Someone rushed for the private address book. Miss Griffith instructed the office boy to go out and find a doctor

– somehow, *anywhere*. In the private address book, Miss Griffith found Sir Edwin Sandeman with an address in Harley Street. Miss Grosvenor, collapsed in a chair, wailed in a voice whose accent was noticeably less Mayfair than usual, 'I made the tea just as usual – really I did – there couldn't have been anything wrong in it.'

'*Wrong* in it?' Miss Griffith paused, her hand on the dial of the telephone. 'Why do you say that?'

'*He* said it – Mr Fortescue – he said it was the tea – '

Miss Griffith's hand hovered irresolutely between Welbeck and 999. Miss Bell, young and hopeful, said: 'We ought to give him some mustard and water – *now*. Isn't there any mustard in the office?'

There was no mustard in the office.

Some short while later Dr Isaacs of Bethnal Green, and Sir Edwin Sandeman met in the elevator just as two different ambulances drew up in front of the building. The telephone and the office boy had done their work.

CHAPTER TWO

Inspector Neele sat in Mr Fortescue's sanctum behind Mr Fortescue's vast sycamore desk. One of his underlings with a notebook sat unobtrusively against the wall near the door.

Inspector Neele had a smart soldierly appearance with crisp brown hair growing back from a rather low forehead. When he uttered the phrase 'just a matter of routine' those addressed were wont to think spitefully: 'And routine is about all *you*'re capable of!' They would have been quite wrong. Behind his unimaginative appearance, Inspector Neele was a highly imaginative thinker, and one of his methods of investigation was to propound to himself fantastic theories of guilt which he applied to such persons as he was interrogating at the time.

Miss Griffith, whom he had at once picked out with an unerring eye as being the most suitable person to give him a succinct account of the events which had led to his being seated where he was, had just left the room having given him an admirable résumé of the morning's happenings. Inspector Neele propounded to himself three separate highly coloured reasons why the faithful doyenne of the typists' room should have poisoned her employer's mid-morning cup of tea, and rejected them as unlikely.

He classified Miss Griffith as (*a*) Not the type of a poisoner, (*b*) Not in love with her employer, (*c*) No pronounced mental instability, (*d*) Not a woman who cherished grudges. That really seemed to dispose of Miss Griffith except as a source of accurate information.

Inspector Neele glanced at the telephone. He was expecting a call from St Jude's Hospital at any moment now.

It was possible, of course, that Mr Fortescue's sudden illness was due to natural causes, but Dr Isaacs of Bethnal Green had not thought so and Sir Edwin Sandeman of Harley Street had not thought so.

Inspector Neele pressed a buzzer conveniently situated at his left hand and demanded that Mr Fortescue's personal secretary should be sent in to him.

Miss Grosvenor had recovered a little of her poise, but not much. She came in apprehensively, with nothing of the swanlike glide about her motions, and said at once defensively:

'I didn't do it!'

Inspector Neele murmured conversationally: 'No?'

He indicated the chair where Miss Grosvenor was wont to place herself, pad in hand, when summoned to take down Mr Fortescue's letters. She sat down now with reluctance and eyed Inspector Neele in alarm. Inspector Neele, his mind playing imaginatively on the themes Seduction? Blackmail? Platinum Blonde in Court? etc., looked reassuring and just a little stupid.

'There wasn't anything wrong with the tea,' said Miss Grosvenor. 'There couldn't have been.'

'*I* see,' said Inspector Neele. 'Your name and address, please?'

'Grosvenor. Irene Grosvenor.'

'How do you spell it?'

'Oh. Like the Square.'

'And your address?'

'14 Rushmoor Road, Muswell Hill.'

Inspector Neele nodded in a satisfied fashion.

'No seduction,' he said to himself. 'No Love Nest. Respectable home with parents. No blackmail.'

Another good set of speculative theories washed out.

'And so it was you who made the tea?' he said pleasantly.

'Well, I had to. I always do, I mean.'

Unhurried, Inspector Neele took her closely through the morning ritual of Mr Fortescue's tea. The cup and saucer and teapot had already been packed up and dispatched to the appropriate quarter for analysis. Now Inspector Neele learned that Irene Grosvenor and only Irene Grosvenor had handled that cup and saucer and teapot. The kettle had been used for making the office tea and had been refilled from the cloakroom tap by Miss Grosvenor.

'And the tea itself?'

'It was Mr Fortescue's own tea, special China tea. It's kept on the shelf in my room next door.'

Inspector Neele nodded. He inquired about sugar and heard that Mr Fortescue didn't take sugar.

The telephone rang. Inspector Neele picked up the receiver. His face changed a little.

'St Jude's?'

He nodded to Miss Grosvenor in dismissal.

'That's all for now, thank you, Miss Grosvenor.'

Miss Grosvenor sped out of the room hurriedly.

Inspector Neele listened carefully to the thin unemotional tones speaking from St Jude's Hospital. As the voice spoke he made a few cryptic signs with a pencil on the corner of the blotter in front of him.

'Died five minutes ago, you say?' he asked. His eye went to the watch on his wrist. *Twelve forty-three*, he wrote on the blotter.

The unemotional voice said that Dr Bernsdorff himself would like to speak to Inspector Neele.

Inspector Neele said, 'Right. Put him through,' which rather scandalized the owner of the voice, who had allowed a certain amount of reverence to seep into the official accents.

There were then various clicks, buzzes, and far-off ghostly murmurs. Inspector Neele sat patiently waiting.

Then without warning a deep bass roar caused him to shift the receiver an inch or two away from his ear.

'Hallo, Neele, you old vulture. At it again with your corpses?'

Inspector Neele and Professor Bernsdorff of St Jude's had been brought together over a case of poisoning just over a year ago and had remained on friendly terms.

'Our man's dead, I hear, doc.'

'Yes. We couldn't do anything by the time he got here.'

'And the cause of death?'

'There will have to be an autopsy, naturally. Very interesting case. Very interesting indeed. Glad I was able to be in on it.'

The professional gusto in Bernsdorff's rich tones told Inspector Neele one thing at least.

'I gather you don't think it was natural death,' he said dryly.

'Not a dog's chance of it,' said Dr Bernsdorff robustly. 'I'm speaking unofficially, of course,' he added with belated caution.

'Of course. Of course. That's understood. He was poisoned?'

'Definitely. And what's more – this is quite unofficial, you understand – just between you and me – I'd be prepared to make a bet on what the poison was.'

'Indeed?'

'Taxine, my boy. Taxine.'

'Taxine? Never heard of it.'

'I know. *Most* unusual. Really delightfully unusual! I don't say I'd have spotted it myself if I hadn't had a case only three or four weeks ago. Couple of kids playing dolls' tea-parties – pulled berries off a yew tree and used them for tea.'

'Is that what it is? Yew berries?'

'Berries or leaves. Highly poisonous. Taxine, of course, is the alkaloid. Don't think I've heard of a case where it was used deliberately. Really *most* interesting and unusual . . . You've no idea, Neele, how tired one gets of the inevitable weed-killer. Taxine is a real treat. Of course, I *may* be wrong – don't quote me, for Heaven's sake – but I don't think so. Interesting for you, too, I should think. Varies the routine!'

'A good time is to be had by all, is that the idea? With the exception of the victim.'

'Yes, yes, poor fellow.' Dr Bernsdorff's tone was perfunctory. 'Very bad luck on him.'

'Did he say anything before he died?'

'Well, one of your fellows was sitting by him with a notebook. He'll have the exact details. He muttered something once about tea – that he'd been given something in his tea at the office – but that's nonsense, of course.'

'Why is it nonsense?' Inspector Neele, who had been reviewing speculatively the picture of the glamorous Miss Grosvenor adding yew berries to a brew of tea, and finding it incongruous, spoke sharply.

'Because the stuff couldn't possibly have worked so soon. I understand the symptoms came on immediately he had drunk the tea?'

165

'That's what they say.'

'Well, there are very few poisons that act as quickly as that, apart from the cyanides, of course – and possibly pure nicotine – '

'And it definitely wasn't cyanide or nicotine?'

'My dear fellow. He'd have been dead before the ambulance arrived. Oh no, there's no question of anything of that kind. I *did* suspect strychnine, but the convulsions were not at all typical. Still unofficial, of course, but I'll stake my reputation it's taxine.'

'How long would that take to work?'

'Depends. An hour. Two hours, three hours. Deceased looked like a hearty eater. If he had had a big breakfast, that would slow things up.'

'Breakfast,' said Inspector Neele thoughtfully. 'Yes, it looks like breakfast.'

'Breakfast with the Borgias.' Dr Bernsdorff laughed cheerfully. 'Well, good hunting, my lad.'

'Thanks, doctor. I'd like to speak to my sergeant before you ring off.'

Again there were clicks and buzzes and far-off ghostly voices. And then the sound of heavy breathing came through, an inevitable prelude to Sergeant Hay's conversation.

'Sir, he said urgently. '*Sir.*'

'Neele here. Did the deceased say anything I ought to know?'

'Said it was the tea. The tea he had at the office. But the M.O. says not . . .'

'Yes, I know about that. Nothing else?'

'No, sir. But there's one thing that's odd. The suit he was wearing – I checked the contents of the pockets. The usual stuff – handkerchief, keys, change, wallet – but there was one thing that's downright peculiar. The right-hand pocket of his jacket. It had *cereal* in it.'

'Cereal?'

'Yes, sir.'

'What do you mean by cereal? Do you mean a breakfast food? Farmer's Glory or Wheatifax. Or do you mean corn or barley – '

'That's right, sir. Grain it was. Looked like rye to me. Quite a lot of it.'

'I see . . . Odd . . . But it might have been a sample – something to do with a business deal.'

'Quite so, sir – but I thought I'd better mention it.'

'Quite right, Hay.'

Inspector Neele sat staring ahead of him for a few moments

166

after he had replaced the telephone receiver. His orderly mind was moving from Phase I to Phase II of the inquiry – from suspicion of poisoning to certainty of poisoning. Professor Bernsdorff's words may have been unofficial, but Professor Bernsdorff was not a man to be mistaken in his beliefs. Rex Fortescue had been poisoned and the poison had probably been administered one to three hours before the onset of the first symptoms. It seemed probable, therefore, that the office staff could be given a clean bill of health.

Neele got up and went into the outer office. A little desultory work was being done but the typewriters were not going at full speed.

'Miss Griffith? Can I have another word with you?'

'Certainly, Mr Neele. Could some of the girls go out to lunch? It's long past their regular time. Or would you prefer that we get something sent in?'

'No. They can go to lunch. But they must return afterwards.'

'Of course.'

Miss Griffith followed Neele back into the private office. She sat down in her composed efficient way.

Without preamble, Inspector Neele said:

'I have heard from St Jude's Hospital. Mr Fortescue died at 12.43.'

Miss Griffith received the news without surprise, merely shook her head.

'I was afraid he was very ill,' she said.

She was not, Neele noted, at all distressed.

'Will you please give me particulars of his home and family?'

'Certainly. I have already tried to get into communication with Mrs Fortescue, but it seems she is out playing golf. She was not expected home to lunch. There is some uncertainty as to which course she is playing on.' She added in an explanatory manner, 'They live at Baydon Heath, you know, which is a centre for three well-known golf courses.'

Inspector Neele nodded. Baydon Heath was almost entirely inhabited by rich city men. It had an excellent train service, was only twenty miles from London and was comparatively easy to reach by car even in the rush of morning and evening traffic.

'The exact address, please, and the telephone number?'

'Baydon Heath 3400. The name of the house is Yewtree Lodge.'

'*What?*' The sharp query slipped out before Inspector Neele could control it. 'Did you say *Yewtree* Lodge?'

'Yes.'

Miss Griffith looked faintly curious, but Inspector Neele had himself in hand again.

'Can you give me particulars of his family?'

'Mrs Fortescue is his second wife. She is much younger than he is. They were married about two years ago. The first Mrs Fortescue has been dead a long time. There are two sons and a daughter of the first marriage. The daughter lives at home and so does the elder son, who is a partner in the firm. Unfortunately he is away in the North of England today on business. He is expected to return tomorrow.'

'When did he go away?'

'The day before yesterday.'

'Have you tried to get in touch with him?'

'Yes. After Mr Fortescue was removed to hospital I rang up the Midland Hotel in Manchester where I thought he might be staying, but he had left early this morning. I believe he was also going to Sheffield and Leicester, but I am not sure about that. I can give you the names of certain firms in those cities whom he might be visiting.'

Certainly an efficient woman, thought the inspector, and if she murdered a man she would probably murder him very efficiently, too. But he forced himself to abandon these speculations and concentrate once more on Mr Fortescue's home front.

'There is a second son you said?'

'Yes. But owing to a disagreement with his father he lives abroad.'

'Are both sons married?'

'Yes. Mr Percival has been married for three years. He and his wife occupy a self-contained flat in Yewtree Lodge, though they are moving into their own house at Baydon Heath very shortly.'

'You were not able to get in touch with Mrs Percival Fortescue when you rang up this morning?'

'She had gone to London for the day.' Miss Griffith went on, 'Mr Lancelot got married less than a year ago. To the widow of Lord Frederick Anstice. I expect you've seen pictures of her. In the *Tatler* – with horses, you know. And at point-to-points.'

Miss Griffith sounded a little breathless and her cheeks were faintly flushed. Neele, who was quick to catch the moods of human beings, realized that this marriage had thrilled the snob and the romantic in Miss Griffith. The aristocracy was the aristocracy to Miss Griffith and the fact that the late Lord Frederick Anstice had had a somewhat unsavoury reputation in sporting circles was almost certainly not known to her. Freddie Anstice had blown his brains out just before an inquiry by the Stewards into the running of one of his horses. Neele remembered something vaguely about his wife. She had been the daughter of an Irish Peer and had been married before to an airman who had been killed in the Battle of Britain.

And now, it seemed, she was married to the black sheep of the Fortescue family, for Neele assumed that the disagreement with his father, referred to primly by Miss Griffith, stood for some disgraceful incident in young Lancelot Fortescue's career.

Lancelot Fortescue! What a name! And what was the other son – Percival? He wondered what the first Mrs Fortescue had been like? She'd had a curious taste in Christian names . . .

He drew the phone towards him and dialled TOL. He asked for Baydon Heath 3400.

Presently a man's voice said:

'Baydon Heath 3400.'

'I want to speak to Mrs Fortescue or Miss Fortescue.'

'Sorry. They aren't in, either of 'em.'

The voice struck Inspector Neele as slightly alcoholic.

'Are you the butler?'

'That's right.'

'Mr Fortescue has been taken seriously ill.'

'I know. They rung up and said so. But there's nothing I can do about it. Mr Val's away up North and Mrs Fortescue's out playing golf. Mrs Val's gone up to London but she'll be back for dinner and Miss Elaine's out with her Brownies.'

'Is there no one in the house I can speak to about Mr Fortescue's illness? It's important.'

'Well – I don't know.' The man sounded doubtful. 'There's Miss Ramsbottom – but she don't ever speak over the phone. Or there's Miss Dove – she's what you might call the 'ousekeeper.'

'I'll speak to Miss Dove, please.'

'I'll try and get hold of her.'

His retreating footsteps were audible through the phone. Inspector Neele heard no approaching footsteps but a minute or two later a woman's voice spoke.

'This is Miss Dove speaking.'

The voice was low and well poised, with clear-cut enunciation. Inspector Neele formed a favourable picture of Miss Dove.

'I am sorry to have to tell you, Miss Dove, that Mr Fortescue died

169

in St Jude's Hospital a short time ago. He was taken suddenly ill in his office. I am anxious to get in touch with his relatives – '

'Of course. I had no idea – ' She broke off. Her voice held no agitation, but it was shocked. She went on: 'It is all most unfortunate. The person you really want to get in touch with is Mr Percival Fortescue. He would be the one to see to all the necessary arrangements. You might be able to get in touch with him at the Midland in Manchester or possibly at the Grand in Leicester. Or you might try Shearer and Bonds of Leicester. I don't know their telephone number, I'm afraid, but I know they are a firm on whom he was going to call and they might be able to inform you where he would be likely to be today. Mrs Fortescue will certainly be in to dinner and she may be in to tea. It will be a great shock to her. It must have been very sudden? Mr Fortescue was quite well when he left here this morning.'

'You saw him before he left?'

'Oh yes. What was it? Heart?'

'Did he suffer from heart trouble?'

'No – no – I don't think so – But I thought as it was so sudden – ' She broke off. 'Are you speaking from St Jude's Hospital? Are you a doctor?'

'No, Miss Dove, I'm not a doctor. I'm speaking from Mr Fortescue's office in the city. I am Detective Inspector Neele of the CID and I shall be coming down to see you as soon as I can get there.'

'Detective Inspector? Do you mean – what *do* you mean?'

'It was a case of sudden death, Miss Dove; and when there is a sudden death we get called to the scene, especially when the deceased man hasn't seen a doctor lately – which I gather was the case?'

It was only the faintest suspicion of a question mark but the young woman responded.

'I know. Percival made an appointment twice for him, but he wouldn't keep it. He was quite unreasonable – they've all been worried – '

She broke off and then resumed in her former assured manner.

'If Mrs Fortescue returns to the house before you arrive, what do you want me to tell her?'

Practical as they make 'em, thought Inspector Neele.

Aloud he said:

'Just tell her that in a case of sudden death we have to make a few inquiries. Routine inquiries.'

He hung up.

CHAPTER THREE

Neele pushed the telephone away and looked sharply at Miss Griffith.

'So they've been worried about him lately,' he said. 'Wanted him to see a doctor. You didn't tell me that.'

'I didn't think of it,' said Miss Griffith, and added: 'He never seemed to me really *ill* – '

'Not ill – but what?'

'Well, just off. Unlike himself. Peculiar in his manner.'

'Worried about something?'

'Oh no, not *worried*. It's *we* who were worried – '

Inspector Neele waited patiently.

'It's difficult to say, really,' said Miss Griffith. 'He had moods, you know. Sometimes he was quite boisterous. Once or twice, frankly, I thought he had been drinking . . . He boasted and told the most extraordinary stories which I'm sure couldn't possibly have been true. For most of the time I've been here he was always very close about his affairs – not giving anything away, you know. But lately he's been quite different, expansive, and positively – well – flinging money about. Most unlike his usual manner. Why, when the office boy had to go to his grandmother's funeral, Mr Fortescue called him in and gave him a five pound note and told him to put it on the second favourite and then roared with laughter. He wasn't – well, he just wasn't like himself. That's all I can say.'

'As though, perhaps, he had something on his mind?'

'Not in the usual meaning of the term. It was as though he were looking forward to something pleasurable – exciting – '

'Possibly a big deal that he was going to pull off?'

Miss Griffith agreed with more conviction.

'Yes – yes, that's much more what I mean. As though everyday

171

things didn't matter any more. He was excited. And some very odd-looking people came to see him on business. People who'd never been here before. It worried Mr Percival dreadfully.'

'Oh, it worried him, did it?'

'Yes. Mr Percival's always been very much in his father's confidence, you see. His father relied on him. But lately – '

'Lately they weren't getting along so well.'

'Well, Mr Fortescue was doing a lot of things that Mr Percival thought unwise. Mr Percival is always very careful and prudent. But suddenly his father didn't listen to him any more and Mr Percival was very upset.'

'And they had a real row about it all?'

Inspector Neele was still probing.

'I don't know about a *row* ... Of course, I realize now Mr Fortescue can't have been himself – shouting like that.'

'Shouted, did he? What did he say?'

'He came right out in the typists' room – '

'So that you all heard?'

'Well – yes.'

'And he called Percival names – abused him – swore at him.'

'What did he say Percival had done?'

'It was more that he hadn't done anything . . . he called him a miserable pettifogging little clerk. He said he had no large outlook, no conception of doing business in a big way. He said: "I shall get Lance home again. He's worth ten of you – *and* he's married well. Lance has got guts even if he did risk a criminal prosecution once – " Oh dear, I oughtn't to have said that!' Miss Griffith, carried away as others before her had been under Inspector Neele's expert handling, was suddenly overcome with confusion.

'Don't worry,' said Inspector Neele comfortingly. 'What's past is past.'

'Oh yes, it was a long time ago. Mr Lance was just young and high-spirited and didn't really realize what he was doing.'

Inspector Neele had heard that view before and didn't agree with it. But he passed on to fresh questions.

'Tell me a little more about the staff here.'

Miss Griffith, hurrying to get away from her indiscretion, poured out information about the various personalities in the firm. Inspector Neele thanked her and then said he would like to see Miss Grosvenor again.

Detective Constable Waite sharpened his pencil. He remarked

172

wistfully that this was a Ritzy joint. His glance wandered appreciatively over the huge chairs, the big desk and the indirect lighting.

'All these people have got Ritzy names, too,' he said. 'Grosvenor – that's something to do with a Duke. And Fortescue – that's a classy name, too.'

Inspector Neele smiled.

'His father's name wasn't Fortescue. Fontescu – and he came from somewhere in Central Europe. I suppose this man thought Fortescue sounded better.'

Detective Constable Waite looked at his superior officer with awe.

'So you know all about him?'

'I just looked up a few things before coming along on the call.'

'Not got a record, had he?'

'Oh no. Mr Fortescue was much too clever for that. He's had certain connections with the black market and put through one or two deals that are questionable to say the least of it, but they've always been just within the law.'

'I see,' said Waite. 'Not a nice man.'

'A twister,' said Neele. 'But we've got nothing on him. The Inland Revenue have been after him for a long time but he's been too clever for them. Quite a financial genius, the late Mr Fortescue.'

'The sort of man,' said Constable Waite, 'who might have enemies?'

He spoke hopefully.

'Oh yes – certainly enemies. But he was poisoned at home, remember. Or so it would seem. You know, Waite, I see a kind of pattern emerging. An old-fashioned familiar kind of pattern. The good boy, Percival. The bad boy, Lance – attractive to women. The wife who's younger than her husband and who's vague about which course she's going to play golf on. It's all very familiar. But there's one thing that sticks out in a most incongruous way.'

Constable Waite asked 'What's that?' just as the door opened and Miss Grosvenor, her poise restored, and once more her glamorous self, inquired haughtily:

'You wished to see me?'

'I wanted to ask you a few questions about your employer – your late employer, perhaps I should say.'

'Poor soul,' said Miss Grosvenor unconvincingly.

'I want to know if you had noticed any difference in him lately.'

'Well, yes. I did, as a matter of fact.'

'In what way?'

'I couldn't really say . . . He seemed to talk a lot of nonsense. I couldn't really believe half of what he said. And then he lost his temper very easily – especially with Mr Percival. Not with me, because of course I *never* argue. I just say, "Yes, Mr Fortescue," whatever peculiar thing he says – said, I mean.'

'Did he – ever – well – make any passes at you?'

Miss Grosvenor replied rather regretfully:

'Well, no, I couldn't exactly say *that*.'

'There's just one other thing, Miss Grosvenor. Was Mr Fortescue in the habit of carrying grain about in his pocket?'

Miss Grosvenor displayed a lively surprise.

'Grain? In his pocket? Do you mean to feed pigeons or something?'

'It could have been for that purpose.'

'Oh, I'm sure he didn't. Mr Fortescue? Feed pigeons? Oh no.'

'Could he have had barley – or rye – in his pocket today for any special reason? A sample, perhaps? Some deal in grain?'

'Oh no. He was expecting the Asiatic Oil people this afternoon. And the President of the Atticus Building Society . . . No one else.'

'Oh well – ' Neele dismissed the subject and Miss Grosvenor with a wave of the hand.

'Lovely legs she's got,' said Constable Waite with a sigh. 'And super nylons – '

'Legs are no help to me,' said Inspector Neele. 'I'm left with what I had before. A pocketful of rye – and no explanation of it.'

CHAPTER FOUR

Mary Dove paused on her way downstairs and looked out through the big window on the stairs. A car had just driven up from which two men were alighting. The taller of the two stood for a moment with his back to the house surveying his surroundings. Mary Dove

174

appraised the two men thoughtfully. Inspector Neele and presumably a subordinate.

She turned from the window and looked at herself in the full-length mirror that hung on the wall where the staircase turned . . . She saw a small demure figure with immaculate white collar and cuffs on a beige grey dress. Her dark hair was parted in the middle and drawn back in two shining waves to a knot in the back of the neck . . . The lipstick she used was a pale rose colour.

On the whole Mary Dove was satisfied with her appearance. A very faint smile on her lips, she went on down the stairs.

Inspector Neele, surveying the house, was saying to himself:

Call it a lodge, indeed! Yewtree Lodge! The affectation of these rich people! The house was what he, Inspector Neele, would call a mansion. He knew what a lodge was. He'd been brought up in one! The lodge at the gates of Hartington Park, that vast unwieldy Palladian house with its twenty-nine bedrooms which had now been taken over by the National Trust. The lodge had been small and attractive from the outside, and had been damp, uncomfortable and devoid of anything but the most primitive form of sanitation within. Fortunately these facts had been accepted as quite proper and fitting by Inspector Neele's parents. They had no rent to pay and nothing whatever to do except open and shut the gates when required, and there were always plenty of rabbits and an occasional pheasant or so for the pot. Mrs Neele had never discovered the pleasure of electric irons, slow combustion stoves, airing cupboards, hot and cold water from taps, and the switching on of light by a mere flick of a finger. In winter the Neeles had an oil lamp and in summer they went to bed when it got dark. They were a healthy family and a happy one, all thoroughly behind the times.

So when Inspector Neele heard the word Lodge, it was his childhood memories that stirred. But this place, this pretentiously named Yewtree Lodge was just the kind of mansion that rich people built themselves and then called it 'their little place in the country'. It wasn't in the country either, according to Inspector Neele's idea of the country. The house was a large solid red-brick structure, sprawling lengthwise rather than upward, with rather too many gables, and a vast number of leaded paned windows. The gardens were highly artificial – all laid out in rose beds and pergolas and pools, and living up to the name of the house with large numbers of clipped yew hedges.

Plenty of yew here for anybody with a desire to obtain the raw

175

material of taxine. Over on the right, behind the rose pergola, there was a bit of actual nature left – a vast yew tree of the kind one associates with churchyards, its branches held up by stakes – like a kind of Moses of the forest world. That tree, the inspector thought, had been there long before the rash of newly built red-brick houses had begun to spread over the countryside. It had been there before the golf courses had been laid out and the fashionable architects had walked round with their rich clients, pointing out the advantages of the various sites. And since it was a valuable antique, the tree had been kept and incorporated in the new set-up and had, perhaps, given its name to the new desirable residence. Yewtree Lodge. And possibly the berries from that very tree –

Inspector Neele cut off these unprofitable speculations. Must get on with the job. He rang the bell.

It was opened promptly by a middle-aged man who fitted in quite accurately with the mental image Inspector Neele had formed of him over the phone. A man with a rather spurious air of smartness, a shifty eye and a rather unsteady hand.

Inspector Neele announced himself and his subordinate and had the pleasure of seeing an instant look of alarm come into the butler's eye . . . Neele did not attach too much importance to that. It might easily have nothing to do with the death of Rex Fortescue. It was quite possibly a purely automatic reaction.

'Has Mrs Fortescue returned yet?'

'No, sir.'

'Nor Mr Percival Fortescue? Nor Miss Fortescue?'

'No, sir.'

'Then I would like to see Miss Dove, please.'

The man turned his head slightly.

'Here's Miss Dove now – coming downstairs.'

Inspector Neele took in Miss Dove as she came composedly down the wide staircase. This time the mental picture did not correspond with the reality. Unconsciously the word housekeeper had conjured up a vague impression of someone large and authoritative dressed in black with somewhere concealed about her a jingle of keys.

The inspector was quite unprepared for the small trim figure descending towards him. The soft dove-coloured tones of her dress, the white collar and cuffs, the neat waves of hair, the faint Mona Lisa smile. It all seemed, somehow, just a little unreal, as though this young woman of under thirty was playing a part: not, he thought, the part of a housekeeper, but the part of Mary Dove. Her appearance was directed towards living up to her name.

She greeted him composedly.

'Inspector Neele?'

'Yes. This is Sergeant Hay. Mr Fortescue, as I told you through the phone, died in St Jude's Hospital at 12.43. It seems likely that his death was the result of something he ate at breakfast this morning. I should be glad therefore if Sergeant Hay could be taken to the kitchen where he can make inquiries as to the food served.'

Her eyes met his for a moment, thoughtfully, then she nodded.

'Of course,' she said. She turned to the uneasily hovering butler. 'Crump, will you take Sergeant Hay out and show him whatever he wants to see.'

The two men departed together. Mary Dove said to Neele.

'Will you come in here?'

She opened the door of a room and preceded him into it. It was a characterless apartment, clearly labelled 'Smoking Room', with panelling, rich upholstery, large stuffed chairs, and a suitable set of sporting prints on the walls.

'Please sit down.'

He sat and Mary Dove sat opposite him. She chose, he noticed, to face the light. An unusual preference for a woman. Still more unusual if a woman had anything to hide. But perhaps Mary Dove had nothing to hide.

'It is very unfortunate,' she said, 'that none of the family is available. Mrs Fortescue may return at any minute. And so may Mrs Val. I have sent wires to Mr Percival Fortescue at various places.'

'Thank you, Miss Dove.'

'You say that Mr Fortescue's death was caused by something he may have eaten for breakfast? Food poisoning, you mean?'

'Possibly.' He watched her.

She said composedly, 'It seems unlikely. For breakfast this morning there were bacon and scrambled eggs, coffee, toast and marmalade. There was also a cold ham on the sideboard, but that had been cut yesterday, and no one felt any ill effects. No fish of any kind was served, no sausages – nothing like that.'

'I see you know exactly what was served.'

'Naturally. I order the meals. For dinner last night – '

'No.' Inspector Neele interrupted her. 'It would not be a question of dinner last night.'

'I thought the onset of food poisoning could sometimes be delayed as much as twenty-four hours.'

'Not in this case . . . Will you tell me exactly what Mr Fortescue ate and drank before leaving the house this morning?'

'He had early tea brought to his room at eight o'clock. Breakfast was at a quarter past nine. Mr Fortescue, as I have told you, had scrambled eggs, bacon, coffee, toast and marmalade.'

'Any cereal?'

'No, he didn't like cereals.'

'The sugar for the coffee – it is lump sugar or granulated?'

'Lump. But Mr Fortescue did not take sugar in his coffee.'

'Was he in the habit of taking any medicines in the morning? Salts? A tonic? Some digestive remedy?'

'No, nothing of that kind.'

'Did you have breakfast with him also?'

'No. I do not take meals with the family.'

'Who was at breakfast?'

'Mrs Fortescue. Miss Fortescue. Mrs Val Fortescue. Mr Percival Fortescue, of course, was away.'

'And Mrs and Miss Fortescue ate the same things for breakfast?'

'Mrs Fortescue has only coffee, orange juice and toast, Mrs Val and Miss Fortescue always eat a hearty breakfast. Besides eating scrambled eggs and cold ham, they would probably have a cereal as well. Mrs Val drinks tea, not coffee.'

Inspector Neele reflected for a moment. The opportunities seemed at least to be narrowing down. Three people and three people only had had breakfast with the deceased, his wife, his daughter and his daughter-in-law. Either of them might have seized an opportunity to add taxine to his cup of coffee. The bitterness of the coffee would have masked the bitter taste of the taxine. There was the early morning tea, of course, but Bernsdorff had intimated that the taste would be noticeable in tea. But perhaps, first thing in the morning, before the senses were alert . . . He looked up to find Mary Dove watching him.

'Your questions about tonic and medicines seem to me rather odd, Inspector,' she said. 'It seems to imply that either there was something wrong with a medicine, or that something had been added to it. Surely neither of those processes could be described as food poisoning.'

Neele eyed her steadily.

'I did not say – definitely – that Mr Fortescue died of food

poisoning. But some kind of poisoning. In fact – just poisoning.'

She repeated softly: 'Poisoning . . .'

She appeared neither startled nor dismayed, merely interested.
Her attitude was of one sampling a new experience.

In fact she said as much, remarking after a moment's reflection:
'I have never had anything to do with a poisoning case before.'

'It's not very pleasant,' Neele informed her dryly.

'No – I suppose not . . .'

She thought about it for a moment and then looked up at him
with a sudden smile.

'I didn't do it,' she said. 'But I suppose everybody will tell
you that!'

'Have you any idea who did do it, Miss Dove?'

She shrugged her shoulders.

'Frankly, he was an odious man. Anybody might have done it.'

'But people aren't poisoned just for being "odious", Miss Dove.
There usually has to be a pretty solid motive.'

'Yes, of course.'

She was thoughtful.

'Do you care to tell me something about the household here?'

She looked up at him. He was a little startled to find her eyes
cool and amused.

'This isn't exactly a statement you're asking me to make, is it? No,
it couldn't be, because your sergeant is busy upsetting the domestic
staff. I shouldn't like to have what I say read out in court – but all
the same I should rather like to say it – unofficially. Off the record,
so to speak?'

'Go ahead then, Miss Dove. I've no witness, as you've already
observed.'

She leaned back, swinging one slim foot and narrowing her
eyes.

'Let me start by saying that I've no feeling of loyalty to my
employers. I work for them because it's a job that pays well and
I insist that it should pay well.'

'I was a little surprised to find you doing this type of job. It struck
me that with your brains and education – '

'I ought to be confined in an office? Or compiling files in a
Ministry? My dear Inspector Neele, this is the perfect racket.
People will pay anything – *anything* – to be spared domestic
worries. To find and engage a staff is a thoroughly tedious job.

Writing to agencies, putting in advertisements, interviewing people, making arrangements for interviews, and finally keeping the whole thing running smoothly – it takes a certain capacity which most of these people haven't got.'

'And suppose your staff, when you've assembled it, runs out on you? I've heard of such things.'

Mary smiled.

'If necessary, I can make the beds, dust the rooms, cook a meal *and* serve it without anyone noticing the difference. Of course I don't advertise that fact. It might give rise to ideas. But I can always be sure of tiding over any little gap. But there aren't often gaps. I work only for the extremely rich who will pay anything to be comfortable. I pay top prices and so I get the best of what's going.'

'Such as the butler?'

She threw him an amused, appreciative glance.

'There's always that trouble with a couple. Crump stays because of Mrs Crump, who is one of the best cooks I've ever come across. She's a jewel and one would put up with a good deal to keep her. Our Mr Fortescue likes his food – liked, I should say. In this household nobody has any scruples and they have plenty of money. Butter, eggs, cream, Mrs Crump can command what she likes. As for Crump, he just makes the grade. His silver's all right, and his waiting at table is not too bad. I keep the key of the wine cellar and a sharp eye on the whisky, and gin, and supervise his valeting.'

Inspector Neele raised his eyebrows.

'The admirable Miss Crichton.'

'I find one must *know* how to do everything oneself. Then – one need never do it. But you wanted to know my impressions of the family.'

'If you don't mind.'

'They are really all quite odious. The late Mr Fortescue was the kind of crook who is always careful to play safe. He boasted a great deal of his various smart dealings. He was rude and overbearing in manner and was a definite bully. Mrs Fortescue, Adele – was his second wife and about thirty years younger than he was. He came across her at Brighton. She was a manicurist on the look-out for big money. She is very good looking – a real sexy piece, if you know what I mean.'

Inspector Neele was shocked but managed not to show it. A girl like Mary Dove ought not to say such things, he felt.

The young lady was continuing composedly:

'Adele married him for his money, of course, and his son, Percival, and his daughter, Elaine, were simply livid about it. They're as nasty as they can be to her, but very wisely she doesn't care or even notice. She knows she's got the old man where she wants him. Oh dear, the wrong tense again. I haven't really grasped yet that he's dead . . .'

'Let's hear about the son.'

'Dear Percival? Val, as his wife calls him. Percival is a mealy-mouthed hypocrite. He's prim and sly and cunning. He's terrified of his father and has always let himself be bullied, but he's quite clever at getting his own way. Unlike his father he's mean about money. Economy is one of his passions. That's why he's been so long about finding a house of his own. Having a suite of rooms here saved his pocket.'

'And his wife?'

'Jennifer's meek and seems very stupid. But I'm not so sure. She was a hospital nurse before her marriage – nursed Percival through pneumonia to a romantic conclusion. The old man was disappointed by the marriage. He was a snob and wanted Percival to make what he called a "good marriage". He despised poor Mrs Val and snubbed her. She dislikes – disliked him a good deal, I think. Her principal interests are shopping and the cinema; her principal grievance is that her husband keeps her short of money.'

'What about the daughter?'

'Elaine? I'm rather sorry for Elaine. She's not a bad sort. One of those great schoolgirls who never grow up. She plays games quite well, and runs Guides and Brownies and all that sort of thing. There was some sort of affair not long ago with a disgruntled young schoolmaster, but Father discovered the young man had communistic ideas and came down on the romance like a ton of bricks.'

'She hadn't got the spirit to stand up to him?'

'*She* had. It was the young man who ratted. A question of money yet again, I fancy. Elaine is not particularly attractive, poor dear.'

'And the other son?'

'I've never seen him. He's attractive, by all accounts, and a thoroughly bad lot. Some little matter of a forged cheque in the past. He lives in East Africa.'

'And was estranged from his father.'

'Yes, Mr Fortescue couldn't cut him off with a shilling because he'd already made him a junior partner in the firm, but he held no

181

communication with him for years, and in fact if Lance was ever mentioned, he used to say: "Don't talk to me of that rascal. He's no son of mine." All the same – '

'Yes, Miss Dove?'

Mary said slowly: 'All the same, I shouldn't be surprised if old Fortescue hadn't been planning to get him back here.'

'What makes you think that?'

'Because, about a month ago, old Fortescue had a terrific row with Percival – he found out something that Percival had been doing behind his back – I don't know what it was – and he was absolutely furious. Percival suddenly stopped being the white-headed boy. He's been quite different lately, too.'

'Mr Fortescue was quite different?'

'No. I meant Percival. He's gone about looking worried to death.'

'Now what about servants? You've already described the Crumps. Who else is there?'

'Gladys Martin is the parlourmaid or waitress, as they like to call themselves nowadays. She does the downstairs rooms, lays the table, clears away and helps Crump wait at table. Quite a decent sort of girl but very nearly half-witted. The adenoidal type.'

Neele nodded.

'The housemaid is Ellen Curtis. Elderly, very crabbed, and very cross, but has been in good service and is a first-class housemaid. The rest is outside help – odd women who come in.'

'And those are the only people living here?'

'There's old Miss Ramsbottom.'

'Who is she?'

'Mr Fortescue's sister-in-law – his first wife's sister. His wife was a good deal older than he was and her sister again was a good deal older than her – which makes her well over seventy. She has a room of her own on the second floor – does her own cooking and all that, with just a woman coming in to clean. She's rather eccentric and she never liked her brother-in-law, but she came here while her sister was alive and stayed on when she died. Mr Fortescue never bothered about her much. She's quite a character, though, is Aunt Effie.'

'And that is all.'

'That's all.'

'So we come to you, Miss Dove.'

'You want particulars? I'm an orphan. I took a secretarial course at the St Alfred's Secretarial College. I took a job as shorthand typist, left it and took another, decided I was in the wrong racket, and started on my present career. I have been with three different employers. After about a year or eighteen months I get tired of a particular place and move on. I have been at Yewtree Lodge just over a year. I will type out the names and addresses of my various employers and give them, with a copy of my references to Sergeant – Hay, is it? Will that be satisfactory?'

'Perfectly, Miss Dove.' Neele was silent for a moment, enjoying a mental image of Miss Dove tampering with Mr Fortescue's breakfast. His mind went back farther, and he saw her methodically gathering yew berries in a little basket. With a sigh he returned to the present and reality. 'Now, I would like to see the girl – er Gladys – and then the housemaid, Ellen.' He added as he rose: 'By the way, Miss Dove, can you give me any idea why Mr Fortescue would be carrying loose grain in his pocket?'

'Grain?' she stared at him with what appeared to be genuine surprise.

'Yes – grain. Does that suggest something to you, Miss Dove?'

'Nothing at all.'

'Who looked after his clothes?'

'Crump.'

'I see. Did Mr Fortescue and Mrs Fortescue occupy the same bedroom?'

'Yes. He had a dressing-room and bath, of course, and so did she . . .' Mary glanced down at her wrist-watch. 'I really think that she ought to be back very soon now.'

The inspector had risen. He said in a pleasant voice:

'Do you know one thing, Miss Dove? It strikes me as very odd that even though there are three golf courses in the immediate neighbourhood, it has yet not been possible to find Mrs Fortescue on one of them before now?'

'It would not be so odd, Inspector, if she did not actually happen to be playing golf at all.'

Mary's voice was dry. The inspector said sharply:

'I was distinctly informed that she was playing golf.'

'She took her golf clubs and announced her intention of doing so. She was driving her own car, of course.'

He looked at her steadily, perceiving the inference.

'Who was she playing with? Do you know?'

'I think it possible that it might be Mr Vivian Dubois.'

Neele contented himself by saying: 'I see.'

'I'll send Gladys in to you. She'll probably be scared to death.' Mary paused for a moment by the door, then she said:

'I should hardly advise you to go too much by all I've told you. I'm a malicious creature.'

She went out. Inspector Neele looked at the closed door and wondered. Whether actuated by malice or not, what she had told him could not fail to be suggestive. If Rex Fortescue had been deliberately poisoned, and it seemed almost certain that that was the case, then the set-up at Yewtree Lodge seemed highly promising. Motives appeared to be lying thick on the ground.

CHAPTER FIVE

The girl who entered the room with obvious unwillingness was an unattractive, frightened-looking girl, who managed to look faintly sluttish in spite of being tall and smartly dressed in a claret-coloured uniform.

She said at once, fixing imploring eyes upon him:

'I didn't do anything. I didn't really. I don't know anything about it.'

'That's all right,' said Neele heartily. His voice had changed slightly. It sounded more cheerful and a good deal commoner in intonation. He wanted to put the frightened rabbit Gladys at her ease.

'Sit down here,' he went on. 'I just want to know about breakfast this morning.'

'I didn't do anything at all.'

'Well, you laid the breakfast, didn't you?'

'Yes, I did that.' Even that admission came unwillingly. She looked both guilty and terrified, but Inspector Neele was used to witnesses who looked like that, He went on cheerfully, trying to put her at her ease, asking questions: who had come down first? And who next?

Elaine Fortescue had been the first down to breakfast. She'd come in just as Crump was bringing in the coffee pot. Mrs Fortescue was down next, and then Mrs Val, and the master last. They waited on themselves. The tea and coffee and the hot dishes were all on hot plates on the sideboard.

He learnt little of importance from her that he did not know already. The food and drink was as Mary Dove had described it. The master and Mrs Fortescue and Miss Elaine took coffee and Mrs Val took tea. Everything had been quite as usual.

Neele questioned her about herself and here she answered more readily. She'd been in private service first and after that in various cafés. Then she thought she'd like to go back to private service and had come to Yewtree Lodge last September. She'd been there two months.

'And you like it?'

'Well, it's all right, I suppose.' She added: 'It's not so hard on your feet – but you don't get so much freedom . . .'

'Tell me about Mr Fortescue's clothes – his suits. Who looked after them? Brushed them and all that?'

Gladys looked faintly resentful.

'Mr Crump's supposed to. But half the time he makes me do it.'

'Who brushed and pressed the suit Mr Fortescue had on today?'

'I don't remember which one he wore. He's got ever so many.'

'Have you ever found grain in the pocket of one of his suits?'

'Grain?' She looked puzzled.

'Rye, to be exact.'

'Rye? That's bread, isn't it? A sort of black bread – got a nasty taste, I always think.'

'That's bread made from rye. Rye is the grain itself. There was some found in the pocket of your master's coat.'

'In his coat pocket?'

'Yes. Do you know how it got there?'

'I couldn't say I'm sure. I never saw any.'

He could get no more from her. For a moment or two he wondered if she knew more about the matter than she was willing to admit. She certainly seemed embarrassed and on the defensive – but on the whole he put it down to a natural fear of the police.

When he finally dismissed her, she asked:

'It's really true, is it. He's dead?'

'Yes, he's dead.'

'Very sudden, wasn't it? They said when they rang up from the office that he'd had a kind of fit.'

'Yes – it was a kind of fit.'

185

Gladys said: 'A girl I used to know had fits. Come on any time, they did. Used to scare me.'

For the moment this reminiscence seemed to overcome her suspicions.

Inspector Neele made his way to the kitchen.

His reception was immediate and alarming. A woman of vast proportions, with a red face armed with a rolling-pin stepped towards him in a menacing fashion.

'Police, indeed,' she said. 'Coming here and saying things like that! Nothing of the kind, I'd have you know. Anything I've sent in the dining-room has been just what it should be. Coming here and saying I poisoned the master. I'll have the law on you, police or no police. No bad food's ever been served in this house.'

It was some time before Inspector Neele could appease the irate artist. Sergeant Hay looked in grinning from the pantry and Inspector Neele gathered that he had already run the gauntlet of Mrs Crump's wrath.

The scene was terminated by the ringing of the telephone.

Neele went out into the hall to find Mary Dove taking the call. She was writing down a message on a pad. Turning her head over her shoulder she said: 'It's a telegram.'

The call concluded, she replaced the receiver and handed the pad on which she had been writing to the inspector. The place of origin was Paris and the message ran as follows:

FORTESCUE YEWTREE LODGE BAYDON HEATH SURREY. SORRY YOUR LETTER DELAYED. WILL BE WITH YOU TOMORROW ABOUT TEATIME. SHALL EXPECT ROAST VEAL FOR DINNER. LANCE.

Inspector Neele raised his eyebrows.

'So the Prodigal Son had been summoned home,' he said.

CHAPTER SIX

At the moment when Rex Fortescue had been drinking his last cup of tea, Lance Fortescue and his wife had been sitting under the trees on the Champs Elysées watching the people walking past.

'It's all very well to say "describe him", Pat. I'm a rotten hand at descriptions. What do you want to know? The Guvnor's a bit of an old crook, you know. But you won't mind that? You must be used to that more or less.'

'Oh, yes,' said Pat. 'Yes – as you say – I'm acclimatized.'

She tried to keep a certain forlornness out of her voice. Perhaps, she reflected, the whole world was really crooked – or was it just that she herself had been unfortunate?

She was a tall, long-legged girl, not beautiful but with a charm that was made up of vitality and a warm-hearted personality. She moved well, and had lovely gleaming chestnut brown hair. Perhaps from a long association with horses, she had acquired the look of a thoroughbred filly.

Crookedness in the racing world she knew about – now, it seemed, she was to encounter crookedness in the financial world. Though for all that, it seemed that her father-in-law, whom she had not yet met, was, as far as the law was concerned, a pillar of rectitude. All these people who went about boasting of 'smart work' were the same – technically they always managed to be within the law. Yet it seemed to her that her Lance, whom she loved, and who had admittedly strayed outside the ringed fence in earlier days, had an honesty that these successful practitioners of the crooked lacked.

'I don't mean,' said Lance, 'that he's a swindler – not anything like that. But he knows how to put over a fast one.'

'Sometimes,' said Pat, 'I feel I hate people who put over fast ones.' She added: 'You're fond of him.' It was a statement, not a question.

Lance considered it for a moment, and then said in a surprised kind of voice:

'Do you know, darling, I believe I am.'

Pat laughed. He turned his head to look at her. His eyes narrowed. What a darling she was! He loved her. The whole thing was worth it for her sake.

'In a way, you know,' he said, 'it's hell going back. City life. Home on the 5.18. It's not my kind of life. I'm far more at home among the down and outs. But one's got to settle down sometime, I suppose. And with you to hold my hand the process may even be quite a pleasant one. And since the old boy has come round, one ought to take advantage of it. I must say I was surprised when I got his letter . . . Percival, of all people, blotting his copybook. Percival, the good little boy. Mind you, Percy was always sly. Yes, he was always sly.'

'I don't think,' said Patricia Fortescue, 'that I'm going to like your brother Percival.'

'Don't let me put you against him. Percy and I never got on – that's all there is to it. I blued my pocket money, he saved his. I had disreputable but entertaining friends, Percy made what's called "worthwhile contacts". Poles apart we were, he and I. I always thought him a poor fish, and he – sometimes, you know, I think he almost hated me. I don't know why exactly . . .'

'I think I can see why.'

'Can you, darling? You're so brainy. You know I've always wondered – it's a fantastic thing to say – but – '

'Well? Say it.'

'I've wondered if it wasn't Percival who was behind that cheque business – you know, when the old man kicked me out – and was he mad that he'd given me a share in the firm and so he couldn't disinherit me! Because the queer thing was that I never forged that cheque – though of course nobody would believe that after that time I swiped funds out of the till and put it on a horse. I was dead sure I could put it back, and anyway it was my own cash in a manner of speaking. But that cheque business – no. I don't know why I've got the ridiculous idea that Percival did that – but I have, somehow.'

'But it wouldn't have done *him* any good? It was paid into your account.'

'I know. So it doesn't make sense, does it?'

Pat turned sharply towards him.

'You mean – he did it to get you chucked out of the firm?'

'I wondered. Oh well – it's a rotten thing to say. Forget it. I wonder what old Percy will say when he sees the Prodigal returned. Those pale, boiled-gooseberry eyes of his will pop right out of his head!'

'Does he know you are coming?'

'I shouldn't be surprised if he didn't know a damned thing! The old man's got rather a funny sense of humour, you know.'

'But what has your brother *done* to upset your father so much?'

'That's what *I'd* like to know. Something must have made the old man livid. Writing off to me the way he did.'

'When was it you got his first letter?'

'Must be four – no five months ago. A cagey letter, but a distinct holding out of the olive branch. "Your elder brother has proved himself unsatisfactory in many ways." "You seem to have sown your wild oats and settled down." "I can promise you that it will be well worth your while financially." "Shall welcome you and your wife." You know, darling, I think my marrying you had a lot to do with it. The old boy was impressed that I'd married into a class above me.'

Pat laughed.

'What? Into the aristocratic riff-raff?'

He grinned. 'That's right. But riff-raff didn't register and aristocracy did. You should see Percival's wife. She's the kind who says "Pass the preserves, please" and talks about a postage stamp.'

Pat did not laugh. She was considering the women of the family into which she had married. It was a point of view which Lance had not taken into account.

'And your sister?' she asked.

'Elaine –? Oh she's all right. She was pretty young when I left home. Sort of an earnest girl – but probably she's grown out of that. Very intense over things.'

It did not sound very reassuring. Pat said:

'She never wrote to you – after you went away?'

'I didn't leave an address. But she wouldn't have, anyway. We're not a devoted family.'

'No.'

He shot a quick look at her.

'Got the wind up? About my family? You needn't. We're not going to live with them, or anything like that. We'll have our own little place, somewhere. Horses, dogs, anything you like.'

'But there will still be the 5.18.'

'For me, yes. To and fro to the city, all togged up. But don't worry, sweet – there are rural pockets, even round London. And lately I've felt the sap of financial affairs rising in me. After all, it's in my blood – from both sides of the family.'

'You hardly remember your mother, do you?'

'She always seemed to me incredibly old. She was old, of course. Nearly fifty when Elaine was born. She wore lots of clinking things and lay on a sofa and used to read me stories about knights and ladies which bored me stiff. Tennyson's "Idylls of the King". I suppose I was fond of her . . . She was very – colourless, you know. I realize that, looking back.'

'You don't seem to have been particularly fond of anybody,' said Pat disapprovingly.

Lance grasped and squeezed her arm.

'I'm fond of you,' he said.

189

CHAPTER SEVEN

Inspector Neele was still holding the telegraph message in his hand when he heard a car drive up to the front door and stop with a careless scrunching of brakes.

Mary Dove, 'That will be Mrs Fortescue now.'

Inspector Neele moved forwards to the front door. Out of the tail of his eye, he saw Mary Dove melt unobtrusively into the background and disappear. Clearly she intended to take no part in the forthcoming scene. A remarkable display of tact and discretion – and also a rather remarkable lack of curiosity. Most women, Inspector Neele decided, would have remained . . .

As he reached the front door he was aware of the butler, Crump, coming forward from the back of the hall. So he had heard the car.

The car was a Rolls Bentley sports model coupé. Two people got out of it and came towards the house. As they reached the door, it opened. Surprised, Adele Fortescue stared at Inspector Neele.

He realized at once that she was a very beautiful woman, and he realized too the force of Mary Dove's comment which had so shocked him at the time. Adele Fortescue *was* a sexy piece. In figure and type she resembled the blonde Miss Grosvenor, but whereas Miss Grosvenor was all glamour without and all respectability within, Adele Fortescue was glamour all through. Her appeal was obvious, not subtle. It said simply to every man 'Here am I. I'm a woman.' She spoke and moved and breathed sex – and yet, within it all, her eyes had a shrewd appraising quality. Adele Fortescue, he thought, liked men – but she would always like money even better.

His eyes went on to the figure behind her who carried her golf clubs. He knew the type very well. It was the type that specialized in the young wives of rich and elderly men. Mr Vivian Dubois, if this was he, had that rather forced masculinity which is, in reality, nothing of the kind. He was the type of man who 'understands' women.

190

'Mrs Fortescue?'

'Yes.' It was a wide blue-eyed gaze. 'But I don't know – '

'I am Inspector Neele. I'm afraid have bad news for you.'

'Do you mean – a burglary – something of that kind?'

'No, nothing of that kind. It is about your husband. He was taken seriously ill this morning.'

'Rex? Ill?'

'We have been trying to get in touch with you since half-past eleven this morning.'

'Where is he? Here? Or in hospital?'

'He was taken to St Jude's Hospital. I'm afraid you must prepare yourself for a shock.'

'You don't mean – he isn't – *dead*.'

She lurched forward a little and clutched his arm. Gravely feeling like someone playing a part in a stage performance, the inspector supported her into the hall. Crump was hovering eagerly.

'Brandy she'll be needing,' he said.

The deep voice of Mr Dubois said:

'That's right, Crump. Get the brandy.' To the inspector he said: 'In here.'

He opened a door on the left. The procession filed in. The inspector and Adele Fortescue, Vivian Dubois, and Crump with a decanter and two glasses.

Adele Fortescue sank on to an easy chair, her eyes covered with her hand. She accepted the glass that the inspector offered and took a tiny sip, then pushed it away, 'I don't want it,' she said. 'I'm all right. But tell me, what was it? A stroke, I suppose? Poor Rex.'

'It wasn't a stroke, Mrs Fortescue.'

'Did you say you were an inspector?' It was Mr Dubois who made the inquiry.

Neele turned to him. 'That's right,' he said pleasantly. 'Inspector Neele of the CID.'

He saw the alarm grow in the dark eyes. Mr Dubois did not like the appearance of an inspector of the CID. He didn't like it at all.

'What's up?' he said. 'Something wrong – eh?'

Quite unconsciously he backed away a little towards the door. Inspector Neele noted the movement.

'I'm afraid,' he said to Mrs Fortescue, 'that there will have to be an inquest.'

'An inquest? Do you mean – what *do* you mean?'

'I'm afraid this is all very distressing for you, Mrs Fortescue.'

The words came smoothly. 'It seemed advisable to find out as soon as possible exactly what Mr Fortescue had to eat or drink before leaving for the office this morning.'

'Do you mean he might have been *poisoned*?'

'Well, yes, it would seem so.'

'I can't believe it. Oh – you mean *food* poisoning.'

Her voice dropped half an octave on the last words. His face wooden, his voice still smooth, Inspector Neele said:

'Madam? What did you think I meant?'

She ignored that question, hurrying on.

'But we've been all right – all of us.'

'You can speak for all the members of the family?'

'Well – no – of course – I can't really.'

Dubois said with a great show of consulting his watch:

'I'll have to push off, Adele. Dreadfully sorry. You'll be all right, won't you? I mean, there are the maids, and the little Dove and all that – '

'Oh, Vivian, don't. Don't go.'

It was quite a wail, and it affected Mr Dubois adversely. His retreat quickened.

'Awfully sorry, old girl. Important engagement. I'm putting up at the Dormy House, by the way, Inspector. If you – er – want me for anything.'

Inspector Neele nodded. He had no wish to detain Mr Dubois. But he recognized Mr Dubois's departure for what it was. Mr Dubois was running away from trouble.

Adele Fortescue said, in an attempt to carry off the sitation:

'It's such a shock, to come back and find the *police* in the house.'

'I'm sure it must be. But you see, it was necessary to act promptly in order to obtain the necessary specimens of foodstuffs, coffee, tea, etc.'

'Tea and coffee? But they're not poisonous? I expect it's the awful bacon we sometimes get. It's quite uneatable sometimes.'

'We shall find out, Mrs Fortescue. Don't worry. You'd be surprised at some of the things that can happen. We once had a case of digitalis poisoning. It turned out that foxglove leaves had been picked in mistake for horseradish.'

'You think something like that could happen here?'

'We shall know better after the autopsy, Mrs Fortescue.'

'The autop- oh I see.' She shivered.

The inspector went on: 'You've got a lot of yew round the house, haven't you, madam. There's no possibility, I suppose, of the berries or leaves having got – mixed up in anything?'

He was watching her closely. She stared at him.

'Yew berries? Are they poisonous?'

The wonder seemed a little too wide-eyed and innocent.

'Children have been known to eat them with unfortunate results.'

Adele clasped her hands to her head.

'I can't bear to talk about it any more. Must I? I want to go and lie down. I can't stand any more. Mr Percival Fortescue will arrange everything – I can't – I can't – it isn't fair to ask me.'

'We are getting in touch with Mr Percival Fortescue as soon as possible. Unfortunately he is away in the North of England.

'Oh yes, I forgot.'

'There's just one thing, Mrs Fortescue. There was a small quantity of grain in your husband's pocket. Could you give me some explanation of that?'

She shook her head. She appeared quite bewildered.

'Would anyone have slipped it in there as a joke?'

'I don't see why it would be a joke?'

Inspector Neele did not see either. He said:

'I won't trouble you any further at present, Mrs Fortescue. Shall I send one of the maids to you? Or Miss Dove?'

'What?' The word came abstractedly. He wondered what she had been thinking about.

She fumbled with her bag and pulled out a handkerchief. Her voice trembled.

'It's so awful,' she said unsteadily. 'I'm only just beginning to take it in. I've really been *numbed* up to now. Poor Rex. Poor dear Rex.'

She sobbed in a manner that was almost convincing.

Inspector Neele watched her respectfully for a moment or two.

'It's been very sudden, I know,' he said. 'I'll send someone to you.'

He went towards the door, opened it and passed through. He paused for a moment before looking back into the room.

Adele Fortescue still held the handkerchief to her eyes. The ends of it hung down but did not quite obscure her mouth. On her lips was a very faint smile.

CHAPTER EIGHT

'I've got what I could, sir.' So Sergeant Hay reported. 'The marmalade, bit of the ham. Samples of tea, coffee and sugar, for what they're worth. Actual brews have been thrown out by now, of course, but there's one point. There was a good lot of coffee left over and they had it in the servants' hall at elevenses – that's important, I should say.'

'Yes, that's important. Shows that if he took it in his coffee, it must have been slipped into the actual cup.'

'By one of those present. Exactly. I've inquired, cautious like, about the yew stuff – berries or leaves – there's been none of it seen about the house. Nobody seems to know anything about the cereal in his pocket, either . . . It just seems daft to them. Seems daft to me, too. He doesn't seem to have been one of those food faddists who'll eat any mortal thing so long as it isn't cooked. My sister's husband's like that. Raw carrots, raw peas, raw turnips. But even he doesn't eat raw grain. Why, I should say it would swell up in your inside something awful.'

The telephone rang and, on a nod from the inspector, Sergeant Hay sprinted off to answer it. Following him, Neele found that it was headquarters on the line. Contact had been made with Mr Percival Fortescue, who was returning to London immediately.

As the inspector replaced the telephone, a car drew up at the front door. Crump went to the door and opened it. The woman who stood there had her arms full of parcels. Crump took them from her.

'Thanks, Crump. Pay the taxi, will you? I'll have tea now. Is Mrs Fortescue or Miss Elaine in?'

The butler hesitated, looking back over his shoulder.

'We've had bad news, ma'am,' he said. 'About the master.'

'About Mr Fortescue?'

Neele came forward. Crump said: 'This is Mrs Percival, sir.'

'What is it? What's happened? An accident?'

194

The inspector looked her over as he replied. Mrs Percival Fortescue was a plump woman with a discontented mouth. Her age he judged to be about thirty. Her questions came with a kind of eagerness. The thought flashed across his mind that she must be very bored.

'I'm sorry to have to tell you that Mr Fortescue was taken to St Jude's Hospital this morning seriously ill and has since died.'

'Died? You mean he's dead?' The news was clearly even more sensational than she had hoped for. 'Dear me – this is a surprise. My husband's away. You'll have to get in touch with him. He's in the North somewhere. I dare say they'll know at the office. He'll have to see to everything. Things always happen at the most awkward moment, don't they.'

She paused for a moment, turning things over in her mind.

'It all depends, I suppose,' she said, 'where they'll have the funeral. Down here, I suppose. Or will it be in London?'

'That will be for the family to say.'

'Of course. I only just wondered.' For the first time she took direct cognisance of the man who was speaking to her.

'Are you from the office?' she asked. 'You're not a doctor, are you?'

'I'm a police officer. Mr Fortescue's death was very sudden and – '

She interrupted him.

'Do you mean he was *murdered*?'

It was the first time that word had been spoken. Neele surveyed her eager questioning face carefully.

'Now why should you think that, madam?'

'Well, people are sometimes. You said sudden. And you're police. Have you seen her about it? What did she say?'

'I don't quite understand to whom you are referring?'

'Adele, of course. I always told Val his father was crazy to go marrying a woman years younger than himself. There's no fool like an old fool. Besotted about that awful creature, he was. And now look what comes of it . . . A nice mess we're all in. Pictures in the paper and reporters coming round.'

She paused, obviously visualizing the future in a series of crude highly coloured pictures. He thought that the prospect was still not wholly unpleasing. She turned back to him.

'What was it? Arsenic?'

In a repressive voice Inspector Neele said:

'The cause of death has yet to be ascertained. There will be an autopsy and an inquest.'

'But you know already, don't you? Or you wouldn't come down here.'

There was a sudden shrewdness in her plump rather foolish face.

'You've been asking about what he ate and drank, I suppose? Dinner last night. Breakfast this morning. And all the drinks, of course.'

He could see her mind ranging vividly over all the possibilities. He said, with caution:

'It seems possible that Mr Fortescue's illness resulted from something he ate at breakfast.'

'Breakfast?' She seemed surprised. 'That's difficult. I don't see how . . .'

She paused and shook her head.

'I don't see how she could have done it, then . . . unless she slipped something into the coffee – when Elaine and I weren't looking . . .'

A quiet voice spoke softly beside them:

'Your tea is all ready in the library, Mrs Val.'

Mrs Val jumped.

'Oh thank you, Miss Dove. Yes, I could do with a cup of tea. Really, I feel quite bowled over. What about you, Mr – Inspector – '

'Thank you, not just now.'

The plump figure hesitated and then went slowly away.

As she disappeared through a doorway, Mary Dove murmured softly:

'I don't think she's ever heard of the term slander.'

Inspector Neele did not reply.

Mary Dove went on:

'Is there anything I can do for you?'

'Where can I find the housemaid, Ellen?'

'I will take you to her. She's just gone upstairs.'

II

Ellen proved to be grim but unafraid. Her sour old face looked triumphantly at the inspector.

'It's a shocking business, sir. And I never thought I'd live to find myself in a house where that sort of thing has been going on. But in a way I can't say that it surprises me. I ought to have given my notice in long ago and that's a fact. I don't like the language that's used in this house, and I don't like the amount of drink that's taken, and I don't approve of the goings on there've been. I've nothing against Mrs Crump, but Crump and that girl Gladys just don't know what proper service is. But it's the goings on that I mind about most.'

'What goings on do you mean exactly?'

'You'll soon hear about them if you don't know already. It's common talk all over the place. They've been seen here, there and everywhere. All this pretending to play golf – or tennis – And I've seen things – with my own eyes – in this house. The library door was open and there they were, kissing and canoodling.'

The venom of the spinster was deadly. Neele really felt it unnecessary to say 'Whom do you mean?' but he said it nevertheless.

'Who should I mean? The mistress – and that man. No shame about it, they hadn't. But if you ask me, the master had got wise to it. Put someone on to watch them, he had. Divorce, that's what it would have come to. Instead, it's come to *this*.'

'When you say this, you mean – '

'You've been asking questions, sir, about what the master ate and drank and who gave it to him. They're in it together, sir, that's what I'd say. He got the stuff from somewhere and she gave it to the master, that was the way of it, I've no doubt.'

'Have you ever seen any yew berries in the house – or thrown away anywhere?'

The small eyes glinted curiously.

'Yew? Nasty poisonous stuff. Never you touch those berries, my mother said to me when I was a child. Was *that* what was used, sir?'

'We don't know yet what was used.'

'I've never seen her fiddling about with yew.' Ellen sounded disappointed. 'No, I can't say I've seen anything of that kind.'

Neele questioned her about the grain found in Fortescue's pocket but here again he drew a blank.

'No, sir. I know nothing about that.'

He went on to further questions, but with no gainful result. Finally he asked if he could see Miss Ramsbottom.

Ellen looked doubtful.

'I could ask her, but it's not everyone she'll see. She's a very old lady, you know, and she's a bit odd.'

The inspector pressed his demand, and rather unwillingly Ellen led him along a passage and up a short flight of stairs to what he thought had probably been designed as a nursery suite.

He glanced out of a passage window as he followed her and saw Sergeant Hay standing by the yew stree talking to a man who was evidently a gardener.

Ellen tapped on a door, and when she received an answer, opened it and said:

'There's a police gentleman here who would like to speak to you, miss.'

The answer was apparently in the affirmative for she drew back and motioned Neele to go in.

The room he entered was almost fantastically overfurnished. The inspector felt rather as though he had taken a step backward into not merely Edwardian but Victorian times. At a table drawn up to a gas fire an old lady was sitting laying out a patience. She wore a maroon-coloured dress and her sparse grey hair was slicked down each side of her face.

Without looking up or discontinuing her game she said impatiently:

'Well, come in, come in. Sit down if you like.'

The invitation was not easy to accept as every chair appeared to be covered with tracts or publications of a religious nature.

As he moved them slightly aside on the sofa Miss Ramsbottom asked sharply:

'Interested in mission work?'

'Well, I'm afraid I'm not very, ma'am.'

'Wrong. You should be. That's where the Christian spirit is nowadays. Darkest Africa. Had a young clergyman here last week. Black as your hat. But a true Christian.'

Inspector Neele found it a little difficult to know what to say.

The old lady further disconcerted him by snapping:

'I haven't got a wireless.'

'I beg your pardon?'

'Oh, I thought perhaps you came about a wireless licence. Or one of these silly forms. Well, man, what is it?'

'I'm sorry to have to tell you, Miss Ramsbottom, that your brother-in-law, Mr Fortescue, was taken suddenly ill and died this morning.'

Miss Ramsbottom continued with her patience without any sign of perturbation, merely remarking in a conversational way:

198

'Struck down at last in his arrogance and sinful pride. Well, it had to come.'

'I hope it's not a shock to you?'

It obviously wasn't but the inspector wanted to hear what she would say.

Miss Ramsbottom gave him a sharp glance over the top of her spectacles and said:

'If you mean I am not distressed, that is quite right. Rex Fortescue was always a sinful man and I never liked him.'

'His death was very sudden – '

'As befits the ungodly,' said the old lady with satisfaction.

'It seems possible that he may have been poisoned – '

The inspector paused to observe the effect he had made.

He did not seem to have made any. Miss Ramsbottom merely murmured: 'Red seven on black eight. Now I can move up the King.'

Struck apparently by the inspector's silence, she stopped with a card poised in her hand and said sharply:

'Well, what did you expect me to say? I didn't poison him if that's what you want to know.'

'Have you any idea who might have done so?'

'That's a very improper question,' said the old lady sharply. 'Living in this house are two of my dead sister's children. I decline to believe that anybody with Ramsbottom blood in them could be guilty of murder. Because it's murder you're meaning, isn't it?'

'I didn't say so, madam.'

'Of course it's murder. Plenty of people have wanted to murder Rex in their time. A very unscrupulous man. And old sins have long shadows, as the saying goes.'

'Have you anyone in particular in mind?'

Miss Ramsbottom swept up the cards and rose to her feet. She was a tall woman.

'I think you'd better go now,' she said.

She spoke without anger but with a kind of cold finality.

'If you want my opinion,' she went on, 'it was probably one of the servants. The butler looks to me a bit of a rascal, and that parlourmaid is definitely subnormal. Good evening.'

Inspector Neele found himself meekly walking out. Certainly a remarkable old lady. Nothing to be got out of her.

He came down the stairs into the square hall to find himself suddenly face to face with a tall dark girl. She was wearing a damp mackintosh and she stared into his face with a curious blankness.

'I've just come back,' she said. 'And they told me – about Father – that he's dead.'

'I'm afraid that's true.'

She pushed out a hand behind her as though blindly seeking for support. She touched an oak chest and slowly, stiffly, she sat down on it.

'Oh no,' she said. 'No . . .'

Slowly two tears ran down her cheeks.

'It's awful,' she said. 'I didn't think that I even liked him . . . I thought I hated him . . . But that can't be so, or I wouldn't mind. I do mind.'

She sat there, staring in front of her, and again tears forced themselves from her eyes and down her cheeks.

Presently she spoke again, rather breathlessly:

'The awful thing is that it makes everything come right. I mean, Gerald and I can get married now. I can do everything that I want to do. But I hate it happening this way. I don't want Father to be dead . . . Oh I don't. Oh Daddy – Daddy . . .'

For the first time since he had come to Yewtree Lodge, Inspector Neele was startled by what seemed to be genuine grief for the dead man.

CHAPTER NINE

'Sounds like the wife to me,' said the assistant commissioner. He had been listening attentively to Inspector Neele's report.

It had been an admirable précis of the case. Short, but with no relevant detail left out.

'Yes,' said the AC. 'It looks like the wife. What do you think yourself, Neele, eh?'

Inspector Neele said that it looked like the wife to him too. He reflected cynically that it usually was the wife – or the husband as the case might be.

'She had the opportunity all right. And motive?' The AC paused. 'There *is* motive?'

'Oh, I think so, sir. This Mr Dubois, you know.'

'Think he was in it, too?'

'No, I shouldn't say that, sir.' Inspector Neele weighed the idea. 'A bit too fond of his own skin for that. He may have guessed what was in her mind, but I shouldn't imagine that he instigated it.'

'No, too careful.'

'Much too careful.'

'Well, we mustn't jump to conclusions, but it seems a good working hypothesis. What about the other two who had opportunity?'

'That's the daughter and the daughter-in-law. The daughter was mixed up with a young man whom her father didn't want her to marry. And he definitely wasn't marrying her unless she had the money. That gives *her* a motive. As to the daughter-in-law, I wouldn't like to say. Don't know enough about her yet. But any of the three of them *could* have poisoned him, and I don't see how anyone else could have done so. The parlour-maid, the butler, the cook, they all handled the breakfast or brought it in, but I don't see how any of them could have been sure of Fortescue himself getting the taxine and nobody else. That is, if it *was* taxine.'

The AC said: 'It was taxine all right. I've just got the preliminary report.'

'That settles that, then,' said Inspector Neele. 'We can go ahead.'

'Servants seem all right?'

'The butler and the parlourmaid both seem nervous. There's nothing uncommon about that. Often happens. The cook's fighting mad and the housemaid was grimly pleased. In fact all quite natural and normal.'

'There's nobody else whom you consider suspicious in any way?'

'No, I don't think so, sir.' Involuntarily, Inspector Neele's mind went back to Mary Dove and her enigmatic smile. There had surely been a faint yet definite look of antagonism. Aloud he said, 'Now that we know it's taxine, there ought to be some evidence to be got as to how it was obtained or prepared.'

'Just so. Well, go ahead, Neele. By the way, Mr Percival Fortescue is here now. I've had a word or two with him and he's waiting to see you. We've located the other son, too. He's in Paris at the Bristol, leaving today. You'll have him met at the airport, I suppose?'

'Yes, sir. That was my idea . . .'

'Well, you'd better see Percival Fortescue now.' The AC chuckled. 'Percy Prim, that's what he is.'

Mr Percival Fortescue was a neat fair man of thirty odd, with pale hair and eyelashes and a slightly pedantic way of speech.

'This has been a terrible shock to me, Inspector Neele, as you can well imagine.'

'It must have been, Mr Fortescue,' said Inspector Neele.

'I can only say that my father was perfectly well when I left home the day before yesterday. This food poisoning, or whatever it was, must have been very sudden?'

'It was very sudden, yes. But it wasn't food poisoning, Mr Fortescue.'

Percival stared and frowned.

'No? So that's why – ' he broke off.

'Your father,' said Inspector Neele, 'was poisoned by the administration of taxine.'

'Taxine? I've never heard of it.'

'Very few people have, I should imagine. It is a poison that takes effect very suddenly and drastically.'

The frown deepened.

'Are you telling me, Inspector, that my father was deliberately poisoned by someone?'

'It would seem so, yes, sir.'

'That's terrible!'

'Yes indeed, Mr Fortescue.'

Percival murmured: 'I understand now their attitude in the hospital – their referring me here.' He broke off. After a pause he went on, 'The funeral?' He spoke interrogatively.

'The inquest is fixed for tomorrow after the post-mortem. The proceedings at the inquest will be purely formal and the inquest will be adjourned.'

'I understand. That is usually the case?'

'Yes, sir. Nowadays.'

'May I ask, have you formed any ideas, any suspicions of who could – Really, I – ' again he broke off.

'It's rather early days for that, Mr Fortescue,' murmured Neele.

'Yes, I suppose so.'

'All the same it would be helpful to us, Mr Fortescue, if you could give us some idea of your father's testamentary dispositions. Or perhaps you could put me in touch with his solicitor.'

'His solicitors are Billingsby, Horsethorpe & Walters of Bedford Square. As far as his will goes, I think I can more or less tell you its main dispositions.'

'If you will be kind enough to do so, Mr Fortescue. It's a routine that has to be gone through, I'm afraid.'

'My father made a new will on the occasion of his marriage two years ago,' said Percival precisely. 'My father left the sum of £100,000 to his wife absolutely and £50,000 to my sister, Elaine. I am his residuary legatee. I am already, of course, a partner in the firm.'

'There was no bequest to your brother, Lancelot Fortescue?'

'No, there is an estrangement of long standing between my father and my brother.'

Neele threw a sharp glance at him – but Percival seemed quite sure of his statement.

'So as the will stands,' said Inspector Neele, 'the three people who stand to gain are Mrs Fortescue, Miss Elaine Fortescue and yourself?'

'I don't think I shall be much of a gainer.' Percival sighed. 'There are death duties, you know, Inspector. And of late my father has been – well, all I can say is, highly injudicious in some of his financial dealings.'

'You and your father have not seen eye to eye lately about the conduct of the business?' Inspector Neele threw out the question in a genial manner.

'I put my point of view to him, but alas – ' Percival shrugged his shoulders.

'Put it rather forcibly, didn't you?' Neele inquired. 'In fact, not to put too fine a point on it, there was quite a row about it, wasn't there?'

'I should hardly say that, Inspector.' A red flush of annoyance mounted to Percival's forehead.

'Perhaps the dispute you had was about some other matter then, Mr Fortescue?'

'There was no dispute, Inspector.'

'Quite sure of that, Mr Fortescue? Well, no matter. Did I understand that your father and brother are still estranged?'

'That is so.'

'Then perhaps you can tell me what this means?'

Neele handed him the telephone message Mary Dove had jotted down.

Percival read it and uttered an exclamation of surprise and annoyance. He seemed both incredulous and angry.

'I can't understand it, I really can't. I can hardly believe it.'

203

'It seems to be true, though, Mr Fortescue. Your brother is arriving from Paris today.'

'But it's extraordinary, quite extraordinary. No, I really *can't* understand it.'

'Your father said nothing to you about it?'

'He certainly did *not*. How outrageous of him. To go behind my back and send for Lance.'

'You've no idea, I suppose, *why* he did such a thing?'

'Of course I haven't. It's all on a par with his behaviour lately – Crazy! Unaccountable. It's got to be stopped – I – '

Percival came to an abrupt stop. The colour ebbed away again from his pale face.

'I'd forgotten – ' he said. 'For the moment I'd forgotten that my father was dead – '

Inspector Neele shook his head sympathetically.

Percival Fortescue prepared to take his departure – as he picked up his hat he said:

'Call upon me if there is anything I can do. But I suppose – ' he paused – 'you will be coming down to Yewtree Lodge?'

'Yes, Mr Fortescue – I've got a man in charge there now.'

Percival shuddered in a fastidious way.

'It will all be most unpleasant. To think such a thing should happen to us – '

He sighed and moved towards the door.

'I shall be at the office most of the day. There is a lot to be seen to here. But I shall get down to Yewtree Lodge this evening.'

'Quite so, sir.'

Percival Fortescue went out.

'Percy Prim,' murmured Neele.

Sergeant Hay who was sitting unobtrusively by the wall looked up and said 'Sir?' interrogatively.

Then as Neele did not reply, he asked, 'What do you make of it all, sir?'

'I don't know,' said Neele. He quoted softly, '"They're all very unpleasant people."'

Sergeant Hay looked somewhat puzzled.

'Alice in Wonderland,' said Neele. 'Don't you know your Alice, Hay?'

'It's a classic, isn't it, sir?' said Hay. 'Third Programme stuff. I don't listen to the Third Programme.'

CHAPTER TEN

It was about five minutes after leaving Le Bourget that Lance Fortescue opened his copy of the continental *Daily Mail*. A minute or two later he uttered a startled exclamation. Pat, in the seat beside him, turned her head inquiringly.

'It's the old man,' said Lance. 'He's dead.'

'Dead! Your father?'

'Yes, he seems to have been taken suddenly ill at the office, was taken to St Jude's Hospital and died there soon after arrival.'

'Darling, I'm so sorry. What was it, a stroke?'

'I suppose so. Sounds like it.'

'Did he ever had a stroke before?'

'No. Not that I know of.'

'I thought people never died from a first one.'

'Poor old boy,' said Lance. 'I never thought I was particularly fond of him, but somehow, now that he's dead . . .'

'Of course you were fond of him.'

'We haven't all got your nice nature, Pat. Oh well, it looks as though my luck's out again, doesn't it.'

'Yes. It's odd that it should happen now. Just when you were on the point of coming home.'

He turned his head sharply towards her.

'Odd? What do you mean by odd, Pat?'

She looked at him with slight surprise.

'Well, a sort of coincidence.'

'You mean that whatever I set out to do goes wrong?'

'No, darling, I didn't mean that. But there is such a thing as a run of bad luck.'

'Yes, I suppose there is.'

Pat said again: 'I'm so sorry.'

When they arrived at Heathrow and were waiting to disembark from the plane, an official of the air company called out in a clear voice:

'Is Mr Lancelot Fortescue abroad?'

'Here,' said Lance.

'Would you just step this way, Mr Fortescue.'

Lance and Pat followed him out of the plane, preceding the other passengers. As they passed a couple in the last seat, they heard the man whisper to his wife:

'Well-known smugglers, I expect. Caught in the act.'

II

'It's fantastic,' said Lance. 'Quite fantastic.' He stared across the table at Detective Inspector Neele.

Inspector Neele nodded his head sympathetically.

'Taxine – yewberries – the whole thing seems like some kind of melodrama. I dare say this sort of thing seems ordinary enough to you, Inspector. All in the day's work. But poisoning, in our family, seems wildly far-fetched.'

'You've no idea then at all,' asked Inspector Neele, 'who might have poisoned your father?'

'Good lord, no. I expect the old man's made a lot of enemies in business, lots of people who'd like to skin him alive, do him down financially – all that sort of thing. But poisoning? Anyway I wouldn't be in the know. I've been abroad for a good many years and have known very little of what's going on at home.'

'That's really what I wanted to ask you about, Mr Fortescue. I understand from your brother that there was an estrangement between you and your father which had lasted for many years. Would you like to tell me the circumstances that led to your coming home at this time?'

'Certainly, Inspector. I heard from my father, let me see it must be about – yes, six months ago now. It was soon after my marriage. My father wrote and hinted that he would like to let bygones be bygones. He suggested that I should come home and enter the firm. He was rather vague in his terms and I wasn't really sure that I wanted to do what he asked. Anyway, the upshot was that I came over to England last – yes, last August, just about three months ago. I went down to see him at Yewtree Lodge and he made me, I must say, a very advantageous offer. I told him that I'd have to think about it and I'd have to consult my wife. He quite understood that. I flew back to East Africa, talked it over with Pat. The upshot was that I decided

206

to accept the old boy's offer. I had to wind up my affairs there, but I agreed to do so before the end of last month. I told him I would wire to him the date of my actual arrival in England.'

Inspector Neele coughed.

'Your arrival back seems to have caused your brother some surprise.'

Lance gave a sudden grin. His rather attractive face lit up with the spirit of pure mischief.

'Don't believe old Percy knew a thing about it,' he said. 'He was away on his holiday in Norway at the time. If you ask me, the old man picked that particular time on purpose. He was going behind Percy's back. In fact I've a very shrewd suspicion that my father's offer to me was actuated by the fact that he had a blazing row with poor old Percy – or Val as he prefers to be called. Val, I think, had been more or less trying to run the old man. Well, the old man would never stand for anything of that kind. What the exact row was about I don't know, but he was furious. And I think he thought it a jolly good idea to get me there and thereby spike poor old Val's guns. For one thing he never liked Percy's wife much and he was rather pleased, in a snobbish way, with my marriage. It would be just his idea of a good joke to get me home and suddenly confront Percy with the accomplished fact.'

'How long were you at Yewtree Lodge on this occasion?'

'Oh, not more than an hour or two. He didn't ask me to stay the night. The whole idea, I'm sure, was a kind of secret offensive behind Percy's back. I don't think he even wanted the servants to report upon it. As I say, things were left that I'd think it over, talk about it to Pat and then write him my decision, which I did. I wrote giving him the approximate date of my arrival, and I finally sent him a telegram yesterday from Paris.'

Inspector Neele nodded.

'A telegram which surprised your brother very much.'

'I bet it did. However, as usual, Percy wins. I've arrived too late.'

'Yes,' said Inspector Neele thoughtfully, 'you've arrived too late.' He went on briskly: 'On the occasion of your visit last August, did you meet any other members of the family?'

'My stepmother was there at tea.'

'You had not met her previously?'

'No.' He grinned suddenly. 'The old boy certainly knew how to pick them. She must be thirty years younger than him at least.'

207

'You will excuse my asking, but did you resent your father's remarriage, or did your brother do so?'

Lance looked surprised.

'I certainly didn't, and I shouldn't think Percy did either. After all, our own mother died when we were about – oh, ten, twelve years old. What I'm really surprised at is that the old man didn't marry again before.'

Inspector Neele murmured:

'It may be considered taking rather a risk to marry a woman very much younger than yourself.'

'Did my dear brother say that to you? It sounds rather like him. Percy is a great master of the art of insinuation. Is that the set up, Inspector? Is my stepmother suspected of poisoning my father?'

Inspector Neele's face became blank.

'It's early days to have any definite ideas about anything, Mr Fortescue,' he said pleasantly. 'Now, may I ask you what your plans are?'

'Plans?' Lance considered. 'I shall have to make new plans, I suppose. Where is the family? All down at Yewtree Lodge?'

'Yes.'

'I'd better go down there straight away.' He turned to his wife. 'You'd better go to an hotel, Pat.'

She protested quickly. 'No, no, Lance, I'll come with you.'

'No, darling.'

'But I want to.'

'Really, I'd rather you didn't. Go and stay at the – oh it's so long since I stayed in London – Barnes's. Barnes's Hotel used to be a nice, quiet sort of place. That's still going, I suppose?'

'Oh, yes, Mr Fortescue.'

'Right, Pat. I'll settle you in there if they've got a room, then I'll go on down to Yewtree Lodge.'

'But why can't I come with you, Lance?'

Lance's face took suddenly a rather grim line.

'Frankly, Pat, I'm not sure of my welcome. It was Father who invited me there, but Father's dead. I don't know who the place belongs to now. Percy, I suppose, or perhaps Adele. Anyway, I'd like to see what reception I get before I bring you there. Besides – '

'Besides what?'

'I don't want to take you to a house where there's a poisoner at large.'

'Oh, what nonsense.'

208

Lance said firmly:

'Where you're concerned, Pat, I'm taking no risks.'

CHAPTER ELEVEN

Mr Dubois was annoyed. He tore Adele Fortescue's letter angrily across and threw it into the waste-paper basket. Then, with a sudden caution, he fished out the various pieces, struck a match and watched them burn to ashes. He muttered under his breath:

'Why have women got to be such damned fools? Surely common prudence . . .' But then, Mr Dubois reflected gloomily, women never had any prudence. Though he had profited by this lack many a time, it annoyed him now. He himself had taken every precaution. If Mrs Fortescue rang up they had instructions to say that he was out. Already Adele Fortescue had rung him up three times, and now she had written. On the whole, writing was far worse. He reflected for a moment or two, then he went to the telephone.

'Can I speak to Mrs Fortescue, please? Yes, Mr Dubois.' A minute or two later he heard her voice.

'Vivian, at last!'

'Yes, yes, Adele, but be careful. Where are you speaking from?'

'From the library.'

'Sure nobody's listening in, in the hall?'

'Why should they?'

'Well, you never know. Are the police still about the house?'

'No, they've gone for the moment, anyhow. Oh, Vivian dear, it's been *awful*.'

'Yes, yes, it must have I'm sure. But look here, Adele, we've got to be careful.'

'Oh, of course, darling.'

'Don't call me darling through the phone. It isn't safe.'

'Aren't you being a little bit panicky, Vivian? After all, everybody says darling nowadays.'

'Yes, yes, that's true enough. But listen. *Don't telephone to me and don't write.*'

'But Vivian – '

'It's just for the present, you understand. *We must be careful.*'

'Oh. All right.' Her voice sounded offended.

'Adele, listen. My letters to you. You did burn them, didn't you?'

There was a momentary hesitation before Adele Fortescue said: 'Of course. I told you I was going to do so.'

'That's all right then. Well I'll ring off now. Don't phone and don't write. You'll hear from me in good time.'

He put the receiver back in its hook. He stroked his cheek thoughtfully. He didn't like that moment's hesitation. Had Adele burnt his letters? Women were all the same. They promised to burn things and then didn't.

Letters, Mr Dubois thought to himself. Women always wanted you to write them letters. He himself tried to be careful but sometimes one could not get out of it. What had he said exactly in the few letters he had written to Adele Fortescue? 'It was the usual sort of gup,' he thought, gloomily. But were there any special words – special phrases that the police could twist to make them say what they wanted them to say. He remembered the Edith Thompson case. His letters were innocent enough, he thought, but he could not be sure. His uneasiness grew. Even if Adele had not already burnt his letters, would she have the sense to burn them now? Or had the police already got hold of them? Where did she keep them, he wondered. Probably in that sitting-room of hers upstairs. That gimcrack little desk, probably sham antique Louis XIV. She had said something to him once about there being a secret drawer in it. Secret drawer! That would not fool the police long. But there were no police about the house now. She had said so. They had been there that morning, and now they had all gone away.

Up to now they had probably been busy looking for possible sources of poison in the food. They would not, he hoped, have got round to a room by room search of the house. Perhaps they would have to ask permission or get a search warrant to do that. It was possible that if he acted now, at once –

He visualized the house clearly in his mind's eye. It would be getting towards dusk. Tea would be brought in, either into the library or into the drawing-room. Everyone would be assembled downstairs and the servants would be having tea in the servants' hall. There would be no one upstairs on the first floor. Easy to walk up through the garden, skirting the yew hedges that provided such admirable cover. Then there was the little door at the side on to the terrace. That was never locked until just before bedtime. One could slip through there and, choosing one's moment, slip upstairs.

Vivian Dubois considered very carefully what it behove him to do next. If Fortescue's death had been put down to a seizure or to a stroke as surely it ought to have been, the position would be very different. As it was – Dubois murmured under his breath: 'Better be safe than sorry.'

II

Mary Dove came slowly down the big staircase. She paused a moment at the window on the half landing, from which she had seen Inspector Neele arrive on the preceding day. Now, as she looked out in the fading light, she noticed a man's figure just disappearing round the yew hedge. She wondered if it was Lancelot Fortescue, the prodigal son. He had, perhaps, dismissed his car at the gate and was wandering round the garden recollecting old times there before tackling a possibly hostile family. Mary Dove felt rather sympathetic towards Lance. A faint smile on her lips, she went on downstairs. In the hall she encountered Gladys, who jumped nervously at the sight of her.

'Was that the telephone I heard just now?' Mary asked. 'Who was it?'

'Oh, that was a wrong number. Thought we were the laundry.' Gladys sounded breathless and rather hurried. 'And before that, it was Mr Dubois. He wanted to speak to the mistress.'

'I see.'

Mary went on across the hall. Turning her head, she said: 'It's teatime, I think. Haven't you brought it in yet?'

Gladys said: 'I don't think it's half-past four yet, is it, miss?'

'It's twenty minutes to five. Bring it in now, will you?'

Mary Dove went on into the library where Adele Fortescue, sitting on the sofa, was staring at the fire, picking with her fingers at a small lace handkerchief. Adele said fretfully:

'Where's tea?'

Mary Dove said: 'It's just coming in.'

A log had fallen out of the fireplace and Mary Dove knelt down at the grate and replaced it with the tongs, adding another piece of wood and a little coal.

211

Gladys went out into the kitchen, where Mrs Crump raised a red and wrathful face from the kitchen table where she was mixing pastry in a large bowl.

'The library bell's been ringing and ringing. Time you took in the tea, my girl.'

'All right, all right, Mrs Crump.'

'What I'll say to Crump tonight,' muttered Mrs Crump. 'I'll tell him off.'

Gladys went on into the pantry. She had not cut any sandwiches. Well, she jolly well wasn't going to cut sandwiches. They'd got plenty to eat without that, hadn't they? Two cakes, biscuits and scones and honey. Fresh black market farm butter. Plenty without her bothering to cut tomato or fois gras sandwiches. She'd got other things to think about. Fair temper Mrs Crump was in, all because Mr Crump had gone out this afternoon. Well, it was his day out, wasn't it? Quite right of him, Gladys thought. Mrs Crump called out from the kitchen:

'The kettle's boiling its head off. Aren't you ever going to make that tea?'

'Coming.'

She jerked some tea without measuring it into the big silver pot, carried it into the kitchen and poured the boiling water on it. She added the teapot and the kettle to the big silver tray and carried the whole thing through to the library where she set it on the small table near the sofa. She went back hurriedly for the other tray with the eatables on it. She carried the latter as far as the hall when the sudden jarring noise of the grandfather clock preparing itself to strike made her jump.

In the library, Adele Fortescue said querulously, to Mary Dove:

'Where *is* everybody this afternoon?'

'I really don't know, Mrs Fortescue. Miss Fortescue came in some time ago. I think Mrs Percival's writing letters in her room.'

Adele said pettishly: 'Writing letters, writing letters. That woman never stops writing letters. She's like all people of her class. She takes an absolute delight in death and misfortune. Ghoulish, that's what I call it. Absolutely ghoulish.'

Mary murmured tactfully: 'I'll tell her that tea is ready.'

Going towards the door she drew back a little in the doorway as Elaine Fortescue came into the room. Elaine said:

'It's cold,' and dropped down by the fireplace, rubbing her hands before the blaze.

Mary stood for a moment in the hall. A large tray with cakes on it was standing on one of the hall chests. Since it was getting dark in the hall, Mary switched on the light. As she did so she thought she heard Jennifer Fortescue walking along the passage upstairs. Nobody, however, came down the stairs and Mary went up the staircase and along the corridor.

Percival Fortescue and his wife occupied a self-contained suite in one wing of the house. Mary tapped on the sitting-room door. Mrs Percival liked you to tap on doors, a fact which always roused Crump's scorn of her. Her voice said briskly:

'Come in.'

Mary opened the door and murmured:

'Tea is just coming in, Mrs Percival.'

She was rather surprised to see Jennifer Fortescue with her outdoor clothes on. She was just divesting herself of a long camel-hair coat.

'I didn't know you'd been out,' said Mary.

Mrs Percival sounded slightly out of breath.

'Oh, I was just in the garden, that's all. Just getting a little air. Really, though, it was too cold. I shall be glad to get down to the fire. The central heating here isn't as good as it might be. Somebody must speak to the gardeners about it, Miss Dove.'

'I'll do so,' Mary promised.

Jennifer Fortescue dropped her coat on a chair and followed Mary out of the room. She went down the stairs ahead of Mary, who drew back a little to give her precedence. In the hall, rather to Mary's surprise, she noticed the tray of eatables was still there. She was about to go out to the pantry and call to Gladys when Adele Fortescue appeared in the door of the library, saying in an irritable voice:

'Aren't we ever going to have anything to eat for tea?'

Quickly Mary picked up the tray and took it into the library, disposing the various things on low tables near the fireplace. She was carrying the empty tray out to the hall again when the front-door bell rang. Setting down the tray, Mary went to the door herself. If this was the prodigal son at last she was rather curious to see him. 'How unlike the rest of the Fortescues,' Mary thought, as she opened the door and looked up into the dark lean face and the faint quizzical twist of the mouth. She said quietly:

'Mr Lancelot Fortescue?'

'Himself.'

Mary peered beyond him.

'Your luggage?'

'I've paid off the taxi. This is all I've got.'

He picked up a medium-sized zip bag. Some faint feeling of surprise in her mind, Mary said:

'Oh, you did come in a taxi. I thought perhaps you'd walked up. And your wife?'

His face set in a rather grim line, Lance said:

'My wife won't be coming. At least, not just yet.'

'I see. Come this way, will you, Mr Fortescue. Everyone is in the library, having tea.'

She took him to the library door and left him there. She thought to herself that Lancelot Fortescue was a very attractive person. A second thought followed the first. Probably a great many other women thought so, too.

III

'Lance!'

Elaine came hurrying forward towards him. She flung her arms round his neck and hugged him with a schoolgirl abandon that Lance found quite surprising.

'Hallo. Here I am.'

He disengaged himself gently.

'This is Jennifer?'

Jennifer Fortescue looked at him with eager curiosity.

'I'm afraid Val's been detained in town,' she said. 'There's so much to see to, you know. All the arrangements to make and everything. Of course it all comes on Val. He has to see to *everything*. You can really have no idea what we're all going through.'

'It must be terrible for you,' said Lance gravely.

He turned to the woman on the sofa, who was sitting with a piece of scone and honey in her hand, quietly appraising him.

'Of course,' cried Jennifer, 'you don't know Adele, do you?'

Lance murmured, 'Oh yes, I do,' as he took Adele Fortescue's hand in his. As he looked down at her, her eyelids fluttered. She set down the scone she was eating with her left hand and just touched the arrangement of her hair. It was a feminine gesture. It marked her recognition of the entry to the room of a personable man. She said in her thick, soft voice:

'Sit down here on the sofa beside me, Lance.' She poured out a cup of tea for him. 'I'm so glad you've come,' she went on. 'We badly need another man in the house.'

Lance said:

'You must let me do everything I can to help.'

'You know – but perhaps you don't know – we've had the police here. They think – they think – ' she broke off and cried out passionately: 'Oh, it's awful! Awful!'

'I know.' Lance was grave and sympathetic. ''As a matter of fact they met me at London Airport.'

'The police met you?'

'Yes.'

'What did they say?'

'Well,' Lance was deprecating. 'They told me what had happened.'

'He was poisoned,' said Adele, 'that's what they think, what they say. Not food poisoning. Real poisoning, by someone. I believe, I really do believe they think it's one of *us*.'

Lance gave her a sudden quick smile.

'That's their pigeon,' he said consolingly. 'It's no good our worrying. What a scrumptious tea! It's a long time since I've seen a good English tea.'

The others fell in with his mood soon enough. Adele said suddenly:

'But your wife – haven't you got a wife, Lance?'

'I've got a wife, yes. She's in London.'

'But aren't you – hadn't you better bring her down here?'

'Plenty of time to make plans,' said Lance. 'Pat – oh, Pat's quite all right where she is.'

Elaine said sharply:

'You don't mean – you don't think – '

Lance said quickly:

'What a wonderful-looking chocolate cake. I must have some.'

Cutting himself a slice, he asked:

'Is Aunt Effie alive still?'

'Oh, yes, Lance. She won't come down and have meals with us or anything, but she's quite well. Only she's getting very peculiar.'

'She always was peculiar,' said Lance. 'I must go up and see her after tea.'

Jennifer Fortescue murmured:

'At her age one does really feel that she ought to be in some

215

kind of a home. I mean somewhere where she will be properly looked after.'

'Heaven help any old ladies' home that got Aunt Effie in their midst,' said Lance. He added, 'Who's the demure piece of goods who let me in?'

Adele looked surprised.

'Didn't Crump let you in? The butler? Oh no, I forgot. It's his day out today. But surely Gladys – '

Lance gave a description. 'Blue eyes, hair parted in the middle, soft voice, butter wouldn't melt in the mouth. What goes on behind it all, I wouldn't like to say.'

'That,' said Jennifer, 'would be Mary Dove.'

Elaine said:

'She sort of runs things for us.'

'Does she, now?'

Adele said:

'She's really very useful.'

'Yes,' said Lance thoughtfully, 'I should think she might be.'

'But what is so nice is,' said Jennifer, 'that she knows her place. She never presumes, if you know what I mean.'

'Clever Mary Dove,' said Lance, and helped himself to another piece of chocolate cake.

CHAPTER TWELVE

'So you've turned up again like a bad penny,' said Miss Ramsbottom.

Lance grinned at her. 'Just as you say, Aunt Effie.'

'Humph!' Miss Ramsbottom sniffed disapprovingly. 'You've chosen a nice time to do it. Your father got himself murdered yesterday, the house is full of police poking about everywhere, grubbing in the dustbins, even. I've seen them out of the window.' She paused, sniffed again, and asked: 'Got your wife with you?'

'No. I left Pat in London.'

'That shows some sense. I shouldn't bring her *here* if I were you. You never know what might happen.'

'To her? To Pat?'

'To anybody,' said Miss Ramsbottom.

Lance Fortescue looked at her thoughtfully.

'Got any ideas about it all, Aunt Effie?' he asked.

Miss Ramsbottom did not reply directly. 'I had an inspector here yesterday asking me questions. He didn't get much change out of me. But he wasn't such a fool as he looked, not by a long way.' She added with some indignation: 'What your grandfather would feel if he knew we had the police in the house – it's enough to make him turn in his grave. A strict Plymouth Brother he was all his life. The fuss there was when he found out I'd been attending Church of England services in the evening! And I'm sure *that* was harmless enough compared to murder.'

Normally Lance would have smiled at this, but his long, dark face remained serious. He said:

'D'you know, I'm quite in the dark after having been away so long. What's been going on here of late?'

Miss Ramsbottom raised her eyes to heaven.

'Godless doings,' she said firmly.

'Yes, yes, Aunt Effie, you would say that anyway. But what gives the police the idea that Dad was killed here, in this house?'

'Adultery is one thing and murder is another,' said Miss Ramsbottom. 'I shouldn't like to think it of her, I shouldn't indeed.'

Lance looked alert. 'Adele?' he asked.

'My lips are sealed,' said Miss Ramsbottom.

'Come on, old dear,' said Lance. 'It's a lovely phrase, but it doesn't mean a thing. Adele had a boy friend? Adele and the boy friend fed him henbane in the morning tea. Is that the set up?'

'I'll trouble you not to joke about it.'

'I wasn't really joking, you know.'

'I'll tell you one thing,' said Miss Ramsbottom suddenly. 'I believe that girl knows something about it.'

'Which girl?' Lance looked surprised.

'The one that sniffs,' said Miss Ramsbottom. 'The one that ought to have brought me up my tea this afternoon, but didn't. Gone out without leave, so they say. I shouldn't wonder if she had gone to the police. Who let you in?'

'Someone called Mary Dove, I understand. Very meek and mild – but not really. Is she the one who's gone to the police?'

'*She* wouldn't go to the police,' said Miss Ramsbottom. 'No – I mean that silly little parlourmaid. She's been twitching and jumping like a rabbit all day. "What's the matter with you?" I said. "Have you got a guilty conscience?" She said: "*I* never did anything – I wouldn't do a thing like that." "I hope you wouldn't," I said to her, "but there's something worrying you now, isn't there?" Then she began to sniff and said she didn't want to get anybody into trouble, she was sure it must be all a mistake. I said to her, I said: "Now, my girl, you speak the truth and shame the devil." That's what I said. "You go to the police," I said, "and tell them anything you know, because no good ever came," I said, "of hushing up the truth, however unpleasant it is." Then she talked a lot of nonsense about she couldn't go to the police, they'd never believe her and what on earth should she say? She ended up by saying anyway she didn't know anything at all.'

'You don't think,' Lance hesitated, 'that she was just making herself important?'

'No, I don't. I think she was scared. I think she saw something or heard something that's given her some idea about the whole thing. It may be important, or it mayn't be of the least consequence.'

'You don't think she herself could've had a grudge against Father and – ' Lance hesitated.

Miss Ramsbottom was shaking her head decidedly.

'She's not the kind of girl your father would have taken the least notice of. No man ever will take much notice of her, poor girl. Ah, well, it's all the better for her soul, that I dare say.'

Lance took no interest in Gladys's soul. He asked:

'You think she may have run along to the police station?'

Aunt Effie nodded vigorously.

'Yes. I think she mayn't like to've said anything to them in this house in case somebody overheard her.'

Lance asked: 'Do you think she may have seen someone tampering with the food?'

Aunt Effie threw him a sharp glance.

'It's possible, isn't it?' she said.

'Yes, I suppose so.' Then he added apologetically: 'The whole thing still seems so wildly improbable. Like a detective story.'

'Percival's wife is a hospital nurse,' said Miss Ramsbottom.

The remark seemed so unconnected with what had gone before that Lance looked at her in a puzzled fashion.

'Hospital nurses are used to handling drugs,' said Miss Ramsbottom.

Lance looked doubtful.

'This stuff – taxine – is it ever used in medicine?'

'They get it from yewberries, I gather. Children eat yewberries sometimes,' said Miss Ramsbottom. 'Makes them very ill, too. I remember a case when I was a child. It made a great impression on me. I never forgot it. Things you remember come in useful sometimes.'

Lance raised his head sharply and stared at her.

'Natural affection is one thing,' said Miss Ramsbottom, 'and I hope I've got as much of it as anyone. But I won't stand for wickedness. Wickedness has to be destroyed.'

II

'Went off without a word to me,' said Mrs Crump, raising her red, wrathful face from the pastry she was now rolling out on the board. 'Slipped out without a word to anybody. Sly, that's what it is. Sly! Afraid she'd be stopped, and I *would* have stopped her if I'd caught her! The idea! There's the master dead, Mr Lance coming home that hasn't been home for years and I said to Crump, I said: "Day out or no day out, I know my duty. There's not going to be cold supper tonight as is usual on a Thursday, but a proper dinner. A gentleman coming home from abroad with his wife, what was formerly married in the aristocracy, things must be properly done." You know me, miss, you know I take a pride in my work.'

Mary Dove, the recipient of these confidences, nodded her head gently.

'And what does Crump say?' Mrs Crump's voice rose angrily. '"It's my day off and I'm goin' off," that's what he says. "And a fig for the aristocracy," he says. No pride in his work, Crump hasn't. So off he goes and I tell Gladys she'll have to manage alone tonight. She just says: "All right, Mrs Crump," then, when my back's turned out *she* sneaks. It wasn't *her* day out, anyway. Friday's *her* day. How we're going to manage now, I don't know! Thank goodness Mr Lance hasn't brought his wife here with him today.'

'We shall manage, Mrs Crump,' Mary's voice was both soothing and authoritative, 'if we just simplify the menu a little.' She outlined a few suggestions. Mrs Crump nodded unwilling acquiescence. 'I shall be able to serve that quite easily,' Mary concluded.

'You mean you'll wait at table yourself, Miss?' Mrs Crump sounded doubtful.

'If Gladys doesn't come back in time.'

'*She* won't come back,' said Mrs Crump. 'Gallivanting off, wasting her money somewhere in the shops. She's got a young man, you know, miss, though you wouldn't think it to look at her. Albert his name is. Going to get married next spring, so she tells me. Don't know what the married state's like, these girls don't. What I've been through with Crump.' She sighed, then said in an ordinary voice: 'What about tea, miss. Who's going to clear it away and wash it up?'

'I'll do that,' said Mary. 'I'll go and do it now.'

The lights had not been turned on in the drawing-room though Adele Fortescue was still sitting on the sofa behind the tea tray.

'Shall I switch the lights on, Mrs Fortescue?' Mary asked. Adele did not answer.

Mary switched on the lights and went across to the window, where she pulled the curtains across. It was only then that she turned her head and saw the face of the woman who had sagged back against the cushions. A half-eaten scone spread with honey was beside her and her tea cup was still half full. Death had come to Adele Fortescue suddenly and swiftly.

III

'Well?' demanded Inspector Neele impatiently.

The doctor said promptly:

'Cyanide – potassium cyanide probably – in the tea.'

'Cyanide,' muttered Neele.

The doctor looked at him with slight curiosity.

'You're taking this hard – any special reason – '

'She was cast as a murderess,' said Neele.

'And she turns out to be a victim. Hm. You'll have to think again, won't you?'

Neele nodded. His face was bitter and his jaw was grimly set.

Poisoned! Right under his nose. Taxine in Rex Fortescue's breakfast coffee, cyanide in Adele Fortescue's tea. Still an intimate family affair. Or so it seemed.

Adele Fortescue, Jennifer Fortescue, Elaine Fortescue and the newly arrived Lance Fortescue had had tea together in the library. Lance had gone up to see Miss Ramsbottom, Jennifer had gone to her own sitting-room to write letters, Elaine had been the last to leave the library. According to her Adele had then been in perfect health and had just been pouring herself out a last cup of tea.

A last cup of tea! Yes, it *had* indeed been her last cup of tea.

And after that a blank twenty minutes, perhaps, until Mary Dove had come into the room and discovered the body.

And during that twenty minutes –

Inspector Neele swore to himself and went out into the kitchen.

Sitting in a chair by the kitchen table, the vast figure of Mrs Crump, her belligerence pricked like a balloon, hardly stirred as he came in.

'Where's that girl? Has she come back yet?'

'Gladys? No – she's not back – Won't be, I suspect, until eleven o'clock.'

'She made the tea, you say, and took it in.'

'I didn't touch it, sir, as God's my witness. And what's more I don't believe Gladys did anything she shouldn't. She wouldn't do a thing like that – not Gladys. She's a good enough girl, sir – a bit foolish like, that's all – not wicked.'

No, Neele did not think that Gladys was wicked. He did not think that Gladys was a poisoner. And in any case the cyanide had not been in the teapot.

'But what made her go off suddenly – like this? It wasn't her day out, you say.'

'No, sir, tomorrow's her day out.'

'Does Crump – '

Mrs Crump's belligerence suddenly revived. Her voice rose wrathfully.

'Don't you go fastening anything on Crump. Crump's out of it. He went off at three o'clock – and thankful I am now that he did. He's as much out of it as Mr Percival himself.'

Percival Fortescue had only just returned from London – to be greeted by the astounding news of this second tragedy.

'I wasn't accusing Crump,' said Neele mildly. 'I just wondered if he knew anything about Gladys's plans.'

'She had her best nylons on,' said Mrs Crump. 'She was up to something. Don't tell me! Didn't cut any sandwiches for tea, either. Oh yes, she was up to something. *I'll* give her a piece of my mind when she comes back.'

When she comes back –

A faint uneasiness possessed Neele. To shake it off he went upstairs to Adele Fortescue's bedroom. A lavish apartment – all

221

rose brocade hanging and a vast gilt bed. On one side of the room was a door into a mirror-lined bathroom with a sunk orchid-pink porcelain bath. Beyond the bathroom, reached by a communicating door, was Rex Fortescue's dressing room. Neele went back into Adele's bedroom, and through the door on the farther side of the room into her sitting-room.

The room was furnished in Empire style with a rose pile carpet. Neele only gave it a cursory glance for that particular room had had his close attention on the preceding day – with special attention paid to the small elegant desk.

Now, however, he stiffened to sudden attention. On the centre of the rose pile carpet was a small piece of caked mud.

Neele went over to it and picked it up. The mud was still damp.

He looked round – there were no footprints visible – only this one isolated fragment of wet earth.

IV

Inspector Neele looked round the bedroom that belonged to Gladys Martin. It was past eleven o'clock – Crump had come in half an hour ago – but there was still no sign of Gladys. Inspector Neele looked round him. Whatever Gladys's training had been, her own natural instincts were slovenly. The bed, Inspector Neele judged, was seldom made, the windows seldom opened. Gladys's personal habits, however, were not his immediate concern. Instead, he went carefully through her possessions.

They consisted for the most part of cheap and rather pathetic finery. There was little that was durable or of good quality. The elderly Ellen, whom he had called upon to assist him, had not been helpful. She didn't know what clothes Gladys had or hadn't. She couldn't say what, if anything, was missing. He turned from the clothes and the under-clothes to the contents of the chest of drawers. There Gladys kept her treasures. There were picture postcards and newspaper cuttings, knitting patterns, hints on beauty culture, dressmaking and fashion advice.

Inspector Neele sorted them neatly into various categories. The picture postcards consisted mainly of views of various places where he presumed Gladys had spent her holidays. Amongs them were three picture postcards signed 'Bert.' Bert, he took to be the 'young man' referred to by Mrs Crump. The first postcard said – in an illiterate

222

hand: 'All the best. Missing you a lot. Yours ever, Bert.' The second said: 'Lots of nice-looking girls here but not one that's a patch on you. Be seeing you soon. Don't forget our date. And remember after that – it's thumbs up and living happy ever after.' The third said merely: 'Don't forget. I'm trusting you. Love, B.'

Next, Neele looked through the newspaper cuttings and sorted them into three piles. There were the dressmaking and beauty hints, there were items about cinema stars to which Gladys had appeared greatly addicted and she had also, it appeared, been attracted by the latest marvels of science. There were cuttings about flying saucers, about secret weapons, about truth drugs used by Russians, and claims for fantastic drugs discovered by American doctors. All the witchcraft, so Neele thought, of our twentieth century. But in all the contents of the room there was nothing to give him a clue to her disappearance. She had kept no diary, not that he had expected that. It was a remote possibility. There was no unfinished letter, no record at all of anything she might have seen in the house which could have had a bearing on Rex Fortescue's death. Whatever Gladys had seen, whatever Gladys had known, there was no record of it. It would still have to be guesswork why the second tea tray had been left in the hall, and Gladys herself had so suddenly vanished.

Sighing, Neele left the room, shutting the door behind him.

As he prepared to descend the small winding stairs he heard a noise of running feet coming along the landing below.

The agitated face of Sergeant Hay looked up at him from the bottom of the stairs. Sergeant Hay was panting a little.

'Sir,' he said urgently. 'Sir! We've found her – '

'Found her?'

'It was the housemaid, sir – Ellen – remembered as she hadn't brought the clothes in from where they were hanging on the line – just round the corner from the back door. So she went out with a torch to take them in and she almost fell over the body – the girl's body – strangled, she was, with a stocking round her throat – been dead for hours, I'd say. And, sir, it's a wicked kind of joke – there was a *clothes peg clipped on her nose* – '

CHAPTER THIRTEEN

An elderly lady travelling by train had bought three morning papers, and each of them as she finished it, folded it and laid it aside, showed the same headline. It was no longer a question now of a small paragraph hidden away in the corner of the papers. There were headlines with flaring announcements of Triple Tragedy at Yewtree Lodge.

The old lady sat very upright, looking out of the window of the train, her lips pursed together, an expression of distress and disapproval on her pink and white wrinkled face. Miss Marple had left St Mary Mead by the early train, changing at the junction and going on to London, where she took a Circle train to another London terminus and thence on to Baydon Heath.

At the station she signalled a taxi and asked to be taken to Yewtree Lodge. So charming, so innocent, such a fluffy and pink and white old lady was Miss Marple that she gained admittance to what was now practically a fortress in a state of siege far more easily than could have been believed possible. Though an army of reporters and photographers were being kept at bay by the police, Miss Marple was allowed to drive in without question, so impossible would it have been to believe that she was anyone but an elderly relative of the family.

Miss Marple paid off the taxi in a careful assortment of small change, and rang the front-door bell. Crump opened it and Miss Marple summed him up with an experienced glance. 'A shifty eye,' she said to herself. 'Scared to death, too.'

Crump saw a tall, elderly lady wearing an old-fashioned tweed coat and skirt, a couple of scarves and a small felt hat with a bird's wing. The old lady carried a capacious handbag and an aged but good-quality suitcase reposed by her feet. Crump recognized a lady when he saw one and said:

'Yes, madam?' in his best and most respectful voice.

'Could I see the mistress of the house, please?' said Miss Marple.

Crump drew back to let her in. He picked up the suitcase and put it carefully down in the hall.

'Well, madam,' he said rather dubiously, 'I don't know who exactly – '

Miss Marple helped him out.

'I have come,' she said, 'to speak about the poor girl who was killed. Gladys Martin.'

'Oh, I see, madam. Well in that case – ' he broke off, and looked towards the library door from which a tall young woman had just emerged. 'This is Mrs Lance Fortescue, madam,' he said.

Pat came forward and she and Miss Marple looked at each other. Miss Marple was aware of a faint feeling of surprise. She had not expected to see someone like Patricia Fortescue in this particular house. Its interior was much as she had pictured it, but Pat did not somehow match with that interior.

'It's about Gladys, madam,' said Crump helpfully.

Pat said rather hesitatingly:

'Will you come in here? We shall be quite alone.'

She led the way into the library and Miss Marple followed her.

'There wasn't anyone specially you wanted to see, was there?' said Pat, 'because perhaps I shan't be much good. You see my husband and I only came back from Africa a few days ago. We don't really know anything much about the household. But I can fetch my sister-in-law or my brother-in-law's wife.'

Miss Marple looked at the girl and liked her. She liked her gravity and her simplicity. For some strange reason she felt sorry for her. A background of shabby chintz and horses and dogs, Miss Marple felt vaguely, would have been much more suitable than this richly furnished interior décor. At the pony show and gymkhanas held locally round St Mary Mead, Miss Marple had met many Pats and knew them well. She felt at home with this rather unhappy-looking girl.

'It's very simple, really,' said Miss Marple, taking off her gloves carefully and smoothing out the fingers of them. 'I read in the paper, you see, about Gladys Martin having been killed. And of course I know all about her. She comes from my part of the country. I trained her, in fact, for domestic service. And since this terrible thing has happened to her, I felt – well, I felt that I ought to come and see if there was anything I could do about it.'

'Yes,' said Pat. 'Of course. I see.'

And she did see. Miss Marple's action appeared to her natural and inevitable.

'I think it's a very good thing you have come,' said Pat. 'Nobody seems to know very much about her. I mean relations and all that.'

'No,' said Miss Marple, 'of course not. She hadn't got any relations. She came to me from the orphanage. St Faith's. A very well-run place though sadly short of funds. We do our best for the girls there, try to give them a good training and all that. Gladys came to me when she was seventeen and I taught her how to wait at table and keep the silver and everything like that. Of course she didn't stay long. They never do. As soon as she got a little experience, she went and took a job in a café. The girls nearly always want to do that. They think it's freer, you know, and a gayer life. Perhaps it may be. I really don't know.'

'I never even saw her,' said Pat. 'Was she a pretty girl?'

'Oh, no,' said Miss Marple, 'not at all. Adenoids, and a good many spots. She was rather pathetically stupid, too. I don't suppose,' went on Miss Marple thoughtfully, 'that she ever made many friends anywhere. She was very keen on men, poor girl. But men didn't take much notice of her and other girls rather made use of her.'

'It sounds rather cruel,' said Pat.

'Yes, my dear,' said Miss Marple, 'life is cruel, I'm afraid. One doesn't really know what to do with the Gladyses. They enjoy going to the pictures and all that, but they're always thinking of impossible things that can't possibly happen to them. Perhaps that's happiness of a kind. But they get disappointed. I think Gladys was disappointed in café and restaurant life. Nothing very glamorous or interesting happened to her and it was just hard on the feet. Probably that's why she came back into private service. Do you know how long she'd been here?'

Pat shook her head.

'Not very long, I should think. Only a month or two.' Pat paused and then went on, 'It seems so horrible and futile that she should have been caught up in this thing. I suppose she'd seen something or noticed something.'

'It was the clothes peg that really worried me,' said Miss Marple in her gentle voice.

'The clothes peg?'

'Yes. I read about it in the papers. I suppose it is true? That when she was found there was a clothes peg clipped on to her nose.'

Pat nodded. The colour rose to Miss Marple's pink cheeks.

'That's what made me so very angry, if you can understand, my dear. It was such a cruel, contemptuous gesture. It gave me a kind of picture of the murderer. To do a thing like that! It's very wicked, you know, to affront human dignity. Particularly if you've already killed.'

Pat said slowly:

'I think I see what you mean.' She got up. 'I think you'd better come and see Inspector Neele. He's in charge of the case and he's here now. You'll like him, I think. He's a very human person.' She gave a sudden, quick shiver. 'The whole thing is such a horrible nightmare. Pointless. Mad. Without rhyme or reason in it.'

'I wouldn't say that, you know,' said Miss Marple. 'No, I wouldn't say that.'

Inspector Neele was looking tired and haggard. Three deaths and the press of the whole country whooping down the trail. A case that seemed to be shaping in well-known fashion had gone suddenly haywire. Adele Fortescue, that appropriate suspect, was now the second victim of an incomprehensible murder case. At the close of that fatal day the assistant commissioner had sent for Neele and the two men had talked far into the night.

In spite of his dismay, or rather behind it, Inspector Neele had felt a faint inward satisfaction. That pattern of the wife and the lover. It had been too slick, too easy. He had always mistrusted it. And now that mistrust of his was justified.

'The whole thing takes on an entirely different aspect,' the AC had said, striding up and down his room and frowning. 'It looks to me, Neele, as though we've got someone mentally unhinged to deal with. First the husband, then the wife. But the very circumstances of the case seem to show that it's an inside job. It's all there, in the family. Someone who sat down to breakfast with Fortescue put taxine in his coffee or on his food, someone who had tea with the family that day put potassium cyanide in Adele Fortescue's cup of tea. Someone trusted, unnoticed, one of the family. Which of 'em, Neele?'

Neele said dryly:

'Percival wasn't there, so that lets him out again. That lets him out again,' Inspector Neele repeated.

The AC looked at him sharply. Something in the repetition had attracted his attention.

'What's the idea, Neele? Out with it, man.'

Inspector Neele looked stolid.

'Nothing, sir. Not so much as an idea. All I say is it was very convenient for him.

227

'A bit too convenient, eh?' The AC reflected and shook his head. 'You think he might have managed it somehow? Can't see how, Neele. No, I can't see how.'

He added: 'And he's a cautious type, too.'

'But quite intelligent, sir.'

'You don't fancy the women. Is that it? Yet the women are indicated. Elaine Fortescue and Percival's wife. They were at breakfast and they were at tea that day. Either of them could have done it. No signs of anything abnormal about them? Well, it doesn't always show. There might be something in their past medical record.'

Inspector Neele did not answer. He was thinking of Mary Dove. He had no definite reason for suspecting her, but that was the way his thoughts lay. There was something unexplained about her, unsatisfactory. A faint, amused antagonism. That had been her attitude after the death of Rex Fortescue. What was her attitude now? Her behaviour and manner were, as always, exemplary. There was no longer, he thought, amusement. Perhaps not even antagonism, but he wondered whether, once or twice, he had not seen a trace of fear. He had been to blame, culpably to blame, in the matter of Gladys Martin. That guilty confusion of hers he had put down to no more than a natural nervousness of the police. He had come across that guilty nervousness so often. In this case it had been something more. Gladys had seen or heard something which had aroused her suspicions. It was probably, he thought, some quite small thing, something so vague and indefinite that she had hardly liked to speak about it. And now, poor little rabbit, she would never speak.

Inspector Neele looked with some interest at the mild, earnest face of the old lady who confronted him now at Yewtree Lodge. He had been in two minds at first how to treat her, but he quickly made up his mind. Miss Marple would be useful to him. She was upright, of unimpeachable rectitude and she had, like most old ladies, time on her hands and an old maid's nose for scenting bits of gossip. She'd get things out of servants, and out of the women of the Fortescue family perhaps, that he and his policemen would never get. Talk, conjecture, reminiscences, repetitions of things said and done, out of it all she would pick the salient facts. So Inspector Neele was gracious.

'It's uncommonly good of you to have come here, Miss Marple,' he said.

'It was my duty, Inspector Neele. The girl had lived in my house.

I feel, in a sense, responsible for her. She was a very silly girl, you know.'

Inspector Neele looked at her appreciatively.

'Yes,' he said, 'just so.'

She had gone, he felt, to the heart of the matter.

'She wouldn't know,' said Miss Marple, 'what she ought to do. If, I mean, something came up. Oh, dear, I'm expressing myself very badly.'

Inspector Neele said that he understood.

'She hadn't got good judgement as to what was important or not, that's what you mean, isn't it?'

'Oh yes, exactly, Inspector.'

'When you say that she was silly – ' Inspector Neele broke off.

Miss Marple took up the theme.

'She was the credulous type. She was the sort of girl who would have given her savings to a swindler, if she'd had any savings. Of course, she never did have any savings because she always spent her money on most unsuitable clothes.'

'What about men?' asked the inspector.

'She wanted a young man badly,' said Miss Marple. 'In fact that's really, I think, why she left St Mary Mead. The competition there is very keen. So few men. She did have hopes of the young man who delivered the fish. Young Fred had a pleasant word for all the girls, but of course he didn't mean anything by it. That upset poor Gladys quite a lot. Still, I gather she did get herself a young man in the end?'

Inspector Neele nodded.

'It seems so. Albert Evans, I gather, his name was. She seems to have met him at some holiday camp. He didn't give her a ring or anything so maybe she made it all up. He was a mining engineer, so she told the cook.'

'That seems *most* unlikely,' said Miss Marple, 'but I dare say it's what he *told* her. As I say, she'd believe anything. You don't connect *him* with this business at all?'

Inspector Neele shook his head.

'No. I don't think there are any complications of that kind. He never seems to have visited her. He sent her a postcard from time to time, usually from a seaport – probably 4th Engineer on a boat on the Baltic run.'

'Well,' said Miss Marple, 'I'm glad she had her little romance. Since her life has been cut short in this way – ' She tightened her lips. 'You know, Inspector, it makes me very, very angry.' And she added, as she had said to Pat Fortescue, 'Especially the clothes peg. That, Inspector, was really wicked.'

Inspector Neele looked at her with interest.

'I know just what you mean, Miss Marple,' he said.

Miss Marple coughed apologetically.

'I wonder – I suppose it would be great presumption on my part – if only I could assist you in my very humble and, I'm afraid, very *feminine* way. This is a wicked murderer, Inspector Neele, and the wicked should not go unpunished.'

'That's an unfashionable belief nowadays, Miss Marple,' Inspector Neele said rather grimly. 'Not that I don't agree with you.'

'There is an hotel near the station, or there's the Golf Hotel,' said Miss Marple tentatively, 'and I believe there's a Miss Ramsbottom in this house who is interested in foreign missions.'

Inspector Neele looked at Miss Marple appraisingly.

'Yes,' he said. 'You've got something there, maybe. I can't say that I've had great success with the lady.'

'It's really very kind of you, Inspector Neele,' said Miss Marple. 'I'm so glad you don't think I'm just a sensation hunter.'

Inspector Neele gave a sudden, rather unexpected smile. He was thinking to himself that Miss Marple was very unlike the popular idea of an avenging fury. And yet, he thought that was perhaps exactly what she was.

'Newspapers,' said Miss Marple, 'are often so sensational in their accounts. But hardly, I fear, as accurate as one might wish.' She looked inquiringly at Inspector Neele. 'If one could be sure of having just the sober facts.'

'They're not particularly sober,' said Neele. 'Shorn of undue sensation, they're as follows. Mr Fortescue died in his office as a result of taxine poisoning. Taxine is obtained from the berries and leaves of yew trees.'

'Very convenient,' Miss Marple said.

'Possibly,' said Inspector Neele, 'but we've no evidence as to that. As yet, that is.' He stressed the point because it was here that he thought Miss Marple might be useful. If any brew or concoction of yewberries had been made in the house, Miss Marple was quite likely to come upon traces of it. She was the sort of old pussy who would make homemade liqueurs, cordials and herb teas herself. She would know methods of making and methods of disposal.

'And Mrs Fortescue?'

'Mrs Fortescue had tea with the family in the library. The last person to leave the room and the tea table was Miss Elaine Fortescue, her step-daughter. She states that as she left the room Mrs Fortescue was pouring herself out another cup of tea. Some twenty minutes or half-hour later Miss Dove, who acts as housekeeper, went in to remove the tea tray. Mrs Fortescue was still sitting on the sofa, dead. Beside her was a tea cup a quarter full and in the dregs of it was potassium cyanide.'

'Which is almost immediate in its action, I believe,' said Miss Marple.

'Exactly.'

'Such dangerous stuff,' murmured Miss Marple. 'One has it to take wasps' nests but I'm always very, very careful.'

'You're quite right,' said Inspector Neele. 'There was a packet of it in the gardener's shed here.'

'Again very convenient,' said Miss Marple. She added, 'Was Mrs Fortescue eating anything?'

'Oh, yes. They'd had quite a sumptuous tea.'

'Cake, I suppose? Bread and butter? Scones, perhaps? Jam? Honey?'

'Yes, there was honey and scones, chocolate cake and swiss roll and various other plates of things.' He looked at her curiously. 'The potassium cyanide was in the tea, Miss Marple.'

'Oh, yes, yes. I quite understand that. I was just getting the whole picture, so to speak. Rather significant, don't you think?'

He looked at her in a slightly puzzled fashion. Her cheeks were pink, her eyes were bright.

'And the third death, Inspector Neele?'

'Well, the facts there seem clear enough, too. The girl, Gladys, took in the tea tray, then she brought the next tray into the hall, but left it there. She'd been rather absent-minded all the day, apparently. After that no one saw her. The cook, Mrs Crump, jumped to the conclusion that the girl had gone out for the evening without telling anybody. She based her belief, I think, on the fact that the girl was wearing a good pair of nylon stockings and her best shoes. There, however, she was proved quite wrong. The girl had obviously remembered suddenly that she had not taken in some clothes that were drying outside on the clothes line. She ran out to fetch them in, had taken down half of them apparently, when somebody took her unawares by slipping a stocking round her neck and – well, that was that.'

'Someone from outside?' said Miss Marple.

'Perhaps,' said Inspector Neele. 'But perhaps someone from inside. Someone who'd been waiting his or her opportunity to get the girl alone. The girl was upset, nervous, when we first questioned her, but I'm afraid we didn't quite appreciate the importance of that.'

'Oh, but how could you,' cried Miss Marple, 'because people so often do look guilty and embarrassed when they are questioned by the police.'

'That's just it. But this time, Miss Marple, it was rather more than that. I think the girl Gladys had seen someone performing some action that seemed to her needed explanation. It can't, I think, have been anything very definite. Otherwise she *would* have spoken out. But I think she did betray the fact to the person in question. That person realized that Gladys was a danger.'

'And so Gladys was strangled and a clothes peg clipped on her nose,' murmured Miss Marple to herself.

'Yes, that's a nasty touch. A nasty, sneering sort of touch. Just a nasty bit of unnecessary bravado.'

Miss Marple shook her head.

'Hardly *unnecessary*. It does all make a pattern, doesn't it?'

Inspector Neele looked at her curiously.

'I don't quite follow you, Miss Marple. What do you mean by a pattern?'

Miss Marple immediately became flustered.

'Well, I mean it does seem – I mean, regarded as a sequence, if you understand – well, one can't get away from facts, can one?'

'I don't think I quite understand.'

'Well, I mean – first we have Mr Fortescue. *Rex* Fortescue. Killed in his office in the city. And then we have Mrs Fortescue, sitting here in the library and having tea. There were scones and *honey*. And then poor Gladys with the clothes peg on her nose. Just to *point* the whole thing. That very charming Mrs Lance Fortescue said to me that there didn't seem to be any rhyme or reason in it, but I couldn't agree with her, because it's the rhyme that strikes one, isn't it?'

Inspector Neele said slowly: 'I don't think – '

Miss Marple went on quickly:

'I expect you're about thirty-five or thirty-six, aren't you, Inspector Neele? I think there was rather a reaction just then, when you were a little boy, I mean, against nursery rhymes. But if one has been

232

brought up on Mother Goose – I mean it is really highly significant, isn't it? What I wondered was,' Miss Marple paused, then appearing to take her courage in her hands went on bravely: 'Of course it is great impertinence I know, on my part, saying this sort of thing to you.'

'Please say anything you like, Miss Marple.'

'Well, that's very kind of you. I shall. Though, as I say, I do it with the utmost diffidence because I know I am very old and rather muddle headed, and I dare say my idea is of no value at all. But what I mean to say is have you gone into the question of blackbirds?'

CHAPTER FOURTEEN

For about ten seconds Inspector Neele stared at Miss Marple with the utmost bewilderment. His first idea was that the old lady had gone off her head.

'Blackbirds?' he repeated.

Miss Marple nodded her head vigorously.

'Yes,' she said, and forthwith recited:

"Sing a song of sixpence, a pocketful of rye,
Four and twenty blackbirds baked in a pie.
When the pie was opened the birds began to sing.
Wasn't that a dainty dish to set before the king?

"The king was in his counting house, counting out his money,
The queen was in the parlour eating bread and honey,
The maid was in the garden hanging out the clothes,
When there came a little dickey bird and nipped off her nose."

'Good Lord,' Inspector Neele said.

'I mean, it does fit,' said Miss Marple. 'It *was* rye in his pocket, wasn't it? One newspaper said so. The others just said cereal, which might mean anything. Farmer's Glory or Cornflakes – or even maize – but it *was* rye?'

Inspector Neele nodded.

'There you are,' said Miss Marple, triumphantly. '*Rex* Fortescue. Rex means *King*. In his *Counting House*. And Mrs Fortescue the Queen in the parlour, eating bread and honey. And so, of course, the murderer had to put that clothes peg on poor Gladys's nose.'

Inspector Neele said:

'You mean the whole set up is crazy?'

'Well, one mustn't jump to conclusions – but it is certainly very *odd*. But you really must make inquiries about blackbirds. Because there must *be* blackbirds!'

It was at this point that Sergeant Hay came into the room saying urgently, 'Sir.'

He broke off at sight of Miss Marple. Inspector Neele, recovering himself, said:

'Thank you, Miss Marple. I'll look into the matter. Since you are interested in the girl, perhaps you would care to look over the things from her room. Sergeant Hay will show you them presently.'

Miss Marple, accepting her dismissal, twittered her way out.

'Blackbirds!' murmured Inspector Neele to himself.

Sergeant Hay stared.

'Yes, Hay, what is it?'

'Sir,' said Sergeant Hay, urgently again. 'Look at this.'

He produced an article wrapped in a somewhat grubby handkerchief.

'Found it in the shrubbery,' said Sergeant Hay. 'Could have been chucked there from one of the back windows.'

He tipped the object down on the desk in front of the inspector, who leaned forward and inspected it with rising excitement. The exhibit was a nearly full pot of marmalade.

The inspector stared at it without speech. His face assumed a peculiarly wooden and stupid appearance. In actual fact this meant that Inspector Neele's mind was racing once more round an imaginary track. A moving picture was enacting itself before the eyes of his mind. He saw a new pot of marmalade, he saw hands carefully removing its cover, he saw a small quantity of marmalade removed, mixed with a preparation of taxine and replaced in the pot, the top smoothed over and the lid carefully replaced. He broke off at this point to ask Sergeant Hay:

'They don't take marmalade out of the pot and put it into fancy pots?'

'No, sir. Got into the way of serving it in its own pot during the war when things were scarce, and it's gone on like that ever since.'

Neele murmured:

'That made it easier, of course.'

'What's more,' said Sergeant Hay, 'Mr Fortescue was the only one that took marmalade for breakfast (and Mr Percival when he was at home). The others had jam or honey.'

Neele nodded.

'Yes,' he said. 'That made it very simple, didn't it?'

After a slight gap the moving picture went on in his mind. It was the breakfast table now. Rex Fortescue stretching out his hand for the marmalade pot, taking out a spoonful of marmalade and spreading it on his toast and butter. Easier, far easier that way than the risk and difficulty of insinuating it into his coffee cup. A foolproof method of administering the poison! And afterwards? Another gap and a picture that was not quite so clear. The replacing of that pot of marmalade by another with exactly the same amount taken from it. And then an open window. A hand and an arm flinging out that pot into the shrubbery. Whose hand and arm?

Inspector Neele said in a businesslike voice:

'Well, we'll have of course to get this analysed. See if there are any traces of taxine. We can't jump to conclusions.'

'No, sir. There may be fingerprints too.'

'Probably not the ones we want,' said Inspector Neele gloomily. 'There'll be Gladys's, of course, and Crump's and Fortescue's own. Then probably Mrs Crump's, the grocer's assistant and a few others! If anyone put taxine in here they'd take care not to go playing about with their own fingers all over the pot. Anyway, as I say, we mustn't jump to conclusions. How do they order marmalade and where is it kept?'

The industrious Sergeant Hay had his answer pat for all these questions.

'Marmalade and jams comes in in batches of six at a time. A new pot would be taken into the pantry when the old one was getting low.'

'That means,' said Neele 'that it could have been tampered with several days before it was actually brought on to the breakfast table. And anyone who was in the house or had access to the house could have tampered with it.'

The term 'access to the house' puzzled Sergeant Hay slightly. He did not see in what way his superior's mind was working.

But Neele was postulating what seemed to him a logical assumption.

If the marmalade had been tampered with *beforehand* – then surely that ruled out *those persons who were actually at the breakfast table on the fatal morning*.

Which opened up some interesting new possibilities.

He planned in his mind interviews with various people – this time with rather a different angle of approach.

He'd keep an open mind . . .

He'd even consider seriously that old Miss Whatshername's suggestions about the nursery rhyme. Because there was no doubt that that nursery rhyme fitted in a rather startling way. It fitted with a point that had worried him from the beginning. The pocketful of rye.

'Blackbirds?' murmured Inspector Neele to himself.

Sergeant Hay stared.

'It's not blackberry jelly, sir,' he said. 'It's *marmalade*.'

II

Inspector Neele went in search of Mary Dove.

He found her in one of the bedrooms on the first floor superintending Ellen, who was denuding the bed of what seemed to be clean sheets. A little pile of clean towels lay on a chair.

Inspector Neele looked puzzled.

'Somebody coming to stay?' he asked.

Mary Dove smiled at him. In contrast to Ellen, who looked grim and truculent, Mary was her usual imperturbable self.

'Actually,' she said, 'the opposite is the case.'

Neele looked inquiringly at her.

'This is the guest room we had prepared for Mr Gerald Wright.'

'Gerald Wright? Who is he?'

'He's a friend of Miss Elaine Fortescue's.' Mary's voice was carefully devoid of inflection.

'He was coming here – when?'

'I believe he arrived at the Golf Hotel the day after Mr Fortescue's death.'

'The day *after*.'

'So Miss Fortescue said.' Mary's voice was still impersonal: 'She told me she wanted him to come and stay in the house – so I had a room prepared. Now – after these other two – tragedies – it seems more suitable that he should remain at the hotel.'

'The Golf Hotel?'

'Yes.'

'Quite,' said Inspector Neele.

Ellen gathered up the sheets and towels and went out of the room.

Mary Dove looked inquiringly at Neele.

'You wanted to see me about something?'

Neele said pleasantly:

'It's becoming important to get exact times very clearly stated. Members of the family all seem a little vague about time – perhaps understandably. You, on the other hand, Miss Dove, I have found extremely accurate in your statements as to times.'

'Again understandably!'

'Yes – perhaps – I must certainly congratulate you on the way you have kept this house going in spite of the – well, panic – these last deaths must have caused.' He paused and then asked curiously: 'How did you do it?'

He had realized, astutely, that the one chink in the armour of Mary Dove's inscrutability was her pleasure in her own efficiency. She unbent slightly now as she answered.

'The Crumps wanted to leave at once, of course.'

'We couldn't have allowed that.'

'I know. But I also told them that Mr Percival Fortescue would be more likely to be – well – generous – to those who had spared him inconvenience.'

'And Ellen?'

'Ellen does not wish to leave.'

'Ellen does not wish to leave,' Neele repeated. 'She has good nerves.'

'She enjoys disasters,' said Mary Dove. 'Like Mrs Percival, she finds in disaster a kind of pleasurable drama.'

'Interesting. Do you think Mrs Percival has – enjoyed the tragedies?'

'No – of course not. That is going too far. I would merely say that it has enabled her to – well – stand up to them – '

'And how have you yourself been affected, Miss Dove?'

Mary Dove shrugged her shoulders.

'It has not been a pleasant experience,' she said dryly.

237

Inspector Neele felt again a longing to break down this cool young woman's defences – to find out what was really going on behind the careful and efficient understatement of her whole attitude.

He merely said brusquely:

'Now – to recapitulate times and places: the last time you saw Gladys Martin was in the hall before tea, and that was at twenty minutes to five?'

'Yes – I told her to bring in tea.'

'You yourself were coming from where?'

'From upstairs – I thought I had heard the telephone a few minutes before.'

'Gladys, presumably, had answered the telephone?'

'Yes. It was a wrong number. Someone who wanted the Baydon Heath Laundry.'

'And that was the last time you saw her?'

'She brought the tea tray into the library about ten minutes or so later.'

'After that Miss Elaine Fortescue came in?'

'Yes, about three or four minutes later. Then I went up to tell Mrs Percival tea was ready.'

'Did you usually do that?'

'Oh no – people came in to tea when they pleased – but Mrs Fortescue asked where everybody was. I thought I heard Mrs Percival coming – but that was a mistake – '

Neele interrupted. Here was something new.

'You mean you heard someone upstairs moving about?'

'Yes – at the head of the stairs, I thought. But no one came down so I went up. Mrs Percival was in her bedroom. She had just come in. She had been out for a walk – '

'Out for a walk – I see. The time being then – '

'Oh – nearly five o'clock, I think – '

'And Mr Lancelot Fortescue arrived – when?'

'A few minutes after I came downstairs again – I thought he had arrived earlier – but – '

Inspector Neele interrupted:

'Why did you think he had arrived earlier?'

'Because I thought I had caught sight of him through the landing window.'

'In the garden, you mean?'

'Yes – I caught a glimpse of someone through the yew hedge – and I thought it would probably be him.'

'This was when you were coming down after telling Mrs Percival Fortescue tea was ready?'

Mary corrected him.

'No – not then – it was earlier – when I came down the first time.'

Inspector Neele stared.

'Are you sure about that, Miss Dove?'

'Yes, I'm perfectly sure. That's why I was surprised to see him – when he actually did ring the bell.'

Inspector Neele shook his head. He kept his inner excitement out of his voice as he said:

'It couldn't have been Lancelot Fortescue you saw in the garden. His train – which was due at 4.28, was nine minutes late. He arrived at Baydon Heath Station at 4.37. He had to wait a few minutes for a taxi – that train is always very full. It was actually nearly a quarter to five (five minutes *after* you had seen the man in the garden) when he left the station and it is a ten-minute drive. He paid off the taxi at the gate here at about five minutes to five at the earliest. No – it wasn't Lancelot Fortescue you saw.'

'I'm sure I did see someone.'

'Yes, you saw someone. It was getting dark. You couldn't have seen the man clearly?'

'Oh no – I couldn't see his face or anything like that – just his build – tall and slender. We were expecting Lancelot Fortescue – so I jumped to the conclusion that that's who it was.'

'He was going – which way?'

'Along behind the yew hedge towards the east side of the house.'

'There is a side door there. Is it kept locked?'

'Not until the house is locked up for the night.'

'Anyone could have come in by that side door without being observed by any of the household.'

Mary Dove considered.

'I think so. Yes.' She added quickly: 'You mean – the person I heard later upstairs could have come in that way? Could have been hiding – upstairs?'

'Something of the kind.'

'But who –?'

'That remains to be seen. Thank you, Miss Dove.'

As she turned to go away Inspector Neele said in a casual voice: 'By the way, you can't tell me anything about *blackbirds*, I suppose?'

For the first time, so it seemed, Mary Dove was taken aback. She turned back sharply.

'I – what did you say?'

'I was just asking you about blackbirds.'

'Do you mean – '

'Blackbirds,' said Inspector Neele.

He had on his most stupid expression.

'You mean that silly business last summer? But surely that can't . . .' She broke off.

Inspector Neele said pleasantly:

'There's been a bit of talk about it, but I was sure I'd get a clear account from you.'

Mary Dove was her calm, practical self again.

'It must, I think, have been some silly, spiteful joke,' she said. 'Four dead blackbirds were on Mr Fortescue's desk in his study here. It was summer and the windows were open, and we rather thought it must have been the gardener's boy, though he insisted he'd never done anything of the kind. But they were actually blackbirds the gardener had shot which had been hanging up by the fruit bushes.'

'And somebody had cut them down and put them on Mr Fortescue's desk?'

'Yes.'

'Any sort of reason behind it – any association with blackbirds?'

Mary shook her head.

'I don't think so.'

'How did Mr Forescue take it? Was he annoyed?'

'Naturally he was annoyed.'

'But not upset in any way?'

'I really can't remember.'

'I see,' said Inspector Neele.

He said no more. Mary Dove once more turned away, but this time, he thought, she went rather unwillingly as though she would have liked to know more of what was in his mind. Ungratefully, all that Inspector Neele felt was annoyance with Miss Marple. She had suggested to him that there would be blackbirds and, sure enough, there the blackbirds were! Not four and twenty of them, that was true. What might be called a token consignment.

That had been as long ago as last summer and where it fitted in Inspector Neele could not imagine. He was not going to let this blackbird bogey divert him from the logical and sober investigation

240

of murder by a sane murderer for a sane reason, but he would be forced from now on to keep the crazier possibilities of the case in mind.

CHAPTER FIFTEEN

'I'm sorry, Miss Fortescue, to bother you again, but I want to be quite, quite clear about this. As far as we know you were the last person – or rather the last person but one – to see Mrs Fortescue alive. It was about twenty-past five when you left the drawing-room?'

'About then,' said Elaine, 'I can't say exactly.' She added defensively: 'One doesn't look at clocks the whole time.'

'No, of course not. During the time that you were alone with Mrs Fortescue after the others had left, what did you talk about?'

'Does it matter what we talked about?'

'Probably not,' said Inspector Neele, 'but it might give me some clue as to what was in Mrs Fortescue's mind.'

'You mean – you think she might have done it herself?'

Inspector Neele noticed the brightening on her face. It would certainly be a very convenient solution as far as the family was concerned. Inspector Neele did not think it was true for a moment. Adele Fortescue was not to his mind a suicidal type. Even if she had poisoned her husband and was convinced the crime was about to be brought home to her, she would not, he thought, have ever thought of killing herself. She would have been sure optimistically that even if she were tried for murder she would be sure to be acquitted. He was not, however, averse to Elaine Fortescue's entertaining the hypothesis. He said, therefore, quite truthfully:

'There's a possibility of it at least, Miss Fortescue. Now perhaps you'll tell me just what your conversation was about?'

'Well, it was really about my affairs.' Elaine hesitated.

'Your affairs being . . .?' he paused questioningly with a genial expression.

'I – a friend of mine had just arrived in the neighbourhood, and I was asking Adele if she would have any objection to – to my asking him to stay here at the house.'

'Ah. And who is this friend?'

'It's a Mr Gerald Wright. He's a schoolmaster. He – he's staying at the Golf Hotel.'

'A very close friend, perhaps?'

Inspector Neele gave an avuncular beam which added at least fifteen years to his age.

'We may expect an interesting announcement shortly, perhaps?'

He felt almost compunction as he saw the awkward gesture of the girl's hand and the flush on her face. She was in love with the fellow all right.

'We – we're not actually engaged and of course we couldn't have it announced just now, but – well, yes I think we do – I mean we are going to get married.'

'Congratulations,' said Inspector Neele pleasantly. 'Mr Wright is staying at the Golf Hotel, you say? How long has he been there?'

'I wired him when Father died.'

'And he came at once. *I* see,' said Inspector Neele.

He used this favourite phrase of his in a friendly and reassuring way.

'What did Mrs Fortescue say when you asked her about his coming here?'

'Oh, she said, all right, I could have anybody I pleased.'

'She was nice about it then?'

'Not exactly nice. I mean, she said – '

'Yes, what else did she say?'

Again Elaine flushed.

'Oh, something stupid about my being able to do a lot better for myself now. It was the sort of thing Adele would say.'

'Ah, well,' said Inspector Neele soothingly, 'relations say these sort of things.'

'Yes, yes, they do. But people often find it difficult to – to appreciate Gerald properly. He's an intellectual, you see, and he's got a lot of unconventional and progressive ideas that people don't like.'

'That's why he didn't get on with your father?'

Elaine flushed hotly.

'Father was very prejudiced and unjust. He hurt Gerald's feelings. In fact, Gerald was so upset by my father's attitude that he went off and I didn't hear from him for weeks.'

242

And probably wouldn't have heard from him now if your father hadn't died and left you a packet of money, Inspector Neele thought. Aloud he said:

'Was there any more conversation between you and Mrs Fortescue?'

'No. No, I don't think so.'

'And that was about twenty-five-past five and Mrs Fortescue was found dead at five minutes to six. You didn't return to the room during that half-hour?'

'No.'

'What were you doing?'

'I – I went out for a short walk.'

'To the Golf Hotel?'

'I – well, yes, but Gerald wasn't in.'

Inspector Neele said 'I see' again, but this time with a rather dismissive effect. Elaine Fortescue got up and said:

'Is that all?'

'That's all, thank you, Miss Fortescue.'

As she got up to go, Neele said casually:

'You can't tell me anything about blackbirds, can you?'

She stared at him.

'Blackbirds? You mean the ones in the pie?'

They *would* be in the pie, the inspector thought to himself. He merely said, 'When was this?'

'Oh! Three or four months ago – and there were some on Father's desk, too. He was furious – '

'Furious, was he? Did he ask a lot of questions?'

'Yes – of course – but we couldn't find out who put them there.'

'Have you any idea why he was so angry?'

'Well – it was rather a horrid thing to do, wasn't it?'

Neele looked thoughtfully at her – but he did not see any signs of evasion in her face. He said:

'Oh, just one more thing, Miss Fortescue. Do you know if your stepmother made a will at any time?'

'I've no idea – I – suppose so. People usually do, don't they?'

'They should do – but it doesn't always follow. Have you made a will yourself, Miss Fortescue?'

'No – no – I haven't – up to now I haven't had anything to leave – now, of course – '

He saw the realization of the changed position come into her eyes.

243

'Yes,' he said. 'Fifty thousand pounds is quite a responsibility – it changes a lot of things, Miss Fortescue.'

II

For some minutes after Elaine Fortescue left the room, Inspector Neele sat staring in front of him thoughtfully. He had, indeed, new food for thought. Mary Dove's statement that she had seen a man in the garden at approximately 4.35 opened up certain new possibilities. That is, of course, if Mary Dove was speaking the truth. It was never Inspector Neele's habit to assume that *anyone* was speaking the truth. But, examine her statement as he might, he could see no real reason why she should have lied. He was inclined to think that Mary Dove was speaking the truth when she spoke of having seen a man in the garden. It was quite clear that that man could not have been Lancelot Fortescue, although her reason for assuming that it was he was quite natural under the circumstances. It had not been Lancelot Fortescue, but it had been a man about the height and build of Lancelot Fortescue, and if there had been a man in the garden at that particular time, moreover a man moving furtively, as it seemed, to judge from the way he had crept behind the yew hedges, then that certainly opened up a line of thought.

Added to this statement of hers, there had been the further statement that she had heard someone moving about upstairs. That, in its turn, tied up with something else. The small piece of mud he had found on the floor of Adele Fortescue's boudoir. Inspector Neele's mind dwelt on the small dainty desk in that room. Pretty little sham antique with a rather obvious secret drawer in it. There had been three letters in that drawer, letters written by Vivian Dubois to Adele Fortescue. A great many love letters of one kind or another had passed through Inspector Neele's hands in the course of his career. He was acquainted with passionate letters, foolish letters, sentimental letters and nagging letters. There had also been cautious letters. Inspector Neele was inclined to classify these three as of the latter kind. Even if read in the divorce court, they could pass as inspired by a merely platonic friendship. Though in this case: 'Platonic friendship my foot!' thought the inspector inelegantly. Neele, when he had found the letters, had sent them up at once to the Yard since at that time the main question was whether the

Public Prosecutor's office thought that there was sufficient evidence to proceed with the case against Adele Fortescue or Adele Fortescue and Vivian Dubois together. Everything had pointed towards Rex Fortescue having been poisoned by his wife with or without her lover's connivance. These letters, though cautious, made it fairly clear that Vivian Dubois was her lover, but there had not been in the wording, so far as Inspector Neele could see, any signs of incitement to crime. There might have been incitement of a spoken kind, but Vivian Dubois would be far too cautious to put anything of that kind down on paper.

Inspector Neele surmised accurately that Vivian Dubois had asked Adele Fortescue to destroy his letters and that Adele Fortescue had told him she had done so.

Well, now they had two more deaths on their hands. And that meant, or should mean, that Adele Fortescue had not killed her husband.

Unless, that is – Inspector Neele considered a new hypothesis – Adele Fortescue had wanted to marry Vivian Dubois and Vivian Dubois had wanted, not Adele Fortescue, but Adele Fortescue's hundred thousand pounds which would come to her on the death of her husband. He had assumed, perhaps, that Rex Fortescue's death would be put down to natural causes. Some kind of seizure or stroke. After all, everybody seemed to be worried over Rex Fortescue's health during the last year. (Parenthetically, Inspector Neele said to himself that he must look into that question. He had a subconscious feeling that it might be important in some way.) To continue, Rex Fortescue's death had not gone according to plan. It had been diagnosed without loss of time as poisoning, and the correct poison named.

Supposing that Adele Fortescue and Vivian Dubois had been guilty, what state would they be in then? Vivian Dubois would have been scared and Adele Fortescue would have lost her head. She might have done or said foolish things. She might have rung up Dubois on the telephone, talking indiscreetly in a way that he would have realized might have been overheard in Yewtree Lodge. What would Vivian Dubois have done next?

It was early as yet to try and answer that question, but Inspector Neele proposed very shortly to make inquiries at the Golf Hotel as to whether Dubois had been in or out of the hotel between the hours of 4.15 and 6 o'clock. Vivian Dubois was tall and dark like Lance Fortescue. He might have slipped through the garden to the side door, made his way upstairs and then what? Looked for the letters and found them gone? Waited there, perhaps, till the coast was clear, then come down into the library when tea was over and Adele Fortescue was alone?

But all this was going to fast –

Neele had questioned Mary Dove and Elaine Fortescue; he must see now what Percival Fortescue's wife had to say.

CHAPTER SIXTEEN

Inspector Neele found Mrs Percival in her own sitting-room upstairs, writing letters. She got up rather nervously when he came in.

'Is there anything – what – are there – '

'Please sit down, Mrs Fortescue. There are only just a few more questions I would like to ask you.'

'Oh, yes. Yes, of course, Inspector. It's all so dreadful, isn't it? So very dreadful.'

She sat down rather nervously in an armchair. Inspector Neele sat down in the small, straight chair near her. He studied her rather more carefully than he had done heretofore. In some ways a mediocre type of woman, he thought – and thought also that she was not very happy. Restless, unsatisfied, limited in mental outlook, yet he thought she might have been efficient and skilled in her own profession of hospital nurse. Though she had achieved leisure by her marriage with a well-to-do man, leisure had not satisfied her. She bought clothes, read novels and ate sweets, but he remembered her avid excitement on the night of Rex Fortescue's death, and he saw in it not so much a ghoulish satisfaction but rather a revelation of the arid deserts of boredom which encompassed her life. Her eyelids fluttered and fell before his searching glance. They gave her the appearance of being both nervous and guilty, but he could not be sure that that was really the case.

'I'm afraid,' he said soothingly, 'we have to ask people questions again and again. It must be very tiresome for you all. I do appreciate that, but so much hangs, you understand, on the exact *timing* of events. You came down to tea rather late, I understand? In fact, Miss Dove came up and fetched you.'

'Yes. Yes, she did. She came and said tea was in. I had no idea it was so late. I'd been writing letters.'

Inspector Neele just glanced over at the writing-desk.

'I see,' he said. 'Somehow or other, I thought you'd been out for a walk.'

'Did she say so? Yes – now I believe you're right. I had been writing letters; then it was so stuffy and my head ached so I went out and – er – went for a walk. Only round the garden.'

'I see. You didn't meet anyone?'

'Meet anyone?' She stared at him. 'What do you mean?'

'I just wondered if you'd seen anybody or anybody had seen you during this walk of yours.'

'I saw the gardener in the distance, that's all.' She was looking at him suspiciously.

'Then you came in, came up here to your room and you were just taking your things off when Miss Dove came to tell you that tea was ready?'

'Yes. Yes, and so I came down.'

'And who was there?'

'Adele and Elaine, and a minute or two later Lance arrived. My brother-in-law, you know. The one who's come back from Kenya.'

'And then you all had tea?'

'Yes, we had tea. Then Lance went up to see Aunt Effie and I came up here to finish my letters. I left Elaine there with Adele.'

He nodded reassuringly.

'Yes. Miss Fortescue seems to have been with Mrs Fortescue for quite five or ten minutes after you left. Your husband hadn't come home yet?'

'Oh no. Percy – Val – didn't get home until about half-past six or seven. He'd been kept up in town.'

'He came back by train?'

'Yes. He took a taxi from the station.'

'Was it unusual for him to come back by train?'

'He does sometimes. Not very often. I think he'd been to places in the city where it's rather difficult to park the car. It was easier for him to take a train home from Cannon Street.'

'I see,' said Inspector Neele. He went on: 'I asked your husband if Mrs Fortescue had made a will before she died. He said he thought not. I suppose you don't happen to have any idea?'

To his surprise Jennifer Fortescue nodded vigorously.

'Oh, yes,' she said. 'Adele made a will. She told me so.'

'Indeed! When was this?'

'Oh, it wasn't very long ago. About a month ago, I think.'

'That's very interesting,' said Inspector Neele.

Mrs Percival leant forward eagerly. Her face now was all animation. She clearly enjoyed exhibiting her superior knowledge.

'Val didn't know about it,' she said. 'Nobody knew. It just happened that I found out about it. I was in the street. I had just come out of the stationer's, then I saw Adele coming out of the solicitor's office. Ansell and Worrall's, you know. In the High Street.'

'Ah,' said Neele, 'the local solicitors?'

'Yes. And I said to Adele: "Whatever have you been doing there?" I said. And she laughed and said: "Wouldn't you like to know?" And then as we walked along together she said: "I'll tell you, Jennifer. I've been making my will." "Well," I said, "why are you doing that, Adele, you're not ill or anything, are you?" And she said no, of course she wasn't ill. She'd never felt better. But everyone ought to make a will. She said she wasn't going to those stuck-up family solicitors in London, Mr Billingsley. She said the old sneak would go round and tell the family. "No," she said, "my will's my own business, Jennifer, and I'll make it my own way and nobody's going to know about it." "Well, Adele," I said, "*I* shan't tell anybody." She said: "It doesn't matter if you do. You won't know what's in it." But I didn't tell anyone. No, not even Percy. I do think women ought to stick together, don't you, Inspector Neele?'

'I'm sure that's a very nice feeling on your part, Mrs Fortescue,' said Inspector Neele diplomatically.

'I'm sure I'm never ill-natured,' said Jennifer. 'I didn't particularly care for Adele, if you know what I mean. I always thought she was the kind of woman who would stick at nothing in order to get what she wanted. Now she's dead, perhaps I misjudged her, poor soul.'

'Well, thank you very much, Mrs Fortescue, for being so helpful to me.'

'You're welcome, I'm sure. I'm only too glad to do anything I can. It's all so very terrible, isn't it? Who is the old lady who's arrived this morning?'

'She's a Miss Marple. She very kindly came here to give us what information she could about the girl Gladys. It seems Gladys Martin was once in service with her.'

'Really? How interesting.'

'There's one other thing, Mrs Percival. Do you know anything about blackbirds?'

Jennifer Fortescue started violently. She dropped her handbag on the floor and bent to pick it up.

'Blackbirds, Inspector? Blackbirds? What kind of blackbirds?'

Her voice was rather breathless. Smiling a little, Inspector Neele said:

'Just blackbirds. Alive or dead or even, shall we say, symbolical?'

Jennifer Fortescue said sharply:

'I don't know what you mean. I don't know what you're talking about.'

'You don't know anything about blackbirds, then, Mrs Fortescue?'

She said slowly:

'I suppose you mean the ones last summer in the pie. All very silly.'

'There were some left on the library table, too, weren't there?'

'It was all a very silly practical joke. I don't know who's been talking to you about it. Mr Fortescue, my father-in-law, was very much annoyed by it.'

'Just annoyed? Nothing more?'

'Oh. I see what you mean. Yes, I suppose – yes, it's true. He asked us if there were any strangers about the place.'

'Strangers!' Inspector Neele raised his eyebrows.

'Well, that's what he said,' said Mrs Percival defensively.

'Strangers,' repeated Inspector Neele thoughtfully. Then he asked: 'Did he seem afraid in any way?'

'Afraid? I don't know what you mean.'

'Nervous. About strangers, I mean.'

'Yes. Yes, he did, rather. Of course I don't remember very well. It was several months ago, you know. I don't think it was anything except a silly practical joke. Crump perhaps. I really do think that Crump is a very unbalanced man, and I'm perfectly certain that he drinks. He's really very insolent in his manner sometimes. I've sometimes wondered if he could have had a grudge against Mr Fortescue. Do you think that's possible, Inspector?'

'Anything's possible,' said Inspector Neele and went away.

Percival Fortescue was in London, but Inspector Neele found Lancelot sitting with his wife in the library. They were playing chess together.

'I don't want to interrupt you,' said Neele, apologetically.

'We're only killing time, Inspector, aren't we, Pat?'

Pat nodded.

'I expect you'll think it's rather a foolish question I'm asking you,' said Neele. 'Do you know anything about blackbirds, Mr Fortescue?'

'Blackbirds?' Lance looked amused. 'What kind of blackbirds? Do you mean genuine birds, or the slave trade?'

Inspector Neele said with a sudden, disarming smile:

'I'm not sure what I mean, Mr Fortescue. It's just that a mention of blackbirds has turned up.'

'Good Lord.' Lancelot looked suddenly alert, 'Not the old Blackbird Mine, I suppose?'

Inspector Neele said sharply:

'The Blackbird Mine? What was that?'

Lance frowned in a puzzled fashion.

'The trouble is, Inspector, that I can't really remember much myself. I just have a vague idea about some shady transaction in my papa's past. Something on the West Coast of Africa. Aunt Effie, I believe, once threw it in his teeth, but I can't remember anything definite about it.'

'Aunt Effie? That will be Miss Ramsbottom, won't it?'

'Yes.'

'I'll go and ask her about it,' said Inspector Neele. He added ruefully: 'She's rather a formidable old lady, Mr Fortescue. Always makes me feel quite nervous.'

Lance laughed.

'Yes. Aunt Effie is certainly a character, but she may be helpful to you, Inspector, if you get on the right side of her. Especially if you're delving into the past. She's got an excellent memory, she takes a positive pleasure in remembering anything that's detrimental in any way.' He added thoughtfully: 'There's something else. I went up to see her, you know, soon after I got back here. Immediately after tea that day, as a matter of fact. And she was talking about Gladys. The maid who got killed. Not that we knew she was dead then, of course. But Aunt Effie was saying she was quite convinced that Gladys knew something that she hadn't told the police.'

'That seems fairly certain,' said Inspector Neele. 'She'll never tell it now, poor girl.'

'No. It seems Aunt Effie had given her good advice as to spilling anything she knew. Pity the girl didn't take it.'

Inspector Neele nodded. Bracing himself for the encounter he penetrated to Miss Ramsbottom's fortress. Rather to his surprise, he found Miss Marple there. The two ladies appeared to be discussing foreign missions.

'I'll go away, Inspector.' Miss Marple rose hurriedly to her feet.

'No need, madam,' said Inspector Neele.

'I've asked Miss Marple to come and stay in the house,' said Miss Ramsbottom. 'No sense in spending money in that ridiculous Golf Hotel. A wicked nest of profiteers, that is. Drinking and card playing all the evening. She'd better come and stay in a decent Christian household. There's a room next door to mine. Dr Mary Peters, the missionary, had it last.'

'It's very, very kind of you,' said Miss Marple, 'but I really think I mustn't intrude in a house of mourning.'

'Mourning? Fiddlesticks,' said Miss Ramsbottom. 'Who'll weep for Rex in this house? Or Adele either? Or is it the police you're worried about? Any objections, Inspector?'

'None from me, madam.'

'There you are,' said Miss Ramsbottom.

'It's very kind of you,' said Miss Marple gratefully. 'I'll go and telephone to the hotel to cancel my booking.' She left the room and Miss Ramsbottom said sharply to the inspector:

'Well, and what do *you* want?'

'I wondered if you could tell me anything about the Blackbird Mine, ma'am.'

Miss Ramsbottom uttered a sudden, shrill cackle of laughter.

'Ha. You've got on to *that*, have you! Took the hint I gave you the other day. Well, what do you want to know about it?'

'Anything you can tell me, madam.'

'I can't tell you much. It's a long time ago now – oh, twenty to twenty-five years maybe. Some concession or other in East Africa. My brother-in-law went into it with a man called MacKenzie. They went out there to investigate the mine together and MacKenzie

251

died out there of fever. Rex came home and said the claim or the concession or whatever you call it was worthless. That's all *I* know.'

'I think you know a little more than that, ma'am,' said Neele persuasively.

'Anything else is hearsay. You don't like hearsay in the law, so I've been told.'

'We're not in court yet, ma'am.'

'Well, *I* can't tell you anything. The MacKenzies kicked up a fuss. That's all I know. They insisted that Rex had swindled MacKenzie. I daresay he did. He was a clever, unscrupulous fellow, but I've no doubt whatever he did it was all legal. They couldn't prove anything. Mrs MacKenzie was an unbalanced sort of woman. She came here and made a lot of threats of revenge. Said Rex had murdered her husband. Silly, melodramatic fuss! I think she was a bit off her head – in fact, I believe she went into an asylum not long after. Came here dragging along a couple of young children who looked scared to death. Said she'd bring up her children to have revenge. Something like that. Tomfoolery, all of it. Well, that's all I can tell you. And mind you, the Blackbird Mine wasn't the only swindle that Rex put over in his lifetime. You'll find a good many more if you look for them. What put you on to the Blackbird? Did you come across some trail leading to the MacKenzies?'

'You don't know what became of the family, ma'am?'

'No idea,' said Miss Ramsbottom. 'Mind you, I don't think Rex would have actually murdered MacKenzie, but he might have left him to die. The same thing before the Lord, but not the same thing before the law. If he did, retribution's caught up with him. The mills of God grind slowly, but they grind exceeding small – you'd better go away now, I can't tell you any more and it's no good your asking.'

'Thank you very much for what you have told me,' said Inspector Neele.

'Send that Marple woman back,' Miss Ramsbottom called after him. 'She's frivolous, like all Church of England people, but she knows how to run a charity in a sensible way.'

Inspector Neele made a couple of telephone calls, the first to Ansell and Worrall and the second to the Golf Hotel, then he summoned Sergeant Hay and told him that he was leaving the house for a short period.

'I've a call to pay at a solicitor's office – after that, you can get me at the Golf Hotel if anything urgent turns up.'

'Yes, sir.'

'And find out anything you can about blackbirds,' added Neele over his shoulder.

'Blackbirds, sir?' Sergeant Hay repeated, thoroughly mystified.

'That's what I said – not blackberry jelly – blackbirds.'

'Very good, sir,' said Sergeant Hay bewilderedly.

CHAPTER SEVENTEEN

Inspector Neele found Mr Ansel the type of solicitor who was more easily intimidated than intimidating. A member of a small and not very prosperous firm, he was anxious not to stand upon his rights but instead to assist the police in every way possible.

Yes, he said, he had made a will for the late Mrs Adele Fortescue. She had called at his office about five weeks previously. It had seemed to him rather a peculiar business but naturally he had not said anything. Peculiar things did happen in a solicitor's business, and of course the inspector would understand that discretion, etc., etc. The inspector nodded to show he understood. He had already discovered Mr Ansell had not transacted any legal business previously for Mrs Fortescue or for any of the Fortescue family.

'Naturally,' said Mr Ansell, 'she didn't want to go to her husband's firm of lawyers about this.'

Shorn of verbiage, the facts were simple. Adele Fortescue had made a will leaving everything of which she died possessed to Vivian Dubois.

'But I gathered,' said Mr Ansell, looking at Neele in an interrogating manner, 'that she hadn't actually much to leave.'

Inspector Neele nodded. At the time Adele Fortescue made her will that was true enough. But since then Rex Fortescue had died, and Adele Fortescue had inherited £100,000 and presumably that £100,000 (less death duties) now belonged to Vivian Edward Dubois.

At the Golf Hotel, Inspector Neele found Vivian Dubois nervously awaiting his arrival. Dubois had been on the point of leaving, indeed his bags were packed, when he had received over the telephone a civil request from Inspector Neele to remain. Inspector Neele had been very pleasant about it, quite apologetic. But behind the conventional words the request had been an order. Vivian Dubois had demurred, but not too much.

He said now:

'I do hope you realize, Inspector Neele, that it is very inconvenient for me to have to stay on. I really have urgent business that needs attending to.'

'I didn't know you were in business, Mr Dubois,' said Inspector Neele, genially.

'I'm afraid none of us can be as leisured as we would like to appear to be nowadays.'

'Mrs Fortescue's death must have been a great shock to you, Mr Dubois. You were great friends, were you not?'

'Yes,' said Dubois, 'she was a charming woman. We played golf quite often together.'

'I expect you'll miss her very much.'

'Yes, indeed.' Dubois sighed. 'The whole thing is really quite, quite terrible.'

'You actually telephoned her, I believe, on the afternoon of her death?'

'Did I? I really cannot remember now.'

'About four o'clock, I understand.'

'Yes, I believe I did.'

'Don't you remember what your conversation was about, Mr Dubois?'

'It wasn't of any significance. I think I asked her how she was feeling and if there was any further news about her husband's death – a more or less conventional inquiry.'

'*I* see,' said Inspector Neele. He added: 'And then you went out for a walk?'

'Er – yes – yes, I – I did, I think. At least, not a walk, I played a few holes of golf.'

Inspector Neele said gently:

'I think not, Mr Dubois . . . Not that particular day . . . The porter here noticed you walking down the road towards Yewtree Lodge.'

Dubois's eyes met his, then shied away again nervously.

'I'm afraid I can't remember, Inspector.'

'Perhaps you actually went to call upon Mrs Fortescue?'

Dubois said sharply:

'No. No, I didn't do that. I never went near the house.'

'Where did you go, then?'

'Oh, I – went on down the road, down as far as the Three Pigeons and then I turned around and came back by the links.'

'You're quite sure you didn't go to Yewtree Lodge?'

'Quite sure, Inspector.'

The inspector shook his head.

'Come, now, Mr Dubois,' he said, 'it's much better to be frank with us, you know. You may have had some quite innocent reason for going there.'

'I tell you I never went to see Mrs Fortescue that day.'

The inspector stood up.

'You know, Mr Dubois,' he said pleasantly, 'I think we'll have to ask you for a statement and you'll be well advised and quite within your rights in having a solicitor present when you are making that statement.'

The colour fled from Mr Dubois's face, leaving it a sickly greenish colour.

'You're threatening me,' he said. 'You're threatening me.'

'No, no, nothing of the kind.' Inspector Neele spoke in a shocked voice. 'We're not allowed to do anything of that sort. Quite the contrary. I'm actually pointing out to you that you have certain rights.'

'I had nothing to do with it at all, I tell you! Nothing to do with it.'

'Come now, Mr Dubois, you were at Yewtree Lodge round about half-past four on that day. Somebody looked out of the window, you know, and saw you.'

'I was only in the garden. I didn't go into the house.'

'Didn't you?' said Inspector Neele. 'Are you sure? Didn't you go in by the side door and up the stairs to Mrs Fortescue's sitting-room on the first floor? You were looking for something, weren't you, in the desk there?'

'*You've* got them, I suppose,' said Dubois sullenly. 'That fool Adele kept them, then – she swore she burnt them – But they don't mean what you think they mean.'

'You're not denying, are you, Mr Dubois, that you were a very *close* friend of Mrs Fortescue's?'

255

'No, of course I'm not. How can I when you've got the letters? All I say is, there's no need to go reading any sinister meaning into them. Don't think for a moment that we – that she – ever thought of getting rid of Rex Fortescue. Good God, I'm not *that* kind of man!'

'But perhaps she was that kind of woman?'

'Nonsense,' cried Vivian Dubois, 'wasn't she killed too?'

'Oh yes, yes.'

'Well, isn't it natural to believe that the same person who killed her husband killed her?'

'It might be. It certainly might be. But there are other solutions. For instance – (this is quite a hypothetical case, Mr Dubois) it's possible that Mrs Fortescue got rid of her husband, and that after his death she became somewhat of a danger to someone else. Someone who had, perhaps, not helped her in what she had done but who had at least encouraged her and provided, shall we say, the *motive* for the deed. She might be, you know, a danger to that particular person.'

Dubois stammered:

'You c-c-can't build up a case against me. You can't.'

'She made a will, you know,' said Inspector Neele. 'She left all her money to you. Everything she possessed.'

'I don't want the money. I don't want a penny of it.'

'Of course, it isn't very much really,' said Inspector Neele. 'There's jewellery and some furs, but I imagine very little actual cash.'

Dubois stared at him, his jaw dropping.

'But I thought her husband – '

He stopped dead.

'Did you, Mr Dubois?' said Inspector Neele, and there was steel now in his voice. 'That's very interesting. I wondered if you knew the terms of Rex Fortescue's will – '

III

Inspector Neele's second interview at the Golf Hotel was with Mr Gerald Wright. Mr Gerald Wright was a thin, intellectual and very superior young man. He was, Inspector Neele noted, not unlike Vivian Dubois in build.

'What can I do for you, Inspector Neele?' he asked.

'I thought you might be able to help us with a little information, Mr Wright.'

'Information? Really? It seems very unlikely.'

'It's in connection with the recent events at Yewtree Lodge. You've heard of them, of course?'

Inspector Neele put a little irony into the question. Mr Wright smiled patronisingly.

'Heard of them,' he said, 'is hardly the right word. The newspapers appear to be full of nothing else. How incredibly bloodthirsty our public press is! What an age we live in! On one side the manufacture of atom bombs, on the other our newspapers delight in reporting brutal murders! But you said you had some questions to ask. Really, I cannot see what they can be. I know nothing about this Yewtree Lodge affair. I was actually in the Isle of Man when Mr Rex Fortescue was killed.'

'You arrived here very shortly afterwards, didn't you, Mr Wright? You had a telegram, I believe, from Miss Elaine Fortescue.'

'Our police know everything, do they not? Yes, Elaine sent for me. I came, of course, at once.'

'And you are, I understand, shortly to be married?'

'Quite right, Inspector Neele. You have no objections, I hope.'

'It is entirely Miss Fortescue's business. I understand the attachment between you dates from some time back? Six or seven months ago, in fact?'

'Quite correct.'

'You and Miss Fortescue became engaged to be married. Mr Fortescue refused to give his consent, informed you that if his daughter married against his wishes he did not propose to give her an income of any kind. Whereupon, I understand, you broke off the engagement and departed.'

Gerald Wright smiled rather pityingly.

'A very crude way of putting things, Inspector Neele. Actually, I was victimized for my political opinions. Rex Fortescue was the worst type of capitalist. Naturally I could not sacrifice my political beliefs and convictions for money.'

'But you have no objections to marrying a wife who has just inherited £50,000?'

Gerald Wright gave a thin satisfied smile.

'Not at all, Inspector Neele. The money will be used for the benefit of the community. But surely you did not come here to discuss with me either my financial circumstances – or my political convictions?'

'No, Mr Wright. I wanted to talk to you about a simple question of fact. As you are aware, Mrs Adele Fortescue died as a result of cyanide poisoning on the afternoon of November the 5th.

'Since you were in the neighbourhood of Yewtree Lodge on that afternoon I thought it possible that you might have seen or heard something that had a bearing on the case.'

'And what leads you to believe that I was, as you call it, in the neighbourhood of Yewtree Lodge at the time?'

'You left this hotel at a quarter-past four on that particular afternoon, Mr Wright. On leaving the hotel you walked down the road in the direction of Yewtree Lodge. It seems natural to suppose that you were going there.'

'I thought of it,' said Gerald Wright, 'but I considered that it would be a rather pointless thing to do. I already had an arrangement to meet Miss Fortescue – Elaine – at the hotel at six o'clock. I went for a walk along a lane that branches off from the main road and returned to the Golf Hotel just before six o'clock. Elaine did not keep her appointment. Quite naturally, under the circumstances.'

'Anybody see you on this walk of yours, Mr Wright?'

'A few cars passed me, I think, on the road. I did not see anyone I knew, if that's what you mean. The lane was little more than a cart-track and too muddy for cars.'

'So between the time you left the hotel at a quarter-past four until six o'clock when you arrived back again, I've only your word for it as to where you were?'

Gerald Wright continued to smile in a superior fashion.

'Very distressing for us both, Inspector, but there it is.'

Inspector Neele said softly:

'Then if someone said they looked out of a landing window and saw you in the garden of Yewtree Lodge at about 4.35 – ' he paused and left the sentence unfinished.

Gerald Wright raised his eyebrows and shook his head.

'Visibility must have been very bad by then,' he said. 'I think it would be difficult for anyone to be sure.'

'Are you acquainted with Mr Vivian Dubois, who is also staying here?'

'Dubois. Dubois? No, I don't think so. Is that the tall, dark man with a pretty taste in suede shoes?'

'Yes. He also was out for a walk that afternoon, and he also left the hotel and walked past Yewtree Lodge. You did not notice him in the road by any chance?'

'No. No. I can't say I did.'

Gerald Wright looked for the first time faintly worried. Inspector Neele said thoughtfully:

'It wasn't really a very nice afternoon for walking, especially after dark in a muddy lane. Curious how energetic everyone seems to have felt.'

IV

On Inspector Neele's return to the house he was greeted by Sergeant Hay with an air of satisfaction.

'I've found out about the blackbirds for you, sir,' he said.

'You have, have you?'

'Yes, sir, in a pie they were. Cold pie was left out for Sunday night's supper. Somebody got at that pie in the larder or somewhere. They'd taken off the crust and they'd taken out the veal and 'am what was inside it, and what d'you think they put in instead? Some stinkin' blackbirds they got out of the gardener's shed. Nasty sort of trick to play, wasn't it?'

'"*Wasn't that a dainty dish to set before the king?*"' said Inspector Neele.

He left Sergeant Hay staring after him.

CHAPTER EIGHTEEN

'Just wait a minute,' said Miss Ramsbottom. 'This patience is going to come out.'

She transferred a king and his various impedimenta into an empty space, put a red seven on a black eight, built up the four, five and six of spades on her foundation heap, made a few more rapid transfers of cards and then leaned back with a sign of satisfaction.

'That's the Double Jester,' she said. 'It doesn't often come out.'

She leaned back in a satisfied fashion, then raised her eyes at the girl standing by the fireplace.

'So you're Lance's wife,' she said.

259

Pat, who had been summoned upstairs to Miss Ramsbottom's presence, nodded her head.

'Yes,' she said.

'You're a tall girl,' said Miss Ramsbottom, 'and you look healthy.'

'I'm very healthy.'

Miss Ramsbottom nodded in a satisfied manner.

'Percival's wife is pasty,' she said. 'Eats too many sweets and doesn't take enough exercise. Well, sit down, child, sit down. Where did you meet my nephew?'

'I met him out in Kenya when I was staying there with some friends.'

'You've been married before, I understand.'

'Yes. Twice.'

Miss Ramsbottom gave a profound sniff.

'Divorce, I suppose.'

'No,' said Pat. Her voice trembled a little. 'They both – died. My first husband was a fighter pilot. He was killed in the war.'

'And your second husband? Let me see – somebody told me. Shot himself, didn't he?'

Pat nodded.

'Your fault?'

'No,' said Pat. 'It wasn't my fault.'

'Racing man, wasn't he?'

'Yes.'

'I've never been on race-course in my life,' said Miss Ramsbottom. 'Betting and card playing – all devices of the devil!'

Pat did not reply.

'I wouldn't go inside a theatre or a cinema,' said Miss Ramsbottom. 'Ah, well, it's a wicked world nowadays. A lot of wickedness was going on in this house, but the Lord struck them down.'

Pat still found it difficult to say anything. She wondered if Lance's Aunt Effie was really quite all there. She was, however, a trifle disconcerted by the old lady's shrewd glance at her.

'How much,' demanded Aunt Effie, 'do you know about the family you've married into?'

'I suppose,' said Pat, 'as much as one ever knows of the family one marries into.'

'H'm, something in that, something in that. Well, I'll tell you this. My sister was a fool, my brother-in-law was a rogue, Percival is a sneak, and your Lance was always the bad boy of the family.'

'I think that's all nonsense,' said Pat robustly.

'Maybe you're right,' said Miss Ramsbottom, unexpectedly. 'You can't just stick labels on people. But don't underestimate Percival. There's a tendency to believe that those who are labelled good are also stupid. Percival isn't the least bit stupid. He's quite clever in a sanctimonious kind of way. I've never cared for him. Mind you, I don't *trust* Lance and I don't *approve* of him, but I can't help being fond of him . . . He's a reckless sort of fellow – always has been. You've got to look after him and see he doesn't go too far. Tell him not to underestimate Percival, my dear. Tell him not to believe everything that Percival says. They're all liars in this house.' The old lady added with satisfaction: 'Fire and brimstone shall be their portion.'

II

Inspector Neele was finishing a telephone conversation with Scotland Yard.

The assistant commissioner at the other end said:

'We ought to be able to get that information for you – by circularizing the various private sanatoriums. Of course she *may* be dead.'

'Probably is. It's a long time ago.'

Old sins cast long shadows. Miss Ramsbottom had said that – said it with a significance, too – as though she was giving him a hint.

'It's a fantastic theory,' said the AC.

'Don't I know it, sir. But I don't feel we can ignore it altogether. Too much fits in – '

'Yes – yes – rye – blackbirds – the man's Christian name – '

Neele said:

'I'm concentrating on the other lines too – Dubois is a possibility – so is Wright – the girl Gladys could have caught sight of either of them outside the side door – she could have left the tea tray in the hall and gone out to see who it was and what they were doing – whoever it was could have strangled her then and there and then carried her body round to the clothes line and put the peg on her nose – '

'A crazy thing to do in all conscience! A nasty one too.'

'Yes, sir. That's what upset the old lady – Miss Marple, I mean. Nice old lady – and very shrewd. She's moved into the house – to be near old Miss Ramsbottom – and I've no doubt she'll get to hear anything that's going.'

'What's your next move, Neele?'

'I've an appointment with the London solicitors. I want to find out a little more about Rex Fortescue's affairs. And though it's old history, I want to hear a little more about the Blackbird Mine.'

III

Mr Billingsley, of Billingsley, Horsethorpe & Walters, was an urbane man whose discretion was concealed habitually by a misleadingly forthcoming manner. It was the second interview that Inspector Neele had had with him, and on this occasion Mr Billingsley's discretion was less noticeable than it had been on the former one. The triple tragedy at Yewtree Lodge had shaken Mr Billingsley out of his professional reserve. He was now only too anxious to put all the facts he could before the police.

'Most extraordinary business, this whole thing,' he said. 'A most extraordinary business. I don't remember anything like it in all my professional career.'

'Frankly, Mr Billingsley,' said Inspector Neele, 'we need all the help we can get.'

'You can count on me, my dear sir. I shall be only too happy to assist you in every way I can.'

'First let me ask you how well you knew the late Mr Fortescue, and how well do you know the affairs of his firm?'

'I knew Rex Fortescue fairly well. That is to say I've known him for a period of, well, sixteen years I should say. Mind you, we are not the only firm of solicitors he employed, not by a long way.'

Inspector Neele nodded. He knew that. Billingsley, Horsethorpe & Walters were what one might describe as Rex Fortescue's reputable solicitors. For his less reputable dealings he had employed several different and slightly less scrupulous firms.

'Now what do you want to know?' continued Mr Billingsley. 'I've told you about his will. Percival Fortescue is the residuary legatee.'

'I'm interested now,' said Inspector Neele, 'in the will of his widow. On Mr Fortescue's death she came into the sum of one hundred thousand pounds, I understand?'

Billingsley nodded his head.

'A considerable sum of money,' he said, 'and I may tell you in confidence, Inspector, that it is one the firm could ill have afforded to pay out.'

'The firm, then, is not prosperous?'

'Frankly,' said Mr Billingsley, 'and strictly between ourselves, it's drifting on to the rocks and has been for the last year and a half.'

'For any particular reason?'

'Why yes. I should say the reason was Rex Fortescue himself. For the last year Rex Fortescue's been acting like a madman. Selling good stock here, buying speculative stuff there, talking big about it all the time in the most extraordinary way. Wouldn't listen to advice. Percival – the son, you know – he came here urging me to use my influence with his father. *He'd* tried, apparently and been swept aside. Well, I did what I could, but Fortescue wouldn't listen to reason. Really, he seems to have been a changed man.'

'But not, I gather, a depressed man,' said Inspector Neele.

'No. no. Quite the contrary Flamboyant, bombastic.'

Inspector Neele nodded. An idea which had already taken form in his mind was strengthened. He thought he was beginning to understand some of the causes of friction between Percival and his father. Mr Billingsley was continuing:

'But it's no good asking me about the wife's will. *I* didn't make any will for her.'

'No. I know that,' said Neele. 'I'm merely verifying that she had something to leave. In short, a hundred thousand pounds.'

'Mr Billingsley was shaking his head violently.

'No, no, my dear sir. You're wrong there.'

'Do you mean the hundred thousand pounds was only left to her for her lifetime?'

'No – no – it was left to her outright. But there was a clause in the will governing that bequest. That is to say, Fortescue's wife did not inherit the sum unless she survived him for one month. That, I may say, is a clause fairly common nowadays. It has come into operation owing to the uncertainties of air travel. If two people are killed in an air accident, it becomes exceedingly difficult to say who was the survivor and a lot of very curious problems arise.'

Inspector Neele was staring at him.

'Then Adele Fortescue had not got a hundred thousand pounds to leave. What happens to that money?'

'It goes back into the firm. Or rather, I should say, it goes to the residuary legatee.'

'And the residuary legatee is Mr Percival Fortescue.'

'That's right,' said Billingsley, 'it goes to Percival Fortescue. And with the state the firm's affairs are in,' he added unguardedly, 'I should say that he'll need it!'

IV

'The things you policemen want to know,' said Inspector Neele's doctor friend.

'Come on, Bob, spill it.'

'Well, as we're alone together you can't quote me, fortunately! But I should say, you know, that your idea's dead right. GPI by the sound of it all. The family suspected it and wanted to get him to see a doctor. He wouldn't. It acts just in the way you describe. Loss of judgment, megalomania, violent fits of irritation and anger – boastfulness – delusions of grandeur – of being a great financial genius. Anyone suffering from that would soon put a solvent firm on the rocks – unless he could be restrained – and that's not so easy to do – especially if the man himself has an idea of what you're after. Yes – I should say it was a bit of luck for your friends that he died.'

'They're no friends of mine,' said Neele. He repeated what he had once said before:

'*They're all very unpleasant people . . .*'

CHAPTER NINETEEN

In the drawing-room at Yewtree Lodge, the whole Fortescue family was assembled. Percival Fortescue, leaning against the mantelpiece, was addressing the meeting.

'It's all very well,' said Percival. 'But the whole position is most unsatisfactory. The police come and go and don't tell us anything. One supposes they're pursuing some line of research. In the meantime everything's at a standstill. One can't make plans, one can't arrange things for the future.'

'It's all so inconsiderate,' said Jennifer. 'And so stupid.'

'There still seems to be this ban against anyone leaving the house,' went on Percival. 'Still, I think among ourselves we might discuss future plans. What about you, Elaine? I gather you're going to marry – what's-his-name – Gerald Wright? Have you any idea when?'

'As soon as possible,' said Elaine.

Percival frowned.

'You mean, in about six months' time?'

'No, I don't. Why should we wait six months?'

'I think it would be more decent,' said Percival.

'Rubbish,' said Elaine. 'A month. That's the longest we'll wait.'

'Well, it's for you to say,' said Percival. 'And what are your plans when you are married, if you have any?'

'We're thinking of starting a school.'

Percival shook his head.

'That's a very risky speculation in these times. What with the shortage of domestic labour, the difficulty of getting an adequate teaching staff – really, Elaine, it sounds all right. But I should think twice about it if I were you.'

'We have thought. Gerald feels that the whole future of this country lies in right education.'

'I am seeing Mr Billingsley the day after tomorrow,' said Percival. 'We've got to go into various questions of finance. He was suggesting that you might like to make this money that's been left to you by Father into a trust for yourself and your children. It's a very sound thing to do nowadays.'

'I don't want to do that,' said Elaine. 'We shall need the money to start up our school. There's a very suitable house we've heard of for sale. It's in Cornwall. Beautiful grounds and quite a good house. It would have to be built on to a good deal – several wings added.'

'You mean – you mean you're going to take all your money out of the business? Really, Elaine, I *don't* think you're wise.'

'Much wiser to take it out than leave it in, I should say,' said Elaine. 'Businesses are going phut all over the place. You said yourself, Val, before Father died, that things were getting into a pretty bad state.'

'One says that sort of thing,' said Percival vaguely, 'but I must say, Elaine, to take out all your capital and sink it in the buying, equipping and running of a school is crazy. If it's not a success, look what happens? You're left without a penny.'

'It *will* be a success,' said Elaine, doggedly.

'I'm with you.' Lance, lying sprawled out in a chair, spoke up encouragingly. 'Have a crack at it, Elaine. In my opinion it'll be a damned odd sort of school, but it's what you want to do – you and Gerald. If you do lose your money you'll at any rate have had the satisfaction of doing what you wanted to do.'

'Just what one might have expected you to say, Lance,' said Percival, acidly.

'I know, I know,' said Lance. 'I'm the spendthrift prodigal son. But I still think I've had more fun out of life than you have, Percy, old boy.'

'It depends on what you call fun,' said Percival coldly. 'Which brings us to your own plans, Lance. I suppose you'll be off again back to Kenya – or Canada – or climbing Mount Everest or something fairly fantastic?'

'Now what makes you think that?' said Lance.

'Well, you've never had much use for a stay-at-home life in England, have you?'

'One changes as one gets older,' said Lance. 'One settles down. D'you know, Percy my boy, I'm quite looking forward to having a crack at being a sober business man.'

'Do you mean . . .'

'I mean I'm coming into the firm with you, old boy.' Lance grinned. 'Oh, you're the senior partner, of course. You've got the lion's share. I'm only a very junior partner. But I *have* got a holding in it that gives me the right to be in on things, doesn't it?'

'Well – yes – of course, if you put it that way. But I can assure you, my dear boy, you'll be very, very bored.'

'I wonder now. I don't believe I shall be bored.'

Percival frowned.

'You don't seriously mean, Lance, that you're coming into the business?'

'Having a finger in the pie? Yes, that's exactly what I am doing.'

Percival shook his head.

'Things are in a very bad way, you know. You'll find that out. It's going to be about all we can do to pay out Elaine her share, if she insists on having it paid out.'

'There you are, Elaine,' said Lance. 'You see how wise you were to insist on grabbing your money while it's still there to grab.'

'Really, Lance,' Percival spoke angrily, 'these jokes of yours are in bad taste.'

'I do think, Lance, you might be more careful what you say,' said Jennifer.

Sitting a little way away near the window, Pat studied them one by one. If this was what Lance had meant by twisting Percival's tail, she could see that he was achieving his object. Percival's neat impassivity was quite ruffled. He snapped again, angrily:

'Are you serious, Lance?'

'Dead serious.'

'It won't work, you know. You'll soon get fed up.'

'Not me. Think what a lovely change it'll be for me. A city office, typists coming and going. I shall have a blonde secretary like Miss Grosvenor – is it Grosvenor? I suppose you've snaffled her. But I shall get one just like her. "Yes, Mr Lancelot; no, Mr Lancelot. Your tea, Mr Lancelot."'

'Oh, don't play the fool,' snapped Percival.

'Why are you so angry, my dear brother? Don't you look forward to having me sharing your city cares?'

'You haven't the least conception of the mess everything's in.'

'No. You'll have to put me wise to all that.'

'First you've got to understand that for the last six months – no, more, a year, Father's not been himself. He's done the most incredibly foolish things, financially. Sold out good stock, acquired various wildcat holdings. Sometimes he's really thrown away money hand over fist. Just, one might say, for the fun of spending it.'

'In fact,' said Lance, 'it's just as well for the family that he had taxine in his tea.'

'That's a very ugly way of putting it, but in essence you're quite right. It's about the only thing that saved us from bankruptcy. But we shall have to be extremely conservative and go very cautiously for a bit.'

Lance shook his head.

'I don't agree with you. Caution never does anyone any good. You must take a few risks, strike out. You must go for something big.'

'I don't agree,' said Percy. 'Caution and economy. Those are our watchwords.'

'Not mine,' said Lance.

'You're only the junior partner, remember,' said Percival.

'All right, all right. But I've got a little say-so all the same.'

Percival walked up and down the room agitatedly.

'It's no good, Lance. I'm fond of you and all that – '

'Are you?' Lance interpolated. Percival did not appear to hear him.'

'. . . but I really don't think we're going to pull together at all. Our outlooks are totally different.'

'That may be an advantage,' said Lance.

'The only sensible thing,' said Percival, 'is to dissolve the partnership.'

'You're going to buy me out – is that the idea?'

'My dear boy, it's the only sensible thing to do, with our ideas so different.'

'If you find it hard to pay Elaine out her legacy, how are you going to manage to pay me my share?'

'Well, I didn't mean in cash,' said Percival. 'We could – er – divide up the holdings.'

'With you keeping the gilt-edged and me taking the worst of the speculative off you, I suppose?'

'They seem to be what you prefer,' said Percival.

Lance grinned suddenly.

'You're right in a way, Percy, old boy. But I can't indulge my own taste entirely. I've got Pat here to think of.'

Both men looked towards her. Pat opened her mouth, then shut it again. Whatever game Lance was playing, it was best that she should not interfere. That Lance was driving at something special, she was quite sure, but she was still a little uncertain as to what his actual object was.

'Line 'em up, Percy,' said Lance, laughing. 'Bogus Diamond Mines, Inaccessible Rubies, the Oil Concessions where no oil is. Do you think I'm quite as big a fool as I look?'

Percival said:

'Of course, some of these holdings are highly speculative, but remember, they *may* turn out immensely valuable.'

'Changed your tune, haven't you?' said Lance, grinning. 'Going to offer me father's latest wildcat acquisition as well as the old Blackbird Mine and things of that kind. By the way, has the inspector been asking you about this Blackbird Mine?'

Percival frowned.

'Yes, he did. I can't imagine what he wanted to know about it. I couldn't tell him much. You and I were children at the time. I just remember vaguely that Father went out there and came back saying the whole thing was no good.'

'What was it – a gold mine?'

'I believe so. Father came back pretty certain that there was no gold there. And, mind you, he wasn't the sort of man to be mistaken.'

'Who got him into it? A man called MacKenzie, wasn't it?'

'Yes. MacKenzie died out there.'

'MacKenzie died out there,' said Lance thoughtfully. 'Wasn't there a terrific scene? I seem to remember . . . Mrs MacKenzie, wasn't it? Came here. Ranted and stormed at Father. Hurled down curses on his head. She accused him, if I remember rightly, of murdering her husband.'

'Really,' said Percival repressively. 'I can't recollect anything of the kind.'

'I remember it, though,' said Lance. 'I was a good bit younger than you, of course. Perhaps that's why it appealed to me. As a child it struck me as full of drama. Where was Blackbird? West Africa wasn't it?'

'Yes, I think so.'

'I must look up the concession sometime,' said Lance, 'when I'm at the office.'

'You can be quite sure,' said Percival, 'that Father made no mistake. If he came back saying there was no gold, there was no gold.'

'You're probably right there,' said Lance. 'Poor Mrs MacKenzie. I wonder what happened to her and to those two kids she brought along. Funny – they must be grown up by now.'

CHAPTER TWENTY

At the Pinewood Private Sanatorium, Inspector Neele, sitting in the visitors' parlour, was facing a grey-haired, elderly lady. Helen MacKenzie was sixty-three, though she looked younger. She had pale blue, rather vacant-looking eyes, and a weak, indeterminate chin. She had a long upper lip which occasionally twitched. She held a large book in her lap and was looking down at it as Inspector

Neele talked to her. In Inspector Neele's mind was the conversation he had just had with Dr Crosbie, the head of the establishment.

'She's a voluntary patient, of course,' said Dr Crosbie, 'not certified.'

'She's not dangerous, then?'

'Oh, no. Most of the time she's as sane to talk to as you or me. It's one of her good periods now so that you'll be able to have a perfectly normal conversation with her.'

Bearing this in mind, Inspector Neele started his first conversational essay.

'It's very kind of you to see me, madam,' he said. 'My name is Neele. I've come to see you about a Mr Fortescue who has recently died. A Mr Rex Fortescue. I expect you know the name.'

Mrs MacKenzie's eyes were fixed on her book. She said:

'I don't know what you're talking about.'

'Mr Fortescue, madam. Mr Rex Fortescue.'

'No,' said Mrs MacKenzie. 'No. Certainly not.'

Inspector Neele was slightly taken aback. He wondered whether this was what Dr Crosbie called being completely normal.

'I think, Mrs MacKenzie, you knew him a good many years ago.'

'Not really,' said Mrs MacKenzie. 'It was yesterday.'

'I see,' said Inspector Neele, falling back upon this formula rather uncertainly. 'I believe,' he went on, 'that you paid him a visit many years ago at his residence, Yewtree Lodge.'

'A very ostentatious house,' said Mrs MacKenzie.

'Yes. Yes, you might call it that. He had been connected with your husband, I believe, over a certain mine in Africa. The Blackbird Mine, I believe it was called.'

'I have to read my book,' said Mrs MacKenzie. 'There's not much time and I have to read my book.'

'Yes, madam. Yes, I quite see that.' There was a pause, then Inspector Neele went on, 'Mr MacKenzie and Mr Fortescue went out together to Africa to survey the mine.'

'It was my husband's mine,' said Mrs MacKenzie. 'He found it and staked a claim to it. He wanted money to capitalize it. He went to Rex Fortescue. If I'd been wiser, if I'd known more, I wouldn't have let him do it.'

'No, I see that. As it was, they went out together to Africa, and there your husband died of fever.'

'I must read my book,' said Mrs MacKenzie.

'Do you think Mr Fortescue swindled your husband over the Blackbird Mine, Mrs MacKenzie?'

Without raising her eyes from the book, Mrs MacKenzie said: 'How stupid you are.'

'Yes, yes, I dare say . . . But you see it's all a long time ago and making inquiries about a thing that is over a long time ago is rather difficult.'

'Who said it was over?'

'I see. You don't think it is over?'

'*No question is ever settled until it is settled right.* Kipling said that. Nobody reads Kipling nowadays, but he was a great man.'

'Do you think the question will be settled right one of these days?'

'Rex Fortescue is dead, isn't he? You said so.'

'He was poisoned,' said Inspector Neele.

Rather disconcertingly, Mrs MacKenzie laughed.

'What nonsense,' she said, 'he died of fever.'

'I'm talking about Mr Rex Fortescue.'

'So am I.' She looked up suddenly and her pale blue eyes fixed his. 'Come now,' she said, 'he died in his bed, didn't he?'

'He died in his bed?'

'He died in St. Jude's Hospital,' said Inspector Neele.

'Nobody knows where my husband died,' said Mrs MacKenzie. 'Nobody knows how he died or where he was buried . . . All anyone knows is what Rex Fortescue *said*. And Rex Fortescue was a liar!'

'Do you think there may have been foul play?'

'Foul play, foul play, fowls lay eggs, don't they?'

'You think that Rex Fortescue was responsible for your husband's death?'

'I had an egg for breakfast this morning,' said Mrs MacKenzie. 'Quite fresh, too. Surprising, isn't it, when one thinks that it was thirty years ago?'

Neele drew a deep breath. It seemed unlikely that he was ever going to get anywhere at this rate, but he persevered.

'Somebody put dead blackbirds on Rex Fortescue's desk about a month or two before he died.'

'That's interesting. That's very, very interesting.'

'Have you any idea, madam, who might have done that?'

'Ideas aren't any help to one. One has to have action. I brought them up for that, you know, to take action.'

'You're talking about your children?'

She nodded her head rapidly.

'Yes. Donald and Ruby. They were nine and seven and left without a father. I told them. I told them every day. I made them swear it every night.'

Inspector Neele leant forward.

'What did you make them swear?'

'That they'd kill him, of course.'

'I see.'

Inspector Neele spoke as though it was the most reasonable remark in the world.

'Did they?'

'Donald went to Dunkirk. He never came back. They sent me a wire saying he was dead: "Deeply regret killed in action." Action, you see, the wrong kind of action.'

'I'm sorry to hear that, madam. What about your daughter?'

'I haven't got a daughter,' said Mrs MacKenzie.

'You spoke of her just now,' said Neele. 'Your daughter, Ruby.'

'Ruby. Yes, Ruby.' She leaned forward. 'Do you know what I've done to Ruby?'

'No, madam. What have you done to her?'

She whispered suddenly:

'Look here at the Book.'

He saw then that what she was holding in her lap was a Bible. It was a very old Bible and as she opened it, on the front page, Inspector Neele saw that various names had been written. It was obviously a family Bible in which the old-fashioned custom had been continued of entering each new birth. Mrs MacKenzie's thin forefinger pointed to the two last names. 'Donald MacKenzie' with the date of his birth, and 'Ruby MacKenzie' with the date of hers. But a thick line was drawn through Ruby MacKenzie's name.

'You see?' said Mrs MacKenzie. 'I struck her out of the Book. I cut her off for ever! The Recording Angel won't find her name there.'

'You cut her name out of the book? Now, why, madam?'

Mrs MacKenzie looked at him cunningly.

'You know why,' she said.

'But I don't. Really, madam, I don't.'

'She didn't keep faith. You know she didn't keep faith.'

'Where is your daughter now, madam?'

'I've told you. I have no daughter. There isn't such a person as Ruby MacKenzie any longer.'

'You mean she's dead?'

272

'Dead?' The woman laughed suddenly. 'It would be better for her if she were dead. Much better. Much, much better.' She sighed and turned restlessly in her seat. Then her manner reverting to a kind of formal courtesy, she said: 'I'm so sorry, but really I'm afraid I can't talk to you any longer. You see, the time is getting very short, and I *must* read my book.'

To Inspector Neele's further remarks Mrs MacKenzie returned no reply. She merely made a faint gesture of annoyance and continued to read her Bible with her finger following the line of the verse she was reading.

Neele got up and left. He had another brief interview with the superintendent.

'Do any of her relations come to see her?' he asked. 'A daughter, for instance?'

'I believe a daughter did come to see her in my predecessor's time, but her visit agitated the patient so much that he advised her not to come again. Since then everything is arranged through solicitors.'

'And you've no idea where this Ruby MacKenzie is now?'

The superintendent shook his head.

'No idea whatsoever.'

'You've no idea whether she's married, for instance?'

'I don't know, all I can do is to give you the address of the solicitors who deal with us.'

Inspector Neele had already tracked down those solicitors. They were unable, or said they were unable, to tell him anything. A trust fund had been established for Mrs MacKenzie which they managed. These arrangements had been made some years previously and they had not seen Miss MacKenzie since.

Inspector Neele tried to get a description of Ruby MacKenzie but the results were not encouraging. So many relations came to visit patients that after a lapse of years they were bound to be remembered dimly, with the appearance of one mixed up with the appearance of another. The matron who had been there for many years seemed to remember that Miss MacKenzie was small and dark. The only other nurse who had been there for any length of time recalled that she was heavily built and fair.

'So there we are, sir,' said Inspector Neele as he reported to the assistant commissioner. 'There's a whole crazy set-up and it fits together. It *must* mean something.'

The AC nodded thoughtfully.

'The blackbirds in the pie tying up with the Blackbird Mine, rye in the dead man's pocket, bread and honey with Adele Fortescue's tea – (not that that is conclusive. After all, anyone might have had bread and honey for tea!) The third murder, that girl strangled with a stocking and a clothes peg nipped on to her nose. Yes, crazy as the set-up is, it certainly can't be ignored.'

'Half a minute, sir,' said Inspector Neele.

'What is it?'

Neele was frowning.

'You know, what you've just said. It didn't ring true. It was wrong somewhere.' He shook his head and sighed. 'No. I can't place it.'

CHAPTER TWENTY-ONE

Lance and Pat wandered round the well-kept grounds surrounding Yewtree Lodge.

'I hope I'm not hurting your feelings, Lance,' Pat murmured, 'if I say this is quite the nastiest garden I've ever been in.'

'It won't hurt my feelings,' said Lance. 'Is it? Really I don't know. It seems to have three gardeners working on it very industriously.'

Pat said:

'Probably that's what's wrong with it. No expense spared, no signs of an individual taste. All the right rhododendrons and all the right bedding out done in the proper season, I expect.'

'Well, what would *you* put in an English garden, Pat, if you had one?'

'My garden,' said Pat, 'would have hollyhocks, lark-spurs and Canterbury bells, no bedding out and none of these horrible yews.'

She glanced up at the dark yew hedges, disparagingly.

'Association of ideas,' said Lance easily.

'There's something awfully frightening about a poisoner,' said Pat. 'I mean it must be a horrid, brooding revengeful mind.'

'So that's how you see it? Funny! I just think of it as businesslike and cold-blooded.'

'I suppose one could look at it that way.' She resumed, with a slight shiver, 'All the same, to do *three* murders . . . Whoever did it *must* be mad.'

'Yes,' said Lance, in a low voice. 'I'm afraid so.' Then breaking out sharply, he said: 'For God's sake, Pat, do go away from here. Go back to London. Go down to Devonshire or up to the Lakes. Go to Stratford-on-Avon or go and look at the Norfolk Broads. The police wouldn't mind your going – you had nothing to do with all this. You were in Paris when the old man was killed and in London when the other two died. I tell you it worries me to death to have you here.'

Pat paused a moment before saying quietly:

'You know who it is, don't you?'

'No, I don't.'

'But you *think* you know . . . That's why you're frightened for me . . . I wish you'd tell me.'

'I can't tell you. I don't know anything. But I wish to God you'd go away from here.'

'Darling,' said Pat. 'I'm not going. I'm staying here. For better, for worse. That's how I feel about it.' She added, with a sudden catch in her voice: 'Only with me it's always for worse.'

'What on earth do you mean, Pat?'

'I bring bad luck. That's what I mean. I bring bad luck to anybody I come in contact with.'

'My dear adorable nitwit, you haven't brought bad luck to me. Look how after I married you the old man sent for me to come home and make friends with him.'

'Yes, and what happened when you did come home? I tell you, I'm unlucky to people.'

'Look here, my sweet, you've got a thing about all this. It's superstition, pure and simple.'

'I can't help it. Some people do bring bad luck. I'm one of them.'

Lance took her by the shoulders and shook her violently. 'You're my Pat and to be married to you is the greatest luck in the world. So get that into your silly head.' Then, calming down, he said in a more sober voice: 'But, seriously, Pat, do be very careful. If there *is* someone unhinged round here, I don't want you to be the one who stops the bullet or drinks the henbane.'

'Or drinks the henbane as you say.'

'When I'm not around, stick to that old lady. What's-her-name Marple. Why do you think Aunt Effie asked her to stay here?'

275

'Goodness knows why Aunt Effie does anything. Lance, how long are *we* going to stay here?'

Lance shrugged his shoulders.

'Difficult to say.'

'I don't think,' said Pat, 'that we're really awfully welcome.' She hesitated as she spoke the words. 'The house belongs to your brother now, I suppose? He doesn't really want us here, does he?'

Lance chuckled suddenly.

'Not he, but he's got to stick us for the present at any rate.'

'And afterwards? What are we going to do, Lance? Are we going back to East Africa or what?'

'Is that what you'd like to do, Pat?'

She nodded vigorously.

'That's lucky,' said Lance, 'because it's what I'd like to do, too. I don't take much to this country nowadays.'

Pat's face brightened.

'How lovely. From what you said the other day, I was afraid you might want to stop here.'

A devilish glint appeared in Lance's eyes.

'You're to hold your tongue about our plans, Pat,' he said. 'I have it in my mind to twist dear brother Percival's tail a bit.'

'Oh, Lance, do be careful.'

'I'll be careful, my sweet, but I don't see why old Percy should get away with everything.'

II

With her head a little on one side looking like an amiable cockatoo, Miss Marple sat in the large drawing-room listening to Mrs Percival Fortescue. Miss Marple looked particularly incongruous in the drawing-room. Her light spare figure was alien to the vast brocaded sofa in which she sat with its many-hued cushions strewn around her. Miss Marple sat very upright because she had been taught to use a back-board as a girl, and not to loll. In a large armchair beside her, dressed in elaborate black, was Mrs Percival, talking away volubly at nineteen to the dozen. 'Exactly,' thought Miss Marple, 'like poor Mrs Emmett, the bank manager's wife.' She remembered how one day Mrs Emmett had come to call and talk about the selling arrangements for Poppy Day, and how after the preliminary business had been settled, Mrs Emmett had suddenly begun to talk and talk and talk. Mrs Emmett occupied rather a difficult position in St Mary Mead. She did not belong to the old guard of ladies in reduced circumstances who lived in neat houses around the church, and who knew intimately all the ramifications of the county families even though they might not be strictly county themselves. Mr Emmett, the bank manager, had undeniably married beneath him and the result was that his wife was in a position of great loneliness since she could not, of course, associate with the wives of the trades people. Snobbery here raised its hideous head and marooned Mrs Emmett on a permanent island of loneliness.

The necessity to talk grew upon Mrs Emmett, and on that particular day it had burst its bounds, and Miss Marple had received the full flood of the torrent. She had been sorry for Mrs Emmett then, and today she was rather sorry for Mrs Percival Fortescue.

Mrs Percival had had a lot of grievances to bear and the relief of airing them to a more or less total stranger was enormous.

'Of course I never want to complain,' said Mrs Percival. 'I've never been of the complaining kind. What I always say is that one must put up with things. What can't be cured must be endured and I'm sure I've never said a word to *anyone*. It's really difficult to know who I *could* have spoken to. In some ways one is very isolated here – very isolated. It's very convenient, of course, and a great saving of expense to have our own set of rooms in this house. But of course it's not at all like having a place of your own. I'm sure you agree.'

Miss Marple said she agreed.

'Fortunately our new house is almost ready to move into. It is a question really of getting the painters and decorators out. These men are so slow. My husband, of course, has been quite satisfied living here. But then it's different for a man. Don't you agree?'

Miss Marple agreed that it was very different for a man. She could say this without a qualm as it was what she really believed. 'The gentlemen' were, in Miss Marple's mind, in a totally different category to her own sex. They required two eggs plus bacon for breakfast, three good nourishing meals a day and were never to be contradicted or argued with before dinner. Mrs Percival went on:

'My husband, you see, is away all day in the city. When he comes home he's just tired and wants to sit down and read. But I, on the contrary, am alone here all day with no congenial company *at all*. I've been perfectly comfortable and all that. Excellent food. But what I do feel one needs is a really pleasant social circle. The people round here are really not my kind. Part of them are what I call a flashy, bridge-playing lot. Not *nice* bridge. I like a hand at bridge myself as well as anyone, but of course, they're all very rich down here. They play for enormously high stakes, and there's a great deal of drinking. In fact, the sort of life that I call really fast society. Then, of course, there's a sprinkling of – well, you can only call them *old pussies* who love to potter round with a trowel and do gardening.'

Miss Marple looked slightly guilty since she was herself an inveterate gardener.

'I don't want to say anything against the dead,' resumed Mrs Percy rapidly, 'but there's no doubt about it, Mr Fortescue, my father-in-law, I mean, made a very foolish second marriage. My – well I can't call her my mother-in-law, she was the same age as I am. The real truth of it is she was man-mad. Absolutely man-mad. And the way she spent money! My father-in-law was an absolute fool about her. Didn't care what bills she ran up. It vexed Percy very much, very much indeed. Percy is always so careful about money matters. He hates waste. And then what with Mr Fortescue being so peculiar and so bad tempered, flashing out in these terrible rages, spending money like water backing wildcat schemes. Well – it wasn't at all nice.'

Miss Marple ventured upon making a remark.

'That must have worried your husband, too?'

'Oh, yes, it did. For the last year Percy's been very worried indeed. It's really made him quite different. His manner, you know, changed even towards me. Sometimes when I talked to him he used not to answer.' Mrs Percy sighed, then went on: 'Then Elaine, my sister-in-law, you know, she's a *very* odd sort of girl. Very out of doors and all that. Not exactly unfriendly, but not sympathetic, you know. She never wanted to go to London and shop, or go to a matinée or anything of that kind. She wasn't even interested in clothes.' Mrs Percival sighed again and murmured: 'But of course I don't want to complain in any way.' A qualm of compunction came over her. She said, hurriedly: 'You must think it most odd, talking to you like this when you are a comparative stranger. But really what with all the strain and shock – I think really it's the shock that matters most. Delayed shock. I feel so nervous, you know that I really – well, I really must speak to *someone*. You remind me so much of a dear old lady, Miss Trefusis James. She fractured her femur when she was seventy-five. It was a very long business nursing her and we became great friends. She gave me a fox fur cape when I left and I did think it was kind of her.'

'I know just how you feel,' said Miss Marple.

And this again was true. Mrs Percival's husband was obviously bored by her and paid very little attention to her, and the poor woman had managed to make no local friends. Running up to London and shopping, matinées and a luxurious house to live in did not make up for the lack of humanity in her relations with her husband's family.

'I hope it's not rude of me to say so,' said Miss Marple in a gentle old lady's voice, 'but I really feel that the late Mr Fortescue cannot have been a very nice man.'

'He wasn't,' said his daughter-in-law. 'Quite frankly my dear, between you and me, he was a detestable old man. I don't wonder – I really don't – that someone put him out of the way.'

'You've no idea at all who – ' began Miss Marple and broke off. 'Oh dear, perhaps this is a question I should not ask – not even an idea who – who – well, who it might have been?'

'Oh, I think it was that horrible man Crump,' said Mrs Percival. 'I've always disliked him very much. He's got a manner, not really rude, you know, but yet it *is* rude. Impertinent, that's more it.'

'Still, there would have to be a motive, I suppose.'

'I really don't know that that sort of person requires much motive. I dare say Mr Fortescue ticked him off about something, and I rather suspect that sometimes he drinks too much. But what I really think is that he's a bit unbalanced, you know. Like that footman, or butler, whoever it was, who went round the house shooting everybody. Of course, to be quite honest with you, I *did* suspect that it was *Adele* who poisoned Mr Fortescue. But now, of course, one can't suspect that since she's been poisoned herself. She may have accused Crump, you know. And then he lost his head and perhaps managed to put something in the sandwiches and Gladys saw him do it and so he killed her too – I think it's really dangerous having him in the house at all. Oh dear, I wish I could get away, but I suppose these horrible policemen won't let one do anything of the kind.' She leant forward impulsively and put a plump hand on Miss Marple's arm. 'Sometimes I feel I must get away – that if it doesn't all stop soon I shall – I shall actually *run away*.'

She leant back studying Miss Marple's face.

'But perhaps – that wouldn't be wise?'

'No – I don't think it would be very wise – the police could soon find you, you know.'

'Could they? Could they really? You think they're clever enough for that?'

'It is very foolish to under-estimate the police. Inspector Neele strikes me as a particularly intelligent man.'

'Oh! I thought he was rather stupid.'

Miss Marple shook her head.

'I can't help feeling' – Jennifer Fortescue hesitated – 'that it's dangerous to stay here.'

'Dangerous for you, you mean?'

'Ye-es – well, yes – '

'Because of something you – know?'

Mrs Percival seemed to take breath.

'Oh no – of course I don't know anything. What should I know? It's just – just that I'm nervous. That man Crump – '

But it was not, Miss Marple thought, of Crump that Mrs Percival Fortescue was thinking – watching the clenching and unclenching of Jennifer's hands. Miss Marple thought that for some reason Jennifer Fortescue was very badly frightened indeed.

CHAPTER TWENTY-TWO

It was growing dark. Miss Marple had taken her knitting over to the window in the library. Looking out of the glass pane she saw Pat Fortescue walking up and down the terrace outside. Miss Marple unlatched the window and called through it.

'Come in, my dear. Do come in. I'm sure it's much too cold and damp for you to be out there without a coat on.'

Pat obeyed the summons. She came in and shut the window and turned on two of the lamps.

'Yes,' she said, 'it's not a very nice afternoon.' She sat down on the sofa by Miss Marple. 'What are you knitting?'

'Oh, just a little matinée coat, dear. For a baby, you know. I always say young mothers can't have too many matinée coats for their babies. It's the second size. I always knit the second size. Babies so soon grow out of the first size.'

Pat stretched out long legs towards the fire.

'It's nice in here today,' she said. 'With the fire and the lamps and you knitting things for babies. It all seems cosy and homely and like England ought to be.'

'It's like England is,' said Miss Marple. 'There are not so many Yewtree Lodges, my dear.'

'I think that's a good thing,' said Pat. 'I don't believe this was ever a happy house. I don't believe anybody was ever happy in it, in spite of all the money they spent and the things they had.'

'No,' Miss Marple agreed. 'I shouldn't say it had been a happy house.'

'I suppose Adele may have been happy,' said Pat. 'I never met her, of course, so I don't know, but Jennifer is pretty miserable and Elaine's been eating her heart out over a young man whom she probably knows in her heart of hearts doesn't care for her. Oh, *how* I want to get away from here!' She looked at Miss Marple and smiled suddenly. 'D'you know,' she said, 'that Lance told me to stick as close to you as I could. He seemed to think I should be safe that way.'

'Your husband's no fool,' said Miss Marple.

'No. Lance isn't a fool. At least, he is in some ways. But I wish he'd tell me exactly what he's afraid of. One thing seems clear enough. Somebody in this house is mad, and madness is always frightening because you don't know how mad people's minds will work. You don't know what they'll do next.'

'My poor child,' said Miss Marple.

'Oh, I'm all right, really. I ought to be tough enough by now.'

Miss Marple said gently:

'You've had a good deal of unhappiness, haven't you, my dear?'

'Oh, I've had some very good times, too. I had a lovely childhood in Ireland, riding, hunting, and a great big, bare, draughty house with lots and lots of sun in it. If you've had a happy childhood, nobody can take that away from you, can they? It was afterwards – when I grew up – that things seemed always to go wrong. To begin with, I suppose, it was the war.'

'Your husband was a fighter pilot, wasn't he?'

'Yes. We'd only been married about a month when Don was shot down.' She stared ahead of her into the fire. 'I thought at first I wanted to die too. It seemed so unfair, so cruel. And yet – in the end – I almost began to see that it had been the best thing. Don was wonderful in the war. Brave and reckless and gay. He had all the qualities that are needed, wanted in a war. But I don't believe, somehow, peace would have suited him. He had a kind of – oh,

281

how shall I put it? – arrogant insubordination. He wouldn't have fitted in or settled down. He'd have fought against things. He was – well, anti-social in a way. No, he wouldn't have fitted in.'

'It's wise of you to see that, my dear.' Miss Marple bent over her knitting, picked up a stitch, counted under her breath, 'Three plain, two purl, slip one, knit two together,' and then said aloud 'And your second husband, my dear?'

'Freddy? Freddy shot himself.'

'Oh dear. How very sad. What a tragedy.'

'We were very happy together,' said Pat. 'I began to realize, about two years after we were married, that Freddy wasn't – well, wasn' always straight. I began to find out the sort of things that were going on. But it didn't seem to matter, between us two, that is. Because you see, Freddy loved me and I loved him. I tried not to know what was going on. That was cowardly of me, I suppose, but I couldn' have changed him you know. You can't change people.'

'No,' said Miss Marple, 'you can't change people.'

'I'd taken him and loved him and married him for what he was and I sort of felt that I just had to – put up with it. Then things went wrong and he couldn't face it, and he shot himself. After h died I went out to Kenya to stay with some friends there. I couldn' stop on in England and go on meeting all – all the old crowd that knew about it all. And out in Kenya I met Lance.' Her face change and softened. She went on looking into the fire, and Miss Marpl looked at her. Presently Pat turned her head and said: 'Tell me Miss Marple, what do you really think of Percival?'

'Well, I've not seen very much of him. Just at breakfast usually That's all. I don't think he very much likes my being here.'

Pat laughed suddenly.

'He's mean, you know. Terribly mean about money. Lanc says he always was. Jennifer complains of it, too. Goes ove the housekeeping accounts with Miss Dove. Complaining of ever item. But Miss Dove manages to hold her own. She's really rathe a wonderful person. Don't you think so?'

'Yes, indeed. She reminds me of Mrs Latimer in my own village St Mary Mead. She ran the WVS, you know, and the Girl Guide and indeed, she ran practically everything there. It wasn't for qui five years that we discovered that – oh, but I mustn't gossip. Nothir is more boring than people talking to you about places and peop whom you've never seen and know nothing about. You must forgiv me, my dear.'

'Is St Mary Mead a very nice village?'

'Well, I don't know what you would call a nice village, my dear. It's quite a *pretty* village. There are some nice people living in it and some extremely unpleasant people as well. Very curious things go on there just as in any other village. Human nature is much the same everywhere, is it not?'

'You go up and see Miss Ramsbottom a good deal, don't you?' said Pat. 'Now she *really* frightens me.'

'Frightens you? Why?'

'Because I think she's crazy. I think she's got religious mania. You don't think she could be – really – *mad*, do you?'

'In what way, mad?'

'Oh, you know what I mean, Miss Marple, well enough. She sits up there and never goes out, and broods about sin. Well, she might have felt in the end that it was her mission in life to execute judgment.'

'Is that what your husband thinks?'

'I don't know what Lance thinks. He won't tell me. But I'm quite sure of one thing – that he believes that it's someone who's mad, and it's someone in the family. Well, Percival's sane enough, I should say. Jennifer's just stupid and rather pathetic. She's a bit nervy but that's all, and Elaine is one of those queer, tempestuous, tense girls. She's desperately in love with this young man of hers and she'll never admit to herself for a moment that he's marrying her for her money.'

'You think he is marrying her for money?'

'Yes, I do. Don't you think so?'

'I should say quite certainly,' said Miss Marple. 'Like young Ellis who married Marion Bates, the rich ironmonger's daughter. She was a very plain girl and absolutely besotted about him. However, it turned out quite well. People like young Ellis and this Gerald Wright are only really disagreeable when they've married a poor girl for love. They are so annoyed with themselves for doing it that they take it out on the girl. But if they marry a rich girl they continue to respect her.'

'I don't see,' went on Pat, frowning, 'how it can be anybody from outside. And so – and so that accounts for the atmosphere that is here. Everyone watching everybody else. Only something's got to happen soon – '

'There won't be any more deaths,' said Miss Marple. 'At least, I shouldn't think so.'

'You can't be sure of that.'

283

'Well, as a matter of fact, I am fairly sure. The murderer's accomplished his purpose, you see.'

'His?'

'Well, his or her. One says his for convenience.'

'You say his or her purpose. What sort of purpose?'

Miss Marple shook her head – she was not yet quite sure herself.

CHAPTER TWENTY-THREE

Once again Miss Somers had just made tea in the typists' room, and once again the kettle had not been boiling when Miss Somers poured the water on to the tea. History repeats itself. Miss Griffith, accepting her cup, thought to herself: 'I really *must* speak to Mr Percival about Somers. I'm sure we can do better. But with all this terrible business going on, one doesn't like to bother him over office details.'

As so often before Miss Griffith said sharply:

'Water not boiling *again*, Somers,' and Miss Somers, going pink, replied in her usual formula:

'Oh, dear, I was sure it was boiling *this* time.'

Further developments on the same line were interrupted by the entrance of Lance Fortescue. He looked round him somewhat vaguely, and Miss Griffith jumped up, came forward to meet him.

'Mr Lance,' she exclaimed.

He swung round towards her and his face lit up in a smile.

'Hallo. Why, it's Miss Griffith.'

Miss Griffith was delighted. Eleven years since he had seen her and he knew her name. She said in a confused voice:

'Fancy your remembering.'

And Lance said easily, with all his charm to the fore:

'Of course I remember.'

A flicker of excitement was running round the typists' room. Miss Somers's troubles over the tea were forgotten. She was gaping at Lance with her mouth slightly open. Miss Bell gazed eagerly over the top of her typewriter and Miss Chase unobtrusively drew out her compact and powdered her nose. Lance Fortescue looked round him.

'So everything's still going on just the same here,' he said.

'Not many changes, Mr Lance. How brown you look and how well! I suppose you must have had a very interesting life abroad.'

'You could call it that,' said Lance, 'but perhaps I am now going to try and have an interesting life in London.'

'You're coming back here to the office?'

'Maybe.'

'Oh, but how delightful.'

'You'll find me very rusty,' said Lance. 'You'll have to show me all the ropes, Miss Griffith.'

Miss Griffith laughed delightedly.

'It will be very nice to have you back, Mr Lance. Very nice indeed.'

Lance threw her an appreciative glance.

'That's sweet of you,' he said, 'that's very sweet of you.'

'We never believed – none of us thought . . .' Miss Griffith broke off and flushed.

Lance patted her on the arm.

'You didn't believe the devil was as black as he was painted? Well, perhaps he wasn't. But that's all old history now. There's no good going back over it. The future's the thing.' He added, 'Is my brother here?'

'He's in the inner office, I think.'

Lance nodded easily and passed on. In the ante-room to the inner sanctum a hard-faced woman of middle age rose behind a desk and said forbiddingly:

'Your name and business, please?'

Lance looked at her doubtfully.

'Are you – Miss Grosvenor?' he asked.

Miss Grosvenor had been described to him as a glamorous blonde. She had indeed appeared so in the pictures that had appeared in the newspapers reporting the inquest on Rex Fortescue. This, surely, could not be Miss Grosvenor.

'Miss Grosvenor left last week. I am Mrs Hardcastle, Mr Percival Fortescue's personal secretary.'

'How like old Percy,' thought Lance. 'To get rid of a glamorous blonde and take on a Gorgon instead. I wonder why? Was it safety or was it because this one comes cheaper?' Aloud he said easily:

'I'm Lancelot Fortescue. You haven't met me yet.'

'Oh, I'm so sorry, Mr Lancelot,' Mrs Hardcastle apologized, 'this is the first time, I think, you've been to the office?'

'The first time but not the last,' said Lance, smiling.

He crossed the room and opened the door of what had been his father's private office. Somewhat to his surprise it was not Percival who was sitting behind the desk there, but Inspector Neele. Inspector Neele looked up from a large wad of papers which he was sorting, and nodded his head.

'Good morning, Mr Fortescue, you've come to take up your duties I suppose.'

'So you've heard I decided to come into the firm?'

'Your brother told me so.'

'He did, did he? With enthusiasm?'

Inspector Neele endeavoured to conceal a smile.

'The enthusiasm was not marked,' he said gravely.

'Poor Percy,' commented Lance.

Inspector Neele looked at him curiously.

'Are you really going to become a City man?'

'You don't think it's likely, Inspector Neele?'

'It doesn't seem quite in character, Mr Fortescue.'

'Why not? I'm my father's son.'

'And your mother's.'

Lance shook his head.

'You haven't got anything there, Inspector. My mother was a Victorian romantic. Her favourite reading was the *Idylls of the King* as indeed you may have deduced from our curious Christian names. She was an invalid and always, I should imagine, out of touch with reality. I'm not like that at all. I have no sentiment, very little sense of romance and I'm a realist first and last.'

'People aren't always what they think themselves to be,' Inspector Neele pointed out.

'No, I suppose that's true,' said Lance.

He sat down in a chair and stretched his long legs out in his own characteristic fashion. He was smiling to himself. Then he said unexpectedly:

'You're shrewder than my brother, Inspector.'

'In what way, Mr Fortescue?'

'I've put the wind up Percy all right. He thinks I'm all set for the City life. He thinks he's going to have my fingers fiddling about his pie. He thinks I'll launch out and spend the firm's money and try and embroil him in wildcat schemes. It would be almost worth doing just for the fun of it! Almost, but not quite. I couldn't really stand an office life, Inspector. I like the open air and some possibilities of adventure. I'd stifle in a place like this.' He added quickly: 'This is off the record, mind. Don't give me away to Percy, will you?'

'I don't suppose the subject will arise, Mr Fortescue.'

'I must have my bit of fun with Percy,' said Lance. 'I want to make him sweat a bit. I've got to get a bit of my own back.'

'That's rather a curious phrase, Mr Fortescue,' said Neele. 'Your own back – for what?'

Lance shrugged his shoulders.

'Oh, it's old history now. Not worth going back over.'

'There was a little matter of a cheque, I understand, in the past. Would that be what you're referring to?'

'How much you know, Inspector!'

'There was no question of prosecution, I understand,' said Neele. 'Your father wouldn't have done that.'

'No. He just kicked me out, that's all.'

Inspector Neele eyed him speculatively, but it was not Lance Fortescue of whom he was thinking, but of Percival. The honest, industrious, parsimonious Percival. It seemed to him that wherever he got in the case he was always coming up against the enigma of Percival Fortescue, a man of whom everybody knew the outer aspects, but whose inner personality was much harder to gauge. One would have said from observing him a somewhat colourless and insignificant character, a man who had been very much under his father's thumb. Percy Prim in fact, as the AC had once said. Neele was trying now, through Lance, to get at a closer appreciation of Percival's personality. He murmured in a tentative manner:

'Your brother seems always to have been very much – well, how shall I put it – under your father's thumb.'

'I wonder.' Lance seemed definitely to be considering the point. 'I wonder. Yes, that would be the effect, I think, given. But I'm not sure that it was really the truth. It's astonishing, you know, when I look back through life, to see how Percy always got his own way without seeming to do so, if you know what I mean.'

Yes, Inspector Neele thought, it was indeed astonishing. He sorted through the papers in front of him, fished out a letter and shoved it across the desk towards Lance.

'This is a letter you wrote last August, isn't it, Mr Fortescue?'

Lance took it, glanced at it and returned it.

'Yes,' he said, 'I wrote it after I got back to Kenya last summer. Dad kept it, did he? Where was it – here in the office?'

'No, Mr Fortescue, it was among your father's papers in Yewtree Lodge.'

The inspector considered it speculatively as it lay on the desk in front of him. It was not a long letter.

Dear Dad,

I've talked things over with Pat and I agree to your proposition. It will take me a little time to get things fixed up here, say about the end of October or beginning of November. I'll let you know nearer the time. I hope we'll pull together better than we used to do. Anyway, I'll do my best. I can't say more. Look after yourself.

Yours, Lance.

'Where did you address this letter, Mr Fortescue. To the office or Yewtree Lodge?'

Lance frowned in an effort of recollection.

'It's difficult. I can't remember. You see it's almost three months now. The office, I think. Yes, I'm almost sure. Here to the office.' He paused a moment before asking with frank curiosity: 'Why?'

'I wondered,' said Inspector Neele. 'Your father did not put it on the file here among his private papers. He took it back with him to Yewtree Lodge, and I found it in his desk there. I wondered why he should have done that.'

Lance laughed.

'To keep it out of Percy's way, I suppose.'

'Yes,' said Inspector Neele, 'it would seem so. Your brother, then, had access to your father's private papers here?'

'Well,' Lance hesitated and frowned, 'not exactly. I mean, I suppose he could have looked through them at any time if he liked, but he wouldn't be . . .'

Inspector Neele finished the sentence for him.

'Wouldn't be supposed to do so?'

Lance grinned broadly. 'That's right. Frankly, it would have been snooping. But Percy, I should imagine, always did snoop.'

Inspector Neele nodded. He also thought it probable that Percival Fortescue snooped. It would be in keeping with what the inspector was beginning to learn of his character.

'And talk of the devil,' murmured Lance, as at that moment the

288

door opened and Percival Fortescue came in. About to speak to the inspector he stopped, frowning, as he saw Lance.

'Hallo,' he said. 'You here? You didn't tell me you were coming here today.'

'I felt a kind of zeal for work coming over me,' said Lance, 'so here I am ready to make myself useful. What do you want me to do?'

Percival said testily:

'Nothing at present. Nothing at all. We shall have to come to some kind of arrangement as to what side of the business you're going to look after. We shall have to arrange for an office for you.'

Lance inquired with a grin:

'By the way, why did you get rid of glamorous Grosvenor, old boy, and replace her by Horsefaced Hetty out there?'

'Really, Lance,' Percival protested sharply.

'Definitely a change for the worse,' said Lance. 'I've been looking forward to the glamorous Grosvenor. Why did you sack her? Thought she knew a bit too much?'

'Of course not. What an idea!' Percy spoke angrily, a flush mounting his pale face. He turned to the inspector. 'You mustn't pay any attention to my brother,' he said coldly. 'He has a rather peculiar sense of humour.' He added: 'I never had a very high opinion of Miss Grosvenor's intelligence. Mrs Hardcastle has excellent references and is most capable besides being very moderate in her terms.'

'Very moderate in her terms,' murmured Lance, casting his eyes towards the ceiling. 'You know, Percy, I don't really approve of skimping over the office personnel. By the way, considering how loyally the staff has stood by us during these last tragic weeks, don't you think we ought to raise their salaries all round?'

'Certainly not,' snapped Percival Fortescue. 'Quite uncalled for and unnecessary.'

Inspector Neele noticed the gleam of devilry in Lance's eyes. Percival, however, was far too much upset to notice it.

'You always had the most extraordinary extravagant ideas,' he stuttered. 'In the state in which this firm has been left, economy is our only hope.'

Inspector Neele coughed apologetically.

'That's one of the things I wanted to talk to you about, Mr Fortescue,' he said to Percival.

'Yes, Inspector?' Percival switched his attention to Neele.

'I want to put certain suggestions before you, Mr Fortescue. I understand that for the past six months or longer, possibly a year, your father's general behaviour and conduct has been a source of increasing anxiety to you.'

'He wasn't well,' said Percival, with finality. 'He certainly wasn't at all well.'

'You tried to induce him to see a doctor but you failed. He refused categorically?'

'That is so.'

'May I ask you if you suspected that your father was suffering from what is familiarly referred to as GPI, General Paralysis of the Insane, a condition with signs of megalomania and irritability which terminates sooner or later in hopeless insanity?'

Percival looked surprised. 'It is remarkably astute of you, Inspector. That is exactly what I did fear. That is why I was so anxious for my father to submit to medical treatment.'

Neele went on:

'In the meantime, until you could persuade your father to do that, he was capable of causing a great deal of havoc to the business?'

'He certainly was,' Percival agreed.

'A very unfortunate state of affairs,' said the inspector.

'Quite terrible. No one knows the anxiety I have been through.'

Neele said gently:

'From the business point of view, your father's death was an extremely fortunate circumstance.'

Percival said sharply:

'You can hardly think I would regard my father's death in that light.'

'It is not a question of how you regard it, Mr Fortescue. I'm speaking merely of a question of fact. Your father died before his finances were completely on the rocks.'

Percival said impatiently:

'Yes, yes. As a matter of actual fact, you are right.'

'It was a fortunate occurrence for your whole family, since they are dependent on this business.'

'Yes. But really, Inspector, I don't see what you're driving at . . .' Percival broke off.

'Oh, I'm not driving at anything, Mr Fortescue,' said Neele. 'I just like getting my facts straight. Now there's another thing. I understood you to say that you'd had no communication of any kind with your brother here since he left England many years ago.'

'Quite so,' said Percival.

'Yes, but it isn't quite so, is it, Mr Fortescue? I mean that last spring when you were so worried about your father's health, you actually wrote to your brother in Africa, told him of your anxiety about your father's behaviour. You wanted, I think, your brother to combine with you in getting your father medically examined and put under restraint, if necessary.'

'I – I – really, I don't see . . .' Percival was badly shaken.

'That is so, isn't it, Mr Fortescue?'

'Well, actually, I thought it only right. After all, Lancelot *was* a junior partner.'

Inspector Neele transferred his gaze to Lance. Lance was grinning.

'You received that letter?' Inspector Neele asked.

Lance Fortescue nodded.

'What did you reply to it?'

Lance's grin widened.

'I told Percy to go and boil his head and to let the old man alone. I said the old man probably knew what he was doing quite well.'

Inspector Neele's gaze went back again to Percival.

'Were those the terms of your brother's answer?'

'I – I – well, I suppose roughly, yes. Far more offensively couched, however.'

'I thought the inspector had better have a bowdlerized version,' said Lance. He went on, 'Frankly, Inspector Neele, that is one of the reasons why, when I got a letter from my father, I came home to see for myself what I thought. In the short interview I had with my father, frankly I couldn't see anything much wrong with him. He was slightly excitable, that was all. He appeared to me perfectly capable of managing his own affairs. Anyway, after I got back to Africa and had talked things over with Pat, I decided that I'd come home and – what shall we say – see fair play.'

He shot a glance at Percival as he spoke.

'I object,' said Percival Fortescue. 'I object strongly to what you are suggesting. I was not intending to victimize my father, I was concerned for his health. I admit that I was also concerned . . .' he paused.

Lance filled the pause quickly.

'You were also concerned for your pocket, eh? For Percy's little pocket.' He got up and all of a sudden his manner changed. 'All right, Percy, I'm through. I was going to string you along a bit by pretending to work here. I wasn't going to let you have things all your own sweet way, but I'm damned if I'm going on with it. Frankly, it

291

makes me sick to be in the same room with you. You've always been a dirty, mean little skunk all your life. Prying and snooping and lying and making trouble. I'll tell you another thing. I can't prove it, but I've always believed it was you who forged that cheque there was all the row about, that got me shot out of here. For one thing it was a damn bad forgery, a forgery that drew attention to itself in letters a foot high. My record was too bad for me to be able to protest effectively, but I often wondered that the old boy didn't realize that if I *had* forged his name I could have made a much better job of it than that.'

Lance swept on, his voice rising. 'Well, Percy, I'm not going on with this silly game. I'm sick of this country, and of the City. I'm sick of little men like you with their pin-stripe trousers and their black coats and their mincing voices and their mean, shoddy financial deals. We'll share out as you suggested, and I'll get back with Pat to a different country – a country where there's room to breathe and move about. You can make your own division of securities. Keep the gilt-edged and the conservative ones, keep the safe two per cent and three per cent and three and a half per cent. Give me father's latest wildcat speculations as you call them. Most of them are probably duds. But I'll bet that one or two of them will pay better in the end than all your playing safe with three per cent Trustee Stocks will do. Father was a shrewd old devil. He took chances, plenty of them. Some of those chances paid five and six and seven hundred per cent. I'll back his judgment and his luck. As for you, you little worm . . .' Lance advanced towards his brother, who retreated rapidly, round the end of the desk towards Inspector Neele. 'All right,' said Lance, 'I'm not going to touch you. You wanted me out of here, you're getting me out of here. You ought to be satisfied.' He added as he strode towards the door: 'You can throw in the old Blackbird Mine concession too, if you like. If we've got the murdering MacKenzies on our trail, I'll draw them off to Africa.' He added as he swung through the doorway. 'Revenge – after all these years – scarcely seems credible. But Inspector Neele seems to take it seriously, don't you, Inspector?'

'Nonsense,' said Percival. 'Such a thing is impossible!'

'Ask him,' said Lance. 'Ask him why he's making all these inquiries into blackbirds and rye in father's pocket.'

Gently stroking his upper lip, Inspector Neele said:

'You remember the blackbirds last summer, Mr Fortescue. There *are* certain grounds for inquiry.'

'Nonsense,' said Percival again. 'Nobody's heard of the MacKenzies for years.'

'And yet,' said Lance, 'I'd almost dare to swear that there's a MacKenzie in our midst. I rather imagine the inspector thinks so, too.'

II

Inspector Neele caught up Lancelot Fortescue as the latter emerged into the street below.

Lance grinned at him rather sheepishly.

'I didn't mean to do that,' he said. 'But I suddenly lost my temper. Oh! well – it would have come to the same before long. I'm meeting Pat at the Savoy – are you coming my way, Inspector?'

'No, I'm returning to Baydon Health. But there's just something I'd like to ask you, Mr Fortescue.'

'Yes!'

'When you came into the inner office and saw me there – you were surprised. Why?'

'Because I didn't expect to see you, I suppose. I thought I'd find Percy there.'

'You weren't told that he'd gone out?'

Lance looked at him curiously.

'No. They said he was in his office.'

'I see – nobody knew he'd gone out. There's no second door out of the inner office – but there is a door leading straight into the corridor from the little ante-chamber – I suppose your brother went out that way – but I'm surprised Mrs Hardcastle didn't tell you so.'

Lance laughed.

'She'd probably been to collect her cup of tea.'

'Yes – yes – quite so.'

Lance looked at him.

'What's the idea, Inspector?'

'Just puzzling over a few little things, that's all, Mr Fortescue – '

In the train on the way down to Baydon Heath, Inspector Neele had singularly little success doing *The Times* crossword. His mind was distracted by various possibilities. In the same way he read the news with only half his brain taking it in. He read of an earthquake in Japan, of the discovery of uranium deposits in Tanganyika, of the body of a merchant seaman washed up near Southampton, and of the imminent strike among the dockers. He read of the latest victims of the cosh and of a new drug that had achieved wonders in advanced cases of tuberculosis.

All these items made a queer kind of pattern in the back of his mind. Presently he returned to the crossword puzzle and was able to put down three clues in rapid succession.

When he reached Yewtree Lodge he had come to a certain decision. He said to Sergeant Hay:

'Where's that old lady? Is she still there?'

'Miss Marple? Oh, yes, she's here still. Great buddies with the old lady upstairs.'

'I see.' Neele paused for a moment and then said: 'Where is she now? I'd like to see her.'

Miss Marple arrived in a few minutes' time, looking rather flushed and breathing fast.

'You want to see me, Inspector Neele? I do hope I haven't kept you waiting. Sergeant Hay couldn't find me at first. I was in the kitchen, talking to Mrs Crump. I was congratulating her on her pastry and how light her hand is, and telling her how delicious the soufflé was last night. I always think, you know, it's better to approach a subject gradually, don't you? At least, I suppose it isn't so easy for you. You more or less have to come almost straight away to the questions you want to ask. But of course for an old lady like me who has all the time in the world, as you might say, it's really *expected* of her that there should be a great deal of unnecessary talk. And the way to a cook's heart, as they say, is through her pastry.'

'What you really wanted to talk to her about,' said Inspector Neele, 'was Gladys Martin?'

Miss Marple nodded.

'Yes. Gladys. You see, Mrs Crump could really tell me a lot about the girl. Not in connection with the murder. I don't mean that. But about her spirits lately and the odd things she said. I don't mean odd in the sense of peculiar. I mean just the odds and ends of conversation.'

'Did you find it helpful?' asked Inspector Neele.

'Yes,' said Miss Marple. 'I found it very helpful indeed. I really think, you know, that things are becoming very much clearer, don't you?'

'I do and I don't,' said Inspector Neele.

Sergeant Hay, he noticed, had left the room. He was glad of it because what he was about to do now was, to say the least of it, slightly unorthodox.

'Look here, Miss Marple,' he said, 'I want to talk to you seriously.'

'Yes, Inspector Neele?'

'In a way,' said Inspector Neele, 'you and I represent different points of view. I admit, Miss Marple, that I've heard something about you at the Yard.' He smiled: 'It seems you're fairly well known there.'

'I don't know how it is,' fluttered Miss Marple, 'but I so often seem to get mixed up in the things that are really *no* concern of mine. Crimes, I mean, and peculiar happenings.'

'You've got a reputation,' said Inspector Neele.

'Sir Henry Clithering, of course,' said Miss Marple, 'is a *very* old friend of mine.'

'As I said before,' Neele went on, 'you and I represent opposite points of view. One might almost call them sanity and insanity.'

Miss Marple put her head a little on one side.

'Now what exactly do you mean by that, I wonder, Inspector?'

'Well, Miss Marple, there's a sane way of looking at things. This murder benefits certain people. One person, I may say, in particular. The second murder benefits the same person. The third murder one might call a murder for safety.'

'But which do you call the third murder?' Miss Marple asked.

Her eyes, a very bright china blue, looked shrewdly at the inspector. He nodded.

'Yes. You've got something there perhaps. You know, the other day when the AC was speaking to me of these murders, something that he said seemed to me to be wrong. That was it. I was thinking, of course, of the nursery rhyme. The King in his counting-house, the Queen in the parlour and the maid hanging out the clothes.'

'Exactly,' said Miss Marple. 'A sequence in that order, but actually Gladys must have been murdered *before* Mrs Fortescue, mustn't she?'

'I think so,' said Neele. 'I take it it's quite certainly so. Her body wasn't discovered till late that night, and of course it was difficult then to say exactly how long she'd been dead. But I think myself that she must almost certainly have been murdered round about five o'clock, because otherwise . . .'

Miss Marple cut in. 'Because otherwise she would certainly have taken the second tray into the drawing-room?'

'Quite so. She took one tray in with the tea on it, she brought the second tray into the hall, and then *something happened*. She saw something or heard something. The question is what that something was. It *might* have been Dubois coming down the stairs from Mrs Fortescue's room. It *might* have been Elaine Fortescue's young man, Gerald Wright, coming in at the side door. Whoever it was lured her away from the tea tray and out into the garden. And once that had happened I don't see any possibility of her death being long delayed. It was cold out and she was only wearing her thin uniform.'

'Of course you're quite right,' said Miss Marple. 'I mean it was never a case of "the maid was in the garden hanging up the clothes". She wouldn't be hanging up clothes at that time of the evening and she wouldn't go out to the clothes line without putting a coat on. That was all camouflage, like the clothes peg, to make the thing fit in with the rhyme.'

'Exactly,' said Inspector Neele, 'crazy. That's where I can't yet see eye to eye with you. I can't – I simply can't swallow this nursery rhyme business.'

'But it *fits*, Inspector. You must agree it fits.'

'It fits,' said Neele heavily, 'but all the same the sequence is wrong. I mean the rhyme definitely suggests that the maid was the third murder. But we know that the Queen was the third murder. Adele Fortescue was not killed until between twenty-five-past five and five minutes to six. By then Gladys must already have been dead.'

'And that's all wrong, isn't it?' said Miss Marple. 'All wrong for the nursery rhyme – that's very significant, isn't it?'

Inspector Neele shrugged his shoulders.

'It's probably splitting hairs. The deaths fulfil the conditions of the rhyme, and I suppose that's all that was needed. But I'm talking now as though I were on your side. I'm going to outline *my* side of the case now, Miss Marple. I'm washing out the blackbirds and the rye and all the rest of it. I'm going by sober facts and common sense and the reasons for which sane people do murders. First, the death of Rex Fortescue, and *who benefits by his death*. Well, it benefits quite a lot of people, but most of all it benefits his son, Percival. His son Percival wasn't at Yewtree Lodge that morning. He couldn't have put poison in his father's coffee or in anything that he ate for breakfast. Or that's what we thought at first.'

'Ah,' Miss Marple's eyes brightened. 'So there *was* a method, was there? I've been thinking about it, you know, a good deal, and I've had several ideas. But of course no evidence or proof.'

'There's no harm in my letting you know,' said Inspector Neele. 'Taxine was added to a new jar of marmalade. That jar of marmalade was placed on the breakfast table and the top layer of it was eaten by Mr Fortescue at breakfast. Later that jar of marmalade was thrown out into the bushes and a similar jar with a similar amount taken out of it was placed in the pantry. The jar in the bushes was found and I've just had the result of the analysis. It shows definite evidence of taxine.'

'So that was it,' murmured Miss Marple. 'So simple and easy to do.'

'Consolidated Investments,' Neele went on, 'was in a bad way. If the firm had had to pay out a hundred thousand pounds to Adele Fortescue under her husband's will, it would, I think, have crashed. If Mrs Fortescue had survived her husband for a month that money would have *had* to be paid out to her. *She* would have had no feeling for the firm or its difficulties. But she didn't survive her husband for a month. She died, and as a result of her death the gainer was the residuary legatee of Rex Fortescue's will. In other words, Percival Fortescue again.

'Always Percival Fortescue,' the inspector continued bitterly. 'And though he *could* have tampered with the marmalade, he couldn't have poisoned his stepmother or strangled Gladys. According to his secretary he was in his city office at five o'clock that afternoon, and he didn't arrive back here until nearly seven.'

'That makes it *very* difficult, doesn't it?' said Miss Marple.

'It makes it impossible,' said Inspector Neele gloomily. 'In other words, Percival is *out*.' Abandoning restraint and prudence, he spoke with some bitterness, almost unaware of his listener. 'Wherever I go, wherever I turn, I always come up against the same person. Percival Fortescue! Yet it *can't* be Percival Fortescue.' Calming himself a little he said: 'Oh, there are other possibilities, other people who had a perfectly good motive.'

'Mr Dubois, of course,' said Miss Marple sharply. 'And that young Mr Wright. I do so agree with you, Inspector. Wherever there is a question of *gain*, one has to be *very suspicious*. The great thing to avoid is having in any way a trustful mind.'

In spite of himself, Neele smiled.

'Always think the worst, eh?' he asked.

It seemed a curious doctrine to be proceeding from this charming and fragile-looking old lady.

'Oh yes,' said Miss Marple fervently. 'I always believe the worst. What is so sad is that one is usually justified in doing so.'

'All right,' said Neele, 'let's think the worst. Dubois could have done it, Gerald Wright could have done it (that is to say if he'd been acting in collusion with Elaine Fortescue and she tampered with the marmalade), Mrs Percival could have done it, I suppose. She was on the spot. But none of the people I have mentioned tie up with the crazy angle. They don't tie up with blackbirds and pockets full of rye. That's *your* theory and it may be that you're right. If so, it boils down to one person, doesn't it? Mrs MacKenzie's in a mental home and has been for a good number of years. She hasn't been messing about with marmalade pots or putting cyanide in the drawing-room afternoon tea. Her son Donald was killed at Dunkirk. That leaves the daugher, Ruby MacKenzie. And if your theory is correct, if this whole series of murders arises out of the old Blackbird Mine business, then Ruby MacKenzie must be here in this house, and there's only one person that Ruby MacKenzie could be.'

'I think, you know,' said Miss Marple, 'that you're being a little too dogmatic.'

Inspector Neele paid no attention.

'Just one person,' he said grimly.

He got up and went out of the room.

II

Mary Dove was in her sitting-room. It was a small, rather austerely furnished room, but comfortable. That is to say Miss Dove herself had made it comfortable. When Inspector Neele tapped at the door Mary Dove raised her head, which had been bent over a pile of tradesmen's books, and said in her clear voice:

'Come in.'

The inspector entered.

'Do sit down, Inspector.' Miss Dove indicated a chair. 'Could you wait just one moment? The total of the fishmonger's account does not seem to be correct and I must check it.'

Inspector Neele sat in silence watching her as she totted up the column. How wonderfully calm and self-possessed the girl was, he thought. He was intrigued, as so often before, by the personality that underlay that self-assured manner. He tried to trace in her features any resemblance to those of the woman he had talked to at the Pinewood Sanatorium. The colouring was not unlike, but he could detect no real facial resemblance. Presently Mary Dove raised her head from her accounts and said:

'Yes, Inspector? What can I do for you?'

Inspector Neele said quietly:

'You know, Miss Dove, there are certain very peculiar features about this case.'

'Yes?'

'To begin with there is the odd circumstance of the rye found in Mr Fortescue's pocket.'

'That was very extraordinary,' Mary Dove agreed. 'You know I really cannot think of any explanation for that.'

'Then there is the curious circumstance of the blackbirds. Those four blackbirds on Mr Fortescue's desk last summer, and also the incident of the blackbirds being substituted for the veal and ham in the pie. You were here, I think, Miss Dove, at the time of both those occurrences?'

'Yes, I was. I remember now. It was most upsetting. It seemed such a very purposeless, spiteful thing to do, especially at the time.'

'Perhaps not entirely purposeless. What do you know, Miss Dove, about the Blackbird Mine?'

'I don't think I've ever heard of the Blackbird Mine.'

'Your name, you told me, is Mary Dove. Is that your real name, Miss Dove?'

Mary raised her eyebrows. Inspector Neele was almost sure that a wary expression had come into her blue eyes.

'What an extraordinary question, Inspector. Are you suggesting that my name is *not* Mary Dove?'

'That is exactly what I am suggesting. I'm suggesting,' said Neele pleasantly, 'that your name is Ruby MacKenzie.'

She stared at him. For a moment her face was entirely blank with neither protest on it nor surprise. There was, Inspector Neele thought, a very definite effect of calculation. After a minute or two she said in a quiet, colourless voice:

'What do you expect me to say?'

'Please answer me. Is your name Ruby MacKenzie?'

'I have told you my name is Mary Dove.'

'Yes, but have you proof of that, Miss Dove?'

'What do you want to see? My birth certificate?'

'That might be helpful or it might not. You might, I mean, be in possession of the birth certificate of *a* Mary Dove. That Mary Dove might be a friend of yours or might be someone who had died.'

'Yes, there are a lot of possibilities, aren't there?' Amusement had crept back into Mary Dove's voice. 'It's really quite a dilemma for you, isn't it, Inspector?'

'They might possibly be able to recognize you at Pinewood Sanatorium,' said Neele.

'Pinewood Sanatorium!' Mary raised her eyebrows. 'What or where is Pinewood Sanatorium?'

'I think you know very well, Miss Dove.'

'I assure you I am quite in the dark.'

'And you deny categorically that you are Ruby MacKenzie?'

'I shouldn't really like to deny *anything*. I think, you know, Inspector, that it's up to you to prove I *am* this Ruby MacKenzie, whoever she is.' There was definite amusement now in her blue eyes, amusement and challenge. Looking him straight in the eyes, Mary Dove said, 'Yes, it's up to you, Inspector. Prove that I'm Ruby MacKenzie if you can.'

CHAPTER TWENTY-FIVE

'The old tabby's looking for you, sir,' said Sergeant Hay in a conspiratorial whisper, as Inspector Neele descended the stairs. 'It appears as how she's got a lot more to say to you.'

'Hell and damnation,' said Inspector Neele.

'Yes, sir,' said Sergeant Hay, not a muscle of his face moving.

He was about to move away when Neele called him back.

'Go over those notes given us by Miss Dove, Hay, notes as to her former employment and situations. Check up on them – and, yes, there are just one or two other things that I would like to know. Put these inquiries in hand, will you?'

He jotted down a few lines on a sheet of paper and gave them to Sergeant Hay, who said:

'I'll get on to it at once, sir.'

Hearing a murmur of voices in the library as he passed, Inspector Neele looked in. Whether Miss Marple had been looking for him or not, she was now fully engaged talking to Mrs Percival Fortescue while her knitting needles clicked busily. The middle of the sentence which Inspector Neele caught was:

'. . . I have really always thought it was a vocation you needed for nursing. It certainly is very noble work.'

Inspector Neele withdrew quietly. Miss Marple had noticed him, he thought, but she had taken no notice of his presence.

She went on in her gentle, soft voice:

'I had such a charming nurse looking after me when I once broke my wrist. She went on from me to nurse Mrs Sparrow's son, a very nice young naval officer. Quite a romance, really, because they became engaged. So romantic I thought it. They were married and were very happy and had two dear little children.' Miss Marple sighed sentimentally. 'It was pneumonia, you know. So much depends on nursing in pneumonia, does it not.'

'Oh, yes,' said Jennifer Fortescue, 'nursing is nearly everything

301

in pneumonia, though of course nowadays M and B works wonders, and it's not the long, protracted battle it used to be.'

'I'm sure you must have been an excellent nurse, my dear,' said Miss Marple. 'That was the beginning of *your* romance, was it not? I mean you came here to nurse Mr Percival Fortescue, did you not?'

'Yes,' said Jennifer. 'Yes, yes – that's how it did happen.'

Her voice was not encouraging, but Miss Marple seemed to take no notice.

'I understand. One should not listen to servants' gossip, of course, but I'm afraid an old lady like myself is always interested to hear about the people in the house. Now what was I saying? Oh, yes. There was another nurse at first, was there not, and she got sent away – something like that. Carelessness, I believe.'

'I don't think it was carelessness,' said Jennifer. 'I believe her father or something was desperately ill, and so I came to replace her.'

'I see,' said Miss Marple. 'And you fell in love and that was that. Yes, very nice indeed, very nice.'

'I'm not so sure about that,' said Jennifer Fortescue. 'I often wish' – her voice trembled – 'I often wish I was back in the wards again.'

'Yes, yes, I understand. You were keen on your profession.'

'I wasn't so much at the time, but now when I think of it – life's so monotonous, you know. Day after day with nothing to do, and Val so absorbed in business.'

Miss Marple shook her head.

'Gentlemen have to work so hard nowadays,' she said. 'There really doesn't seem any leisure, no matter how much money there is.'

'Yes, it makes it very lonely and dull for a wife sometimes. I often wish I'd never come here,' said Jennifer. 'Oh, well, I dare say it serves me right. I ought never to have done it.'

'Ought never to have done what, my dear?'

'I ought never to have married Val. Oh, well – ' she sighed abruptly. 'Don't let's talk of it any more.'

Obligingly Miss Marple began to talk about the new skirts that were being worn in Paris.

II

'So kind of you not to interrupt just now,' said Miss Marple when, having tapped at the door of the study, Inspector Neele had told her to come in. 'There were just one or two little points, you know, that I wanted to verify.' She added reproachfully: 'We didn't really finish our talk just now.'

'I'm so sorry, Miss Marple.' Inspector Neele summoned up a charming smile. 'I'm afraid I was rather rude. I summoned you to a consultation and did all the talking myself.'

'Oh, that's quite all right,' said Miss Marple immediately, 'because, you see, I wasn't really quite ready then to put all *my* cards on the table. I mean I wouldn't like to make any accusation unless I was absolutely sure about it. Sure, that is, in *my own mind*. And I *am* sure, now.'

'You're sure about what, Miss Marple?'

'Well, certainly about who killed Mr Fortescue. What you told me about the marmalade, I mean, just clinches the matter. Showing *how*, I mean, as well as *who*, and well within the mental capacity.'

Inspector Neele blinked a little.

'I'm so sorry,' said Miss Marple, perceiving this reaction on his part, 'I'm afraid I find it difficult sometimes to make myself perfectly clear.'

'I'm not quite sure yet, Miss Marple, what we're talking about.'

'Well, perhaps,' said Miss Marple, 'we'd better begin all over again. I mean if you could spare the time. I would rather like to put my own point of view before you. You see, I've talked a good deal to people, to old Miss Ramsbottom and to Mrs Crump and to her husband. He, of course, is a liar, but that doesn't really matter because, if you know liars are liars, it comes to the same thing. But I did want to get the telephone calls clear and the nylon stockings and all that.'

Inspector Neele blinked again and wondered what he had let himself in for and why he had ever thought that Miss Marple might be a desirable and clear-headed colleague. Still, he thought to himself, however muddle-headed she was, she might have picked up some useful bits of information. All Inspector Neele's success in his profession had come from listening well. He was prepared to listen now.

'Please tell me all about it, Miss Marple,' he said, 'but start at the beginning, won't you.'

'Yes, of course,' said Miss Marple, 'and the beginning is Gladys. I mean I came here because of Gladys. And you very kindly let me look through all her things. And what with that and the nylon stockings and the telephone calls and one thing and another, it did come out perfectly clear. I mean about Mr Fortescue and the taxine.'

'You have a theory?' asked Inspector Neele, 'as to who put the taxine into Mr Fortescue's marmalade.'

'It isn't a theory,' said Miss Marple. 'I know.'

For the third time Inspector Neele blinked.

'It was Gladys, of course,' said Miss Marple.

CHAPTER TWENTY-SIX

Inspector Neele stared at Miss Marple and slowly shook his head.

'Are you saying,' he said incredulously, 'that Gladys Martin deliberately murdered Rex Fortescue? I'm sorry, Miss Marple, but I simply don't believe it.'

'No, of course she didn't *mean* to murder him,' said Miss Marple, 'but she did it all the same! You said yourself that she was nervous and upset when you questioned her. And that she looked guilty.'

'Yes, but not guilty of *murder*.'

'Oh, no, I agree. As I say, she didn't *mean* to murder anybody, but she put the taxine in the marmalade. She didn't think it was poison, of course.'

'What *did* she think it was?' Inspector Neele's voice still sounded incredulous.

'I rather imagine she thought it was a truth drug,' said Miss Marple. 'It's very interesting, you know, and very instructive – the things these girls cut out of papers and keep. It's always been the same, you know, all through the ages. Recipes for beauty, for attracting the man you love. And witchcraft and charms and marvellous happenings. Nowadays they're mostly lumped together under the heading of Science. Nobody believes in magicians any more, nobody believes that anyone can come along and wave a wand and turn you into a frog. But if you read in the paper that by injecting certain glands scientists can alter your vital tissues and you'll develop froglike characteristics, well, everybody would believe that. And having read in the papers about truth drugs, of course

Gladys would believe it absolutely when he told her that that's what it was.'

'When who told her?' said Inspector Neele.

'Albert Evans,' said Miss Marple. 'Not of course that that is *really* his name. But anyway he met her last summer at a holiday camp, and he flattered her up and made love to her, and I should imagine told her some story of injustice or persecution, or something like that. Anyway, the point was that Rex Fortescue had to be made to confess what he had done and make restitution. I don't *know* this, of course, Inspector Neele, but I'm pretty sure about it. He got her to take a post here, and it's really very easy nowadays with the shortage of domestic staff, to obtain a post where you want one. Staffs are changing the whole time. They then arranged a date together. You remember on that last postcard he said: "Remember our date." That was to be the great day they were working for. Gladys would put the drug that he gave her into the top of the marmalade, so that Mr Fortescue would eat it at breakfast and she would also put the rye in his pocket. I don't know what story he told her to account for the rye, but as I told you from the beginning, Inspector Neele, Gladys Martin was a *very* credulous girl. In fact, there's hardly anything she wouldn't believe if a personable young man put it to her the right way.'

'Go on,' said Inspector Neele in a dazed voice.

'The idea probably was,' continued Miss Marple, 'that Albert was going to call upon him at the office that day, and that by that time the truth drug would have worked, and that Mr Fortescue would have confessed everything and so on and so on. You can imagine the poor girl's feelings when she heard that Mr Fortescue was dead.'

'But, surely,' Inspector Neele objected, 'she would have told?'

Miss Marple asked sharply:

'What was the first thing she said to you when you questioned her?'

'She said: "I didn't do it,"' Inspector Neele said.

'Exactly,' said Miss Marple, triumphantly. 'Don't you see that's exactly what she *would* say? If she broke an ornament, you know, Gladys would always say: "I didn't do it, Miss Marple. I can't think *how* it happened." They can't help it, poor dears. They're very upset at what they've done and their great idea is to avoid blame. You don't think that a nervous young woman who had murdered someone when she didn't mean to murder him is going to admit it, do you? That would have been *quite* out of character.'

'Yes,' Neele said, 'I suppose it would.'

305

He ran his mind back over his interview with Gladys. Nervous, upset, guilty, shifty-eyed, all those things. They might have had a small significance, or a big one. He could not really blame himself for having failed to come to the right conclusion.

'Her first idea, as I say,' went on Miss Marple, 'would be to deny it all. Then in a confused way she would try to sort it all out in her mind. Perhaps Albert hadn't known how strong the stuff was, or he'd made a mistake and given her too much of it. She'd think of excuses for him and explanations. She'd hope he'd get in touch with her, which, of course, he did. By telephone.'

'Do you know that?' asked Neele sharply.

Miss Marple shook her head.

'No. I admit I'm assuming it. But there were unexplained calls that day. That is to say, people rang up and, when Crump or Mrs Crump answered, the phone was hung up. That's what he'd do, you know. Ring up and wait until Gladys answered the phone, and then he'd make an appointment with her to meet him.'

'I see,' said Neele. 'You mean she had an appointment to meet him on the day she died.'

Miss Marple nodded vigorously.

'Yes, that was indicated. Mrs Crump was right about one thing. The girl had on her best nylon stockings and her good shoes. She was going to meet someone. Only she wasn't going *out* to meet him. He was coming to Yewtree Lodge. That's why she was on the look-out that day and flustered and late with tea. Then, as she brought the second tray into the hall, I think she looked along the passage to the side door, and saw him there, beckoning to her. She put the tray down and went out to meet him.'

'And then he strangled her,' said Neele.

Miss Marple pursed her lips together. 'It would only take a minute,' she said, 'but he couldn't risk her talking. She had to die, poor, silly, credulous girl. And then – he put a clothes peg on her nose!' Stern anger vibrated the old lady's voice. 'To make it fit in with the rhyme. The rye, the blackbirds, the counting-house, the bread and honey, and the clothes peg – the nearest he could get to a little dicky bird that nipped off her nose – '

'And I suppose at the end of it all he'll go to Broadmoor and we shan't be able to hang him because he's crazy!' said Neele slowly.

'I think you'll hang him all right,' said Miss Marple. 'And he's not crazy, Inspector, not for a moment!'

Inspector Neele looked hard at her.

'Now see here, Miss Marple, you've outlined a theory to me. Yes – yes – although you say you *know*, it's only a *theory*. You're saying that a man is responsible for these crimes, who called himself Albert Evans, who picked up the girl Gladys at a holiday camp and used her for his own purposes. This Albert Evans was someone who wanted revenge for the old Blackbird Mine business. You're suggesting, aren't you, that Mrs MacKenzie's son, Don MacKenzie, didn't die at Dunkirk. That he's still alive, that he's behind all this?'

But to Inspector Neele's surprise, Miss Marple was shaking her head violently.

'Oh no!' she said, 'oh *no*! I'm not suggesting that *at all*. Don't you see, Inspector Neele, all this blackbird business is really a complete *fake*. It was *used*, that was all, used by somebody who heard about the blackbirds – the ones in the library and in the pie. The blackbirds were genuine enough. They were put there by someone who knew about the old business, who wanted revenge for it. But only the revenge of trying to frighten Mr Fortescue or to make him uncomfortable. I don't believe, you know, Inspector Neele, that children can really be brought up and taught to wait and brood and carry out revenge. Children, after all, have got a lot of *sense*. But anyone whose father had been swindled and perhaps left to die might be willing to play a malicious trick on the person who was supposed to have done it. That's what happened, I think. And the killer used it.'

'The killer,' said Inspector Neele. 'Come now, Miss Marple, let's have your ideas about the killer. Who was he?'

'You won't be surprised,' said Miss Marple. 'Not really. Because you'll see, as soon as I tell you who he is, or rather who I think he is, for one must be accurate must one not? – you'll see that he's just the type of person who *would* commit these murders. He's sane, brilliant and quite unscrupulous. And he did it, of course, for money, probably for a good deal of money.'

'Percival Fortescue?' Inspector Neele spoke almost imploringly, but he knew as he spoke that he was wrong. The picture of the man that Miss Marple had built up for him had no resemblance to Percival Fortescue.

'Oh, no,' said Miss Marple. 'Not Percival. Lance.'

CHAPTER TWENTY-SEVEN

'It's impossible,' said Inspector Neele.

He leaned back in his chair and watched Miss Marple with fascinated eyes. As Miss Marple had said, he was not surprised. His words were a denial, not of probability, but of possibility. Lance Fortescue fitted the description: Miss Marple had outlined it well enough. But Inspector Neele simply could not see how Lance could be the answer.

Miss Marple leaned forward in her chair and gently, persuasively, and rather in the manner of someone explaining the simple facts of arithmetic to a small child, outlined her theory.

'He's always been like that, you see. I mean, he's always been *bad*. Bad all through, although with it he's always been *attractive*. Especially attractive to *women*. He's got a brilliant mind and he'll take risks. He's always taken risks and because of his charm people have always believed the best and not the worst about him. He came home in the summer to see his father. I don't believe for a moment that his father wrote to him or sent for him – unless, of course, you've got actual evidence to that effect.' She paused inquiringly.

Neele shook his head. 'No,' he said, 'I've no evidence of his father sending for him. I've got a letter that Lance is supposed to have written to him after being here. But Lance could quite easily have slipped that among his father's papers in the study here the day he arrived.'

'Sharp of him,' said Miss Marple, nodding her head. 'Well, as I say, he probably flew over here and attempted a reconciliation with his father, but Mr Fortescue wouldn't have it. You see, Lance had recently got married and the small pittance he was living on, and which he had doubtless been supplementing in various dishonest ways, was not enough for him any more. He was very much in love with Pat (who is a dear, sweet girl) and he wanted a respectable, settled life with her – nothing shifty. And that, from his point of view, meant having a lot of money. When he was at

Yewtree Lodge he must have heard about these blackbirds. Perhaps his father mentioned them. Perhaps Adele did. He jumped to the conclusion that MacKenzie's daughter was established in the house and it occurred to him that she would make a very good scapegoat for murder. Because, you see, when he realized that he couldn't get his father to do what he wanted, he must have cold-bloodedly decided that murder it would have to be. He may have realized that his father wasn't – er, very well – and have feared that by the time his father died there would have been a complete crash.'

'He knew about his father's health all right,' said the inspector.

'Ah – that explains a good deal. Perhaps the coincidence of his father's Christian name being *Rex* together with the blackbird incident suggested the idea of the nursery rhyme. Make a crazy business of the whole thing – and tie it up with that old revenge threat of the MacKenzies. Then, you see, he could dispose of Adele, too, and that hundred thousand pounds going out of the firm. But there would have to be a third character, the "maid in the garden hanging up the clothes" – and I suppose that suggested the whole wicked plan to him. An innocent accomplice whom he could silence before she could talk. And that would give him what he wanted – a genuine alibi for the first murder. The rest was easy. He arrived here from the station just before five o'clock, which was the time when Gladys brought the second tray into the hall. He came to the side door, saw her and beckoned to her. Strangling her and carrying her body round the house to where the clothes lines were would only have taken three or four minutes. Then he rang the front-door bell, was admitted to the house, and joined the family for tea. After tea he went up to see Miss Ramsbottom. When he came down, he slipped into the drawing-room, found Adele alone there drinking a last cup of tea and sat down by her on the sofa, and while he was talking to her, he managed to slip the cyanide into her tea. It wouldn't be difficult, you know. A little piece of white stuff, like sugar. He might have stretched out his hand to the sugar basin and taken a lump and apparently dropped it into her cup. He'd laugh and say: "Look, I've dropped more sugar into your tea." She'd say she didn't mind, stir it and drink it. It would be as easy and audacious as that. Yes, he's an audacious fellow.'

Inspector Neele said slowly:

'It's actually possible – yes. But I cannot see – really, Miss Marple, I cannot see – what he stood to gain by it. Granted that unless old Fortescue died the business would soon be on the rocks, is Lance's share big enough to cause him to plan three murders? I don't think so. I really don't think so.'

'That *is* a little difficult,' admitted Miss Marple. 'Yes, I agree with you. That does present difficulties. I suppose . . .' She hesitated, looking at the inspector. 'I suppose – I am so very ignorant in financial matters – but I suppose it is really true that the Blackbird Mine *is* worthless?'

Neele reflected. Various scraps fitted together in his mind. Lance's willingness to take the various speculative or worthless shares off Percival's hands. His parting words today in London that Percival had better get rid of the Blackbird and its hoodoo. A gold mine. A worthless gold mine. But perhaps the mine had *not* been worthless. And yet, somehow, that seemed unlikely. Old Rex Fortescue was hardly likely to have made a mistake on that point, although of course there might have been soundings recently. Where *was* the mine? West Africa, Lance had said. Yes but somebody else – was it Miss Ramsbottom – had said it was in *East* Africa. Had Lance been deliberately misleading when he said West instead of East? Miss Ramsbottom was old and forgetful, and yet *she* might have been right and not Lance. East Africa. Lance had just come from East Africa. Had he perhaps some recent knowledge?

Suddenly with a click another piece fitted into the inspector's puzzle. Sitting in the train, reading *The Times*. *Uranium deposits found in Tanganyika*. Supposing that the uranium deposits were on the site of the old Blackbird? That would explain everything. Lance had come to have knowledge of that, being on the spot, and with uranium deposits there, there was a fortune to be grasped. An enormous fortune! He sighed. He looked at Miss Marple.

'How do you think,' he asked reproachfully, 'that I'm ever going to be able to prove all this?'

Miss Marple nodded at him encouragingly, as an aunt might have encouraged a bright nephew who was going in for a scholarship exam.

'You'll prove it,' she said. 'You're a very, *very* clever man, Inspector Neele. I've seen that from the first. Now you know who it is you ought to be able to get the evidence. At that holiday camp, for instance, they'll recognize his photograph. He'll find it hard to explain why he stayed there for a week calling himself Albert Evans.'

Yes, Inspector Neele thought, Lance Fortescue was brilliant and unscrupulous – but he was foolhardy, too. The risks he took were just a little too great.

Neele thought to himself, 'I'll get him!' Then, doubt sweeping over him, he looked at Miss Marple.

'It's all pure assumption, you know,' he said.

'Yes – but you are sure, aren't you?'

'I suppose so. After all, I've known his kind before.'

The old lady nodded.

'Yes – that matters so much – that's really why *I'm* sure.'

Neele looked at her playfully.

'Because of your knowledge of criminals.'

'Oh no – of course not. Because of Pat – a dear girl – and the kind that always marries a bad lot – that's really what drew my attention to him at the start – '

'I may be sure – in my own mind,' said the inspector, 'but there's a lot that needs explaining – the Ruby MacKenzie business for instance. I could swear that – '

Miss Marple interrupted:

'And you're quite right. But you've been thinking of the wrong person. Go and talk to Mrs Percy.'

II

'Mrs Fortescue,' said Inspector Neele, 'do you mind telling me your name before you were married.'

'Oh!' Jennifer gasped. She looked frightened.

'You needn't be nervous madam,' said Inspector Neele, 'but it's much better to come out with the truth. I'm right, I think, in saying that your name before you were married was Ruby MacKenzie?'

'My – well, oh well – oh dear – well, why shouldn't it be?' said Mrs Percival Fortescue.

'No reason at all,' said Inspector Neele gently, and added: 'I was talking to your mother a few days ago at Pinewood Sanatorium.'

'She's very angry with me,' said Jennifer. 'I never go and see her now because it only upsets her. Poor Mumsy, she was so devoted to Dad, you know.'

'And she brought you up to have very melodramatic ideas of revenge?'

'Yes,' said Jennifer. 'She kept making us swear on the Bible that we'd never forget and that we'd kill him one day. Of course, once

311

I'd gone into hospital and started my training, I began to realize that her mental balance wasn't what it should be.'

'You yourself must have felt revengeful though, Mrs Fortescue?'

'Well, of course I did. Rex Fortescue practically murdered my father! I don't mean he actually shot him, or knifed him or anything like that. But I'm quite certain that he *did* leave Father to die. That's the same thing, isn't it?'

'It's the same thing morally – yes.'

'So I did want to pay him back,' said Jennifer. 'When a friend of mine came to nurse his son I got her to leave and to propose my replacing her. I don't know exactly what I meant to do . . . I didn't, really I didn't, Inspector, I never meant to *kill* Mr Fortescue. I had some idea, I think, of nursing his son so badly that the son would die. But of course, if you *are* a nurse by profession you can't do that sort of thing. Actually I had quite a job pulling Val through. And then he got fond of me and asked me to marry him and I thought, "Well, really that's a far more sensible revenge than anything else." I mean, to marry Mr Fortescue's eldest son and get the money he swindled Father out of back that way. I think it was a far more sensible way.'

'Yes, indeed,' said Inspector Neele, 'far more sensible.' He added, 'It was you, I suppose, who put the blackbirds on the desk and in the pie?'

Mrs Percival flushed.

'Yes. I suppose it was silly of me really . . . But Mr Fortescue had been talking about suckers one day and boasting of how he'd swindled people – got the best of them. Oh, in quite a *legal* way. And I thought I'd just like to give him – well, a kind of fright. And it *did* give him a fright! He was awfully upset.' She added anxiously, 'But I didn't do anything *else*! I didn't really, Inspector. You don't – you don't honestly think I would *murder* anyone, do you?'

Inspector Neele smiled.

'No,' he said, 'I don't.' He added: 'By the way, have you given Miss Dove any money lately?'

Jennifer's jaw dropped.

'How did you know?'

'We know a lot of things,' said Inspector Neele and added to himself: 'And guess a good many, too.'

Jennifer continued, speaking rapidly:

'She came to me and said that you'd accused her of being Ruby MacKenzie. She said if I'd get hold of five hundred pounds she'd

312

let you go on thinking so. She said if you knew that I was Ruby MacKenzie, I'd be suspected of murdering Mr Fortescue and my stepmother. I had an awful job getting the money, because of course I couldn't tell Percival. He doesn't know about me. I had to sell my diamond engagement ring and a very beautiful necklace Mr Fortescue gave me.'

'Don't worry, Mrs Percival,' said Inspector Neele, 'I think we can get your money back for you.'

III

It was on the following day that Inspector Neele had another interview with Miss Mary Dove.

'I wonder, Miss Dove,' he said, 'if you'd give me a cheque for five hundred pounds payable to Mrs Percival Fortescue.'

He had the pleasure of seeing Mary Dove lose countenance for once.

'The silly fool told you, I suppose,' she said

'Yes. Blackmail, Miss Dove, is rather a serious charge.'

'It wasn't exactly blackmail, Inspector. I think you'd find it hard to make out a case of blackmail against me. I was just doing Mrs Percival a special service to oblige her.'

'Well, if you'll give me that cheque, Miss Dove, we'll leave it like that.'

Mary Dove got her cheque book and took out her fountain pen.

'It's very annoying,' she said with a sigh. 'I'm particularly hard up at the moment.'

'You'll be looking for another job soon, I suppose?'

'Yes. This one hasn't turned out quite according to plan. It's all been very unfortunate from my point of view.'

Inspector Neele agreed.

'Yes, it put you in rather a difficult position, didn't it? I mean, it was quite likely that at any moment we might have to look into your antecedents.'

Mary Dove, cool once more, allowed her eyebrows to rise.

'Really, Inspector, my past is quite blameless, I assure you.'

'Yes, it is,' Inspector Neele agreed, cheerfully. 'We've nothing against you at all, Miss Dove. It's a curious coincidence, though, that in the last three places which you have filled so admirably, there have happened to be robberies about three months after you left. The thieves have seemed remarkably well informed as to where mink coats, jewels, etc., were kept. Curious coincidence, isn't it?'

'Coincidences do happen, Inspector.'

'Oh, yes,' said Neele. 'They happen. But they mustn't happen too often, Miss Dove. I dare say,' he added, 'that we may meet again in the future.'

'I hope' – said Mary Dove – 'I don't mean to be rude, Inspector Neele – but I hope we don't.'

CHAPTER TWENTY-EIGHT

Miss Marple smoothed over the top of her suitcase, tucked in an end of woolly shawl and shut the lid down. She looked round her bedroom. No, she had left nothing behind. Crump came in to fetch down her luggage. Miss Marple went into the next room to say goodbye to Miss Ramsbottom.

'I'm afraid,' said Miss Marple, 'that I've made a very poor return for your hospitality. I hope you will be able to forgive me some day.'

'Hah,' said Miss Ramsbottom.

She was as usual playing patience.

'Black knave, red queen,' she observed, then she darted a shrewd, sideways glance at Miss Marple. 'You found out what you wanted to, I suppose,' she said.

'Yes.'

'And I suppose you've told that police inspector all about it? Will he be able to prove a case?'

'I'm almost sure he will,' said Miss Marple. 'It may take a little time.'

'I'm not asking you any questions,' said Miss Ramsbottom. 'You're a shrewd woman. I knew that as soon as I saw you. I don't blame you for what you've done. Wickedness is wickedness and has got to be punished. There's a bad streak in this family. It didn't come from our side, I'm thankful to say. Elvira, my sister, was a fool. Nothing worse.

'Black knave,' repeated Miss Ramsbottom, fingering the card. 'Handsome, but a black heart. Yes, I was afraid of it. Ah, well, you can't always help loving a sinner. The boy always had a way with him. Even got round me . . . Told a lie about the time he left me that day. I didn't contradict him, but I wondered . . . I've wondered ever since. But he was Elvira's boy – I couldn't bring myself to say anything. Ah well, you're a righteous woman, Jane Marple, and right must prevail. I'm sorry for his wife, though.'

'So am I,' said Miss Marple.

In the hall Pat Fortescue was waiting to say goodbye.

'I wish you weren't going,' she said. 'I shall miss you.'

'It's time for me to go,' said Miss Marple. 'I've finished what I came here to do. It hasn't been – altogether pleasant. But it's important, you know, that wickedness shouldn't triumph.'

Pat looked puzzled.

'I don't understand.'

'No, my dear. But perhaps you will, some day. If I might venture to advise, if anything ever – goes wrong in your life – I think the happiest thing for you would be to go back to where you were happy as a child. Go back to Ireland, my dear. Horses and dogs. All that.'

Pat nodded.

'Sometimes I wish I'd done just that when Freddy died. But if I had' – her voice changed and softened – 'I'd never have met Lance.'

Miss Marple sighed.

'We're not staying here, you know,' said Pat. 'We're going back to East Africa as soon as everything's cleared up. I'm so glad.'

'God bless you, dear child,' said Miss Marple. 'One needs a great deal of courage to get through life. I think you have it.'

She patted the girl's hand and, releasing it, went through the front door to the waiting taxi.

II

Miss Marple reached home late that evening.

Kitty – the latest graduate from St Faith's Home – let her in and greeted her with a beaming face.

'I've got a herring for your supper, miss. I'm so glad to see you home – you'll find everything very nice in the house. Regular spring cleaning I've had.'

'That's very nice, Kitty – I'm glad to be home.'

Six spiders webs on the cornice, Miss Marple noted. These girls never raised their heads! She was none the less too kind to say so.

'Your letters is on the hall table, miss. And there's one as went to Daisymead by mistake. Always doing that, aren't they? Does look a bit alike, Dane and Daisy, and the writing's so bad I don't wonder this time. They've been away there and the house shut up, they only got back and sent it round today. Said as how they hoped it wasn't important.'

Miss Marple picked up her correspondence. The letter to which Kitty had referred was on top of the others. A faint chord of remembrance stirred in Miss Marple's mind at the sight of the blotted scrawled handwriting. She tore it open.

DEAR MADAM,

I hope as you'll forgive me writing this but I really don't know what to do indeed I don't and I never meant no harm. Dear madam, you'll have seen the newspapers it was murder they say but it wasn't me that did it, not really, because I would never do anything wicked like that and I know as how he wouldn't either. Albert, I mean. I'm telling this badly, but you see we met last summer and was going to be married only Bert hadn't got his rights, he'd been done out of them, swindled by this Mr Fortescue who's dead. And Mr Fortescue he just denied everything and of course everybody believed him and not Bert because he was rich and Bert was poor. But Bert had a friend who works in a place where they make these new drugs and there's what they call a truth drug you've read about it perhaps in the paper and it makes people speak the truth whether they want to or not. Bert was going to see Mr Fortescue in his office on Nov. 5th and taking a lawyer with him and I was to be sure to give him the drug at breakfast that morning and then it would work just right for when they came and he'd admit as all what Bert said was quite true. Well, madam, I put it in the marmalade but now he's dead and I think as how it must have been too strong but it wasn't Bert's fault because Bert would never do a thing like that but I can't tell the police because maybe they'd think Bert did it on purpose which I know he didn't. Oh, madam, I don't know what to do or what to say and the police are here in the house and it's awful and they ask you questions and look at you so stern and I don't know what to do and I haven't heard from Bert. Oh, madam,

316

don't like to ask it of you but if you could only come here and help me they'd listen to you and you were always so kind to me, and I didn't mean anything wrong and Bert didn't either. If you could only help us. Yours respectfully,
GLADYS MARTIN.
P. S. – I'm enclosing a snap of Bert and me. One of the boys took it at the camp and give it me. Bert doesn't know I've got it – he hates being snapped. But you can see, madam, what a nice boy he is.

Miss Marple, her lips pursed together, stared down at the photograph. The pair pictured there were looking at each other. Miss Marple's eyes went from Gladys's pathetic adoring face, the mouth slightly open, to the other face – the dark handsome smiling face of Lance Fortescue.

The last words of the pathetic letter echoed in her mind:
You can see what a nice boy he is.

The tear rose in Miss Marple's eyes. Succeeding pity, there came anger – anger against a heartless killer.

And then, displacing both these emotions, there came a surge of triumph – the triumph some specialist might feel who has successfully reconstructed an extinct animal from a fragment of jawbone and a couple of teeth.

The Mirror Crack'd
From side to Side

To MARGARET RUTHERFORD
in Admiration

Out flew the web and floated wide;
The mirror crack'd from side to side:
"The curse is come upon me," cried
The Lady of Shalott

Alfred Tennyson

CHAPTER ONE

Miss Jane Marple was sitting by her window. The window looked over her garden, once a source of pride to her. That was no longer so. Nowadays she looked out of the window and winced. Active gardening had been forbidden her for some time now. No stooping, no digging, no planting – at most a little light pruning. Old Laycock who came three times a week, did his best, no doubt. But his best, such as it was (which was not much) was only the best according to *his* lights, and not according to those of his employer. Miss Marple knew exactly what she wanted done, and when she wanted it done, and instructed him duly. Old Laycock then displayed his particular genius which was that of enthusiastic agreement and subsequent lack of performance.

'That's right, missus. We'll have them mecosoapies there and the Canterburys along the wall and as you say it ought to be got on with first thing next week.'

Laycock's excuses were always reasonable, and strongly resembled those of Captain George's in *Three Men in a Boat* for avoiding going to sea. In the captain's case the wind was always wrong, either blowing off shore or in shore, or coming from the unreliable west, or the even more treacherous east. Laycock's was the weather. Too dry – too wet – waterlogged – a nip of frost in the air. Or else something of great importance had to come first (usually to do with cabbages or brussels sprouts of which he liked to grow inordinate quantities). Laycock's own principles of gardening were simple and no employer, however knowledgeable, could wean him from them.

They consisted of a great many cups of tea, sweet and strong, as an encouragement to effort, a good deal of sweeping up of leaves in the autumn, and a certain amount of bedding out of his own favourite plants, mainly asters and salvias – to 'make a nice show', as he put it, in summer. He was all in favour of syringeing roses for green-fly, but was slow to get around to it, and a demand for deep trenching for sweet peas was usually countered by the remark that you ought to see his own sweet peas! A proper treat last year, and no fancy stuff done beforehand.

To be fair, he was attached to his employers, humoured their fancies in horticulture (so far as no actual hard work was involved) but vegetables he knew to be the real stuff of life; a nice Savoy, or a bit of curly kale; flowers were fancy stuff such as ladies liked to go in for, having nothing better to do with their time. He showed his affection by producing presents of the aforementioned asters, salvias, lobelia edging, and summer chrysanthemums.

'Been doing some work at them new houses over at the Development. Want their gardens laid out nice, they do. More plants than they needed so I brought along a few, and I've put 'em in where them old-fashioned roses ain't looking so well.'

Thinking of these things, Miss Marple averted her eyes from the garden, and picked up her knitting.

One had to face the fact: St Mary Mead was *not* the place it had been. In a sense, of course, nothing was what it had been. You could blame the war (both the wars) or the younger generation, or women going out to work, or the atom bomb, or just the Government – but what one really meant was the simple fact that one was growing old. Miss Marple, who was a very sensible lady, knew that quite well. It was just that, in a queer way, she felt it more in St Mary Mead, because it had been her home for so long.

St Mary Mead, the old world core of it, was still there. The Blue Boar was there, and the church and the vicarage and the little nest of Queen Anne and Georgian houses, of which hers was one. Miss Hartnell's house was still there, and also Miss Hartnell, fighting progress to the last gasp. Miss Wetherby had passed on and her house was now inhabited by the bank manager and his family, having been given a face-lift by the painting of doors and windows a bright royal blue. There were new people in most of the other old houses, but the houses themselves were little changed in appearances since the people who had bought them had done so because they liked what the house agent called 'old world charm'. They just added another bathroom, and spent a good deal of money on plumbing, electric cookers, and dish-washers.

But though the houses looked much as before, the same could hardly be said of the village street. When shops changed hands there, it was with a view to immediate and intemperate modernization. The fishmonger was unrecognizable with new super windows behind which the refrigerated fish gleamed. The butcher had remained

324

conservative – good meat is good meat, if you have the money to pay for it. If not, you take the cheaper cuts and the tough joints and like it! Barnes, the grocer, was still there, unchanged, for which Miss Hartnell and Miss Marple and others daily thanked Heaven. So *obliging*, comfortable chairs to sit in by the counter, and cosy discussions as to cuts of bacon, and varieties of cheese. At the end of the street, however, where Mr Toms had once had his basket shop stood a glittering new supermarket – anathema to the elderly ladies of St Mary Mead.

'Packets of things one's never even *heard* of,' exclaimed Miss Hartnell. 'All these great packets of breakfast cereal instead of cooking a child a proper breakfast of bacon and eggs. *And* you're expected to take a basket *yourself* and go round looking for things – it takes a quarter of an hour sometimes to find all one wants – and usually made up in inconvenient sizes, too much or too little. And then a long queue waiting to pay as you go out. Most tiring. Of course it's all very well for the people from the Development – '

At this point she stopped.

Because, as was now usual, the sentence came to an end there. The Development, Period, as they would say in modern terms. It had an entity of its own, and a capital letter.

II

Miss Marple uttered a sharp exclamation of annoyance. She'd dropped a stitch again. Not only that, she must have dropped it some time ago. Not until now, when she had to decrease for the neck and count the stitches, had she realized the fact. She took up a spare pin, held the knitting sideways to the light and peered anxiously. Even her new spectacles didn't seem to do any good. And that, she reflected, was because obviously there came a time when oculists, in spite of their luxurious waiting-rooms, the up-to-date instruments, the bright lights they flashed into your eyes, and the very high fees they charged, couldn't do anything much more for you. Miss Marple reflected with some nostalgia on how good her eyesight had been a few (well, not perhaps a *few*) years ago. From the vantage-point of her garden, so admirably placed to see all that was going on in St Mary Mead, how little had escaped her noticing eye! And with the help of her bird glasses – (an interest in birds was *so* useful!) – she had been able to see – She broke off there and let her thoughts run back over the past. Ann Protheroe in her summer frock going along to the Vicarage garden. And Colonel Protheroe – poor man – a very tiresome and unpleasant man, to be sure – but to be murdered like that – She shook her head and went on to thoughts of Griselda, the vicar's pretty young wife. Dear Griselda – such a faithful friend – a Christmas card every year. That attractive baby of hers was a strapping young man now, and with a very good job. Engineering, was it? He always *had* enjoyed taking his mechanical trains to pieces. Beyond the Vicarage, there had been the stile and the field path with Farmer Giles's cattle beyond in the meadows where now – now . . .

The Development.

And why not? Miss Marple asked herself sternly. These things had to be. The houses were necessary, and they were very well built, or so she had been told. 'Planning,' or whatever they called it. Though why everything had to be called a Close she couldn't imagine. Aubrey Close and Longwood Close, and Grandison Close and all the rest of them. Not really Closes at all. Miss Marple knew what a Close was perfectly. Her uncle had been a Canon of Chichester Cathedral. As a child she had gone to stay with him in the Close.

It was like Cherry Baker who always called Miss Marple's old-world overcrowded drawing-room the 'lounge'. Miss Marple corrected her gently, 'It's the drawing-room, Cherry.' And Cherry, because she was young and kind, endeavoured to remember, though it was obvious to her 'drawing-room' was a very funny word to use – and 'lounge' came slipping out. She had of late, however, compromised on 'living-room'. Miss Marple liked Cherry very much. Her name was Mrs Baker and she came from the Development. She was one of the detachment of young wives who shopped at the supermarket and wheeled prams about the quiet streets of St Mary Mead. They were all smart and well turned out. Their hair was crisp and curled. They laughed and talked and called to one another. They were like a happy flock of birds. Owing to the insidious snares of Hire Purchase, they were always in need of ready money, though their husbands all earned good wages; and so they came and did housework or cooking. Cherry was a quick and efficient cook, she was an intelligent girl, took telephone calls correctly and was quick to spot inaccuracies in the tradesmen's books. She was not much given to turning mattresses, and as far as washing up went Miss Marple always now passed the pantry door with her head turned away so as not to observe Cherry's method which was that of thrusting everything into the sink together and letting loose a snowstorm of detergent on it. Miss Marple had quietly removed her old Worcester teaset from daily circulation and put it in the corner cabinet whence it only emerged on special occasions. Instead she had purchased a modern service with a pattern of pale grey on white and no gilt on it whatsoever to be washed away in the sink.

How different it had been in the past . . . Faithful Florence, for instance, that grenadier of a parlourmaid – and there had been Amy and Clara and Alice, those 'nice little maids' – arriving from St Faith's Orphanage, to be 'trained', and then going on to better paid jobs elsewhere. Rather simple, some of them had been, and frequently adenoidal, and Amy distinctly moronic. They had gossiped and chattered with the other maids in the village and walked out with the fishmonger's assistant, or the under-gardener at the Hall, or one of Mr Barnes the grocer's numerous assistants. Miss Marple's mind went back over them affectionately thinking of all the little woolly coats she had knitted for their subsequent offspring. They had not been very good with the telephone, and no good at all at arithmetic. On the other hand, they knew how to wash up, and how to make a bed. They had had skills, rather than education. It was odd that nowadays it should be the educated girls who went in for all the domestic chores. Students from abroad, girls *au pair*, university students in the vacation, young married women like Cherry Baker, who lived in spurious Closes on new building developments.

There were still, of course, people like Miss Knight. This last thought came suddenly as Miss Knight's tread overhead made the lustres on the mantelpiece tinkle warningly. Miss Knight had obviously had her afternoon rest and would now go out for her afternoon walk. In a moment she would come to ask Miss Marple if she could get her anything in the town. The thought of Miss Knight brought the usual reaction to Miss Marple's mind. Of course, it was very generous of dear Raymond (her nephew) and nobody could be kinder than Miss Knight, and of course that attack of bronchitis *had* left her very weak, and Dr Haydock had said very firmly that she must not go on sleeping alone in the house with only someone coming in daily, but – She stopped there. Because it was no use going on with the thought which was 'If only it could have been someone other than Miss Knight.' But there wasn't much choice for elderly ladies nowadays. Devoted maidservants had gone out of fashion. In real illness you could have a proper hospital nurse, at vast expense and procured with difficulty, or you could go to hospital. But after the critical phase of illness had passed, you were down to the Miss Knights.

There wasn't, Miss Marple reflected, anything wrong about the Miss Knights other than the fact that they were madly irritating. They were full of kindness, ready to feel affection towards their charges, to humour them, to be bright and cheerful with them and in general to treat them as slightly mentally afflicted children.

'But I,' said Miss Marple to herself, 'although I may be old, am *not* a mentally retarded child.'

At this moment, breathing rather heavily, as was her custom, Miss Knight bounced brightly into the room. She was a big, rather flabby woman of fifty-six with yellowing grey hair very elaborately arranged, glasses, a long thin nose, and below it a good-natured mouth and a weak chin.

'Here we are!' she exclaimed with a kind of beaming boisterousness, meant to cheer and enliven the sad twilight of the aged. 'I hope *we've* had our little snooze?'

'*I* have been knitting,' Miss Marple replied, putting some emphasis on the pronoun, 'and,' she went on, confessing her weakness with distaste and shame, 'I've dropped a stitch.'

'Oh dear, dear,' said Miss Knight. 'Well, we'll soon put that right, won't we?'

'*You* will,' said Miss Marple. '*I*, alas, am unable to do so.'

The slight acerbity of her tone passed quite unnoticed. Miss Knight, as always, was eager to help.

'There,' she said after a few moments. 'There you are, dear. Quite all right now.'

Though Miss Marple was perfectly agreeable to be called 'dear' (and even 'ducks') by the woman at the greengrocer or the girl at the paper shop, it annoyed her intensely to be called 'dear' by Miss Knight. Another of those things that elderly ladies have to bear. She thanked Miss Knight politely.

'And now I'm just going out for my wee toddle,' said Miss Knight humorously. 'Shan't be long.'

'Please don't dream of hurrying back,' said Miss Marple politely and sincerely.

'Well, I don't like to leave you too long on your own, dear, in case you get moped.'

'I assure you I am quite happy,' said Miss Marple. 'I probably shall have' (she closed her eyes) 'a little nap.'

'That's right, dear. Anything I can get you?'

Miss Marple opened her eyes and considered.

'You might go into Longdon's and see if the curtains are ready. And perhaps another skein of the blue wool from Mrs Wisley. And a box of blackcurrant lozenges at the chemist's. And change my book at the library – but don't let them give you anything that isn't on my list. This last one was too terrible. I couldn't read it.' She held out *The Spring Awakens*.

'Oh dear dear! Didn't you like it? I thought you'd love it. Such a pretty story.'

'And if it isn't too far for you, perhaps you wouldn't mind going as far as Halletts and see if they have one of those up-and-down egg whisks – *not* the turn-the-handle kind.'

(She knew very well they had nothing of the kind, but Halletts was the farthest shop possible.)

'If all this isn't too much – ' she murmured.

But Miss Knight replied with obvious sincerity.

'Not at all. I shall be delighted.'

Miss Knight loved shopping. It was the breath of life to her. One met acquaintances, and had the chance of a chat, one gossiped with the assistants, and had the opportunity of examining various articles in the various shops. And one could spend quite a long time engaged in these pleasant occupations without any guilty feeling that it was one's duty to hurry back.

So Miss Knight started off happily, after a last glance at the frail old lady resting so peacefully by the window.

After waiting a few minutes in case Miss Knight should return for a shopping bag, or her purse, or a handkerchief (she was a great forgetter and returner), and also to recover from the slight mental fatigue induced by thinking of so many unwanted things to ask Miss Knight to get, Miss Marple rose briskly to her feet, cast aside her knitting and strode purposefully across the room and into the hall. She took down her summer coat from its peg, a stick from the hall stand and exchanged her bedroom slippers for a pair of stout walking shoes. Then she left the house by the side door.

'It will take her at least an hour and a half,' Miss Marple estimated to herself. 'Quite that – with all the people from the Development doing their shopping.'

Miss Marple visualized Miss Knight at Longdon's making abortive inquiries re curtains. Her surmises were remarkably accurate. At this moment Miss Knight was exclaiming, 'Of course, I felt quite sure in

329

my own mind they wouldn't be ready yet. But of course I said I'd come along and see when the old lady spoke about it. Poor old dears, they've got so little to look forward to. One must humour them. And she's a sweet old lady. Failing a little now, it's only to be expected – their faculties get dimmed. Now that's a pretty material you've got there. Do you have it in any other colours?'

A pleasant twenty minutes passed. When Miss Knight had finally departed, the senior assistant remarked with a sniff, 'Failing, is she? I'll believe that when I see it for myself. Old Miss Marple has always been as sharp as a needle, and I'd say she still is.' She then gave her attention to a young woman in tight trousers and a sail-cloth jersey who wanted plastic material with crabs on it for bathroom curtains.

'Emily Waters, that's who she reminds me of,' Miss Marple was saying to herself, with the satisfaction it always gave her to match up a human personality with one known in the past. 'Just the same bird brain. Let me see, what happened to Emily?'

Nothing much, was her conclusion. She had once nearly got engaged to a curate, but after an understanding of several years the affair had fizzled out. Miss Marple dismissed her nurse attendant from her mind and gave her attention to her surroundings. She had traversed the garden rapidly only observing as it were from the corner of her eye that Laycock had cut down the old-fashioned roses in a way more suitable to hybrid teas, but she did not allow this to distress her, or distract her from the delicious pleasure of having escaped for an outing entirely on her own. She had a happy feeling of adventure. She turned to the right, entered the Vicarage gate, took the path through the Vicarage garden and came out on the right of way. Where the stile had been there was now an iron swing gate giving on to a tarred asphalt path. This led to a neat little bridge over the stream and on the other side of the stream where once there had been meadows with cows, there was the Development.

CHAPTER TWO

With the feeling of Columbus setting out to discover a new world, Miss Marple passed over the bridge, continued on to the path and within four minutes was actually in Aubrey Close.

Of course Miss Marple had seen the Development from the Market Basing Road, that is, had seen from afar its Closes and rows of neat well-built houses, with their television masts and their blue and pink and yellow and green painted doors and windows. But until now it had only had the reality of a map, as it were. She had not been in it and of it. But now she was here, observing the brave new world that was springing up, the world that by all accounts was foreign to all she had known. It was like a neat model built with child's bricks. It hardly seemed real to Miss Marple.

The people, too, looked unreal. The trousered young women, the rather sinister-looking young men and boys, the exuberant bosoms of the fifteen-year-old girls. Miss Marple couldn't help thinking that it all looked terribly depraved. Nobody noticed her much as she trudged along. She turned out of Aubrey Close and was presently in Darlington Close. She went slowly and as she went she listened avidly to the snippets of conversation between mothers wheeling prams, to the girls addressing young men, to the sinister-looking Teds (she supposed they were Teds) exchanging dark remarks with each other. Mothers came out on doorsteps calling to their children who, as usual, were busy doing all the things they had been told not to do. Children, Miss Marple reflected gratefully, never changed. And presently she began to smile, and noted down in her mind her usual series of recognitions.

That woman is just like Carry Edwards – and the dark one is just like that Hooper girl – she'll make a mess of her marriage just like Mary Hooper did. Those boys – the dark one is just like Edward Leeke, a lot of wild talk but no harm in him – a nice boy really – the fair one is Mrs Bedwell's Josh all over again. Nice boys, both of them. The one like Gregory Binns

331

won't do very well, I'm afraid. I expect he's got the same sort of mother . . .

She turned a corner into Walsingham Close and her spirits rose every moment.

The new world was the same as the old. The houses were different, the streets were called Closes, the clothes were different, the voices were different, but the human beings were the same as they always had been. And though using slightly different phraseology, the subjects of conversation were the same.

By dint of turning corners in her exploration, Miss Marple had rather lost her sense of direction and had arrived at the edge of the housing estate again. She was now in Carrisbrook Close, half of which was still 'under construction'. At the first floor window of a nearly finished house a young couple were standing. Their voices floated down as they discussed the amenities.

'You must admit it's a nice position, Harry.'

'Other one was just as good.'

'This one's got two more rooms.'

'And you've got to pay for them.'

'Well, I *like* this one.'

'You would!'

'Ow, don't be such a spoil-sport. You know what Mum said.'

'Your Mum never stops saying.'

'Don't you say nothing against Mum. Where'd I have been without her? And she might have cut up nastier than she did. She could have taken you to court.'

'Oh, come off it, Lily.'

'It's a good view of the hills. You can almost see – ' She leaned far out, twisting her body to the left. 'You can almost see the reservoir – '

She leant farther still, not realizing that she was resting her weight on loose boards that had been laid across the sill. They slipped under the pressure of her body, sliding outwards, carrying her with them. She screamed, trying to regain her balance.

'Harry – '

The young man stood motionless – a foot or two behind her. He took one step backwards –

Desperately, clawing at the wall, the girl righted herself. 'Oo!' She let out a frightened breath. 'I near as nothing fell out. Why didn't you get hold of me?'

'It was all so quick. Anyway you're all right.'

332

'That's all you know about it. I nearly went, I tell you. And look at the front of my jumper, it's all mussed.'

Miss Marple went on a little way, then on impulse, she turned back.

Lily was outside in the road waiting for the young man to lock up the house.

Miss Marple went up to her and spoke rapidly in a low voice.

'If I were you, my dear, I shouldn't marry that young man. You want someone whom you can rely upon if you're in danger. You must excuse me for saying this to you – but I feel you ought to be warned.'

She turned away and Lily stared after her.

'Well, of all the – '

Her young man approached.

'What was she saying to you, Lil?'

Lily opened her mouth – then shut it again.

'Giving me the gipsy's warning if you want to know.'

She eyed him in a thoughtful manner.

Miss Marple in her anxiety to get away quickly, turned a corner, stumbled over some loose stones and fell.

A woman came running out of one of the houses.

'Oh dear, what a nasty spill! I hope you haven't hurt yourself?'

With almost excessive goodwill she put her arms round Miss Marple and tugged her to her feet.

'No bones broken, I hope? There we are. I expect you feel rather shaken.'

Her voice was loud and friendly. She was a plump squarely built woman of about forty, brown hair just turning grey, blue eyes, and a big generous mouth that seemed to Miss Marple's rather shaken gaze to be far too full of white shining teeth.

'You'd better come inside and sit down and rest a bit. I'll make you a cup of tea.'

Miss Marple thanked her. She allowed herself to be led through the blue-painted door and into a small room full of bright cretonne-covered chairs and sofas.

'There you are,' said her rescuer, establishing her on a cushioned arm-chair. 'You sit quiet and I'll put the kettle on.'

She hurried out of the room which seemed rather restfully quiet after her departure. Miss Marple took a deep breath. She was not really hurt, but the fall had shaken her. Falls at her age were not to be encouraged. With luck, however, she thought guiltily, Miss

333

Knight need never know. She moved her arms and legs gingerly. Nothing broken. If she could only get home all right. Perhaps, after a cup of tea –

The cup of tea arrived almost as the thought came to her. Brought on a tray with four sweet biscuits on a little plate.

'There you are.' It was placed on a small table in front of her. 'Shall I pour it out for you? Better have plenty of sugar.'

'No sugar, thank you.'

'You must have sugar. Shock, you know. I was abroad with ambulances during the war. Sugar's wonderful for shock.' She put four lumps in the cup and stirred vigorously. 'Now you get that down, and you'll feel as right as rain.'

Miss Marple accepted the dictum.

'A kind woman,' she thought. 'She reminds me of someone – now who is it?'

'You've been very kind to me,' she said, smiling.

'Oh, that's nothing. The little ministering angel, that's me. I love helping people.' She looked out of the window as the latch of the outer gate clicked. 'Here's my husband home. Arthur – we've got a visitor.'

She went out into the hall and returned with Arthur who looked rather bewildered. He was a thin pale man, rather slow in speech.

'This lady fell down – right outside our gate, so of course I brought her in.'

'Your wife is very kind, Mr – '

'Badcock's the name.'

'Mr Badcock, I'm afraid I've given her a lot of trouble.'

'Oh, no trouble to Heather. Heather enjoys doing things for people.' He looked at her curiously. 'Were you on your way anywhere in particular?'

'No, I was just taking a walk. I live in St Mary Mead, the house beyond the Vicarage. My name is Marple.'

'Well, I never!' exclaimed Heather. 'So *you're* Miss Marple. I've heard about you. You're the one who does all the murders.'

'Heather! What *do* you – '

'Oh, you know what I mean. Not actually *do* murders – find out about them. That's right, isn't it?'

Miss Marple murmured modestly that she *had* been mixed up in murders once or twice.

'I heard there have been murders here, in this village. They were talking about it the other night at the Bingo Club. There was one at Gossington Hall. I wouldn't buy a place where there'd been a murder. I'd be sure it was haunted.'

'The murder wasn't committed in Gossington Hall. A dead body was brought there.'

'Found in the library on the hearthrug, that's what they said?' Miss Marple nodded.

'Did you ever? Perhaps they're going to make a film of it. Perhaps that's why Marina Gregg has bought Gossington Hall.'

'Marina Gregg?'

'Yes. She and her husband. I forget his name – he's a producer, I think, or a director – Jason something. But Marina Gregg, she's lovely, isn't she? Of course she hasn't been in so many pictures of late years – she was ill for a long time. But I still think there's never anybody like her. Did you see her in *Carmenella*. And *The Price of Love*, and *Mary of Scotland*? She's not so young any more, but she'll always be a wonderful actress. I've always been a terrific fan of hers. When I was a teenager I used to dream about her. The big thrill of my life was when there was a big show in aid of the St John Ambulance in Bermuda, and Marina Gregg came to open it. I was mad with excitement, and then on the very day I went down with a temperature and the doctor said I couldn't go. But I wasn't going to be beaten. I didn't actually feel too bad. So I got up and put a lot of make-up on my face and went along. I was introduced to her and she talked to me for quite three minutes and gave me her autograph. It was wonderful. I've never forgotten that day.'

Miss Marple stared at her.

'I hope there were no – unfortunate after-effects?' she said anxiously.

Heather Badcock laughed.

'None at all. Never felt better. What I say is, if you want a thing you've got to take risks. I always do.'

She laughed again, a happy strident laugh.

Arthur Badcock said admiringly. 'There's never any holding Heather. She always gets away with things.'

'Alison Wilde,' murmured Miss Marple, with a nod of satisfaction.

'Pardon?' said Mr Badcock.

'Nothing. Just someone I used to know.'

Heather looked at her inquiringly.

'You reminded me of her, that is all.'

'Did I? I hope she was nice.'

335

'She was very nice indeed,' said Miss Marple slowly. 'Kind, healthy, full of life.'

'But she had her faults, I suppose?' laughed Heather. 'I have.'

'Well, Alison always saw her own point of view so clearly that she didn't always see how things might appear to, or affect, other people.'

'Like the time you took in that evacuated family from a condemned cottage and they went off with all our teaspoons,' Arthur said.

'But Arthur! – I couldn't have turned them away. It wouldn't have been kind.'

'They were family spoons,' said Mr Badcock sadly. 'Georgian. Belonged to my mother's grandmother.'

'Oh, do forget those old spoons, Arthur. You do harp so.'

'I'm not very good at forgetting, I'm afraid.'

Miss Marple looked at him thoughtfully.

'What's your friend doing now?' asked Heather of Miss Marple with kindly interest.

Miss Marple paused a moment before answering.

'Alison Wilde? Oh – she died.'

CHAPTER THREE

'I'm glad to be back,' said Mrs Bantry. 'Although, of course, I've had a wonderful time.'

Miss Marple nodded appreciatively, and accepted a cup of tea from her friend's hand.

When her husband, Colonel Bantry, had died some years ago, Mrs Bantry had sold Gossington Hall and the considerable amount of land attached to it, retaining for herself what had been the East Lodge, a charming porticoed little building replete with inconvenience, where even a gardener had refused to live. Mrs Bantry had added to it the essentials of modern life, a built-on kitchen of the latest type, a new water supply from the main, electricity, and bathroom. This had all cost her a great deal, but not nearly so much as an attempt to live at Gossington Hall would have done. She had also retained the essentials of privacy, about three quarters of an acre of garden nicely ringed with trees, so that, as she explained. 'Whatever they do with Gossington I shan't really see it or worry.'

For the last few years she had spent a good deal of the year travelling about, visiting children and grandchildren in various parts of the globe, and coming back from time to time to enjoy the privacies of her own home. Gossington Hall itself had changed hands once or twice. It had been run as a guest house, failed, and been bought by four people who had shared it as four roughly divided flats and subsequently quarrelled. Finally the Ministry of Health had bought it for some obscure purpose for which they eventually did not want it. The Ministry had now resold it – and it was this sale which the two friends were discussing.

'I have heard rumours, of course,' said Miss Marple.

'Naturally,' said Mrs Bantry. 'It was even said that Charlie Chaplin and all his children were coming to live here. That would have been wonderful fun; unfortunately there isn't a word of truth in it. No, it's definitely Marina Gregg.'

'How very lovely she was,' said Miss Marple with a sigh. 'I always remember those early films of hers. *Bird of Passage* with that handsome Joel Roberts. And the Mary, Queen of Scots film. And of course it was very sentimental, but I *did* enjoy *Comin' thru the Rye*. Oh dear, that was a long time ago.'

'Yes,' said Mrs Bantry. 'She must be – what do you think? Forty-five? Fifty?'

Miss Marple thought nearer fifty.

'Has she been in anything lately? Of course I don't go very often to the cinema nowadays.'

'Only small parts, I think,' said Mrs Bantry. 'She hasn't been a star for quite a long time. She had that bad nervous breakdown. After one of her divorces.'

'Such a lot of husbands they all have,' said Miss Marple. 'It must really be quite tiring.'

'It wouldn't suit *me*,' said Mrs Bantry. 'After you've fallen in love with a man and married him and got used to his ways and settled down comfortably – to go and throw it all up and start again! It seems to me madness.'

'I can't presume to speak,' said Miss Marple with a little spinsterish cough, 'never having married. But it seems, you know, a *pity*.'

'I suppose they can't help it really,' said Mrs Bantry vaguely. 'With the kind of lives they have to live. So public, you know.

337

I met her,' she added. 'Marina Gregg, I mean, when I was in California.'

'What was she like?' Miss Marple asked with interest.

'Charming,' said Mrs Bantry. 'So natural and unspoiled.' She added thoughtfully, 'It's like a kind of livery really.'

'What is?'

'Being unspoiled and natural. You learn how to do it, and then you have to go on being it all the time. Just think of the hell of it – never to be able to chuck something, and say, "Oh, for the Lord's sake stop bothering me." I dare say that in sheer self-defence you have to have drunken parties or orgies.'

'She's had five husbands, hasn't she?' Miss Marple asked.

'At least. An early one that didn't count, and then a foreign Prince or Count, and then another film star, Robert Truscott, wasn't it? That was built up as a great romance. But it only lasted four years. And then Isidore Wright, the playwright. That was rather serious and quiet, and she had a baby – apparently she'd always longed to have a child – she's even half-adopted a few strays – anyway this was the real thing. Very much built up. Motherhood with a capital M. And then, I believe, it was an imbecile, or queer or something – and it was after that, that she had this breakdown and started to take drugs and all that, and threw up her parts.'

'You seem to know a lot about her,' said Miss Marple.

'Well, naturally,' said Mrs Bantry. 'When she bought Gossington I was interested. She married the present man about two years ago, and they say she's quite all right again now. He's a producer – or do I mean a director? I always get mixed. He was in love with her when they were quite young, but he didn't amount to very much in those days. But now, I believe, he's got quite famous. What's his name now? Jason – Jason something – Jason Hudd, no Rudd, that's it. They've bought Gossington because it's handy for' – she hesitated – 'Elstree?' she hazarded.

Miss Marple shook her head.

'I don't think so,' she said. 'Elstree's in North London.'

'It's the fairly new studios. Hellingforth – that's it. Sounds so Finnish, I always think. About six miles from Market Basing. She's going to do a film on Elizabeth of Austria, I believe.'

'What a lot you know,' said Miss Marple. 'About the private lives of film stars. Did you learn it all in California?'

'Not really,' said Mrs Bantry. 'Actually I get it from the extraordinary magazines I read at my hairdresser's. Most of the stars I don't even know by name, but as I said because Marina Gregg and her husband have bought Gossington, I was interested. Really the things those magazines say! I don't suppose half of it is true – probably not a quarter. I *don't* believe Marina Gregg is a nymphomaniac, I *don't* think she drinks, probably she doesn't even take drugs, and quite likely she just went away to have a nice rest and didn't have a nervous breakdown at all! – but it's true that she is coming here to live.'

'Next week, I heard,' said Miss Marple.

'As soon as that? I know she's lending Gossington for a big fête on the twenty-third in aid of the St John Ambulance Corps. I suppose they've done a lot to the house?'

'Practically everything,' said Miss Marple. 'Really it would have been much simpler, and probably cheaper, to have pulled it down and built a new house.'

'Bathrooms, I suppose?'

'Six new ones, I hear. And a palm court. And a pool. And what I believe they call picture windows, and they've knocked your husband's study and the library into one to make a music room.'

'Arthur will turn in his grave. You know how he hated music. Tone deaf, poor dear. His face, when some kind friend took us to the opera! He'll probably come back and haunt them.' She stopped and then said abruptly. 'Does anyone ever hint that Gossington might be haunted?'

Miss Marple shook her head.

'It isn't,' she said with certainty.

'That wouldn't prevent people saying it was,' Mrs Bantry pointed out.

'Nobody ever has said so.' Miss Marple paused and then said. 'People aren't really foolish, you know. Not in villages.'

Mrs Bantry shot her a quick look. 'You've always stuck to that, Jane. And I won't say that you're not right.'

She suddenly smiled.

'Marina Gregg asked me, very sweetly and delicately, if I wouldn't find it very painful to see my old home occupied by strangers. I assured her that it wouldn't hurt me at all. I don't think she quite believed me. But after all, as you know, Jane, Gossington wasn't our home. We weren't brought up there as children – that's what really counts. It was just a house with a nice bit of shooting and fishing attached, that we bought when Arthur retired. We thought of it, I remember, as a house that would be nice and easy to run! How we can ever have thought that, I can't imagine! All those staircases and passages. Only four servants! *Only*! Those were the days, ha ha!' She added suddenly: 'What's all this about your falling down? That Knight woman ought not to let you go out by yourself.'

'It wasn't poor Miss Knight's fault. I gave her a lot of shopping to do and then I – '

'Deliberately gave her the slip? I see. Well, you shouldn't do it, Jane. Not at your age.'

'How did you hear about it?'

Mrs Bantry grinned.

'You can't keep any secrets in St Mary Mead. You've often told me so. Mrs Meavy told me.'

'Mrs Meavy?' Miss Marple looked at sea.

'She comes in daily. She's from the Development.'

'Oh, the Development.' The usual pause happened.

'What were you doing in the Development?' asked Mrs Bantry, curiously.

'I just wanted to see it. To see what the people were like.'

'And what did you think they were like?'

'Just the same as everyone else. I don't quite know if that was disappointing or reassuring.'

'Disappointing, I should think.'

'No. I think it's reassuring. It makes you – well – recognize certain types – so that when anything occurs – one will understand quite well why and for what reason.'

'Murder, do you mean?'

Miss Marple looked shocked.

'I don't know why you should assume that I think of murder *all* the time.'

'Nonsense, Jane. Why don't you come out boldly and call yourself a criminologist and have done with it?'

'Because I am nothing of the sort,' said Miss Marple with spirit. 'It is simply that I have a certain knowledge of human nature – that is only natural after having lived in a small village all my life.'

'You probably have something there,' said Mrs Bantry thought-fully, 'though most people wouldn't agree, of course. Your nephew Raymond always used to say this place was a complete backwater.'

'Dear Raymond,' said Miss Marple indulgently. She added: 'He's always been so kind. He's paying for Miss Knight, you know.'

The thought of Miss Knight induced a new train of thought and she arose and said: 'I'd better be going back now, I suppose.'

'You didn't walk all the way here, did you?'

'Of course not. I came in Inch.'

This somewhat enigmatic pronouncement was received with complete understanding. In days very long past, Mr Inch had been the proprietor of two cabs, which met trains at the local station and which were also hired by the local ladies to take them 'calling', out to tea parties, and occasionally, with their daughters, to such frivolous entertainments as dances. In the fullness of time Inch, a cheery red-faced man of seventy odd, gave place to his son – known as 'young Inch' (he was then aged forty-five) though old Inch still continued to drive such elderly ladies as considered his son too young and irresponsible. To keep up with the times, young Inch abandoned horse vehicles for motor cars. He was not very good with machinery and in due course a certain Mr Bardwell took over from him. The name Inch persisted. Mr Bardwell in due course sold out to Mr Roberts, but in the telephone book *Inch's Taxi Service* was still the official name, and the older ladies of the community continued to refer to their journeys as going somewhere 'in Inch', as though they were Jonah and Inch was a whale.

II

'Dr Haydock called,' said Miss Knight reproachfully. 'I told him you'd gone to tea with Mrs Bantry. He said he'd call in again tomorrow.'

She helped Miss Marple off with her wraps.

'And now, I expect, we're tired out,' she said accusingly.

'*You* may be,' said Miss Marple. '*I* am not.'

'You come and sit cosy by the fire,' said Miss Knight, as usual paying no attention. ('You don't need to take much notice of what the old dears say. I just humour them.') 'And how would we fancy a nice cup of Ovaltine? Or Horlicks for a change?'

Miss Marple thanked her and said she would like a small glass of dry sherry. Miss Knight looked disapproving.

'I don't know what the doctor would say to that, I'm sure,' she said, when she returned with the glass.

'We will make a point of asking him tomorrow morning,' said Miss Marple.

On the following morning Miss Knight met Dr Haydock in the hall, and did some agitated whispering.

341

The elderly doctor came into the room rubbing his hands, for it was a chilly morning.

'Here's our doctor to see us,' said Miss Knight gaily. 'Can I take your gloves, Doctor?'

'They'll be all right here,' said Haydock, casting them carelessly on a table. 'Quite a nippy morning.'

'A little glass of sherry perhaps?' suggested Miss Marple.

'I heard you were taking to drink. Well, you should never drink alone.'

The decanter and the glasses were already on a small table by Miss Marple. Miss Knight left the room.

Dr Haydock was a very old friend. He had semi-retired, but came to attend certain of his old patients.

'I hear you've been falling about,' he said as he finished his glass. 'It won't do, you know, not at your age. I'm warning you. And I hear you didn't want to send for Sandford.'

Sandford was Haydock's partner.

'That Miss Knight of yours sent for him anyway – and she was quite right.'

'I was only bruised and shaken a little. Dr Sandford said so. I could have waited quite well until you were back.'

'Now look here, my dear. I can't go on for ever. And Sandford, let me tell you, has better qualifications than I have. He's a first class man.'

'The young doctors are all the same,' said Miss Marple. 'They take your blood pressure, and whatever's the matter with you, you get some kind of mass produced variety of new pills. Pink ones, yellow ones, brown ones. Medicine nowadays is just like a supermarket – all packaged up.'

'Serve you right if I prescribed leeches, and black draught, and rubbed your chest with camphorated oil.'

'I do that myself when I've got a cough,' said Miss Marple with spirit, 'and very comforting it is.'

'We don't like getting old, that's what it is,' said Haydock gently. 'I hate it.'

'You're quite a young man compared to me,' said Miss Marple. 'And I don't really mind getting old – not that in itself. It's the lesser indignities.'

'I think I know what you mean.'

'Never being alone! The difficulty of getting out for a few minutes by oneself. And even my knitting – such a comfort that has always been, and I really am a good knitter. Now I drop stitches all the time – and quite often I don't even know I've dropped them.'

Haydock looked at her thoughtfully.

Then his eyes twinkled.

'There's always the opposite.'

'Now what do you mean by that?'

'If you can't knit, what about unravelling for a change? Penelope did.'

'I'm hardly in her position.'

'But unravelling's rather in your line, isn't it?'

He rose to his feet.

'I must be getting along. What I'd prescribe for you is a nice juicy murder.'

'That's an outrageous thing to say!'

'Isn't it? However, you can always make do with the depth the parsley sank into the butter on a summer's day. I always wondered about that. Good old Holmes. A period piece, nowadays, I suppose. But he'll never be forgotten.'

Miss Knight bustled in after the doctor had gone.

'There,' he said, 'we look *much* more cheerful. Did the doctor recommend a tonic?'

'He recommended me to take an interest in murder.'

'A nice detective story?'

'No,' said Miss Marple. 'Real life.'

'Goodness,' exclaimed Miss Knight. 'But there's not likely to be a murder in this quiet spot.'

'Murders,' said Miss Marple, 'can happen anywhere. And do.'

'At the Development, perhaps?' mused Miss Knight. 'A lot of those Teddy-looking boys carry knives.'

But the murder, when it came, was not at the Development.

CHAPTER FOUR

Mrs Bantry stepped back a foot or two, surveyed herself in the glass, made a slight adjustment to her hat (she was not used to wearing hats), drew on a pair of good quality leather gloves and left the lodge, closing the door carefully behind her. She had the most pleasurable anticipations of what lay in front of her. Some three weeks had passed since her talk with Miss Marple. Marina Gregg and her husband had arrived at Gossington Hall and were now more or less installed there.

There was to be a meeting there this afternoon of the main persons involved in the arrangements for the fête in aid of the St John Ambulance. Mrs Bantry was not among those on the committee, but she had received a note from Marina Gregg asking her to come and have tea beforehand. It had recalled their meeting in California and had been signed, 'Cordially, Marina Gregg.' It had been handwritten, not typewritten. There is no denying that Mrs Bantry was both pleased and flattered. After all, a celebrated film star is a celebrated film star and elderly ladies, though they may be of local importance, are aware of their complete unimportance in the world of celebrities. So Mrs Bantry had the pleased feeling of a child for whom a special treat had been arranged.

As she walked up the drive Mrs Bantry's keen eyes went from side to side registering her impressions. The place had been smartened up since the days when it had passed from hand to hand. 'No expense spared,' said Mrs Bantry to herself, nodding in satisfaction. The drive afforded no view of the flower garden and for that Mrs Bantry was just as pleased. The flower garden and its special herbaceous border had been her own particular delight in the far-off days when she had lived at Gossington Hall. She permitted regretful and nostalgic memories of her irises. The best iris garden of any in the country, she told herself with a fierce pride.

Faced by a new front door in a blaze of new paint she pressed the bell. The door was opened with gratifying promptness by what was undeniably an Italian butler. She was ushered by him straight to the room which had been Colonel Bantry's library. This, as she had already heard, had been thrown into one with the study. The result was impressive. The walls were panelled, the floor was parquet. At one end was a grand piano and halfway along the wall was a superb record player. At the other end of the room was a small island, as it were, which comprised Persian rugs, a tea-table and some chairs. By the tea-table sat Marina Gregg, and leaning against the mantelpiece was what Mrs Bantry at first thought to be the ugliest man she had ever seen.

Just a few moments previously when Mrs Bantry's hand had been advanced to press the bell, Marina Gregg had been saying in a soft, enthusiastic voice, to her husband:

'This place is right for me, Jinks, just right. It's what I've always wanted. *Quiet*. English quiet and the English countryside. I can see myself living here, living here all my life if need be. And we'll adopt the English way of life. We'll have afternoon tea every afternoon with China tea and my lovely Georgian tea service. And we'll look out of the window on those lawns and that English herbaceous border. I've come *home* at last, that's what I feel. I feel that I can settle down here, that I can be quiet and happy. It's going to be home, this place. That's what I feel. *Home*.'

And Jason Rudd (known to his wife as Jinks) had smiled at her. It was an acquiescent smile, indulgent, but it held its reserve because, after all, he had heard it very often before. Perhaps this time it would be true. Perhaps this *was* the place that Marina Gregg might feel at home. But he knew her early enthusiasms so well. She was always so sure that at last she had found exactly what she wanted. He said in his deep voice:

'That's grand, honey. That's just grand. I'm glad you like it.'

'Like it? I adore it. Don't you adore it too?'

'Sure,' said Jason Rudd. 'Sure.'

It wasn't too bad, he reflected to himself. Good, solidly built, rather ugly Victorian. It had, he admitted, a feeling of solidity and security. Now that the worst of its fantastic inconveniences had been ironed out, it would be quite reasonably comfortable to live in. Not a bad place to come back to from time to time. With luck, he thought, Marina wouldn't start taking a dislike to it for perhaps two years to two years and a half. It all depended.

Marina said, sighing softly:

'It's so wonderful to feel well again. Well and strong. Able to cope with things.'

And he said again: 'Sure, honey, sure.'

And it was at that moment that the door opened and the Italian butler had ushered in Mrs Bantry.

Marina Gregg's welcome was all that was charming. She came forward, hands outstretched, saying how delightful it was to meet Mrs Bantry again. And what a coincidence that they should have met that time in San Fransisco and that two years later she and Jinks should actually buy the house that had once belonged to Mrs Bantry. And she did hope, she really did hope that Mrs Bantry wouldn't mind terribly the way they'd pulled the house about and done things to it and she hoped she wouldn't feel that they were terrible intruders living here.

'Your coming to live here is one of the most exciting things that has ever happened to this place,' said Mrs Bantry cheerfully and she looked towards the mantelpiece. Whereupon, almost as an after-thought, Marina Gregg said:

'You don't know my husband, do you? Jason, this is Mrs Bantry.'

Mrs Bantry looked at Jason Rudd with some interest. Her first impression that this was one of the ugliest men she had ever seen became qualified. He had interesting eyes. They were, she thought, more deeply sunk in his head than any eyes she had seen. Deep quiet pools, said Mrs Bantry to herself, and felt like a romantic lady novelist. The rest of his face was distinctly craggy, almost ludicrously out of proportion. His nose jutted upwards and a little red paint would have transformed it into the nose of a clown very easily. He had, too, a clown's big sad mouth. Whether he was at this moment in a furious temper or whether he always looked as though he were in a furious temper she did not quite know. His voice when he spoke was unexpectedly pleasant. Deep and slow.

'A husband,' he said, 'is always an afterthought. But let me say with my wife that we're very glad to welcome you here. I hope you don't feel that it ought to be the other way about.'

'You must get it out of your head,' said Mrs Bantry, 'that I've been driven forth from my old home. It never *was* my old home. I've been congratulating myself ever since I sold it. It was a most inconvenient house to run. I liked the garden but the house became more and more of a worry. I've had a perfectly splendid time ever since travelling abroad and going and seeing my married daughters and my grandchildren and my friends in all different parts of the world.'

'Daughters,' said Marina Gregg, 'you have daughters and sons?'

'Two sons and two daughters,' said Mrs Bantry, 'and pretty widely spaced. One in Kenya, one in South Africa. One near Texas and the other, thank goodness, in London.'

'Four,' said Marina Gregg. 'Four – and grandchildren?'

'Nine up to date,' said Mrs Bantry. 'It's great fun being a grand-mother. You don't have any of the worry of parental responsibility. You can spoil them in the most unbridled way – '

Jason Rudd interrupted her. 'I'm afraid the sun catches your eyes,' he said, and went to a window to adjust the blind. 'You must tell us all about this delightful village,' he said as he came back.

He handed her a cup of tea.

'Will you have a hot scone or a sandwich, or this cake? We have an Italian cook and she makes quite good pastry and cakes. You see we have quite taken to your English afternoon tea.'

'Delicious tea too,' said Mrs Bantry, sipping the fragrant bever-age.

Marina Gregg smiled and looked pleased. The sudden nervous movement of her fingers which Jason Rudd's eyes had noticed a minute or two previously, was stilled again. Mrs Bantry looked at her hostess with great admiration. Marina Gregg's heyday had been before the rise to supreme importance of vital statistics. She could not have been described as Sex Incarnate, or 'The Bust' or 'The Torso'. She had been long and slim and willowy. The bones of her face and head had had some of the beauty associated with those of Garbo. She had brought personality to her pictures rather than mere sex. The sudden turn of her head, the opening of the deep lovely eyes, the faint quiver of her mouth, all these were what brought to one suddenly that feeling of breath-taking loveliness that comes not from regularity of feature but from sudden magic of the flesh that catches the onlooker unawares. She still had this quality though it was not now so easily apparent. Like many film and stage actresses she had what seemed to be a habit of turning off personality at will. She could retire into herself, be quiet, gentle, aloof, disappointing to an eager fan. And then suddenly the turn of the head, the movement of the hands, the sudden smile and the magic was there.

One of her greatest pictures had been *Mary, Queen of Scots*, and it was of her performance in that picture that Mrs Bantry was reminded now as she watched her. Mrs Bantry's eye switched to the husband. He too was watching Marina. Off guard for a moment, his

347

face expressed clearly his feelings. 'Good Lord,' said Mrs Bantry to herself, 'the man adores her.'

She didn't know why she should feel so surprised. Perhaps because film stars and their love affairs and their devotion were so written up in the Press, that one never expected to see the real thing with one's own eyes. On an impulse she said:

'I do hope you'll enjoy it here and that you'll be able to stay here some time. Do you expect to have the house for long?'

Marina opened wide surprised eyes as she turned her head. 'I want to stay here always,' she said. 'Oh, I don't mean that I shan't have to go away a lot. I shall, of course. There's a possibility of making a film in North Africa next year although nothing's settled yet. No, but this will be my home. I shall come back here. I shall always be able to come back here.' She sighed. 'That's what's so wonderful. To have found a *home* at last.'

'I see,' said Mrs Bantry, but at the same time she thought to herself, 'All the same I don't believe for a moment that it *will* be like that. I don't believe you're the kind that can ever settle down.'

Again she shot a quick surreptitious glance at Jason Rudd. He was not scowling now. Instead he was smiling, a sudden very sweet and unexpected smile, but it was a sad smile. 'He knows it too,' thought Mrs Bantry.

The door opened and a woman came in. 'Bartletts want you on the telephone, Jason,' she said.

'Tell them to call back.'

'They said it was urgent.'

He sighed and rose. 'Let me introduce you to Mrs Bantry,' he said. 'Ella Zielinsky, my secretary.'

'Have a cup of tea, Ella,' said Marina as Ella Zielinsky acknowledged the introduction with a smiling 'pleased to meet you.'

'I'll have a sandwich,' said Ella. 'I don't go for China tea.'

Ella Zielinsky was at a guess thirty-five. She wore a well cut suit, a ruffled blouse and appeared to breathe self-confidence. She had short-cut black hair and a wide forehead.

'You used to live here, so they tell me,' she said to Mrs Bantry.

'It's a good many years ago now,' said Mrs Bantry. 'After my husband's death I sold it and it's passed through several hands since then.'

'Mrs Bantry really says she doesn't hate the things we've done to it,' said Marina.

'I should be frightfully disappointed if you hadn't,' said Mrs Bantry.

'I came up here all agog. I can tell you the most splendid rumours have been going around the village.'

'Never knew how difficult it was to get hold of plumbers in this country,' said Miss Zielinsky, champing a sandwich in a businesslike way. 'Not that that's been really my job,' she went on.

'Everything is your job,' said Marina, 'and you know it is, Ella. The domestic staff and the plumbing and arguing with the builders.'

'They don't seem ever to have heard of a picture window in this country.'

Ella looked towards the window. 'It's a nice view, I must admit.'

'A lovely old-fashioned rural English scene,' said Marina. 'This house has got *atmosphere*.'

'It wouldn't look so rural if it wasn't for the trees,' said Ella Zielinsky. 'That housing estate down there grows while you look at it.'

'That's new since my time,' said Mrs Bantry.

'You mean there was nothing but the village when you lived here?'

Mrs Bantry nodded.

'It must have been hard to do your shopping.'

'I don't think so,' said Mrs Bantry. 'I think it was frightfully easy.'

'I understand having a flower garden,' said Ella Zielinsky, 'but you folk over here seem to grow all your vegetables as well. Wouldn't it be much easier to buy them – there's a supermarket?'

'It's probably coming to that,' said Mrs Bantry, with a sigh. 'They don't taste the same, though.'

'Don't spoil the atmosphere, Ella,' said Marina.

The door opened and Jason looked in. 'Darling,' he said to Marina, 'I hate to bother you but would you mind? They just want your private view about this.'

Marina sighed and rose. She trailed languidly towards the door. 'Always something,' she murmured. 'I'm so sorry, Mrs Bantry. I don't really think that this will take longer than a minute or two.'

'Atmosphere,' said Ella Zielinsky, as Marina went out and closed the door. 'Do you think the house has got atmosphere?'

'I can't say I ever thought of it that way,' said Mrs Bantry. 'It was just a house. Rather inconvenient in some ways and very nice and cosy in other ways.'

'That's what I should have thought,' said Ella Zielinsky. She cast a quick direct look at Mrs Bantry. 'Talking of atmosphere, when did the murder take place here?'

'No murder ever took place here,' said Mrs Bantry.

'Oh come now. The stories I've heard. There are always stories, Mrs Bantry. On the hearthrug, right there, wasn't it?' said Miss Zielinsky nodding towards the fireplace.

'Yes,' said Mrs Bantry. 'That was the place.'

'So there *was* a murder?'

Mrs Bantry shook her head. 'The murder didn't take place here. The girl who had been killed was brought here and planted in this room. She'd nothing to do with us.'

Miss Zielinsky looked interested.

'Possibly you had a bit of difficulty making people believe that?' she remarked.

'You're quite right there,' said Mrs Bantry.

'When did you find it?'

'The housemaid came in in the morning,' said Mrs Bantry, 'with early morning tea. We had housemaids then, you know.'

'I know,' said Miss Zielinksy, 'wearing print dresses that rustled.'

'I'm not sure about the print dress,' said Mrs Bantry, 'it may have been overalls by then. At any rate, she burst in and said there was a body in the library. I said "nonsense", then I woke up my husband and we came down to see.'

'And there it was,' said Miss Zielinsky. 'My, the way things happen.' She turned her head sharply towards the door and then back again. 'Don't talk about it to Miss Gregg, if you don't mind,' she said. 'It's not good for her, that sort of thing.'

'Of course. I won't say a word,' said Mrs Bantry. 'I never do talk about it, as a matter of fact. It all happened so long ago. But won't she – Miss Gregg I mean – won't she hear it anyway?'

'She doesn't come very much in contact with reality,' said Ella Zielinsky. 'Film stars can lead a fairly insulated life, you know. In fact very often one has to take care that they do. Things upset them. Things upset *her*. She's been seriously ill the last year or two, you know. She only started making a comeback a year ago.'

'She seems to like the house,' said Mrs Bantry, 'and to feel she will be happy here.'

'I expect it'll last a year or two,' said Ella Zielinsky.

'Not longer than that?'

'Well, I rather doubt it. Marina is one of those people, you know,

350

who are always thinking they've found their heart's desire. But life isn't as easy as that, is it?'

'No,' said Mrs Bantry forcefully, 'it isn't.'

'It'll mean a lot to him if she's happy here,' said Miss Zielinsky. She ate two more sandwiches in an absorbed, rather gobbling fashion in the manner of one who crams food into themselves as though they had an important train to catch. 'He's a genius, you know,' she went on. 'Have you seen any of the pictures he's directed?'

Mrs Bantry felt slightly embarrassed. She was of the type of woman who when she went to the cinema went entirely for the picture. The long lists of casts, directors, producers, photography and the rest of it passed her by. Very frequently, indeed, she did not even notice the names of the stars. She was not, however, anxious to call attention to this failing on her part.

'I get mixed up,' she said.

'Of course he's got a lot to contend with,' said Ella Zielinsky. 'He's got her as well as everything else and she's not easy. You've got to keep her happy, you see; and it's not really easy, I suppose, to keep people happy. Unless – that is – they – they are – ' she hesitated.

'Unless they're the happy kind,' suggested Mrs Bantry, 'Some people,' she added thoughtfully, 'enjoy being miserable.'

'Oh, Marina isn't like that,' said Ella Zielinsky, shaking her head. 'It's more that her ups and downs are so violent. You know – far too happy one moment, far too pleased with everything and delighted with everything and how wonderful she feels. Then of course some little thing happens and down she goes to the opposite extreme.'

'I suppose that's temperament,' said Mrs Bantry vaguely.

'That's right,' said Ella Zielinsky. 'Temperament. They've all got it, more or less, but Marina Gregg has got it more than most people. Don't we know it! The stories I could tell you!' She ate the last sandwich. 'Thank God I'm only the social secretary.'

CHAPTER FIVE

The throwing open of the grounds of Gossington Hall for the benefit of the St John Ambulance Association was attended by a quite unprecedented number of people. Shilling admission fees mounted up in a highly satisfactory fashion. For one thing, the weather was good, a clear sunny day. But the preponderant attraction was undoubtedly the enormous local curiosity to know exactly what these 'film people' had done to Gossington Hall. The most extravagant assumptions were entertained. The swimming pool in particular caused immense satisfaction. Most people's ideas of Hollywood stars were of sun-bathing by a pool in exotic surroundings and in exotic company. That the climate of Hollywood might be more suited to swimming pools than that of St Mary Mead failed to be considered. After all, England always has one fine hot week in the summer and there is always one day that the Sunday papers publish articles on How to Keep Cool, How to Have Cool Suppers and How to Make Cool Drinks. The pool was almost exactly what everyone had imagined it might be. It was large, its waters were blue, it had a kind of exotic pavilion for changing and was surrounded with a highly artificial plantation of hedges and shrubs. The reactions of the multitude were exactly as might have been expected and hovered over a wide range of remarks.

'O-oh, isn't it lovely!'

'Two penn'orth of splash here, all right!'

'Reminds me of that holiday camp I went to.'

'Wicked luxury *I* call it. It oughtn't to be allowed.'

'Look at all that fancy marble. It must have cost the earth!'

'Don't see why these people think they can come over here and spend all the money they like.'

'Perhaps this'll be on the telly sometime. That'll be fun.'

Even Mr Sampson, the oldest man in St Mary Mead, boasting proudly of being ninety-six though his relations insisted firmly that he was only eighty-six, had staggered along supporting his rheumatic legs with a stick, to see this excitement. He gave it his highest praise: 'Ah, there'll be a lot of wickedness here, I don't doubt. Naked men and women drinking and smoking what they call in the papers them reefers. There'll be all that, I expect. Ah yes,' said Mr Sampson with enormous pleasure, 'there'll be a lot of wickedness.'

It was felt that the final seal of approval had been set on the afternoon's entertainment. For an extra shilling people were allowed to go into the house, and study the new music room, the drawing-room, the completely unrecognizable dining-room, now done in dark oak and Spanish leather, and a few other joys.

'Never think this was Gossington Hall, would you, now?' said Mr Sampson's daughter-in-law.

Mrs Bantry strolled up fairly late and observed with pleasure that the money was coming in well and that the attendance was phenomenal.

The large marquee in which tea was being served was jammed with people. Mrs Bantry hoped the buns were going to go round. There seemed some very competent women, however, in charge. She herself made a bee-line for the herbaceous border and regarded it with a jealous eye. No expense had been spared on the herbacous border, she was glad to note, and it was a proper herbaceous border, well planned and arranged and expensively stocked. No personal labours had gone into it, she was sure of that. Some good gardening firm had been given the contract, no doubt. But aided by *carte blanche* and the weather, they had turned out a very good job.

Looking round her, she felt there was a faint flavour of a Buckingham Palace garden party about the scene. Everybody was craning to see all they could see, and from time to time a chosen few were led into one of the more secret recesses of the house. She herself was presently approached by a willowy young man with long wavy hair.

'Mrs Bantry? You *are* Mrs Bantry?'

'I'm Mrs Bantry, yes.'

'Hailey Preston.' He shook hands with her. 'I work for Mr Rudd. Will you come up to the second floor? Mr and Mrs Rudd are asking a few special friends up there.'

Duly honoured Mrs Bantry followed him. They went in through what had been called in her time the garden door. A red cord cordoned off the bottom of the main stairs. Hailey Preston unhooked it and she passed through. Just in front of her Mrs Bantry observed

Councillor and Mrs Allcock. The latter who was stout was breathing heavily.

'Wonderful what they've done, isn't it, Mrs Bantry?' panted Mrs Allcock. 'I'd like to have a look at the bathrooms, I must say, but I suppose I shan't get the chance.' Her voice was wistful.

At the top of the stairs Marina Gregg and Jason Rudd were receiving this specially chosen élite. What had once been a spare bedroom had been thrown into the landing so as to make a wide lounge-like effect. Giuseppe the butler was officiating with drinks.

A stout man in livery was announcing guests.

'Councillor and Mrs Allcock,' he boomed.

Marina Gregg was being, as Mrs Bantry had described her to Miss Marple, completely natural and charming. She could already hear Mrs Allcock saying later: '– and so *unspoiled*, you know, in spite of being so famous.'

How very nice of Mrs Allcock to come, *and* the Councillor, and she did hope they'd enjoy their afternoon. 'Jason please look after Mrs Allcock.'

Councillor and Mrs Allcock were passed on to Jason and drinks.

'Oh, Mrs Bantry, it *is* nice of you to come.'

'I wouldn't have missed it for the world,' said Mrs Bantry and moved on purposefully towards the Martinis.

The young man called Hailey Preston ministered to her in a tender manner and then made off, consulting a little list in his hand, to fetch, no doubt, more of the Chosen to the Presence. It was all being managed very well, Mrs Bantry thought, turning, Martini in hand, to watch the next arrivals. The vicar, a lean, ascetic man, was looking vague and slightly bewildered. He said earnestly to Marina Gregg:

'Very nice of you to ask me. I'm afraid, you know, I haven't got a television set myself, but of course I – er – I – well, of course my young people keep me up to the mark.'

Nobody knew what he meant. Miss Zielinsky, who was also on duty, administered a lemonade to him with a kindly smile. Mr and Mrs Badcock were next up the stairs. Heather Badcock, flushed and triumphant, came a little ahead of her husband.

'Mr and Mrs Badcock,' boomed the man in livery.

'Mrs Badcock,' said the vicar, turning back, lemonade in his hand, 'the indefatigable secretary of the association. She's one of our hardest workers. In fact I don't know what the St John would do without her.'

'I'm sure you've been wonderful,' said Marina.

'You don't remember me?' said Heather, in an arch manner. 'How should you, with all the hundreds of people you meet. And anyway, it was years ago. In Bermuda of all places in the world. I was there with one of our ambulance units. Oh, it's a long time ago now.'

'Of course,' said Marina Gregg, once more all charm and smiles.

'I remember it all so well,' said Mrs Badcock, 'I was thrilled, you know, absolutely thrilled. I was only a girl at the time. To think there was a chance of seeing Marina Gregg in the flesh – oh! I was a mad fan of yours always.'

'It's too kind of you, really too kind of you,' said Marina sweetly, her eyes beginning to hover faintly over Heather's shoulder towards the next arrivals.

'I'm not going to detain you,' said Heather – 'but I must – '

'Poor Marina Gregg,' said Mrs Bantry to herself. 'I suppose this kind of thing is always happening to her! The patience they need!'

Heather was continuing in a determined manner with her story.

Mrs Allcock breathed heavily at Mrs Bantry's shoulder.

'The changes they've made here! You wouldn't believe till you saw for yourself. What it must have *cost* . . .'

'I – didn't feel really ill – and I thought I just must – '

'This is vodka,' Mrs Allcock regarded her glass suspiciously. 'Mr Rudd asked if I'd like to try it. Sounds very Russian. I don't think I like it very much . . .'

'– I said to myself: I won't be beaten! I put a lot of make-up on my face – '

'I suppose it would be rude if I just put it down somewhere.' Mrs Allcock sounded desperate.

Mrs Bantry reassured her gently.

'Not at all. Vodka ought really to be thrown straight down the throat' – Mrs Allcock looked startled – 'but that needs practice. Put it down on the table and get yourself a Martini from that tray the butler's carrying.'

She turned back to hear Heather Badcock's triumphant peroration.

'I've never forgotten how wonderful you were that day. It was a hundred times worth it.'

Marina's response was this time not so automatic. Her eyes which had wavered over Heather Badcock's shoulder, now seemed to be fixed on the wall midway up the stairs. She was staring and there was something so ghastly in her expression that Mrs Bantry half took a step forward. Was the woman going to faint? What on earth could she be seeing that gave her that basilisk look? But before she could reach Marina's side the latter had recovered herself. Her eyes, vague and unfocussed, returned to Heather and the charm of manner was turned on once more, albeit a shade mechanically.

'What a nice little story. Now, what will you have to drink? Jason! A cocktail?'

'Well, really I usually have a lemonade or orange juice.'

'You must have something better than that,' said Marina. 'This is a feast day, remember.'

'Let me persuade you to an American daiquiri,' said Jason, appearing with a couple in his hand. 'They're Marina's favourites, too.'

He handed one to his wife.

'I shouldn't drink any more,' said Marina, 'I've had three already.' But she accepted the glass.

Heather took her drink from Jason. Marina turned away to meet the next person who was arriving.

Mrs Bantry said to Mrs Allcock, 'Let's go and see the bathrooms.'

'Oh, do you think we can? Wouldn't it look rather rude?'

'I'm sure it wouldn't,' said Mrs Bantry. She spoke to Jason Rudd. 'We want to explore your wonderful new bathrooms, Mr Rudd. May we satisfy this purely domestic curiosity?'

'Sure,' said Jason, grinning. 'Go and enjoy yourselves, girls. Draw yourselves baths if you like.'

Mrs Allcock followed Mrs Bantry along the passage.

'That was ever so kind of you, Mrs Bantry. I must say I wouldn't have dared myself.'

'One has to dare if one wants to get anywhere,' said Mrs Bantry.

They went along the passage, opening various doors. Presently 'Ahs' and 'Ohs' began to escape Mrs Allcock and two other women who had joined the party.

'I do like the pink one,' said Mrs Allcock. 'Oh, I like the pink one a lot.'

'I like the one with the dolphin tiles,' said one of the other women.

Mrs Bantry acted the part of hostess with complete enjoyment. For a moment she had really forgotten that the house no longer belonged to her.

'All those showers!' said Mrs Allcock with awe. 'Not that I really *like* showers. I never know how you keep your head dry.'

'It'd be nice to have a peep into the bedrooms,' said one of the other women, wistfully, 'but I suppose it'd be a bit *too* nosy. What do *you* think?'

'Oh, I don't think we could do *that*,' said Mrs Allcock. They both looked hopefully at Mrs Bantry.

'Well,' said Mrs Bantry, 'no, I suppose we oughtn't to – ' then she took pity on them, 'But – I don't think anyone would know if we have one peep.' She put her hand on a door-handle.

But that had been attended to. The bedrooms were locked. Everyone was very disappointed.

'I suppose they've got to have some privacy,' said Mrs Bantry kindly.

They retraced their steps along the corridors. Mrs Bantry looked out of one of the landing windows. She noted below her Mrs Meavy (from the Development) looking incredibly smart in a ruffled organdie dress. With Mrs Meavy, she noticed, was Miss Marple's Cherry, whose last name for the moment Mrs Bantry could not remember. They seemed to be enjoying themselves and were laughing and talking.

Suddenly the house felt to Mrs Bantry old, worn-out and highly artificial. In spite of its new gleaming paint, its alterations, it was in essence a tired old Victorian mansion. 'I was wise to go,' thought Mrs Bantry. 'Houses are like everything else. There comes a time when they've just had their day. This has had its day. It's been given a face lift, but I don't really think it's done it any good.'

Suddenly a slight rise in the hum of voices reached her. The two women with her started forward.

'What's happening?' said one. 'It sounds as though something's happening.'

They stepped back along the corridor towards the stairs. Ella Zielinksy came rapidly along and passed them. She tried a bedroom door and said quickly, 'Oh, damn. Of course they've locked them all.'

'Is anything the matter?' asked Mrs Bantry.

'Someone's taken ill,' said Miss Zielinsky shortly.

'Oh dear, I'm sorry. Can I do anything?'

'I suppose there's a doctor here somewhere?'

'I haven't seen any of our local doctors,' said Mrs Bantry, 'but there's almost sure to be one here.'

'Jason's telephoning,' said Ella Zielinsky, 'but she seems pretty bad.'

'Who is it?' asked Mrs Bantry.

'A Mrs Badcock, I think.'

'Heather Badcock? But she looked so well just now.'

Ella Zielinksy said impatiently, 'She's had a seizure, or a fit, or something. Do you know if there's anything wrong with her heart or anything like that?'

'I don't really know anything about her,' said Mrs Bantry. 'She's new since my day. She comes from the Development.'

'The Development? Oh, you mean that housing estate. I don't even know where her husband is or what he looks like.'

'Middle-aged, fair, unobtrusive,' said Mrs Bantry. 'He came with her so he must be about somewhere.'

Ella Zielinsky went into a bathroom. 'I don't know really what to give her,' she said. 'Sal volatile, do you think, something like that?'

'Is she faint?' said Mrs Bantry.

'It's more than that,' said Ella Zielinsky.

'I'll see if there's anything I can do,' said Mrs Bantry. She turned away and walked rapidly back towards the head of the stairs. Turning a corner she cannoned into Jason Rudd.

'Have you seen Ella?' he said, 'Ella Zielinsky?'

'She went along there into one of the bathrooms. She was looking for something. Sal volatile – something like that.'

'She needn't bother,' said Jason Rudd.

Something in his tone struck Mrs Bantry. She looked up sharply. 'Is it bad?' she said, 'really bad?'

'You could call it that,' said Jason Rudd. 'The poor woman's dead.'

'Dead!' Mrs Bantry was really shocked. She said, as she had said before, 'But she looked so well just now.'

'I know. I know,' said Jason. He stood there, scowling. 'What a thing to happen!'

CHAPTER SIX

'Here we are,' said Miss Knight, settling a breakfast tray on the bed-table beside Miss Marple. 'And how are we this morning? I see we've got our curtains pulled back,' she added with a slight note of disapproval in her voice.

'I wake early,' said Miss Marple. 'You probably will, when you're my age,' she added.

'Mrs Bantry rang up,' said Miss Knight, 'about half an hour ago. She wanted to talk to you but I said she'd better ring up again after you'd had your breakfast. I wasn't going to disturb you at that hour, before you'd even had a cup of tea or anything to eat.'

'When my friends ring up,' said Miss Marple, 'I prefer to be told.'

'I'm sorry, I'm sure,' said Miss Knight, 'but it seemed to me very inconsiderate. When you've had your nice tea and your boiled egg and your toast and butter, we'll see.'

'Half an hour ago,' said Miss Marple, thoughtfully, 'that would have been – let me see – eight o'clock.'

'Much too early,' reiterated Miss Knight.

'I don't believe Mrs Bantry would have rung me up then unless it was for some particular reason,' said Miss Marple thoughtfully. 'She doesn't usually ring up in the early morning.'

'Oh well, dear, don't fuss your head about it,' said Miss Knight soothingly. 'I expect she'll be ringing up again very shortly. Or would you like me to get her for you?'

'No thank you,' said Miss Marple. 'I prefer to eat my breakfast while it's hot.'

'Hope I haven't forgotten anything,' said Miss Knight, cheerfully.

But nothing had been forgotten. The tea had been properly made with boiling water, the egg had been boiled exactly three and three-quarter minutes, the toast was evenly browned, the butter was arranged in a nice little pat and the small jar of honey stood beside it. In many ways undeniably Miss Knight was a treasure. Miss Marple ate her breakfast and enjoyed it. Presently the whirr of a vacuum cleaner began below. Cherry had arrived.

Competing with the whirr of the vacuum cleaner was a fresh tuneful voice singing one of the latest popular tunes of the day. Miss Knight, coming in for the breakfast tray, shook her head.

'I really wish that young woman wouldn't go singing all over the house,' she said. 'It's not what I call respectful.'

Miss Marple smiled a little. 'It would never enter Cherry's head that she would have to be respectful,' she remarked 'Why should she?'

Miss Knight sniffed and said, 'Very different to what things used to be.'

'Naturally,' said Miss Marple. 'Times change. That is a thing which has to be accepted.' She added, 'Perhaps you'll ring up Mrs Bantry now and find out what it was she wanted.'

Miss Knight bustled away. A minute or two later there was a rap on the door and Cherry entered. She was looking bright and excited and extremely pretty. A plastic overall rakishly patterned with sailors and naval emblems was tied round her dark blue dress.

'Your hair looks nice,' said Miss Marple.

'Went for a perm yesterday,' said Cherry. 'A bit stiff still, but it's going to be all right. I came up to see if you'd heard the news.'

'What news?' said Miss Marple.

'About what happened at Gossington Hall yesterday. You know there was a big do there for the St John Ambulance?'

Miss Marple nodded. 'What happened?' she asked.

'Somebody died in the middle of it. A Mrs Badcock. Lives round the corner from us. I don't suppose you'd know her.'

'Mrs Badcock?' Miss Marple sounded alert. 'But I do know her. I think – yes, that was the name – she came out and picked me up when I fell down the other day. She was very kind.'

'Oh, Heather Badcock's kind all right,' said Cherry. 'Overkind, some people say. They call it interfering. Well, anyway, she up and died. Just like that.'

'Died! But what of?'

'Search me,' said Cherry. 'She'd been taken into the house because of her being the secretary of the St John Ambulance, I suppose. She and the mayor and a lot of others. As far as I heard, she had a glass of something and about five minutes later she was took bad and died before you could snap your fingers.'

'What a shocking occurrence,' said Miss Marple. 'Did she suffer from heart trouble?'

'Sound as a bell, so they say,' Cherry said. 'Of course, you never know, do you? I suppose you can have something wrong with your heart and nobody knowing about it. Anyway, I can tell you this. They've not sent her home.'

Miss Marple looked puzzled. 'What do you mean, not sent her home?'

'The body,' said Cherry, her cheerfulness unimpaired. 'The doctor said there'd have to be an autopsy. Postmortem – whatever you call it. He said he hadn't attended her for anything and there was nothing to show the cause of death. Looks funny to me,' she added.

'Now what do you mean by funny?' said Miss Marple.

'Well.' Cherry considered. 'Funny. As though there was something behind it.'

'Is her husband terribly upset?'

'Looks as white as a sheet. Never saw a man as badly hit, to look at – that is to say.'

Miss Marple's ears, long attuned to delicate nuances, led her to cock her head slightly on one side like an inquisitive bird.

'Was he so very devoted to her?'

'He did what she told him and gave her her own way,' said Cherry, 'but that doesn't always mean you're devoted, does it? It may mean you haven't got the courage to stick up for yourself.'

'You didn't like her?' asked Miss Marple.

'I hardly know her really,' said Cherry. 'Knew her, I mean. I don't – didn't – dislike her. But she's just not my type. Too interfering.'

'You mean inquisitive, nosy?'

'No, I don't,' said Cherry. 'I don't mean that at all. She was a very kind woman and she was always doing things for people. And she was always quite sure she knew the best thing to do. What they thought about it wouldn't have mattered. I had an aunt like that. Very fond of seed cake herself and she used to bake seed cakes for people and take them to them, and she never troubled to find out whether they liked seed cake or not. There are people can't bear it, just can't stand the flavour of caraway. Well, Heather Badcock was a bit like that.'

'Yes,' said Miss Marple thoughtfully, 'yes, she would have been. I knew someone a little like that. Such people,' she added, 'live dangerously – though they don't know it themselves.'

Cherry stared at her. 'That's a funny thing to say. I don't quite get what you mean.'

Miss Knight bustled in. 'Mrs Bantry seems to have gone out,' she said. 'She didn't say where she was going.'

'I can guess where she's going,' said Miss Marple. 'She's coming here. I shall get up now,' she added.

II

Miss Marple had just ensconced herself in her favourite chair by the window when Mrs Bantry arrived. She was slightly out of breath.

'I've got plenty to tell you, Jane,' she said.

'About the fête?' asked Miss Knight, 'you went to the fête yesterday, didn't you? I was there myself for a short time early in the afternoon. The tea tent was very crowded. An astonishing lot of people seemed to be there. I didn't catch a glimpse of Marina Gregg, though, which was rather disappointing.'

She flicked a little dust off a table and said brightly, 'Now I'm sure you two want to have a nice little chat together,' and went out of the room.

'She doesn't seem to know anything about it,' said Mrs Bantry. She fixed her friend with a keen glance. 'Jane, I believe you *do* know.'

'You mean about the death yesterday?'

'You always know everything,' said Mrs Bantry. 'I cannot think how.'

'Well, really dear,' said Miss Marple, 'in the same way one always has known everything. My daily helper, Cherry Baker, brought the news. I expect the butcher will be telling Miss Knight presently.'

'And what do you think of it?' said Mrs Bantry.

'What do I think of what?' said Miss Marple.

'Now don't be aggravating, Jane, you know perfectly what I mean. There's this woman – whatever her name is – '

'Heather Badcock,' said Miss Marple.

'She arrives full of life and spirit. I was there when she came. And about a quarter of an hour later she sits down in a chair, says she doesn't feel well, gasps a bit and dies. What do you think of *that*?'

'One mustn't jump to conclusions,' said Miss Marple. 'The point is, of course, what did a medical man think of it?'

Mrs Bantry nodded. 'There's to be an inquest and a post-mortem,' she said. 'That shows what they think of it, doesn't it?'

'Not necessarily,' said Miss Marple. 'Anyone may be taken ill and die suddenly and they have to have a post-mortem to find out the cause.'

'It's more than that,' said Mrs Bantry.

'How do you know?' said Miss Marple.

'Dr Sandford went home and rang up the police.'

'Who told you that?' said Miss Marple, with great interest.

'Old Briggs,' said Mrs Bantry. 'At least, he didn't tell me. You know he goes down after hours in the evening to see to Dr Sandford's garden, and he was clipping something quite close to the study and he heard the doctor ringing up the police station in Much Benham. Briggs told his daughter and his daughter mentioned it to the postwoman and she told me,' said Mrs Bantry.

Miss Marple smiled. 'I see,' she said, 'that St Mary Mead has not changed very much from what it used to be.'

'The grape vine is much the same,' agreed Mrs Bantry. 'Well, now, Jane, tell me what you think?'

'One thinks, of course, of the husband,' said Miss Marple reflectively. 'Was he there?'

'Yes, he was there. You don't think it would be suicide,' said Mrs Bantry.

'Certainly not suicide,' said Miss Marple decisively. 'She wasn't the type.'

'How did you come across her, Jane?'

'It was the day I went for a walk to the Development, and fell down near her house. She was kindness itself. She was a very kind woman.'

'Did you see the husband? Did he look as though he'd like to poison her?'

'You know what I mean,' Mrs Bantry went on as Miss Marple showed some slight signs of protesting. 'Did he remind you of Major Smith or Bertie Jones or someone you've known years ago who did poison a wife, or tried to?'

'No,' said Miss Marple, 'he didn't remind me of anyone I know.' She added, 'But she did.'

'Who – Mrs Badcock?'

'Yes,' said Miss Marple, 'she reminded me of someone called Alison Wilde.'

'And what was Alison Wilde like?'

'She didn't know at all,' said Miss Marple slowly, 'what the world was like. She didn't know what people were like. She'd never thought about them. And so, you see, she couldn't guard against things happening to her.'

'I don't really think I understand a word of what you're saying,' said Mrs Bantry.

'It's very difficult to explain exactly,' said Miss Marple, apologetically. 'It comes really from being self-centred and I don't mean selfish by that,' she added. 'You can be kind and unselfish and even thoughtful. But if you're like Alison Wilde, you never really know what you may be doing. And so you never know what may happen to you.'

'Can't you make that a little clearer?' said Mrs Bantry.

'Well, I suppose I could give you a sort of figurative example. This isn't anything that actually happened, it's just something I'm inventing.'

'Go on,' said Mrs Bantry.

'Well, supposing you went into a shop, say, and you knew the proprietress had a son who was the spivvy young juvenile delinquent type. He was there listening while you told his mother about some money you had in the house, or some silver or a piece of jewellery. It was something you were excited and pleased about and you wanted to talk about it. And you also perhaps mention an evening that you were going out. You even say that you never lock the house. You're interested in what you're saying, what you're telling her, because it's so very much in your mind. And then, say, on that particular evening you come home because you've forgotten something and there's this bad lot of a boy in the house, caught in the act, and he turns round and coshes you.'

'That might happen to almost anybody nowadays,' said Mrs Bantry.

'Not quite,' said Miss Marple, 'most people have a sense of protection. They realise when it's unwise to say or do something because of the person or persons who are taking in what you say, and because of the kind of character that those people have. But as I say, Alison Wilde never thought of anybody else but herself – She was the sort of person who tells you what they've done and what they've seen and what they've felt and what they've heard. They never mention what any other people said or did. Life is a kind of one-way track – just their own progress through it. Other people seem to them just like – like wall-paper in a room.' She paused and then said, 'I think Heather Badcock was that kind of person.'

Mrs Bantry said, 'You think she was the sort of person who might have butted into something without knowing what she was doing?'

'And without realising that it was a dangerous thing to do,' said Miss Marple. She added, 'It's the only reason I can possibly think of why she should have been killed. If of course,' added Miss Marple, 'we are right in assuming that murder *has* been committed.'

'You don't think she was blackmailing someone?' Mrs Bantry suggested.

'Oh, no,' Miss Marple assured her. 'She was a kind, good woman. She'd never have done anything of *that* kind.' She added vexedly, 'The whole thing seems to me very unlikely. I suppose it can't have been – '

'Well?' Mrs Bantry urged her.

'I just wondered if it might have been the wrong murder,' said Miss Marple thoughtfully.

The door opened and Dr Haydock breezed in, Miss Knight twittering behind him.

'Ah, at it already, I see,' said Dr Haydock, looking at the two ladies. 'I came in to see how your health was,' he said to Miss Marple, 'but I needn't ask. I see you've begun to adopt the treatment that I suggested.'

'Treatment, Doctor?'

Dr Haydock pointed a finger at the knitting that lay on the table beside her. 'Unravelling,' he said. 'I'm right, aren't I?'

Miss Marple twinkled very slightly in a discreet, old-fashioned kind of way.

'You will have your joke, Doctor Haydock,' she said.

'You can't pull the wool over my eyes, my dear lady. I've known you too many years. Sudden death at Gossington Hall and all the tongues of St Mary Mead are wagging. Isn't that so? Murder suggested long before anybody even knows the result of the inquest.'

'When is the inquest to be held?' asked Miss Marple.

'The day after tomorrow,' said Dr Haydock, 'and by that time,' he said, 'you ladies will have reviewed the whole story, decided on the verdict and decided on a good many other points too, I expect. Well,' he added, 'I shan't waste my time here. It's no good wasting time on a patient that doesn't need my ministrations. Your cheeks are pink, your eyes are bright, you've begun to enjoy yourself. Nothing like having an interest in life. I'll be on my way.' He stomped out again.

'I'd rather have him than Sandford any day,' said Mrs Bantry.

'So would I,' said Miss Marple. 'He's a good friend, too,' she added thoughtfully. 'He came, I think, to give me the go-ahead sign.'

'Then it *was* murder,' said Mrs Bantry. They looked at each other. 'At any rate, the doctors think so.'

Miss Knight brought in cups of coffee. For once in their lives, both ladies were too impatient to welcome this interruption. When Miss Knight had gone Miss Marple started immediately.

'Now then, Dolly, you were there – '

'I practically saw it happen,' said Mrs Bantry, with modest pride.

'Splendid,' said Miss Marple. 'I mean – well, you know what I mean. So you can tell me just exactly what happened from the moment she arrived.'

'I'd been taken into the house,' said Mrs Bantry. 'Snob status.'

'Who took you in?'

'Oh, a willowy-looking young man. I think he's Marina Gregg's secretary or something like that. He took me in, up the staircase. They were having a kind of reunion reception committee at the top of the stairs.'

'On the landing?' said Miss Marple, surprised.

'Oh, they've altered all that. They've knocked the dressing-room and bedroom down so that you've got a big sort of alcove, practically a room. It's very attractive looking.'

'I see. And who was there?'

'Marina Gregg, being natural and charming, looking lovely in a sort of willowy grey-green dress. And the husband, of course, and that woman Ella Zielinsky I told you about. She's their social secretary. And there were about – oh, eight or ten people I should think. Some of them I knew, some of them I didn't. Some I think were from the studios – the ones I didn't know. There was the vicar and Doctor Sandford's wife. He wasn't there himself until later, and Colonel and Mrs Clittering and the High Sheriff. And I think there was someone from the press there. And a young woman with a big camera taking photographs.'

Miss Marple nodded.

'Go on.'

'Heather Badcock and her husband arrived just after me. Marina Gregg said nice things to me, then to somebody else, oh yes, – the vicar – and then Heather Badcock and her husband came. She's the secretary, you know, of the St John Ambulance. Somebody said something about that and how hard she worked and how valuable she

366

was. And Marina Gregg said some pretty things. Then Mrs Badcock, who struck me, I must say, Jane, as rather a tiresome sort of woman, began some long rigmarole of how years before she'd met Marina Gregg somewhere. She wasn't awfully tactful about it since she urged exactly how long ago and the year it was and everything like that. I'm sure that actresses and film stars and people don't really like being reminded of the exact age they are. Still, she wouldn't think of that I suppose.'

'No,' said Miss Marple, 'she wasn't the kind of woman who would have thought of that. Well?'

'Well, there was nothing particular in that except for the fact that Marina Gregg didn't do her usual stuff.'

'You mean she was annoyed?'

'No, no, I don't mean that. As a matter of fact I'm not at all sure that she heard a word of it. She was staring, you know, over Mrs Badcock's shoulder and when Mrs Badcock had finished her rather silly story of how she got out of a bed of sickness and sneaked out of the house to go and meet Marina and get her autograph, there was a sort of odd silence. Then I saw her face.'

'Whose face? Mrs Badcock's?'

'No. Marina Gregg's. It was as though she hadn't heard a word the Badcock woman was saying. She was staring over her shoulder right at the wall opposite. Staring with – I can't explain it to you – '

'But do try, Dolly,' said Miss Marple, 'because I think perhaps that this might be important.'

'She had a kind of frozen look,' said Mrs Bantry, struggling with words, 'as though she'd seen something that – oh dear me, how hard it is to describe things. Do you remember the Lady of Shalott? *The mirror crack'd from side to side*: "*The doom has come upon me*," *cried the Lady of Shalott*. Well, that's what she looked like. People laugh at Tennyson nowadays, but the Lady of Shalott always thrilled me when I was young and it still does.'

'She had a frozen look,' repeated Miss Marple thoughtfully. 'And she was looking *over* Mrs Badcock's shoulder at the wall. What was on the wall?'

'Oh! A picture of some kind, I think,' said Mrs Bantry. 'You know, Italian. I think it was a copy of a Bellini Madonna, but I'm not sure. A picture where the Virgin is holding up a laughing child.'

Miss Marple frowned. 'I can't see that a *picture* could give her that expression.'

'Especially as she must see it every day,' agreed Mrs Bantry.

367

'There were people coming up the stairs still, I suppose?'

'Oh yes, there were.'

'Who were they, do you remember?'

'You mean she might have been looking at one of the people coming up the stairs?'

'Well, it's possible, isn't it?' said Miss Marple.

'Yes – of course – Now let me see. There was the mayor, all dressed up too with his chains and all, and his wife, and there was a man with long hair and one of those funny beards they wear nowadays. Quite a young man. And there was the girl with the camera. She'd taken her position on the stairs so as to get photos of people coming up and having their hands shaken by Marina, and – let me see, two people I didn't know. Studio people, I think, and the Grices from Lower Farm. There may have been others, but that's all I can remember now.'

'Doesn't sound very promising,' said Miss Marple. 'What happened next?'

'I think Jason Rudd nudged her or something because all of a sudden she seemed to pull herself together and she smiled at Mrs Badcock, and she began to say all the usual things. You know, sweet, unspoilt, natural, charming, the usual bag of tricks.'

'And then?'

'And then Jason Rudd gave them drinks.'

'What kind of drinks?'

'Daiquiris, I think. He said they were his wife's favourites. He gave one to her and one to the Badcock woman.'

'That's very interesting,' said Miss Marple. 'Very interesting indeed. And what happened after that?'

'I don't know, because I took a gaggle of women to look at the bathrooms. The next thing I knew was when the secretary woman came rushing along and said someone had been taken ill.'

CHAPTER SEVEN

The inquest, when it was held, was short and disappointing. Evidence of identification was given by the husband, and the only other evidence was medical. Heather Badcock had died as a result of four grains of hy-ethyl-dexyl-barbo-quindelorytate, or, let us be frank, some such name. There was no evidence to show how the drug was administered.

The inquest was adjourned for a fortnight.

After it was concluded, Detective-Inspector Frank Cornish joined Arthur Badcock.

'Could I have a word with you, Mr Badcock?'

'Of course, of course.'

Arthur Badcock looked more like a chewed-out bit of string than ever. 'I can't understand it,' he muttered. 'I simply can't understand it.'

'I've got a car here,' said Cornish. 'We'll drive back to your house, shall we? Nicer and more private there.'

'Thank you, sir. Yes, yes, I'm sure that would be much better.'

They drew up at the neat little blue-painted gate of No. 3 Arlington Close. Arthur Badcock led the way and the inspector followed him. He drew out his latch-key but before he had inserted it into the door, it was opened from inside. The woman who opened it stood back looking slightly embarrassed. Arthur Badcock looked startled.

'Mary,' he said.

'I was just getting you ready some tea, Arthur. I thought you'd need it when you came back from the inquest.'

'That's very kind of you, I'm sure,' said Arthur Badcock gratefully. Er – ' he hesitated. 'This is Inspector Cornish, Mrs Bain, She's a neighbour of mine.'

'I see,' said Inspector Cornish.

'I'll get another cup,' said Mrs Bain.

She disappeared and rather doubtfully Arthur Badcock showed

the inspector into the bright cretonne-covered sitting-room to the right of the hall.

'She's very kind,' said Arthur Badcock. 'Very kind always.'

'You've known her a long time?'

'Oh, no. Only since we came here.'

'You've been here two years, I believe, or is it three?'

'Just about three now,' said Arthur. 'Mrs Bain only got here six months ago,' he explained. 'Her son works near here and so, after her husband's death, she came down to live here and he boards with her.'

Mrs Bain appeared at this point bringing the tray from the kitchen. She was a dark, rather intense-looking woman of about forty years of age. She had gipsy colouring that went with her dark hair and eyes. There was something a little odd about her eyes. They had a watchful look. She put down the tray on the table and Inspector Cornish said something pleasant and non-committal. Something in him, some professional instinct, was on the alert. The watchful look in the woman's eyes, the slight start she had given when Arthur introduced him had not passed unnoticed. He was familiar with that slight uneasiness in the presence of the kind of natural alarm and distrust as of those who might have offended unwittingly against the majesty of the law, but there was a second kind. And it was the second kind that he felt sure was present here. Mrs Bain, he thought, had had at some time some connection with the police, something that had left her wary and ill at ease. He made a mental note to find out a little more about Mary Bain. Having set down the tea tray, and refused to partake herself saying she had to get home, she departed.

'Seems a nice woman,' said Inspector Cornish.

'Yes, indeed. She's very kind, a very good neighbour, a very sympathetic woman,' said Arthur Badcock.

'Was she a great friend of your wife?'

'No. No, I wouldn't say that. They were neighbourly and on pleasant terms. Nothing special about it though.'

'I see. Now, Mr Badcock, we want as much information as we can from you. The findings of the inquest have been a shock to you, I expect?'

'Oh, they have, Inspector. Of course I realized that you must think something was wrong and I almost thought so myself because Heather has always been such a healthy woman. Practically never a day's illness. I said to myself, "There must be something wrong."

370

But it seems so incredible, if you understand what I mean, Inspector. Really quite incredible. What is this stuff – this Bi-ethyl-hex – ' he came to a stop.

'There is an easier name for it,' said the inspector. 'It's sold under a trade name, the trade name of Calmo. Ever come across it?'

Arthur Badcock shook his head, perplexed.

'It's more used in America than here,' said the inspector. 'They prescribe it very freely over there, I understand.'

'What's it for?'

'It induces, or so I understand, a happy and tranquil state of mind,' said Cornish. 'It's prescribed for those under strain; suffering anxiety, depression, melancholy, sleeplessness and a good many other things. The properly prescribed dose is not dangerous, but overdoses are not to be advised. It would seem that your wife took something like six times the ordinary dose.'

Badcock stared. 'Heather never took anything like that in her life,' he said. 'I'm sure of it. She wasn't one for taking medicines anyway. She was never depressed or worried. She was one of the most cheerful women you could possibly imagine.'

The inspector nodded. 'I see. And no doctor had prescribed anything of this kind for her?'

'No. Certainly not. I'm sure of that.'

'Who was her doctor?'

'She was on Dr Sim's panel, but I don't think she's been to him once since we've been here.'

Inspector Cornish said thoughtfully, 'So she doesn't seem the kind of woman to have been likely to need such a thing, or to have taken it?'

'She didn't, Inspector, I'm sure she didn't. She must have taken it by a mistake of some kind.'

'It's a very difficult mistake to imagine,' said Inspector Cornish. 'What did she have to eat and drink that afternoon?'

'Well, let me see. For lunch – '

'You needn't go back as far as lunch,' said Cornish. 'Given in such quantity the drug would act quickly and suddenly. Tea. Go back to tea.'

'Well, we went into the marquee in the grounds. It was a terrible scrum in there, but we managed in the end to get a bun each and a cup of tea. We finished it as quickly as possible because it was very hot in the marquee and we came out again.'

'And that's all she had, a bun and a cup of tea there?'

371

'That's right, sir.'

'And after that you went into the house. Is that right?'

'Yes. The young lady came and said that Miss Marina Gregg would be very pleased to see my wife if she would like to come into the house. Of course my wife was delighted. She had been talking about Marina Gregg for days. Everybody was excited. Oh well, you know that, Inspector, as well as anyone does.'

'Yes, indeed,' said Cornish. 'My wife was excited, too. Why, from all around people were paying their shilling to go in and see Gossington Hall and what had been done there, and hoped to catch a glimpse of Marina Gregg herself.'

'The young lady took us into the house,' said Arthur Badcock, 'and up the stairs. That's where the party was. On the landing up there. But it looked quite different from what it used to look like, so I understand. It was more like a room, a sort of big hollowed out place with chairs and tables with drinks on them. There were about ten or twelve people there, I suppose.'

Inspector Cornish nodded. 'And you were received there – by whom?'

'By Miss Marina Gregg herself. Her husband was with her. I've forgotten his name now.'

'Jason Rudd,' said Inspector Cornish.

'Oh, yes, not that I noticed him at first. Well, anyway, Miss Gregg greeted Heather very nicely and seemed very pleased to see her, and Heather was talking and telling a story of how she'd once met Miss Gregg years ago in the West Indies and everything seemed as right as rain.'

'Everything seemed as right as rain,' echoed the inspector. 'And then?'

'And then Miss Gregg said what would we have? And Miss Gregg's husband, Mr Rudd, got Heather a kind of cocktail, a dickery or something like that.'

'A daiquiri.'

'That's right, sir. He brought two. One for her and one for Miss Gregg.'

'And you, what did you have?'

'I had a sherry.'

'I see. And you three stood there drinking together?'

'Well, not quite like that. You see there were more people coming up the stairs. There was the mayor, for one, and some other people – an American gentleman and lady, I think – so we moved off a bit.'

'And your wife drank her daiquiri then?'

'Well, no, not then, she didn't.'

'Well, if she didn't drink it then, when did she drink it?'

Arthur Badcock stood frowning in remembrance. 'I think – she set it down on one of the tables. She saw some friends there. I think it was someone to do with the St John Ambulance who'd driven over there from Much Benham or somewhere like that. Anyway they got to talking together.'

'And when did she drink her drink?'

Arthur Badcock again frowned. 'It was a little after that,' he said. 'It was getting rather more crowded by then. Somebody jogged Heather's elbow and her glass got spilt.'

'What's that?' Inspector Cornish looked up sharply. 'Her glass was spilt?'

'Yes, that's how I remember it . . . She'd picked it up and I think she took a little sip and made rather a face. She didn't really like cocktails, you know, but all the same she wasn't going to be downed by that. Anyway, as she stood there, somebody jogged her elbow and the glass spilled over. It went down her dress and I think it went on Miss Gregg's dress too. Miss Gregg couldn't have been nicer. She said it didn't matter at all and it would make no stain and she gave Heather her handkerchief to wipe up Heather's dress, and then she passed over the drink she was holding and said, 'Have this, I haven't touched it yet.'

'She handed over her own drink, did she?' said the inspector. 'You're quite sure of that?'

Arthur Badcock paused a moment while he thought. 'Yes, I'm quite sure of that,' he said.

'And your wife took the drink?'

'Well, she didn't want to at first, sir. She said "Oh no, I couldn't do that" and Miss Gregg laughed and said, "I've had far too much to drink already."'

'And so your wife took that glass and did what with it?'

'She turned away a little and drank it, rather quickly, I think. And then we walked a little way along the corridor looking at some of the pictures and the curtains. Lovely curtain stuff it was, like nothing we'd seen before. Then I met a pal of mine, Councillor Allcock, and I was just passing the time of day with him when I looked round and saw Heather was sitting on a chair looking rather odd, so I came to her and said, "What's the matter?" She said she felt a little queer.'

373

'What kind of queerness?'

'I don't know, sir. I didn't have time. Her voice sounded very queer and thick and her head was rolling a little. All of a sudden she made a great half gasp and her head fell forward. She was dead, sir, dead.'

CHAPTER EIGHT

'St Mary Mead, you say?' Chief-Inspector Craddock looked up sharply.

The assistant commissioner was a little surprised.

'Yes,' he said, 'St Mary Mead. Why? Does it – '

'Nothing really,' said Dermot Craddock.

'It's quite a small place, I understand,' went on the other. 'Though of course there's a great deal of building development going on there now. Practically all the way from St Mary Mead to Much Benham, I understand. Hellingforth Studios,' he added, 'are on the other side of St Mary Mead, towards Market Basing.' He was still looking slightly inquiring. Dermot Craddock felt that he should perhaps explain.

'I know someone living there,' he said. 'At St Mary Mead. An old lady. A very old lady by now. Perhaps she's dead, I don't know. But if not – '

The assistant commissioner took his subordinate's point, or at any rate he thought he did.

'Yes,' he said, 'it would give you an "in" in a way. One needs a bit of local gossip. The whole thing is a curious business.'

'The County have called us in?' Dermot asked.

'Yes. I've got the chief constable's letter here. They don't seem to feel that it's necessarily a local affair. The largest house in the neighbourhood, Gossington Hall, was recently sold as a residence for Marina Gregg, the film star, and her husband. They're shooting a film at their new studios, at Hellingforth, in which she is starring. A fête was held in the grounds in aid of the St John Ambulance. The dead woman – her name is Mrs Heather Badcock – was the local secretary of this and had done most of the administrative work for the fête. She seems to have been a competent, sensible person, well liked locally.'

'One of those bossy women?' suggested Craddock.

'Very possibly,' said the assistant commissioner. 'Still in my experience, bossy women seldom get themselves murdered. I can't think why not. When you come to think of it, it's rather a pity. There was a record attendance at the fête, it seems, good weather, everything running to plan. Marina Gregg and her husband held a kind of small private reception in Gossington Hall. About thirty or forty people attended this. The local notables, various people connected with the St John Ambulance Association, several friends of Marina Gregg herself, and a few people connected with the studios. All very peaceful, nice and happy. But, fantastically and improbably, Heather Badcock was poisoned there.'

Dermot Craddock said thoughtfully, 'An odd place to choose.'

'That's the chief constable's point of view. If anyone wanted to poison Heather Badcock, why choose that particular afternoon and circumstances? Hundreds of much simpler ways of doing it. A risky business anyway, you know, to slip a dose of deadly poison into a cocktail in the middle of twenty or thirty people milling about. Somebody ought to have seen something.'

'It definitely was in the drink?'

'Yes, it was definitely in the drink. We have the particulars here. One of those inexplicable names that doctors delight in, but actually a fairly common prescription in America.'

'In America. I see.'

'Oh, this country too. But these things are handed out much more freely on the other side of the Atlantic. Taken in small doses, beneficial.'

'Supplied on prescription or can it be bought freely?'

'No. You have to have a prescription.'

'Yes, it's odd,' said Dermot. 'Heather Badcock have any connection with these film people?'

'None whatever.'

'Any member of her own family at this do?'

'Her husband.'

'Her husband,' said Dermot thoughtfully.

'Yes, one always thinks that way,' agreed his superior officer, 'but the local man – Cornish, I think his name is – doesn't seem to think there's anything in that, although he does report that Badcock seemed ill at ease and nervous, but he agrees that respectable people

375

often are like that when interviewed by the police. They appear to have been quite a devoted couple.'

'In other words, the police there don't think it's their pigeon. Well, it ought to be interesting. I take it I'm going down there, sir?'

'Yes. Better get there as soon as possible, Dermot. Who do you want with you?'

Dermot considered for a moment or two.

'Tiddler, I think,' he said thoughtfully. 'He's a good man and, what's more, he's a film star. That might come in useful.'

The assistant commissioner nodded. 'Good luck to you,' he said.

II

'Well!' exclaimed Miss Marple, going pink with pleasure and surprise. 'Thus is a surprise. How are you, my dear boy – though you're hardly a boy now. What are you – a Chief-Inspector or this new thing they call a Commander?'

Dermot explained his present rank.

'I suppose I need hardly ask what you are doing down here,' said Miss Marple. 'Our local murder is considered worthy of the attention of Scotland Yard.'

'They handed it over to us,' said Dermot, 'and so, naturally, as soon as I got down here I came to headquarters.'

'Do you mean – ' Miss Marple fluttered a little.

'Yes, Aunty,' said Dermot disrespectfully. 'I mean you.'

'I'm afraid,' said Miss Marple regretfully, 'I'm very much out of things nowadays. I don't get out much.'

'You get out enough to fall down and be picked up by a woman who's going to be murdered ten days later,' said Dermot Craddock.

Miss Marple made the kind of noise that would once have been written down as 'tut-tut'.

'I don't know where you hear these things,' she said.

'You should know,' said Dermot Craddock. 'You told me yourself that in a village everybody knows everything.

'And just off the record,' he added, 'did you think she was going to be murdered as soon as you looked at her?'

'Of course not, of course not,' exclaimed Miss Marple. 'What an idea!'

'You didn't see that look in her husband's eye that reminded you of Harry Simpson or David Jones or somebody you've known years ago, and subsequently pushed his wife off a precipice.'

'No, I did *not*!' said Miss Marple. 'I'm sure Mr Badcock would never do a wicked thing of that kind. At least,' she added thoughtfully, 'I'm nearly sure.'

'But human nature being what it is – ' murmured Craddock, wickedly.

'Exactly,' said Miss Marple. She added, 'I daresay, after the first natural grief, he won't miss her very much . . .'

'Why? Did she bully him?'

'Oh no,' said Miss Marple, 'but I don't think that she – well, she wasn't a considerate woman. Kind, yes. Considerate – no. She would be fond of him and look after him when he was ill and see to his meals and be a good housekeeper, but I don't think she would ever – well, that she would ever even know what he might be feeling or thinking. That makes rather a lonely life for a man.'

'Ah,' said Dermot, 'and is his life less likely to be lonely in future?'

'I expect he'll marry again,' said Miss Marple. 'Perhaps quite soon. And probably, which is such a pity, a woman of much the same type. I mean he'll marry someone with a stronger personality than his own.'

'Anyone in view?' asked Dermot.

'Not that I know of,' said Miss Marple. She added regretfully, 'But I know so little.'

'Well, what do you *think*?' urged Dermot Craddock. 'You've never been backward in thinking things.'

'I think,' said Miss Marple, unexpectedly, 'that you ought to go and see Mrs Bantry.'

'Mrs Bantry? Who is she? One of the film lot?'

'No,' said Miss Marple, 'she lives in the East Lodge at Gossington. She was at the party that day. She used to own Gossington at one time. She and her husband, Colonel Bantry.'

'She was at the party. And she saw something?'

'I think she must tell you herself what it was she saw. You mayn't think it has any bearing on the matter, but I think it might be – just might be – suggestive. Tell her I sent you to her and – ah yes, perhaps you'd better just mention the Lady of Shalott.'

Dermot Craddock looked at her with his head just slightly on one side.

'The Lady of Shalott,' he said. 'Those are the code words, are they?'

'I don't know that I should put it that way,' said Miss Marple, 'but it will remind her of what I mean.'

Dermot Craddock got up. 'I shall be back,' he warned her.

'That is very nice of you,' said Miss Marple. 'Perhaps if you have time, you would come and have tea with me one day. If you still drink tea,' she added rather wistfully. 'I know that so many young people nowadays only go out to drinks and things. They think that afternoon tea is a very outmoded affair.'

'I'm not as young as all that,' said Dermot Craddock. 'Yes, I'll come and have tea with you one day. We'll have tea and gossip and talk about the village. Do you know any of the film stars, by the way, or any of the studio lot?'

'Not a thing,' said Miss Marple, 'except what I hear,' she added.

'Well, you usually hear a good deal,' said Dermot Craddock. 'Goodbye. It's been very nice to see you.'

III

'Oh, how do you do?' said Mrs Bantry, looking slightly taken aback when Dermot Craddock had introduced himself and explained who he was. 'How very exciting to see you. Don't you always have sergeants with you?'

'I've got a sergeant down here, yes,' said Craddock. 'But he's busy.'

'On routine enquiries?' asked Mrs Bantry, hopefully.

'Something of the kind,' said Dermot gravely.

'And Jane Marple sent you to me,' said Mrs Bantry, as she ushered him into her small sitting-room. 'I was just arranging some flowers,' she explained. 'It's one of those days when flowers won't do anything you want them to. They fall out, or stick up where they shouldn't stick up or won't lie down where you want them to lie down. So I'm thankful to have a distraction, and especially such an exciting one. So it really was murder, was it?'

'Did you think it was murder?'

'Well, it could have been an accident, I suppose,' said Mrs Bantry, 'Nobody's said anything definite, officially, that is. Just that rather silly piece about no evidence to show by whom or in what way the poison was administered. But, of course, we all talk about it as murder.'

'And about who did it?'

'That's the odd part of it,' said Mrs Bantry. 'We don't. Because I really don't see who *can* have done it.'

'You mean as a matter of definite physical fact you don't see who could have done it?'

'Well, no, not that. I suppose it would have been difficult but not impossible. No, I mean, I don't see who could have *wanted* to do it.'

'Nobody, you think, could have wanted to kill Heather Badcock?'

'Well, frankly,' said Mrs Bantry, 'I can't imagine *anybody* wanting to kill Heather Badcock. I've seen her quite a few times, on local things, you know. Girl guides and the St John Ambulance, and various parish things. I found her a rather trying sort of woman. Very enthusiastic about everything and a bit given to over-statement, and just a little bit of a gusher. But you don't want to murder people for that. She was the kind of woman who in the old days if you'd seen her approaching the front door, you'd have hurried out to say to your parlourmaid – which was an institution we had in those days, and very useful too – and told her to say "not at home" or "not at home to visitors," if she had conscientious scruples about the truth.'

'You mean that one might take pains to avoid Mrs Badcock, but one would have no urge to remove her permanently.'

'Very well put,' said Mrs Bantry, nodding approval.

'She had no money to speak of,' mused Dermot, 'so nobody stood to gain by her death. Nobody seems to have disliked her to the point of hatred. I don't suppose she was blackmailing anybody?'

'She wouldn't have dreamed of doing such a thing, I'm sure,' said Mrs Bantry. 'She was the conscientious and high-principled kind.'

'And her husband wasn't having an affair with someone else?'

'I shouldn't think so,' said Mrs Bantry. 'I only saw him at the party. He looked like a bit of chewed string. Nice but wet.'

'Doesn't leave much, does it?' said Dermot Craddock. 'One falls back on the assumption she knew something.'

'Knew something?'

'To the detriment of somebody else.'

Mrs Bantry shook her head again. 'I doubt it,' she said. 'I doubt it very much. She struck me as the kind of woman who if she had known anything about anyone, couldn't have helped talking about it.'

379

'Well, that washes that out,' said Dermot Craddock, 'so we'll come, if we may, to my reasons for coming to see you. Miss Marple, for whom I have the greatest admiration and respect, told me that I was to say to you the Lady of Shalott.'

'Oh, *that*!' said Mrs Bantry.

'Yes,' said Craddock. '*That*! Whatever it is.'

'People don't read much Tennyson nowadays,' said Mrs Bantry.

'A few echoes come back to me,' said Dermot Craddock. 'She looked out to Camelot, didn't she?

> Out flew the web and floated wide;
> The Mirror crack'd from side to side;
> "The curse has come upon me," cried
> The Lady of Shalott.'

'Exactly. She did,' said Mrs Bantry.

'I beg your pardon. Who did? Did what?'

'Looked like that,' said Mrs Bantry.

'Who looked like what?'

'Marina Gregg.'

'Ah, Marina Gregg. When was this?'

'Didn't Jane Marple tell you?'

'She didn't tell me anything. She sent me to you.'

'That's tiresome of her,' said Mrs Bantry, 'because she can always tell things better than I can. My husband always used to say that I was so abrupt that he didn't know what I was talking about. Anyway, it may have been only my fancy. But when you see anyone looking like that you can't help remembering it.'

'Please tell me,' said Dermot Craddock.

'Well, it was at the party. I call it a party because what can one call things? But it was just a sort of reception up at the top of the stairs where they've made a kind of recess. Marina Gregg was there and her husband. They fetched some of us in. They fetched me, I suppose, because I once owned the house, and they fetched Heather Badcock and her husband because she'd done all the running of the fête, and the arrangements. And we happened to go up the stairs at about the same time, so I was standing there, you see, when I noticed it.'

'Quite. When you noticed what?'

'Well, Mrs Badcock went into a long spiel as people do when they meet celebrities. You know, how wonderful it was, and what a thrill and they'd always hoped to see them. And she went into a long story of how she'd once met her years ago and how exciting it had been. And I thought, in my own mind, you know, what a bore it must be for these poor celebrities to have to say all the right things. And then I noticed that Marina Gregg wasn't saying the right things. She was just staring.'

'Staring – at Mrs Badcock?'

'No – no, it looked as though she'd forgotten Mrs Badcock altogether. I mean, I don't believe she'd even heard what Mrs Badcock was saying. She was just staring with what I call this Lady of Shalott look, as though she'd seen something awful. Something frightening, something that she could hardly believe she saw and couldn't bear to see.'

'The curse has come upon me?' suggested Dermot Craddock.

'Yes, just that. That's why I call it the Lady of Shalott look.'

'But what was she looking *at*, Mrs Bantry?'

'Well, I wish I knew,' said Mrs Bantry.

'She was at the top of the stairs, you say?'

'She was looking over Mrs Badcock's head – no, more over one shoulder, I think.'

'Straight at the middle of the staircase?'

'It might have been a little to one side.'

'And there were people coming up the staircase?'

'Oh yes, I should think about five or six people.'

'Was she looking at one of these people in particular?'

'I can't possibly tell,' said Mrs Bantry. 'You see, I wasn't facing that way. I was looking at *her*. My back was to the stairs. I thought perhaps she was looking at one of the pictures.'

'But she must know the pictures quite well if she's living in the house.'

'Yes, yes, of course. No, I suppose she must have been looking at one of the people. I wonder which.'

'We have to try and find out,' said Dermot Craddock. 'Can you remember at all who the people were?'

'Well, I know the mayor was one of them with his wife. There was someone who I think was a reporter, with red hair, because I was introduced to him later, but I can't remember his name. I never hear names. Galbraith – something like that. Then there was a big black man. I don't mean a negro – I just mean very dark, forceful looking. And an actress with him. A bit overblonde and the minky kind. And old General Barnstaple from Much Benham.

381

He's practically ga-ga now, poor old boy. I don't think *he* could have been anybody's doom. Oh! and the Grices from the farm.'

'Those are all the people you can remember?'

'Well, there may have been others. But you see I wasn't – well, I mean I wasn't noticing particularly. I know that the mayor and General Barnstaple and the Americans did arrive about that time. And there were people taking photographs. One I think was a local man, and there was a girl from London, an arty-looking girl with long hair and a rather large camera.'

'And you think it was one of those people who brought that look to Marina Gregg's face?'

'I didn't really think anything,' said Mrs Bantry with complete frankness. 'I just wondered what on earth made her look like that and then I didn't think of it any more. But afterwards one remembers about these things. But of course,' added Mrs Bantry with honesty, 'I *may* have imagined it. After all, she may have had a sudden toothache or a safety pin run into her or a sudden violent colic. The sort of thing where you try to go on as usual and not to show anything, but your face can't help looking awful.'

Dermot Craddock laughed. 'I'm glad to see you're a realist, Mrs Bantry,' he said. 'As you say, it may have been something of that kind. But it's certainly just one interesting little fact that might be a pointer.'

He shook his head and departed to present his official credentials in Much Benham.

CHAPTER NINE

'So locally you've drawn a blank?' said Craddock, offering his cigarette case to Frank Cornish.

'Completely,' said Cornish. 'No enemies, no quarrels, on good terms with her husband.'

'No question of another woman or another man?'

The other shook his head. 'Nothing of that kind. No hint of scandal anywhere. She wasn't what you'd call the sexy kind. She was on a lot of committees and things like that and there were some small local rivalries, but nothing beyond that.'

'There wasn't anyone else the husband wanted to marry? No one in the office where he worked?'

'He's in Biddle & Russell, the estate agents and valuers. There's Florrie West with adenoids, and Miss Grundle, who is at least fifty and as plain as a haystack – nothing much there to excite a man. Though for all that I shouldn't be surprised if he *did* marry again soon.'

Craddock looked interested.

'A neighbour,' explained Cornish. 'A widow. When I went back with him from the inquest she'd gone in and was making him tea and looking after him generally. He seemed surprised and grateful. If you ask me, she's made up her mind to marry him, but he doesn't know it yet, poor chap.'

'What sort of a woman is she?'

'Good looking,' admitted the other. 'Not young but handsome in a gipsyish sort of way. High colour. Dark eyes.'

'What's her name?'

'Bain. Mrs Mary Bain. Mary Bain. She's a widow.'

'What'd her husband do?'

'No idea. She's got a son working near here who lives with her. She seems a quiet, respectable woman. All the same, I've a feeling I've seen her before.' He looked at his watch. 'Ten to twelve. I've made an appointment for you at Gossington Hall at twelve o'clock. We'd best be going.'

II

Dermot Craddock's eyes, which always looked gently inattentive, were in actuality making a close mental note of the features of Gossington Hall. Inspector Cornish had taken him there, had delivered him over to a young man called Hailey Preston, and had then taken a tactful leave. Since then, Dermot Craddock had been gently nodding at Mr Preston. Hailey Preston, he gathered, was a kind of public relations or personal assistant, or private secretary, or more likely, a mixture of all three, to Jason Rudd. He talked. He talked freely and at length without much modulation and managing miraculously not to repeat himself too often. He was a pleasant young man, anxious that his own views, reminiscent of those of Dr Pangloss

383

that all was for the best in the best of all possible worlds, should be shared by anyone in whose company he happened to be. He said several times and in different ways what a terrible shame this had been, how worried everyone had been, how Marina was absolutely prostrated, how Mr Rudd was more upset than he could possibly say, how it absolutely beat anything that a thing like that should happen, didn't it? Possibly there might have been some kind of allergy to some particular kind of substance? He just put that forward as an idea – allergies were extraordinary things. Chief-Inspector Craddock was to count on every possible co-operation that Hellingforth Studios or any of their staff could give. He was to ask any questions he wanted, go anywhere he liked. If they could help in any way they would do so. They all had had the greatest respect for Mrs Badcock and appreciated her strong social sense and the valuable work she had done for the St John Ambulance Association.

He then started again, not in the same words but using the same motifs. No one could have been more eagerly co-operative. At the same time he endeavoured to convey how very far this was from the cellophane world of studios; and Mr Jason Rudd and Miss Marina Gregg, or any of the people in the house who surely were going to do their utmost to help in any way they possibly could. Then he nodded gently some forty-four times. Dermot Craddock took advantage of the pause to say:

'Thank you very much.'

It was said quietly but with a kind of finality that brought Mr Hailey Preston up with a jerk. He said:

'Well –' and paused inquiringly.

'You said I might ask questions?'

'Sure. Sure. Fire ahead.'

'Is this the place where she died?'

'Mrs Badcock?'

'Mrs Badcock. Is this the place?'

'Yes, sure. Right here. At least, well actually I can show you the chair.'

They were standing on the landing recess. Hailey Preston walked a short way along the corridor and pointed out a rather phony-looking oak arm-chair.

'She was sitting right there,' he said. 'She said she didn't feel well. Someone went to get her something, and then she just died, right there.'

'I see.'

'I don't know if she'd seen a physician lately. If she'd been warned that she had anything wrong with her heart – '

'She had nothing wrong with her heart,' said Dermot Craddock. 'She was a healthy woman. She died of six times the maximum dose of a substance whose official name I will not try to pronounce but which I understand is generally known as Calmo.'

'I know, I know,' said Hailey Preston. 'I take it myself sometimes.'

'Indeed? That's very interesting. You find it has a good effect?'

'Marvellous. Marvellous. It bucks you up *and* it soothes you down, if you understand what I mean. Naturally,' he added, 'you would have to take it in the proper dosage.'

'Would there be supplies of this substance in the house?'

He knew the answer to the question, but he put it as though he did not. Hailey Preston's answer was frankness itself.

'Loads of it, I should say. There'll be a bottle of it in most of the bathroom cupboards here.'

'Which doesn't make our task easier.'

'Of course,' said Hailey Preston, 'she might have used the stuff herself and taken a dose, and as I say, had an allergy.'

Craddock looked unconvinced – Hailey Preston sighed and said:

'You're quite definite about the dosage?'

'Oh yes. It was a lethal dose and Mrs Badcock did not take any such things herself. As far as we can make out the only things she ever took were bicarbonate of soda or aspirin.' Hailey Preston shook his head and said, 'That sure gives us a problem. Yes, it sure does.'

'Where did Mr Rudd and Miss Gregg receive their guests?'

'Right here.' Hailey Preston went to the spot at the top of the stairs.

Chief-Inspector Craddock stood beside him. He looked at the wall opposite him. In the centre was an Italian Madonna and child. A good copy, he presumed, of some well-known picture. The blue-robed Madonna held aloft the infant Jesus and both child and mother were laughing. Little groups of people stood on either side, their eyes upraised to the child. One of the more pleasing Madonnas, Dermot Craddock thought. To the right and left of this picture were two narrow windows. The whole effect was very charming but it seemed to him that there was emphatically nothing there that would cause a woman to look like the Lady of Shalott whose doom had come upon her.

'People, of course, were coming up the stairs?' he asked.

'Yes. They came in driblets, you know. Not too many at once. I shepherded up some, Ella Zielinsky, that's Mr Rudd's secretary, brought some of the others. We wanted to make it all pleasant and informal.'

'Were you here yourself at the time Mrs Badcock came up?'

'I'm ashamed to tell you, Chief-Inspector Craddock, that I just can't remember. I had a list of names, I went out and I shepherded people in. I introduced them, saw to drinks, then I'd go out and come up with the next batch. At the time I didn't know this Mrs Badcock by sight, and she wasn't one of the ones on my list to bring up.'

'What about a Mrs Bantry?'

'Ah yes, she's the former owner of this place, isn't she?' I believe she, and Mrs Badcock and her husband, *did* come up about the same time.' He paused. 'And the mayor came just about then. He had a big chain on and a wife with yellow hair, wearing royal blue with frills. I remember all of them. I didn't pour drinks for any of them because I had to go down and bring up the next lot.'

'Who did pour drinks for them?'

'Why, I can't exactly say. There were three or four of us on duty. I know I went down the stairs just as the mayor was coming up.'

'Who else was on the stairs as you went down, if you can remember?'

'Jim Galbraith, one of the newspaper boys who was covering this, three or four others whom I didn't know. There were a couple of photographers, one of the locals, I don't remember his name, and an arty girl from London, who rather specialises in queer angle shots. Her camera was set right up in that corner so that she could get a view of Miss Gregg receiving. Ah, now let me think, I rather fancy that that was when Ardwyck Fenn arrived.'

'And who is Ardwyck Fenn?'

Hailey Preston looked shocked. 'He's a big shot, Chief-Inspector. A very big shot in the Television and Moving Picture world. We didn't even know he was in this country.'

'His turning up was a surprise?'

'I'll say it was,' said Preston. 'Nice of him to come and quite unexpected.'

'Was he an old friend of Miss Gregg's and Mr Rudd's?'

'He was an old friend of Marina's a good many years ago when she was married to her second husband. I don't know how well Jason knew him.'

'Anyway, it was a pleasant surprise when he arrived?'

'Sure it was. We were all delighted.'

Craddock nodded and passed from that to other subjects. He made meticulous inquiries about the drinks, their ingredients, how they were served, who served them, what servants and hired servants were on duty. The answers seemed to be, as Inspector Cornish had already hinted was the case that, although any one of thirty people *could* have poisoned Heather Badcock with the utmost ease, yet at the same time any one of the thirty might have been seen doing so! It was, Craddock reflected, a big chance to take.

'Thank you,' he said at last, 'now I would like, if I may, to speak to Miss Marina Gregg.'

Hailey Preston shook his head.

'I'm sorry,' he said. 'I really am sorry but that's right out of the question.'

Craddock's eyebrows rose.

'Surely!'

'She's prostrated. She's absolutely prostrated. She's got her own physician here looking after her. He wrote out a certificate. I've got it here. I'll show it to you.'

Craddock took it and read it.

'I see,' he said. He asked, 'Does Marina Gregg always have a physician in attendance?'

'They're very high strung, all these actors and actresses. It's a big strain, this life. It's usually considered desirable in the case of the big shots that they should have a physician who understands their constitution and their nerves. Maurice Gilchrist has a very big reputation. He's looked after Miss Gregg for many years now. She's had a great deal of illness, as you may have read, in the last four years. She was hospitalized for a very long time. It's only about a year ago that she got her strength and health back.'

'I see.'

Hailey Preston seemed relieved that Craddock was not making any more protests.

'You'll want to see Mr Rudd?' he suggested. 'He'll be – ' he looked at his watch, '– he'll be back from the studios in about ten minutes if that's all right for you.'

'That'll do admirably,' said Craddock. 'In the meantime is Dr Gilchrist in the house?'

'He is.'

'Then I'd like to talk to him.'

'Why, certainly. I'll fetch him right away.'

387

The young man bustled away. Dermot Craddock stood thought-fully at the top of the stairs. Of course this frozen look that Mrs Bantry had described might have been entirely Mrs Bantry's imagination. She was, he thought, a woman who would jump to conclusions. At the same time he thought it quite likely that the conclusion to which she had jumped was a just one. Without going so far as to look like the Lady of Shalott seeing doom coming down upon her, Marina Gregg might have seen something that vexed or annoyed her. Something that had caused her to have been negligent to a guest to whom she was talking. Somebody had come up those stairs, perhaps, who could be described as an unexpected guest – an unwelcome guest?

He turned at the sound of footsteps. Hailey Preston was back and with him was Dr Maurice Gilchrist. Dr Gilchrist was not at all as Dermot Craddock had imagined him. He had no suave bedside manner, neither was he theatrical in appearance. He seemed on the face of it, a blunt, hearty, matter-of-fact man. He was dressed in tweeds, slightly florid tweeds to the English idea. He had a thatch of brown hair and observant, keen dark eyes.

'Doctor Gilchrist? I am Chief-Inspector Dermot Craddock. May I have a word or two with you in private?'

The doctor nodded. He turned along the corridor and went along it almost to the end, then he pushed the door open and invited Craddock to enter.

'No one will disturb us here,' he said.

It was obviously the doctor's own bedroom, a very comfortably appointed one. Dr Gilchrist indicated a chair and then sat down himself.

'I understand,' said Craddock, 'that Miss Marina Gregg, according to you, is unable to be interviewed. What's the matter with her, Doctor?'

Gilchrist shrugged his shoulders very slightly.

'Nerves,' he said. 'If you were to ask her questions now she'd be in a state bordering on hysteria within ten minutes. I can't permit that. If you like to send your police doctor to see me, I'd be willing to give him my views. She was unable to be present at the inquest for the same reason.'

'How long,' asked Craddock, 'is such a state of things likely to continue?'

Dr Gilchrist looked at him and smiled. It was a likeable smile.

'If you want my opinion,' he said, 'a human opinion, that is, not

388

a medical one, any time within the next forty-eight hours, and she'll be not only willing, but asking to see you! She'll be wanting to ask questions. She'll be wanting to answer your questions. They're like that!' He leaned forward. 'I'd like to try and make you understand if I can, Chief-Inspector, a little bit what makes these people act the way they do. The motion picture life is a life of continuous strain, and the more successful you are, the greater the strain. You live always, all day, in the public eye. When you're on location, when you're working, it's hard monotonous work with long hours. You're there in the morning, you sit and you wait. You do your small bit, the bit that's being shot over and over again. If you're rehearsing on the stage you'd be rehearsing as likely as not a whole act, or at any rate a part of an act. The thing would be in sequence, it would be more or less human and credible. But when you're shooting a picture everything's taken out of sequence. It's a monotonous, grinding business. It's exhausting. You live in luxury, of course, you have soothing drugs, you have baths and creams and powders and medical attention, you have relaxations and parties and people, but you're always in the public eye. You can't enjoy yourself quietly. You can't really – *ever relax*.'

'I can understand that,' said Dermot. 'Yes, I can understand.'

'And there's another thing,' went on Gilchrist. 'If you adopt this career, and especially if you're any good at it, you are a certain kind of person. You're a person – or so I've found in my experience with a skin too few – a person who is plagued the whole time with diffidence. A terrible feeling of inadequacy, of apprehension that you can't do what's required of you. People say that actors and actresses are vain. That isn't true. They're not *conceited* about themselves; they're *obsessed* with themselves, yes, but they need reassurance the whole time. They *must* be continually reassured. Ask Jason Rudd. He'll tell you the same. You have to make them feel they can do it, to assure them they can do it, take them over and over again over the same thing encouraging them the whole time until you get the effect you want. But they are always doubtful of themselves. And that makes them, in an ordinary human, unprofessional word: nervy. Damned nervy! A mass of nerves. And the worse their nerves are the better they are at the job.'

'That's interesting,' said Craddock. 'Very interesting.' He paused, adding: 'Though I don't see quite why you – '

'I'm trying to make you understand Marina Gregg,' said Maurice Gilchrist. 'You've seen her pictures, no doubt.'

389

'She's a wonderful actress,' said Dermot, 'wonderful. She has a personality, a beauty, a sympathy.'

'Yes,' said Gilchrist, 'she has all those, and she's had to work like the devil to produce the effects that she has produced. In the process her nerves get shot to pieces, and she's not actually a strong woman physically. Not as strong as you need to be. She's got one of those temperaments that swing to and fro between despair and rapture. She can't help it. She's made that way. She's suffered a great deal in her life. A large part of the suffering has been her own fault, but some of it hasn't. None of her marriages has been happy, except, I'd say, this last one. She's married to a man now who loves her dearly and who's loved her for years. She's sheltering in that love and she's happy in it. At least, at the moment she's happy in it. One can't say how long all that will last. The trouble with her is that either she thinks that at last she's got to that spot or place or that moment in her life where everything's like a fairy tale come true, that nothing can go wrong, that she'll never be unhappy again; or else she's down in the dumps, a woman whose life is ruined, who's never known love and happiness and who never will again.' He added dryly, 'If she could only stop half-way between the two it'd be wonderful for her; and the world would lose a fine actress.'

He paused, but Dermot Craddock did not speak. He was wondering why Maurice Gilchrist was saying what he did. Why this close detailed analysis of Marina Gregg? Gilchrist was looking at him. It was as though he was urging Dermot to ask one particular question. Dermot wondered very much what the question was that he ought to ask. He said at last slowly, with the air of one feeling his way:

'She's been very much upset by this tragedy happening here?'

'Yes,' said Gilchrist, 'she has.'

'Almost unnaturally so?'

'That depends,' said Dr Gilchrist.

'On what does it depend?'

'On her reason for being so upset.'

'I suppose,' said Dermot, feeling his way, 'that it was a shock, a sudden death happening like that in the midst of a party.'

He saw very little response in the face opposite him 'Or might it,' he said, 'be something more than that?'

'You can't tell, of course,' said Dr Gilchrist, 'how people are going to react. You can't tell however well you know them. They can always surprise you. Marina might have taken this in her stride. She's a soft-hearted creature. She might say, "Oh, poor, poor woman, how

390

tragic. I wonder how it could have happened." She could have been sympathetic without really caring. After all deaths do occasionally occur at studio parties. Or she might, if there wasn't anything very interesting going on, choose – choose unconsciously, mind you – to dramatize herself over it. She might decide to throw a scene. Or there might be some quite different reason.'

Dermot decided to take the bull by the horns. 'I wish,' he said, 'you would tell me what you really think?'

'I don't know,' said Dr Gilchrist, 'I can't be sure.' He paused and then said, 'There's professional etiquette, you know. There's the relationship between doctor and patient.'

'She has told you something?'

'I don't think I could go as far as that.'

'Did Marina Gregg know this woman, Heather Badcock? Had she met her before?'

'I don't think she knew her from Adam,' said Dr Gilchrist. 'No. That's not the trouble. If you ask me it's nothing to do with Heather Badcock.'

Dermot said. 'This stuff, this Calmo. Does Marina Gregg ever use it herself?'

'Lives on it, pretty well,' said Dr Gilchrist. 'So does everyone else around here,' he added. 'Ella Zielinsky takes it, Hailey Preston takes it, half the boiling takes it – it's the fashion at this moment. They're all much the same, these things. People get tired of one and they try a new one that comes out and they think it's wonderful, and that it makes all the difference.'

'And does it make all the difference?'

'Well,' said Gilchrist, 'it makes *a* difference. It does its work. It calms you or it peps you up, makes you feel you could do things which otherwise you might fancy that you couldn't. I don't prescribe them more than I can help, but they're not dangerous taken properly. They help people who can't help themselves.'

'I wish I knew,' said Dermot Craddock, 'what it is that you are trying to tell me.'

'I'm trying to decide,' said Gilchrist, 'what is my duty. There are two duties. There's the duty of a doctor to his patient. What his patient says to him is confidential and must be kept so. But there's another point of view. You can fancy that there is a danger to a patient. You have to take steps to avoid that danger.'

He stopped. Craddock looked at him and waited.

'Yes,' said Dr Gilchrist. 'I think I know what I must do. I must

391

ask you, Chief-Inspector Craddock, to keep what I am telling you confidential. Not from your colleagues, of course. But as far as regards the outer world, particularly in the house here. Do you agree?'

'I can't bind myself,' said Craddock, 'I don't know what will arise. In general terms, yes, I agree. That is to say, I imagine that any piece of information you gave me I should prefer to keep to myself and my colleagues.'

'Now listen,' said Gilchrist, 'this mayn't mean anything at all. Women say anything when they're in the state of nerves Marina Gregg is now. I'm telling you something which she said to me. There may be nothing in it at all.'

'What did she say?' asked Craddock.

'She broke down after this thing happened. She sent for me. I gave her a sedative. I stayed there beside her, holding her hand, telling her to calm down, telling her things were going to be all right. Then, just before she went off into unconsciousness she said, "It was meant for *me*, Doctor."'

Craddock stared. 'She said that, did she? And afterwards – the next day?'

'She never alluded to it again. I raised the point once. She evaded it. She said, "Oh, you must have made a mistake. I'm sure I never said anything like that. I expect I was half doped at the time."'

'But you think she meant it?'

'She meant it all right,' said Gilchrist. 'That's not to say that it is so,' he added warningly. 'Whether someone meant to poison her or meant to poison Heather Badcock I don't know. You'd probably know better than I would. All I do say is that Marina Gregg definitely thought and believed that that dose was meant for her.'

Craddock was silent for some moments. Then he said, 'Thank you, Doctor Gilchrist. I appreciate what you have told me and I realise your motive. If what Marina Gregg said to you was founded on fact it may mean, may it not, that there is still danger to her?'

'That's the point,' said Gilchrist. 'That's the whole point.'

'Have you any reason to believe that that might be so?'

'No, I haven't.'

'No idea what her reason for thinking so was?'

'No.'

'Thank you.'

Craddock got up. 'Just one thing more, Doctor. Do you know if she said the same thing to her husband?'

392

Slowly Gilchrist shook his head. 'No,' he said, 'I'm quite sure of that. She didn't tell her husband.'

His eyes met Dermot's for a few moments then he gave a brief nod of his head and said, 'You don't want me any more? All right. I'll go back and have a look at the patient. You shall talk to her as soon as it's possible.'

He left the room and Craddock remained, pursing his lips up and whistling very softly beneath his breath.

CHAPTER TEN

'Jason's back now,' said Hailey Preston. 'Will you come with me, Chief-Inspector, I'll take you to his room.'

The room which Jason Rudd used partly for office and partly for a sitting-room, was on the first floor. It was comfortably but not luxuriously furnished. It was a room which had little personality and no indication of the private tastes or predilection of its user. Jason Rudd rose from the desk at which he was sitting, and came forward to meet Dermot. It was wholly unnecessary, Dermot thought, for the room to have a personality; the user of it had so much. Hailey Preston had been an efficient and voluble gasbag. Gilchrist had force and magnetism. But here was a man whom, as Dermot immediately admitted to himself, it would not be easy to read. In the course of his career, Craddock had met and summed up many people. By now he was fully adept in realising the potentialities and very often reading the thoughts of most of the people with whom he came in contact. But he felt at once that one would be able to gauge only as much of Jason Rudd's thoughts as Jason Rudd himself permitted. The eyes, deepset and thoughtful, perceived but would not easily reveal. The ugly, rugged head spoke of an excellent intellect. The clown's face could repel you or attract you. Here, thought Dermot Craddock, to himself, is where I sit and listen and take very careful notes.

'Sorry, Chief-Inspector, if you've had to wait for me. I was held up by some small complication over at the Studios. Can I offer you a drink?'

'Not just now, thank you, Mr Rudd.'

The clown's face suddenly crinkled into a kind of ironic amusement.

'Not the house to take a drink in, is that what you're thinking?'

'As a matter of fact it wasn't what I was thinking.'

'No, no I suppose not. Well, Chief-Inspector, what do you want to know? What can I tell you?'

'Mr Preston has answered very adequately all the questions I have put to him.'

'And that has been helpful to you?'

'Not as helpful as I could wish.'

Jason Rudd looked inquiring.

'I've also seen Dr Gilchrist. He informs me that your wife is not yet strong enough to be asked questions.'

'Marina,' said Jason Rudd, 'is very sensitive. She's subject, frankly, to nervous storms. And murder at such close quarters is, as you will admit, likely to produce a nerve storm.'

'It is not a pleasant experience,' Dermot Craddock agreed, dryly.

'In any case I doubt if there is anything my wife could tell you that you could not learn equally well from me. I was standing beside her when the thing happened, and frankly I would say that I am a better observer than my wife.'

'The first question I would like to ask,' said Dermot, '(and it is a question that you have probably answered already but for all that I would like to ask again), had you or your wife any previous acquaintance with Heather Badcock?'

Jason Rudd shook his head.

'None whatever. I certainly have never. seen the woman before in my life. I had two letters from her on behalf of the St John Ambulance Association, but I had not met her personally until about five minutes before her death.'

'But she claimed to have met your wife?'

Jason Rudd nodded.

'Yes, some twelve or thirteen years ago, I gather. In Bermuda. Some big garden party in aid of ambulances, which Marina opened for them, I think, and Mrs Badcock, as soon as she was introduced, burst into some long rigmarole of how although she was in bed with 'flu, she had got up and had managed to come to this affair and had asked for and got my wife's autograph.'

Again the ironical smile crinkled his face.

394

'That, I may say, is a very common occurrence, Chief-Inspector. Large mobs of people are usually lined up to obtain my wife's autograph and it is a moment that they treasure and remember. Quite understandably, it is an event in their lives. Equally naturally it is not likely that my wife would remember one out of a thousand or so autograph hunters. She had, quite frankly, no recollection of ever having seen Mrs Badcock before.'

'That I can well understand,' said Craddock. 'Now I have been told, Mr Rudd, by an onlooker that your wife was slightly *distraite* during the few moments that Heather Badcock was speaking to her. Would you agree that such was the case?'

'Very possibly,' said Jason Rudd. 'Marina is not particularly strong. She was, of course, used to what I may describe as her public social work, and could carry out her duties in that line almost automatically. But towards the end of a long day she was inclined occasionally to flag. This may have been such a moment. I did not, I may say, observe anything of the kind myself. No, wait a minute, that is not quite true. I do remember that she was a little slow in making her reply to Mrs Badcock. In fact I think I nudged her very gently in the ribs.'

'Something had perhaps distracted her attention?' said Dermot.

'Possibly, but it may have been just a momentary lapse through fatigue.'

Dermot Craddock was silent for a few minutes. He looked out of the window where the view was the somewhat sombre one over the woods surrounding Gossington Hall. He looked at the pictures on the walls, and finally he looked at Jason Rudd. Jason Rudd's face was attentive but nothing more. There was no guide to his feelings. He appeared courteous and completely at ease, but he might, Craddock thought, be actually nothing of the kind. This was a man of very high mental calibre. One would not, Dermot thought, get anything out of him that he was not prepared to say unless one put one's cards on the table. Dermot took his decision. He would do just that.

'Has it occurred to you, Mr Rudd, that the poisoning of Heather Badcock may have been entirely accidental? That the real intended victim was your wife?'

There was a silence. Jason Rudd's face did not change its expression. Dermot waited. Finally Jason Rudd gave a deep sigh and appeared to relax.

'Yes,' he said quietly, 'you're quite right, Chief-Inspector. I have been sure of it all along.'

'But you have said nothing to that effect, not to Inspector Cornish, not at the inquest?'

'No.'

'Why not, Mr Rudd?'

'I could answer you very adequately by saying that it was merely a belief on my part unsupported by any kind of evidence. The facts that led me to deduce it, were facts equally accessible to the law which was probably better qualified to decide than I was. I knew nothing about Mrs Badcock personally. She might have enemies, someone might have decided to administer a fatal dose to her on this particular occasion, though it would seem a very curious and far-fetched decision. But it might have been chosen conceivably for the reason that at a public occasion of this kind the issues would be more confused, the number of strangers present would be considerable and just for that reason it would be more difficult to bring home to the person in question the commission of such a crime. All that is true, but I am going to be frank with you, Chief-Inspector. That was *not* my reason for keeping silent. I will tell you what the reason was. I didn't want my wife to suspect for one moment that it was she who had narrowly escaped dying by poison.'

'Thank you for your frankness,' said Dermot. 'Not that I quite understand your motive in keeping silent.'

'No? Perhaps it is a little difficult to explain. You would have to know Marina to understand. She is a person who badly needs happiness and security. Her life has been highly successful in the material sense. She has won renown artistically but her personal life has been one of deep unhappiness. Again and again she has thought that she has found happiness and was wildly and unduly elated thereby, and has had her hopes dashed to the ground. She is incapable, Mr Craddock, of taking a rational, prudent view of life. In her previous marriages she has expected, like a child reading a fairy story, to live happy ever afterwards.'

Again the ironic smile changed the ugliness of the clown's face into a strange, sudden sweetness.

'But marriage is not like that, Chief-Inspector. There can be no rapture continued indefinitely. We are fortunate indeed if we can achieve a life of quiet content, affection, and serene and sober happiness.' He added. 'Perhaps you are married, Chief-Inspector?'

Dermot Craddock shook his head.

'I have not so far that good, or bad fortune,' he murmured.

'In our world, the moving picture world, marriage is a fully occupational hazard. Film stars marry often. Sometimes happily, sometimes disastrously, but seldom permanently. In that respect I should not say that Marina has had any undue cause to complain, but to one of her temperament things of that kind matter very deeply. She imbued herself with the idea that she was unlucky, that nothing would ever go right for her. She has always been looking desperately for the same things, love, happiness, affection, security. She was wildly anxious to have children. According to some medical opinion, the very strength of that anxiety frustrated its object. One very celebrated physician advised the adoption of a child. He said it is often the case that when an intense desire for maternity is assuaged by having adopted a baby, a child is born naturally shortly afterwards. Marina adopted no less than three children. For a time she got a certain amount of happiness and serenity, but it was not the real thing. You can imagine her delight when eleven years ago she found she was going to have a child. Her pleasure and delight were quite indescribable. She was in good health and the doctors assured her that there was every reason to believe that everything would go well. As you may or may not know, the result was tragedy. The child, a boy, was born mentally deficient, imbecile. The result was disastrous. Marina had a complete breakdown and was severely ill for years, confined to a sanatorium. Though her recovery was slow she did recover. Shortly after that we married and she began once more to take an interest in life and to feel that perhaps she could be happy. It was difficult at first for her to get a worth while contract for a picture. Everyone was inclined to doubt whether her health would stand the strain. I had to battle for that.' Jason Rudd's lips set firmly together. 'Well, the battle was successful. We have started shooting the picture. In the meantime we bought this house and set about altering it. Only about a fortnight ago Marina was saying to me how happy she was, and how she felt at last she was going to be able to settle down to a happy home life, her troubles behind her. I was a little nervous because, as usual, her expectations were too optimistic. But there was no doubt that she was happy. Her nervous symptoms disappeared, there was a calmness and a quietness about her that I had never seen before. Everything was going well until –' he paused. His voice became suddenly bitter. 'Until this happened! That woman had to die – *here*! That in itself was shock enough. I couldn't risk – I was determined not to risk – Marina's knowing that an attempt had been made on *her* life. That would have been a second, perhaps fatal, shock. It might have precipitated another mental collapse.'

He looked directly at Dermot.

'Do you understand – now?'

'I see your point of view,' said Craddock, 'but forgive me, isn't there one aspect that you are neglecting? You give me your conviction that an attempt was made to poison your wife. Doesn't that danger still remain? If a poisoner does not succeed, isn't it likely that the attempt may be repeated?'

'Naturally I've considered that,' said Jason Rudd, 'but I am confident that, being forewarned so to speak, I can take all reasonable precautions for my wife's safety. I shall watch over her and arrange that others shall watch over her. The great thing, I feel, is that she herself should not know that any danger threatened her.'

'And you think,' said Dermot cautiously, 'that she does *not* know?'

'Of course not. She has no idea.'

'You're sure of that?'

'Certain. Such an idea would never occur to her.'

'But it occurred to you,' Dermot pointed out.

'That's very different,' said Jason Rudd. 'Logically it was the only solution. But my wife isn't logical, and to begin with she could not possibly imagine that anyone would want to do away with her. Such a possibility would simply not occur to her mind.'

'You may be right,' said Dermot slowly, 'but that leaves us now with several other questions. Again, let me put this bluntly. Whom do you suspect?'

'I can't tell you.'

'Excuse me, Mr Rudd, do you mean by that you can't or that you won't?'

Jason Rudd spoke quickly. 'Can't. Can't every time. It seems to me just as impossible as it would seem to her that anyone would dislike her enough – should have a sufficient grudge against her – to do such a thing. On the other hand, on the sheer, downright evidence of the facts, that is exactly what must have occurred.'

'Will you outline the facts to me as you see them?'

'If you like. The circumstances are quite clear. I poured out two daiquiri cocktails from an already prepared jug. I took them to Marina and Mrs Badcock. What Mrs Badcock did I do not know. She moved on, I presume, to speak to someone she knew. My wife had her drink in her hand. At that moment the mayor and his wife

398

were approaching. She put down her glass, as yet untouched, and greeted them. Then there were more greetings. An old friend we'd not seen for years, some other locals and one or two people from the studios. During that time the glass containing the cocktail stood on the table which was situated at that time behind us since we had both moved forward a little to the top of the stairs. One or two photographs were taken of my wife talking to the mayor, which we hoped would please the local population, at the special request of the representatives of the local newspaper. While this was being done I brought some fresh drinks to a few of the last arrivals. During that time my wife's glass must have been poisoned. Don't ask me *how* it was done, it cannot have been easy to do. On the other hand, it is startling, if anyone has the nerve to do an action openly and unconcernedly, how little people are likely to notice it! You ask me if I have suspicions; all I can say is that at least one of about twenty people *might* have done it. People, you see, were moving about in little groups, talking, occasionally going off to have a look at the alterations which had been done to the house. There was movement, continual movement. I've thought and I've thought, I've racked my brains but there is nothing, absolutely *nothing* to direct my suspicions to any particular person.'

He paused and gave an exasperated sigh.

'I understand,' said Dermot. 'Go on, please.'

'I dare say you've heard the next part before.'

'I should like to hear it again from you.'

'Well, I had come back towards the head of the stairs. My wife had turned towards the table and was just picking up her glass. There was a slight exclamation from Mrs Badcock. Somebody must have jogged her arm and the glass slipped out of her fingers and was broken on the floor. Marina did the natural hostess's act. Her own skirt had been slightly touched with the liquid. She insisted no harm was done, used her own handkerchief to wipe Mrs Badcock's skirt and insisted on her having her own drink. If I remember she said "I've had far too much already." So that was that. But I can assure you of this. The fatal dose could not have been added *after* that for Mrs Badcock immediately began to drink from the glass. As you know, four or five minutes later she was dead. I wonder – how I wonder – what the poisoner must have felt when he realised how badly his scheme had failed . . .'

'All this occurred to you at the time?'

'Of course not. At the time I concluded, naturally enough, this woman had had some kind of a seizure. Perhaps heart, coronary thrombosis, something of that sort. It never occurred to me that *poisoning* was involved. Would it occur to you – would it occur to anybody?'

'Probably not,' said Dermot. 'Well your account is clear enough and you seem sure of your facts. You say you have no suspicion of any particular person. I can't quite accept that, you know.'

'I assure you it's the truth.'

'Let us approach it from another angle. Who is there who could wish to harm your wife? It all sounds melodramatic if you put it this way, but what enemies had she got?'

Jason Rudd made an expressive gesture.

'Enemies? Enemies? It's so hard to define what one means by an enemy. There's plenty of envy and jealousy in the world my wife and I occupy. There are always people who say malicious things, who'll start a whispering campaign, who will do someone they are jealous of a bad turn if the opportunity occurs. But that doesn't mean that any of those people is a murderer, or indeed even a likely murderer. Don't you agree?'

'Yes, I agree. There must be something beyond petty dislikes or envies. Is there anyone whom your wife has injured, say, in the past?'

Jason Rudd did not rebut this easily. Instead he frowned.

'Honestly, I don't think so,' he said at last, 'and I may say I've given a lot of thought to that point.'

'Anything in the nature of a love affair, an association with some man?'

'There have of course been affairs of that kind. It may be considered, I suppose, that Marina has occasionally treated some man badly. But there is nothing to cause any lasting illwill. I'm sure of it.'

'What about women? Any woman who has had a lasting grudge against Miss Gregg?'

'Well,' said Jason Rudd, 'you can never tell with women. I can't think of any particular one offhand.'

'Who'd benefit financially by your wife's death?'

'Her will benefits various people but not to any large extent. I suppose the people who'd benefit, as you put it, financially, would be myself as her husband from another angle, possibly the star who might replace her in this film. Though, of course, the film might be abandoned altogether. These things are very uncertain.'

'Well, we need not go into all that now,' said Dermot.

'And I have your assurance that Marina will not be told that she is in possible danger?'

'We shall have to go into that matter,' said Dermot. 'I want to impress upon you that you are taking quite a considerable risk there. However, the matter will not arise for some days since your wife is still under medical care. Now there is one more thing I would like you to do. I would like you to write down for me as accurately as you can every single person who was in that recess at the top of the stairs, or whom you saw coming up the stairs at the time of the murder.'

'I'll do my best, but I'm rather doubtful. You'd do far better to consult my secretary, Ella Zielinsky. She has a most accurate memory and also lists of the local lads who were there. If you'd like to see her now – '

'I would like to talk to Miss Ella Zielinsky very much,' said Dermot.

CHAPTER ELEVEN

Surveying Dermot Craddock unemotionally through her large horn-rimmed spectacles, Ella Zielinsky seemed to him almost too good to be true. With quiet businesslike alacrity she whipped out of a drawer a typewritten sheet and passed it across to him.

'I think I can be fairly sure that there are no omissions,' she said. 'But it is just possible that I may have included one or two names – local names they will be – who were not actually there. That is to say who may have left earlier or who may not have been found and brought up. Actually, I'm pretty sure that it is correct.'

'A very efficient piece of work if I may say so,' said Dermot.

'Thank you.'

'I suppose – I am quite an ignoramus in such things – that you have to attain a high standard of efficiency in your job?'

'One has to have things pretty well taped, yes.'

'What else does your job comprise? Are you a kind of liaison officer, so to speak, between the studios and Gossington Hall?'

'No. I've nothing to do with the studios, actually, though of course I naturally take messages from there on the telephone or send them. My job is to look after Miss Gregg's social life, her public and private engagements, and to supervise in some degree the running of the house.'

'You like the job?'

'It's extremely well paid and I find it reasonably interesting. I didn't however bargain for murder,' she added dryly.

'Did it seem very incredible to you?'

'So much so that I am going to ask you if you are really sure it *is* murder?'

'Six times the dose of di-ethyl-mexine etc. etc., could hardly be anything else.'

'It might have been an accident of some kind.'

'And how would you suggest such an accident could have occurred?'

'More easily than you'd imagine, since you don't know the set-up. This house is simply full of drugs of all kinds. I don't mean dope when I say drugs. I mean properly prescribed remedies, but, like most of these things, what they call, I understand, the lethal dose is not very far removed from the therapeutic dose.'

Dermot nodded.

'These theatrical and picture people have the most curious lapses in their intelligence. Sometimes it seems to me that the more of an artistic genius you are, the less common sense you have in everday life.'

'That may well be.'

'What with all the bottles, cachets, powders, capsules, and little boxes that they carry about with them; what with popping in a tranquilliser here and a tonic there and a pep pill somewhere else, don't you think it would be easy enough that the whole thing might get mixed up?'

'I don't see how it could apply in this case.'

'Well, I think it could. Somebody, one of the guests, may have wanted a sedative, or a reviver, and whipped out his or her little container which they carry around and possibly because they hadn't remembered the dose because they hadn't had one for some time, might have put too much in a glass. Then their mind was distracted and they went off somewhere, and let's say this Mrs What's-her-name

402

comes along, thinks it's her glass, picks it up and drinks it. That's surely a more feasible idea than anything else?'

'You don't think that all those possibilities haven't been gone into, do you?'

'No, I suppose not. But there were a lot of people there and a lot of glasses standing about with drinks in them. It happens often enough, you know, that you pick up the wrong glass and drink out of it.'

'Then you don't think that Heather Badcock was deliberately poisoned? You think that she drank out of somebody else's glass?'

'I can't imagine anything more likely to happen.'

'In that case,' said Dermot speaking carefully, 'it would have had to be Marina Gregg's glass. You realise that? Marina handed her her own glass.'

'Or what she thought was her own glass,' Ella Zielinsky corrected him. 'You haven't talked to Marina yet, have you? she's extremely vague. She'd pick up any glass that looked as though it were hers, and drink it. I've seen her do it again and again.'

'She takes Calmo?'

'Oh yes, we all do.'

'You too, Miss Zielinsky?'

'I'm driven to it sometimes,' said Ella Zielinsky. 'These things are rather imitative, you know.'

'I shall be glad,' said Dermot, 'when I am able to talk to Miss Gregg. She – er – seems to be prostrated for a very long time.'

'That's just throwing a temperament,' said Ella Zielinksy. 'She just dramatizes herself a good deal, you know. She'd never take murder in her stride.'

'As you manage to do, Miss Zielinsky?'

'When everybody about you is in a continual state of agitation,' said Ella dryly, 'it develops in you a desire to go to the opposite extreme.'

'You learn to take a pride in not turning a hair when some shocking tragedy occurs?'

She considered. 'It's not a really nice trait, perhaps. But I think if you didn't develop that sense you'd probably go round the bend yourself.'

'Was Miss Gregg – is Miss Gregg a difficult person to work for?'

It was something of a personal question but Dermot Craddock regarded it as a kind of test. If Ella Zielinsky raised her eyebrows and tacitly demanded what this had to do with the murder of

Mrs Badcock, he would be forced to admit that it had nothing to do with it. But he wondered if Ella Zielinsky might perhaps enjoy telling him what she thought of Marina Gregg.

'She's a great artist. She's got a personal magnetism that comes over on the screen in the most extraordinary way. Because of that one feels it's rather a privilege to work with her. Taken purely personally, of course, she's hell!'

'Ah,' said Dermot.

'She's no kind of moderation, you see. She's up in the air or down in the dumps and everything is always terrifically exaggerated, and she changes her mind and there are an enormous lot of things that one must never mention or allude to because they upset her.'

'Such as?'

'Well, naturally, mental breakdown, or sanatoriums for mental cases. I think it is quite to be understood that she should be sensitive about that. And anything to do with children.'

'Children? In what way?'

'Well, it upsets her to see children, or to hear of people being happy with children. If she hears someone is going to have a baby or has just had a baby, it throws her into a state of misery at once. She can never have another child herself, you see, and the only one she did have is batty. I don't know if you knew that?'

'I had heard it, yes. It's all very sad and unfortunate. But after a good many years you'd think she'd forget about it a little.'

'She doesn't. It's an obsession with her. She broods on it.'

'What does Mr Rudd feel about it?'

'Oh, it wasn't his child. It was her last husband's, Isidore Wright's.'

'Ah yes, her last husband. Where is he now?'

'He married again and lives in Florida,' said Ella Zielinsky promptly.

'Would you say that Marina Gregg had made many enemies in her life?'

'Not unduly so. Not more than most, that is to say. There are always rows over other women or other men or over contracts or jealousy – all of those things.'

'She wasn't as far as you know afraid of anyone?'

'Marina? *Afraid* of anyone? I don't think so. Why? Should she be?'

'I don't know,' said Dermot. He picked up the list of names. 'Thank you very much, Miss Zielinsky. If there's anything else I want to know I'll come back. May I?'

'Certainly. I'm only too anxious – we're all only too anxious – to do anything we can to help.'

II

'Well, Tom, what have you got for me?'

Detective-Sergeant Tiddler grinned appreciatively. His name was not Tom, it was William, but the combination of Tom Tiddler had always been too much for his colleagues.

'What gold and silver have you picked up for me?' continued Dermot Craddock.

The two were staying at the Blue Boar and Tiddler had just come back from a day spent at the studios.

'The proportion of gold is very small,' said Tiddler. 'Not much gossip. No startling rumours. One or two suggestions of suicide.'

'Why suicide?'

'They thought she might have had a row with her husband and be trying to make him sorry. That line of country. But that she didn't really mean to go so far as doing herself in.'

'I can't see that that's a very helpful line,' said Dermot.

'No, of course it isn't. They know nothing about it, you see. They don't know anything except what they're busy on. It's all highly technical and there's an atmosphere of "the show must go on," or as I suppose one ought to say the picture must go on, or the shooting must go on. I don't know any of the right terms. All they're concerned about is when Marina Gregg will get back to the set. She's mucked up a picture once or twice before by staging a nervous breakdown.'

'Do they like her on the whole?'

'I should say they consider her the devil of a nuisance but for all that they can't help being fascinated by her when she's in the mood to fascinate them. Her husband's besotted about her, by the way.'

'What do they think of him?'

'They think he's the finest director or producer or whatever it is that there's ever been.'

'No rumours of his being mixed up with some other star or some woman of some kind?'

Tom Tiddler stared. 'No,' he said, 'no. Not a hint of such a thing. Why, do you think there might be?'

'I wondered,' said Dermot. 'Marina Gregg is convinced that that lethal dose was meant for her.'

'Is she now? Is she right?'

'Almost certainly, I should say,' Dermot replied. 'But that's not the point. The point is that she hasn't told her husband so, only her doctor.'

'Do you think she would have told him if – '

'I just wondered,' said Craddock, 'whether she might have had at the back of her mind an idea that her husband had been responsible. The doctor's manner was a little peculiar. I may have imagined it but I don't think I did.'

'Well, there were no such rumours going about at the studios,' said Tom. 'You hear that sort of thing soon enough.'

'She herself is not embroiled with any other man?'

'No, she seems to be devoted to Rudd.'

'No interesting snippets about her past?'

Tiddler grinned. 'Nothing to what you can read in a film magazine any day of the week.'

'I think I'll have to read a few,' said Dermot, 'to get the atmosphere.'

'The things they say and hint!' said Tiddler.

'I wonder,' said Dermot thoughtfully, 'if my Miss Marple reads film magazines.'

'Is that the old lady who lives in the house by the church?'

'That's right.'

'They say she's sharp,' said Tiddler. 'They say there's nothing goes on here that Miss Marple doesn't hear about. She may not know much about the film people, but she ought to be able to give you the low-down on the Badcocks all right.'

'It's not as simple as it used to be,' said Dermot. 'There's a new social life springing up here. A housing estate, big building development. The Badcocks are fairly new and come from there.'

'I didn't hear much about the locals, of course,' said Tiddler. 'I concentrated on the sex life of film stars and such things.'

'You haven't brought back very much,' grumbled Dermot. 'What about Marina Gregg's past, anything about that?'

'Done a bit of marrying in her time but not more than most. Her first husband didn't like getting the chuck, so they said, but he was a very ordinary sort of bloke. He was a realtor or something like that. What is a realtor, by the way?'

'I think it means in the real estate business.'

'Oh well, anyway, he didn't line up as very glamorous so she got rid of him and married a foreign count or prince. That lasted hardly any time at all but there don't seem to be any bones broken. She just shook him off and teamed up with number three. Film Star Robert Truscott. That was said to be a passionate love match. His wife didn't much like letting go of him, but she had to take it in the end. Big alimony. As far as I can make out everybody's hard up because they've got to pay so much alimony to all their ex-wives.'

'But it went wrong?'

'Yes. She was the broken-hearted one, I gather. But another big romance came along a year or two later. Isidore Somebody – a playwright.'

'It's an exotic life,' said Dermot. 'Well, we'll call it a day now. Tomorrow we've got to get down to a bit of hard work.'

'Such as?'

'Such as checking a list I've got here. Out of twenty-odd names we ought to be able to do *some* elimination and out of what's left we'll have to look for X.'

'Any idea who X is?'

'Not in the least. If it isn't Jason Rudd, that is.' He added with a wry and ironic smile, 'I shall have to go to Miss Marple and get briefed on local matters.'

CHAPTER TWELVE

Miss Marple was pursuing her own methods of research.

'It's very kind, Mrs Jameson, very kind of you indeed. I can't tell you how grateful I am.'

'Oh, don't mention it, Miss Marple. I'm sure I'm glad to oblige you. I suppose you'll want the latest ones?'

'No, no, not particularly,' said Miss Marple. 'In fact I think I'd rather have some of the old numbers.'

'Well, here you are then,' said Mrs Jameson, 'there's a nice armful and I can assure you we shan't miss them. Keep them as long as you like. Now it's too heavy for you to carry. Jenny, how's your perm doing?'

'She's all right, Mrs Jameson. She's had her rinse and now she's having a good dry-out.'

'In that case, dear, you might just run along with Miss Marple here, and carry these magazines for her. No, really, Miss Marple, it's no trouble at all. Always pleased to do anything we can for you.'

How kind people were, Miss Marple thought, especially when they'd known you practically all their lives. Mrs Jameson, after long years of running a hairdressing parlour had steeled herself to going as far in the cause of progress as to repaint her sign and call herself 'DIANE. Hair Stylist.' Otherwise the shop remained much as before and catered in much the same way to the needs of its clients. It turned you out with a nice firm perm: it accepted the task of shaping and cutting for the younger generation and the resultant mess was accepted without too much recrimination. But the bulk of Mrs Jameson's clientele was a bunch of solid, stick in the mud middle-aged ladies who found it extremely hard to get their hair done the way they wanted it anywhere else.

'Well, I never,' said Cherry the next morning, as she prepared to run a virulent Hoover round the lounge as she still called it in her mind. 'What's all this?'

'I am trying,' said Miss Marple, 'to instruct myself a little in the moving picture world.'

She laid aside *Movie News* and picked up *Amongst the Stars*.

'It's really very interesting. It reminds one so much of so many things.'

'Fantastic lives they must lead,' said Cherry.

'Specialised lives,' said Miss Marple. 'Highly specialised. It reminds me very much of the things a friend of mine used to tell me. She was a hospital nurse. The same simplicity of outlook and all the gossip and the rumours. And goodlooking doctors causing any amount of havoc.'

'Rather sudden, isn't it, this interest of yours?' said Cherry.

'I'm finding it difficult to knit nowadays,' said Miss Marple. 'Of course the print of these *is* rather small, but I can always use a magnifying glass.'

Cherry looked on curiously.

'You're always surprising me,' she said. 'The things you take an interest in.'

'I take an interest in everything,' said Miss Marple.

'I mean taking up new subjects at your age.'

Miss Marple shook her head.

'They aren't really new subjects. It's human nature I'm interested in, you know, and human nature is much the same whether it's film stars or hospital nurses or people in St Mary Mead or,' she added thoughtfully, 'people who live in the Development.'

'Can't see much likeness between me and a film star,' said Cherry laughing, 'more's the pity. I suppose it's Marina Gregg and her husband coming to live at Gossington Hall that set you off on this.'

'That and the very sad event that occurred there,' said Miss Marple.

'Mrs Badcock, you mean? It was bad luck that.'

'What do you think of it in the – ' Miss Marple paused with the 'D' hovering on her lips. 'What do you and your friends think about it?' she amended the question.

'It's a queer do,' said Cherry. 'Looks as though it were murder, doesn't it, though of course the police are too cagey to say so outright. Still, that's what it looks like.'

'I don't see what else it could be,' said Miss Marple.

'It couldn't be suicide,' agreed Cherry, 'not with Heather Badcock.'

'Did you know her well?'

'No, not really. Hardly at all. She was a bit of a nosy parker you know. Always wanting you to join this, join that, turn up for meetings at so-and-so. Too much energy. Her husband got a bit sick of it sometimes, I think.'

'She doesn't seem to have had any real enemies.'

'People used to get a bit fed up with her sometimes. The point is, I don't see who could have murdered her unless it was her husband. And he's a very meek type. Still, the worm will turn, or so they say. I've always heard that Crippen was ever so nice a man and that man, Haigh, who pickled them all in acid – they say he couldn't have been more charming! So one never knows, does one?'

'Poor Mr Badcock,' said Miss Marple.

'And people say he was upset and nervy at the fête that day – before it happened, I mean – but people always say that kind of thing afterwards. If you ask me, he's looking better now than he's looked for years. Seems to have got a bit more spirit and go in him.'

'Indeed?' said Miss Marple.

'Nobody *really* thinks he did it,' said Cherry. 'Only if he didn't,

409

who did? I can't help thinking myself it must have been an accident of some kind. Accidents do happen. You think you know all about mushrooms and go out and pick some. One fungus gets in among them and there you are, rolling about in agony and lucky if the doctor gets to you in time.'

'Cocktails and glasses of sherry don't seem to lend themselves to accident,' said Miss Marple.

'Oh, I don't know,' said Cherry. 'A bottle of something or other could have got in by mistake. Somebody I knew took a dose of concentrated D.D.T. once. Horribly ill they were.'

'Accident,' said Miss Marple thoughtfully. 'Yes, it certainly seems the best solution. I must say I can't believe that in the case of Heather Badcock it *could* have been deliberate murder. I won't say it's impossible. Nothing is impossible, but it doesn't seem like it. No, I think the truth lies somewhere here.' She rustled her magazines and picked up another one.

'You mean you're looking for some special story about someone?'

'No,' said Miss Marple. 'I'm just looking for odd mentions of people and a way of life and something – some little something that might help.' She returned to her perusal of the magazines and Cherry removed her vacuum cleaner to the upper floor. Miss Marple's face was pink and interested, and being slightly deaf now, she did not hear the footsteps that came along the garden path towards the drawing-room window. It was only when a slight shadow fell on the page that she looked up. Dermot Craddock was standing smiling at her.

'Doing your homework, I see,' he remarked.

'Inspector Craddock, how very nice to see you. And how kind to spare time to come and see me. Would you like a cup of coffee, or possibly a glass of sherry?'

'A glass of sherry would be splendid,' said Dermot. 'Don't you move,' he added. 'I'll ask for it as I come in.'

He went round by the side door and presently joined Miss Marple.

'Well,' he said, 'is that bumph giving you ideas?'

'Rather too many ideas,' said Miss Marple. 'I'm not often shocked, you know, but this does shock me a little.'

'What, the private lives of film stars?'

'Oh no,' said Miss Marple, 'not *that*! That all seems to be *most* natural, given the circumstances and the money involved and the opportunities for propinquity. Oh, no, that's natural enough. I mean the way they're written about. I'm rather old-fashioned, you know, and I feel that that really shouldn't be allowed.'

'It's news,' said Dermot Craddock, 'and some pretty nasty things can be said in the way of fair comment.'

'I know,' said Miss Marple. 'It makes me sometimes very angry. I expect you think it's silly of me reading all these. But one does so badly want to be *in* things and of course sitting here in the house I can't really know as much about things as I would like to.'

'That's just what I thought,' said Dermot Craddock, 'and that's why I've come to tell you about them.'

'But, my dear boy, excuse me, would your superiors really approve of that?'

'I don't see why not,' said Dermot. 'Here,' he added, 'I have a list. A list of people who were there on that landing during the short time of Heather Badcock's arrival until her death. We've eliminated a lot of people, perhaps precipitately, but I don't think so. We've eliminated the mayor and his wife and Alderman somebody and his wife and a great many of the locals, though we've kept in the husband. If I remember rightly you were always very suspicious of husbands.'

'They are often the obvious suspects,' said Miss Marple, apologetically, 'and the obvious is so often right.'

'I couldn't agree with you more,' said Cruddock.

'But which husband, my dear boy, are you referring to?'

'Which one do you think?' asked Dermot. He eyed her sharply.

Miss Marple looked at him.

'Jason Rudd?' she asked.

'Ah!' said Craddock. 'Your mind works just as mine does. I don't think it was Arthur Badcock, because you see, I don't think that Heather Badcock was meant to be killed. I think the intended victim was Marina Gregg.'

'That would seem almost certain, wouldn't it?' said Miss Marple.

'And so,' said Craddock, 'as we both agree on that, the field widens. To tell you who was there on that day, what they saw or said they saw, and where they were or said they were, is only a thing you could have observed for yourself if you'd been there. So my superiors, as you call them, couldn't possibly object to my discussing that with you, could they?'

'That's very nicely put, my dear boy,' said Miss Marple.

411

'I'll give you a little précis of what I was told and then we'll come to the list.'

He gave a brief résumé of what he had heard, and then he produced his list.

'It must be one of these,' he said. 'My godfather, Sir Henry Clithering, told me that you once had a club here. You called it the Tuesday Night Club. You all dined with each other in turn and then someone would tell a story – a story of some real life happening which had ended in mystery. A mystery of which only the teller of the tale knew the answer. And every time, so my godfather told me, you guessed right. So I thought I'd come along and see if you'd do a bit of guessing for me this morning.'

'I think that is rather a frivolous way of putting it,' said Miss Marple, reproving, 'but there is one question I should like to ask.'

'Yes?'

'What about the children?'

'The children? There's only one. An imbecile child in a sanatorium in America. Is that what you mean?'

'No,' said Miss Marple, 'that's not what I mean. It's very sad of course. One of those tragedies that seem to happen and there's no one to blame for it. No, I meant the children that I've seen mentioned in some article here.' She tapped the papers in front of her. 'Children that Marina Gregg adopted. Two boys, I think, and a girl. In one case a mother with a lot of children and very little money to bring them up in this country, wrote to her, and asked if she couldn't take a child. There was a lot of very silly false sentiment written about that. About the mother's unselfishness and the wonderful home and education and future the child was going to have. I can't find out much about the other two. One I think was a foreign refugee and the other was some American child. Marina Gregg adopted them at different times. I'd like to know what's happened to them.'

Dermot Craddock looked at her curiously. 'It's odd that you should think of that,' he said. 'I did just vaguely wonder about those children myself. But how do you connect them up?'

'Well,' said Miss Marple, 'as far as I can hear or find out, they're not living with her now, are they?'

'I expect they were provided for,' said Craddock. 'In fact, I think that the adoption laws would insist on that. There was probably money settled on them in trust.'

'So when she got – tired of them,' said Miss Marple with a very faint pause before the word 'tired,' 'they were dismissed!

412

After being brought up in luxury with every advantage. Is that it?'

'Probably,' said Craddock. 'I don't know exactly.' He continued to look at her curiously.

'Children feel things, you know,' said Miss Marple, nodding her head. 'They feel things more than the people around them ever imagine. The sense of hurt, of being rejected, of not belonging. It's a thing that you don't get over just because of advantages. Education is no substitute for it, or comfortable living, or an assured income, or a start in a profession. It's the sort of thing that might rankle.'

'Yes. But all the same, isn't it rather far-fetched to think that – well, what exactly do you think?'

'I haven't got as far as that,' said Miss Marple. 'I just wondered where they were now and how old they would be now? Grown up, I should imagine, from what I've read here.'

'I could find out, I suppose,' said Dermot Craddock slowly.

'Oh, I don't want to bother you in any way, or even to suggest that my little idea's worth while at all.'

'There's no harm,' said Dermot Craddock, 'in having that checked up on.' He made a note in his little book. 'Now do you want to look at my little list?'

'I don't really think I should be able to do anything useful about that. You see, I wouldn't know who the people were.'

'Oh, I could give you a running commentary,' said Craddock. 'Here we are. *Jason Rudd, husband*, (husbands always highly suspicious). Everyone says that Jason Rudd adores her. That is suspicious in itself, don't you think?'

'Not necessarily,' said Miss Marple with dignity.

'He's been very active in trying to conceal the fact that his wife was the object of attack. He hasn't hinted any suspicion of such a thing to the police. I don't know why he thinks we're such asses as not to think of it for ourselves. We've considered it from the first. But anyway, that's his story. He was afraid that knowledge of that fact might get to his wife's ears and that she'd go into a panic about it.'

'Is she the sort of woman who goes into panics?'

'Yes, she's neurasthenic, throws temperaments, has nervous breakdowns, gets in states.'

'That might not mean any lack of courage,' Miss Marple objected.

'On the other hand,' said Craddock, 'if she knows quite well that she was the object of attack, it's also possible that she may know who did it.'

'You mean she knows who did it – but does not want to disclose the fact?'

'I just say it's a possibility, and if so, one rather wonders why not? It looks as though the motive, the root of the matter, was something she didn't want to come to her husband's ear.'

'That is certainly an interesting thought,' said Miss Marple.

'Here are a few more names. The secretary, Ella Zielinsky. An extremely competent and efficient young woman.'

'In love with the husband, do you think?' asked Miss Marple.

'I should think definitely,' answered Craddock, 'but why should you think so?'

'Well, it so often happens,' said Miss Marple. 'And therefore not very fond of poor Marina Gregg, I expect?'

'Therefore possible motive for murder,' said Craddock.

'A lot of secretaries and employees are in love with their employers' husbands,' said Miss Marple, 'but very, very few of them try to poison them.'

'Well, we must allow for exceptions,' said Craddock. 'Then there were two local and one London photographer, and two members of the Press. None of them seems likely but we will follow them up. There was the woman who was formerly married to Marina Gregg's second or third husband. She didn't like it when Marina Gregg took her husband away. Still, that's about eleven or twelve years ago. It seems unlikely that she'd make a visit here at this juncture on purpose to poison Marina because of that. Then there's a man called Ardwyck Fenn. He was once a very close friend of Marina Gregg's. He hasn't seen her for years. He was not known to be in this part of the world and it was a great surprise when he turned up on this occasion.'

'She would be startled then when she saw him?'

'Presumably yes.'

'Startled – and possibly frightened.'

'"*The doom has come upon me*,"' said Craddock. 'That's the idea. Then there was young Hailey Preston dodging about that day, doing his stuff. Talks a good deal but definitely heard nothing, saw nothing and knew nothing. Almost too anxious to say so. Does anything there ring a bell?'

'Not exactly,' said Miss Marple. 'Plenty of interesting possibilities. But I'd still like to know a little more about the children.'

He looked at her curiously. 'You've got quite a bee in your bonnet about that, haven't you?' he said. 'All right, I'll find out.'

414

'I suppose it couldn't possibly have been the mayor?' said Inspector Cornish wistfully.

He tapped the paper with the list of names on it with his pencil. Dermot Craddock grinned.

'Wishful thinking?' he asked.

'You could certainly call it that,' said Cornish. 'Pompous, canting old hypocrite!' he went on. 'Everybody's got it in for him. Throws his weight about, ultra sanctimonious, *and* neck deep in graft for years past!'

'Can't you ever bring it home to him?'

'No,' said Cornish. 'He's too slick for that. He's always just on the right side of the law.'

'It's tempting, I agree,' said Dermot Craddock, 'but I think you'll have to banish that rosy picture from your mind, Frank.'

'I know, I know,' said Cornish. 'He's a possible, but a wildly improbable. Who else have we got?'

Both men studied the list again. There were still eight names on it.

'We're pretty well agreed,' said Craddock, 'that there's nobody missed out from here?' There was a faint question in his voice. Cornish answered it.

'I think you can be pretty sure that's the lot. After Mrs Bantry came the vicar, and after that the Badcocks. There were then eight people on the stairs. The mayor and his wife, Joshua Grice and wife from Lower Farm. Donald McNeil of the Much Benham *Herald & Argus*. Ardwyck Fenn, U.S.A., Miss Lola Brewster, U.S.A., Moving Picture Star. There you are. In addition there was an arty photographer from London with a camera set up on the angle of the stairs. If, as you suggest, this Mrs Bantry's story of Marina Gregg having a "frozen look" was occasioned by someone she saw on the stairs, you've got to take your pick among that lot. Mayor regretfully out. Grices out – never been away from St Mary Mead I should say.

That leaves four. Local journalist unlikely, photographer girl had been there for half an hour already, so why should Marina react so late in the day? What does that leave?'

'Sinister strangers from America,' said Craddock with a faint smile.

'You've said it.'

'They're our best suspects by far, I agree,' said Craddock. 'They turned up unexpectedly. Ardwyck Fenn was an old flame of Marina's whom she had not seen for years. Lola Brewster was once married to Marina Gregg's third husband, who got a divorce from her in order to marry Marina. It was not, I gather, a very amicable divorce.'

'I'd put her down as Suspect Number One,' said Cornish.

'Would you, Frank? After a lapse of about fifteen years or so, and having remarried twice herself since then?'

Cornish said that you never knew with women. Dermot accepted that as a general dictum, but remarked that it seemed odd to him to say the least of it.

'But you agree that it lies between them?'

'Possibly. But I don't like it very much. What about the hired help who were serving the drinks?'

'Discounting the "frozen look" we've heard so much about? Well, we've checked up in a general way. Local catering firm from Market Basing had the job – for the fête, I mean. Actually in the house, there was the butler, Giuseppe, in charge; and two local girls from the studios canteen. I know both of them. Not over bright, but harmless.'

'Pushing it back at me, are you? I'll go and have a word with the reporter chap. He might have seen something helpful. Then to London. Ardwyck Fenn, Lola Brewster – and the photographer girl – what's her name? – Margot Bence. She also might have seen something.'

Cornish nodded. 'Lola Brewster is my best bet,' he said. He looked curiously at Craddock. 'You don't seem as sold on her as I am.'

'I'm thinking of the difficulties,' said Dermot slowly.

'Difficulties?'

'Of putting poison into Marina's glass without anybody seeing her.'

'Well, that's the same for everybody, isn't it? It was a mad thing to do.'

'Agreed it was a mad thing to do, but it would be a madder thing for someone like Lola Brewster than for anybody else.'

'Why?' asked Cornish.

'Because she was a guest of importance. She's a somebody, a big name. Everyone would be looking at her.'

'True enough,' Cornish admitted.

'The locals would nudge each other and whisper and stare, and after Marina Gregg and Jason Rudd greeted her she'd have been passed on for the secretaries to look after. It wouldn't be easy, Frank. However adroit you were, you couldn't be sure *someone* wouldn't see you. That's the snag there, and it's a big snag.'

'As I say, isn't that snag the same for everybody?'

'No,' said Craddock. 'Oh no. Far from it. Take the butler now, Giuseppe. He's busy with the drinks and glasses, with pouring things out, with handing them. He could put a pinch or a tablet or two of Calmo in a glass easily enough.'

'Giuseppe?' Frank Cornish reflected. 'Do you think he did?'

'No reason to believe so,' said Craddock, 'but we might find a reason. A nice solid bit of motive, that is to say. Yes, he could have done it. Or one of the catering staff could have done it – unfortunately they weren't on the spot – a pity.'

'Someone might have managed to get himself or herself deliberately planted in the firm for the purpose.'

'You mean it might have been as premeditated as all that?'

'We don't know anything about it yet,' said Craddock, vexedly. 'We absolutely don't know the first thing about it. Not until we can prise what we want to know out of Marina Gregg, or out of her husband. They *must* know or suspect – but they're not telling. And we don't know yet *why* they're not telling. We've a long way to go.'

He paused and then resumed: 'Discounting the "frozen look" which may have been pure coincidence, there are other people who could have done it fairly easily. The secretary woman, Ella Zielinsky. She was also busy with glasses, with handing things to people. Nobody would be watching *her* with any particular interest. The same applies to that willow wand of a young man – I've forgotten his name. Hailey – Hailey Preston? That's right. There would have been a good opportunity for either of them. In fact if either of them *had* wanted to do away with Marina Gregg it would have been far safer to do so on a public occasion.'

'Anyone else?'

'Well, there's always the husband,' said Craddock.

'Back to the husbands again,' said Cornish, with a faint smile.

'We thought it was that poor devil, Badcock, before we realised that Marina was the intended victim. Now we've transferred our suspicions to Jason Rudd. He seems devoted enough though, I must say.'

'He has the reputation of being so,' said Craddock, 'but one never knows.'

'If he wanted to get rid of her, wouldn't divorce be much easier?'

'It would be far more usual,' agreed Dermot, 'but there may be a lot of ins and outs to this business that we don't know yet.'

The telephone rang. Cornish took up the receiver.

'What? Yes? Put them through. Yes, he's here.' He listened for a moment then put his hand over the receiver and looked at Dermot. 'Miss Marina Gregg,' he said, 'is feeling very much better. She is quite ready to be interviewed.'

'I'd better hurry along,' said Dermot Craddock, 'before she changes her mind.'

II

At Gossington Hall Dermot Craddock was received by Ella Zielinsky. She was, as usual, brisk and efficient.

'Miss Gregg is waiting for you, Mr Craddock,' she said.

Dermot looked at her with some interest. From the beginning he had found Ella Zielinsky an intriguing personality. He had said to himself, 'A poker face if I ever saw one.' She had answered any questions he had asked with the utmost readiness. She had shown no signs of keeping anything back, but what she really thought or felt or even knew about the business, he still had no idea. There seemed to be no chink in the armour of her bright efficiency. She might know more than she said she did; she might know a good deal. The only thing he was sure of – and he had to admit to himself that he had no reasons to adduce for that surety – was that she was in love with Jason Rudd. It was, as he had said, an occupational disease of secretaries. It probably meant nothing. But the fact did at least suggest a motive and he was sure, quite sure, that she was concealing something. It might be love, it might be hate. It might, quite simply, be guilt. She might have taken her opportunity that afternoon, or she might have deliberately planned what she was going to do. He could see her in the part quite easily, as far as the execution of it went. Her swift but unhurried movements, moving here and there, looking after guests, handing glasses to one or another, taking glasses away, her eyes marking the spot where Marina had put her glass down on the table. And then, perhaps at the very moment when Marina had been greeting the arrivals from the States, with surprise and joyous cries and everybody's eyes turned towards their meeting, she could have quietly and unobtrusively dropped the fatal dose into that glass. It would require audacity, nerve, swiftness. She would have had all those. Whatever she had done, she would not have looked guilty whilst she was doing it. It would have been a simple, brilliant crime, a crime that could hardly fail to be successful. But chance had ruled otherwise. In the rather crowded floorspace someone had joggled Heather Badcock's arm. Her drink had been spilt, and Marina, with her natural impulsive grace, had quickly proffered her own glass, standing there untouched. And so the wrong woman had died.

A lot of pure theory, and probably hooey at that, said Dermot Craddock to himself at the same time as he was making polite remarks to Ella Zielinsky.

'One thing I wanted to ask you, Miss Zielinsky. The catering was done by a Market Basing firm, I understand?'

'Yes.'

'Why was that particular firm chosen?'

'I really don't know,' said Ella. 'That doesn't lie amongst my duties. I know Mr Rudd thought it would be more tactful to employ somebody local rather than to employ a firm from London. The whole thing was really quite a small affair from our point of view.'

'Quite.' He watched her as she stood frowning a little and looking down. A good forehead, a determined chin, a figure which could look quite voluptuous if it was allowed to do so, a hard mouth, an acquisitive mouth. The eyes? He looked at them in surprise. The lids were reddened. He wondered. Had she been crying? It looked like it. And yet he could have sworn she was not the type of young woman to cry. She looked up at him, and as though she read his thoughts, she took out her handkerchief and blew her nose heartily.

'You've got a cold,' he said.

'Not a cold. Hay-fever. It's an allergy of some kind, really. I always get at it this time of year.'

There was a low buzz. There were two phones in the room, one on the table and one on another table in the corner. It was the latter

419

one that was beginning to buzz. Ella Zielinsky went over to it and picked up the receiver.

'Yes,' she said, 'he's here. I'll bring him up at once.' She put the receiver down again. 'Marina's ready for you,' she said.

III

Marina Gregg received Craddock in a room on the first floor, which was obviously her own private sitting-room opening out of her bedroom. After the accounts of her prostration and her nervous state, Dermot Craddock had expected to find a fluttering invalid. But although Marina was half reclining on a sofa her voice was vigorous and her eyes were bright. She had very little make-up on, but in spite of this she did not look her age, and he was struck very forcibly by the subdued radiance of her beauty. It was the exquisite line of cheek and jawbone, the way the hair fell loosely and naturally to frame her face. The long sea-green eyes, the pencilled eyebrows, owing something to art but more to nature, and the warmth and sweetness of her smile, all had a subtle magic. She said:

'Chief-Inspector Craddock? I've been behaving disgracefully. I do apologize. I just let myself go to pieces after this awful thing. I could have snapped out of it but I didn't. I'm ashamed of myself.' The smile came, rueful, sweet, turning up the comers of the mouth. She extended a hand and he took it.

'It was only natural,' he said, 'that you should feel upset.'

'Well, everyone was upset,' said Marina. 'I'd no business to make out it was worse for me than anyone else.'

'Hadn't you?'

She looked at him for a minute and then nodded. 'Yes,' she said, 'you're very perceptive. Yes, I had.' She looked down and with one long forefinger gently stroked the arm of the sofa. It was a gesture he had noticed in one of her films. It was a meaningless gesture, yet it seemed fraught with significance. It had a kind of musing gentleness.

'I'm a coward,' she said, her eyes still cast down. 'Somebody wanted to kill me and I didn't want to die.'

'Why do you think someone wanted to kill you?'

Her eyes opened wide. 'Because it was my glass – *my* drink – that had been tampered with. It was just a mistake that that poor stupid woman got it. That's what's so horrible and so tragic. Besides – '

420

'Yes, Miss Gregg?'

She seemed a little uncertain about saying more.

'You had other reasons perhaps for believing that you were the intended victim?'

She nodded.

'What reasons, Miss Gregg?'

She paused a minute longer before saying, 'Jason says I must tell you all about it.'

'You've confided in him then?'

'Yes . . . I didn't want to at first – but Dr Gilchrist put it to me that I must. And then I found that he thought so too. He'd thought it all along but – it's rather funny really' – rueful smile curled her lips again – 'he didn't want to alarm me by telling me. Really!' Marina sat up with a sudden vigorous movement. 'Darling Jinks! Does he think I'm a complete fool?'

'You haven't told me yet, Miss Gregg, why you should think anyone wanted to kill you.'

She was silent for a moment and then with a sudden brusque gesture, she stretched out for her handbag, opened it, took out a piece of paper and thrust it into his hand. He read it. Typed on it was one line of writing.

Don't think you'll escape next time.

Craddock said sharply, 'When did you get this?'

'It was on my dressing-table when I came back from the bath.'

'So someone in the house – '

'Not necessarily. Someone could have climbed up the balcony outside my window and pushed it through there. I think they meant it to frighten me still more, but actually it didn't. I just felt furiously angry and sent word to you to come and see me.'

Dermot Craddock smiled. 'Possibly a rather unexpected result for whoever sent it. Is this the first kind of message like that you've had?'

Again Marina hesitated. Then she said, 'No, it isn't.'

'Will you tell me about any other?'

'It was three weeks ago, when we first came here. It came to the studio, not here. It was quite ridiculous. It was just a message. Not typewritten that time. In capital letters. It said, "Prepare to die."'

She laughed. There was perhaps a very faint tinge of hysteria in the laugh. The mirth was genuine enough. 'It was so silly,' she said. 'Of

421

course one often gets crank messages, threats, things like that. I thought it was probably religious you know. Someone who didn't approve of film actresses. I just tore it up and threw it into the waste-paper basket.'

'Did you tell anyone about it, Miss Gregg?'

Marina shook her head. 'No, I never said a word to anyone. As a matter of fact, we were having a bit of worry at the moment about the scene we were shooting. I just couldn't have thought of anything but that at the moment. Anyway, as I say, I thought it was either a silly joke or one of those religious cranks who write and disapprove of play-acting and things like that.'

'And after that, was there another?'

'Yes. On the day of the fête. One of the gardeners brought it to me, I think. He said someone had left a note for me and was there any answer? I thought perhaps it had to do with the arrangements. I just tore it open. It said "Today will be your last day on earth." I just crumpled it up and said, "No answer." Then I called the man back and asked him who gave it to him. He said it was a man with spectacles on a bicycle. Well, I mean, what could you think about that? I thought it was more silliness. I didn't think – I didn't think for a moment, it was a real genuine threat.'

'Where's that note now, Miss Gregg?'

'I've no idea. I was wearing one of those coloured Italian silk coats and I think, as far as I remember, that I crumpled it up and shoved it into the pocket of it. But it's not there now. It probably fell out.'

'And you've no idea who wrote these silly notes, Miss Gregg? Who inspired them? Not even now?'

Her eyes opened widely. There was a kind of innocent wonder in them that he took note of. He admired it, but he did not believe in it.

'How can I tell? How can I possibly tell?'

'I think you might have quite a good idea, Miss Gregg.'

'I haven't. I assure you I haven't.'

'You're a very famous person,' said Dermot. 'You've had great successes. Successes in your profession, and personal successes, too. Men have fallen in love with you, wanted to marry you, have married you. Women have been jealous and envied you. Men have been in love with you and been rebuffed by you. It's a pretty wild field, I agree, but I should think you must have *some* idea who could have written these notes.'

422

'It could have been anybody.'

'No, Miss Gregg, it couldn't have been *anybody*. It could possibly have been one of quite a lot of people. It could be someone quite humble, a dresser, an electrician, a servant; or it could be someone among the ranks of your friends, or so-called friends. But you must have some idea. Some name, more than one name, perhaps, to suggest.'

The door opened and Jason Rudd came in. Marina turned to him. She swept out an arm appealingly.

'Jinks, darling, Mr Craddock is insisting that I must know who wrote those horrid notes. And I don't. You know I don't. Neither of us knows. We haven't got the least idea.'

'Very urgent about that,' thought Craddock. 'Very urgent. Is Marina Gregg afraid of what her husband might say?'

Jason Rudd, his eyes dark with fatigue and the scowl on his face deeper than usual, came over to join them. He took Marina's hand in his.

'I know it sounds unbelievable to you, Inspector,' he said, 'but honestly neither Marina nor I have any idea about this business.'

'So you're in the happy position of having no enemies, is that it?' The irony was manifest in Dermot's voice.

Jason Rudd flushed a little. 'Enemies? That's a very biblical word, Inspector. In that sense, I can assure you I can think of no enemies. People who dislike one, would like to get the better of one, would do a mean turn to one if they could, in malice and uncharitableness, yes. But it's a long step from that to putting an overdose of poison in a drink.'

'Just now, in speaking to your wife, I asked her who could have written or inspired those letters. She said she didn't know. When we come to the actual action, it narrows it down. *Somebody actually put the poison in that glass*. And that's a fairly limited field, you know.'

'I saw nothing,' said Jason Rudd.

'I certainly didn't,' said Marina. 'Well, I mean – if I had seen anyone putting anything in my glass, I wouldn't have drunk the stuff, would I?'

'I can't help believing, you know,' said Dermot Craddock gently, 'that you do know a little more than you're telling me.'

'It's not *true*,' said Marina. 'Tell him that that isn't true, Jason.'

'I assure you,' said Jason Rudd, 'that I am completely and absolutely at a loss. The whole thing's fantastic. I might believe

423

it was a joke – a joke that had somehow gone wrong – that had proved dangerous, done by a person who never dreamt that it would be dangerous . . .'

There was a slight question in his voice, then he shook his head. 'No. I see that idea doesn't appeal to you.'

'There's one more thing I should like to ask you,' said Dermot Craddock. 'You remember Mr and Mrs Badcock's arrival, of course. They came immediately after the vicar. You greeted them, I understand, Miss Gregg, in the same charming way as you had received all your guests. But I am told by an eye-witness that immediately after greeting them you looked over Mrs Badcock's shoulder and that you saw something which seemed to alarm you. Is that true, and if so, what was it?'

Marina said quickly, 'Of course it isn't true. Alarm me – what should have alarmed me?'

'That's what we want to know,' said Dermot Craddock patiently. 'My witness is very insistent on the point, you know.'

'Who was your witness? What did he or she say she saw?'

'You were looking at the staircase,' said Dermot Craddock. 'There were people coming up the staircase. There was a journalist, there was Mr Grice and his wife, elderly residents in this place, there was Mr Ardwyck Fenn who had just arrived from the States and there was Miss Lola Brewster. Was it the sight of one of those people that upset you, Miss Gregg?'

'I tell you I wasn't upset.' She almost barked the words.

'And yet your attention wavered from greeting Mrs Badcock. She had said something to you which you left unanswered because you were staring past her at something else.'

Marina Gregg took hold on herself. She spoke quickly and convincingly.

'I can explain, I really can. If you knew anything about acting you'd be able to understand quite easily. There comes a moment, even when you know a part well – in fact it usually happens when you *do* know a part well – when you go on with it mechanically. Smiling, making the proper movements and gestures, saying the words with the usual inflexions. But your mind isn't on it. And quite suddenly there's a horrible blank moment when you don't know where you are, where you've got to in the play, what your next lines are! Drying up, that's what we call it. Well, that's what happened to me. I'm not terribly strong, as my husband will tell you. I've had rather a strenuous time, and a good deal of nervous

424

apprehension about this film. I wanted to make a success of this fête and to be nice and pleasant and welcoming to everybody. But one does say the same things over and over again, mechanically, to the people who are always saying the same things to you. You know, how they've always wanted to meet you. How they once saw you outside a theatre in San Francisco – or travelled in a plane with you. Something silly really, but one has to be nice about it and say things. Well, as I'm telling you, one does that automatically. One doesn't need to think what to say because one's said it so often before. Suddenly, I think, a wave of tiredness came over me. My brain went blank. Then I realized that Mrs Badcock had been telling me a long story which I hadn't really heard at all, and was now looking at me in an eager sort of way and that I hadn't answered her or said any of the proper things. It was just tiredness.'

'Just tiredness,' said Dermot Craddock slowly. 'You insist on that, Miss Gregg?'

'Yes, I do. I can't see why you don't believe me.'

Dermot Craddock turned towards Jason Rudd. 'Mr Rudd,' he said, 'I think you're more likely to understand my meaning than your wife is. I am concerned, very much concerned, for your wife's safety. There has been an attempt on her life, there have been threatening letters. That means, doesn't it, that there is someone who was here on the day of the fête and possibly is still here, someone in very close touch with this house and what goes on in it. That person, whoever it is, may be slightly insane. It's not just a question of threats. Threatened men live long, as they say. The same goes for women. But whoever it was didn't stop at threats. A deliberate attempt was made to poison Miss Gregg. Don't you see in the whole nature of things, that the attempt is bound to be repeated? There's only one way to achieve safety. That is to give me all the clues you possibly can. I don't say that you *know* who that person is, but I think that you must be able to give a guess or to have a vague idea. Won't you tell me the truth? Or if, which is possible, you yourself do not know the truth, won't you urge your wife to do so. It's in the interests of her own safety that I'm asking you.'

Jason Rudd turned his head slowly. 'You hear what Inspector Craddock says, Marina,' he said. 'It's possible, as he says, that you may know something that I do not. If so, for God's sake, don't be foolish about it. If you've the least suspicion of *anyone*, tell it to us now.'

'But I haven't.' Her voice rose in a wail. 'You must believe me.'

'Who were you afraid of that day?' asked Dermot.

'I wasn't afraid of anyone.'

'Listen, Miss Gregg, of the people on the stairs or coming up it, there were two friends whom you were surprised to see, whom you had not seen for a long time and whom you did not expect to see that day. Mr Ardwyck Fenn and Miss Brewster. Had you any special emotions when you suddenly saw them coming up the stairs? You didn't know they were coming, did you?'

'No, we'd no idea they were even in England,' said Jason Rudd.

'I was delighted,' said Marina, 'absolutely delighted!'

'Delighted to see Miss Brewster?'

'Well – ' she shot him a quick, faintly suspicious glance.

Craddock said, 'Lola Brewster was, I believe, originally married to your third husband Robert Truscott?'

'Yes, that's so.'

'He divorced her in order to marry you.'

'Oh, everyone knows about that,' said Marina Gregg impatiently. 'You needn't think it's anything you've found out. There was a bit of a rumpus at the time, but there wasn't any bad feeling about it in the end.'

'Did she make threats against you?'

'Well – in a way, yes. But, oh dear, I wish I could explain. No one takes those sort of threats *seriously*. It was at a party, she'd had a lot of drink. She might have taken a pot-shot at me with a pistol if she'd had one. But luckily she didn't. All that was *years* ago! None of these things last, these emotions! They don't, really they don't. That's true, isn't it, Jason?'

'I'd say it was true enough,' said Jason Rudd, 'and I can assure you, Mr Craddock, that Lola Brewster had no opportunity on the day of the fête of poisoning my wife's drink. I was close beside her most of the time. The idea that Lola would suddenly, after a long period of friendliness, come to England, and arrive at our house all prepared to poison my wife's drink – why the whole idea's absurd.'

'I appreciate your point of view,' said Craddock.

'It's not only that, it's a matter of *fact* as well. She was nowhere near Marina's glass.'

'And your other visitor – Ardwyck Fenn?'

There was, he thought, a very slight pause before Jason Rudd spoke.

426

'He's a very old friend of ours,' he said. 'We haven't seen him for a good many years now, though we occasionally correspond. He's quite a big figure in American Television.'

'Was he an old friend of yours too?' Dermot Craddock asked Marina.

Her breath came rather quickly as she replied. 'Yes, oh yes. He – he was quite a friend of mine always, but I've rather lost sight of him of late years.' Then with a sudden quick rush of words, she went on, 'If you think that I looked up and saw Ardwyck and was frightened of him, it's nonsense. It's absolute *nonsense*. Why should I be frightened of him, what reason would I have to be frightened of him? We were great friends. I was just very, very pleased when I suddenly saw him. It was a delightful surprise, as I told you. Yes, a delightful surprise.' She raised her head, looking at him, her face vivid and defiant.

'Thank you, Miss Gregg,' said Craddock quietly. 'If you should feel inclined at any moment to take me a little further into your confidence I should strongly advise you to do so.'

CHAPTER FOURTEEN

Mrs Bantry was on her knees. A good day for hoeing. Nice dry soil. But hoeing wouldn't do everything. Thistles now, and dandelions. She dealt vigorously with these pests.

She rose to her feet, breathless but triumphant, and looked out over the hedge on to the road. She was faintly surprised to see the dark-haired secretary whose name she couldn't remember coming out of the public call box that was situated near the bus stop on the other side of the road.

What was her name now. It began with a B – or was it an R? No, *Zielinsky*, that was it. Mrs Bantry remembered just in time, as Ella crossed the road into the drive past the Lodge.

'Good morning, Miss Zielinsky,' she called in a friendly tone.

Ella Zielinsky jumped. It was not so much a jump, as a shy – the shy of a frightened horse. It surprised Mrs Bantry.

'Good morning,' said Ella, and added quickly: 'I came down to telephone. There's something wrong with our line today.'

Mrs Bantry felt more surprise. She wondered why Ella Zielinsky bothered to explain her action. She responded civilly. 'How annoying for you. Do come in and telephone any time you want to.'

'Oh – thank you very much . . .' Ella was interrupted by a fit of sneezing.

'You've got hay-fever,' said Mrs Bantry with immediate diagnosis. 'Try weak bicarbonate of soda and water.'

'Oh, that's all right. I have some very good patent stuff in an atomizer. Thank you all the same.'

She sneezed again as she moved away, walking briskly up the drive.

Mrs Bantry looked after her. Then her eyes returned to her garden. She looked at it in a dissatisfied fashion. Not a weed to be seen anywhere.

'Othello's occupation's gone,' Mrs Bantry murmured to herself confusedly. 'I dare say I'm a nosy old woman but I would like to know if – '

A moment of irresolution and then Mrs Bantry yielded to temptation. She was going to be a nosy old woman and the hell with it! She strode indoors to the telephone, lifted the receiver and dialled it. A brisk transatlantic voice spoke.

'Gossington Hall.'

'This is Mrs Bantry, at the East Lodge.'

'Oh, good morning, Mrs Bantry. This is Hailey Preston. I met you on the day of the fête. What can I do for you?'

'I thought perhaps I could do something for you. If your telephone's out of order – '

His astonished voice interrupted her.

'Our telephone out of order? There's been nothing wrong with it. Why did you think so?'

'I must have made a mistake,' said Mrs Bantry. 'I don't always hear very well,' she explained unblushingly.

She put the receiver back, waited a minute, then dialled once more.

'Jane? Dolly here.'

'Yes, Dolly. What is it?'

'Well, it seems rather *odd*. The secretary woman was dialling from the public call box in the road. She took the trouble to explain to me quite unnecessarily that she was doing so because the line at

428

Gossington Hall was out of order. But I've rung up there, and it *isn't* . . .'

She paused, and waited for intelligence to pronounce.

'Indeed,' said Miss Marple thoughtfully. 'Interesting.'

'For what reason, do you think?'

'Well, clearly, she didn't want to be overheard – '

'Exactly.'

'And there might be quite a number of reasons for that.'

'Yes.'

'Interesting,' said Miss Marple again.

II

Nobody could have been more ready to talk than Donald McNeil. He was an amiable red-headed young man. He greeted Dermot Craddock with pleasure and curiosity.

'How are you getting along,' he asked cheerfully, 'got any little special tit-bit for me?'

'Not as yet. Later perhaps.'

'Stalling as usual. You're all the same. Affable oysters! Haven't you come to the stage yet of inviting someone to come and "assist you in your inquiries"?'

'I've come to you,' said Dermot Craddock with a grin.

'Is there a nasty double entendre in that remark? Are you really suspicious that I murdered Heather Badcock and do you think I did it in mistake for Marina Gregg or that I meant to murder Heather Badcock and do you think I did it in mistake for Marina Gregg or that I meant to murder Heather Badcock all the time?'

'I haven't suggested anything,' said Craddock.

'No, no, you wouldn't do that, would you? You'd be very correct. All right. Let's go into it. I was there. I had opportunity but had I any motive? Ah, that's what you'd like to know. What was my motive?'

'I haven't been able to find one so far,' said Craddock.

'That's very gratifying. I feel safer.'

'I'm just interested in what you may have seen that day.'

'You've had that already. The local police had that straight away. It's humiliating. There I was on the scene of a murder. I practically *saw* the murder committed, must have done, and yet I've no idea who did it. I'm ashamed to confess that the first *I* knew about it was

429

seeing the poor, dear woman sitting on a chair gasping for breath and then pegging out. Of course it made a very good eye-witness account. It was a good scoop for me – and all that. But I'll confess to you that I feel humiliated that I don't know more. I ought to know more. And you can't kid me that the dose was meant for Heather Badcock. She was a nice woman who talked too much, but nobody gets murdered for that – unless of course they give away secrets. But I don't think anybody would ever have told Heather Badcock a secret. She wasn't the kind of woman who'd have been interested in other people's secrets. My view of her is of a woman who invariably talked about *herself*.'

'That seems to be the generally accepted view,' agreed Craddock.

'So we come to the famous Marina Gregg. I'm sure there are lots of wonderful motives for murdering Marina. Envy and jealousy and love tangles – all the stuff of drama. But who did it? Someone with a screw loose, I presume. There! You've had my valuable opinion. Is that what you wanted?'

'Not that alone. I understand that you arrived and came up the stairs about the same time as the vicar and the mayor.'

'Quite correct. But that wasn't the first time I'd arrived. I'd been there earlier.'

'I didn't know that.'

'Yes. I was on a kind of roving commission, you know, going here and there. I had a photographer with me. I'd gone down to take a few local shots of the mayor arriving and throwing a hoopla and putting in a peg for buried treasure and that kind of thing. Then I went back up again, not so much on the job, as to get a drink or two. The drink was good.'

'I see. Now can you remember who else was on the staircase when you went up?'

'Margot Bence from London was there with her camera.'

'You know her well?'

'Oh I just run against her quite often. She's a clever girl, who makes a success of her stuff. She takes all the fashionable things – First Nights, Gala Performances – specializes in photographs from unusual angles. Arty! She was in a corner of the half landing very well placed for taking anyone who came up and for taking the greetings going on at the top. Lola Brewster was just ahead of me on the stairs. Didn't know her at first. She's got a new rust-red hair-do. The very latest Fiji Islander type. Last time I saw her it was lank waves falling round her face and chin in a nice shade of auburn.

There was a big dark man with her, American. I don't know who he was but he looked important.'

'Did you look at Marina Gregg herself at all as you were coming up?'

'Yes, of course I did.'

'She didn't look upset or as though she'd had a shock or was frightened?'

'It's odd you should say that. I *did* think for a moment or two she was going to faint.'

'I see,' said Craddock thoughtfully. 'Thanks. There's nothing else you'd like to tell me?'

McNeil gave him a wide innocent stare.

'What could there be?'

'I don't trust you,' said Craddock.

'But you seem quite sure I didn't do it. Disappointing. Suppose I turn out to be her first husband. Nobody knows who he was except that he was so insignificant that even his name's been forgotten.'

Dermot grinned.

'Married from your prep school?' he asked. 'Or possibly in rompers! I must hurry. I've got a train to catch.'

III

There was a neatly docketed pile of papers on Craddock's desk at New Scotland Yard. He gave a perfunctory glance through them, then threw a question over his shoulder.

'Where's Lola Brewster staying?'

'At the Savoy, sir. Suite 1800. She's expecting you.'

'And Ardwyck Fenn?'

'He's at the Dorchester. First floor, 190.'

'Good.'

He picked up some cablegrams and read through them again before shoving them into his pocket. He smiled a moment to himself over the last one. 'Don't say I don't do my stuff, Aunt Jane,' he murmured under his breath.

He went out and made his way to the Savoy.

In Lola Brewster's suite Lola went out of her way to welcome him effusively. With the report he had just read in his mind, he studied her carefully. Quite a beauty still, he thought, in a lush kind of way, what you might call a trifle over-blown, perhaps, but they still liked

431

them that way. A completely different type, of course, from Marina Gregg. The amenities over, Lola pushed back her Fiji Islander hair, drew her generous lipsticked mouth into a provocative pout, and flickering blue eyelids over wide brown eyes, said:

'Have you come to ask me a lot more horrible questions? Like that local inspector did.'

'I hope they won't be too horrible, Miss Brewster.'

'Oh, but I'm sure they will be, and I'm sure the whole thing must have been some terrible mistake.'

'Do you really think so?'

'Yes. It's all such nonsense. Do you really mean that someone tried to poison Marina? Who on earth would poison Marina? She's an absolute sweetie, you know. Everybody loves her.'

'Including you?'

'I've always been devoted to Marina.'

'Oh come now, Miss Brewster, wasn't there a little trouble about eleven or twelve years ago?'

'Oh that.' Lola waved it away. 'I was terribly nervy and distraught, and Rob and I had been having the most frightful quarrels. We were neither of us normal at the moment. Marina just fell wildly in love with him and rushed him off his feet, the poor pet.'

'And you minded very much?'

'Well, I thought I did, Inspector. Of course I see now it was one of the best things that ever happened for me. I was really worried about the *children*, you know. Breaking up our home. I'm afraid I'd already realized that Rob and I were incompatible. I expect you know I got married to Eddie Groves as soon as the divorce went through? I think really I'd been in love with him for a long time, but of course I didn't want to break up my marriage, because of the children. It's so important, isn't it, that children should have a *home*?'

'Yet people say that actually you were terribly upset.'

'Oh, people always say things,' said Lola vaguely.

'You said quite a lot, didn't you, Miss Brewster? You went about threatening to shoot Marina Gregg, or so I understand.'

'I've told you one *says* things. One's *supposed* to say things like that. Of course I wouldn't really shoot *anyone*.'

'In spite of taking a pot-shot at Eddie Groves some few years later?'

'Oh, that was because we'd had an argument,' said Lola. 'I lost my temper.'

432

'I have it on very good authority, Miss Brewster, that you said
– and these are your exact words or so I'm told,' (he read from a
note-book) – 'That bitch needn't think she'll get away with it. If I
don't shoot her now I'll wait and get her in some other way. I don't
care how long I wait, years if need be, but I'll get even with her in
the end.'

'Oh, I'm sure I never said anything of the kind,' Lola laughed.

'I'm sure, Miss Brewster, that you did.'

'People exaggerate so.' A charming smile broke over her face. 'I
was just mad at the moment, you know,' she murmured confidentially. 'One says all sorts of things when one's mad with people. But
you don't really think I'd wait fourteen years and come across to
England, and look up Marina and drop some deadly poison into
her cocktail glass within three minutes of seeing her again?'

Dermot Craddock didn't really think so. It seemed to him wildly
improbable. He merely said:

'I'm only pointing out to you, Miss Brewster, that there had been
threats in the past and that Marina Gregg was certainly startled and
frightened to see someone who came up the stairs that day. Naturally
one feels that that someone must have been you.'

'But darling Marina was delighted to see me! She kissed me and
exclaimed how wonderful it was. Oh really, Inspector, I do think
you're being very, very silly.'

'In fact, you were all one big happy family?'

'Well, that's really much more true than all the things you've been
thinking.'

'And you've no ideas that could help us in any way? No ideas
who might have killed her?'

'I tell you nobody would have wanted to kill Marina. She's a very
silly woman anyway. Always making terrible fusses about her health,
and changing her mind and wanting this, that and the other, and when
she's got it being dissatisfied with it! I can't think why people are as
fond of her as they are. Jason's always been absolutely mad about
her. What that man has to put up with! But there it is. Everybody
puts up with Marina, puts themselves out for her. Then she gives
them a sad, sweet smile and thanks them! And apparently that makes
them feel that all the trouble is worth while. I really don't know how
she does it. You'd better put the idea that somebody wanted to kill
her right out of your head.'

'I should like to,' said Dermot Craddock. 'Unfortunately I can't
put it out of my head because, you see, it happened.'

'What do you mean, *it happened*, nobody has killed Marina, have they?'

'No. But the attempt was made.'

'I don't believe it for a moment! I expect whoever it was meant to kill the other woman all the time – the one who *was* killed. I expect someone comes into money when she dies.'

'She hadn't any money, Miss Brewster.'

'Oh well, there was some other reason. Anyway, I shouldn't worry about Marina if I were you. Marina is *always* all right!'

'Is she? She doesn't look a very happy woman to me.'

'Oh, that's because she makes such a song and dance about everything. Unhappy love affairs. Not being able to have any children.'

'She adopted some children, didn't she?' said Dermot with a lively remembrance of Miss Marple's urgent voice.

'I believe she did once. It wasn't a great success I believe. She does these impulsive things and then wishes she hadn't.'

'What happened to the children she adopted?'

'I've no idea. They just sort of vanished after a bit. She got tired of them, I suppose, like everything else.'

'I see,' said Dermot Craddock.

IV

Next – the Dorchester. Suite 190.

'Well, Chief-Inspector – ' Ardwyck Fenn looked down at the card in his hand.

'Craddock.'

'What can I do for you?'

'I hope you won't mind if I ask you a few questions.'

'Not at all. It's this business at Much Benham. No – what's the actual name, St Mary Mead?'

'Yes. That's right. Gossington Hall.'

'Can't think what Jason Rudd wanted to buy a place like that for. Plenty of good Georgian houses in England – or even Queen Anne. Gossington Hall is a purely Victorian mansion. Where's the attraction in that, I wonder?'

'Oh, there's some attraction – for some people, that is, in Victorian stability.'

'Stability? Well, perhaps you've got something there. Marina, I suppose, had a feeling for stability. It's a thing she never had herself, poor girl, so I suppose that's why she always covets it. Perhaps this place will satisfy her for a bit.'

'You know her well, Mr Fenn?'

Ardwyck Fenn shrugged his shoulders.

'Well? I don't know that I'd say that. I've known her over a long period of years. Known her off and on, that is to say.'

Craddock looked at him appraisingly. A dark man, heavily built, shrewd eyes behind thick glasses, heavy jowl and chin, Ardwyck Fenn went on:

'The idea is, I gather, from what I read in the newspapers, that this Mrs Whatever-her-name-was, was poisoned by mistake. That the dose was intended for Marina. Is that right?'

'Yes. That's it. The dose was in Marina Gregg's cocktail. Mrs Badcock spilt hers and Marina handed over her drink to her.'

'Well that seems pretty conclusive. I really can't think, though, who would want to poison Marina. Especially as Lynette Brown wasn't there.'

'Lynette Brown?' Craddock looked slightly at sea.

Ardwyck Fenn smiled. 'If Marina breaks this contract, throws up the part – Lynette will get it and it would mean a good deal to Lynette to get it. But for all that, I don't imagine she'd send some emissary along with poison. Much too melodramatic an idea.'

'It seems a little far-fetched,' said Dermot dryly.

'Ah, you'd be surprised what women will do when they're ambitious,' said Ardwyck Fenn. 'Mind you, death mayn't have been intended. It may have been just to give her a fright – Enough to knock her out but not to finish her.'

Craddock shook his head. 'It wasn't a borderline dose,' he said.

'People make mistakes in doses, quite big ones.'

'Is this really your theory?'

'Oh no, it isn't. It was only a suggestion. I've no theory. I was only an innocent bystander.'

'Was Marina Gregg very surprised to see you?'

'Yes, it was a complete surprise to her.' He laughed amusedly. 'Just couldn't believe her eyes when she saw me coming up the stairs. She gave me a very nice welcome, I must say.'

'You hadn't seen her for a long time?'

'Not for four or five years, I should say.'

'And some years before that there was a time when you and she were very close friends, I believe?'

'Are you insinuating anything in particular by that remark, Inspector Craddock?'

There was very little change in the voice but there was something there that had not been there before. A hint of steel, of menace. Dermot felt suddenly that this man would be a very ruthless opponent.

'It would be as well, I think,' said Ardwyck Fenn, 'that you said exactly what you do mean.'

'I'm quite prepared to do so, Mr Fenn. I have to inquire into the past relations of everyone who was there on that day with Marina Gregg. It seems to have been a matter of common gossip that at the time I have just referred to, you were wildly in love with Marina Gregg.'

Ardwyck Fenn shrugged his shoulders.

'One has these infatuations, Inspector. Fortunately, they pass.'

'It is said that she encouraged you and that later she turned you down and that you resented the fact.'

'It is said – it is said! I suppose you read all that in *Confidential*?'

'It has been told me by quite well informed and sensible people.'

Ardwyck Fenn threw back his head, showing the bull-like line of his neck.

'I had a yen for her at one time, yes,' he admitted. 'She was a beautiful and attractive woman and still is. To say that I ever threatened her is going a little too far. I'm never pleased to be thwarted, Chief-Inspector, and most people who thwart me tend to be sorry that they have done so. But that principle applies mainly in my business life.'

'You did, I believe, use your influence to have her dropped from a picture that she was making?'

Fenn shrugged his shoulders.

'She was unsuitable for the role. There was conflict between her and the director. I had money in that picture and I had no intention of jeopardizing it. It was, I assure you, purely a business transaction.'

'But perhaps Marina Gregg did not think so?'

'Oh, naturally she did not think so. She would always think that anything like that was personal.'

'She actually told certain friends of hers that she was afraid of you, I believe?'

436

'Did she? How childish. I expect she enjoyed the sensation.'

'You think there was no need for her to be afraid of you?'

'Of course not. Whatever personal disappointment I might have had, I soon put it behind me. I've always gone on the principle that where women are concerned there are as good fish in the sea as ever came out of it.'

'A very satisfactory way to go through life, Mr Fenn.'

'Yes, I think it is.'

'You have a wide knowledge of the moving picture world?'

'I have financial interests in it.'

'And therefore you are bound to know a lot about it?'

'Perhaps.'

'You are a man whose judgement would be worth listening to. Can you suggest to me any person who is likely to have such a deep grudge against Marina Gregg that they would be willing to do away with her?'

'Probably a dozen,' said Ardwyck Fenn, 'that is to say, if they hadn't got to do anything about it personally. If it was a mere matter of pressing a button in a wall, I dare say there'd be a lot of willing fingers.'

'You were there that day. You saw her and talked to her. Do you think that amongst any of the people who were around you in that brief space of time – from when you arrived to the moment when Heather Badcock died – do you think that amongst them you can suggest – only suggest, mind you, I'm asking you for nothing more than a guess – anyone who might poison Marina Gregg?'

'I wouldn't like to say,' said Ardwyck Fenn.

'That means that you have some idea?'

'It means that I have nothing to say on that subject. And that, Chief-Inspector Craddock, is all you'll get out of me.'

CHAPTER FIFTEEN

Dermot Craddock looked down at the last name and address he had written down in his note-book. The telephone number had been rung twice for him but there had been no response. He tried it now once more. He shrugged his shoulders, got up and decided to go and see for himself.

Margot Bence's studio was in a cul-de-sac off the Tottenham Court Road. Beyond the name on a plate on the side of a door, there was little to identify it, and certainly no form of advertizing. Craddock groped his way to the first floor. There was a large notice here painted in black on a white board. 'Margot Bence, Personality Photographer. Please enter.'

Craddock entered. There was a small waiting-room but nobody in charge of it. He stood there hesitating, then cleared his throat in a loud and theatrical manner. Since that drew no attention he raised his voice.

'Anybody here?'

He heard a flap of slippers behind a velvet curtain, the curtain was pushed aside and a young man with exuberant hair and a pink and white face, peered round it.

'Terribly sorry, my dear,' he said. 'I didn't hear you. I had an absolutely new idea and I was just trying it out.'

He pushed the velvet curtain farther aside and Craddock followed him into an inner room. This proved to be unexpectedly large. It was clearly the working studio. There were cameras, lights, arc-lights, piles of drapery, screens on wheels.

'Such a mess,' said the young man, who was almost as willowy as Hailey Preston. 'But one finds it very hard to work, I think, unless one *does* get into a mess. Now what were you wanting to see us about?'

'I wanted to see Miss Margot Bence.'

'Ah, Margot. Now what a pity. If you'd been half an hour earlier you'd have found her here. She's gone off to produce some photographs of models for *Fashion Dream*. You should have rung up, you know, to make an appointment. Margot's terribly busy these days.'

'I did ring up. There was no reply.'

'Of course,' said the young man. 'We took the receiver off. I remember now. It disturbed us.' He smoothed down a kind of lilac smock that he was wearing. 'Can I do anything for you? Make an appointment? I do a lot of Margot's business arrangements for her. You wanted to arrange for some photography somewhere? Private or business?'

'From that point of view, neither,' said Dermot Craddock. He handed his card to the young man.

'How perfectly rapturous,' said the young man. 'C.I.D.! I believe, you know, I've seen pictures of you. Are you one of the Big Four or the Big Five, or is it perhaps the Big Six nowadays? There's so much crime about, they'd have to increase the numbers, wouldn't they? Oh dear, is that disrespectful? I'm afraid it is. I didn't mean to be disrespectful at all. Now, what do you want Margot for – not to arrest her, I hope.'

'I just wanted to ask her one or two questions.'

'She doesn't do indecent photographs or anything like that,' said the young man anxiously. 'I hope nobody's been telling you any stories of that kind because it isn't true. Margot's very artistic. She does a lot of stage work and studio work. But her studies are terribly, terribly pure – almost prudish, I'd say.'

'I can tell you quite simply why I want to speak to Miss Bence,' said Dermot. 'She was recently an eye-witness of a crime that took place near Much Benham, at a village called St Mary Mead.'

'Oh, my dear, of *course*! I know about *that*. Margot came back and told me all about it. Hemlock in the cocktails, wasn't it? Something of that kind. So *bleak* it sounded! But all mixed up with the St John Ambulance which doesn't seem so bleak, does it? But haven't you already asked Margot questions about that – or was it somebody else?'

'One always finds there are more questions, as the case goes on,' said Dermot.

'You mean it develops. Yes, I can quite see that. Murder develops. Yes, like a photograph, isn't it?'

'It's very much like photography really,' said Dermot. 'Quite a good comparison of yours.'

'Well, it's very nice of you to say so, I'm sure. Now about Margot.

439

Would you like to get hold of her right away?'

'If you can help me to do so, yes.'

'Well, at the moment,' said the young man, consulting his watch, 'at the moment she'll be outside Keats' house at Hampstead Heath. My car's outside. Shall I run you up there?'

'That would be very kind of you, Mr – '

'Jethroe,' said the young man, 'Johnny Jethroe.'

As they went down the stairs Dermot asked:

'Why Keats' house?'

'Well, you know we don't pose fashion photographs in the studio any more. We like them to seem natural, blown about by the wind. And if possible some rather unlikely background. You know, an Ascot frock against Wandsworth Prison, or a frivolous suit outside a poet's house.'

Mr Jethroe drove rapidly but skilfully up Tottenham Court Road, through Camden Town and finally to the neighbourhood of Hampstead Heath. On the pavement near Keats' house a pretty little scene was being enacted. A slim girl, wearing diaphanous organdie, was standing clutching an immense black hat. On her knees, a little way behind her, a second girl was holding the first girl's skirt well pulled back so that it clung around her knees and legs. In a deep hoarse voice a girl with a camera was directing operations.

'For goodness' sake, Jane, get your *behind* down. It's showing behind her right knee. Get down *flatter*. That's it. No, more to the left. That's right. Now you're masked by the bush. That'll do. Hold it. We'll have one more. Both hands on the back of the hat this time. Head up. Good – now turn round, Elsie. Bend over. More. Bend! *Bend*, you've got to pick up that cigarette case. That's right. That's *heaven*! Got it! Now move over to the left. Same pose, only just turn your head over your shoulder. So.'

'I can't see what you want to go taking photographs of my behind for,' said the girl called Elsie rather sulkily.

'It's a lovely behind, dear. It looks smashing,' said the photographer. 'And when you turn your head your chin comes up like the rising moon over a mountain. I don't think we need bother with any more.'

'Hi – Margot,' said Mr Jethroe.

She turned her head. 'Oh, it's you. What are you doing here?'

'I brought someone along to see you. Chief-Inspector Craddock, C.I.D.'

The girl's eyes turned swiftly on to Dermot. He thought they had a wary, searching look but that, as he well knew, was nothing extra-ordinary. It was a fairly common reaction to detective-inspectors. She was a thin girl, all elbows and angles, but was an interesting shape for all that. A heavy curtain of black hair fell down either side of her face. She looked dirty as well as sallow and not particularly prepossessing, to his eyes. But he acknowledged that there was character there. She raised her eyebrows which were slightly raised by art already and remarked:

'And what can I do for you, Detective-Inspector Craddock?'

'How do you do, Miss Bence. I wanted to ask you if you would be so kind as to answer a few questions about that very unfortunate business at Gossington Hall, near Much Benham. You went there, if I remember, to take some photographs.'

The girl nodded. 'Of course. I remember quite well.' She shot him a quick searching look. 'I didn't see you there. Surely it was somebody else. Inspector – Inspector – '

'Inspector Cornish?' said Dermot.

'That's right.'

'We were called in later.'

'You're from Scotland Yard?'

'Yes.'

'You butted in and took over from the local people. Is that it?'

'Well, it isn't quite a question of butting in, you know. It's up to the Chief Constable of the County to decide whether he wants to keep it in his own hands or whether he thinks it'll be better handled by us.'

'What makes him decide?'

'It very often turns on whether the case has a local background or whether it's a more – universal one. Sometimes, perhaps, an international one.'

'And he decided, did he, that this was an international one?'

'Transatlantic, perhaps, would be a better word.'

'They've been hinting that in the papers, haven't they? Hinting that the killer, whoever he was, was out to get Marina Gregg and got some wretched local woman by mistake. Is that true or is it a bit of publicity for their film?'

'I'm afraid there isn't much doubt about it, Miss Bence.'

'What do you want to ask me? Have I got to come to Scotland Yard?'

He shook his head. 'Not unless you like. We'll go back to your studio if you prefer.'

441

'All right, let's do that. My car's just up the street.'

She walked rapidly along the footpath. Dermot went with her. Jethroe called after them.

'So long darling, I won't butt in. I'm sure you and the Inspector are going to talk big secrets.' He joined the two models on the pavement and began an animated discussion with them.

Margot got into the car, unlocked the door on the other side, and Dermot Craddock got in beside her. She said nothing at all during the drive back to Tottenham Court Road. She turned down the cul-de-sac and at the bottom of it drove through an open doorway.

'Got my own parking place here,' she remarked. 'It's a furniture depository place really, but they rent me a bit of space. Parking a car is one of the big headaches in London, as you probably know only too well, though I don't suppose you deal with traffic, do you?'

'No, that's not one of my troubles.'

'I should think murder would be infinitely preferable,' said Margot Bence.

She led the way back to the studio, motioned him to a chair, offered him a cigarette and sank down on the large pouffe opposite him. From behind the curtain of dark hair she looked at him in a sombre questioning way.

'Shoot, stranger,' she said.

'You were taking photographs on the occasion of this death, I understand.'

'Yes.'

'You'd been engaged professionally?'

'Yes. They wanted someone to do a few specialized shots. I do quite a lot of that stuff. I do some work for film studios sometimes, but this time I was just taking photographs of the fête, and afterwards a few shots of special people being greeted by Marina Gregg and Jason Rudd. Local notabilities or other personalities. That sort of thing.'

'Yes. I understand that. You had your camera on the stairs, I understand?'

'A part of the time, yes. I got a very good angle from there. You get people coming up the stairs below you and you could swivel round and get Marina shaking hands with them. You could get a lot of different angles without having to move much.'

'I know, of course, that you answered some questions at the time

442

as to whether you'd seen anything unusual, anything that might be helpful. They were general questions.'

'Have you got more specialized ones?'

'A little more specialized, I think. You had a good view of Marina Gregg from where you were standing?'

She nodded. 'Excellent.'

'And of Jason Rudd?'

'Occasionally. But he was moving about more. Drinks and things and introducing people to one another. The locals to the celebrities. That kind of thing, I should imagine. I didn't see this Mrs Baddeley – '

'Badcock.'

'Sorry, Badcock. I didn't see her drink the fatal draught or anything like that. In fact I don't think I really know which she was.'

'Do you remember the arrival of the mayor?'

'Oh, yes. I remember the mayor all right. He had on his chain and his robes of office. I got one of him coming up the stairs – a close-up – rather a cruel profile, and then I got him shaking hands with Marina.'

'Then you can fix that time at least in your mind. Mrs Badcock and her husband came up the stairs to Marina Gregg immediately in front of him.'

She shook her head. 'Sorry. I still don't remember her.'

'That doesn't matter so much. I presume that you had a pretty good view of Marina Gregg and that you had your eyes on her and were pointing the camera at her fairly often.'

'Quite right. Most of the time. I'd wait till I got just the right moment.'

'Do you know a man called Ardwyck Fenn by sight?'

'Oh yes. I know him well enough. Television network – films too.'

'Did you take a photograph of him?'

'Yes. I got him coming up with Lola Brewster.'

'That would be just after the mayor?'

She thought a minute then agreed. 'Yes, about then.'

'Did you notice that about that time Marina Gregg seemed to feel suddenly ill? Did you notice any unusual expression on her face?'

Margot Bence leant forward, opened a cigarette box and took out a cigarette. She lit it. Although she had not answered Dermot did not press her. He waited, wondering what it was she was turning over in her mind. She said at last, abruptly:

'Why do you ask me that?'

'Because it's a question to which I am very anxious to have an answer – a reliable answer.'

'Do you think my answer's likely to be reliable?'

'Yes I do, as a matter of fact. You must have the habit of watching people's faces very closely, waiting for certain expressions, certain propitious moments.'

She nodded her head.

'Did you see anything of that kind?'

'Somebody else saw it too, did they?'

'Yes. More than one person, but it's been described rather differently.'

'How did the other people describe it?'

'One person has told me that she was taken faint.'

Margot Bence shook her head slowly.

'Someone else said that she was startled.' He paused a moment then went on, 'and somebody else describes her as having a frozen look on her face.'

'Frozen,' said Margot Bence thoughtfully.

'Do you agree to that last statement?'

'I don't know. Perhaps.'

'It was put rather more fancifully still,' said Dermot. 'In the words of the late poet, Tennyson. "The mirror crack'd from side to side: 'The doom has come upon me,' cried the Lady of Shalott."'

'There wasn't any mirror,' said Margot Bence, 'but if there had been it might have cracked.' She got up abruptly. 'Wait,' she said. 'I'll do something better than describe it to you. I'll show you.'

She pushed aside the curtain at the far end and disappeared for some moments. He could hear her uttering impatient mutterings under her breath.

'What hell it is,' she said as she emerged again, 'one never can find things when one wants them. I've got it now though.'

She came across to him and put a glossy print into his hand. He looked down at it. It was a very good photograph of Marina Gregg. Her hand was clasped in the hand of a woman standing in front of her, and therefore with her back to the camera. But Marina Gregg was not looking at the woman. Her eyes stared not quite into the camera but slightly obliquely to the left. The interesting thing to Dermot Craddock was that the face expressed nothing whatever. There was no fear on it, no pain. The woman portrayed there was staring at *something*, something she saw, and the emotion it aroused in her was so great that she was phsyically unable to express it by any kind of facial expression. Dermot Craddock had seen such a look once on a man's face, a man who a second later had been shot dead . . .

'Satisfied?' asked Margot Bence.

Craddock gave a deep sigh. 'Yes, thank you. It's hard, you know, to make up one's mind if witnesses are exaggerating, if they are imagining they see things. But that's not so in this case. There *was* something to see and she saw it.' He asked, 'Can I keep this picture?'

'Oh, yes you can have the print. I've got the negative.'

'You didn't send it to the Press?'

Margot Bence shook her head.

'I rather wonder why you didn't. After all, it's rather a dramatic photograph. Some paper might have paid a good price for it.'

'I wouldn't care to do that,' said Margot Bence. 'If you look into somebody's soul by accident, you feel a bit embarrassed about cashing in.'

'Did you know Marina Gregg at all?'

'No.'

'You come from the States, don't you?'

'I was born in England. I was trained in America though. I came over here, oh, about three years ago.'

Dermot Craddock nodded. He had known the answers to his questions. They had been waiting for him among the other lists of information on his office table. The girl seemed straightforward enough. He asked:

'Where did you train?'

'Reingarden Studios. I was with Andrew Quilp for a time. He taught me a lot.'

'Reingarden Studios and Andrew Quilp.' Dermot Craddock was suddenly alert. The names struck a chord of remembrance.

'You lived in Seven Springs, didn't you?'

She looked amused.

'You seem to know a lot about me. Have you been checking up?'

'You're a very well-known photographer, Miss Bence. There have been articles written about you, you know. Why did you come to England?'

She shrugged her shoulders.

'Oh, I like a change. Besides as I told you, I was born in England although I went to the States as a child.'

'Quite a young child, I think.'

'Five years old if you're interested.'

'I am interested. I think, Miss Bence, you could tell me a little more than you have done.'

Her face hardened. She stared at him.

'What do you mean by that?'

Dermot Craddock looked at her and risked it. It wasn't much to go on. Reingarden Studios and Andrew Quilp and the name of one town. But he felt rather as if old Miss Marple were at his shoulder egging him on.

'I think you knew Marina Gregg better than you say.'

She laughed. 'Prove it. You're imagining things.'

'Am I? I don't think I am. And it *could* be proved, you know, with a little time and care. Come now, Miss Bence, hadn't you better admit the truth? Admit that Marina Gregg adopted you as a child and that you lived with her for four years.'

She drew her breath in sharply with a hiss.

'You nosy bastard!' she said.

It startled him a little, it was such a contrast to her former manner. She got up, shaking her black head of hair.

'All right, all right, it's true enough! Yes Marina Gregg took me over to America with her. My mother had eight kids. She lived in a slum somewhere. She was one of hundreds of people, I suppose, who wrote to any film actress that they happen to see or hear about, spilling a hard luck story, begging her to adopt the child a mother couldn't give advantages to. Oh, it's such a sickening business, all of it.'

'There were three of you,' said Dermot. 'Three children adopted at different times from different places.'

'That's right. Me and Rod and Angus. Angus was older than I was, Rod was practically a baby. We had a wonderful life. Oh, a wonderful life! All the advantages!' Her voice rose mockingly. 'Clothes and cars and a wonderful house to live in and people to look after us, good schooling and teaching, and delicious food. Everything piled on! And she herself, our "Mom." "Mom" in inverted commas, playing her part, crooning over us, being photographed with us! Ah, such a pretty sentimental picture.'

'But she really wanted children,' said Dermot Craddock. 'That was real enough, wasn't it? It wasn't just a publicity stunt.'

'Oh, perhaps. Yes, I think that was true. She wanted children. But she didn't want *us*! Not really. It was just a glorious bit of

play-acting. *"My family." "So lovely to have a family of my own."*
And Izzy let her do it. He ought to have known better.'
'Izzy was Isidore Wright?'
'Yes, her third husband or her fourth, I forget which. He was
a wonderful man really. He understood her, I think, and he was
worried sometimes about us. He was kind to us, but he didn't pretend
to be a father. He didn't feel like a father. He only cared really about
his own writing. I've read some of his things since. They're sordid
and rather cruel, but they're powerful. I think people will call him
a great writer one day.'
'And this went on until when?'
Margot Bence's smile curved suddenly. 'Until she got sick of that
particular bit of play-acting. No, that's not quite true . . . She found
she was going to have a child of her own.'
She laughed with sudden bitterness. 'Then we'd had it! We weren't
wanted any more. We'd done very well as little stopgaps, but she
didn't care a damn about us really, not a damn. Oh, she pensioned
us off very prettily. With a home and a foster-mother and money for
our education and a nice little sum to start us off in the world. Nobody
can say that she didn't behave correctly and handsomely. But she'd
never wanted *us* – all she wanted was a child of her own.'
'You can't blame her for that,' said Dermot gently.
'I don't blame her for wanting a child of her own, no! But what
about us? She took us away from our own parents, from the place
where we belonged. My mother sold me for a mess of pottage,
if you like, but she didn't sell me for advantage to herself. She
sold me because she was a damn' silly woman who thought I'd get
"advantages" and "education" and have a wonderful life. She thought
she was doing the best for me. Best for me? If she only knew.'
'You're still very bitter, I see.'
'No, I'm not bitter now. I've got over that. I'm bitter because I'm
remembering, because I've gone back to those days. We were all
pretty bitter.'
'All of you?'
'Well, not Rod. Rod never cared about anything. Besides he was
rather small. But Angus felt like I did, only I think he was more
revengeful. He said that when he was grown up he would go and
kill that baby she was going to have.'
'You knew about the baby?'
'Oh, of course I knew. And everyone knows what happened. She
went crazy with rapture about having it and then when it was born

it was an idiot! Serve her right. Idiot or no idiot, she didn't want *us* back again.'

'You hate her very much.'

'Why shouldn't I hate her? She did the worst thing to me that anyone can do to anyone else. Let them believe that they're loved and wanted and then show them that it's all a sham.'

'What happened to your two – I'll call them brothers, for the sake of convenience.'

'Oh, we all drifted apart later. Rod's farming somewhere in the Middle West. He's got a happy nature, and always had, Angus? I don't know. I lost sight of him.'

'Did he continue to feel regretful?'

'I shouldn't think so,' said Margot. 'It's not the sort of thing you can go on feeling. The last time I saw him, he said he was going on the stage. I don't know whether he did.'

'*You've* remembered, though,' said Dermot.

'Yes. I've remembered,' said Margot Bence.

'Was Marina Gregg surprised to see you on that day or did she make the arrangements for your photography on purpose to please you?'

'She?' The girl smiled scornfully. 'She knew nothing about the arrangements. I was curious to see her, so I did a bit of lobbying to get the job. As I say I've got some influence with studio people. I wanted to see what she looked like nowadays.' She stroked the surface of the table. 'She didn't even recognize me. What do you think of that? I was with her for four years. From five years old to nine and she didn't recognize me.'

'Children change,' said Dermot Craddock, 'they change so much that you'd hardly know them. I have a niece I met the other day and I assure you I'd have passed her in the street.'

'Are you saying that to make me feel better? I don't care really. Oh, what the hell, let's be honest. I do care. I did. She had a magic, you know. Marina! A wonderful calamitous magic that took hold of you. You can hate a person and still mind.'

'You didn't tell her who you were?'

She shook her head. 'No, I didn't tell her. That's the last thing I'd do.'

'Did you try and poison her, Miss Bence?'

Her mood changed. She got up and laughed.

'What ridiculous questions you do ask! But I suppose you have to. It's part of your job. No. I can assure you I didn't kill her.'

448

'That isn't what I asked you, Miss Bence.'

She looked at him, frowning, puzzled.

'Marina Gregg,' he said, 'is still alive.'

'For how long?'

'What do you mean by that?'

'Don't you think it's likely, Inspector, that someone will try again, and this time – this time, perhaps – they'll succeed?'

'Precautions will be taken.'

'Oh, I'm sure they will. The adoring husband will look after her, won't he, and make sure that no harm comes to her?'

He was listening carefully to the mockery in her voice.

'What did you mean when you said you didn't ask me that?' she said, harking back suddenly.

'I asked you if you tried to kill her. You replied that you didn't kill her. That's true enough, but *someone* died, *someone* was killed.'

'You mean I tried to kill Marina and instead I killed Mrs What's-her-name. If you'd like me to make it quite clear, I *didn't* try to poison Marina and I *didn't* poison Mrs Badcock.'

'But you know perhaps who did?'

'I don't know anything, Inspector, I assure you.'

'But you have some idea?'

'Oh, one always has ideas.' She smiled at him, a mocking smile. 'Among so many people it might be, mightn't it, the black-haired robot of a secretary, the elegant Hailey Preston, servants, maids, a masseur, the hairdresser, someone at the studios, so many people – *and one of them mightn't be what he or she pretended to be.*'

Then as he took an unconscious step towards her she shook her head vehemently.

'Relax, Inspector,' she said. 'I'm only teasing you. *Somebody's* out for Marina's blood, but who it is I've no idea. Really. I've no idea at all.'

CHAPTER SIXTEEN

At No. 16 Aubrey Close, young Mrs Baker was talking to her husband. Jim Baker, a big good-looking blond giant of a man, was intent on assembling a model construction unit.

'Neighbours!' said Cherry. She gave a toss of her black curly head. 'Neighbours!' she said with venom.

She carefully lifted the frying pan from the stove, then neatly shot its contents on to two plates, one rather fuller than the other. She placed the fuller one before her husband.

'Mixed grill,' she announced.

Jim looked up and sniffed appreciatively.

'That's something like,' he said. 'What is today? My birthday?'

'You have to be well nourished,' said Cherry.

She was looking very pretty in a cerise and white striped apron with little frills on it. Jim Baker shifted the component parts of a strato-cruiser to make room for his meal. He grinned at his wife and asked:

'Who says so?'

'My Miss Marple for one!' said Cherry. 'And if it comes to that,' she added, sitting down opposite Jim and pulling her plate towards her, 'I should say *she* could do with a bit more solid nourishment herself. That old cat of a White Knight of hers, gives her nothing but carbohydrates. It's all she can think of! A "nice custard," a "nice bread and butter pudding," a "nice macaroni cheese." Squashy puddings with pink sauce. And gas, gas, gas, all day. Talks her head off she does.'

'Oh well,' said Jim vaguely, 'it's invalid diet, I suppose.'

'Invalid diet!' said Cherry and snorted. 'Miss Marple isn't an invalid – she's just *old*. Always interfering, too.'

'Who, Miss Marple?'

'No. That Miss Knight. Telling me how to do things! She even tries to tell me how to cook! I know a lot more about cooking than she does.'

'You're tops for cooking, Cherry,' said Jim appreciatively.

'There's something *to* cooking,' said Cherry, 'something you can get your teeth into.'

Jim laughed. 'I'm getting my teeth into this all right. Why did your Miss Marple say that I needed nourishing? Did she think I looked run-down, the other day when I came in to fix the bathroom shelf?'

Cherry laughed. 'I'll tell you what she said to me. She said, "You've got a handsome husband, my dear. A *very* handsome husband." Sounds like one of those period books they read aloud on the telly.'

'I hope you agreed with her?' said Jim with a grin.

'I said you were all right.'

'All right indeed! That's a nice lukewarm way of talking.'

'And then she said "You must take care of your husband, my dear. Be sure you *feed* him properly. Men need plenty of good meat meals, well cooked."'

'Hear, hear!'

'And she told me to be sure and prepare fish food for you and not to buy ready-made pies and things and slip them in the oven to warm up. Not that I do that often,' added Cherry virtuously.

'You can't do it too seldom for me,' said Jim. 'They don't taste a bit the same.'

'So long as you notice what you eat,' said Cherry, 'and aren't so taken up with those strato-cruisers and things you're always building. And don't tell me you brought that set as a Christmas present for your nephew Michael. You bought it so that you could play with it yourself.'

'He's not quite old enough for it yet,' said Jim apologetically.

'And I suppose you're going on dithering about with it all the evening. What about some music? Did you get that new record you were talking about?'

'Yes, I did. Tchaikovski 1812.'

'That's the loud one with the battle, isn't it?' said Cherry. She made a face. 'Our Mrs Hartwell won't half like that! Neighbours! I'm fed up with neighbours. Always grousing and complaining. I don't know which is the worst. The Hartwells or the Barnabys. The Hartwells start rapping on the wall as early as twenty to eleven sometimes. It's a bit thick! After all even the telly and the B.B.C. go on later than that. Why *shouldn't* we have a bit of music if we like? And always asking us to turn it down low.'

'You can't turn these things down low,' said Jim with authority. 'You don't get the *tone* unless you've got the volume. Everyone knows that. It's absolutely recognized in musical circles. And what about their cat – always coming over into our garden, digging up the beds, just when I've got it nice.'

'I tell you what, Jim. I'm fed up with this place.'

'You didn't mind your neighbours up in Huddersfield,' remarked Jim.

'It wasn't the same there,' said Cherry. 'I mean, you're all independent there. If you're in trouble, somebody'd give you a hand and you'd give a hand to them. But you don't interfere. There's something about a new estate like this that makes people look sideways at their neighbours. Because we're all new I suppose. The amount of back-biting and tale-telling and writing to the council and one thing and another round here beats me! People in real towns are too busy for it.'

'You may have something there, my girl.'

'D'you like it here, Jim?'

'The job's all right. And after all, this is a brand new house. I wish there was a bit more room in it so that I could spread myself a bit more. It would be fine if I could have a workshop.'

'I thought it was lovely at first,' said Cherry, 'but now I'm not so sure. The house is all right and I love the blue paint and the bathroom's nice, but I don't like the people and the *feeling* round here. Did I tell you that Lily Price and that Harry of hers have broken off? It was a funny business that day in that house they went to look over. You know when she more or less fell out of the window. She said Harry just stood there like a stuck pig.'

'I'm glad she's broken off with him. He's a no-good if I ever saw one,' said Jim.

'No good marrying a chap just because a baby's on the way,' said Cherry. 'He didn't want to marry her, you know. He's not a very nice fellow. Miss Marple said he wasn't,' she added thoughtfully. 'She spoke to Lily about him. Lily thought she was crackers.'

'Miss Marple? I didn't know she'd ever seen him?'

'Oh yes, she was round here walking the day she fell down and Mrs Badcock picked her up and took her into her house. Do you think Arthur and Mrs Bain will make a match of it?'

Jim frowned as he picked up a bit of strato-cruiser and consulted the instructional diagram.

'I do wish you'd listen when I'm talking,' said Cherry.

452

'What did you say?'

'Arthur Badcock and Mary Bain.'

'For the Lord's sake, Cherry, his wife's only just dead! You women! I've heard he's in a terrible state of nerves still – jumps if you speak to him.'

'I wonder why . . . I shouldn't have thought he'd take it that way, would you?'

'Can you clear off this end of the table a bit?' said Jim, relinquishing even a passing interest in the affairs of his neighbours. 'Just so that I can spread some of these pieces out a bit.'

Cherry heaved an exasperated sigh.

'To get any attention round here, you have to be a super jet, or a turbo prop,' she said bitterly. 'You and your construction models!'

She piled the tray with the remains of supper and carried it over to the sink. She decided not to wash up, a necessity of daily life she always put off as long as possible. Instead, she piled everything into the sink, haphazard, slipped on a corduroy jacket and went out of the house, pausing to call over her shoulder:

'I'm just going to slip along to see Gladys Dixon. I want to borrow one of her *Vogue* patterns.'

'All right, old girl.' Jim bent over his model.

Casting a venomous look at her next-door neighbour's front door as she passed, Cherry went round the corner into Blenheim Close and stopped at No. 16. The door was open and Cherry tapped on it and went into the hall calling out:

'Is Gladdy about?'

'Is that you, Cherry?' Mrs Dixon looked out of the kitchen. 'She's upstairs in her room, dressmaking.'

'Right. I'll go up.'

Cherry went upstairs to a small bedroom in which Gladys, a plump girl with a plain face, was kneeling on the floor, her cheeks flushed, and several pins in her mouth, tacking up a paper pattern.

'Hallo, Cherry. Look, I got a lovely bit of stuff at Harper's sale at Much Benham. I'm going to do that cross-over pattern with frills again, the one I did in Terylene before.'

'That'll be nice,' said Cherry.

Gladys rose to her feet, panting a little.

'Got indigestion now,' she said.

'You oughtn't to do dressmaking right after supper,' said Cherry, 'bending over like that.'

'I suppose I ought to slim a bit,' said Gladys. She sat down on the bed.

'Any news from the studios?' asked Cherry, always avid for film news.

'Nothing much. There's a lot of talk still. Marina Gregg came back on the set yesterday – and she created something frightful.'

'What about?'

'She didn't like the taste of her coffee. You know, they have coffee in the middle of the morning. She took one sip and said there was something wrong with it. Which was nonsense, of course. There couldn't have been. It comes in a jug straight from the canteen. Of course I always put hers in a special china cup, rather posh – different from the others – but it's the same coffee. So there couldn't have been anything wrong with it, could there?'

'Nerves, I suppose,' said Cherry. 'What happened?'

'Oh, nothing. Mr Rudd just calmed everyone down. He's wonderful that way. He took the coffee from her and poured it down the sink.'

'That seems to be rather stupid,' said Cherry slowly.

'Why – what do you mean?'

'Well, if there *was* anything wrong with it – now nobody will ever know.'

'Do you think there really might have been?' asked Gladys looking alarmed.

'Well – ' Cherry shrugged her shoulders, '– there was something wrong with her cocktail the day of the fête, wasn't there, so why not the coffee? If at first you don't succeed, try, try, try again.'

Gladys shivered.

'I don't half like it, Cherry,' she said. 'Somebody's got it in for her all right. She's had more letters, you know, threatening her – and there was that bust business the other day.'

'What bust business?'

'A marble bust. On the set. It's a corner of a room in some Austrian palace or other. Funny name like Shotbrown. Pictures and china and marble busts. This one was up on a bracket – suppose it hadn't been pushed back enough. Anyway, a heavy lorry went past out in the road and jarred it off – right on to the chair where Marina sits for her big scene with Count Somebody-or-other. Smashed to smithereens! Lucky they weren't shooting at the time. Mr Rudd, he said not to say a word to her, and he put another chair there, and when she came yesterday and asked why the chair had been changed, he said

454

the other chair was the wrong period, and this gave a better angle for the camera. But he didn't half like it – I can tell you that.'

The two girls looked at each other.

'It's exciting in a way,' said Cherry slowly. 'And yet – it isn't . . .'

'I think I'm going to give up working in the canteen at the studios,' said Gladys.

'Why? Nobody wants to poison you or drop marble busts on your head!'

'No. But it's not always the person who's meant to get done in who gets done in. It may be someone else. Like Heather Badcock that day.'

'True enough,' said Cherry.

'You know,' said Gladys, 'I've been thinking. I was at the Hall that day, helping. I was quite close to them at the time.'

'When Heather died?'

'No, when she spilt the cocktail. All down her dress. A lovely dress it was, too, royal blue nylon taffeta. She'd got it quite new for the occasion. And it was funny.'

'What was funny?'

'I didn't think anything of it at the time. But it does seem funny when I think it over.'

Cherry looked at her expectantly. She accepted the adjective 'funny' in the sense that it was meant. It was not intended humorously.

'For goodness' sake, what was funny?' she demanded.

'I'm almost sure she did it on purpose.'

'Spilt the cocktail on purpose?'

'Yes. And I do think that was funny, don't you?'

'On a brand new dress? I don't believe it.'

'I wonder now,' said Gladys, 'what Arthur Badcock will do with all Heather's clothes. That dress would clean all right. Or I could take out half a breadth, it's a lovely full skirt. Do you think Arthur Badcock would think it very awful of me if I wanted to buy it off him? It would need hardly any alteration – and it's lovely stuff.'

'You wouldn't – ' Cherry hesitated – 'mind?'

'Mind what?'

'Well – having a dress that a woman had died in – I mean died that way . . .'

Gladys stared at her.

'I hadn't thought of that,' she admitted. She considered for a moment or two. Then she cheered up.

'I can't see that it really matters,' she said. 'After all, every time you buy something second-hand, somebody's usually worn it who has died, haven't they?'

'Yes. But it's not quite the same.'

'I think you're being fanciful,' said Gladys. 'It's a lovely bright shade of blue, and really expensive stuff. About that funny business,' she continued thoughtfully, 'I think I'll go up to the hall tomorrow morning on my way to work and have a word with Mr Giuseppe about it.'

'Is he the Italian butler?'

'Yes. He's awfully handsome. Flashing eyes. He's got a terrible temper. When we go and help there, he chivvies us girls something terrible.' She giggled. 'But none of us really mind. He can be awfully nice sometimes . . . Anyway, I might just tell him about it, and ask him what I ought to do.'

'I don't see that you've got anything to tell,' said Cherry.

'Well, it was funny,' said Gladys, defiantly clinging to her favourite adjective.

'*I* think,' said Cherry, 'that you just want an excuse to go and talk to Mr Giuseppe – and you'd better be careful, my girl. You know what these wops are like! Affiliation orders all over the place. Hot-blooded and passionate, that's what these Italians are.'

Gladys sighed ecstatically.

Cherry looked at her friend's fat slightly spotted face and decided that her warnings were unnecessary. Mr Giuseppe, she thought, would have better fish to fry elsewhere.

II

'Aha!' said Dr Haydock, 'unravelling, I see.'

He looked from Miss Marple to a pile of fluffy white fleecy wool.

'You advised me to try unravelling if I couldn't knit,' said Miss Marple.

'You seem to have been very thorough about it.'

'I made a mistake in the pattern right at the beginning. That made the whole thing go out of proportion, so I've had to unravel it all. It's a very elaborate pattern, you see.'

'What are elaborate patterns to you? Nothing at all.'

'I ought really, I suppose, with my bad eyesight, to stick to plain knitting.'

'You'd find that very boring. Well, I'm flattered that you took my advice.'

'Don't I always take your advice, Doctor Haydock?'

'You do when it suits you,' said Dr Haydock.

'Tell me, Doctor, was it really knitting you had in mind when you gave me that advice?'

He met the twinkle in her eyes and twinkled back at her.

'How are you getting on with unravelling the murder?' he asked.

'I'm afraid my faculties aren't quite what they were,' said Miss Marple, shaking her head with a sigh.

'Nonsense,' said Dr Haydock. 'Don't tell me you haven't formed *some* conclusions.'

'Of course I have formed conclusions. Very definite ones.'

'Such as?' asked Haydock inquiringly.

'If the cocktail glass was tampered with that day – and I don't see quite how that could have been done – '

'Might have had the stuff ready in an eye-dropper,' suggested Haydock.

'You are so professional,' said Miss Marple admiringly. 'But even then it seems to me so very peculiar that nobody saw it happen.'

'Murder should not only be done, but be *seen* done! Is that it?'

'You know exactly what I mean,' said Miss Marple.

'That was a chance the murderer had to take,' said Haydock.

'Oh quite so. I'm not disputing *that* for a moment. But there were, I have found by inquiry and adding up the persons, at least eighteen to twenty people on the spot. It seems to me that amongst twenty people *somebody* must have seen that action occur.'

Haydock nodded. 'One would think so, certainly. But obviously no one did.'

'I wonder,' said Miss Marple thoughtfully.

'What have you got in mind exactly?'

'Well, there are three possibilities. I'm assuming that at least one person *would* have seen something. One out of twenty. I think it's only reasonable to assume that.'

'I think you're begging the question,' said Haydock, 'and I can see looming ahead one of those terrible exercises in probability where six men have white hats and six men have black and you have to work it out by mathematics how likely it is that the hats will get mixed up and in what proportion. If you start thinking about things like that you would go round the bend. Let me assure you of that!'

457

'I wasn't thinking of anything like that,' said Miss Marple. 'I was just thinking of what is likely – '

'Yes,' said Haydock thoughtfully, 'you're very good at that. You always have been.'

'It *is* likely, you know,' said Miss Marple, 'that out of twenty people one at least should be an observant one.'

'I give in,' said Haydock. 'Let's have the three possibilities.'

'I'm afraid I'll have to put them in rather sketchily,' said Miss Marple. 'I haven't quite thought it out. Inspector Craddock, and probably Frank Cornish before him, will have questioned everybody who was there so the natural thing would be that whoever saw anything of the kind would have said so at once.'

'Is that one of the possibilities?'

'No, of course it isn't,' said Miss Marple, 'because it hasn't happened. What you have to account for is if one person *did* see something why didn't that person say so?'

'I'm listening.'

'Possibility One,' said Miss Marple, her cheeks going pink with animation. 'The person who saw it didn't realise what they had seen. That would mean, of course, that it would have to be rather a stupid person. Someone, let us say, who can use their eyes but not their brain. The sort of person who, if you asked them. 'Did you see anyone put anything in Marina Gregg's glass?" would answer, "Oh, no," but if you said "Did you see anyone put their hand over the top of Marina Gregg's glass" would say "Oh, yes, of course I did."'

Haydock laughed. 'I admit,' he said, 'that one never quite allows for the moron in our midst. All right, I grant you Possibility One. The moron saw it, the moron didn't grasp what the action meant. And the second possibility?'

'This one's far-fetched, but I do think it *is* just a possibility. It might have been a person whose action in putting something in a glass was natural.'

'Wait, wait, explain that a little more clearly.'

'It seems to me nowadays,' said Miss Marple, 'that people are always adding things to what they eat and drink. In my young days it was considered to be very bad manners to take medicines with one's meals. It was on a par with blowing your nose at the dinner table. It just wasn't *done*. If you *had* to take pills or capsules, or a spoonful of something, you went out of the room to do so. That's not the case now. When staying with my nephew Raymond, I observed some of his guests seemed to arrive with quite a quantity of little

458

bottles of pills and tablets. They take them with food, or before food, or after food. They keep aspirins and such things in their handbags and take them the whole time – with cups of tea or with their after-dinner coffee. You understand what I mean?'

'Oh, yes,' said Dr Haydock, 'I've got your meaning now and it's interesting. You mean that someone – ' he stopped. 'Let's have it in your own words.'

'I meant,' said Miss Marple, 'that it would be quite possible, audacious but possible, for someone to pick up that glass which as soon as it was in her or her hand, of course, would be assumed to be his or her own drink and to add whatever was added quite *openly*. In that case, you see, people wouldn't think twice of it.'

'He – or she – couldn't be sure of that, though,' Haydock pointed out.

'No,' agreed Miss Marple, 'it would be a gamble, a risk – but it *could* happen. And then,' she went on, 'there's the third possibility.

'Possibility One, a moron,' said the doctor. 'Possibility Two, a gambler – what's Possibility Three?'

'Somebody saw what happened, and has held their tongue deliberately.'

Haydock frowned. 'For what reason?' he asked. 'Are you suggesting blackmail? If so – '

'If so,' said Miss Marple, 'it's a very dangerous thing to do.'

'Yes, indeed.' He looked sharply at the placid old lady with the white fleecy garment on her lap. 'Is the third possibility the one you consider the most probable one?'

'No,' said Miss Marple, 'I wouldn't go so far as that. I have, at the moment, insufficient grounds. Unless,' she added carefully, 'someone else gets killed.'

'Do you think someone else is going to get killed?'

'I hope not,' said Miss Marple, 'I trust and pray not. But it so often happens, Doctor Haydock. That's the sad and frightening thing. It so often happens.'

CHAPTER SEVENTEEN

Ella put down the telephone receiver, smiled to herself and came out of the public telephone box. She was pleased with herself.

'Chief-Inspector God Almighty Craddock!' she said to herself. 'I'm twice as good as he is at the job. Variations on the theme of: "Fly, all is discovered!"'

She pictured to herself with a good deal of pleasure the reactions recently suffered by the person at the other end of the line. That faint menacing whisper coming through the receiver. '*I saw you . . .*'

She laughed silently, the corners of her mouth curving up in a feline cruel line. A student of psychology might have watched her with some interest. Never until the last few days had she had this feeling of power. She was hardly aware herself of how much the heady intoxication of it affected her . . .

'Damn that old woman,' thought Ella. She could feel Mrs Bantry's eyes following her as she walked up the drive.

A phrase came into her head for no particular reason.

The pitcher goes to the well once too often . . .

Nonsense. Nobody could suspect that it was she who had whispered those menacing words . . .

She sneezed.

'Damn this hay-fever,' said Ella Zielinsky.

When she came into her office, Jason Rudd was standing by the window.

He wheeled round.

'I couldn't think where you were.'

'I had to go and speak to the gardener. There were – ' she broke off as she caught sight of his face.

She asked sharply: 'What is it?'

His eyes seemed set deeper in his face than ever. All the gaiety of the clown was gone. This was a man under strain. She had seen him under strain before but never looking like this.

She said again: 'What is it?'

He held a sheet of paper out to her. 'It's the analysis of that coffee. The coffee that Marina complained about and wouldn't drink.'

'You sent it to be analysed?' She was startled. 'But you poured it away down the sink. I saw you.'

His wide mouth curled up in a smile. 'I'm pretty good at sleight of hand, Ella,' he said. 'You didn't know that, did you? Yes, I poured most of it away but I kept a little and I took it along to be analysed.'

She looked down at the paper in her hand.

'*Arsenic*.' She sounded incredulous.

'Yes, arsenic.'

'So Marina was right about it tasting bitter?'

'She wasn't right about that. Arsenic has no taste. But her instinct was quite right.'

'And we thought she was just being hysterical!'

'She is hysterical! Who wouldn't be? She has a woman drop dead at her feet practically. She gets threatening notes – one after another – there's not been anything today, has there?'

Ella shook her head.

'Who plants the damned things? Oh well, I suppose it's easy enough – all these open windows. Anyone could slip in.'

'You mean we ought to keep the house barred and locked? But it's such hot weather. There's a man posted in the grounds, after all.'

'Yes, and I don't want to frighten her more than she's frightened already. Threatening notes don't matter two hoots. But arsenic, Ella, arsenic's different . . .'

'Nobody could tamper with food here in the house.'

'Couldn't they, Ella? Couldn't they?'

'Not without being seen. No unauthorized person – '

He interrupted.

'People will do things for money, Ella.'

'Hardly murder!'

'Even that. And they mightn't realize it *was* murder . . . The servants . . .'

'I'm sure the servants are all right.'

'Giuseppe now. I doubt if I'd trust Giuseppe very far if it came to the question of money . . . He's been with us some time, of course, but – '

'Must you torture yourself like this, Jason?'

He flung himself down in the chair. He leaned forward, his long arms hanging down between his knees.

461

'What to do?' he said slowly and softly. 'My God, what to do?'

Ella did not speak. She sat there watching him.

'She was happy here,' said Jason. He was speaking more to himself than to Ella. He stared down between his knees at the carpet. If he had looked up, the expression on her face might perhaps have surprised him.

'She was happy,' he said again. 'She hoped to be happy and she *was* happy. She was saying so that day, the day Mrs What's-her-name – '

'Bantry?'

'Yes. The day Mrs Bantry came to tea. She said it was "so peaceful." She said that at last she'd found a place where she could settle down and be happy and feel secure. My goodness, secure!'

'Happy ever after?' Ella's voice held a slight tone of irony. 'Yes, put like that, it sounds just like a fairy story.'

'At any rate she believed it.'

'But you didn't,' said Ella. 'You never thought it *would* be like that?'

Jason Rudd smiled. 'No. I didn't go the whole hog. But I did think for a while, a year – two years – there might be a period of calm and content. It might have made a new woman of her. It might have given her confidence in herself. She can be happy, you know. When she is happy she's like a child. Just like a child. And now – *this* had to happen to her.'

Ella moved restlessly. 'Things have to happen to all of us,' she said brusquely. 'That's the way life is. You just have to take it. Some of us can, some of us can't. She's the kind that can't.'

She sneezed.

'Your hay-fever bad again?'

'Yes. By the way, Giuseppe's gone to London.'

Jason looked faintly surprised.

'To London? Why?'

'Some kind of family trouble. He's got relations in Soho, and one of them's desperately ill. He went to Marina about it and she said it was all right, so I gave him the day off. He'll be back sometime tonight. You don't mind do you?'

'No,' said Jason, 'I don't mind . . .'

He got up and walked up and down.

'If I could take her away . . . now . . . at once.'

'Scrap the picture? But just think.'

His voice rose.

'I can't think of anything but Marina. Don't you understand? She's in danger. That's all I can think about.'

She opened her mouth impulsively, then closed it.

She gave another muffled sneeze and rose.

'I'd better get my atomizer.'

She left the room and went to her bedroom, a word echoing in her mind.

Marina . . . Marina . . . Marina . . . Always Marina . . .

Fury rose up in her. She stilled it. She went into the bathroom and picked up the spray she used.

She inserted the nozzle into one nostril and squeezed.

The warning came a second too late . . . Her brain recognized the unfamiliar odour of bitter almonds . . . but not in time to paralyse the squeezing fingers.

CHAPTER EIGHTEEN

Frank Cornish replaced the receiver.

'Miss Brewster is out of London for the day,' he announced.

'Is she now?' said Craddock.

'Do you think she – '

'I don't know. I shouldn't think so, but I don't know. Ardwyck Fenn?'

'Out. I left word for him to ring you. And Margot Bence, Personality Photographer, has got an assignment somewhere in the country. Her pansy partner didn't know where – or said he didn't. And the butler's hooked it to London.'

'I wonder,' said Craddock thoughtfully, 'if the butler has hooked it for good. I always suspect dying relatives. Why was he suddenly anxious to go to London today?'

'He could have put the cyanide in the atomizer easily enough before he left.'

'Anybody could.'

'But I think he's indicated. It could hardly be someone from outside.'

'Oh, yes, it could. You'd have to judge your moment. You could leave a car in one of the side drives, wait until everyone is in the dining-room, say, and slip in through a window and upstairs. The shrubberies come close up to the house.'

'Damn' risky.'

'This murderer doesn't mind taking risks, you know. That's been apparent all along.'

'We've had a man on duty in the grounds.'

'I know. One man wasn't enough. So long as it was a question of these anonymous letters I didn't feel so much urgency. Marina Gregg herself is being well guarded. It never occurred to me that anyone else was in danger. I – '

The telephone rang. Cornish took the call.

'It's the Dorchester. Mr Ardwyck Fenn is on the line.'

He preffered the receiver to Craddock who took it.

'Mr Fenn? This is Craddock here.'

'Ah, yes. I heard you had rung me. I have been out all day.'

'I am sorry to tell you, Mr Fenn, that Miss Zielinsky died this morning – of cyanide poisoning.'

'Indeed? I am shocked to hear it. An accident? Or not an accident?'

'Not an accident. Prussic acid had been put in an atomizer she was in the habit of using.'

'I see. Yes, I see . . .' There was a short pause. 'And why, may I ask, should you ring me about this distressing occurrence?'

'You knew Miss Zielinsky, Mr Fenn?'

'Certainly I knew her. I have known her for some years. But she was not an intimate friend.'

'We hoped that you could, perhaps, assist us?'

'In what way?'

'We wondered if you could suggest any motive for her death. She is a stranger in this country. We know very little about her friends and associates and the circumstances of her life.'

'I would suggest that Jason Rudd is the person to question about that.'

'Naturally. We have done so. But there might be an off-chance that you might know something about her that he does not.'

'I'm afraid that is not so. I know next to nothing about Ella Zielinsky except that she was a most capable young woman, and first-class at her job. About her private life I know nothing at all.'

'So you have no suggestions to make?'

464

Craddock was ready for the decisive negative, but to his surprise it did not come. Instead there was a pause. He could hear Ardwyck Fenn breathing rather heavily at the other end.

'Are you still there, Chief-Inspector?'

'Yes, Mr Fenn. I'm here.'

'I have decided to tell you something that may be of assistance to you. When you hear what it is, you will realize that I have every reason to keep it to myself. But I judge that in the end that might be unwise. The facts are these. A couple of days ago I received a telephone call. A voice spoke to me in a whisper. It said – I am quoting now – *I saw you . . . I saw you put the tablets in the glass . . . You didn't know there had been an eye-witness, did you? That's all for now – very soon you will be told what you have to do.*'

Craddock uttered an ejaculation of astonishment.

'Surprising, was it not, Mr Craddock? I will assure you categorically that the accusation was entirely unfounded. I did *not* put tablets in anybody's glass. I defy anyone to prove that I did. The suggestion is utterly absurd. But it would seem, would it not, that Miss Zielinsky was embarking on black mail.'

'You recognized her voice?'

'You cannot recognize a whisper. But it was Ella Zielinsky all right.'

'How do you know?'

'The whisperer sneezed heavily before ringing off. I knew that Miss Zielinsky suffered from hay-fever.'

'And you think – what?'

'I think that Miss Zielinsky got hold of the wrong person at her first attempt. It seems to me possible that she was more successful later. Blackmail can be a dangerous game.'

Craddock pulled himself together.

'I must thank you for your statement, Mr Fenn. As a matter of form, I shall have to check upon your movements today.'

'Naturally. My chauffeur will be able to give you precise information.'

Craddock rang off and repeated what Fenn had said. Cornish whistled.

'Either that lets him out completely. Or else – '

'Or else it's a magnificent piece of bluff. It could be. He's the kind of man who has the nerve for it. If there's the least chance that Ella Zielinsky left a record of her suspicions, then this taking of the bull by the horns is a magnificent bluff.'

465

'And his alibi?'

'We've come across some very good faked alibis in our time,' said Craddock. 'He could afford to pay a good sum for one.'

II

It was past midnight when Giuseppe returned to Gossington. He took a taxi from Much Benham, as the last train on the branch line to St Mary Mead had gone.

He was in very good spirits. He paid off the taxi at the gate, and took a short cut through the shrubbery. He opened the back door with his key. The house was dark and silent. Giuseppe shut and bolted the door. As he turned to the stair which led to his own comfortable suite of bed and bath, he noticed that there was a draught. A window open somewhere, perhaps. He decided not to bother. He went upstairs smiling and fitted a key into his door. He always kept his suite locked. As he turned the key and pushed the door open, he felt the pressure of a hard round ring in his back. A voice said, 'Put your hands up and don't scream.'

Giuseppe threw his hands up quickly. He was taking no chances. Actually there was no chance to take.

The trigger was pressed – once – twice.

Giuseppe fell forward . . .

Bianca lifted her head from her pillow.

Was that a shot . . . She was almost sure she had heard a shot . . . She waited some minutes. Then she decided she had been mistaken and lay down again.

CHAPTER NINETEEN

'It's too dreadful,' said Miss Knight. She put down her parcels and gasped for breath.

'Something has happened?' asked Miss Marple.

'I really don't like to tell you about it, dear, I really don't. It might be a shock to you.'

'If you don't tell me,' said Miss Marple, 'somebody else will.'

'Dear, dear, that's true enough,' said Miss Knight. 'Yes, that's terribly true. Everybody talks too much, they say. And I'm sure there's a lot in that. I never repeat anything myself. Very careful I am.'

'You were saying,' said Miss Marple, 'that something rather terrible had happened?'

'It really quite bowled me over,' said Miss Knight. 'Are you sure you don't feel the draught from that window, dear?'

'I like a little fresh air,' said Miss Marple.

'Ah, but we mustn't catch cold, must we?' said Miss Knight archly. 'I'll tell you what. I'll just pop out and make you a nice egg-nog. We'd like that, wouldn't we?'

'I don't know whether *you* would like it,' said Miss Marple. '*I* should be delighted for you to have it if you would like it.'

'Now, now,' said Miss Knight, shaking her finger, 'so fond of our joke, aren't we?'

'But you were going to tell me something,' said Miss Marple.

'Well, you mustn't worry about it,' said Miss Knight, 'and you mustn't let it make you nervous in any way, because I'm sure it's nothing to do with *us*. But with all these American gangsters and things like that, well I suppose it's nothing to be surprised about.'

'Somebody else has been killed,' said Miss Marple, 'is that it?'

'Oh, that's very sharp of you, dear. I don't know what should put such a thing into your head.'

'As a matter of fact,' said Miss Marple thoughtfully, 'I've been expecting it.'

'Oh, really!' exclaimed Miss Knight.

'Somebody always sees something,' said Miss Marple, 'only sometimes it takes a little while for them to realize what it is they have seen. Who is it who's dead?'

'The Italian butler. He was shot last night.'

'I see,' said Miss Marple thoughtfully. 'Yes, very likely, of course, but I should have thought that he'd have realized before now the importance of what he saw – '

'Really!' exclaimed Miss Knight, 'you talk as though you knew all about it. Why should he have been killed?'

'I expect,' said Miss Marple, thoughtfully, 'that he tried to blackmail somebody.'

'He went to London yesterday, they say.'

'Did he now,' said Miss Marple, 'that's very interesting, and suggestive too, I think.'

Miss Knight departed to the kitchen intent on the concoction of nourishing beverages. Miss Marple remained sitting thoughtfully till disturbed by the loud aggressive humming of the vacuum cleaner, assisted by Cherry's voice singing the latest favourite ditty of the moment, 'I Said To You and You Said To Me.'

Miss Knight popped her head round the kitchen door.

'Not quite so much noise, please, Cherry,' she said. 'You don't want to disturb Miss Marple, do you? You mustn't be thoughtless, you know.'

She shut the kitchen door again as Cherry remarked, either to herself or the world at large, 'And who said you could call me Cherry, you old jelly-bag?' The vacuum continued to whine while Cherry sang in a more subdued voice. Miss Marple called in a high clear voice:

'Cherry, come here a minute.'

Cherry switched off the vacuum and opened the drawingroom door.

'I didn't mean to disturb you by singing, Miss Marple.'

'Your singing is much pleasanter than the horrid noise that vacuum makes,' said Miss Marple, 'but I know one has to go with the times. It would be no use on earth asking any of you young people to use the dustpan and brush in the old-fashioned way.'

'What, get down on my knees with a dustpan and brush?' Cherry registered alarm and surprise.

'Quite unheard of, I know,' said Miss Marple. 'Come in and shut the door. I called you because I wanted to talk to you.'

Cherry obeyed and came towards Miss Marple looking inquiringly at her.

'We've not much time,' said Miss Marple. 'That old – Miss Knight I mean – will come in any moment with an egg drink of some kind.'

'Good for you, I expect. It'll pep you up,' said Cherry encouragingly.

'Had you heard,' asked Miss Marple, 'that the butler at Gossington Hall was shot last night?'

'What, the wop?' demanded Cherry.

'Yes. His name is Giuseppe, I understand.'

'No,' said Cherry, 'I hadn't heard *that*. I heard that Mr Rudd's secretary had a heart attack yesterday, and somebody said she was actually dead – but I suspect that was just a rumour. Who told you about the butler?'

'Miss Knight came back and told me.'

'Of course I haven't seen anyone to speak to this morning,' said Cherry, 'not before coming along here. I expect the news has only just got round. Was he bumped off?' she demanded.

'That seems to be assumed,' said Miss Marple, 'whether rightly or wrongly I don't quite know.'

'This is a wonderful place for talk,' said Cherry. 'I wonder if Gladys got to see him or not,' she added thoughtfully.

'Gladys?'

'Oh, a sort of friend of mine. She lives a few doors away. Works in the canteen at the studios.'

'And she talked to you about Giuseppe?'

'Well, there was something that struck her as a bit funny and she was going to ask him what he thought about it. But if you ask me it was just an excuse – she's a bit sweet on him. Of course he's quite handsome and Italians do have a way with them – I told her to be careful about him, though. You know what Italians are.'

'He went to London yesterday,' said Miss Marple, 'and only returned in the evening I understand.'

'I wonder if she managed to get to see him before he went.'

'Why did she want to see him, Cherry?'

'It was just something which she felt was a bit funny,' said Cherry.

Miss Marple looked at her inquiringly. She was able to take the word 'funny' at the valuation it usually had for the Gladyses of the neighbourhood.

'She was one of the girls who helped at the party there,' explained Cherry. 'The day of the fête. You know, when Mrs Badcock got hers.'

'Yes?' Miss Marple was looking more alert than ever, much as a fox terrier might look at a waiting rat-hole.

'And there was something that she saw that struck her as a bit funny.'

'Why didn't she go to the police about it?'

'Well, she didn't really think it meant anything, you see,' explained Cherry. 'Anyway she thought she'd better ask Mr Giuseppe first.'

'What was it that she saw that day?'

'Frankly,' said Cherry, 'what she told me seemed nonsense! I've wondered, perhaps, if she was just putting me off – and what

469

she was going to see Mr Giuseppe about was something quite different.'

'What *did* she say?' Miss Marple was patient and pursuing.

Cherry frowned. 'She was talking about Mrs Badcock and the cocktail and she said she was quite near her at the time. And she said she did it herself.'

'Did what herself?'

'Spilt her cocktail all down her dress, and ruined it.'

'You mean it was clumsiness?'

'No, not clumsiness. Gladys said she did it on *purpose* – that she *meant* to do it. Well, I mean, that doesn't make sense, does it, however you look at it?'

Miss Marple shook her head, perplexed. 'No,' she said. 'Certainly not – no, I can't see any sense in that.'

'She'd got on a new dress too,' said Cherry. 'That's how the subject came up. Gladys wondered whether she'd be able to buy it. Said it ought to clean all right but she didn't like to go and ask Mr Badcock herself. She's very good at dressmaking, Gladys is, and she said it was lovely stuff. Royal blue artificial taffeta; and she said even if the stuff *was* ruined where the cocktail stained it, she could take out a seam – half a breadth say – because it was one of those full skirts.'

Miss Marple considered this dressmaking problem for a moment and then set it aside.

'But you think your friend Gladys might have been keeping something back?'

'Well, I just wondered because I don't see if that's all she saw – Heather Badcock deliberately spilling her cocktail over herself – I don't see that there'd be anything to ask Mr Giuseppe *about*, do you?'

'No, I don't,' said Miss Marple. She sighed. 'But it's always interesting when one doesn't see,' she added. 'If you don't see what a thing means you must be looking at it wrong way round, unless of course you haven't got full information. Which is probably the case here.' She sighed. 'It's a pity she didn't go straight to the police.'

The door opened and Miss Knight bustled in holding a tall tumbler with a delicious pale yellow froth on top.

'Now here you are, dear,' she said, 'a nice little treat. We're going to enjoy this.'

She pulled forward a little table and placed it beside her employer. Then she turned a glance on Cherry. 'The vacuum cleaner,' she said

470

coldly, 'is left in a most difficult position in the hall. I nearly fell over it. *Anyone* might have an accident.'

'Right-ho,' said Cherry. 'I'd better get on with things.'

She left the room.

'Really,' said Miss Knight, 'that Mrs Baker! I'm continually having to speak to her about something or other. Leaving vacuum cleaners all over the place and coming in here chattering to you when you want to be quiet.'

'I called her in,' said Miss Marple. 'I wanted to speak to her.'

'Well, I hope you mentioned the way the beds are made,' said Miss Knight. 'I was quite shocked when I came to turn down your bed last night. I had to make it all over again.'

'That was very kind of you,' said Miss Marple.

'Oh, I never grudge being helpful,' said Miss Knight. 'That's why I'm here, isn't it. To make a certain person we know as comfortable and happy as possible. Oh dear, dear,' she added, 'you've pulled out a lot of your knitting again.'

Miss Marple leaned back and closed her eyes. 'I'm going to have a little rest,' she said. 'Put the glass here – thank you. And please don't come in and disturb me for at least three-quarters of an hour.'

'Indeed I won't, dear,' said Miss Knight. 'And I'll tell that Mrs Baker to be very quiet.'

She bustled out purposefully.

II

The good-looking young American glanced round him in a puzzled way.

The ramifications of the housing estate perplexed him.

He addressed himself politely to an old lady with white hair and pink cheeks who seemed to be the only human being in sight.

'Excuse me, m'am, but could you tell me where to find Blenheim Close?'

The old lady considered him for a moment. He had just begun to wonder if she was deaf, and had prepared himself to repeat his demand in a louder voice, when she spoke.

'Along here to the right, then turn left, second to the right again, and straight on. What number do you want?'

'No. 16.' He consulted a small piece of paper. 'Gladys Dixon.'

'That's right,' said the old lady. 'But I believe she works at the

Hellingforth Studios. In the canteen. You'll find her there if you want her.'

'She didn't turn up this morning,' explained the young man. 'I want to get hold of her to come up to Gossington Hall. We're very shorthanded there today.'

'Of course,' said the old lady. 'The butler was shot last night, wasn't he?'

The young man was slightly staggered by this reply.

'I guess news gets round pretty quickly in these parts,' he said.

'It does indeed,' said the old lady. 'Mr Rudd's secretary died of some kind of seizure yesterday, too, I understand.' She shook her head. 'Terrible. Quite terrible. What are we coming to?'

CHAPTER TWENTY

A little later in the day yet another visitor found his way to 16 Blenheim Close. Detective-Sergeant William (Tom) Tiddler.

In reply to his sharp knock on the smart yellow painted door, it was opened to him by a girl of about fifteen. She had long straggly fair hair and was wearing tight black pants and an orange sweater.

'Miss Gladys Dixon live here?'

'You want Gladys? You're unlucky. She isn't here.'

'Where is she? Out for the evening?'

'No. She's gone away. Bit of a holiday like.'

'Where's she gone to?'

'That's telling,' said the girl.

Tom Tiddler smiled at her in his most ingratiating manner. 'May I come in? Is your mother at home?'

'Mum's out at work. She won't be in until half past seven. But she can't tell you any more than I can. Gladys has gone off for a holiday.'

'Oh, I see. When did she go?'

'This morning. All of a sudden like. Said she'd got the chance of a free trip.'

'Perhaps you wouldn't mind giving me her address.'

472

The fair-haired girl shook her head. 'Haven't got an address,' she said. 'Gladys said she'd send us her address as soon as she knew where she was going to stay. As like as not she won't though,' she added. 'Last summer she went to Newquay and never sent us as much as a postcard. She's slack that way and besides, she says, why do mothers have to bother all the time?'

'Did somebody stand her this holiday?'

'Must have,' said the girl. 'She's pretty hard up at the moment. Went to the sales last week.'

'And you've no idea at all who gave her this trip or – er – paid for her going there?'

The fair girl bristled suddenly.

'Now don't get any wrong ideas. Our Gladys isn't that sort. She and her boyfriend may like to go to the same place for holidays in August, but there's nothing wrong about it. She pays for herself. So don't you get ideas, mister.'

Tiddler said meekly that he wouldn't get ideas but he would like the address if Gladys Dixon should send a postcard.

He returned to the station with the result of his various inquiries. From the studios, he had learnt that Gladys Dixon had rung up that day and said she wouldn't be able to come to work for about a week. He had also learned some other things.

'No end of a shemozzle there's been there lately,' he said. 'Marina Gregg's been having hysterics most days. Said some coffee she was given was poisoned. Said it tasted bitter. Awful state of nerves she was in. Her husband took it and threw it down the sink and told her not to make so much fuss.'

'Yes?' said Craddock. It seemed plain there was more to come.

'But word went round as Mr Rudd didn't throw it all away. He kept some and had it analysed and it *was* poison.'

'It sounds to me,' said Craddock, 'very unlikely. I'll have to ask him about that.'

II

Jason Rudd was nervous, irritable.

'Surely, Inspector Craddock,' he said, 'I was only doing what I had a perfect right to do.'

'If you suspected anything was wrong with that coffee, Mr Rudd, it would have been much better if you'd turned it over to us.'

'The truth of it is that I didn't suspect for a moment that anything was wrong with it.'

'In spite of your wife saying that it tasted odd?'

'Oh, that!' A faintly rueful smile came to Rudd's face. 'Ever since the date of the fête everything that my wife has eaten or drunk has tasted odd. What with that and the threatening notes that have been coming – '

'There have been more of them?'

'Two more. One through the window down there. The other one was slipped in the letter-box. Here they are if you would like to see them.'

Craddock looked. They were printed, as the first one had been. One ran:

It won't be long now. Prepare yourself.

The other had a rough drawing of a skull and crossbones and below it was written: *This means you, Marina.*

Craddock's eyebrows rose.

'Very childish,' he said.

'Meaning you discount them as dangerous?'

'Not at all,' said Craddock. 'A murderer's mind usually is childish. You've really no idea at all, Mr Rudd, who sent these?'

'Not the least,' said Jason. 'I can't help feeling it's more like a macabre joke than anything else. It seemed to me perhaps – ' he hesitated.

'Yes, Mr Rudd?'

'It could be somebody local, perhaps, who – who had been excited by the poisoning on the day of the fête. Someone perhaps, who has a grudge against the acting profession. There are rural pockets where acting is considered to be one of the devil's weapons.'

'Meaning that you think Miss Gregg is not actually threatened? But what about this business of the coffee?'

'I don't even know how you got to hear about that,' said Rudd with some annoyance.

Craddock shook his head.

'Everyone's talked about that. It always comes to one's ears sooner or later. But you should have come to us. Even when you got the result of the analysis you didn't let us know, did you?'

'No,' said Jason. 'No, I didn't. But I had other things to think about. Poor Ella's death for one thing. And now this business of Giuseppe. Inspector Craddock, when can I get my wife away from here? She's half frantic.'

'I can understand that. But there will be the inquests to attend.'

'You do realize that her life is still in danger?'

'I hope not. Every precaution will be taken – '

'Every precaution! I've heard that before, I think . . . I must get her away from here, Craddock. I *must*.'

III

Marina was lying on the chaise-longue in her bedroom, her eyes closed. She looked grey with strain and fatigue.

Her husband stood there for a moment looking at her. Her eyes opened.

'Was that that Craddock man?'

'Yes.'

'What did he come about? Ella?'

'Ella – and Giuseppe.'

Marina frowned.

'Giuseppe? Have they found out who shot him?'

'Not yet.'

'It's all a nightmare . . . Did he say we could go away?'

'He said – not yet.'

'Why not? We must. Didn't you make him see that I can't go on waiting day after day for someone to kill me. It's fantastic.'

'Every precaution will be taken.'

'They said that before. Did it stop Ella being killed? Or Giuseppe? Don't you see, they'll get me in the end . . . There was something in my coffee that day at the studio. I'm sure there was . . . if only you hadn't poured it away! If we'd kept it, we could have had it analysed or whatever you call it. We'd have known for sure . . .'

'Would it have made you happier to know for sure?'

She stared at him, the pupils of her eyes widely dilated.

'I don't see what you mean. If they'd known for sure that someone was trying to poison me, they'd have let us leave here, they'd have let us get away.'

'Not necessarily.'

'But I can't go on like this! I can't . . . I can't . . . You must help me, Jason. You must do *something*. I'm frightened. I'm so terribly frightened . . . There's an enemy here. And I don't know who it is . . . It might be anyone – anyone. At the studios – or here in the house. Someone who hates me – but why?' . . . why? . . . Someone

475

who wants me dead . . . But who is it? Who is it? I thought – I was almost sure – it was Ella. But now – '

'You thought it was Ella?' Jason sounded astonished. 'But why?'

'Because she hated me – oh yes she did. Don't men ever see these things? She was madly in love with you. I don't believe you had the least idea of it. But it can't be Ella, because Ella's dead. Oh, Jinks, Jinks – do help me – get me away from here – let me go somewhere safe . . . safe . . .'

She sprang up and walked rapidly up and down, turning and twisting her hands.

The director in Jason was full of admiration for those passionate, tortured movements. I must remember them, he thought. For Hedda Gabler, perhaps? Then, with a shock, he remembered that it was his wife he was watching.

'It's all right, Marina – all right. I'll look after you.'

'We must go away from this hateful house – at once. I hate this house – hate it.'

'Listen, we can't go away immediately.'

'Why not? Why *not*?'

'Because,' said Rudd, 'deaths cause complications . . . and there's something else to consider. Will running away do any good?'

'Of course it will. We'll get away from this person who hates me.'

'If there's anyone who hates you that much, they could follow you easily enough.'

'You mean – you mean – I shall *never* get away? I shall never be safe again?'

'Darling – it will be all right. I'll look after you. I'll keep you safe.'

She clung to him.

'Will you, Jinks? Will you see that nothing happens to me?'

She sagged against him, and he laid her down gently on the chaise-longue.

'Oh, I'm a coward,' she murmured, 'a coward . . . if I knew *who* it was – and why? . . . Get me my pills – the yellow ones – not the brown. I must have something to calm me.'

'Don't take too many, for God's sake, Marina.'

'All right – all right . . . Sometimes they don't have any effect any more . . .' She looked up in his face.

She smiled, a tender exquisite smile.

'You'll take care of me, Jinks? Swear you'll take care of me . . .'

'Always,' said Jason Rudd. 'To the bitter end.'

Her eyes opened wide.

'You looked so – so odd when you said that.'

'Did I? How did I look?'

'I can't explain. Like – like a clown laughing at something terribly sad, that no one else has seen . . .'

CHAPTER TWENTY-ONE

It was a tired and depressed Inspector Craddock who came to see Miss Marple the following day.

'Sit down and be comfortable,' she said. 'I can see you've had a very hard time.'

'I don't like to be defeated,' said Inspector Craddock. 'Two murders within twenty-four hours. Ah well, I'm poorer at my job than I thought I was. Give me a nice cup of tea, Aunt Jane, with some thin bread and butter and soothe me with your earliest remembrances of St Mary Mead.'

Miss Marple clicked with her tongue in a sympathetic manner.

'Now it's no good talking like that, my dear boy, and I don't think bread and butter is *at all* what you want. Gentlemen, when they've had a disappointment, want something stronger than tea.'

As usual, Miss Marple said the word 'gentlemen' in the way of someone describing a foreign species.

'I should advise a good stiff whisky and soda,' she said.

'Would you really, Aunt Jane? Well, I won't say no.'

'And I shall get it for you myself,' said Miss Marple, rising to her feet.

'Oh, no, don't do that. Let me. Or what about Miss What's-her-name?'

'We don't want Miss Knight fussing about in here,' said Miss Marple. 'She won't be bringing my tea for another twenty minutes so that gives us a little peace and quiet. Clever of you to come to the window and not through the front door. Now we can have a nice quiet little time by ourselves.'

She went to a corner cupboard, opened it and produced a bottle, a syphon of soda and a glass.

'You are full of surprises,' said Dermot Craddock. 'I'd no idea that's what you kept in your corner cupboard. Are you quite sure you're not a secret drinker, Aunt Jane?'

'Now, now,' Miss Marple admonished him. 'I have never been an advocate of teetotalism. A little strong drink is always advisable on the premises in case there is a shock or an accident. Invaluable at such times. Or, of course, if a gentleman should arrive suddenly. There!' said Miss Marple, handing him her remedy with an air of quiet triumph. 'And you don't need to joke any more. Just sit quietly there and relax.'

'Wonderful wives there must have been in your young days,' said Dermot Craddock.

'I'm sure, my dear boy, you would find the young lady of the type you refer to as a very inadequate helpmeet nowadays. Young ladies were not encouraged to be intellectual and very few of them had university degrees or any kind of academic distinction.'

'There are things that are preferable to academic distinctions,' said Dermot. 'One of them is knowing when a man wants whisky and soda and giving it to him.'

Miss Marple smiled at him affectionately.

'Come,' she said, 'tell me all about it. Or as much as you are allowed to tell me.'

'I think you probably know as much as I do. And very likely you have something up your sleeve. How about your dog's-body, your dear Miss Knight? What about her having committed the crime?'

'Now why should Miss Knight have done such a thing?' demanded Miss Marple surprised.

'Because she's the most unlikely person,' said Dermot. 'It so often seems to hold good when you produce your answer.'

'Not at all,' said Miss Marple with spirit. 'I have said over and over again, not only to you, my dear Dermot – if I may call you so – that it is always the *obvious* person who has done the crime. One thinks so often of the wife or the husband and so very often it *is* the wife or the husband.'

'Meaning Jason Rudd?' He shook his head. 'That man adores Marina Gregg.'

'I was speaking generally,' said Miss Marple, with dignity. 'First we had Mrs Badcock apparently murdered. One asked oneself who could have done such a thing and the first answer would naturally be the husband. So one had to examine that possibility. Then we decided that the real object of the crime was Marina Gregg and there again we have to look for the person most intimately connected with Marina Gregg, starting as I say with the husband. Because there is no doubt about it that husbands do, very frequently, want to make away with their wives, though sometimes, of course, they only *wish* to make away with their wives and do not actually do so. But I agree with you, my dear boy, that Jason Rudd really cares with all his heart for Marina Gregg. It *might* be very clever acting, though I can hardly believe that. And one certainly cannot see a motive of any kind for his doing away with her. If he wanted to marry somebody else there could, I should say, be nothing more simple. Divorce, if I may say so, seems second nature to film stars. A practical advantage does not seem to arise either. He is not a poor man by any means. He has his own career, and is, I understand, most successful in it. So we must go farther afield. But it certainly is difficult. Yes, very difficult.'

'Yes,' said Craddock, 'it must hold particular difficulties for you because of course this film world is entirely new to you. You don't know the local scandals and all the rest of it.'

'I know a little more than you may think,' said Miss Marple. 'I have studied very closely vaious numbers of *Confidential*, *Film Life*, *Film Talk* and *Film Topics*.'

Dermot Craddock laughed. He couldn't help it.

'I must say,' he said, 'it tickles me to see you sitting there and telling me what your course of literature has been.'

'I found it very interesting,' said Miss Marple. 'They're not particularly well written, if I may say so. But it really is disappointing in a way that it is all so much the same as it used to be in my young days. *Modern Society* and *Tit Bits* and all the rest of them. A lot of gossip. A lot of scandal. A great preoccupation with who is in love with whom, and all the rest of it. Really, you know, practically exactly the same sort of thing goes on in St Mary Mead. And in the Development too. Human nature, I mean, is just the same everywhere. One comes back, I think, to the question of who could have been likely to want to kill Marina Gregg, to want to so much that having failed once they sent threatening letters and made repeated attempts to do so. Someone perhaps a little – ' very gently she tapped her forehead.

'Yes,' said Craddock, 'that certainly seems indicated. And of course it doesn't always show.'

'Oh, I know,' agreed Miss Marple, fervently. 'Old Mrs Pike's second boy, Alfred, *seemed* perfectly rational and normal. Almost painfully prosaic, if you know what I mean, but actually, it seems, he had the most abnormal psychology, or so I understand. Really positively dangerous. He seems quite happy and contented, so Mrs Pike told me, now that he is in Fairways Mental Home. They understand him there, and the doctors think him a most interesting case. That of course pleases him very much. Yes, it all ended quite happily, but she had one or two very near escapes.'

Craddock revolved in his mind the possibility of a parallel between someone in Marina Gregg's entourage and Mrs Pike's second son.

'The Italian butler,' continued Miss Marple, 'the one who was killed. He went to London, I understand, on the day of his death. Does anyone know what he did there – if you are allowed to tell me, that is,' she added conscientiously.

'He arrived in London at eleven-thirty in the morning,' said Craddock, 'and what he did in London nobody knows until a quarter or two he visited his bank and made a deposit of five hundred pounds in cash. I may say that there was no confirmation of his story that he went to London to visit an ill relative or a relative who had got into trouble. None of his relatives there had seen him.'

Miss Marple nodded her head appreciatively.

'Five hundred pounds,' she said. 'Yes, that's quite an interesting sum, isn't it. I should imagine it would be the first instalment of a good many other sums, wouldn't you?'

'It looks that way,' said Craddock.

'It was probably all the ready money the person he was threatening could raise. He may even have pretended to be satisfied with that or he may have accepted it as a down payment and the victim may have promised to raise further sums in the immediate future. It seems to knock out the idea that Marina Gregg's killer could have been someone in humble circumstances who had a private vendetta against her. It would also knock out, I should say, the idea of someone who'd obtained work as a studio helper or attendant or a servant or a gardener. Unless' – Miss Marple pointed out – 'such a person may have been the active agent whereas the employing agent may not have been in the neighbourhood. Hence the visit to London.'

'Exactly. We have in London Ardwyck Fenn, Lola Brewster and Margot Bence. All three were present at the party. All three of them could have met Giuseppe at an arranged meeting-place somewhere in London between the hours of eleven and a quarter to two. Ardwyck Fenn was out of his office during those hours. Lola Brewster had left her suite to go shopping. Margot Bence was not in her studio. By the way – '

'Yes?' said Miss Marple, 'have you something to tell me?'

'You asked me,' said Dermot, 'about the children. The children that Marina Gregg adopted before she knew she could have a child of her own.'

'Yes I did.'

Craddock told her what he had learned.

'Margot Bence,' said Miss Marple softly. 'I had a feeling, you know, that it had something to do with children . . .'

'I can't believe that after all these years – '

'I know, I know. One never can. But do you really, my dear Dermot, know very much about children? Think back to your own childhood. Can't you remember some incident, some happening that caused you grief, or a passion quite incommensurate with its real importance? Some sorrow or passionate resentment that has really never been equalled since? There was such a book, you know, written by that brilliant writer. Mr Richard Hughes. I forget the name of it but it was about some children who had been through a hurricane. Oh yes – the hurricane in Jamaica. What made a vivid impression on them was their cat rushing madly through the house. It was the only thing they remembered. But the whole of the horror and excitement and fear that they had experienced was bound up in that one incident.'

'It's odd you should say that,' said Craddock thoughtfully.

'Why, has it made you remember something?'

'I was thinking of when my mother died. I was five I think. Five or six. I was having dinner in the nursery, jam roll pudding. I was very fond of jam roll pudding. One of the servants came in and said to my nursery governess, "Isn't it awful? There's been an accident and Mrs Craddock has been killed." . . . Whenever I think of my mother's death, d'you know what I see?'

'What?'

'A plate with jam roll pudding on it, and I'm staring at it. Staring at it and I can see as well now as then, how the jam oozed out of it at one side. I didn't cry or say anything. I remember just sitting there as though I'd been frozen stiff, staring at the pudding. And d'you know, even now if I see in a shop or a restaurant or in anyone's

481

house a portion of jam roll pudding, a whole wave of horror and misery and despair comes over me. Sometimes for a moment I don't remember *why*. Does that seem very crazy to you?'

'No,' said Miss Marple, 'it seems entirely natural. It's very interesting, that. It's given me a sort of idea . . .'

The door opened and Miss Knight appeared bearing the tea tray.

'Dear, dear,' she exclaimed, 'and so we've got a visitor, have we? How very nice. How do you do, Inspector Craddock. I'll just fetch another cup.'

'Don't bother,' Dermot called after her. 'I've had a drink instead.'

Miss Knight popped her head back round the door.

'I wonder – could you just come here a minute, Mr Craddock?'

Dermot joined her in the hall. She went to the dining-room and shut the door.

'You will be careful, won't you,' she said.

'Careful? In what way, Miss Knight?'

'Our old dear in there. You know, she's so interested in everything but it's not very good for her to get excited over murders and nasty things like that. We don't want her to brood and have bad dreams. She's very old and frail, and she really must lead a very sheltered life. She always has, you know. I'm sure all this talk of murders and gangsters and things like that is very, very bad for her.'

Dermot looked at her with faint amusement.

'I don't think,' he said gently, 'that anything that you or I could say about murders is likely unduly to excite or shock Miss Marple. I can assure you, my dear Miss Knight, that Miss Marple can contemplate murder and sudden death and indeed crime of all kinds with the utmost equanimity.'

He went back to the drawing-room, and Miss Knight, clucking a little in an indignant manner, followed him. She talked briskly during tea with an emphasis on political news in the paper and the most cheerful subjects she could think of. When she finally removed the tea tray and shut the door behind her, Miss Marple drew a deep breath.

'At last we've got some peace,' she said. 'I hope I shan't murder that woman some day. Now listen, Dermot, there are some things I want to know.'

'Yes? What are they?'

'I want to go over very carefully what happened on the day of the fête. Mrs Bantry has arrived, and the vicar shortly after her.

Then come Mr and Mrs Badcock and on the stairs at that time were the mayor and his wife, this man Ardwyck Fenn, Lola Brewster, a reporter from the *Herald & Argus* of Much Benham, and this photographer girl, Margot Bence. Margot Bence, you said, had her camera at an angle on the stairs, and was taking photographs of the proceedings. Have you seen any of those photographs?'

'Actually I brought one to show you.'

He took from his pocket an unmounted print. Miss Marple looked at it steadfastly. Marina Gregg with Jason Rudd a little behind her to one side, Arthur Badcock, his hand to his face, looking slightly embarrassed, was standing back, whilst his wife had Marina Gregg's hand in hers and was looking up at her and talking. Marina was not looking at Mrs Badcock. She was staring over her head looking, it seemed, full into the camera, or possibly just slightly to the left of it.

'*Very* interesting,' said Miss Marple. 'I've had descriptions, you know, of what this look was on her face. A frozen look. Yes, that describes it quite well. A look of doom. I'm not really so sure about that. It's more a kind of paralysis of feeling rather than apprehension of doom. Don't you think so? I wouldn't say it was actually fear, would you, although fear of course might take you that way. It might paralyse you. But I don't think it was fear. I think rather that it was *shock*. Dermot, my dear boy, I want you to tell me, if you've got notes of it, what exactly Heather Badcock said to Marina Gregg on that occasion. I know roughly the gist of it, of course, but how near can you get to the actual *words*. I suppose you had accounts of it from different people.'

Dermot nodded.

'Yes. Let me see. Your friend, Mrs Bantry, then Jason Rudd and I think Arthur Badcock. As you say they varied a little in wording, but the gist of them was the same.'

'I know. It's the variations that I want. I think it might help us.'

'I don't see how,' said Dermot, 'though perhaps you do. Your friend, Mrs Bantry, was probably the most definite on the point. As far as I remember – wait – I carry a good many of my jottings around with me.'

He took out a small note-book from his pocket, looked through it to refresh his memory.

'I haven't got the exact words here,' he said, 'but I made a rough note. Apparently Mrs Badcock was very cheerful, rather arch, and delighted with herself. She said something like "I can't tell you how

483

wonderful this is for me. You won't remember but years ago in Bermuda – I got up from bed when I had chicken pox and came along to see you and you gave me an autograph and it's one of the proudest days of my life which I have never forgotten."'

'I see,' said Miss Marple, 'she mentioned the place but not the date, did she?'

'Yes.'

'And what did Rudd say?'

'Jason Rudd? He said that Mrs Badcock told his wife that she'd got up from bed when she had the 'flu and had come to meet Marina and she still had her autograph. It was a shorter account than your friend's but the gist of it was the same.'

'Did he mention the time and place?'

'No. I don't think he did. I think he said roughly that it was some ten or twelve years ago.'

'I see. And what about Mr Badcock?'

'Mr Badcock said that Heather was extremely excited and anxious to meet Marina Gregg, that she was a great fan of Marina Gregg's and that she'd told him that once when she was ill as a girl she managed to get up and meet Miss Gregg and get her autograph. He didn't go into any close particulars, as it was evidently in the days before he was married to his wife. He impressed me as not thinking the incident of much importance.'

'I see,' said Miss Marple. 'Yes, I see . . .'

'And what do you see?' asked Craddock.

'Not quite as much as I'd like to yet,' said Miss Marple, honestly, 'but I have a sort of feeling if I only knew why she'd ruined her new dress – '

'Who – Mrs Badcock?'

'Yes. It seems to me such a very odd thing – such an inexplicable one unless – of course – Dear me, I think I must be *very* stupid!'

Miss Knight opened the door and entered, switching the light on as she did so.

'I think we want a little light in here,' she said brightly.

'Yes,' said Miss Marple, 'you are so right, Miss Knight. That is exactly what we did want. A little light. I think, you know, that at last we've got it.'

The tête-à-tête seemed ended and Craddock rose to his feet.

'There only remains one thing,' he said, 'and that is for you to tell me just what particular memory from your own past is agitating your mind now.'

'Everyone always teases me about that,' said Miss Marple, 'but I must say that I was reminded just for a moment of the Lauristons' parlourmaid.'

'The Lauriston's parlourmaid?' Craddock looked completely mystified.

'She had, of course, to take messages on the telephone,' said Miss Marple, 'and she wasn't very good at it. She used to get the general *sense* right, if you know what I mean, but the way she wrote it down used to make quite nonsense of it sometimes. I suppose really, because her grammar was so bad. The result was that some very unfortunate incidents occurred. I remember one in particular. A Mr Burroughs, I think it was, rang up and said he had been to see Mr Elvaston about the fence being broken down but he said that the fence wasn't his business at all to repair. It was on the other side of the property and he said he would like to know if that was really the case before proceeding further as it would depend on whether he was liable or not and it was important for him to know the proper lie of the land before instructing solicitors. A very obscure message, as you see. It confused rather than enlightened.'

'If you're talking about parlourmaids,' said Miss Knight with a little laugh, 'that must have been a *very* long time ago. I've never heard of a parlourmaid for many years now.'

'It was a good many years ago,' said Miss Marple, 'but nevertheless human nature was very much the same then as it is now. Mistakes were made for very much the same reasons. Oh dear,' she added, 'I *am* thankful that that girl is safely in Bournemouth.'

'The girl? What girl?' asked Dermot.

'That girl who did dressmaking and went up to see Giuseppe that day. What was her name – Gladys something.'

'Gladys Dixon?'

'Yes, that's the name.'

'She's in *Bournemouth*, do you say? How on earth do you know that?'

'I know,' said Miss Marple, 'because I sent her there.'

'What?' Dermot stared at her. 'You? Why?'

'I went out to see her,' said Miss Marple, 'and I gave her some money and told her to take a holiday and not to write home.'

'Why on earth did you do that?'

'Because I didn't want her to be killed, of course,' said Miss Marple, and blinked at him placidly.

CHAPTER TWENTY-TWO

'Such a sweet letter from Lady Conway,' Miss Knight said two days later as she deposited Miss Marple's breakfast tray. 'You remember my telling you about her? Just a little, you know – ' she tapped her forehead – 'wanders sometimes. And her memory's bad. Can't recognize her relations always and tells them to go away.'

'That might be shrewdness really,' said Miss Marple, 'rather than a loss of memory.'

'Now, now,' said Miss Knight, 'aren't we being naughty to make suggestions like that? She's spending the winter at the Belgrave Hotel at Llandudno. *Such* a nice residential hotel. Splendid grounds and a very nice glassed-in terrace. She's most anxious for me to come and join her there.' She sighed.

Miss Marple sat herself upright in bed.

'But please,' she said, 'if you are wanted – if you are needed there and would like to go – '

'No, no, I couldn't hear of it,' cried Miss Knight. 'Oh, no, I never meant anything like that. Why, what would Mr Raymond West say? He explained to me that being here might turn out to be a permanency. I should *never* dream of not fulfilling my obligations. I was only just mentioning the fact in passing, so don't worry, dear,' she added, patting Miss Marple on the shoulder. 'We're not going to be deserted! no, no, indeed we're not! we're going to be looked after and cosseted and made very happy and comfortable always.'

She went out of the room. Miss Marple sat with an air of determination, staring at her tray and failing to eat anything. Finally she picked up the receiver of the telephone and dialled with vigour.

'Dr Haydock?'

'Yes?'

'Jane Marple here.'

'And what's the matter with you? In need of my professional services?'

'No,' said Miss Marple. 'But I want to see you as soon as possible.'

When Dr Haydock came, he found Miss Marple still in bed waiting for him.

'You look the picture of health,' he complained.

'That is why I wanted to see you,' said Miss Marple. 'To tell you that I am perfectly well.'

'An unusual reason for sending for the doctor.'

'I'm quite strong, I'm quite fit, and it's absurd to have anybody living in the house. So long as someone comes every day and does the cleaning and all that I don't see any need at all for having someone living here permanently.'

'I dare say you don't, but I do,' said Dr Haydock.

'It seems to me you're turning into a regular old fussbudget,' said Miss Marple unkindly.

'And don't call me names!' said Dr Haydock. 'You're a very healthy woman for your age; you were pulled down a bit by bronchitis which isn't good for the elderly. But to stay alone in a house at your age is a risk. Supposing you fall down the stairs one evening or fall out of bed or slip in the bath. There you'd lie and nobody'd know about it.'

'One can imagine anything,' said Miss Marple. 'Miss Knight might fall down the stairs and I'd fall over her rushing out to see what had happened.'

'It's no good your bullying me,' said Dr Haydock. 'You're an old lady and you've got to be looked after in a proper manner. If you don't like this woman you've got, change her and get somebody else.'

'That's not always so easy,' said Miss Marple.

'Find some old servant of yours, someone that you like, and who's lived with you before. I can see this old hen irritates you. She'd irritate me. There must be some old servant somewhere. That nephew of yours is one of the best-selling authors of the day. He'd make it worth her while if you found the right person.'

'Of course dear Raymond would do anything of that kind. He is most generous,' said Miss Marple. 'But it's not so easy to find the right person. Young people have their own lives to live, and so many of my faithful old servants, I am sorry to say, are dead.'

'Well, you're not dead,' said Dr Haydock, 'and you'll live a good deal longer if you take proper care of yourself.'

He rose to his feet.

'Well,' he said. 'No good my stopping here. You look as fit as a fiddle. I shan't waste time taking your blood pressure or feeling your pulse or asking you questions. You're thriving on all this local excitement, even if you can't get about to poke your nose in as much as you'd like to do. Goodbye, I've got to go now and do some real doctoring. Eight to ten cases of German measles, half a dozen whooping coughs, and a suspected scarlet fever as well as my regulars!'

Dr Haydock went out breezily – but Miss Marple was frowning . . . Something that he had said . . . what was it? Patients to see . . . the usual village ailments . . . village ailments? Miss Marple pushed her breakfast tray farther away with a purposeful gesture. Then she rang up Mrs Bantry.

'Dolly? Jane here. I want to ask you something. Now pay attention. Is it true that you told Inspector Craddock that Heather Badcock told Marina Gregg a long pointless story about how she had chicken pox and got up in spite of it to go and meet Marina and get her autograph?'

'That was it more or less.'

'*Chicken pox*?'

'Well, something like that. Mrs Allcock was talking to me about Vodka at the time, so I wasn't really listening closely.'

'You're sure,' Miss Marple took a breath, 'that she didn't say whooping cough?'

'Whooping cough?' Mrs Bantry sounded astounded. 'Of course not. She wouldn't have had to powder her face and do it up for whooping cough.'

'I see – that's what you went by – her special mention of make-up?'

'Well, she laid stress on it – she wasn't the making-up kind. But I think you're right, it wasn't chicken pox . . . Nettlerash, perhaps.'

'You only say that,' said Miss Marple coldly, 'because you once had nettlerash yourself and couldn't go to a wedding. You're hopeless, Dolly, quite hopeless.'

She put the receiver down with a bang, cutting off Mrs Bantry's astonished protest of 'Really, Jane.'

Miss Marple made a ladylike noise of vexation like a cat sneezing to indicate profound disgust. Her mind reverted to the problem of her own domestic comfort. Faithful Florence? Could faithful Florence, that grenadier of a former parlourmaid be persuaded to leave her comfortable small house and come back to St Mary Mead to look

488

after her erstwhile mistress? Faithful Florence had always been very devoted to her. But faithful Florence was very attached to her own little house. Miss Marple shook her head vexedly. A gay rat-tat-tat sounded at the door. On Miss Marple's calling 'Come in' Cherry entered.

'Come for your tray,' she said. 'Has anything happened? You're looking rather upset, aren't you?'

'I feel so helpless,' said Miss Marple. 'Old and helpless.'

'Don't worry,' said Cherry, picking up the tray. 'You're very far from helpless. You don't know the things I hear about you in this place! Why practically everybody in the Development knows about you now. All sorts of extraordinary things you've done. *They* don't think of you as the old and helpless kind. It's *she* puts it into your head.'

'She?'

Cherry gave a vigorous nod of her head backwards towards the door behind her.

'Pussy, pussy,' she said. 'Your Miss Knight. Don't you let her get you down.'

'She's very kind,' said Miss Marple, 'really *very* kind,' she added, in the tone of one who convinces herself.

'Care killed the cat, they say,' said Cherry. 'You don't want kindness rubbed into your skin, so to speak, do you?'

'Oh, well,' said Miss Marple sighing, 'I suppose we all have our troubles.'

'I should say we do,' said Cherry. 'I oughtn't to complain but I feel sometimes that if I live next door to Mrs Hartwell any longer there's going to be a regrettable incident. Sour-faced old cat, always gossiping and complaining. Jim's pretty fed up too. He had a first-class row with her last night. Just because we had *The Messiah* on a bit loud! You can't object to *The Messiah*, can you? I mean, it's religious.'

'Did she object?'

'She created something terrible, said Cherry. 'Banged on the wall and shouted and one thing and another.'

'Do you have to have your music turned on so loud?' asked Miss Marple.

'Jim likes it that way,' said Cherry. 'He says you don't get the tone unless you have full volume.'

'It might,' suggested Miss Marple, 'be a *little* trying for anyone if they *weren't* musical.'

'It's these houses being semi-detached,' said Cherry. 'Thin as anything, the walls. I'm not so keen really on all this new building, when you come to think of it. It looks all very prissy and nice but you can't express your personality without somebody being down on you like a ton of bricks.'

Miss Marple smiled at her.

'You've got a lot of personality to express, Cherry,' she said.

'D'you think so?' Cherry was pleased and she laughed. 'I wonder,' she began. Suddenly she looked embarrassed. She put down the tray and came back to the bed.

'I wonder if you'd think it cheek if I asked you something? I mean – you've only got to say "out of the question" and that's that.'

'Something you want me to do?'

'Not quite. It's those rooms over the kitchen. They're never used nowadays, are they?'

'No.'

'Used to be a gardener and wife there once, so I heard. But that's old stuff. What I wondered – what Jim and I wondered – is if we could have them. Come and live here, I mean.'

Miss Marple stared at her in astonishment.

'But your beautiful new house in the Development?'

'We're both fed up with it. We like gadgets, but you can have gadgets anywhere – get them on H.P. and there would be a nice lot of room here, especially if Jim could have the room over the stables. He'd fix it up like new, and he could have all his construction models there, and wouldn't have to clear them away all the time. And if we had our stereogram there too, you'd hardly hear it.'

'Are you really serious about this, Cherry?'

'Yes, I am. Jim and I, we've talked about it a lot. Jim could fix things for you any time – you know, plumbing or a bit of carpentry, and I'd look after you every bit as well as your Miss Knight does. I know you think I'm a bit slap-dash – but I'd try and take trouble with the beds and the washing-up – and I'm getting quite a dab hand at cooking. Did Beef Stroganoff last night, it's quite easy, really.'

Miss Marple contemplated her.

Cherry was looking like an eager kitten – vitality and joy of life radiated from her. Miss Marple thought once more of faithful Florence. Faithful Florence would, of course, keep the house far better. (Miss Marple put no faith in Cherry's promise.) But she was at least sixty-five – perhaps more. And would she really want to be uprooted? She might accept that out of very real devotion for

490

Miss Marple. But did Miss Marple really want sacrifices made for her? Wasn't she already suffering from Miss Knight's conscientious devotion to duty?

Cherry, however inadequate her housework, *wanted* to come. And she had qualities that to Miss Marple at this moment seemed of supreme importance.

Warm-heartedness, vitality, and a deep interest in everything that was going on.

'I don't want, of course,' said Cherry, 'to go behind Miss Knight's back in any way.'

'Never mind about Miss Knight,' said Miss Marple, coming to a decision. 'She'll go off to someone called Lady Conway at a hotel in Llandudno – and enjoy herself thoroughly. We'll have to settle a lot of details, Cherry, and I shall want to talk to your husband – but if you really think you'd be happy . . .'

'It'd suit us down to the ground,' said Cherry. 'And you really can rely on me doing things properly. I'll even use the dustpan and brush if you like.'

Miss Marple laughed at this supreme offer.

Cherry picked up the breakfast tray again.

'I must get cracking. I got here late this morning – hearing about poor Arthur Badcock.'

'Arthur Badcock? What happened to him?'

'Haven't you heard? He's up at the police-station now,' said Cherry. 'They asked him if he'd come and "assist them with their inquiries" and you know what that always means.'

'When did this happen?' demanded Miss Marple.

'This morning,' said Cherry. 'I suppose,' she added, 'that it got out about his once having been married to Marina Gregg.'

'What!' Miss Marple sat up again. 'Arthur Badcock was once married to Marina Gregg?'

'That's the story,' said Cherry. 'Nobody had any idea of it. It was Mr Upshaw put it about. He's been to the States once or twice on business for his firm and so he knows a lot of gossip from over there. It was a long time ago, you know. Really before she'd begun her career. They were only married a year or two and then she won a film award and of course he wasn't good enough for her then, so they had one of these easy American divorces and he just faded out, as you might say. He's the fading out kind, Arthur Badcock. He wouldn't make a fuss. He changed his name and came back to England. It's all ever so long ago. You wouldn't think anything like

491

that mattered nowadays, would you? Still, there it is. It's enough for the police to go on, I suppose.'

'Oh, no,' said Miss Marple. 'Oh *no*. This mustn't happen. If I could only think what to do – Now, let me see.' She made a gesture to Cherry. 'Take the tray away, Cherry, and send Miss Knight up to me. I'm going to get up.'

Cherry obeyed. Miss Marple dressed herself with fingers that fumbled slightly. It irritated her when she found excitement of any kind affecting her. She was just hooking up her dress when Miss Knight entered.

'Did you want me? Cherry said – '

Miss Marple broke in incisively.

'Get Inch,' she said.

'I beg your pardon,' said Miss Knight, startled.

'Inch,' said Miss Marple, 'get Inch. Telephone for him to come at once.'

'Oh, oh I see. You mean the taxi people. But his name's Roberts, isn't it?'

'To me,' said Miss Marple, 'he is Inch and always will be. But anyway get him. He's to come here at once.'

'You want to go for a little drive?'

'Just get him, can you?' said Miss Marple, 'and hurry, please.'

Miss Knight looked at her doubtfully and proceeded to do as she was told.

'We are feeling all right, dear, aren't we?' she said anxiously.

'We are both feeling very well,' said Miss Marple, 'and I am feeling *particularly* well. Inertia does not suit me, and never has. A practical course of action, that is what I have been wanting for a long time.'

'Has that Mrs Baker been saying something that has upset you?'

'Nothing has upset me,' said Miss Marple. 'I feel particularly well. I am annoyed with myself for being stupid. But really, until I got a hint from Dr Haydock this morning – now I wonder if I remember rightly. Where is that medical book of mine?' She gestured Miss Knight aside and walked firmly down the stairs. She found the book she wanted in a shelf in the drawing-room. Taking it out she looked up the index, murmured. 'Page 210,' turned to the page in question, read for a few moments then nodded her head, satisfied.

'Most remarkable,' she said, 'most curious. I don't suppose anybody would ever have thought of it. I didn't myself, until the two things came together, so to speak.'

Then she shook her head, and a little line appeared between her eyes. If only there was *someone* . . .

She went over in her mind the various accounts she had been given of that particular scene . . .

Her eyes widened in thought. There was someone – but would he, she wondered, be any good? One never knew with the vicar. He was quite unpredictable.

Nevertheless she went to the telephone and dialled.

'Good morning, Vicar, this is Miss Marple.'

'Oh, yes, Miss Marple – anything I can do for you?'

'I wonder if you could help me on a small point. It concerns the day of the fête when poor Mrs Badcock died. I believe you were standing quite near Miss Gregg when Mr and Mrs Badcock arrived.'

'Yes – yes – I was just before them, I think. Such a tragic day.'

'Yes, indeed. And I believe that Mrs Badcock was recalling to Miss Gregg that they had met before in Bermuda. She had been ill in bed and had got up specially.'

'Yes, yes, I do remember.'

'And do you remember if Mrs Badcock mentioned the illness she was suffering from?'

'I think now – let me see – yes, it was measles – at least not real measles – German measles – a much less serious disease. Some people hardly feel ill at all with it. I remember my cousin Caroline . . .'

Miss Marple cut off reminiscences of Cousin Caroline by saying firmly: 'Thank you so much, Vicar,' and replacing the receiver.

There was an awed expression on her face. One of the great mysteries of St Mary Mead was what made the vicar remember certain things – only outstripped by the greater mystery of what the vicar could manage to forget!

'The taxi's here, dear,' said Miss Knight, bustling in. 'It's a very old one, and not too clean I should say. I don't really like you driving in a thing like that. You might pick up some germ or other.'

'Nonsense,' said Miss Marple. Setting her hat firmly on her head and buttoning up her summer coat, she went out to the waiting taxi.

'Good morning, Roberts,' she said.

'Good morning, Miss Marple. You're early this morning. Where do you want to go?'

'Gossington Hall, please,' said Miss Marple.

493

'I'd better come with you, hadn't I, dear,' said Miss Knight. 'It won't take a minute just to slip an outdoor shoes.'

'No, thank you,' said Miss Marple, firmly. 'I'm going by myself. Drive on, Inch. I mean Roberts.'

Mr Roberts drove on, merely remarking:

'Ah, Gossington Hall. Great changes there and everywhere nowadays. All that development. Never thought anything like that'd come to St Mary Mead.'

Upon arrival at Gossington Hall Miss Marple rang the bell and asked to see Mr Jason Rudd.

Giuseppe's successor, a rather shaky-looking elderly man, conveyed doubt.

'Mr Rudd,' he said, 'does not see anybody without an appointment, madam. And today especially – '

'I have no appointment,' said Miss Marple, 'but I will wait,' she added.

She stepped briskly past him into the hall and sat down on a hall chair.

'I'm afraid it will be quite impossible this morning, madam.'

'In that case,' said Miss Marple, 'I shall wait until this afternoon.'

Baffled, the new butler retired. Presently a young man came to Miss Marple. He had a pleasant manner and a cheerful, slightly American voice.

'I've seen you before,' said Miss Marple. 'In the Development. You asked me the way to Blenheim Close.'

Hailey Preston smiled good-naturedly. 'I guess you did your best, but you misdirected me badly.'

'Dear me, did I?' said Miss Marple. 'So many Closes, aren't there. Can I see Mr Rudd?'

'Why, now, that's too bad,' said Hailey Preston. 'Mr Rudd's a busy man and he's – er – fully occupied this morning and really can't be disturbed.'

'I'm sure he's very busy,' said Miss Marple. 'I came here quite prepared to wait.'

'Why, I'd suggest now,' said Hailey Preston, 'that you should tell me what it is you want. I deal with all these things for Mr Rudd, you see. Everyone has to see me first.'

'I'm afraid,' said Miss Marple, 'that I want to see Mr Rudd himself. And,' she added, 'I shall wait here until I do.'

She settled herself more firmly in the large oak chair.

Hailey Preston hesitated, started to speak, finally turned away and went upstairs.

He returned with a large man in tweeds.

'This is Dr Gilchrist. Miss – er – '

'Miss Marple.'

'So you're Miss Marple,' said Dr Gilchrist. He looked at her with a good deal of interest.

Hailey Preston slipped away with celerity.

'I've heard about you,' said Dr Gilchrist. 'From Dr Haydock.'

'Dr Haydock is a very old friend of mine.'

'He certainly is. Now you want to see Mr Jason Rudd? Why?'

'It is necessary that I should,' said Miss Marple.

Dr Gilchrist's eyes appraised her.

'And you're camping here until you do?' he asked.

'Exactly.'

'You would, too,' said Dr Gilchrist. 'In that case I will give you a perfectly good reason why you cannot see Mr Rudd. His wife died last night in her sleep.'

'Dead!' exclaimed Miss Marples. 'How?'

'An overdose of sleeping stuff. We don't want the news to leak out to the Press for a few hours. So I'll ask you to keep this knowledge to yourself for the moment.'

'Of course. Was it an accident?'

'That is definitely my view,' said Gilchrist.

'But it could be suicide.'

'It could – but most unlikely.'

'Or someone could have given it to her?'

Gilchrist shrugged his shoulders.

'A most remote contingency. And a thing,' he added firmly, 'that would be quite impossible to prove.'

'I see,' said Miss Marple. She took a deep breath. 'I'm sorry, but it's more necessary than ever that I should see Mr Rudd.'

Gilchrist looked at her.

'Wait here,' he said.

CHAPTER TWENTY-THREE

Jason Rudd looked up as Gilchrist entered.

'There's an old dame downstairs,' said the doctor; 'looks about a hundred. Wants to see you. Won't take no and says she'll wait. She'll wait till this afternoon, I gather, or she'll wait till this evening and she's quite capable, I should say, of spending the night here. She's got something she badly wants to say to you. I'd see her if I were you.'

Jason Rudd looked up from his desk. His face was white and strained.

'Is she mad?'

'No. Not in the least.'

'I don't see why I – Oh, all right – send her up. What does it matter.'

Gilchrist nodded, went out of the room and called to Hailey Preston.

'Mr Rudd can spare you a few minutes now, Miss Marple,' said Hailey Preston, appearing again by her side.

'Thank you. That's very kind of him,' said Miss Marple as she rose to her feet. 'Have you been with Mr Rudd long?' she asked.

'Why, I've worked with Mr Rudd for the last two and a half years. My job is public relations generally.'

'I see.' Miss Marple looked at him thoughtfully. 'You remind me very much,' she said, 'of someone I knew called Gerald French.'

'Indeed? What did Gerald French do?'

'Not very much,' said Miss Marple, 'but he was a very good talker.' She sighed. 'He had had an unfortunate past.'

'You don't say,' said Hailey Preston, slightly ill at ease. 'What kind of a past?'

'I won't repeat it,' said Miss Marple. 'He didn't like it talked about.'

Jason Rudd rose from his desk and looked with some surprise at the slender elderly lady who was advancing towards him.

'You wanted to see me?' he said. 'What can I do for you?'

'I am very sorry about your wife's death,' said Miss Marple. 'I can see it has been a great grief to you and I want you to believe that I should not intrude upon you now or offer you sympathy unless it was absolutely necessary. But there are things that need badly to be cleared up unless an innocent man is going to suffer.'

'An innocent man? I don't understand you.'

'Arthur Badcock,' said Miss Marple. 'He is with the police now, being questioned.'

'Questioned in connection with my wife's death? But that's absurd, absolutely absurd. He's never been near the place. He didn't even know her.'

'I think he knew her,' said Miss Marple. 'He was married to her once.'

'Arthur *Badcock*? But – he was – he was Heather Badcock's husband. Aren't you perhaps –' he spoke kindly and apologetically – 'Making a little mistake?'

'He was married to both of them,' said Miss Marple. 'He was married to your wife when she was very young, before she went into pictures.'

Jason Rudd shook his head.

'My wife was first married to a man called Alfred Beadle. He was in real estate. They were not suited and they parted almost immediately.'

'Then Alfred Beadle changed his name to Badcock,' said Miss Marple. 'He's in a real estate firm here. It's odd how some people never seem to like to change their job and want to go on doing the same thing. I expect really that's why Marina Gregg felt that he was no use to her. He couldn't have kept up with her.'

'What you've told me is most surprising.'

'I can assure you that I am not romancing or imagining things. What I am telling you is sober fact. These things get round very quickly in a village, you know, though they take a little longer,' she added, 'in reaching the Hall.'

'Well,' Jason Rudd stalled, uncertain what to say, then he accepted the position, 'and what do you want me to do for you, Miss Marple?' he asked.

'I want, if I may, to stand on the stairs at the spot where you and your wife received guests on the day of the fête.'

He shot a quick doubtful glance at her. Was this, after all, just

497

another sensation-seeker? But Miss Marple's face was grave and composed.

'Why certainly,' he said, 'if you want to do so. Come with me.'

He led her to the staircase head and paused in the hollowed-out bay at the top of it.

'You've made a good many changes in the house since the Bantrys were here,' said Miss Marple. 'I like this. Now, let me see. The tables would be about here, I suppose, and you and your wife would be standing – '

'My wife stood here.' Jason showed her the place. 'People came up the stairs, she shook hands with them and passed them on to me.'

'She stood here,' said Miss Marple.

She moved over and took her place where Marina Gregg had stood. She remained there quite quietly without moving. Jason Rudd watched her. He was perplexed but interested. She raised her right hand slightly as though shaking, looked down the stairs as though to see people coming up it. Then she looked straight ahead of her. On the wall half-way up the stairs was a large picture, a copy of an Italian Old Master. On either side of it were narrow windows, one giving out on the garden and the other giving on to the end of the stables and the weathercock. But Miss Marple looked at neither of these. Her eyes were fixed on the picture itself.

'Of course you always hear a thing right the first time,' she said. 'Mrs Bantry told me that your wife stared at the picture and her face "froze," as she put it.' She looked at the rich red and blue robes of the Madonna, a Madonna with her head slightly back, laughing up at the Holy Child that she was holding up in her arms. 'Giacomo Bellini's "Laughing Madonna",' she said. 'A religious picture, but also a painting of a happy mother with her child. Isn't that so Mr Rudd?'

'I would say so, yes.'

'I understand now,' said Miss Marple. 'I understand quite well. The whole thing is really very simple, isn't it?' She looked at Jason Rudd.

'Simple?'

'I think you know how simple it is,' said Miss Marple. There was a peal on the bell below.

'I don't think,' said Jason Rudd, 'I quite understand.' He looked down the stairway. There was a sound of voices.

'I know that voice,' said Miss Marple, 'it's Inspector Craddock's voice, isn't it?'

'Yes, it seems to be Inspector Craddock.'

'He wants to see you, too. Would you mind very much if he joined us?'

'Not at all as far as I am concerned. Whether he will agree – '

'I think he will agree,' said Miss Marple. 'There's really not much time now to be lost is there? We've got to the moment when we've got to understand just how everything happened.'

'I thought you said it was simple,' said Jason Rudd.

'It was so simple,' said Miss Marple, 'that one just couldn't see it.'

The decayed butler arrived at this moment up the stairs.

'Inspector Craddock is here, sir,' he said.

'Ask him to join us here, please,' said Jason Rudd.

The butler disappeared again and a moment or two later Dermot Craddock came up the stairs.

'You!' he said to Miss Marple, 'how did you get here?'

'I came in Inch,' said Miss Marple, producing the usual confused effect that that remark always caused.

From slightly behind her Jason Rudd rapped his forehead interrogatively. Dermot Craddock shook his head.

'I was saying to Mr Rudd,' said Miss Marple, '– has the butler gone away – '

Dermot Craddock cast a look down the stairs.

'Oh, yes,' he said, 'he's not listening. Sergeant Tiddler will see to that.'

'Then that is all right,' said Miss Marple. 'We could of course have gone into a room to talk, but I prefer it like this. Here we are on the spot where the thing happened, which makes it so much easier to understand.'

'You are talking,' said Jason Rudd, 'of the day of the fête here, the day when Heather Badcock was poisoned.'

'Yes,' said Miss Marple, 'and I'm saying that it is all very simple if one only looks at it in the proper way. It all began, you see, with Heather Badcock being the kind of person she was. It was inevitable, really, that something of that kind should happen some day to Heather.'

'I don't understand what you mean,' said Jason Rudd. 'I don't understand at all.'

'No, it has to be explained a little. You see, when my friend, Mrs Bantry who was here, described the scene to me, she quoted a poem that was a great favourite in my youth, a poem of dear

499

Lord Tennyson's. "The Lady of Shalott".' She raised her voice a little.

> 'The mirror crack'd from side to side:
> "The Curse is come upon me," cried
> The Lady of Shalott.

That's what Mrs Bantry saw, or thought she saw, though actually she misquoted and said doom instead of curse – perhaps a better word in the circumstances. She saw your wife speaking to Heather Badcock and heard Heather Badcock speaking to your wife and she saw this look of doom on your wife's face.'

'Haven't we been over that a great many times?' said Jason Rudd.

'Yes, but we shall have to go over it once more,' said Miss Marple. 'There was that expression on your wife's face and she was looking not at Heather Badcock but at that picture. At a picture of a laughing, happy mother holding up a happy child. The mistake was that though there *was* doom foreshadowed in Marina Gregg's face, it was not on *her* the doom would come. The doom was to come upon Heather. Heather was doomed from the first moment that she began talking and boasting of an incident in the past.'

'Could you make yourself a little clearer?' said Dermot Craddock.

Miss Marple turned to him.

'Of course I will. This is something that you know nothing about. You couldn't know about it, because nobody has told you what it was Heather Badcock actually said.'

'But they have,' protested Dermot. 'They've told me over and over again. Several people have told me.'

'Yes,' said Miss Marple, 'but you don't know because, you see, Heather Badcock didn't tell it to *you*.'

'She hardly could tell it to me seeing she was dead when I arrived here,' said Dermot.

'Quite so,' said Miss Marple. 'All you know is that she was ill but she got up from bed and came along to a celebration of some kind where she met Marina Gregg and spoke to her and asked for an autograph and was given one.'

'I know,' said Craddock with slight impatience. 'I've heard all that.'

'But you didn't hear the one operative phrase, because no one

500

thought it was important,' said Miss Marple. 'Heather Badcock was ill in bed – with *German measles.*'

'German measles? What on earth has that got to do with it?'

'It's a very slight illness, really,' said Miss Marple. 'It hardly makes you feel ill at all. You have a rash which is easy to cover up with powder, and you have a little fever, but not very much. You feel quite well enough to go out and see people if you want to. And of course in repeating all this the fact that it was German measles didn't strike people particularly. Mrs Bantry, for instance, just said that Heather had been ill in bed and mentioned chicken pox and nettlerash. Mr Rudd here said that it was 'flu, but of course he did that on purpose. But I think myself that what Heather Badcock said to Marina Gregg was that she had had German measles and got up from bed and went off to meet Marina. And that's really the answer to the whole thing, because, you see, German measles is extremely infectious. People catch it very easily. And there's one thing about it which you've got to remember. If a woman contracts it in the first four months of – ' Miss Marple spoke the next word with a slight Victorian modesty '– of – er – pregnancy, it may have a terribly serious effect. It may cause an unborn child to be born blind or to be born mentally affected.'

She turned to Jason Rudd.

'I think I am correct in saying, Mr Rudd, that your wife had a child who was born mentally afflicted and that she has never really recovered from the shock. She had always wanted a child and when at last the child came, this was the tragedy that happened. A tragedy she has never forgotten, that she has not allowed herself to forget and which ate into her as a kind of deep sore, an obsession.'

'It's quite true,' said Jason Rudd. 'Marina developed German measles early on in her pregnancy and was told by the doctor that the mental affliction of her child was due to that cause. It was not a case of inherited insanity or anything of that kind. He was trying to be helpful but I don't think it helped her much. She never knew how, or when or from whom she had contracted the disease.'

'Quite so,' said Miss Marple, 'she never knew until one afternoon here when a perfectly strange woman came up those stairs and told her the fact – told her, what was more – with a great deal of pleasure! With an air of being proud of what she'd done! *She* thought she'd been resourceful and brave and shown a lot of spirit in getting up from her bed, covering her face with make-up, and going along to meet the actress on whom she had such a crush and obtaining her autograph.

501

It's a thing she has boasted of all through her life. Heather Badcock meant no harm. She never did mean harm but there is no doubt that people like Heather Badcock (and like my old friend Alison Wilde), are capable of doing a lot of harm because they lack – not kindness, they have kindness – but any real consideration for the way their actions may affect other people. She thought always of what an action meant to *her*, never sparing a thought to what it might mean to somebody else.'

Miss Marple nodded her head gently.

'So she died, you see, for a simple reason out of her own past. You must imagine what that moment meant to Marina Gregg. I think Mr Rudd understands it very well. I think she had nursed all those years a kind of hatred for the unknown person who had been the cause of her tragedy. And here suddenly she meets that person face to face. And a person who is gay, jolly and pleased with herself. It was too much for her. If she had had time to think, to calm down, to be persuaded to relax – but she gave herself no time. Here was this woman who had destroyed her happiness and destroyed the sanity and health of her child. She wanted to punish her. She wanted to kill her. And unfortunately the means were to hand. She carried with her that well-known specific, Calmo. A somewhat dangerous drug because you had to be careful of the exact dosage. It was very easy to do. She put the stuff into her own glass. If by any chance anyone noticed what she was doing they were probably so used to her pepping herself up or soothing herself down in any handy liquid that they'd hardly notice it. It's possible that one person did see her, but I rather doubt it. I think that Miss Zielinsky did no more than guess. Marina Gregg put her glass down on the table and presently she managed to jog Heather Badcock's arm so that Heather Badcock spilt her own drink all down her new dress. And that's where the element of puzzle has come into the matter, owing to the fact that people cannot remember to use their pronouns properly.

'It reminds me so much of that parlourmaid I was telling you about,' she added to Dermot. 'I only had the account, you see, of what Gladys Dixon said to Cherry which simply was that she was worried about the ruin of Heather Badcock's dress with the cocktail spilt down it. What seemed so funny, she said, was that she did it on purpose. But the "she" that Glady's referred to was not Heather Badcock, it was Marina Gregg. As Gladys said: She did it on purpose! She jogged Heather's arm. Not by accident but because she *meant* to do so. We do know that she must have been

502

standing very close to Heather because we have heard that she mopped up both Heather's dress and her own before pressing her cocktail on Heather. It was really,' said Miss Marple meditatively, 'a very perfect murder; because, you see, it was committed on the spur of the moment without pausing to think or reflect. She wanted Heather Badcock dead and a few minutes later Heather Badcock *was* dead. She didn't realize, perhaps, the seriousness of what she'd done and certainly not the danger of it until afterwards. But she realized it then. She was afraid, horribly afraid. Afraid that someone had seen her dope her own glass, that someone had seen her deliberately jog Heather's elbow, afraid that someone would accuse her of having poisoned Heather. She could see only one way out. To insist that the murder had been aimed at *her*, that *she* was the prospective victim. She tried that idea first on her doctor. She refused to let him tell her husband because I think she knew that her husband would not be deceived. She did fantastic things. She wrote notes to herself and arranged to find them in extraordinary places and at extraordinary moments. She doctored her own coffee at the studios one day. She did things that could really have been seen through fairly easily if one had happened to be thinking that way. They were seen through by one person.'

She looked at Jason Rudd.

'This is only a theory of yours,' said Jason Rudd.

'You can put it that way, if you like,' said Miss Marple, 'but you know quite well, don't you, Mr Rudd, that I'm speaking the truth. You know, because you knew from the first. You knew because you heard that mention of German measles. You knew and you were frantic to protect her. But you didn't realize how much you would have to protect her from. You didn't realize that it was not only a question of hushing up one death, the death of a woman whom you might say quite fairly had brought her death on herself. But there were other deaths – the death of Giuseppe, a blackmailer, it is true, but a human being. And the death of Ella Zielinsky of whom I expect you were fond. You were frantic to protect Marina and also to prevent her from doing more harm. All you wanted was to get her safely away somewhere. You tried to watch her all the time, to make sure that nothing more should happen.'

She paused, and then coming nearer to Jason Rudd, she laid a gentle hand on his arm.

'I am very sorry for you,' she said, 'very sorry. I do realize the agony you've been through. You cared for her so much, didn't you?'

Jason Rudd turned slightly away.

'That,' he said, 'is, I believe, common knowledge.'

'She was such a beautiful creature,' said Miss Marple gently. 'She had such a wonderful gift. She had a great power of love and hate but no stability. That's what's so sad for anyone, to be born with no stability. She couldn't let the past go and she could never see the future as it really was, only as she imagined it to be. She was a great actress and a beautiful and very unhappy woman. What a wonderful Mary, Queen of Scots, she was! I shall never forget her.'

Sergeant Tiddler appeared suddenly on the stairs.

'Sir,' he said, 'can I speak to you a moment?'

Craddock turned.

'I'll be back,' he said to Jason Rudd, then he went towards the stairs.

'Remember,' Miss Marple called after him, 'poor Arthur Badcock had nothing to do with this. He came to the fête because he wanted to have a glimpse of the girl he had married long ago. I should say she didn't even recognize him. Did she?' she asked Jason Rudd.

Jason Rudd shook his head.

'I don't think so. She certainly never said anything to me. I don't think,' he added thoughtfully, 'she would recognize him.'

'Probably not,' said Miss Marple. 'Anyway,' she added, 'he's quite innocent of wanting to kill her or anything of that kind. Remember that,' she added to Dermot Craddock as he went down the stairs.

'He's not been in any real danger, I can assure you,' said Craddock, 'but of course when we found out that he had actually been Miss Marina Gregg's first husband we naturally had to question him on the point. Don't worry about him, Aunt Jane,' he added in a low murmur, then he hurried down the stairs.

Miss Marple turned to Jason Rudd. He was standing there like a man in a daze, his eyes far away.

'Would you allow me to see her?' said Miss Marple.

He considered her for a moment or two, then he nodded.

'Yes, you can see her. You seem to – understand her very well.'

He turned and Miss Marple followed him. He preceded her into the big bedroom and drew the curtains slightly aside.

Marina Gregg lay in the great white shell of the bed – her eyes closed, her hands folded.

So, Miss Marple thought, might the Lady of Shalott have lain in the boat that carried her down to Camelot. And there, standing musing, was a man with a rugged, ugly face, who might pass as a Lancelot of a later day.

Miss Marple said gently, 'It's very fortunate for her that she – took an overdose. Death was really the only way of escape left to her. Yes – very fortunate she took that overdose – or – *was given it*?'

His eyes met hers, but he did not speak.

He said brokenly, 'She was – so lovely – and she had suffered so much.'

Miss Marple looked back again at the still figure.

She quoted softly the last lines of the peom:

> 'He said: "She has a lovely face;
> God in His mercy lend her grace,
> The Lady of Shalott."'

They Do It With Mirrors

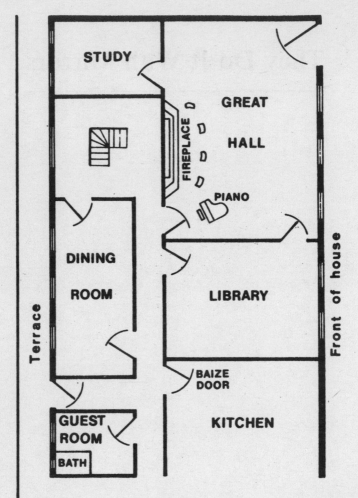

Plan of Stonygates

To Mathew Prichard

CHAPTER ONE

Mrs Van Rydock moved a little back from the mirror and sighed.

'Well, that'll have to do,' she murmured. 'Think it's all right, Jane?'

Miss Marple eyed the Lanvanelli creation appraisingly.

'It seems to me a very beautiful gown,' she said.

'The gown's all right,' said Mrs Van Rydock and sighed.

'Take if off, Stephanie,' she said.

The elderly maid with the grey hair and the small pinched mouth eased the gown carefully up over Mrs Van Rydock's upstretched arms.

Mrs Van Rydock stood in front of the glass in her peach satin slip. She was exquisitely corseted. Her still shapely legs were encased in fine nylon stockings. Her face, beneath a layer of cosmetics and constantly toned up by massage, appeared almost girlish at a slight distance. Her hair was less grey than tending to hydrangea blue and was perfectly set. It was practically impossible when looking at Mrs Van Rydock to imagine what she would be like in a natural state. Everything that money could do had been done for her – reinforced by diet, massage, and constant exercises.

Ruth Van Rydock looked humorously at her friend.

'Do you think most people would guess, Jane, that you and I are practically the same age?'

Miss Marple responded loyally.

'Not for a moment, I'm sure,' she said reassuringly. 'I'm afraid, you know, that *I* look every minute of *my* age!'

Miss Marple was white-haired, with a soft pink and white wrinkled face and innocent china blue eyes. She looked a very sweet old lady. Nobody would have called Mrs Van Rydock a sweet old lady.

'I guess you do, Jane,' said Mrs Van Rydock. She grinned suddenly, 'And so do I. Only not in the same way. "Wonderful how that old hag keeps her figure." That's what they say of me. But they know I'm an old hag all right! And, my God, do I feel like one!'

She dropped heavily on to the satin quilted chair.

'That's all right, Stephanie,' she said. 'You can go.'

Stephanie gathered up the dress and went out.

'Good old Stephanie,' said Ruth Van Rydock. 'She's been with me for over thirty years now. She's the only woman who knows what I really look like! Jane, I want to talk to you.'

Miss Marple leant forward a little. Her face took on a receptive expression. She looked, somehow, an incongruous figure in the ornate bedroom of the expensive hotel suite. She was dressed in rather dowdy black, carried a large shopping bag and looked every inch a lady.

'I'm worried, Jane. About Carrie Louise.'

'Carrie Louise?' Miss Marple repeated the name musingly. The sound of it took her a long way back.

The pensionnat in Florence. Herself, the pink and white English girl from a Cathedral Close. The two Martin girls, Americans, exciting to the English girl because of their quaint ways of speech and their forthright manner and vitality. Ruth, tall, eager, on top of the world; Carrie Louise, small, dainty, wistful.

'When did you see her last, Jane?'

'Oh! not for many many years. It must be twenty-five at least. Of course we still send cards at Christmas.'

Such an odd thing, friendship! She, young Jane Marple, and the two Americans. Their ways diverging almost at once, and yet the old affection persisting; occasional letters, remembrances at Christmas. Strange that Ruth whose home – or rather homes – had been in America should be the sister whom she had seen the more often of the two. No, perhaps not strange. Like most Americans of her class, Ruth had been cosmopolitan, every year or two she had come over to Europe, rushing from London to Paris, on to the Riviera, and back again, and always keen to snatch a few moments wherever she was with her old friends. There had been many meetings like this one. In Claridge's, or the Savoy, or the Berkeley, or the Dorchester. A *recherché* meal, affectionate reminiscences, and a hurried and affectionate goodbye. Ruth had never had time to visit St Mary Mead. Miss Marple had not, indeed, ever expected it. Everyone's life has a *tempo*. Ruth's was *presto* whereas Miss Marple's was content to be *adagio*.

So it was American Ruth whom she had seen most of, whereas Carrie Louise who lived in England, she had not now seen for over twenty years. Odd, but quite natural, because when one lives in the same country there is no need to arrange meetings with old friends. One assumes that, sooner or later, one will see them without contrivance. Only, if you move in different spheres, that does not happen. The paths of Jane Marple and Carrie Louise did not cross. It was as simple as that.

'Why are you worried about Carrie Louise, Ruth?' asked Miss Marple.

'In a way that's what worries me most! I just don't know.'

'She's not ill?'

'She's very delicate – always has been. I wouldn't say she'd been any worse than usual – considering that she's getting on just as we all are.'

'Unhappy?'

'Oh *no*.'

No, it wouldn't be that, thought Miss Marple. It would be difficult to imagine Carrie Louise unhappy – and yet there were times in her life when she must have been. Only – the picture did not come clearly. Bewildered – yes – incredulous – yes – but violent grief – no.

Mrs Van Rydock's words came appositely.

'Carrie Louise,' she said, 'has always lived right out of this world. She doesn't know what it's like. Maybe it's *that* that worries me.'

'Her circumstances,' began Miss Marple, then stopped, shaking her head. 'No,' she said.

'No, it's she herself,' said Ruth Van Rydock. 'Carrie Louise was always the one of us who had ideals. Of course it was the fashion when we were young to have ideals – we all had them, it was the proper thing for young girls. You were going to nurse lepers, Jane, and I was going to be a nun. One gets over all that nonsense. Marriage, I suppose one might say, knocks it out of one. Still, take it by and large, I haven't done badly out of marriage.'

Miss Marple thought that Ruth was expressing it mildly. Ruth had been married three times, each time to an extremely wealthy man, and the resultant divorces had increased her bank balance without in the least souring her disposition.

'Of course,' said Mrs Van Rydock, 'I've always been tough. Things don't get me down. I've not expected too much of life and certainly not expected too much of men – and I've done very well out of it – and no hard feelings. Tommy and I are still excellent friends, and Julius often asks me my opinion about the market.' Her face darkened. 'I believe that's what worries me about Carrie Louise – she's always had a tendency, you know, to marry *cranks*.'

'Cranks?'

'People with ideals. Carrie Louise was always a pushover for ideals. There she was, as pretty as they make them, just seventeen and listening with her eyes as big as saucers to old Gulbrandsen holding forth about his plans for the human race. Over fifty, and she married him, a widower with a family of grown-up children – all because of his philanthropic ideas. She used to sit listening to him spellbound. Just like Desdemona and Othello. Only fortunately there was no Iago about to mess things up – and anyway Gulbrandsen wasn't coloured. He was a Swede or a Norwegian or something.'

Miss Marple nodded thoughtfully. The name of Gulbrandsen had an international significance. A man who with shrewd business acumen and perfect honesty had built up a fortune so colossal that really philanthropy had been the only solution to the disposal of it. The name still held significance. The Gulbrandsen Trust, the Gulbrandsen Research Fellowships, the Gulbrandsen Administrative Almshouses, and best known of all the vast educational College for the sons of working men.

'She didn't marry him for his money, you know,' said Ruth, '*I* should have if I'd married him at all. But not Carrie Louise. I don't know what would have happened if he hadn't died when she was thirty-two. Thirty-two's a very nice age for a widow. She's got experience, but she's still adaptable.'

The spinster listening to her, nodded gently whilst her mind revived, tentatively, widows she had known in the village of St Mary Mead.

'I was really happiest about Carrie Louise when she was married to Johnnie Restarick. Of course *he* married her for her money – or if not exactly that, at any rate he wouldn't have married her if she hadn't had any. Johnnie was a selfish, pleasure-loving, lazy hound, but that's so much safer than a crank. All Johnnie wanted was to live soft. He wanted Carrie Louise to go to the best dressmakers and have yachts and cars and enjoy herself with him. That kind of man is so very *safe*. Give him comfort and luxury and he'll purr like a cat and be absolutely charming to you. I never took that scene designing and theatrical stuff of his very seriously. But Carrie Louise was thrilled by it – saw it all as Art with a capital A and really forced him back into those surroundings, and then that dreadful Yugoslavian woman got hold of him and just swept him off with her. He didn't really want to go. If Carrie Louise had waited and been sensible, he would have come back to her.'

'Did she care very much?' asked Miss Marple.

'That's the funny thing. I don't really believe she did. She was absolutely sweet about it all – but then she would be. She *is* sweet. Quite anxious to divorce him so that he and that creature could get married. And offering to give those two boys of his by his first marriage a home with her because it would be more settled for them. So there poor Johnnie was – he *had* to marry the woman and she led him an awful six months and then drove him over a precipice in a car in a fit of rage. They *said* it was an accident, but *I* think it was just temper!'

Mrs Van Rydock paused, took up a mirror and gazed at her face searchingly. She picked up her eyebrow tweezers and pulled out a hair.

'And what does Carrie Louise do next but marry this man Lewis Serrocold. Another crank! Another man with ideals! Oh, I don't say he isn't devoted to her – I think he is – but he's bitten by that same bug of wanting to improve everybody's lives for them. And really, you know, nobody can do that but yourself.'

'I wonder,' said Miss Marple.

'Only, of course, there's a fashion in these things, just like there is in clothes. (My dear, have you seen what Christian Dior is trying to make us wear in the way of skirts?) Where was I? Oh yes, Fashion. Well there's a fashion in philanthropy too. It used to be education in Gulbrandsen's day. But that's out of date now. The State has stepped in. Everyone expects education as a matter of right – and doesn't think much of it when they get it! Juvenile Delinquency – that's what is the rage nowadays. All these young criminals and potential criminals. Everyone's mad about them. You should see Lewis Serrocold's eyes sparkle behind those thick glasses of his. Crazy with enthusiasm! One of those men of enormous will power who like living on a banana and a piece of toast and put all their energies into a Cause. And Carrie Louise eats it up – just as she always did. But I don't like it, Jane. They've had meetings of the Trustees and the whole place has been turned over to this new idea. It's a training establishment now for these juvenile criminals, complete with psychiatrists and psychologists and all the rest of it. There Lewis and Carrie Louise are, living there, surrounded by these boys – who aren't perhaps quite normal. And the place stiff with occupational therapists and teachers and enthusiasts, half of *them* quite mad. Cranks, all the lot of them, and my little Carrie Louise in the middle of it all!'

515

She paused – and stared helplessly at Miss Marple.

Miss Marple said in a faintly puzzled voice:

'But you haven't told me yet, Ruth, what you are really afraid of.'

'I tell you, I don't *know*! And *that*'s what worries me. I've just been down there – for a flying visit. And I felt all along that there was something wrong. In the atmosphere – in the house – I know I'm not mistaken. I'm sensitive to atmosphere, always have been. Did I ever tell you how I urged Julius to sell out of Amalgamated Cereals before the crash came? And wasn't I right? Yes, something is *wrong* down there. But I don't know why or what – if it's these dreadful young jailbirds – or if it's nearer home. I can't say what it is. There's Lewis just living for his ideas and not noticing anything else, and Carrie Louise, bless her, never seeing or hearing or thinking anything except what's a lovely sight, or a lovely sound, or a lovely thought. It's sweet but it isn't *practical*. There *is* such a thing as evil – and I want you, Jane, to go down there right away and find out just exactly what's the matter.'

'*Me*?' exclaimed Miss Marple. 'Why me?'

'Because you've got a nose for that sort of thing. You always had. You've always been a sweet innocent-looking creature, Jane, and all the time underneath nothing has ever surprised you, you always believe the worst.'

'The worst is so often true,' murmured Miss Marple.

'Why you have such a poor idea of human nature, I can't think – living in that sweet peaceful village of yours, so old world and pure.'

'You have never lived in a village, Ruth. The things that go on in a pure peaceful village would probably surprise you.'

'Oh I daresay. My point is that they don't surprise *you*. So you *will* go down to Stonygates and find out what's wrong, won't you?'

'But, Ruth dear, that would be a most difficult thing to do.'

'No, it wouldn't. I've thought it all out. If you won't be absolutely mad at me, I've prepared the ground already.'

Mrs Van Rydock paused, eyed Miss Marple rather uneasily, lighted a cigarette, and plunged rather nervously into explanation.

'You'll admit, I'm sure, that things have been difficult in this country since the war, for people with small fixed incomes – for people like you, that is to say, Jane.'

'Oh yes, indeed. But for the kindness, the really great kindness of my nephew Raymond, I don't know really where I should be.'

'Never mind your nephew,' said Mrs Van Rydock. 'Carrie Louise knows nothing about your nephew – or if she does, she knows him as a writer and has no idea that he's your nephew. The point, as I put it to Carrie Louise, is that it's just too bad about dear Jane. Really sometimes hardly enough to eat, and of course, far too proud ever to appeal to old friends. One couldn't, I said, suggest *money* – but a nice long rest in lovely surroundings, with an old friend and with plenty of nourishing food, and no cares or worries' – Ruth Van Rydock paused and then added defiantly, 'Now go on – be mad at me if you want to be.'

Miss Marple opened her china blue eyes in gentle surprise.

'But why should I be mad at you, Ruth? A very ingenious and plausible approach. I'm sure Carrie Louise responded.'

'She's writing to you. You'll find the letter when you get back. Honestly, Jane, you don't feel that I've taken an unpardonable liberty? You won't mind – '

She hesitated and Miss Marple put her thoughts deftly into words.

'Going to Stonygates as an object of charity – more or less under false pretences? Not in the least – if it is *necessary*. You think it is necessary – and I am inclined to agree with you.'

Mrs Van Rydock stared at her.

'But why? What have you heard?'

'I haven't heard anything. It's just your conviction. You're not a fanciful woman, Ruth.'

'No, but I haven't anything definite to go upon.'

'I remember,' said Miss Marple thoughtfully, 'one Sunday morning at church – it was the second Sunday in Advent – sitting behind Grace Lamble and feeling more and more worried about her. Quite sure, you know, that something was wrong – badly wrong – and yet being quite unable to say why. A most disturbing feeling and very very definite.'

'And was there something wrong?'

'Oh yes. Her father, the old Admiral, had been *very* peculiar for some time, and the very next day he went for her with the coal hammer, roaring out that she was Antichrist masquerading as his daughter. He nearly killed her. They took him away to the asylum and she eventually recovered after months in hospital – but it was a very near thing.'

'And you'd actually had a premonition that day in church?'

'I wouldn't call it a premonition. It was founded on *fact* – these things usually are, though one doesn't always recognize it at the time. She was wearing her Sunday hat the wrong way round. Very significant, really, because Grace Lamble was a most precise woman, not at all vague or absent-minded – and the circumstances under which she would not notice which way her hat was put on to go to church were really extremely limited. Her father, you see, had thrown a marble paperweight at her and it had shattered the looking-glass. She had caught up her hat, put it on, and hurried out of the house. Anxious to keep up appearances and for the servants not to hear anything. She put down these actions, you see, to "dear Papa's Naval temper," she didn't realize that his mind was definitely unhinged. Though she ought to have realized it clearly enough. He was always complaining to her of being spied upon and of enemies – all the usual symptoms, in fact.'

Mrs Van Rydock gazed respectfully at her friend.

'Maybe, Jane,' she said, 'that St Mary Mead of yours isn't quite the idyllic retreat that I've always imagined it.'

'Human nature, dear, is very much the same everywhere. It is more difficult to observe it closely in a city, that is all.'

'And you'll go to Stonygates?'

'I'll go to Stonygates. A little unfair, perhaps, on my nephew Raymond. To let it be thought that he does not assist me, I mean. Still, the dear boy is in Mexico for six months. And by that time it should all be over.'

'What should all be over?'

'Carrie Louise's invitation will hardly be for an indefinite stay. Three weeks, perhaps – a month. That should be ample.'

'For you to find out what is wrong?'

'For me to find out what is wrong.'

'My, Jane,' said Mrs Van Rydock, 'you've got a lot of confidence in yourself, haven't you?'

Miss Marple looked faintly reproachful.

'*You* have confidence in me, Ruth. Or so you say . . . I can only assure you that I shall endeavour to justify your confidence.'

CHAPTER TWO

Before catching her train back to St Mary Mead (Wednesday special cheap day return), Miss Marple, in a precise and businesslike fashion, collected certain data.

'Carrie Louise and I have corresponded after a fashion, but it has largely been a matter of Christmas cards or calendars. It's just the facts I should like, Ruth dear – and also some idea as to whom exactly I shall encounter in the household at Stonygates.'

'Well, you know about Carrie Louise's marriage to Gulbrandsen. There were no children and Carrie Louise took that very much to heart. Gulbrandsen was a widower, and had three grown-up sons. Eventually they adopted a child. Pippa, they called her – a lovely little creature. She was just two years old when they got her.'

'Where did she come from? What was her background?'

'Really, now, Jane, I can't remember – if I ever heard, that is. An Adoption Society, maybe? Or some unwanted child that Gulbrandsen had heard about. Why? Do you think it's important?'

'Well, one always likes to know the background, so to speak. But please go on.'

'The next thing that happened was that Carrie Louise found that she was going to have a baby after all. I understand from doctors that that quite often happens.'

Miss Marple nodded.

'I believe so.'

'Anyway, it did happen, and in a funny kind of way, Carrie Louise was almost disconcerted, if you can understand what I mean. Earlier, of course, she'd have been wild with joy. As it was, she'd given such a devoted love to Pippa that she felt quite apologetic to Pippa for putting her nose out of joint, so to speak. And then Mildred, when she arrived, was really a very unattractive child. Took after the Gulbrandsens – who were solid and worthy – but definitely homely. Carrie Louise was always so anxious to make no difference between the adopted child and her own child that I think she rather

519

tended to overindulge Pippa and pass over Mildred. Sometimes I think that Mildred resented it. However I didn't see them often. Pippa grew up a very beautiful girl and Mildred grew up a plain one. Eric Gulbrandsen died when Mildred was fifteen and Pippa eighteen. At twenty Pippa married an Italian, the Marchese di San Severiano – oh, quite a genuine Marchese – not an adventurer, or anything like that. She was by way of being an heiress (naturally, or San Severiano wouldn't have married her – you know what Italians are!). Gulbrandsen left an equal sum in trust for both his own and his adopted daughter. Mildred married a Canon Strete – a nice man but given to colds in the head. About ten or fifteen years older than she was. Quite a happy marriage, I believe.

'He died a year ago and Mildred has come back to Stonygates to live with her mother. But that's getting on too fast, I've skipped a marriage or two. I'll go back to them. Pippa married her Italian. Carrie Louise was quite pleased about the marriage. Guido had beautiful manners and was very handsome, and he was a fine sportsman. A year later Pippa had a daughter and died in childbirth. It was a terrible tragedy and Guido San Severiano was very cut up. Carrie Louise went to and fro between Italy and England a good deal, and it was in Rome that she met Johnnie Restarick and married him. The Marchese married again and he was quite willing for his little daughter to be brought up in England by her exceedingly wealthy grandmother. So they all settled down at Stonygates, Johnnie Restarick and Carrie Louise, and Johnnie's two boys, Alexis and Stephen (Johnnie's first wife was a Russian) and the baby Gina. Mildred married her Canon soon afterwards. Then came all this business of Johnnie and the Yugoslavian woman and the divorce. The boys still came to Stonygates for their holidays and were devoted to Carrie Louise, and then in 1938, I think it was, Carrie Louise married Lewis.'

Mrs Van Rydock paused for breath.

'You've not met Lewis?'

Miss Marple shook her head.

'No, I think I last saw Carrie Louise in 1928. She very sweetly took me to Covent Garden – to the Opera.'

'Oh yes. Well, Lewis was a very suitable person for her to marry. He was the head of a very celebrated firm of chartered accountants. I think he met her first over some questions of the finances of the Gulbrandsen Trust and the College. He was well off, just about her own age, and a man of absolutely upright life. But he *was* a crank.

He was absolutely rabid on the subject of the redemption of young criminals.'

Ruth Van Rydock sighed.

'As I said just now, Jane, there are fashions in philanthropy. In Gulbrandsen's time it was education. Before that it was soup kitchens – '

Miss Marple nodded.

'Yes, indeed. Port wine jelly and calf's head broth taken to the sick. My mother used to do it.'

'That's right. Feeding the body gave way to feeding the mind. Everyone went mad on educating the lower classes. Well, that's passed. Soon, I expect, the fashionable thing to do will be not to educate your children, preserve their illiteracy carefully until they're eighteen. Anyway the Gulbrandsen Trust and Education Fund was in some difficulties because the State was taking over its functions. Then Lewis came along with his passionate enthusiasm about constructive training for juvenile delinquents. His attention had been drawn to the subject first in the course of his profession – auditing accounts where ingenious young men had perpetrated frauds. He was more and more convinced that juvenile delinquents were not subnormal – that they had excellent brains and abilities and only needed right direction.'

'There is something in that,' said Miss Marple. 'But it is not entirely true. I remember – '

She broke off and glanced at her watch.

'Oh dear – I mustn't miss the 6.30.'

Ruth Van Rydock said urgently:

'And you will go to Stonygates?'

Gathering up her shopping bag and her umbrella Miss Marple said:

'If Carrie Louise asks me – '

'She will ask you. You'll go? Promise, Jane?'

Jane Marple promised.

CHAPTER THREE

Miss Marple got out of the train at Market Kindle station. A kindly fellow passenger handed out her suitcase after her, and Miss Marple, clutching a string bag, a faded leather handbag and some miscellaneous wraps, uttered appreciative twitters of thanks.

'So kind of you, I'm sure . . . So difficult nowadays – not many porters. I get so flustered when I travel.'

The twitters were drowned by the booming noise of the station announcer saying loudly but indistinctly that the 3.18 was standing at Platform 1, and was about to proceed to various unidentifiable stations.

Market Kindle was a large empty windswept station with hardly any passengers or railway staff to be seen on it. Its claim to distinction lay in having six platforms and a bay where a very small train of one carriage was puffing importantly.

Miss Marple, rather more shabbily dressed than was her custom (so lucky that she hadn't given away the old speckledy), was peering around her uncertainly when a young man came up to her.

'Miss Marple?' he said. His voice had an unexpectedly dramatic quality about it, as though the utterance of her name were the first words of a part he was playing in amateur theatricals. 'I've come to meet you – from Stonygates.'

Miss Marple looked gratefully at him, a charming helpless-looking old lady with, if he had chanced to notice it, very shrewd blue eyes. The personality of the young man did not quite match his voice. It was less important, one might almost say insignificant. His eyelids had a trick of fluttering nervously.

'Oh thank you,' said Miss Marple. 'There's just this suitcase.'

She noticed that the young man did not pick up her suitcase himself. He flipped a finger at a porter who was trundling some packing cases past on a trolley.

'Bring it out, please,' he said, and added importantly, 'for Stonygates.'

The porter said cheerfully:

'Rightyho. Shan't be long.'

Miss Marple fancied that her new acquaintance was not too pleased about this. It was as if Buckingham Palace had been dismissed as no more important than 3 Laburnum Road.

He said, 'The railways get more impossible every day!'

Guiding Miss Marple towards the exit,' he said: 'I'm Edgar Lawson. Mrs Serrocold asked me to meet you. I help Mr Serrocold in his work.'

There was again the faint insinuation that a busy and important man had, very charmingly, put important affairs on one side out of chivalry to his employer's wife.

And again the impression was not wholly convincing – it had a theatrical flavour.

Miss Marple began to wonder about Edgar Lawson.

They came out of the station and Edgar guided the old lady to where a rather elderly Ford V. 8 was standing.

He was just saying 'Will you come in front with me, or would you prefer the back?' when there was a diversion.

A new gleaming two-seater Rolls Bentley came purring into the station yard and drew up in front of the Ford. A very beautiful young woman jumped out of it and came across to them. The fact that she wore dirty corduroy slacks and a simple shirt open at the neck seemed somehow to enhance the fact that she was not only beautiful but expensive.

'There you are, Edgar. I thought I wouldn't make it in time. I see you've got Miss Marple. I came to meet her.' She smiled dazzlingly at Miss Marple, showing a row of lovely teeth in a sunburnt southern face. 'I'm Gina,' she said. 'Carrie Louise's granddaughter. What was your journey like? Simply foul? What a nice string bag. I *love* string bags. I'll take it and the coats and then you can get in better.'

Edgar's face flushed. He protested.

'Look here, Gina, I came to meet Miss Marple. It was all arranged . . .'

Again the teeth flashed in that wide lazy smile.

'Oh I know, Edgar, but I suddenly thought it would be nice if I came along. I'll take her with me and you can wait and bring her cases up.'

She slammed the door on Miss Marple, ran round to the other side, jumped in the driving seat, and they purred swiftly out of the station.

Looking back, Miss Marple noticed Edgar Lawson's face.

'I don't think, my dear,' she said, 'that Mr Lawson is very pleased.'

Gina laughed.

'Edgar's a frightful idiot,' she said. 'Always so pompous about things. You'd really think he *mattered*!'

Miss Marple asked, 'Doesn't he matter?'

'Edgar?' There was an unconscious note of cruelty in Gina's scornful laugh. 'Oh, he's bats anyway.'

'Bats?'

'They're all bats at Stonygates,' said Gina. 'I don't mean Lewis and Grandam and me and the boys – and not Miss Bellever, of course. But the others. Sometimes I feel *I'm* going a bit bats myself living there. Even Aunt Mildred goes out on walks and mutters to herself all the time – and you don't expect a Canon's widow to do that, do you?'

They swung out of the station approach and accelerated up the smooth surfaced empty road. Gina shot a swift sideways glance at her companion.

'You were at school with Grandam, weren't you? It seems so queer.'

Miss Marple knew perfectly what she meant. To youth it seems very odd to think that age was once young and pigtailed and struggled with decimals and English literature.

'It must,' said Gina with awe in her voice, and obviously not meaning to be rude, 'have been a *very* long time ago.'

'Yes, indeed,' said Miss Marple. 'You feel that more with me than you do with your grandmother, I expect?'

Gina nodded. 'It's cute of you saying that. Grandam, you know, gives one a curiously ageless feeling.'

'It is a long time since I've seen her. I wonder if I shall find her much changed.'

'Her hair's grey, of course,' said Gina vaguely. 'And she walks with a stick because of her arthritis. It's got much worse lately. I suppose that – ' she broke off, and then asked: 'Have you been to Stonygates before?'

'No, never. I've heard a great deal about it, of course.'

'It's pretty ghastly, really,' said Gina cheerfully. 'A sort of Gothic monstrosity. What Steve calls Best Victorian Lavatory period. But it's fun, too, in a way. Only of course everything's madly earnest, and you tumble over psychiatrists everywhere underfoot. Enjoying

524

themselves madly. Rather like Scout-masters, only worse. The young criminals are rather pets, some of them. One showed me how to diddle locks with a bit of wire and one angelic-faced boy gave me a lot of points about coshing people.'

Miss Marple considered this information thoughtfully.

'It's the thugs I like best,' said Gina. 'I don't fancy the queers so much. Of course Lewis and Dr Maverick think they're *all* queer – I mean they think it's repressed desires and disordered home life and their mothers getting off with soldiers and all that. I don't really see it myself because some people have had awful home lives and yet have managed to turn out quite all right.'

'I'm sure it is all a very difficult problem,' said Miss Marple.

Gina laughed, again showing her magnificent teeth.

'It doesn't worry me much. I suppose some people have these sort of urges to make the world a better place. Lewis is quite dippy about it all – he's going to Aberdeen next week because there's a case coming up in the police court – a boy with five previous convictions.'

'The young man who met me at the station? Mr Lawson. He helps Mr Serrocold, he told me. Is he his secretary?'

'Oh Edgar hasn't brains enough to be a secretary. He's a *case*, really. He used to stay at hotels and pretend he was a V.C. or a fighter pilot and borrow money and then do a flit. I think he's just a rotter. But Lewis goes through a routine with them all. Makes them feel one of the family and gives them jobs to do and all that to encourage their sense of responsibility. I daresay we shall be murdered by one of them one of these days.' Gina laughed merrily.

Miss Marple did not laugh.

They turned in through some imposing gates where a Commissionaire was standing on duty in a military manner and drove up a drive flanked with rhododendrons. The drive was badly kept and the grounds seemed neglected.

Interpreting her companion's glance, Gina said, 'No gardeners during the war, and since we haven't bothered. But it does look rather terrible.'

They came round a curve and Stonygates appeared in its full glory. It was, as Gina had said, a vast edifice of Victorian Gothic – a kind of temple to Plutocracy. Philanthropy had added to it in various wings and outbuildings which, while not positively dissimilar in style, had robbed the structure as a whole of any cohesion or purpose.

'Hideous, isn't it?' said Gina affectionately. 'There's Grandam on the terrace. I'll stop here and you can go and meet her.'

525

Miss Marple advanced along the terrace towards her old friend.

From a distance, the slim little figure looked curiously girlish in spite of the stick on which she leaned and her slow and obviously rather painful progress. It was as though a young girl was giving an exaggerated imitation of old age.

'Jane,' said Mrs Serrocold.

'Dear Carrie Louise.'

Yes, unmistakably Carrie Louise. Strangely unchanged, strangely youthful still, although, unlike her sister, she used no cosmetics or artificial aids to youth. Her hair was grey, but it had always been of a silvery fairness and the colour had changed very little. Her skin had still a rose leaf pink and white appearance, though now it was a crumpled rose leaf. Her eyes had still their starry innocent glance. She had the slender youthful figure of a girl and her head kept its eager birdlike tilt.

'I do blame myself,' said Carrie Louise in her sweet voice, 'for letting it be so long. *Years* since I saw you, Jane dear. It's just lovely that you've come at last to pay us a visit here.'

From the end of the terrace Gina called:

'You ought to come in, Grandam. It's getting cold and Jolly will be furious.'

Carrie Louise gave her little silvery laugh.

'They all fuss about me so,' she said. 'They rub it in that I'm an old woman.'

'And you don't feel like one.'

'No, I don't, Jane. In spite of all my aches and pains and I've got plenty. Inside I go on feeling just a chit like Gina. Perhaps everyone does. The glass shows them how old they are and they just don't believe it. It seems only a few months ago that we were at Florence. Do you remember Fraulein Schweich and her boots?'

The two elderly women laughed together at events that had happened nearly half a century ago.

They walked together to a side door. In the doorway a gaunt elderly lady met them. She had an arrogant nose, a short haircut and wore stout well-cut tweeds.

She said fiercely:

'It's absolutely crazy of you, Cara, to stay out so late. You're absolutely incapable of taking care of yourself. What will Mr Serrocold say?'

'Don't scold me, Jolly,' said Carrie Louise pleadingly.

She introduced Miss Bellever to Miss Marple.

'This is Miss Bellever, who is simply everything to me. Nurse, dragon, watchdog, secretary, housekeeper and very faithful friend.'

Juliet Bellever sniffed, and the end of her big nose turned rather pink, a sign of emotion.

'I do what I can,' she said gruffly. 'This is a crazy household. You simply can't arrange any kind of planned routine.'

'Darling Jolly, of course you can't. I wonder why you ever try. Where are you putting Miss Marple?'

'In the Blue Room. Shall I take her up?' asked Miss Bellever.

'Yes, please do, Jolly. And then bring her down to tea. It's in the library today, I think.'

The Blue Room had heavy curtains of a rich faded blue brocade that must have been, Miss Marple thought, about fifty years old. The furniture was mahogany, big and solid, and the bed was a vast mahogany fourposter. Miss Bellever opened a door into a connecting bathroom. This was unexpectedly modern, orchid in colouring and with much dazzling chromium.

She observed grimly:

'John Restarick had ten bathrooms put into the house when he married Cara. The plumbing is about the only thing that's ever been modernized. He wouldn't hear of the rest being altered – said the whole place was a perfect Period Piece. Did you ever know him at all?'

'No, I never met him. Mrs Serrocold and I have met very seldom though we have always corresponded.'

'He was an agreeable fellow,' said Miss Bellever. 'No good, of course! A complete rotter. But pleasant to have about the house. Great charm. Women liked him far too much. That was his undoing in the end. Not really Cara's type.'

She added with a brusque resumption of her practical manner:

'The housemaid will unpack for you. Do you want a wash before tea?'

Receiving an affirmative answer, she said that Miss Marple would find her waiting at the top of the stairs.

Miss Marple went into the bathroom and washed her hands and dried them a little nervously on a very beautiful orchid-coloured face towel. Then she removed her hat and patted her soft white hair into place.

Opening her door, she found Miss Bellever waiting for her, and was conducted down the big gloomy staircase and across a vast dark hall and into a room where bookshelves went up

527

to the ceiling and a big window looked out over an artificial lake.

Carrie Louise was standing by the window and Miss Marple joined her.

'What a very imposing house this is,' said Miss Marple. 'I feel quite lost in it.'

'Yes, I know. It's ridiculous, really. It was built by a prosperous iron master – or something of that kind. He went bankrupt not long after. I don't wonder really. There were about fourteen living-rooms – all enormous. I've never seen what people *can* want with more than one sitting-room. And all those huge bedrooms. Such a lot of unnecessary space. Mine is terribly overpowering – and quite a long way to walk from the bed to the dressing table. And great heavy dark crimson curtains.'

'You haven't had it modernized and redecorated?'

Carrie Louise looked vaguely surprised.

'No. On the whole it's very much as it was when I first lived here with Eric. It's been repainted, of course, but they always do it the same colour. Those things don't really matter, do they? I mean I shouldn't have felt justified in spending a lot of money on that kind of thing when there are so many things that are so much more important.'

'Have there been no changes at all in the house?'

'Oh – yes – heaps of them. We've just kept a kind of block in the middle of the house as it was – the Great Hall and the rooms off and over. They're the best ones and Johnnie – my second husband – was lyrical over them and said they should never be touched or altered – and of course he was an artist and a designer and he knew about these things. But the East and West wings have been completely remodelled. All the rooms partitioned off and divided up, so that we have offices, and bedrooms for the teaching staff, and all that. The boys are all in the College building – you can see it from here.'

Miss Marple looked out towards where large red brick buildings showed through a belt of sheltered trees. Then her eyes fell on something nearer at hand, and she smiled a little.

'What a very beautiful girl Gina is,' she said.

Carrie Louise's face lit up.

'Yes, isn't she?' she said softly. 'It's so lovely to have her back here again. I sent her to America at the beginning of the war – to Ruth. Did Ruth talk about her at all?'

'No. At least she did just mention her.'

Carrie Louise sighed.

'Poor Ruth! She was frightfully upset over Gina's marriage. But I've told her again and again that I don't blame her in the least. Ruth doesn't realize, as I do, that the old barriers and class shibboleths are gone – or at any rate are going.

'Gina was doing her war work – and she met this young man. He was a Marine and had a very good war record. And a week later they were married. It was all far too quick, of course, no time to find out if they were really suited to each other – but that's the way of things nowadays. Young people belong to their generation. We may think they're unwise in many of their doings, but we have to accept their decisions. Ruth, though, was terribly upset.'

'She didn't consider the young man suitable?'

'She kept saying that one didn't know anything about him. He came from the Middle West and he hadn't any money – and naturally no profession. There are hundreds of boys like that everywhere – but it wasn't Ruth's idea of what was right for Gina. However, the thing was done. I was so glad when Gina accepted my invitation to come over here with her husband. There's so much going on here – jobs of every kind, and if Walter wants to specialize in medicine or get a degree or anything he could do it in this country. After all, this is Gina's home. It's delightful to have her back, to have someone so warm and gay and alive in the house.'

Miss Marple nodded and looked out of the window again at the two young people standing near the lake.

'They're a remarkably handsome couple, too,' she said. 'I don't wonder Gina fell in love with him!'

'Oh, but that – that isn't Wally.' There was, quite suddenly, a touch of embarrassment, or restraint, in Mrs Serrocold's voice. 'That's Steve – the younger of Johnnie Restarick's two boys. When Johnnie – when he went away, he'd no place for the boys in the holidays, so I always had them here. They look on this as their home. And Steve's here permanently now. He runs our dramatic branch. We have a theatre, you know, and plays – we encourage all the artistic instincts. Lewis says that so much of this juvenile crime is due to exhibitionism, most of the boys have had such a thwarted unhappy home life, and these hold-ups and burglaries make them feel heroes. We urge them to write their own plays and act in them and design and paint their own scenery. Steve is in charge of the theatre. He's so keen and enthusiastic. It's wonderful what life he's put into the whole thing.'

'I see,' said Miss Marple slowly.

Her long-distance sight was good (as many of her neighbours knew to their cost in the village of St Mary Mead) and she saw very clearly the dark handsome face of Stephen Restarick as he stood facing Gina, talking eagerly. Gina's face she could not see, since the girl had her back to them, but there was no mistaking the expression in Stephen Restarick's face.

'It isn't any business of mine,' said Miss Marple, 'but I suppose you realize, Carrie Louise, that he's in love with her.'

'Oh no – ' Carrie Louise looked troubled. 'Oh no, I do hope not.'

'You were always up in the clouds, Carrie Louise. There's not the least doubt about it.'

CHAPTER FOUR

Before Mrs Serrocold could say anything, her husband came in from the hall carrying some open letters in his hand.

Lewis Serrocold was a short man, not particularly impressive in appearance, but with a personality that immediately marked him out. Ruth had once said of him that he was more like a dynamo than a human being. He usually concentrated entirely on what was immediately occupying his attention and paid no attention to the objects or persons who were surrounding them.

'A bad blow, dearest,' he said. 'That boy, Jackie Flint. Back at his tricks again. And I really did think he meant to go straight this time if he got a proper chance. He was most earnest about it. You know we found he'd always been keen on railways – and both Maverick and I thought that if he got a job on the railways he'd stick to it and make good. But it's the same story. Petty thieving from the parcels office. Not even stuff he could want or sell. That shows that it *must* be psychological. We haven't really got to the root of the trouble. But I'm not giving up.'

'Lewis – this is my old friend, Jane Marple.'

'Oh how d'you do,' said Mr Serrocold absently. 'So glad – they'll prosecute, of course. A nice lad, too, not too many brains, but a really nice boy. Unspeakable home he came from. I – '

He suddenly broke off, and the dynamo was switched on to the guest.

'Why, Miss Marple, I'm so delighted you've come to stay with us for a while. It will make such a great difference to Caroline to have a friend of old days with whom she can exchange memories. She has in many ways a grim time here – so much sadness in the stories of these poor children. We do hope you'll stay with us a very long time.'

Miss Marple felt the magnetism and realized how attractive it would have been to her friend. That Lewis Serrocold was a man who would always put causes before people she did not doubt for a moment. It might have irritated some women, but not Carrie Louise.

Lewis Serrocold sorted out another letter.

'At any rate we've *some* good news. This is from the Wiltshire and Somerset Bank. Young Morris is doing extremely well. They're thoroughly satisfied with him and in fact are promoting him next month. I always knew that all he needed was responsibility – that, and a thorough grasp of the handling of money and what it means.'

He turned to Miss Marple.

'Half these boys don't *know* what money is. It represents to them going to the pictures or to the dogs, or buying cigarettes – and they're clever with figures and find it exciting to juggle them round. Well, I believe in – what shall I say? – rubbing their noses in the stuff – train them in accountancy, in figures – show them the whole inner romance of money, so to speak. Give them skill and then responsibility – let them handle it officially. Our greatest successes have been that way – only two out of thirty-eight have let us down. One's head cashier in a firm of druggists – a really responsible position – '

He broke off to say: 'Tea's in, dearest,' to his wife.

'I thought we were having it here. I told Jolly.'

'No, it's in the Hall. The others are there.'

'I thought they were all going to be out.'

Carrie Louise linked her arm through Miss Marple's and they went into the Great Hall. Tea seemed a rather incongruous meal in its surroundings. The tea things were piled haphazard on a tray – white utility cups mixed with the remnants of what had been Rockingham and Spode tea services. There was a loaf of

531

bread, two pots of jam, and some cheap and unwholesome-looking cakes.

A plump middle-aged woman with grey hair sat behind the tea table and Mrs Serrocold said:

'This is Mildred, Jane. My daughter Mildred. You haven't seen her since she was a tiny girl.'

Mildred Strete was the person most in tune with the house that Miss Marple had so far seen. She looked prosperous and dignified. She had married late in her thirties a Canon of the Church of England and was now a widow. She looked exactly like a Canon's widow, respectable and slightly dull. She was a plain woman with a large unexpressive face and dull eyes. She had been, Miss Marple reflected, a very plain little girl.

'And this is Wally Hudd – Gina's husband.'

Wally was a big young man with hair brushed up on his head and a sulky expression. He nodded awkwardly and went on cramming cake into his mouth.

Presently Gina came in with Stephen Restarick. They were both very animated.

'Gina's got a wonderful idea for that backcloth,' said Stephen. 'You know, Gina, you've got a very definite flair for theatrical designing.'

Gina laughed and looked pleased. Edgar Lawson came in and sat down by Lewis Serrocold. When Gina spoke to him, he made a pretence of not answering.

Miss Marple found it all a little bewildering and was glad to go to her room and lie down after tea.

There were more people still at dinner, a young Dr Maverick who was either a psychiatrist or a psychologist – Miss Marple was rather hazy about the difference – and whose conversation, dealing almost entirely with the jargon of his trade, was practically unintelligible to her. There were also two spectacled young men who held posts on the teaching side, and a Mr Baumgarten, who was an occupational therapist, and three intensely bashful youths who were doing their 'house guest' week. One of them, a fairhaired lad with very blue eyes was, Gina informed her in a whisper, the expert with the 'cosh.'

The meal was not a particularly appetizing one. It was indifferently cooked and indifferently served. A variety of costumes were worn. Miss Bellever wore a high black dress, Mildred Strete wore evening dress and a woollen cardigan over it. Carrie Louise had on a short dress of grey wool – Gina was resplendent in a kind of peasant get up.

Wally had not changed, nor had Stephen Restarick, Edgar Lawson had on a neat dark blue suit. Lewis Serrocold wore the conventional dinner jacket. He ate very little and hardly seemed to notice what was on his plate.

After dinner Lewis Serrocold and Dr Maverick went away to the latter's office. The occupational therapist and the schoolmasters went away to some lair of their own. The three 'cases' went back to the college. Gina and Stephen went to the theatre to discuss Gina's idea for a set. Mildred knitted an indeterminate garment and Miss Bellever darned socks. Wally sat in a chair gently tilted backwards and stared into space. Carrie Louise and Miss Marple talked about old days. The conversation seemed strangely unreal.

Edgar Lawson alone seemed unable to find a niche. He sat down and then got up restlessly.

'I wonder if I ought to go to Mr Serrocold,' he said rather loudly. 'He may need me.'

Carrie Louise said gently, 'Oh I don't think so. He was going to talk over one or two points with Dr Maverick this evening.'

'Then I certainly won't butt in! I shouldn't dream of going where I wasn't wanted. I've already wasted time today going down to the station when Mrs Hudd meant to go herself.'

'She ought to have told you,' said Carrie Louise. 'But I think she just decided at the last moment.'

'You do realize, Mrs Serrocold, that she made me look a complete fool! A complete fool!'

'No, no,' said Carrie Louise, smiling. 'You mustn't have these ideas.'

'I know I'm not needed or wanted . . . I'm perfectly aware of *that*. If things had been different – if I'd had my proper place in life it would be very different. Very different indeed. It's no fault of mine that I haven't got my proper place in life.'

'Now, Edgar,' said Carrie Louise. 'Don't work yourself up about nothing. Jane thinks it was very kind of you to meet her. Gina always has these sudden impulses – she didn't mean to upset you.'

'Oh yes, she did. It was done on purpose – to humiliate me – '

'Oh Edgar – '

'You don't know half of what's going on, Mrs Serrocold. Well, I won't say any more now except goodnight.'

Edgar went out, shutting the door with a slam behind him.

Miss Bellever snorted:

'Atrocious manners.'

'He's so sensitive,' said Carrie Louise vaguely.

Mildred Strete clicked her needles and said sharply:

'He really is a most odious young man. You shouldn't put up with such behaviour, Mother.'

'Lewis says he can't help it.'

Mildred said sharply:

'Everyone can help behaving rudely. Of course I blame Gina very much. She's so completely scatterbrained in everything she undertakes. She does nothing but make trouble. One day she encourages the young man and the next day she snubs him. What can you expect?'

Wally Hudd spoke for the first time that evening.

He said:

'That guy's crackers. That's all there is to it! Crackers!'

II

In her bedroom that night Miss Marple tried to review the pattern of Stonygates, but it was as yet too confused. There were currents and cross-currents here – but whether they could account for Ruth Van Rydock's uneasiness it was impossible to tell. It did not seem to Miss Marple that Carrie Louise was affected in any way by what was going on round her. Stephen was in love with Gina. Gina might or might not be in love with Stephen. Walter Hudd was clearly not enjoying himself. These were incidents that might and did occur in all places and at most times. There was, unfortunately, nothing exceptional about them. They ended in the divorce court and everybody hopefully started again – when fresh tangles were created. Mildred Strete was clearly jealous of Gina and disliked her. That, Miss Marple thought, was very natural.

She thought over what Ruth Van Rydock had told her. Carrie Louise's disappointment at not having a child – the adoption of little Pippa – and then the discovery that, after all, a child was on the way.

'Often happens like that,' Miss Marple's doctor had told her. Relief of tension, maybe, and then Nature can do its work.'

He had added that it was usually hard lines on the adopted child.

But that had not been so in this case. Both Gulbrandsen and his wife had adored little Pippa. She had made her place too firmly in their hearts to be lightly set aside. Gulbrandsen was already a father. Paternity meant nothing new to him. Carrie Louise's maternal yearnings had been assuaged by Pippa. Her pregnancy had been uncomfortable and the actual birth difficult and prolonged. Possibly Carrie Louise, who had never cared for reality, did not enjoy her first brush with it.

There remained two little girls growing up, one pretty and amusing, the other plain and dull. Which again, Miss Marple thought, was quite natural. For when people adopt a baby girl, they choose a pretty one. And though Mildred might have been lucky and taken after the Martins who had produced handsome Ruth and dainty Carrie Louise, Nature elected that she should take after the Gulbrandsens, who were large and stolid and uncompromisingly plain.

Moreover, Carrie Louise was determined that the adopted child should never feel her position, and in making sure of this she was over-indulgent to Pippa and sometimes less than fair to Mildred.

Pippa had married and gone away to Italy, and Mildred for a time had been the only daughter of the house. But then Pippa had died and Carrie Louise had brought Pippa's baby back to Stonygates, and once more Mildred had been out of it. There had been the new marriage – the Restarick boys. In 1934 Mildred had married Canon Strete, a scholarly antiquarian about fifteen years her senior and had gone away to live in the South of England. Presumably she had been happy – but one did not really know. There had been no children. And now here she was, back again in the same house where she had been brought up. And once again, Miss Marple thought, not particularly happy in it.

Gina, Stephen, Wally, Mildred, Miss Bellever who liked an ordered routine and was unable to enforce it. Lewis Serrocold who was clearly blissfully and wholeheartedly happy; an idealist able to translate his ideals into practical measures. In none of these personalities did Miss Marple find what Ruth's words had led her to believe she might find. Carrie Louise seemed secure, remote at the heart of the whirlpool – as she had been all her life. What then, in that atmosphere, had Ruth felt to be wrong . . .? Did she, Jane Marple, feel it also?

What of the outer personalities of the whirlpool – the occupational therapists, the schoolmasters, earnest, harmless young men, confident young Dr Maverick, the three pink-faced innocent-eyed young delinquents – Edgar Lawson . . .

And here, just before she fell asleep, Miss Marple's thoughts

535

stopped and revolved speculatively round the figure of Edgar Lawson. Edgar Lawson reminded her of someone or something. There *was* something a little wrong about Edgar Lawson – perhaps more than a little. Edgar Lawson was maladjusted – that was the phrase, wasn't it? But surely that didn't, and couldn't touch Carrie Louise?'

Mentally, Miss Marple shook her head.

What worried her was something more than that.

CHAPTER FIVE

Gently eluding her hostess the next morning, Miss Marple went out into the gardens. Their condition distressed her. They had once been an ambitiously set out achievement. Clumps of rhododendrons, smooth slopes of lawns, massed borders of herbaceous plants, clipped boxhedges surrounding a formal rose garden. Now all was largely derelict, the lawns raggedly mown, the borders full of weeds with tangled flowers struggling through them, the paths moss-covered and neglected. The kitchen gardens, on the other hand, enclosed by red brick walls, were prosperous and well stocked. That, presumably, was because they had a utility value. So, also, a large portion of what had once been lawn and flower garden, was now fenced off and laid out in tennis courts and a bowling green.

Surveying the herbaceous border, Miss Marple clicked her tongue vexedly and pulled up a flourishing plant of groundsel.

As she stood with it in her hand, Edgar Lawson came into view. Seeing Miss Marple, he stopped and hesitated. Miss Marple had no mind to let him escape. She called him briskly. When he came, she asked him if he knew where any gardening tools were kept.

Edgar said vaguely that there was a gardener somewhere who would know.

'It's such a pity to see this border so neglected,' twittered Miss Marple. 'I'm so fond of gardens.' And since it was not her intention that Edgar should go in search of any necessary implement she went on quickly:

'It's about all an old and useless woman can find to do. Now I don't suppose *you* ever bother your head about gardens, Mr Lawson. You have so much real and important work to do. Being in a responsible position here, with Mr Serrocold. You must find it all most interesting.'

He answered quickly, almost eagerly:

'Yes – yes – it is interesting.'

'And you must be of the greatest assistance to Mr Serrocold.'

His face darkened.

'I don't know. I can't be sure. It's what's *behind* it all – '

He broke off. Miss Marple watched him thoughtfully. A pathetic undersized young man in a neat dark suit. A young man that few people would look at twice, or remember if they did look . . .

There was a garden seat nearby and Miss Marple drifted towards it and sat. Edgar stood frowning in front of her.

'I'm sure,' said Miss Marple brightly, 'that Mr Serrocold relics on you a *great* deal.'

'I don't know,' said Edgar. 'I really don't know.' He frowned and almost absently sat down beside her. 'I'm in a very difficult position.'

'Of course,' said Miss Marple.

The young man Edgar sat staring in front of him.

'This is all highly confidential,' he said suddenly.

'Of course,' said Miss Marple.

'If I had my rights – '

'Yes?'

'I might as well tell you . . . You won't let it go any further I'm sure?'

'Oh no.' She noticed he did not wait for her disclaimer.

'My father – actually, my father is a very important man.'

This time there was no need to say anything. She had only to listen.

'Nobody knows except Mr Serrocold. You see, it might prejudice my father's position if the story got out.' He turned to her. He smiled. A sad dignified smile. 'You see, *I'm Winston Churchill's son.*'

'Oh,' said Miss Marple. 'I *see.*'

And she did see. She remembered a rather sad story in St Mary Mead – and the way it had gone.

Edgar Lawson went on, and what he said had the familiarity of a stage scene.

'There were reasons. My mother wasn't free. Her own husband

was in an asylum – there could be no divorce – no question of marriage. I don't really blame them. At least, I think I don't . . . He's done, always, everything he could. Discreetly, of course. And that's where the trouble has arisen. He's got enemies – and they're against me, too. They've managed to keep us apart. They watch me. Wherever I go, they spy on me. And they make things go wrong for me.'

Miss Marple shook her head.

'Dear, dear,' she said.

'In London I was studying to be a doctor. They tampered with my exams – they altered the answers. They *wanted* me to fail. They followed me about the streets. They told things about me to my landlady. They hound me wherever I go.'

'Oh, but you can't be sure of that,' said Miss Marple soothingly.

'I tell you I *know*! Oh they're very cunning. I never get a glimpse of them or find out who they are. But I shall find out . . . Mr Serrocold took me away from London and brought me down here. He was kind – very kind. But even here, you know, I'm not *safe*. They're here too. Working against me. Making the others dislike me. Mr Serrocold says that isn't true – but Mr Serrocold doesn't know. Or else – I wonder – sometimes I've thought – '

He broke off. He got up.

'This is all confidential,' he said. 'You do understand that, don't you? But if you notice anyone *following* me – *spying*, I mean – you might let me know *who it is*!'

He went away, then – neat, pathetic, insignificant. Miss Marple watched him and wondered . . .

A voice spoke.

'Nuts,' it said. 'Just nuts.'

Walter Hudd was standing beside her. His hands were thrust deep in his pockets and he was frowning as he stared after Edgar's retreating figure.

'What kind of a joint is this, anyway?' he said. 'They're all bughouse, the whole lot of them.'

Miss Marple said nothing and Walter went on:

'That Edgar guy – what do you make of him? Says his father's really Lord Montgomery. Doesn't seem likely to me. Not *Monty*! Not from all I've heard about him.'

'No,' said Miss Marple. 'It doesn't seem very likely.'

'He told Gina something quite different – some bunk about being really the heir to the Russian throne – said he was some Grand

Duke's son or other. Hell, doesn't the chap know who his father really was?'

'I should imagine not,' said Miss Marple. 'That is probably just the trouble.'

Walter sat down beside her, dropping his body on to the seat with a slack movement. He repeated his former statement.

'They're all bughouse here.'

'You don't like being at Stonygates?'

The young man frowned.

'I simply don't *get* it – that's all! I don't get it. Take this place – the house – the whole set-up. They're rich, these people. They don't need dough – they've got it. And look at the way they live. Cracked antique china and cheap plain stuff all mixed up. No proper upper-class servants – just some casual hired help. Tapestries and drapes and chair-covers all satin and brocade and stuff – and it's falling to pieces! Big silver tea urns and what do you know – all yellow and tarnished for want of cleaning. Mrs Serrocold just doesn't care. Look at that dress she had on last night. Darned under the arms, nearly worn out – and yet she could go to a store and order what she liked. Bond Street or wherever it is. Dough? They're rolling in dough.'

He paused and sat, deliberating.

'I understand being poor. There's nothing much wrong with it. If you're young and strong and ready to work. I never had much money, but I was all set to get where I wanted. I was going to open a garage. I'd got a bit of money put by. I talked to Gina about it. She listened. She seemed to understand. I didn't know much about her. All those girls in uniform, they look about the same. I mean you can't tell from looking at them who's got dough and who hasn't. I thought she was a cut above me, perhaps, education and all that. But it didn't seem to matter. We fell for each other. We got married. I'd got my bit put by and Gina had some too, she told me. We were going to set up a gas station back home – Gina was willing. Just a couple of crazy kids we were – mad about each other. Then that snooty aunt of Gina's started making trouble . . . And Gina wanted to come here to England to see her grandmother. Well, that seemed fair enough. It was her home, and I was curious to see England anyway. I'd heard a lot about it. So we came. Just a visit – that's what I thought.'

The frown became a scowl.

'But it hasn't turned out like that. We're caught up in this crazy business. Why don't we stay here – make our home here – that's what they say? Plenty of jobs for me. Jobs! I don't want a job feeding candy to gangster kids and helping them play at kids' games . . . what's the sense of it all? This place could be swell – *really* swell. Don't people who've got money understand their luck? Don't they understand that most of the world can't have a swell place like this and that they've got one? Isn't it plain crazy to kick your luck when you've got it? I don't mind working if I've got to. But I'll work the way I like and at what I like – and I'll work to get somewhere. This place makes me feel I'm tangled up in a spider's web. And Gina – I can't make Gina out. She's not the same girl I married over in the States. I can't – dang it all – I can't even *talk* to her now. Oh hell!'

Miss Marple said gently:

'I quite see your point of view.'

Wally shot a swift glance at her.

'You're the only one I've shot my mouth off to so far. Most of the time I shut up like a clam. Don't know what it is about you – you're English right enough, really English – but in the durndest way you remind me of my Aunt Betsy back home.'

'Now that's very nice.'

'A lot of sense she had,' Wally continued reflectively. 'Looked as frail as though you could snap her in two, but actually she was tough – yes, sir, I'll say she was tough.'

He got up.

'Sorry talking to you this way,' he apologized. For the first time, Miss Marple saw him smile. It was a very attractive smile, and Wally Hudd was suddenly transfigured from an awkward sulky boy into a handsome and appealing young man. 'Had to get things off my chest, I suppose. But too bad picking on you.'

'Not at all, my dear boy,' said Miss Marple. 'I have a nephew of my own – only, of course, a great deal older than you are.'

Her mind dwelt for a moment on the sophisticated modern writer Raymond West. A greater contrast to Walter Hudd could not have been imagined.

'You've got other company coming,' said Walter Hudd. 'That dame doesn't like me. So I'll quit. So long, ma'am. Thanks for the talk.'

He strode away and Miss Marple watched Mildred Strete coming across the lawn to join her.

II

'I see you've been victimized by that terrible young man,' said Mrs Strete, rather breathlessly, as she sank down on the seat. 'What a tragedy that is.'

'A tragedy?'

'Gina's marriage. It all came about from sending her off to America. I told mother at the time it was most unwise. After all, this is quite a quiet district. We had hardly any raids here. I do so dislike the way many people gave way to panic about their families – and themselves, too, very often.'

'It must have been difficult to decide what was right to do,' said Miss Marple thoughtfully. 'Where children were concerned, I mean. With the prospect of possible invasion, it might have meant their being brought up under a German régime – as well as the danger of bombs.'

'All nonsense,' said Mrs Strete, 'I never had the least doubt that we should win. But mother has always been quite unreasonable where Gina is concerned. The child was always spoilt and indulged in every way. There was absolutely no need to take her away from Italy in the first place.'

'Her father raised no objection, I understand?'

'Oh San Severiano! You know what Italians are. Nothing matters to them but money. He married Pippa for her money, of course.'

'Dear me. I always understood he was very devoted to her and was quite inconsolable at her death.'

'He pretended to be, no doubt. Why mother ever countenanced her marrying a foreigner, I can't imagine. Just the usual American pleasure in a title, I suppose.'

Miss Marple said mildly:

'I always thought that dear Carrie Louise was almost too unworldly in her attitude to life.'

'Oh, I know. I've no patience with it. Mother's fads and whims and idealistic projects. You've no idea, Aunt Jane, of all that it has meant. I can speak with knowledge, of course. I was brought up in the middle of it all.'

It was with a very faint shock that Miss Marple heard herself addressed as Aunt Jane. And yet that had been the convention of those times. Her Christmas presents to Carrie Louise's children were always labelled 'With love from Aunt Jane,' and as 'Aunt Jane' they thought of her, when they thought of her at all. Which was not, Miss Marple supposed, very often.

She looked thoughtfully at the middle-aged woman sitting beside her. At the pursed tight mouth, the deep lines from the nose down, the hands tightly pressed together.

She said gently:

'You must have had – a difficult childhood.'

Mildred Strete turned eager grateful eyes to her.

'Oh I'm so glad that somebody appreciates that. People don't really know what children go through. Pippa, you see, was the pretty one. She was older than I was, too. It was always she who got all the attention. Both father and mother encouraged her to push herself forward – not that she needed any encouragement – to show off. I was always the quiet one. I was shy – Pippa didn't know what shyness was. A child can suffer a great deal, Aunt Jane.'

'I know that,' said Miss Marple.

'"Mildred's so stupid" – that's what Pippa used to say. But I was younger than she was. Naturally I couldn't be expected to keep up with her in lessons. And it's very unfair on a child when her sister is always put in front of her.

'"What a lovely little girl," people used to say to Mamma. They never noticed *me*. And it was Pippa that Papa used to joke and play with. Someone ought to have seen how hard it was on *me*. All the notice and attention going to her. I wasn't old enough to realize that it's *character* that matters.'

Her lips trembled, then hardened again.

'And it was unfair – really unfair – I was their own child. Pippa was only adopted. *I* was the daughter of the house. She was – nobody.'

'Probably they were extra indulgent to her on that account,' said Miss Marple.

'They liked her best,' said Mildred Strete. And added: 'A child whose own parents didn't want her – or more probably illegitimate.'

She went on:

'It's come out in Gina. There's bad blood there. Blood will tell. Lewis can have what theories he likes about environment. Bad blood does tell. Look at Gina.'

'Gina is a very lovely girl,' said Miss Marple.

'Hardly in behaviour,' said Mrs Strete. 'Everyone but mother notices how she is carrying on with Stephen Restarick. Quite

542

disgusting, I call it. Admittedly she made a very unfortunate marriage, but marriage is marriage and one should be prepared to abide by it. After all, she chose to marry that dreadful young man.'

'Is he so dreadful?'

'Oh dear Aunt Jane! He really looks to me quite like a gangster. And so surly and rude. He hardly opens his mouth. And he always looks so raw and uncouth.'

'He is unhappy, I think,' said Miss Marple mildly.

'I really don't know why he should be – apart from Gina's behaviour, I mean. Everything has been done for him here. Lewis has suggested several ways in which he could try to make himself useful – but he prefers to skulk about doing nothing.'

She burst out: 'Oh this whole place is impossible – quite impossible. Lewis thinks of nothing but these horrible young criminals. And mother thinks of nothing but him. Everything Lewis does is right. Look at the state of the garden – the weeds – the overgrowth. And the house – nothing properly done. Oh I know a domestic staff is difficult nowadays, but it can be got. It's not as though there were any shortage of money. It's just that nobody *cares*. If it were *my* house – ' She stopped.

'I'm afraid,' said Miss Marple, 'that we have all to face the fact that conditions are different. These large establishments are a great problem. It must be sad for you, in a way, to come back here and find everything so different. Do you really prefer living here to – well – somewhere of your own?'

Mildred Strete flushed.

'After all, it's my home,' she said. 'It was my father's house. Nothing can alter that. I've a right to be here if I choose. And I do choose. If only mother were not so impossible! She won't even buy herself proper clothes. It worries Jolly a lot.'

'I was going to ask you about Miss Bellever.'

'Such a comfort having her here. She adores mother. She's been with her a long time now – she came in John Restarick's time. And was wonderful, I believe, during the whole sad business. I expect you heard that he ran away with a dreadful Yugoslavian woman – a most abandoned creature. She'd had any amount of lovers, I believe. Mother was very fine and dignified about it all. Divorced him as quietly as possible. Even went so far as to have the Restarick boys for their holidays – quite unnecessary, really, other arrangements could have been made. It would have been unthinkable, of course, to have let them go to their father and that woman. Anyway, mother had them here . . . And Miss Bellever stood by all through things and was a tower of strength. I sometimes think she makes mother even more vague than she need be, by doing all the practical things herself. But I really don't know what mother would do without her.'

She paused and then remarked in a tone of surprise:

'Here is Lewis. How odd. He seldom comes out in the garden.'

Mr Serrocold came towards them in the same single-minded way that he did everything. He appeared not to notice Mildred, because it was only Miss Marple who was in his mind.

'I'm so sorry,' he said. 'I wanted to take you round our institution and show you everything. Caroline asked me to. Unfortunately I have to go off to Liverpool. The case of that boy and the railway parcels office. But Maverick will take you. He'll be here in a few minutes. I shan't be back until the day after tomorrow. It will be splendid if we can get them not to prosecute.'

Mildred Strete got up and walked away. Lewis Serrocold did not notice her go. His earnest eyes gazed at Miss Marple through thick glasses.

'You see,' he said, 'the Magistrates nearly always take the wrong view. Sometimes they're too severe, but sometimes they're too lenient. If these boys get a sentence of a few months it's no deterrent – they get a kind of a kick out of it, even. Boast about it to their girl friends. But a severe sentence often sobers them. They realize that the game isn't worth it. Or else it's better not to serve a prison sentence at all. Corrective training – constructional training like we have here – '

Miss Marple interrupted him.

'Mr Serrocold,' she said. 'Are you quite satisfied about young Mr Lawson. Is he – is he quite normal?'

A disturbed expression appeared on Lewis Serrocold's face.

'I do hope he's not relapsing. What has he been saying?'

'He told me that he was Winston Churchill's son – '

'Of course – of course. The usual statements. He's illegitimate, as you've probably guessed, poor lad, and of very humble beginnings. He was a case recommended to me by a Society in London. He'd assaulted a man in the street who he said was spying on him. All very typical – Dr Maverick will tell you. I went into his case history. Mother was of a poor class but a respectable family in Plymouth. Father a sailor – she didn't even know his name . . . Child brought up in difficult circumstances. Started romancing about his father and later about himself. Wore uniform and decorations he wasn't entitled to – all quite typical. But Maverick considers the prognosis hopeful. If we can give him confidence in himself. I've given him responsibility here, tried to make him appreciate that it's not a man's birth that matters but what he *is*. I've tried to give him confidence in his own ability. The improvement was marked. I was very happy about him. And now you say – '

He shook his head.

'Mightn't he be dangerous, Mr Serrocold?'

'Dangerous? I don't think he has shown any suicidal tendencies.'

'I wasn't thinking of suicide. He talked to me of enemies – of persecution. Isn't that, forgive me – a dangerous sign?'

'I don't really think it has reached such a pitch. But I'll speak to Maverick. So far, he has been hopeful – very hopeful.'

He looked at his watch.

'I must go. Ah, here is our dear Jolly. She will take charge of you.'

Miss Bellever, arriving briskly, said, 'The car is at the door, Mr Serrocold. Dr Maverick rang through from the Institute. I said I would bring Miss Marple over. He will meet us at the gates.'

'Thank you. I must go. My brief case?'

'In the car, Mr Serrocold.'

Lewis Serrocold hurried away. Looking after him, Miss Bellever said:

'Some day that man will drop dead in his tracks. It's against human nature never to relax or rest. He only sleeps four hours a night.'

'He is very devoted to this cause,' said Miss Marple.

'Never thinks of anything else,' said Miss Bellever grimly. 'Never dreams of looking after his wife or considering her in any way. She's a sweet creature, as you know, Miss Marple, and she ought to have love and attention. But nothing's thought of or considered here except a lot of whining boys and young men who want to live easily and dishonestly and don't care about the idea of doing a little hard work. What about the decent boys from decent homes? Why isn't something done for them? Honesty just isn't interesting to cranks like Mr Serrocold and Dr Maverick and all the bunch of half-baked sentimentalists we've got here. I and my brothers were brought up the hard way, Miss Marple, and we weren't encouraged to whine. Soft, that's what the world is nowadays!'

They had crossed the garden and passed through a palisaded

gate and had come to the arched gate which Eric Gulbrandsen had erected as an entrance to his College, a sturdily built, hideous, red brick building.

Dr Maverick, looking, Miss Marple decided, distinctly abnormal himself, came out to meet them.

'Thank you, Miss Bellever,' he said. 'Now, Miss – er – oh yes, Miss Marple – I'm sure you're going to be interested in what we're doing here. In our splendid approach to this great problem. Mr Serrocold is a man of great insight – great vision. And we've got Sir John Stillwell behind us – my old chief. He was at the Home Office until he retired and his influence turned the scales in getting this started. It's a *medical* problem – that's what we've got to get the legal authorities to understand. Psychiatry came into its own in the war. The one positive good that did come out of it – Now first of all I want you to see our initial approach to the problem. Look up – '

Miss Marple looked up at the words carved over the large arched doorway:

RECOVER HOPE ALL YE WHO ENTER HERE

'Isn't that splendid! Isn't that just the right note to strike. You don't want to scold these lads – or punish them. That's what they're hankering after half the time, punishment. We want to make them feel what fine fellows they are.'

'Like Edgar Lawson?' said Miss Marple.

'Interesting case, that. Have you been talking to him?'

'He has been talking to me,' said Miss Marple. She added apologetically, 'I wondered if, perhaps, he isn't a little *mad*?'

Dr Maverick laughed cheerfully.

'We're all mad, dear lady,' he said as he ushered her in through the door. 'That's the secret of existence. We're all a little mad.'

CHAPTER SIX

On the whole it was rather an exhausting day.

Enthusiasm in itself can be extremely wearing, Miss Marple thought. She felt vaguely dissatisfied with herself and her own reactions. There was a pattern here – perhaps several patterns, and yet she herself could obtain no clear glimpse of it or them. Any vague disquietude she felt centred round the pathetic but inconspicuous personality of Edgar Lawson. If she could only find in her memory the right parallel.

Painstakingly she rejected the curious behaviour of Mr Selkirk's delivery van – the absent-minded postman – the gardener who worked on Whit Monday – and that very curious affair of the summer weight combinations.

Something that she could not quite put her finger on was wrong about Edgar Lawson – something that went beyond the observed and admitted facts. But for the life of her, Miss Marple did not see how that wrongness, whatever it was, affected her friend Carrie Louise. In the confused patterns of life at Stonygates people's troubles and desires impinged on each other. But none of them (again as far as she could see) impinged on Carrie Louise.

Carrie Louise . . . Suddenly Miss Marple realized that it was she alone, except for the absent Ruth, who used that name. To her husband, she was Caroline. To Miss Bellever, Cara. Stephen Restarick usually addressed her as Madonna. To Wally she was formally Mrs Serrocold, and Gina elected to address her as Grandam – a mixture, she had explained, of Grande Dame and Grandmamma.

Was there some significance, perhaps, in the various names that were found for Caroline Louise Serrocold? Was she to all of them a symbol and not quite a real person?

When on the following morning Carrie Louise, dragging her feet a little as she walked, came and sat down on the garden seat beside her friend and asked her what she was thinking about, Miss Marple replied promptly:

'You, Carrie Louise.'

'What about me?'

'Tell me honestly – is there anything here that worries you?'

'Worries me?' The woman raised wondering clear blue eyes. 'But Jane, what should worry me?'

'Well, most of us have worries.' Miss Marple's eyes twinkled a little. 'I have. Slugs, you know – and the difficulty of getting linen properly darned – and not being able to get sugar candy for making my damson gin. Oh, lots of little things – it seems unnatural that you shouldn't have any worries at all.'

'I suppose I must have really,' said Mrs Serrocold vaguely. 'Lewis works too hard, and Stephen forgets his meals slaving at the theatre, and Gina is very jumpy – but I've never been able to alter people – I don't see how you can. So it wouldn't be any good worrying, would it?'

'Mildred's not very happy, either, is she?'

'Oh no,' said Carrie Louise. 'Mildred never is happy. She wasn't as a child. Quite unlike Pippa, who was always radiant.'

'Perhaps,' suggested Miss Marple, 'Mildred had cause not to be happy?'

Carrie Louise said quietly:

'Because of being jealous? Yes, I daresay. But people don't really need a cause for feeling what they do feel. They're just made that way. Don't you think so, Jane?'

Miss Marple thought briefly of Miss Moncrieff, a slave to a tyrannical invalid mother. Poor Miss Moncrieff who longed for travel and to see the world. And of how St Mary Mead in a decorous way had rejoiced when Mrs Moncrieff was laid in the churchyard and Miss Moncrieff, with a nice little income, was free at last. And of how Miss Moncrieff, starting on her travels, had got no farther than Hyères where, calling to see one of 'mother's oldest friends,' she had been so moved by the plight of an elderly hypochondriac that she had cancelled her travel reservations and taken up her abode in the villa to be bullied, over-worked, and to long wistfully, once more, for the joys of a wider horizon.

Miss Marple said:

'I expect you're right, Carrie Louise.'

'Of course my being so free from cares is partly due to Jolly. Dear Jolly. She came to me when Johnnie and I were just married and was wonderful from the first. She takes care of me as though I were a baby and quite helpless. She'd do anything for me. I feel quite ashamed sometimes. I really believe Jolly would murder someone for me, Jane. Isn't that an awful thing to say?'

'She's certainly very devoted,' agreed Miss Marple.

'She gets so indignant.' Mrs Serrocold's silvery laugh rang out. 'She'd like me to be always ordering wonderful clothes, and surrounding myself with luxuries, and she thinks everybody ought to put me first and to dance attendance on me. She's the one person who's absolutely unimpressed by Lewis's enthusiasm. All our poor boys are in her view pampered young criminals and not worth taking trouble over. She thinks this place is damp and bad for my rheumatism, and that I ought to go to Egypt or somewhere warm and dry.'

'Do you suffer much from rheumatism?'

'It's got much worse lately. I find it difficult to walk. Horrid cramps in my legs. Oh well – ' again there came that bewitching elfin smile, 'age must tell.'

Miss Bellever came out of the french windows and hurried across to them.

'A telegram, Cara, just come over the telephone. *Arriving this afternoon, Christian Gulbrandsen.*'

'Christian?' Carrie Louise looked very surprised. 'I'd no idea he was in England.'

'The oak suite, I suppose?'

'Yes, please, Jolly. Then there will be no stairs.'

Miss Bellever nodded and turned back to the house.

'Christian Gulbrandsen is my stepson,' said Carrie Louise. 'Eric's eldest son. Actually he's two years older than I am. He's one of the trustees of the Institute – the principal trustee. How very annoying that Lewis is away. Christian hardly ever stays longer than one night. He's an immensely busy man. And there are sure to be so many things they would want to discuss.'

Christian Gulbrandsen arrived that afternoon in time for tea. He was a big heavy-featured man, with a slow methodical way of talking. He greeted Carrie Louise with every sign of affection.

'And how is our little Carrie Louise? You do not look a day older. Not a day.'

His hands on her shoulders – he stood smiling down at her. A hand tugged his sleeve.

'Christian!'

'Ah,' he turned – 'it is Mildred? How are you, Mildred?'

'I've not really been at all well lately.'

549

'That is bad. That is bad.'

There was a strong resemblance between Christian Gulbrandsen and his half-sister Mildred. There was nearly thirty years' difference in age and they might easily have been taken for father and daughter. Mildred herself seemed particularly pleased by his arrival. She was flushed and talkative, and had talked repeatedly during the day of 'my brother,' 'my brother Christian,' 'my brother Mr Gulbrandsen.'

'And how is little Gina?' said Gulbrandsen, turning to that young woman. 'You and your husband are still here, then?'

'Yes. We've quite settled down, haven't we, Wally?'

'Looks like it,' said Wally.

Gulbrandsen's small shrewd eyes seemed to sum up Wally quickly. Wally, as usual, looked sullen and unfriendly.

'So here I am with all the family again,' said Gulbrandsen.

His voice displayed a rather determined geniality – but in actual fact, Miss Marple thought, he was not feeling particularly genial. There was a grim set to his lips and a certain preoccupation in his manner.

Introduced to Miss Marple, he swept a keen look over her as though measuring and appraising this newcomer.

'We'd no idea you were in England, Christian,' said Mrs Serrocold.

'No, I came over rather unexpectedly.'

'It is too bad that Lewis is away. How long can you stay?'

'I meant to go tomorrow. When will Lewis be back?'

'Tomorrow afternoon or evening.'

'It seems then that I must stay another night.'

'If you'd only let us know – '

'My dear Carrie Louise, my arrangements, they were made very suddenly.'

'You will stay to see Lewis?'

'Yes, it is necessary that I see Lewis.'

Miss Bellever said to Miss Marple: 'Mr Gulbrandsen and Mr Serrocold are both trustees of the Gulbrandsen Institute. The others are the Bishop of Cromer and Mr Gilfoy.'

Presumably, then, it was on business concerned with the Gulbrandsen Institute that Christian Gulbrandsen had come to Stonygates. It seemed to be assumed so by Miss Bellever and everyone else. And yet Miss Marple wondered.

Once or twice the old man cast a thoughtful puzzled look at Carrie Louise when she was not aware of it – a look that puzzled Carrie

550

Louise's watching friend. From Carrie Louise he shifted his gaze to the others, examining them one and all with a kind of covert appraisal that seemed distinctly odd.

After tea, Miss Marple withdrew tactfully from the others to the library, but rather to her surprise when she had settled herself with her knitting, Christian Gulbrandsen came in and sat down beside her.

'You are a very old friend, I think, of our dear Carrie Louise?' he said.

'We were at school together in Italy, Mr Gulbrandsen. Many many years ago.'

'Ah yes. And you are fond of her?'

'Yes, indeed,' said Miss Marple warmly.

'So, I think, is everyone. Yes, I truly think that. It should be so. For she is a very dear and enchanting person. Always, since my father married her, I and my brothers have loved her very much. She has been to us like a very dear sister. She was a faithful wife to my father and loyal to all his ideas. She has never thought of herself, but put the welfare of others first.'

'She has always been an idealist,' said Miss Marple.

'An idealist? Yes. Yes, that is so. And therefore it may be that she does not truly appreciate the evil that there is in the world.'

Miss Marple looked at him, surprised. His face was very stern.

'Tell me,' he said. 'How is her health?'

Again Miss Marple felt surprised.

'She seems to me very well – apart from arthritis – or rheumatism.'

'Rheumatism? Yes. And her heart? Her heart is good?'

'As far as I know.' Miss Marple was still more surprised. 'But until yesterday I had not seen her for many years. If you want to know the state of her health, you should ask somebody in the house here. Miss Bellever, for instance.'

'Miss Bellever – Yes, Miss Bellever. Or Mildred?'

'Or, as you say, Mildred.'

Miss Marple was faintly embarrassed.

Christian Gulbrandsen was staring at her very hard.

'There is not between the mother and daughter a very great sympathy, would you say?'

'No, I don't think there is.'

'I agree. It is a pity – her only child, but there it is. Now this Miss Bellever, you think, is really attached to her?'

'Very much so.'

'And Carrie Louise leans on this Miss Bellever?'

'I think so.'

Christian Gulbrandsen was frowning. He spoke as though more to himself than to Miss Marple.

'There is the little Gina – but she is so young. It is difficult – ' He broke off. 'Sometimes,' he said simply, 'it is hard to know what is best to be done. I wish very much to act for the best. I am particularly anxious that no harm and no unhappiness should come to that dear lady. But it is not easy – not easy at all.'

Mrs Strete came into the room at that moment.

'Oh, there you are, Christian. We were wondering where you were. Dr Maverick wants to know if you would like to go over anything with him.'

'That is the new young doctor here? No – no, I will wait until Lewis returns.'

'He's waiting in Lewis's study. Shall I tell him – '

'I will have a word with him myself.'

Gulbrandsen hurried out. Mildred Strete stared after him and then stared at Miss Marple.

'I wonder if anything is wrong. Christian is very unlike himself . . . Did he say anything – '

'He only asked me about your mother's health.'

'Her health? Why should he ask you about that?'

Mildred spoke sharply, her large square face flushing unbecomingly.

'I really don't know.'

'Mother's health is perfectly good. Surprisingly so for a woman of her age. Much better than mine as far as that goes.' She paused a moment before saying: 'I hope you told him so?'

'I don't really know anything about it,' said Miss Marple. 'He asked me about her heart.'

'Her *heart*?'

'Yes.'

'There's nothing wrong with mother's heart. Nothing at all!'

'I'm delighted to hear you say so, my dear.'

'What on earth put all these queer ideas into Christian's head?'

'I've no idea,' said Miss Marple.

CHAPTER SEVEN

The next day passed uneventfully to all appearances, yet to Miss Marple it seemed that there were signs of an inner tension. Christian Gulbrandsen spent his morning with Dr Maverick in going round the Institute and in discussing the general results of the Institute's policy. In the early afternoon Gina took him for a drive, and after that Miss Marple noticed that he induced Miss Bellever to show him something in the gardens. It seemed to her that it was a pretext for ensuring a *tête-à-tête* with that grim woman. And yet, if Christian Gulbrandsen's unexpected visit had only to do with business matters, why this wish for Miss Bellever's company, since the latter dealt only with the domestic side of Stonygates?

But in all this, Miss Marple could tell herself that she was being fanciful. The one really disturbing incident of the day happened about four o'clock. She had rolled up her knitting and had gone out in the garden to take a little stroll before tea. Rounding a straggling rhododendron she came upon Edgar Lawson, who was striding along muttering to himself and who nearly ran into her.

He said, 'I beg your pardon,' hastily, but Miss Marple was startled by the queer staring expression of his eyes.

'Aren't you feeling well, Mr Lawson?'

'Well? How should I be feeling well? I've had a shock – a terrible shock.'

'What kind of a shock?'

The young man gave a swift glance past her, and then a sharp uneasy glance to either side. His doing so gave Miss Marple a nervous feeling.

'Shall I tell you?' He looked at her doubtfully. 'I don't know. I don't really *know*. I've been so spied upon.'

Miss Marple made up her mind. She took him firmly by the arm.

'If we walk down this path . . . There, now, there are no trees or bushes near. Nobody can overhear.'

'No – no, you're right.' He drew a deep breath, bent his head and almost whispered his next words. 'I've made a discovery. A terrible discovery.'

Edgar Lawson began to shake all over. He was almost weeping.

'To have trusted someone! To have believed . . . and it was lies – all lies. Lies to keep me from finding out the truth. I can't bear it. It's too wicked. You see, he was the one person I trusted, and now to find out that all the time he's been at the bottom of it all. It's *he* who's been my enemy! It's *he* who has been having me followed about and spied upon. But he can't get away with it any more. I shall speak out. I shall tell him I know what he has been doing.'

'Who is "he"?' demanded Miss Marple.

Edgar Lawson drew himself up to his full height. He might have looked pathetic and dignified. But actually he only looked ridiculous.

'I'm speaking of my father.'

'Viscount Montgomery – or do you mean Winston Churchill?'

Edgar threw her a glance of scorn.

'They let me think that – just to keep me from guessing the truth. But I know now. I've got a friend – a real friend. A friend who tells me the truth and lets me know just how I've been deceived. Well, my father will have to reckon with *me*. I'll throw his lies in his face! I'll challenge him with the truth. We'll see what he's got to say to that.'

And suddenly breaking away, Edgar went off at a run and disappeared in the park.

Her face grave, Miss Marple went back to the house.

'We're all a little mad, dear lady,' Dr Maverick had said.

But it seemed to her that in Edgar's case it went rather further than that.

II

Lewis Serrocold arrived back at six-thirty. He stopped the car at the gates and walked to the house through the park. Looking out of her window, Miss Marple saw Christian Gulbrandsen go out to meet him and the two men, having greeted one another, turned and paced to and fro up and down the terrace.

Miss Marple had been careful to bring her bird glasses with her.

At this moment she brought them into action. Was there, or was there not, a flight of siskins by that far clump of trees?

She noted as the glasses swept down before rising that both men were looking seriously disturbed. Miss Marple leant out a little farther. Scraps of conversation floated up to her now and then. If either of the men should look up, it would be quite clear that an enraptured bird watcher had her attention fixed on a point far removed from their conversation.

'. . . how to spare Carrie Louise the knowledge – ' Gulbrandsen was saying.

The next time they passed below, Lewis Serrocold was speaking.

'if it *can* be kept from her. I agree that it is she who must be considered . . .'

Other faint snatches came to the listener.

'– Really serious – ' '– not justified – ' '– too big a responsibility to take – ' '– we should, perhaps, take outside advice – '

Finally Miss Marple heard Christian Gulbrandsen say:

'Ach, it grows cold. We must go inside.'

Miss Marple drew her head in through the window with a puzzled expression. What she had heard was too fragmentary to be easily pieced together – but it served to confirm that vague apprehension that had been gradually growing upon her and about which Ruth Van Rydock had been so positive.

Whatever was wrong at Stonygates, it definitely affected Carrie Louise.

III

Dinner that evening was a somewhat constrained meal. Both Gulbrandsen and Lewis were absent-minded and absorbed in their own thoughts. Walter Hudd glowered even more than usual, and for once Gina and Stephen seemed to have little to say either to each other or to the company at large. Conversation was mostly sustained by Dr Maverick, who had a lengthy technical discussion with Mr Baumgarten, one of the Occupational Therapists.

When they moved into the hall after dinner, Christian Gulbrandsen excused himself almost at once. He said he had an important letter to write.

'So if you will forgive me, dear Carrie Louise, I will go now to my room.'

555

'You have all you want there? Jolly?'

'Yes, yes. Everything. A typewriter, I asked, and one has been put there. Miss Bellever has been most kind and attentive.'

He left the Great Hall by the door on the left which led past the foot of the main staircase and along a corridor, at the end of which was a suite of bedroom and bathroom.

When he had gone out Carrie Louise said:

'Not going down to the theatre tonight, Gina?'

The girl shook her head. She went over and sat by the window overlooking the front drive and the court.

Stephen glanced at her, then strolled over to the big grand piano. He sat down at it and strummed very softly – a queer melancholy little tune. The two Occupational Therapists, Mr Baumgarten and Mr Lacy, and Dr Maverick, said goodnight and left. Walter turned on the switch of a reading lamp and with a crackling noise half the lights in the hall went out.

He growled.

'That darned switch is always faulty. I'll go and put a new fuse in.'

He left the Hall and Carrie Louise murmured, 'Wally's so clever with electrical gadgets and things like that. You remember how he fixed that toaster?'

'It seems to be all he does do here,' said Mildred Strete. 'Mother, have you taken your tonic?'

Miss Bellever looked annoyed.

'I declare I completely forgot tonight.' She jumped up and went into the dining-room, returning presently with a small glass containing a little rose-coloured fluid.

Smiling a little, Carrie Louise held out an obedient hand.

'Such horrid stuff and nobody lets me forget it,' she said, making a wry face.

And then, rather unexpectedly, Lewis Serrocold said: 'I don't think I should take it tonight, my dear. I'm not sure it really agrees with you.'

Quietly, but with that controlled energy always so apparent in him, he took the glass from Miss Bellever and put it down on the big oak Welsh dresser.

Miss Bellever said sharply:

'Really, Mr Serrocold, I can't agree with you there. Mrs Serrocold has been very much better since – '

She broke off and turned sharply.

The front door was pushed violently open and allowed to swing to with a crash. Edgar Lawson came into the big dim Hall with the air of a star performer making a triumphal entry.

He stood in the middle of the floor and struck an attitude.

It was almost ridiculous – but not quite ridiculous.

Edgar said theatrically:

'So I have found you, O mine enemy!'

He said it to Lewis Serrocold.

Mr Serrocold looked mildly astonished.

'Why, Edgar, what is the matter?'

'You can say that to me – you!' You know what's the matter. You've been deceiving me, spying on me, working with my enemies against me.'

Lewis took him by the arm.

'Now, now, my dear lad, don't excite yourself. Tell me all about it quietly. Come into my office.'

He led him across the Hall and through a door on the right, closing it behind him. After he had done so, there was another sound, the sharp sound of a key being turned in the lock.

Miss Bellever looked at Miss Marple, the same idea in both their minds. *It was not Lewis Serrocold who had turned the key*.

Miss Bellever said sharply: 'That young man is just about to go off his head in my opinion. It isn't safe.'

Mildred said: 'He's a most unbalanced young man – and absolutely ungrateful for everything that's been done for him – you ought to put your foot down, Mother.'

With a faint sigh Carrie Louise murmured:

'There's no harm in him really. He's fond of Lewis. He's very fond of him.'

Miss Marple looked at her curiously. There had been no fondness in the expression that Edgar had turned on Lewis Serrocold a few moments previously, very far from it. She wondered, as she wondered before, if Carrie Louise deliberately turned her back on reality.

Gina said sharply:

'He had something in his pocket. Edgar, I mean. Playing with it.'

Stephen murmured as he took his hands from the keys:

'In a film it would certainly have been a revolver.'

Miss Marple coughed.

'I think you know,' she said apologetically, 'it *was* a revolver.'

557

From behind the closed door of Lewis's office the sound of voices had been plainly discernible. Now, suddenly, they became clearly audible. Edgar Lawson shouted whilst Lewis Serrocold's voice kept its even reasonable note.

'Lies – lies – lies, all lies. *You*'re my father. I'm *your* son. You've deprived me of my rights. *I* ought to own this place. You hate me – you want to get rid of me!'

There was a soothing murmur from Lewis and then the hysterical voice rose still higher. It screamed out foul epithets. Edgar seemed rapidly losing control of himself. Occasional words came from Lewis – 'calm – just be calm – you know none of this is true – ' But they seemed not to soothe, but on the contrary to enrage the young man still further.

Insensibly everyone in the hall was silent, listening intently to what went on behind the locked door of Lewis's study.

'I'll make you listen to me,' yelled Edgar. 'I'll take that supercilious expression off your face. I'll have revenge, I tell you. Revenge for all you've made me suffer.'

The other voice came curtly, unlike Lewis's usual unemotional tones.

'Put that revolver down!'

Gina cried sharply:

'Edgar will kill him. He's crazy. Can't we get the police or something?'

Carrie Louise, still unmoved, said softly:

'There's no need to worry, Gina. Edgar loves Lewis. He's just dramatizing himself, that's all.'

Edgar's voice sounded through the door in a laugh that Miss Marple had to admit sounded definitely insane.

'Yes, I've got a revolver – and it's loaded. No, don't speak, don't move. You're going to hear me out. It's you who started this conspiracy against me and now you're going to pay for it.'

What sounded like the report of a firearm made them all start, but Carrie Louise said:

'It's all right, it's outside – in the park somewhere.'

Behind the locked door, Edgar was raving in a high screaming voice.

'You sit there looking at me – looking at me – pretending to be unmoved. Why don't you get down on your knees and beg for mercy? I'm going to shoot, I tell you. I'm going to shoot you dead! I'm your son – your unacknowledged despised son – you wanted me hidden away, out of the world altogether, perhaps. You set your spies to follow me – to hound me down – you plotted against me. You, my father! My father. I'm only a bastard, aren't I? Only a bastard. You went on filling me up with lies. Pretending to be kind to me, and all the time – all the time – You're not fit to live. I won't let you live.'

Again there came a stream of obscene profanity. Somewhere during the scene Miss Marple was conscious of Miss Bellever saying:

'We must *do* something,' and leaving the Hall.

Edgar seemed to pause for breath and then he shouted out:

'You're going to die – to *die*. You're going to die *now*. Take *that*, you devil, and *that*!'

Two sharp cracks rang out – not in the park this time, but definitely behind the locked door.

Somebody, Miss Marple thought it was Mildred, cried out:

'Oh God, what shall we do?'

There was a thud from inside the room and then a sound, almost more terrible than what had gone before, the sound of slow heavy sobbing.

Somebody strode past Miss Marple and started shaking and rattling the door.

It was Stephen Restarick.

'Open the door. Open the door,' he shouted.

Miss Bellever came back into the Hall. In her hand she held an assortment of keys.

'Try some of these,' she said breathlessly.

At that moment the fused lights came on again. The Hall sprang into life again after its eerie dimness.

Stephen Restarick began trying the keys.

They heard the inside key fall out as he did so.

Inside that wild desperate sobbing went on.

Walter Hudd, coming lazily back into the Hall, stopped dead and demanded:

'Say, what's going on round here?'

Mildred said tearfully:

'That awful crazy young man has shot Mr Serrocold.'

'Please.' It was Carrie Louise who spoke. She got up and came across to the study door. Very gently she pushed Stephen Restarick aside. 'Let me speak to him.'

She called – very softly – 'Edgar . . . Edgar . . . let me in, will you? Please, Edgar.'

They heard the key fitted into the lock. It turned and the door was slowly opened.

But it was not Edgar who opened it. It was Lewis Serrocold. He was breathing hard as though he had been running, but otherwise he was unmoved.

'It's all right, dearest,' he said. 'Dearest, it's quite all right.'

'We thought you'd been shot,' said Miss Bellever gruffly.

Lewis Serrocold frowned. He said with a trifle of asperity:

'Of course I haven't been shot.'

They could see into the study by now. Edgar Lawson had collapsed by the desk. He was sobbing and gasping. The revolver lay on the floor where it had dropped from his hand.

'But we heard the shots,' said Mildred.

'Oh yes, he fired twice.'

'And he missed you?'

'Of course he missed me,' snapped Lewis.

Miss Marple did not consider that there was any of course about it. The shots must have been fired at fairly close range.

Lewis Serrocold said irritably:

'Where's Maverick? It's Maverick we need.'

Miss Bellever said:

'I'll get him. Shall I ring up the police as well?'

'Police? Certainly not.'

'Of course we must ring up the police,' said Mildred. 'He's dangerous.'

'Nonsense,' said Lewis Serrocold. 'Poor lad. Does he look dangerous?'

At the moment he did not look dangerous. He looked young and pathetic and rather repulsive.

His voice had lost its carefully acquired accent.

'I didn't mean to do it,' he groaned. 'I dunno what came over me – talking all that stuff – I must have been mad.'

Mildred sniffed.

'I really must have been mad. I didn't mean to. Please, Mr Serrocold, I really didn't mean to.'

Lewis Serrocold patted him on the shoulder.

'That's all right, my boy. No damage done.'

'I might have killed you, Mr Serrocold.'

Walter Hudd walked across the room and peered at the wall behind the desk.

'The bullets went in here,' he said. His eye dropped to the desk and the chair behind it. 'Must have been a near miss,' he said grimly.

'I lost my head. I didn't rightly know what I was doing. I thought he'd done me out of my rights. I thought – '

Miss Marple put in the question she had been wanting to ask for some time.

'Who told you,' she asked, 'that Mr Serrocold was your father?'

Just for a second a sly expression peeped out of Edgar's distracted face. It was there and gone in a flash.

'Nobody,' he said. 'I just got it into my head.'

Walter Hudd was staring down at the revolver where it lay on the floor.

'Where the hell did you get that gun?' he demanded.

'Gun?' Edgar stared down at it.

'Looks mighty like my gun,' said Walter. He stooped down and picked it up. 'By heck, it *is*! You took it out of my room, you creeping louse, you.'

Lewis Serrocold interposed between the cringing Edgar and the menacing American.

'All this can be gone into later,' he said. 'Ah, here's Maverick. Take a look at him, will you, Maverick?'

Dr Maverick advanced upon Edgar with a kind of professional zest.

'This won't do, Edgar,' he said. 'This won't do, you know.'

'He's a dangerous lunatic,' said Mildred sharply. 'He's been shooting off a revolver and raving. He only just missed my stepfather.'

Edgar gave a little yelp and Dr Maverick said reprovingly:

'Careful, please, Mrs Strete.'

'I'm sick of all this. Sick of the way you all go on here! I tell you this man's a lunatic.'

With a bound Edgar wrenched himself away from Dr Maverick and fell to the floor at Serrocold's feet.

'Help me. Help me. Don't let them take me away and shut me up. Don't let them . . .'

An unpleasing scene, Miss Marple thought.

Mildred said angrily, 'I tell you he's – '

Her mother said soothingly:

'Please Mildred. Not now. He's suffering.'

Walter muttered:

'Suffering cripes. They're all cuckoo round here.'

'I'll take charge of him,' said Dr Maverick. 'You come with me,

Edgar. Bed and a sedative – and we'll talk everything out in the morning. Now you trust me, don't you?'

Rising to his feet and trembling a little, Edgar looked doubtfully at the young doctor and then at Mildred Strete.

'She said – I was a lunatic.'

'No, no, you're not a lunatic.'

Miss Bellever's footsteps rang purposefully across the Hall. She came in with her lips pursed together and a flushed face.

'I've telephoned the police,' she said grimly. 'They will be here in a few minutes.'

Carrie Louise cried, 'Jolly!' in tones of dismay.

Edgar uttered a wail.

Lewis Serrocold frowned angrily.

'I told you, Jolly, I did *not* want the police summoned. This is a medical matter.'

'That's as may be,' said Miss Bellever. 'I've my own opinion. But I had to call the police. Mr Gulbrandsen's been shot dead.'

CHAPTER EIGHT

It was a moment or two before anyone took in what she was saying.

Carrie Louise said incredulously:

'Christian shot? Dead? Oh, surely, that's impossible.'

'If you don't believe me,' said Miss Bellever, pursing her lips, and addressing not so much Carrie Louise, as the assembled company, 'go and look for yourselves.'

She was angry. And her anger sounded in the crisp sharpness of her voice.

Slowly, unbelievingly, Carrie Louise took a step towards the door. Lewis Serrocold put a hand on her shoulder.

'No, dearest, let me go.'

He went out through the doorway. Dr Maverick, with a doubtful glance at Edgar, followed him. Miss Bellever went with them.

Miss Marple gently urged Carrie Louise into a chair. She sat down, her eyes looking hurt and stricken.

'Christian – shot?' she said again.

It was the bewildered hurt tone of a child.

Walter Hudd remained close to Edgar Lawson, glowering down at him. In his hand he held the gun that he had picked up from the floor.

Mrs Serrocold said in a wondering voice:

'But who could possibly want to shoot *Christian*?'

It was not a question that demanded an answer.

Walter muttered under his breath:

'Nuts! The whole lot of them.'

Stephen had moved protectively closer to Gina. Her young startled face was the most vivid thing in the room.

Suddenly the front door opened and a rush of cold air together with a man in a big overcoat came in.

The heartiness of his greeting seemed incredibly shocking.

'Hallo, everybody, what's going on tonight? A lot of fog on the road. I had to go dead slow.'

For a startled moment, Miss Marple thought that she was seeing double. Surely the same man could not be standing by Gina and coming in by the door. Then she realized that it was only a likeness and not, when you looked closely, such a very strong likeness. The two men were clearly brothers with a strong family resemblance, but no more.

Where Stephen Restarick was thin to the point of emaciation the newcomer was sleek. The big coat with the astrakhan collar fitted the sleekness of body snugly. A handsome young man, and one who bore upon him the authority and good humour of success.

But Miss Marple noted one thing about him. His eyes, as he entered the hall, looked immediately at Gina.

He said, a little doubtfully:

'You *did* expect me? You got my wire?'

He was speaking now to Carrie Louise. He came towards her.

Almost mechanically, she put her hand out to him. He took it and kissed it gently. It was an affectionate act of homage, not a mere theatrical courtesy.

She murmured:

'Of course, Alex dear – of course. Only, you see – things have been happening – '

'Happening?'

Mildred gave the information, gave it with a kind of grim relish that Miss Marple found distasteful.

563

'Christian Gulbrandsen,' she said. 'My brother Christian Gulbrandsen has been found shot dead.'

'Good God,' Alex registered a more than life-size dismay. 'Suicide, do you mean?'

Carrie Louise moved swiftly.

'Oh no,' she said. 'It couldn't be suicide. Not *Christian*! Oh no.'

'Uncle Christian would never shoot himself, I'm sure,' said Gina.

Alex Restarick looked from one person to the other. From his brother Stephen he received a short confirmative nod. Walter Hudd stared back at him with faint resentment. Alex's eyes rested on Miss Marple with a sudden frown. It was as though he had found some unwanted prop on a stage set.

He looked as though he would like her explained. But nobody explained her, and Miss Marple continued to look an old, fluffy and sweetly bewildered old lady.

'When? asked Alex. 'When did this happen, I mean?'

'Just before you arrived,' said Gina. 'About – oh three or four minutes ago, I suppose. Why, of course, we actually heard the shot. Only we didn't notice it – not really.'

'Didn't notice it? Why not?'

'Well, you see, there were other things going on . . .' Gina spoke rather hesitantly.

'Sure were,' said Walter with emphasis.

Juliet Bellever came into the Hall by the door from the library.

'Mr Serrocold suggests that we should all wait in the library. It would be convenient for the police. Except for Mrs Serrocold. You've had a shock, Cara. I've ordered some hot bottles to be put in your bed. I'll take you up and – '

Rising to her feet, Carrie Louise shook her head.

'I must see Christian first,' she said.

'Oh no, dear. Don't upset yourself – '

Carrie Louise put her very gently to one side.

'Dear Jolly – you don't understand.' She looked round and said, 'Jane?'

Miss Marple had already moved towards her.

'Come with me, will you, Jane.'

They moved together towards the door. Dr Maverick, coming in, almost collided with them.

Miss Bellever exclaimed:

'Dr Maverick. Do stop her. So foolish.'

Carrie Louise looked calmly at the young doctor. She even gave a tiny smile.

Dr Maverick said: 'You want to go and – see him?'

'I must.'

'I see.' He stood aside. 'If you feel you must, Mrs Serrocold. But afterwards, please go and lie down and let Miss Bellever look after you. At the moment you do not feel the shock, but I assure you that you will do so.'

'Yes. I expect you are right. I will be quite sensible. Come, Jane.'

The two women moved out through the door, past the foot of the main staircase and along the corridor, past the dining-room on the right and the double doors leading to the kitchen quarters on the left, past the side door to the terrace and on to the door that gave admission to the Oak suite that had been allotted to Christian Gulbrandsen. It was a room furnished as a sitting-room more than a bedroom, with a bed in an alcove to one side and a door leading into a dressing-room and bathroom.

Carrie Louise stopped on the threshold. Christian Gulbrandsen had been sitting at the big mahogany desk with a small portable typewriter open in front of him. He sat there now, but slumped sideways in the chair. The high arms of the chair prevented him from slipping to the floor.

Lewis Serrocold was standing by the window. He had pulled the curtain a little aside and was gazing out into the night.

He looked round and frowned.

'My dearest, you shouldn't have come.'

He came towards her and she stretched out a hand to him. Miss Marple retreated a step or two.

'Oh yes, Lewis. I had to – see him. One has to know just exactly how things are.'

She walked slowly towards the desk.

Lewis said warningly:

'You mustn't touch anything. The police must have things left exactly as we found them.'

'Of course. He was shot deliberately by someone, then?'

'Oh yes.' Lewis Serrocold looked a little surprised that the question had even been asked. 'I thought – you knew that?'

'I did really. Christian would not commit suicide, and he was such a competent person that it could not possibly have been an accident. That only leaves' – she hesitated a moment – 'murder.'

She walked up behind the desk and stood looking down at the dead man. There was sorrow and affection in her face.

'Dear Christian,' she said. 'He was always good to me.'

Softly, she touched the top of his head with her fingers.

'Bless you and thank you, dear Christian,' she said.

Lewis Serrocold said with something more like emotion than Miss Marple had ever seen in him before:

'I wish to God I could have spared you this, Caroline.'

His wife shook her head gently.

'You can't really spare anyone anything,' she said. 'Things always have to be faced sooner or later. And therefore it had better be sooner. I'll go and lie down now. I suppose you'll stay here, Lewis, until the police come?'

'Yes.'

Carrie Louise turned away and Miss Marple slipped an arm round her.

CHAPTER NINE

Inspector Curry and his entourage found Miss Bellever alone in the Great Hall when they arrived.

She came forward efficiently.

'I am Juliet Bellever, companion and secretary to Mrs Serrocold.'

'It was you who found the body and telephoned to us?'

'Yes. Most of the household are in the library – through that door there. Mr Serrocold remained in Mr Gulbrandsen's room to see that nothing was disturbed. Dr Maverick, who first examined the body, will be here very shortly. He had to take a – case over to the other wing. Shall I lead the way?'

'If you please.'

'Competent woman,' thought the Inspector to himself. 'Seems to have got the whole thing taped.'

He followed her along the corridor.

For the next twenty minutes the routine of police procedure was duly set in motion. The photographer took the necessary pictures.

The police surgeon arrived and was joined by Dr Maverick. Half an hour later, the ambulance had taken away the mortal remains of Christian Gulbrandsen, and Inspector Curry started his official interrogation.

Lewis Serrocold took him into the library, and he glanced keenly round the assembled people, making brief notes in his mind. An old lady with white hair, a middle-aged lady, the good looking girl he'd seen driving her car round the countryside, that sulky looking American husband of hers. A couple of young men who were mixed up in the outfit somewhere or other and the capable woman, Miss Bellever, who'd phoned him and met him on arrival.

Inspector Curry had already thought out a little speech and he now delivered it as planned.

'I'm afraid this is all very upsetting to you,' he said, 'and I hope not to keep you too long this evening. We can go into things more thoroughly tomorrow. It was Miss Bellever who found Mr Gulbrandsen dead, and I'll ask Miss Bellever to give me an outline of the general situation as that will save too much repetition. Mr Serrocold, if you want to go up to your wife, please do, and when I have finished with Miss Bellever, I should like to talk to you. Is that all quite clear? Perhaps there is some small room where – '

Lewis Serrocold said: 'My office, Jolly?'

Miss Bellever nodded, and said: 'I was just going to suggest it.'

She led the way across the Great Hall, and Inspector Curry and his attendant Sergeant followed her.

Miss Bellever arranged them and herself suitably. It might have been she and not Inspector Curry who was in charge of the investigation.

The moment had come, however, when the initiative passed to him. Inspector Curry had a pleasant voice and manner. He looked quiet and serious and just a little apologetic. Some people made the mistake of underrating him. Actually he was as competent in his way as Miss Bellever was in hers. But he preferred not to make a parade of the fact.

He cleared his throat.

'I've had the main facts from Mr Serrocold. Mr Christian Gulbrandsen was the eldest son of the late Eric Gulbrandsen, the founder of the Gulbrandsen Trust and Fellowships . . . and all the rest of it. He was one of the trustees of this place and he arrived here unexpectedly yesterday. That is correct?'

'Yes.'

567

Inspector Curry was pleased by her conciseness. He went on:

'Mr Serrocold was away in Liverpool. He returned this evening by the 6.30 train.'

'Yes.'

'After dinner this evening, Mr Gulbrandsen announced his intention of working in his own room and left the rest of the party here after coffee had been served. Correct?'

'Yes.'

'Now, Miss Bellever, please tell me in your own words how you came to discover him dead.'

'There was a rather unpleasant incident this evening. A young man, a psychopathic case, became very unbalanced and threatened Mr Serrocold with a revolver. They were locked in this room. The young man eventually fired the revolver – you can see the bullet holes in the wall there. Fortunately Mr Serrocold was unhurt. After firing the shots, this young man went completely to pieces. Mr Serrocold sent me to find Dr Maverick. I got through on the house phone but he was not in his room. I found him with one of his colleagues and gave him the message and he came here at once. On my own way back I went to Mr Gulbrandsen's room. I wanted to ask him if there was anything he would like – hot milk, or whisky, before settling for the night. I knocked, but there was no response, so I opened the door. I saw that Mr Gulbrandsen was dead. I then rang you up.'

'What entrances and exits are there to the house? And how are they secured? Could anyone have come in from outside without being heard or seen?'

'Anyone could have come in by the side door to the terrace. That is not locked until we all go to bed, as people come in and out that way to go to the College buildings.'

'And you have, I believe, between two hundred and two hundred and fifty juvenile delinquents in the College?'

'Yes. But the College buildings are well secured and patrolled. I should say it was most unlikely that anyone could leave the College unsponsored.'

'We shall have to check up on that, of course. Had Mr Gulbrandsen given any cause for – shall we say, rancour? Any unpopular decisions as to policy?'

Miss Bellever shook her head.

'Oh no, Mr Gulbrandsen had nothing whatever to do with the running of the College, or with administrative matters.'

'What was the purpose of his visit?'

'I have no idea.'

'But he was annoyed to find Mr Serrocold absent, and immediately decided to wait until he returned?'

'Yes.'

'So his business here was definitely with Mr Serrocold?'

'Yes. But it would be – because it would be almost certainly business to do with the Institute.'

'Yes, presumably that is so. Did he have a conference with Mr Serrocold?'

'No, there was no time. Mr Serrocold only arrived just before dinner this evening.'

'But after dinner, Mr Gulbrandsen said he had important letters to write and went away to do so. He didn't suggest a session with Mr Serrocold?'

Miss Bellever hesitated.

'No. No, he didn't.'

'Surely that was rather odd – if he had waited on at inconvenience to himself to see Mr Serrocold?'

'Yes, it was odd.'

The oddness of it seemed to strike Miss Bellever for the first time.

'Mr Serrocold did not accompany him to his room?'

'No. Mr Serrocold remained in the Hall.'

'And you have no idea at what time Mr Gulbrandsen was killed?'

'I think it is possible that we heard the shot. If so, it was at twenty-three minutes past nine.'

'You heard a shot? And it did not alarm you?'

'The circumstances were peculiar.'

She explained in rather more detail the scene between Lewis Serrocold and Edgar Lawson which had been in progress.

'So it occurred to no one that the shot might actually have come from within the house?'

'No. No, I certainly don't think so. We were all so relieved, you know, that the shot didn't come from in here.'

Miss Bellever added rather grimly:

'You don't expect murder and attempted murder in the same house on the same night.'

Inspector Curry acknowledged the truth of that.

'All the same,' said Miss Bellever, suddenly, 'you know, I believe that's what made me go along to Mr Gulbrandsen's room later. I did mean to ask him if he would like anything, but it was a kind of excuse to reassure myself that everything was all right.'

Inspector Curry stared at her for a moment.

'What made you think it mightn't be all right?'

'I don't know. I think it was the shot outside. It hadn't meant anything at the time. But afterwards it came back into my mind. I told myself that it was only a backfire from Mr Restarick's car – '

'Mr Restarick's car?'

'Yes. Alex Restarick. He arrived by car this evening – he arrived just after all this happened.'

'I see. When you discovered Mr Gulbrandsen's body, did you touch anything in the room?'

'Of course not.' Miss Bellever sounded reproachful. 'Naturally I knew that nothing must be touched or moved. Mr Gulbrandsen had been shot through the head but there was no firearm to be seen, so I knew it was murder.'

'And just now, when you took us into the room, everything was exactly as it had been when you found the body?'

Miss Bellever considered. She sat back screwing up her eyes. She had Inspector Curry thought, one of those photographic memories.

'One thing was different,' she said. 'There was nothing in the typewriter.'

'You mean,' said Inspector Curry, 'that when you first went in Mr Gulbrandsen had been writing a letter on the typewriter, and that that letter had since been removed?'

'Yes, I'm almost sure that I saw the white edge of the paper sticking up.'

'Thank you, Miss Bellever. Who else went into that room before we arrived?'

'Mr Serrocold, of course. He remained there when I came to meet you. And Mrs Serrocold and Miss Marple went there. Mrs Serrocold insisted.'

'Mrs Serrocold and Miss Marple,' said Inspector Curry. 'Which is Miss Marple?'

'The old lady with white hair. She was a school friend of Mrs Serrocold's. She came on a visit about four days ago.'

'Well, thank you, Miss Bellever. All that you have told us is quite clear. I'll go into things with Mr Serrocold now. Ah, but perhaps – Miss Marple's an old lady, isn't she? I'll just have a word with her first and then she can go off to bed. Rather cruel to keep an old lady like that up,' said Inspector Curry virtuously. 'This must have been a shock to her.'

'I'll tell her, shall I?'

'If you please.'

Miss Bellever went out. Inspector Curry looked at the ceiling. 'Gulbrandsen?' he said. 'Why Gulbrandsen? Two hundred odd maladjusted youngsters on the premises. No reason any of them shouldn't have done it. Probably one of them did. But why Gulbrandsen? The stranger within the gates.'

Sergeant Lake said: 'Of course we don't know everything yet.'

Inspector Curry said:

'So far, we don't know anything at all.'

He jumped up and was gallant when Miss Marple came in. She seemed a little flustered and he hurried to put her at her ease.

'Now don't upset yourself, m'am.' The old ones like M'am, he thought. To them, police officers were definitely of the lower classes and should show respect to their betters. 'This is all very distressing, I know. But we've just got to get the facts clear. Get it all clear.'

'Oh yes, I know,' said Miss Marple. 'So difficult, isn't it? To be clear about anything, I mean. Because if you're looking at one thing, you can't be looking at another. And one so often looks at the wrong thing, though whether because one happens to do so or because you're meant to, it's very hard to say. Misdirection, the conjurers call it. So clever, aren't they? And I never *have* known how they manage with a bowl of goldfish – because really that cannot fold up small, can it?'

Inspector Curry blinked a little and said soothingly:

'Quite so. Now, m'am, I've had an account of this evening's events from Miss Bellever. A most anxious time for all of you, I'm sure.'

'Yes, indeed. It was all so *dramatic*, you know.'

'First this to-do between Mr Serrocold and' – he looked down at a note he had made – 'this Edgar Lawson.'

'A very odd young man,' said Miss Marple. 'I have felt all along that there was something wrong about him.'

'I'm sure you have,' said Inspector Curry. 'And then, after that excitement was over, there came Mr Gulbrandsen's death. I understand that you went with Mrs Serrocold to see the – er – the body.'

'Yes, I did. She asked me to come with her. We are very old friends.'

'Quite so. And you went along to Mr Gulbrandsen's room.

571

Did you touch anything while you were in the room, either of you?'

'Oh no. Mr Serrocold warned us not to.'

'Did you happen to notice, ma'm, whether there was a letter or a piece of paper, say, in the typewriter?'

'There wasn't,' said Miss Marple promptly. 'I noticed that at once because it seemed to me odd. Mr Gulbrandsen was sitting there at the typewriter so he must have been typing something. Yes, I thought it very odd.'

Inspector Curry looked at her sharply. He said:

'Did you have much conversation with Mr Gulbrandsen while he was here?'

'Very little.'

'There is nothing especial – or significant that you can remember?'

Miss Marple considered.

'He asked me about Mrs Serrocold's health. In particular, about her heart.'

'Her heart? Is there something wrong with her heart?'

'Nothing whatever, I understand.'

Inspector Curry was silent for a moment or two, then he said:

'You heard a shot this evening during the quarrel between Mr Serrocold and Edgar Lawson?'

'I didn't actually hear it myself. I am a little deaf, you know. But Mrs Serrocold mentioned it as being outside in the park.'

'Mr Gulbrandsen left the party immediately after dinner, I understand?'

'Yes, he said he had letters to write.'

'He didn't show any wish for a business conference with Mr Serrocold?'

'No.'

Miss Marple added:

'You see, they'd already had one little talk.'

'They had? When? I understood that Mr Serrocold only returned home just before dinner.'

'That's quite true, but he walked up through the park, and Mr Gulbrandsen went out to meet him and they walked up and down the terrace together.'

'Who else knows this?'

'I shouldn't think anybody else,' said Miss Marple. 'Unless, of course, Mr Serrocold told Mrs Serrocold. I just happened to be looking out of my window – at some birds.'

572

'Birds?'

'Birds,' Miss Marple added after a moment or two: 'I thought, perhaps, they might be siskins.'

Inspector Curry was uninterested in siskins.

'You didn't,' he said delicately, 'happen to – er – overhear anything of what they said?'

Innocent china blue eyes met his.

'Only fragments, I'm afraid,' said Miss Marple gently.

'And those fragments?'

Miss Marple was silent for a moment, then she said:

'I do not know the actual subject of their conversation, but their immediate concern was to keep whatever it was from the knowledge of Mrs Serrocold. To spare her – that was how Mr Gulbrandsen put it, and Mr Serrocold said, "I agree that it is she who must be considered." They also mentioned a "big responsibility" and that they should, perhaps, "take outside advice."'

She paused.

'I think you know, you had better ask Mr Serrocold himself about all this.'

'We shall do so, m'am. Now there is nothing else that struck you as unusual this evening?'

Miss Marple considered.

'It was all so unusual if you know what I mean – '

'Quite so. Quite so.'

Something flickered into Miss Marple's memory.

'There was one rather unusual incident. Mr Serrocold stopped Mrs Serrocold from taking her medicine. Miss Bellever was quite put out about it.'

She smiled in a deprecating fashion.

'But that, of course, is such a little thing . . .'

'Yes, of course. Well, thank you, Miss Marple.'

As Miss Marple went out of the room, Sergeant Lake said:

'She's old, but she's sharp . . .'

CHAPTER TEN

Lewis Serrocold came into the office and immediately the whole focus of the room shifted. He turned to close the door behind him, and in doing so he created an atmosphere of privacy. He walked over and sat down, not in the chair Miss Marple had just vacated, but in his own chair behind the desk. Miss Bellever had settled Inspector Curry in a chair drawn up to one side of the desk, as though unconsciously she had reserved Lewis Serrocold's chair against his coming.

When he had sat down, Lewis Serrocold looked at the two police officers thoughtfully. His face looked drawn and tired. It was the face of a man who was passing through a severe ordeal, and it surprised Inspector Curry a little because, though Christian Gulbrandsen's death must undeniably have been a shock to Lewis Serrocold, yet Gulbrandsen had not been a close friend or relation, only a rather remote connection by marriage.

In an odd way, the tables seemed to have been turned. It did not seem as though Lewis Serrocold had come into the room to answer police questioning. It seemed rather that Lewis Serrocold had arrived to preside over a court of inquiry. It irritated Inspector Curry a little.

He said briskly:

'Now, Mr Serrocold – '

Lewis Serrocold still seemed lost in thought. He said with a sigh: 'How difficult it is to know the right thing to do.'

Inspector Curry said:

'I think *we* will be the judges of that, Mr Serrocold. Now about Mr Gulbrandsen, he arrived unexpectedly, I understand?'

'Quite unexpectedly.'

'You did not know he was coming.'

'I had not the least idea of it.'

'And you have no idea of why he came?'

Lewis Serrocold said quietly:

'Oh yes, I know why he came. He told me.'

574

'When?'

'I walked up from the station. He was watching from the house and came out to meet me. It was then that he explained what had brought him here.'

'Business connected with the Gulbrandsen Institute, I suppose?'

'Oh no, it was nothing to do with the Gulbrandsen Institute.'

'Miss Bellever seemed to think it was.'

'Naturally. That would be the assumption. Gulbrandsen did nothing to correct that impression. Neither did I.'

'Why, Mr Serrocold?'

Lewis Serrocold said slowly:

'Because it seemed to both of us important that no hint should arise as to the real purpose of his visit.'

'What was the real purpose?'

Lewis Serrocold was silent for a minute or two. He sighed.

'Gulbrandsen came over here regularly twice a year for meetings of the trustees. The last meeting was only a month ago. Consequently he was not due to come over again for another five months. I think, therefore, that anyone might realize that the business that brought him must definitely be urgent business, but I still think that the normal assumption would be that it *was* a business visit, and that the matter, however urgent – would be a Trust matter. As far as I know, Gulbrandsen did nothing to contradict that impression – or thought he didn't. Yes, perhaps that is nearer the truth – he thought he didn't.'

'I'm afraid, Mr Serrocold, that I don't quite follow you.'

Lewis Serrocold did not answer at once. Then he said gravely:

'I fully realize that with Gulbrandsen's death – which was murder, undeniably murder, I have got to put all the facts before you. But frankly, I am concerned for my wife's happiness and peace of mind. It is not for me to dictate to you, Inspector, but if you can see your way to keeping certain things from her as far as possible I shall be grateful. You see, Inspector Curry, Christian Gulbrandsen came here expressly to tell me that he believed my wife was being slowly and cold-bloodedly poisoned.'

'What?'

Curry leaned forward incredulously.

Serrocold nodded.

'Yes, it was, as you can imagine, a tremendous shock to me. I had had no suspicion of such a thing myself, but as soon as Christian told me, I realized that certain symptoms my wife had complained

575

of lately were quite compatible with that belief. What she took to be rheumatism, leg cramps, pain, and occasional sickness. All that fits in very well *with the symptoms of arsenical poisoning*.'

'Miss Marple told us that Christian Gulbrandsen asked her about the condition of Mrs Serrocold's heart.'

'Did he now? That's interesting. I suppose he thought that a heart poison would be used since it paved the way to a sudden death without undue suspicion. But I think myself that arsenic is more likely.'

'You definitely think, then, that Christian Gulbrandsen's suspicions were well founded?'

'Oh yes, I think so. For one thing, Gulbrandsen would hardly come to me with such a suggestion unless he was fairly sure of his facts. He was a cautious and hard-headed man, difficult to convince, but very shrewd.'

'What was his evidence?'

'We had no time to go into that. Our interview was a hurried one. It served only the purpose of explaining his visit, and a mutual agreement that nothing whatever should be said to my wife about the matter until we were sure of our facts.'

'And whom did he suspect of administering poison?'

'He did not say, and actually I don't think he knew. He *may* have suspected. I think now that he probably did suspect – otherwise why should he be killed?'

'But he mentioned no name to you?'

'He mentioned no name. We agreed that we must investigate the matter thoroughly, and he suggested inviting the advice and co-operation of Dr Galbraith, the Bishop of Cromer. Dr Galbraith is a very old friend of the Gulbrandsens and is one of the trustees of the Institute. He is a man of great wisdom and experience and would be of infinite help and comfort to my wife if – if it was necessary to tell her of our suspicions. We meant to rely on his advice as to whether or not to consult the police.'

'Quite extraordinary,' said Curry.

'Gulbrandsen left us after dinner to write to Dr Galbraith. He was actually in the act of typing a letter to him when he was shot.'

'How do you know?'

Lewis said calmly:

'Because I took the letter out of the typewriter. I have it here.'

From his breast pocket, he drew out a folded typewritten sheet of paper and handed it to Curry.

576

The latter said sharply:

'You shouldn't have taken this, or touched anything in the room.'

'I touched nothing else. I know that I committed an unpardonable offence in your eyes in moving this, but I had a very strong reason. I felt certain that my wife would insist on coming into the room and I was afraid that she might read something of what is written here. I admit myself in the wrong, but I am afraid I would do the same again. I would do anything – *anything* – to save my wife unhappiness.'

Inspector Curry said no more for the moment. He read the typewritten sheet.

Dear Dr Galbraith. If it is at all possible, I beg that you will come to Stonygates as soon as you receive this. A crisis of extraordinary gravity has arisen and I am at a loss how to deal with it. I know how deep your affection is for our dear Carrie Louise, and how grave your concern will be for anything that affects her. How much has she got to know? How much can we keep from her? Those are the questions that I find difficult to answer.

Not to beat about the bush, I have reason to believe that that sweet and innocent lady is being slowly poisoned. I first suspected this when –

Here the letter broke off abruptly.

Curry said:

'And when he had reached this point Christian Gulbrandsen was shot?'

'Yes.'

'But why on earth was this letter in the typewriter?'

'I can only conceive of two reasons – one, that the murderer had no idea to whom Gulbrandsen was writing and what was the subject of the letter. Secondly – he may not have had time. He may have heard someone coming and only had just time to escape unobserved.'

'And Gulbrandsen gave you no hint as to whom he suspected – if he did suspect anyone?'

There was, perhaps, a very slight pause before Lewis answered.

'None whatever.'

He added, rather obscurely:

'Christian was a very fair man.'

'How do you think this poison, arsenic or whatever it may be – was or is being administered?'

'I thought over that whilst I was changing for dinner and it seemed to me that the most likely vehicle was some medicine, a tonic, that my wife was taking. As regards food, we all partake of the same dishes and my wife has nothing specially prepared for her. But anyone could add arsenic to the medicine bottle.'

'We must take the medicine and have it analysed.'

Lewis said quietly:

'I already have a sample of it. I took it this evening before dinner.'

From a drawer in the desk he took out a small corked bottle with a red fluid in it.

Inspector Curry said with a curious glance:

'You think of everything, Mr Serrocold.'

'I believe in acting promptly. Tonight, I stopped my wife from taking her usual dose. It is still in a glass on the oak dresser in the Hall – the bottle of tonic itself is in the dining-room.'

Curry leaned forward across the desk. He lowered his voice and spoke confidentially and without officialdom.

'You'll excuse me, Mr Serrocold, but just *why* are you so anxious to keep this from your wife? Are you afraid she'd panic? Surely, for her own sake, it would be as well if she were warned.'

'Yes – yes, that may well be so. But I don't think you quite understand. Without knowing my wife Caroline, it would be difficult. My wife, Inspector Curry, is an idealist, a completely trustful person. Of her it may truly be said that she sees no evil, hears no evil, and speaks no evil. It would be inconceivable to her that anyone could wish to kill her. But we have to go farther than that. It is not just "anyone." It is a case – surely you see that – of someone possibly very near and dear to her . . .'

'So that's what you think?'

'We have got to face facts. Close at hand we have a couple of hundred warped and stunted personalities who have expressed themselves often enough by crude and senseless violence. But by the very nature of things, none of *them* can be suspect in this case. A slow poisoner is someone living in the intimacy of family life. Think of the people who are here in this house; her husband, her daughter, her granddaughter, her granddaughter's husband, her stepson whom she regards as her own son, Miss Bellever her devoted companion and friend of many years. All very near and dear to her – and yet the suspicion must arise – is it one of them?'

Curry said slowly:

'There *are* outsiders – '

'Yes, in a sense. There is Dr Maverick, one or two of the staff

578

are often with us, there are the servants – but frankly, what possible motive could they have?'

Inspector Curry said:

'And there's young – what is his name again – Edgar Lawson?'

'Yes. But he has only been down here as a casual visitor just lately. He has no possible motive. Besides, he is deeply attached to Caroline – just as everyone is.'

'But he's unbalanced. What about this attack on you tonight?'

Serrocold waved it aside impatiently.

'Sheer childishness. He had no intention of harming me.'

'Not with these two bullet holes in the wall? He shot at you, didn't he?'

'He didn't mean to hit me. It was play-acting, no more.'

'Rather a dangerous form of play-acting, Mr Serrocold.'

'You don't understand. You must talk to our psychiatrist, Dr Maverick. Edgar is an illegitimate child. He has consoled himself for his lack of a father and a humble origin by pretending to himself that he is the son of a celebrated man. It's a well-known phenomenon, I assure you. He was improving, improving very much. Then, for some reason, he had a set-back. He identified me as his "father" and made a melodramatic attack, waving a revolver and uttering threats. I was not in the least alarmed. When he had actually fired the revolver, he broke down and sobbed and Dr Maverick took him away and gave him a sedative. He'll probably be quite normal tomorrow morning.'

'You don't wish to bring a charge against him?'

'That would be the worst thing possible – for him, I mean.'

'Frankly, Mr Serrocold, it seems to me he ought to be under restraint. People who go about firing off revolvers to bolster up their egos –! One has to think of the community, you know.'

'Talk to Dr Maverick on the subject,' urged Lewis. 'He'll give you the professional point of view. In any case,' he added, 'poor Edgar certainly did not shoot Gulbrandsen. He was in here threatening to shoot *me*.'

'That's the point I was coming to, Mr Serrocold. We've covered the outside. Anyone, it seems, could have come in from *outside*, and shot Mr Gulbrandsen, since the terrace door was unlocked. But there is a narrower field *inside* the house, and in view of what you have been telling me, it seems to me that very close attention must be paid to that. It seems possible that, with the exception of old Miss – er – yes, Marple, who happened to be looking out of her bedroom window, no one was aware that you and Christian Gulbrandsen had already had a private interview. If so, Gulbrandsen may have been shot to prevent him communicating his suspicions to you. Of course it is too early to say as yet what other motives may exist. Mr Gulbrandsen was a wealthy man, I presume?'

'Yes, he was a very wealthy man. He has sons and daughters and grandchildren – all of them will probably benefit by his death. But I do not think that any of his family are in this country, and they are all solid and highly respectable people. As far as I know, there are no black sheep amongst them.'

'Had he any enemies?'

'I should think it most unlikely. He was – really, he was not that type of man.'

'So it boils down, doesn't it, to this house and the people in it? Who from *inside* the house could have killed him?'

Lewis Serrocold said slowly:

'That is difficult for me to say. There are the servants and the members of my household and our guests. They are, from your point of view, all possibilities, I suppose. I can only tell you that, as far as I know, everyone except the servants was in the Great Hall when Christian left it, and whilst I was there, nobody left it.'

'Nobody at all?'

'I think' – Lewis frowned in an effort of remembrance – 'oh yes. Some of the lights fused – Mr Walter Hudd went to see to it.'

'That's the young American gentleman?'

'Yes – of course I don't know what took place after Edgar and I came in here.'

'And you can't give me anything nearer than that, Mr Serrocold?'

Lewis Serrocold shook his head.

'No, I'm afraid I can't help you. It's – it's all quite inconceivable.'

Inspector Curry sighed. He said: 'Mr Gulbrandsen was shot with a small automatic pistol. Do you know if anyone in the house has such a weapon?'

'I have no idea, I should think it most unlikely.'

Inspector Curry sighed again. He said:

'You can tell the party that they can all go to bed. I'll talk to them tomorrow.'

When Serrocold had left the room, Inspector Curry said to Lake:

'Well – what do you think?'

'Knows – or thinks he knows, who did it,' said Lake.

'Yes. I agree with you. And he doesn't like it a bit . . .'

CHAPTER ELEVEN

Gina greeted Miss Marple with a rush as the latter came down to breakfast the next morning.

'The police are here again,' she said. 'They're in the library this time. Wally is absolutely fascinated by them. He can't understand their being so quiet and so remote. I think he's really quite thrilled by the whole thing. I'm not. I hate it. I think it's horrible. Why do you think I'm so upset? Because I'm half Italian?'

'Very possible. At least perhaps it explains why you don't mind showing what you feel.'

Miss Marple smiled just a little as she said this.

'Jolly's frightfully cross,' said Gina, hanging on Miss Marple's arm and propelling her into the dining-room. 'I think really because the police are in charge and she can't exactly "run" them like she runs everybody else.

'Alex and Stephen,' continued Gina severely, as they came into the dining-room where the two brothers were finishing their breakfast, 'just don't care.'

'Gina dearest,' said Alex, 'you are most unkind. Good morning, Miss Marple. I care intensely. Except for the fact that I hardly knew your Uncle Christian, I'm far and away the best suspect. You do realize that, I hope.'

'Why?'

'Well, I was driving up to the house at about the right time, it seems. And they've been checking up on things, and it seems that I took too much time between the lodge and the house – time enough, the implication is, to leave the car, run round the house, go in through the side door, shoot Christian and rush out and back to the car again.'

'And what were you really doing?'

'I thought little girls were taught quite young not to ask indelicate

581

questions. Like an idiot, I stood for several minutes taking in the fog effect in the headlights and thinking what I'd use to get that effect on a stage. For my new "Limehouse" ballet.'

'But you can tell them that!'

'Naturally. But you know what policemen are like. They say "thank you" very civilly and write it all down, and you've no idea *what* they are thinking except that one does feel they have rather sceptical minds.'

'It would amuse me to see you in a spot, Alex,' said Stephen with his thin, rather cruel smile. 'Now, *I'm* quite all right! I never left the Hall last night.'

Gina cried, 'But they couldn't possibly think it was one of *us*!'

Her dark eyes were round and dismayed.

'Don't say it must have been a tramp, dear,' said Alex, helping himself lavishly to marmalade. 'It's so hackneyed.'

Miss Bellever looked in at the door and said:

'Miss Marple, when you have finished your breakfast, will you go to the library?'

'You again,' said Gina. 'Before any of us.'

She seemed a little injured.

'Hi, what was that?' asked Alex.

'Didn't hear anything,' said Stephen.

'It was a pistol shot.'

'They've been firing shots in the room where Uncle Christian was killed,' said Gina. 'I don't know why. And outside too.'

The door opened again and Mildred Strete came in. She was wearing black with some onyx beads.

She murmured good morning without looking at anyone and sat down.

In a hushed voice she said:

'Some tea, please, Gina. Nothing much to eat – just some toast.'

She touched her nose and her eyes delicately with the handkerchief she held in one hand. Then she raised her eyes and looked in an unseeing way at the two brothers. Stephen and Alex became uncomfortable. Their voices dropped to almost a whisper and presently they got up and left.

Mildred Strete said, whether to the universe or Miss Marple was not quite certain, 'Not even a black tie!'

'I don't suppose,' said Miss Marple apologetically, 'that they knew beforehand that a murder was going to happen.'

Gina made a smothered sound and Mildred Strete looked sharply at her.

'Where's Walter this morning?' she asked.

Gina flushed.

'I don't know. I haven't seen him.'

She sat there uneasily like a guilty child.

Miss Marple got up.

'I'll go to the library now,' she said.

II

Lewis Serrocold was standing by the window in the library.

There was no one else in the room.

He turned as Miss Marple came in and came forward to meet her, taking her hand in his.

'I hope,' he said, 'that you are not feeling the worse for the shock. To be at close quarters with what is undoubtedly murder must be a great strain on anyone who has not come in contact with such a thing before.'

Modesty forbade Miss Marple to reply that she was, by now, quite at home with murder. She merely said that life in St Mary Mead was not quite so sheltered as outside people believed.

'Very nasty things go on in a village, I assure you,' she said. 'One has an opportunity of studying things there that one would never have in a town.'

Lewis Serrocold listened indulgently, but with only half an ear.

He said very simply: 'I want your help.'

'But of course, Mr Serrocold.'

'It is a matter that affects my wife – affects Caroline. I think that you are really attached to her?'

'Yes, indeed. Everyone is.'

'That is what I believed. It seems that I am wrong. With the permission of Inspector Curry, I am going to tell you something that no one else as yet knows. Or perhaps I should say what only one person knows.'

Briefly, he told her what he had told Inspector Curry the night before.

Miss Marple looked horrified.

'I can't believe it, Mr Serrocold. I really can't believe it.'

'That is what I felt when Christian Gulbrandsen told me.'

'I should have said that dear Carrie Louise had not got an enemy in the world.'

'It seems incredible that she should have. But you see the implication? Poisoning – slow poisoning – is an intimate family matter. It must be one of our closely-knit little household – '

'If it is *true*. Are you sure that Mr Gulbrandsen was not mistaken?'

'Christian was not mistaken. He is too cautious a man to make such a statement without foundation. Besides, the police took away Caroline's medicine bottle and a separate sample of its contents. There was arsenic in both of them – and arsenic was not prescribed. The actual quantitative tests will take longer – but the actual fact of arsenic being present is established.'

'Then her rheumatism – the difficulty in walking – all that – '

'Yes, leg cramps are typical, I understand. Also, before you came, Caroline has had one or two severe attacks of a gastric nature – I never dreamed until Christian came – '

He broke off. Miss Marple said softly: 'So Ruth was right!'

'Ruth?'

Lewis Serrocold sounded surprised. Miss Marple flushed.

'There is something I have not told you. My coming here was not entirely fortuitous. If you will let me explain – I'm afraid I tell things so badly. Please have patience.'

Lewis Serrocold listened whilst Miss Marple told him of Ruth's unease and urgency.

'Extraordinary,' he commented. 'I had no idea of this.'

'It was all so vague,' said Miss Marple. 'Ruth herself didn't know why she had this feeling. There must be a reason – in my experience there always is – but "something wrong" was as near as she could get.'

Lewis Serrocold said grimly:

'Well, it seems that she was right. Now, Miss Marple, you see how I am placed. Am I to tell Carrie Louise of this?'

Miss Marple said quickly: 'Oh no,' in a distressed voice, and then flushed and stared doubtfully at Lewis. He nodded.

'So you feel as I do? As Christian Gulbrandsen did. Should we feel like that with an ordinary woman?'

'Carrie Louise is *not* an ordinary woman. She lives by her trust, by her belief in human nature – oh dear, I am expressing myself very badly. But I do feel that until we know who – '

'Yes, that is the crux. But you do see, Miss Marple, that there is a risk in saying nothing – '

'And so you want me to – how shall I put it? – watch over her?'

'You see, you are the only person whom I can trust,' said Lewis Serrocold simply. 'Everyone here *seems* devoted. But are they? Now your attachment goes back many years.'

'And also I only arrived a few days ago,' said Miss Marple pertinently.

Lewis Serrocold smiled.

'Exactly.'

'It is a very mercenary question,' said Miss Marple apologetically. 'But who exactly would benefit if dear Carrie Louise were to die?'

'Money!' said Lewis bitterly. 'It always boils down to money, doesn't it?'

'Well, I really think it must be in this case. Because Carrie Louise is a very sweet person with a great deal of charm, and one cannot really imagine anyone disliking her. She couldn't, I mean, have an *enemy*. So then it does boil down, as you put it, to a question of money, because as you don't need me to tell you, Mr Serrocold, people will quite often do anything for money.'

'I suppose so, yes.'

He went on: 'Naturally Inspector Curry has already taken up that point. Mr Gilfoy is coming down from London today and can give detailed information. Gilfoy, Gilfoy, Jaimes and Gilfoy are a very eminent firm of lawyers. This Gilfoy's father was one of the original trustees, and they drew up both Caroline's will and the original will of Eric Gulbrandsen. I will put it in simple terms for you – '

'Thank you,' said Miss Marple gratefully. 'So mystifying the law, I always think.'

'Eric Gulbrandsen, after endowment of the College and various fellowships and trusts and other charitable bequests, and having settled an equal sum on his daughter Mildred and on his adopted daughter Pippa (Gina's mother), left the remainder of his vast fortune in trust, the income from it to be paid to Caroline for her lifetime.'

'And after her death?'

'After her death it was to be divided equally between Mildred and Pippa – or their children if they themselves had predeceased Caroline.'

'So that in fact it goes to Mrs Strete and to Gina.'

'Yes. Caroline has also quite a considerable fortune of her own –

though not in the Gulbrandsen class. Half of this she made over to me four years ago. Of the remaining amount, she left ten thousand pounds to Juliet Bellever, and the rest equally divided between Alex and Stephen Restarick, her two stepsons.'

'Oh dear,' said Miss Marple. 'That's bad. That's very bad.'

'You mean?'

'It means everyone in the house had a financial motive.'

'Yes. And yet, you know, I can't believe that any of these people would do murder. I simply can't . . . Mildred is her daughter – and already quite well provided for. Gina is devoted to her grandmother. She is generous and extravagant, but has no acquisitive feelings. Jolly Bellever is fanatically devoted to Caroline. The two Restaricks care for Caroline as though she were really their mother. They have no money of their own to speak of, but quite a lot of Caroline's income has gone towards financing their enterprises – especially so with Alex. I simply can't believe either of those two would deliberately poison her for the sake of inheriting money at her death. I just can't believe any of it, Miss Marple.'

'There's Gina's husband, isn't there?'

'Yes,' said Lewis gravely. 'There is Gina's husband.'

'You don't really know much about him. And one can't help seeing that he's a very unhappy young man.'

Lewis sighed.

'He hasn't fitted in here – no. He's no interest in or sympathy for what we're trying to do. But after all, why should he? He's young, crude, and he comes from a country where a man is esteemed by the success he makes of life.'

'Whilst here we are so very fond of failures,' said Miss Marple.

Lewis Serrocold looked at her sharply and suspiciously.

She flushed a little and murmured rather incoherently:

'I think sometimes, you know, one can overdo things the other way . . . I mean the young people with a good heredity, and brought up wisely in a good home – and with grit and pluck and the ability to get on in life – well, they are really, when one comes down to it – the sort of people a country *needs*.'

Lewis frowned and Miss Marple hurried on, getting pinker and pinker and more and more incoherent.

'Not that I don't appreciate – I do indeed – you and Carrie Louise – a really noble work – real compassion – and one should have compassion – because after all it's what people *are* that counts – good and bad luck – and much more expected (and rightly) of the lucky ones. But I do think sometimes one's sense of proportion – oh, I don't mean *you*, Mr Serrocold. Really I don't know *what* I mean – but the English *are* rather odd that way. Even in war, so much prouder of their defeats and their retreats than of their victories. Foreigners never can understand why we're so proud of Dunkirk. It's the sort of thing they'd prefer not to mention themselves. But we always seem to be almost embarrassed by a victory – and treat it as though it weren't quite nice to boast about it. And look at all our poets! The Charge of the Light Brigade, and the little *Revenge* went down in the Spanish Main. It's really a very odd characteristic when you come to think of it!'

Miss Marple drew a fresh breath.

'What I really mean is that everything here must seem rather peculiar to young Walter Hudd.'

'Yes,' Lewis allowed. 'I see your point. And Walter has certainly a fine war record. There's no doubt about his bravery.'

'Not that that helps,' said Miss Marple candidly. 'Because war is one thing, and everyday life is quite another. And actually to commit a murder, I think you do need bravery – or perhaps, more often, just conceit. Yes, conceit.'

'But I would hardly say that Walter Hudd had a sufficient motive.'

'Wouldn't you?' said Miss Marple. 'He hates it here. He wants to get away. He wants to get Gina away. And if it's really money he wants, it would be important for Gina to get all the money before she – er – definitely forms an attachment to someone else.'

'An attachment to someone else,' said Lewis, in an astonished voice.

Miss Marple wondered at the blindness of enthusiastic social reformers.

'That's what I said. Both the Restaricks are in love with her, you know.'

'Oh, I don't think so,' said Lewis absently.

He went on:

'Stephen's invaluable to us – quite invaluable. The way he's got those lads coming along – keen – interested. They gave a splendid show last month. Scenery, costumes, everything. It just shows, as I've always said to Maverick, that it's lack of drama in their lives that leads these boys to crime. To dramatize yourself is a child's natural instinct. Maverick says – ah yes, Maverick – '

Lewis broke off.

'I want Maverick to see Inspector Curry about Edgar. The whole thing is so ridiculous really.'

'What do you really know about Edgar Lawson, Mr Serrocold?'

'Everything,' said Lewis positively. 'Everything, that is, that one needs to know. His background, upbringing – his deep-seated lack of confidence in himself – '

Miss Marple interrupted.

'Couldn't Edgar Lawson have poisoned Mrs Serrocold?' she asked.

'Hardly. He's only been here a few weeks. And anyway, it's ridiculous! Why should Edgar want to poison my wife? What could he possibly gain by doing so?'

'Nothing material, I know. But he might have – some *odd* reason. He *is* odd, you know.'

'You mean unbalanced?'

'I suppose so. No, I don't – not quite. What I mean is, he's all *wrong*.'

It was not a very lucid exposition of what she felt. Lewis Serrocold accepted the words at their face value.

'Yes,' he said with a sigh. 'He's all wrong, poor lad. And he was showing such marked improvement. I can't really understand why he had this sudden set-back . . .'

Miss Marple leaned forward eagerly.

'Yes, that's what I wondered. If – '

She broke off as Inspector Curry came into the room.

CHAPTER TWELVE

Lewis Serrocold went away, and Inspector Curry sat down and gave Miss Marple a rather peculiar smile.

'So Mr Serrocold has been asking you to act as watch dog,' he said.

'Well, yes,' she added apologetically: 'I hope you don't mind – '

'*I* don't mind. I think it's a very good idea. Does Mr Serrocold know just how well qualified you are for the post?'

'I don't quite understand, Inspector.'

'I see. He thinks you're just a very nice elderly lady who was at school with his wife.' He shook his head at her. 'We know you're a bit more than that, Miss Marple, aren't you? Crime is right down your street. Mr Serrocold only knows one aspect of crime – the promising beginners. Makes me a bit sick, sometimes. Daresay I'm wrong and old-fashioned. But there are plenty of good decent lads about, lads who could do with a start in life. But there, honesty has to be its own reward – millionaires don't leave trust funds to help the worthwhile. Well – well, don't pay any attention to me. I'm old-fashioned. I've seen boys – and girls – with everything against them, bad homes, bad luck, every disadvantage, and they've had the grit to win through. That's the kind I shall leave my packet to, if I ever have one. But then, of course, that's what I never shall have. Just my pension and a nice bit of garden.'

He nodded his head at Miss Marple.

'Superintendent Blacker told me about you last night. Said you'd had a lot of experience of the seamy side of human nature. Well now, let's have your point of view. Who's the nigger in the woodpile? The G.I. husband?'

'That,' said Miss Marple, 'would be very convenient for everybody.'

Inspector Curry smiled softly to himself.

'A G.I. pinched my best girl,' he said reminiscently. 'Naturally, I'm prejudiced. His manner doesn't help. Let's have the amateur point of view. Who's been secretly and systematically poisoning Mrs Serrocold?'

'Well,' said Miss Marple judicially, 'one is always inclined, human nature being what it is, to think of the *husband*. Or if it's the other way round, the wife. That's the first assumption, don't you think, in a poisoning case?'

'I agree with you every time,' said Inspector Curry.

'But really – in this case – ' Miss Marple shook her head. 'No, frankly – I can *not* seriously consider Mr Serrocold. Because you see, Inspector, he really *is* devoted to his wife. Naturally he would make a parade of being so – but it isn't a parade. It's very quiet, but it's genuine. He loves his wife, and I'm quite certain that he wouldn't poison her.'

'To say nothing of the fact that he wouldn't have any motive for doing so. She's made over her money to him already.'

'Of course,' said Miss Marple primly, 'there are other reasons for a gentleman wanting his wife out of the way. An attachment to a young woman, for instance. But I really don't see any signs of it in this case. Mr Serrocold does not act as though he had any romantic preoccupation. I'm really afraid,' she sounded quite regretful about it, 'we shall have to wash him out.'

'Regrettable, isn't it?' said the Inspector. He grinned. 'And anyway, he couldn't have killed Gulbrandsen. It seems to me that there's no doubt that the one thing hinges on the other. Whoever is poisoning Mrs Serrocold killed Gulbrandsen to prevent him spilling the beans. What we've got to get at now is who had an opportunity to kill Gulbrandsen last night. And our prize suspect – there's no doubt about it – is young Walter Hudd. It was he who switched on a reading lamp which resulted in a fuse going, thereby giving him the opportunity to leave the Hall and go to the fuse box. The fuse box is in the kitchen passage which opens off from the main corridor. It was during his absence from the Great Hall that the shot was heard. So that's suspect No. 1 perfectly placed for committing the crime.'

'And suspect No. 2?' asked Miss Marple.

'Suspect No. 2 is Alex Restarick, who was alone in his car between the lodge and the house and took too long getting there.'

'Anybody else?' Miss Marple leaned forward eagerly – remembering to add: 'It's very kind of you to tell me all this.'

'It's not kindness,' said Inspector Curry. 'I've got to have your help. You put your finger on the spot when you said "Anybody else?" Because there I've got to depend on *you*. You were there, in the Hall last night, and you can tell me *who left it* . . .'

'Yes – yes, I ought to be able to tell you . . . But can I? You see – the circumstances – '

'You mean that you were all listening to the argument going on behind the door of Mr Serrocold's study.'

Miss Marple nodded vehemently.

'Yes, you see we were all really very frightened. Mr Lawson looked – he really did – quite demented. Apart from Mrs Serrocold, who seemed quite unaffected, we all feared that he would do a mischief to Mr Serrocold. He was shouting, you know, and saying the most terrible things – we could hear them quite plainly – and what with that and with most of the lights being out – I didn't really notice anything else.'

'You mean that whilst that scene was going on, anybody could have slipped out of the Hall, gone along the corridor, shot Mr Gulbrandsen and slipped back again?'

'I think it would have been possible . . .'

'Could you say definitely that anybody was in the Great Hall the whole time?'

Miss Marple considered.

'I could say that Mrs Serrocold was – because I was watching her. She was sitting quite close to the study door, and she never moved from her seat. It surprised me, you know, that she was able to remain so calm.'

'And the others?'

'Miss Bellever went out – but I think – I am almost sure – that that was *after* the shot. Mrs Strete? I really don't know. She was sitting behind me, you see. Gina was over by the far window. I *think* she remained there the whole time but of course I cannot be sure. Stephen was at the piano. He stopped playing when the quarrel began to get heated – '

'We mustn't be misled by the time you heard the shot,' said Inspector Curry. 'That's a trick that's been done before now, you know. Fake up a shot so as to fix the time of a crime, and fix it wrong. *If* Miss Bellever had cooked up something of that kind (far fetched – but you never know) then she'd leave as she did, openly, after the shot was heard. No, we can't go by the shot. The limits are between when Christian Gulbrandsen left the Hall to the moment when Miss Bellever found him dead, and we can only eliminate those people who were known not to have had opportunity. That gives us Lewis Serrocold and young Edgar Lawson in the study, and Mrs Serrocold in the Hall. It's very unfortunate, of course, that Gulbrandsen should be shot on the same evening that this schemozzle happened between Serrocold and this young Lawson.'

'Just unfortunate, you think?' murmured Miss Marple.

'Oh? What do you think?'

'It occurred to me,' murmured Miss Marple, 'that it might have been *contrived*.'

'So that's your idea?'

'Well, everybody seems to think it very odd that Edgar Lawson should quite suddenly have a relapse, so to speak. He'd got this curious complex, or whatever the term is, about his unknown father. Winston Churchill and Viscount Montgomery – all quite likely in his state of mind. Just any famous man he happened to think of. But suppose somebody puts it into his head that it's Lewis Serrocold who is really his father, that it's Lewis Serrocold who has been persecuting him – that he ought by rights to be the Crown Prince as it were of Stonygates. In his weak mental state he'll accept the idea – work himself up into a frenzy, and sooner or later will make the kind of scene he did make. And what a wonderful cover *that* will be! Everybody will have their attention fixed on the dangerous situation that is developing – especially if somebody has thoughtfully supplied him with a revolver.'

'Hm, yes. Walter Hudd's revolver.'

'Oh yes,' said Miss Marple, 'I'd thought of that. But you know, Walter is uncommunicative and he's certainly sullen and ungracious, but I don't really think he's *stupid*.'

'So you don't think it's Walter?'

'I think everybody would be very relieved if it *was* Walter. That sounds very unkind, but it's because he is an outsider.'

'What about his wife?' asked Inspector Curry. 'Would she be relieved?'

Miss Marple did not answer. She was thinking of Gina and Stephen Restarick standing together as she had seen them on her first day. And she thought of the way Alex Restarick's eyes had gone straight to Gina as he had entered the Hall last night. What was Gina's own attitude?

II

Two hours later Inspector Curry tilted back his chair, stretched himself and sighed.

'Well,' he said, 'we've cleared a good deal of ground.'

Sergeant Lake agreed.

'The servants are out,' he said. 'They were together all through the critical period – those that sleep here. The ones that don't live in had gone home.'

Curry nodded. He was suffering from mental fatigue.

He had interviewed physio-therapists, members of the teaching staff, and what he called to himself the 'two young lags,' whose turn it had been to dine with the family that night. All their stories dovetailed and checked. He could write them off. Their activities and habits were communal. There were no lonely souls among them. Which was useful for the purposes of alibis. Curry had kept Dr Maverick, who was, as far as he could judge, the chief person in charge of the Institute, to the end.

592

'But we'll have him in now, Lake.'

So the young doctor bustled in, neat and spruce and rather inhuman looking behind his pince-nez.

Maverick confirmed the statements of his staff, and agreed with Curry's findings. There had been no slackness, no loophole in the College impregnability. Christian Gulbrandsen's death could not be laid to the account of the 'young patients,' as Curry almost called them, so hypnotized had he become by the fervent medical atmosphere.

'But patients are exactly what they are, Inspector,' said Dr Maverick with a little smile.

It was a superior smile, and Inspector Curry would not have been human if he had not resented it just a little.

He said professionally:

'Now as regards your own movements, Dr Maverick? Can you give me an account of them?'

'Certainly. I have jotted them down for you with approximate times.'

Dr Maverick had left the Great Hall at fifteen minutes after nine, with Mr Lacy and Dr Baumgarten. They had gone to Dr Baumgarten's rooms, where they had all three remained discussing certain courses of treatment until Miss Bellever had come hurrying in and asked Dr Maverick to go to the Great Hall. That was at approximately half-past nine. He had gone at once to the Hall and had found Edgar Lawson in a state of collapse.

Inspector Curry stirred a little.

'Just a minute, Dr Maverick. Is this young man, in your opinion, definitely a mental case?'

Dr Maverick smiled the superior smile again.

'We are all mental cases, Inspector Curry.'

Tomfool answer, thought the Inspector. He knew quite well *he* wasn't a mental case, whatever Dr Maverick might be!

'Is he responsible for his actions? He knows what he is doing, I suppose?'

'Perfectly.'

'Then when he fired that revolver at Mr Serrocold it was definitely attempted murder.'

'No, no, Inspector Curry. Nothing of *that* kind.'

'Come now, Dr Maverick. I've seen the two bullet holes in the wall. They must have gone dangerously near to Mr Serrocold's head.'

'Perhaps. But Lawson had no intention of killing Mr Serrocold or even of wounding him. He is very fond of Mr Serrocold.'

'It seems a curious way of showing it.'

Dr Maverick smiled again. Inspector Curry found that smile very trying.

'Everything one does is intentional. Every time you, Inspector, forget a name or a face it is because, unconsciously, you *wish* to forget it.'

Inspector Curry looked unbelieving.

'Every time you make a slip of the tongue, that slip has a meaning. Edgar Lawson was standing a few feet away from Mr Serrocold. He could easily have shot him dead. Instead, he missed him. Why did he miss him? Because he *wanted* to miss him. It is as simple as that. Mr Serrocold was never in any danger – and Mr Serrocold himself was quite aware of that fact. He understood Edgar's gesture for exactly what it was – a gesture of defiance and resentment against a universe that has denied him the simple necessities of a child's life – security and affection.'

'I think I'd like to see this young man.'

'Certainly if you wish. His outburst last night has had a cathartic effect. There is a great improvement today. Mr Serrocold will be very pleased.'

Inspector Curry stared hard at him, but Dr Maverick was serious as always.

Curry sighed.

'Do you have any arsenic?' he asked.

'Arsenic?' The question took Dr Maverick by surprise. It was clearly unexpected. 'What a very curious question. Why arsenic?'

'Just answer the question, please.'

'No, I have no arsenic of any kind in my possession.'

'But you have some drugs?'

'Oh certainly. Sedatives. Morphia – the barbiturates. The usual things.'

'Do you attend Mrs Serrocold?'

'No. Dr Gunter of Market Kimble is the family physician. I hold a medical degree, of course, but I practise purely as a psychiatrist.'

'I see. Well, thank you very much, Dr Maverick.'

As Dr Maverick went out, Inspector Curry murmured to Lake that psychiatrists gave him a pain in the neck.

'We'll get on to the family now,' he said. 'I'll see young Walter Hudd first.'

594

Walter Hudd's attitude was cautious. He seemed to be studying the police officer with a slightly wary expression. But he was quite co-operative.

There was a good deal of defective wiring in Stonygates – the whole electric system was very old-fashioned. They wouldn't stand for a system like that in the States.

'It was installed, I believe, by the late Mr Gulbrandsen when electric light was a novelty,' said Inspector Curry with a faint smile.'

'I'll say so! Sweet old feudal English and never been brought up to date.'

The fuse which controlled most of the lights in the Great Hall had gone, and he had gone out to the fuse-box to see about it. In due course he got it repaired and came back.

'How long were you away?'

'Why that I couldn't say for sure. The fuse-box is in an awkward place. I had to get steps and a candle. I was maybe ten minutes – perhaps a quarter of an hour.'

'Did you hear a shot?'

'Why no, I didn't hear anything like that. There are double doors through to the kitchen quarters and one of them is lined with a kind of felt.'

'I see. And when you came back into the Hall, what did you see?'

'They were all crowded round the door into Mr Serrocold's study. Mrs Strete said that Mr Serrocold had been shot – but actually that wasn't so. Mr Serrocold was quite all right. The boob had missed him.'

'You recognized the revolver?'

'Sure I recognized it! It was mine.'

'When did you see it last?'

'Two or three days ago.'

'Where did you keep it?'

'In the drawer in my room.'

'Who knew that you kept it there?'

'I wouldn't know who knows what in this house.'

'What do you mean by that, Mr Hudd?'

'Aw, they're all nuts!'

'When you came into the Hall, was everybody else there?'

'What d'you mean by everybody?'

'The same people who were there when you went to repair the fuse.'

'Gina was there . . . and the old lady with white hair – and Miss Bellever . . . I didn't notice particularly – but I should say so.'

'Mr Gulbrandsen arrived quite unexpectedly the day before yesterday, did he not?'

'I guess so. It wasn't his usual routine, I understand.'

'Did anyone seem upset by his arrival?'

Walter Hudd took a moment or two before he answered:

'Why no, I wouldn't say so.'

Once more there was a touch of caution in his manner.

'Have you any idea why he came?'

'Their precious Gulbrandsen Trust I suppose. The whole set-up here is crazy.'

'You have these "set-ups" as you call it, in the States.'

'It's one thing to endow a scheme, and another to give it the personal touch as they do here. I had enough of psychiatrists in the Army. This place is stiff with them. Teaching young thugs to make raffia baskets and carve pipe-racks. Kids' games! It's sissy!'

Inspector Curry did not comment on this criticism. Possibly he agreed with it.

He said, eying Walter carefully:

'So you have no idea who could have killed Mr Gulbrandsen?'

'One of the bright boys from the College practising his technique, I'd say.'

'No, Mr Hudd, that's out. The College, in spite of its carefully produced atmosphere of freedom, is none the less a place of detention and is run on those lines. Nobody can run in and out of it after dark and commit murders.'

'I wouldn't put it past them! Well – if you want to fix it nearer home, I'd say your best bet was Alex Restarick.'

'Why do you say that?'

'He had the opportunity. He drove up through the grounds alone in his car.'

'And why should he kill Christian Gulbrandsen?'

Walter shrugged his shoulders.

'I'm a stranger. I don't know the family set-ups. Maybe the old boy had heard something about Alex and was going to spill the beans to the Serrocolds.'

'With what results?'

'They might cut off the dough. He can use dough – uses a good deal of it by all accounts.'

'You mean – in theatrical enterprises?'

'That's what he calls it?'

'Do you suggest it was otherwise?'

Again Walter Hudd shrugged his shoulders.

'I wouldn't know,' he said.

CHAPTER THIRTEEN

Alex Restarick was voluble. He also gestured with his hands.

'I know, I know! I'm the ideal suspect. I drive down here alone and on the way to the house, I get a creative fit. I can't expect you to understand. How should you?'

'I might,' Curry put in drily, but Alex Restarick swept on.

'It's just one of those things! They come upon you there's no knowing when or how. An effect – an idea – and everything else goes to the winds! I'm producing *Limehouse Nights* next month. Suddenly – last night – the set-up was wonderful . . . *The* perfect lighting. Fog – and the headlights cutting through the fog and being thrown back – and reflecting dimly a tall pile of buildings. Everything helped! The shots – the running footsteps – and the chug-chugging of the electric power engine – could have been a launch on the Thames. And I thought – that's it – but what am I going to use to get just these effects? – and – '

Inspector Curry broke in.

'You heard shots? Where?'

'Out of the fog, Inspector.' Alex waved his hands in the air – plump well-kept hands. 'Out of the fog. That was the wonderful part about it.'

'It didn't occur to you that anything was wrong?'

'Wrong? Why should it?'

'Are shots such a usual occurrence?'

'Ah, I knew you wouldn't understand! The shots fitted into the scene I was creating. I *wanted* shots. Danger – opium – crazy business. What did I care what they were really? Backfires from a lorry on the road? A poacher after rabbits?'

'They snare rabbits mostly round here.'

Alex swept on:

'A child letting off fireworks? I didn't even think about them *as*
– shots. I was in Limehouse – or rather at the back of the stalls –
looking at Limehouse.'

'How many shots?'

'I don't know,' said Alex petulantly. 'Two or three. Two close
together, I do remember that.'

Inspector Curry nodded.

'And the sound of running footsteps, I think you said? Where
were they?'

'They came to me out of the fog. Somewhere near the house.'

Inspector Curry said gently:

'That would suggest that the murderer of Christian Gulbrandsen
came from *outside*.'

'Of course. Why not? You don't really suggest, do you, that he
came from inside the house?'

Still very gently Inspector Curry said:

'We have to think of everything.'

'I suppose so,' said Alex Restarick generously. 'What a soul-
destroying job yours must be, Inspector! The details, the times
and places, the pettifogging *pettiness* of it. And in the end – what
good is it all? Does it bring the wretched Christian Gulbrandsen
back to life?'

'There's quite a satisfaction in getting your man, Mr Restarick.'

'The Wild Western touch!'

'Did you know Mr Gulbrandsen well?'

'Not well enough to murder him, Inspector. I had met him, off
and on, since I lived here as a boy. He made brief appearances from
time to time. One of our captains of industry. The type does not
interest me. He has quite a collection, I believe, of Thorwaldsen's
statuary – ' Alex shuddered. 'That speaks for itself, does it not? My
God, these rich men!'

Inspector Curry eyed him meditatively. Then he said: 'Do you
take any interest in poisons, Mr Restarick?'

'In poisons? My dear man, he was surely not poisoned first and
shot afterwards. That would be too madly detective story.'

'He was not poisoned. But you haven't answered my question.'

'Poison has a certain appeal . . . It has not the crudeness of the
revolver bullet or the blunt weapon. I have no special knowledge
of the subject, if that is what you mean.'

'Have you ever had arsenic in your possession?'

598

'In sandwiches – after the show? The idea has its allurements. You don't know Rose Glidon? These actresses who think they have a name! No I have never thought of arsenic. One extracts it from weed killer or flypapers, I believe.'

'How often are you down here, Mr Restarick?'

'It varies, Inspector. Sometimes not for several weeks. But I try to get down for weekends whenever I can. I always regard Stonygates as my true home.'

'Mrs Serrocold has encouraged you to do so?'

'What I owe Mrs Serrocold can never be repaid. Sympathy, understanding, affection – '

'And quite a lot of solid cash as well, I believe?'

Alex looked faintly disgusted.

'She treats me as a son, and she has belief in my work.'

'Has she ever spoken to you about her will?'

'Certainly. But may I ask what is the point of all these questions, Inspector? There is nothing wrong with Mrs Serrocold.'

'There had better not be,' said Inspector Curry grimly.

'Now what can you possibly mean by that?'

'If you don't know, so much the better,' said Inspector Curry. 'And if you do – I'm warning you.'

When Alex had gone Sergeant Lake said:

'Pretty bogus, would you say?'

Curry shook his head.

'Difficult to say. He may have genuine creative talent. He may just like living soft and talking big. One doesn't know. Heard running footsteps, did he? I'd be prepared to bet he made that up.'

'For any particular reason?'

'Definitely for a particular reason. We haven't come to it yet, but we will.'

'After all, sir, one of those smart lads may have got out of the College buildings unbeknownst. Probably a few cat burglars amongst them, and if so – '

'That's what we're meant to think. Very convenient. But if that's so, Lake, I'll eat my new soft hat.'

II

'I was at the piano,' said Stephen Restarick. 'I'd been strumming softly when the row blew up. Between Lewis and Edgar.'

'What did you think of it?'

'Well – to tell the truth I didn't really take it seriously. The poor beggar has these fits of venom. He's not really loopy, you know. All this nonsense is a kind of blowing off steam. The truth is, we all get under his skin – particularly Gina, of course.'

'Gina? You mean Mrs Hudd? Why does she get under his skin?'

'Because she's a woman – and a very beautiful woman, and because she thinks he's funny! She's half Italian, you know, and the Italians have that unconscious vein of cruelty. They've no compassion for anyone who's old or ugly, or peculiar in any way. They point with their fingers and jeer. That's what Gina did, metaphorically speaking. She'd no use for young Edgar. He was ridiculous, pompous, and at bottom fundamentally unsure of himself. He wanted to impress, and he only succeeded in looking silly. It wouldn't mean anything to her that the poor fellow suffered a lot.'

'Are you suggesting that Edgar Lawson is in love with Mrs Hudd?' asked Inspector Curry.

Stephen replied cheerfully:

'Oh yes. As a matter of fact we all are, more or less! She likes us that way.'

'Does her husband like it?'

'He takes a dim view. He suffers, too, poor fellow. The thing can't last, you know. Their marriage, I mean. It will break up before long. It was just one of these war affairs.'

'This is all very interesting,' said the Inspector. 'But we're getting away from our subject, which is the murder of Christian Gulbrandsen.'

'Quite,' said Stephen. 'But I can't tell you anything about it. I sat at the piano, and I didn't leave the piano until dear Jolly came in with some rusty old keys and tried to fit one to the lock of the study door.'

'You stayed at the piano. Did you continue to play the piano?'

'A gentle obbligato to the life and death struggle in Lewis's study? No, I stopped playing when the tempo rose. Not that I had any doubts as to the outcome. Lewis has what I can only describe as a dynamic eye. He could easily break up Edgar just by looking at him.'

'Yet Edgar Lawson fired two shots at him.'

Stephen shook his head gently.

'Just putting on an act, that was. Enjoying himself. My dear mother used to do it. She died or ran away with someone when I was four, but I remember her blazing off with a pistol if anything

600

upset her. She did it at a night club once. Made a pattern on the wall. She was an excellent shot. Quite a bit of trouble she caused. She was a Russian dancer, you know.'

'Indeed. Can you tell me, Mr Restarick, who left the Hall yesterday evening whilst you were there – during the relevant time?'

'Wally – to fix the lights. Juliet Bellever to find a key to fit the study door. Nobody else, as far as I know.'

'Would you have noticed if somebody did?'

Stephen considered.

'Probably not. That is, if they just tiptoed out and back again. It was so dark in the Hall – and there was the fight to which we were all listening avidly.'

'Is there anyone you are sure *was* there the whole time?'

'Mrs Serrocold – yes, and Gina. I'd swear to them.'

'Thank you, Mr Restarick.'

Stephen went towards the door. Then he hesitated and came back.

'What's all this,' he said, 'about arsenic?'

'Who mentioned arsenic to you?'

'My brother.'

'Ah – yes.'

Stephen said:

'Has somebody been giving Mrs Serrocold arsenic?'

'Why should you mention Mrs Serrocold?'

'I've read of the symptoms of arsenical poisoning. Peripheral neuritis, isn't it? It would square more or less with what she's been suffering from lately. And then Lewis snatching away her tonic last night. Is *that* what's been going on here?'

'The matter is under investigation,' said Inspector Curry in his most official manner.

'Does she know about it herself?'

'Mr Serrocold was particularly anxious that she should not be – alarmed.'

'Alarmed isn't the right word, Inspector. Mrs Serrocold is never alarmed . . . Is that what lies behind Christian Gulbrandsen's death? Did he find out she was being poisoned – but how could he find out? Anyway, the whole thing seems most improbable. It doesn't make sense.'

'It surprises you very much, does it, Mr Restarick?'

'Yes, indeed. When Alex spoke to me I could hardly believe it.'

'Who, in your opinion, would be likely to administer arsenic to Mrs Serrocold?'

For a moment a grin appeared upon Stephen Restarick's handsome face.

'Not the usual person. You can wash out the husband. Lewis Serrocold's got nothing to gain. And also he worships that woman. He can't bear her to have an ache in her little finger.'

'Who then? Have you any idea?'

'Oh yes. I'd say it was a certainty.'

'Explain, please.'

Stephen shook his head.

'It's a certainty psychologically speaking. Not in any other way. No evidence of any kind. And you probably wouldn't agree.'

Stephen Restarick went out nonchalantly, and Inspector Curry drew cats on the sheet of paper in front of him.

He was thinking three things. A, that Stephen Restarick thought a good deal of himself; B, that Stephen Restarick and his brother presented a united front; and C, that Stephen Restarick was a handsome man where Walter Hudd was a plain one.

He wondered about two other things – what Stephen meant by 'psychologically speaking' and whether Stephen could possibly have seen Gina from his seat at the piano. He rather thought not.

III

Into the Gothic gloom of the library, Gina brought an exotic glow. Even Inspector Curry blinked a little at the radiant young woman who sat down, leaned forward over the table and said expectantly, 'Well?'

Inspector Curry, observing her scarlet shirt and dark green slacks, said drily:

'I see you're not wearing mourning, Mrs Hudd?'

'I haven't got any,' said Gina. 'I know everyone is supposed to have a little black number and wear it with pearls. But I don't. I hate black. I think it's hideous, and only receptionists and housekeepers and people like that ought to wear it. Anyway Christian Gulbrandsen wasn't really a relation. He's my grandmother's stepson.'

'And I suppose you didn't know him very well?'

Gina shook her head.

'He came here three or four times when I was a child, but then

602

in the war I went to America, and I only came back here to live about six months ago.'

'You have definitely come back here to live? You're not just on a visit?'

'I haven't really thought,' said Gina.

'You were in the Great Hall last night, when Mr Gulbrandsen went to his room?'

'Yes. He said goodnight and went away. Grandam asked if he had everything he wanted and he said yes – that Jolly had fixed him up fine. Not those words, but that kind of thing. He said he had letters to write.'

'And then?'

Gina described the scene between Lewis and Edgar Lawson. It was the same story that Inspector Curry had by now heard many times, but it took an added colour, a new gusto, under Gina's handling. It became drama.

'It was Wally's revolver,' she said. 'Fancy Edgar's having the guts to go and pinch it out of his room. I'd never have believed he'd have the guts.'

'Were you alarmed when they went into the study and Edgar Lawson locked the door?'

'Oh no,' said Gina, opening her enormous brown eyes very wide. 'I loved it. It was so ham, you know, and so madly theatrical. Everything Edgar does is always ridiculous. One can't take him seriously for a moment.'

'He did fire the revolver, though?'

'Yes. We all thought then that he'd shot Lewis after all.'

'And did you enjoy that?' Inspector Curry could not refrain from asking.

'Oh no, I was terrified, then. Everyone was, except Grandam. She never turned a hair.'

'That seems rather remarkable.'

'Not really. She's that kind of person. Not quite in this world. She's the sort of person who never believes *anything* bad can happen. She's sweet.'

'During all this scene, who was in the Hall?'

'Oh we were all there. Except Uncle Christian, of course.'

'Not *all*, Mrs Hudd. People went in and out.'

'Did they?' asked Gina vaguely.

'Your husband, for instance, went out to fix the lights.'

'Yes. Wally's great at fixing things.'

'During his absence, a shot was heard, I understand. A shot that you all thought came from the Park?'

'I don't remember that . . . Oh yes, it was just after the lights had come on again and Wally had come back.'

'Did anyone else leave the Hall?'

'I don't think so. I don't remember.'

'Where were you sitting, Mrs Hudd?'

'Over by the window.'

'Near the door to the library?'

'Yes.'

'Did you yourself leave the Hall at all?'

'Leave? With all the excitement? Of course not.'

Gina sounded scandalized by the idea.

'Where were the others sitting?'

'Mostly round the fireplace, I think. Aunt Mildred was knitting and so was Aunt Jane – Miss Marple, I mean – Grandam was just sitting.'

'And Mr Stephen Restarick?'

'Stephen? He was playing the piano to begin with. I don't know where he went later.'

'And Miss Bellever?'

'Fussing about, as usual. She practically never sits down. She was looking for keys or something.'

She said suddenly:

'What's all this about Grandam's tonic? Did the chemist make a mistake in making it up or something?'

'Why should you think that?'

'Because the bottle's disappeared, and Jolly's been fussing round madly looking for it, in no end of a stew. Alex told her the police had taken it away. Did you?'

Instead of replying to the question, Inspector Curry said:

'Miss Bellever was upset, you say?'

'Oh! Jolly always fusses,' said Gina carelessly. 'She likes fussing. Sometimes I wonder how Grandam can stand it.'

'Just one last question, Mrs Hudd. You've no ideas yourself as to who killed Christian Gulbrandsen and why?'

'One of the queers did it, I should think. The thug ones are really quite sensible. I mean they only cosh people so as to rob a till or get money or jewellery – not just for fun. But one of the queers – you know, what they call mentally maladjusted – might do it for fun, don't you think? Because I can't see what other reason there could be for killing Uncle Christian except fun, do you? At least I don't mean fun, exactly – but – '

'You can't think of a motive?'

'Yes, that's what I mean,' said Gina gratefully. 'He wasn't robbed or anything, was he?'

'But you know, Mrs Hudd, the College buildings were locked and barred. Nobody could get out from there without a pass.'

'Don't you believe it,' Gina laughed merrily. 'Those boys could get out from anywhere! They've taught me a lot of tricks.'

'She's a lively one,' said Lake when Gina had departed. 'First time I've seen her close to. Lovely figure, hasn't she. Sort of a foreign figure, if you know what I mean.'

Inspector Curry threw him a cold glance. Sergeant Lake said hastily that she was a merry one. 'Seems to have enjoyed it all, as you might say.'

'Whether Stephen Restarick is right or not about her marriage breaking up, I notice that she went out of her way to mention that Walter Hudd was back in the Great Hall before that shot was heard.'

'Which, according to everyone else, isn't so?'

'Exactly.'

'She didn't mention Miss Bellever leaving the Hall to look for keys, either.'

'No,' said the Inspector thoughtfully, 'she didn't . . .'

CHAPTER FOURTEEN

Mrs Strete fitted into the library very much better than Gina Hudd had done. There was nothing exotic about Mrs Strete. She wore black with an onyx brooch, and she wore a hairnet over carefully arranged grey hair.

She looked, Inspector Curry reflected, exactly as the relict of a Canon of the Established Church should look – which was almost odd, because so few people ever did look like what they really were.

Even the tight line of her lips had an ascetic ecclesiastical flavour. She expressed Christian Endurance, and possibly Christian Fortitude. But not, Curry thought, Christian Charity.

Moreover it was clear that Mrs Strete was offended.

'I should have thought that you could have given me *some* idea of when you would want me, Inspector. I have been forced to sit around waiting all the morning.'

It was, Curry judged, her sense of importance that was hurt. He hastened to pour oil on the troubled waters.

'I'm very sorry, Mrs Strete. Perhaps you don't quite know how we set about these things. We start, you know, with the less important evidence – get it out of the way, so to speak. It's valuable to keep to the last a person on whose judgment we can rely – a good observer – by whom we can check what has been told us up to date.'

Mrs Strete softened visibly.

'Oh I see. I hadn't quite realized . . .'

'Now you're a woman of mature judgment, Mrs Strete. A woman of the world. And then this is your home – you're the daughter of the house, and you can tell me all about the people who are in it.'

'I can certainly do that,' said Mildred Strete.

'So you see that when we come to the question of who killed Christian Gulbrandsen, you can help us a great deal.'

'But is there any question? Isn't it perfectly obvious who killed my brother?'

Inspector Curry leant back in his chair. His hand stroked his small neat moustache.

'Well – we have to be careful,' he said. 'You think it's obvious?'

'Of course. That dreadful American husband of poor Gina's. He's the only stranger here. We know absolutely nothing about him. He's probably one of these dreadful American gangsters.'

'But that wouldn't quite account for his killing Christian Gulbrandsen, would it? Why should he?'

'Because Christian had found out something about him. That's what he came here for so soon after his last visit.'

'Are you sure of that, Mrs Strete?'

'Again it seems to me quite obvious. He let it be thought his visit was in connection with the Trust – but that's nonsense. He was here for that only a month ago. And nothing of importance has arisen since. So he must have come on some private business. He saw Walter on his last visit, and he may have recognized him – or perhaps made inquiries about him in the States – naturally

606

he has agents all over the world – and found out something really damaging. Gina is a very silly girl. She always has been. It is just like her to marry a man she knows nothing about – she's always been man mad! A man wanted by the police, perhaps, or a man who's already married, or some bad character in the underworld. But my brother Christian wasn't an easy man to deceive. He came here, I'm sure, to settle the whole business. Expose Walter and show him up for what he is. And so, naturally, Walter shot him.'

Inspector Curry, adding some out-sized whiskers to one of the cats on his blotting pad, said:

'Ye – es.'

'Don't you agree with me that that's what *must* have happened?'

'It could be – yes,' admitted the Inspector.

'What other solution could there be? Christian had no enemies. What I can't understand is why you haven't already arrested Walter?'

'Well, you see, Mrs Strete, we have to have evidence.'

'You could probably get that easily enough. If you wired to America – '

'Oh yes, we shall check up on Mr Walter Hudd. You can be sure of that. But until we can prove motive, there's not very much to go upon. There's opportunity, of course – '

'He went out just after Christian, pretending the lights had fused – '

'They did fuse.'

'He could easily arrange that.'

'True.'

'That gave him his excuse. He followed Christian to his room, shot him and then repaired the fuse and came back to the Hall.'

'His wife says he came back before you heard the shot from outside.'

'Not a bit of it! Gina would say anything. The Italians are never truthful. And she's a Roman Catholic, of course.'

Inspector Curry side-stepped the ecclesiastical angle.

'You think his wife was in it with him?'

Mildred Strete hesitated for a moment.

'No – no, I don't think that.' She seemed rather disappointed not to think so. She went on: 'That must have been partly the motive – to prevent Gina's learning the truth about him. After all, Gina is his bread and butter.'

'And a very beautiful girl.'

'Oh yes. I've always said Gina is good looking. A very common

607

type in Italy, of course. But if you ask me, it's *money* that Walter Hudd is after. That's why he came over here and has settled down living on the Serrocolds.'

'Mrs Hudd is very well off, I understand?'

'Not at present. My father settled the same sum on Gina's mother as he did on me. But of course she took her husband's nationality (I believe the law is altered now) and what with the war and his being a Fascist, Gina has very little of her own. My mother spoils her, and her American aunt, Mrs Van Rydock, spent fabulous sums on her and bought her everything she wanted during the war years. Nevertheless, from Walter's point of view, he can't lay his hands on much until my mother's death, when a very large fortune will come to Gina.'

'And to you, Mrs Strete.'

A faint colour came into Mildred Strete's cheek.

'And to me, as you say. My husband and myself always lived quietly. He spent very little money except on books – he was a great scholar. My own money has almost doubled itself. It is more than enough for my simple needs. Still one can always use money for the benefit of others. Any money that comes to me, I shall regard as a sacred trust.'

'But it won't be in a Trust, will it?' said Curry, wilfully misunderstanding. 'It will come to you absolutely.'

'Oh yes – in that sense. Yes, it will be mine absolutely.'

Something in the ring of that last word made Inspector Curry raise his head sharply. Mrs Strete was not looking at him. Her eyes were shining, and her long thin mouth was curved in a triumphant smile.

Inspector said in a considering voice:

'So in your view – and of course you've had ample opportunities of judging – Master Walter Hudd wants the money that will come to his wife when Mrs Serrocold dies. By the way, she's not very strong, is she, Mrs Strete?'

'My mother has always been delicate.'

'Quite so. But delicate people often live as long or longer than people who have robust health.'

'Yes, I suppose they do.'

'You haven't noticed your mother's health failing just lately?'

'She suffers from rheumatism. But then one must have something as one grows older. I've no sympathy with people who make a fuss over inevitable aches and pains.'

608

'Does Mrs Serrocold make a fuss?'

Mildred Strete was silent for a moment. She said at last:

'She does not make a fuss herself, but she is used to being made a fuss of. My stepfather is far too solicitous. And as for Miss Bellever, she makes herself positively ridiculous. In any case, Miss Bellever has had a very bad influence in this house. She came here many years ago, and her devotion to my mother, though admirable in itself, has really become somewhat of an infliction. She literally tyrannizes over my mother. She runs the whole house and takes far too much upon herself. I think it annoys Lewis sometimes. I should never be surprised if he told her to go. She has no tact – no tact whatever, and it is trying for a man to find his wife completely dominated by a bossy woman.'

Inspector Curry nodded his head gently.

'I see . . . I see . . .'

He watched her speculatively.

'There's one thing I don't quite get, Mrs Strete. The position of the two Restarick brothers?'

'More foolish sentiment. Their father married my poor mother for her money. Two years afterwards he ran away with a Jugoslavian singer of the lowest morals. He was a very unworthy person. My mother was soft-hearted enough to be sorry for these two boys. Since it was out of the question for them to spend their holidays with a woman of such notorious morals, she more or less adopted them. They have been hangers-on here ever since. Oh yes, we've plenty of spongers in this house, I can tell you that.'

'Alex Restarick had an opportunity of killing Christian Gulbrandsen. He was in his car alone – driving from the Lodge to the house – what about Stephen?'

'Stephen was in the Hall with us. I don't approve of Alex Restarick – he is getting to look very coarse, and I imagine he leads an irregular life – but I don't really see him as a murderer. Besides, why should he kill my brother?'

'That's what we always come back to, isn't it?' said Inspector Curry genially. 'What did Christian Gulbrandsen know – about someone – that made it necessary for that someone to kill him?'

'Exactly,' said Mrs Strete triumphantly. 'It *must* be Walter Hudd.'

'Unless it's someone nearer home.'

Mildred said sharply:

'What did you mean by that?'

Inspector Curry said slowly:

'Mr Gulbrandsen seemed very concerned about Mrs Serrocold's health whilst he was here.'

Mrs Strete frowned.

'Men always fuss over mother because she looks fragile. I think she likes them to! Or else Christian had been listening to Juliet Bellever.'

'You're not worried about your mother's health yourself, Mrs Strete?'

'No. I hope I'm sensible. Naturally mother is not young – '

'And death comes to all of us,' said Inspector Curry. 'But not ahead of its appointed time. That's what we have to prevent.'

He spoke meaningfully. Mildred Strete flared into sudden animation.

'Oh it's wicked – wicked. No one else here really seems to care. Why should they? I'm the only person who was a blood relation to Christian. To mother, he was only a grown-up stepson. To Gina, he isn't really any relation at all. But he was my own brother.'

'Half-brother,' suggested Inspector Curry.

'Half-brother, yes. But we were both Gulbrandsens in spite of the difference in age.'

Curry said gently:

'Yes – yes, I see your point . . .'

Tears in her eyes, Mildred Strete marched out. Curry looked at Lake.

'So she's quite sure it's Walter Hudd,' he said. 'Won't entertain for a moment the idea of its being anybody else.'

'And she may be right.'

'She certainly may. Wally fits. Opportunity – and motive. Because if he wants money quick, his wife's mother would have to die. So Wally tampers with her tonic, and Christian Gulbrandsen sees him do it – or hears about it in some way. Yes, it fits very nicely.'

He paused and said:

'By the way, Mildred Strete likes money . . . She mayn't spend it, but she likes it. I'm not sure why . . . She may be a miser – with a miser's passion. Or she may like the power that money gives. Money for benevolence, perhaps? She's a Gulbrandsen. She may want to emulate Father.'

'Complex, isn't it?' said Sergeant Lake, and scratched his head.

Inspector Curry said:

'We'd better see this screwy young man Lawson, and after that we'll go to the Great Hall and work out who was where – and if –

610

and why – and when . . . We've heard one or two rather interesting things this morning.'

II

It was very difficult, Inspector Curry thought, to get a true estimate of someone from what other people said.

Edgar Lawson had been described by a good many different people that morning, but looking at him now, Curry's own impressions were almost ludicrously different.

Edgar did not impress him as 'queer' or 'dangerous,' or 'arrogant' or even as 'abnormal.' He seemed a very ordinary young man, very much cast down and in a state of humility approaching that of Uriah Heep's. He looked young and slightly common and rather pathetic.

He was only too anxious to talk and to apologize.

'I know I've done very wrong. I don't know what came over me – really I don't. Making that scene and kicking up such a row. And actually shooting off a pistol. At Mr Serrocold too, who's been so good to me and so patient, too.'

He twisted his hands nervously. They were rather pathetic hands, with bony wrists.

'If I've got to be had up for it, I'll come with you at once. I deserve it. I'll plead guilty.'

'No charge has been made against you,' said Inspector Curry crisply. 'So we've no evidence on which to act. According to Mr Serrocold, letting off the pistol was an accident.'

'That's because he's so good. There never was a man as good as Mr Serrocold! He's done everything for me. And I go and repay him by acting like this.'

'What made you act as you did?'

Edgar looked embarrassed.

'I made a fool of myself.'

Inspector Curry said drily:

'So it seems. You told Mr Serrocold in the presence of witnesses that you had discovered that he was your father. Was that true?'

'No, it wasn't.'

'What put that idea into your head? Did someone suggest it to you?'

'Well, it's a bit hard to explain.'

Inspector Curry looked at him thoughtfully, then said in a kindly voice:

'Suppose you try. *We* don't want to make things hard for you.'

'Well, you see, I had a rather hard time of it as a kid. The other boys jeered at me. Because I hadn't got a father. Said I was a little bastard – which I was, of course. Mum was usually drunk and she had men coming in all the time. My father was a foreign seaman, I believe. The house was always filthy, and it was all pretty fair hell. And then I got to thinking, supposing my Dad had been not just some foreign sailor, but someone important – and I used to make up a thing or two. Kid stuff first – changed at birth – really the rightful heir – that sort of thing. And then I went to a new school and I tried it on once or twice hinting things. Said my father was really an Admiral in the Navy. I got to believing it myself. I didn't feel so bad then.'

He paused and then went on:

'And then – later – I thought up some other ideas. I used to stay at hotels and told a lot of silly stories about being a fighter pilot – or about being in Military Intelligence. I got all sort of mixed up. I didn't seem able to stop telling lies.

'Only I didn't really try to get money by it. It was just swank so as to make people think a bit more of me. I didn't want to be dishonest. Mr Serrocold will tell you – and Dr Maverick – they've got all the stuff about it.'

Inspector Curry nodded. He had already studied Edgar's case history and his police record.

'Mr Serrocold got me clear in the end and brought me down here. He said he needed a secretary to help him – and I did help him! I really did. Only the others laughed at me. They were always laughing at me.'

'What others? Mrs Serrocold?'

'No, not Mrs Serrocold. She's a lady – she's always gentle and kind. No, but Gina treated me like dirt. And Stephen Restarick. And Mrs Strete looked down on me for not being a gentleman. So did Miss Bellever – and what's she? She's a paid companion, isn't she?'

Curry noted the signs of rising excitement.

'So you didn't find them very sympathetic?'

Edgar said passionately:

'It was because of me being a bastard. If I'd had a proper father they wouldn't have gone on like that.'

'So you appropriated a couple of famous fathers?'

Edgar blushed.

'I always seem to get to telling lies,' he muttered.

'And finally you said Mr Serrocold was your father. Why?'

'Because that would stop them once for all, wouldn't it? If *he* was my father they couldn't do anything to me.'

'Yes. But you accused him of being your enemy – of persecuting you.'

'I know – ' He rubbed his forehead. 'I got things all wrong. There are times when I don't – when I don't get things quite right. I get muddled.'

'And you took the revolver from Mr Walter Hudd's room?'

Edgar looked puzzled.

'Did I? Is that where I got it?'

'Don't you remember where you got it?'

Edgar said:

'I meant to threaten Mr Serrocold with it. I meant to frighten him. It was kid stuff all over again.'

Inspector Curry said patiently:

'How did you get the revolver?'

'You just said – out of Walter's room.'

'You remember doing that now?'

'I must have got it from his room. I couldn't have got hold of it any other way, could I?'

'I don't know,' said Inspector Curry. 'Somebody – might have given it to you?'

Edgar was silent – his face a blank.

'Is that how it happened?'

Edgar said passionately:

'I don't remember. I was so worked up. I walked about the garden in a red mist of rage. I thought people were spying on me, watching me, trying to hound me down. Even that nice white-haired old lady . . . I can't understand it all now. I feel I must have been mad. I don't remember where I was and what I was doing half the time!'

'Surely you remember who told you Mr Serrocold was your father?'

Edgar gave the same blank stare.

'Nobody told me,' he said sullenly. 'It just came to me.'

Inspector Curry sighed. He was not satisfied. But he judged he could make no further progress at present.

'Well, watch your step in future,' he said.

'Yes, sir. Yes indeed I will.'

As Edgar went, Inspector Curry slowly shook his head.

'These pathological cases are the devil!'

'D'you think he's mad, sir?'

'Much less mad than I'd imagined. Weak-headed, boastful, a liar – yet a certain pleasant simplicity about him. Highly suggestible I should imagine . . .'

'You think someone did suggest things to him?'

'Oh yes, old Miss Marple was right there. She's a shrewd old bird. But I wish I knew who it was. He won't tell. If we only knew that . . . Come on, Lake, let's have a thorough reconstruction of the scene in the Hall.'

III

'That fixes it pretty well.'

Inspector Curry was sitting at the piano. Sergeant Lake was in a chair by the window overlooking the lake.

Curry went on:

'If I'm half-turned on the piano stool, watching the study door, I can't see you.'

Sergeant Lake rose softly and edged quietly through the door to the library.

'All this side of the room was dark. The only lights that were on were the ones beside the study door. No, Lake, I didn't see you go. Once in the library, you could go out through the other door to the corridor – two minutes to run along to the oak suite, shoot Gulbrandsen and come back through the library to your chair by the window.

'The women by the fire have their backs to you. Mrs Serrocold was sitting *here* – on the right of the fireplace, near the study door. Everyone agrees she didn't move and she's the only one who's in the line of direct vision. Miss Marple was here. She was looking past Mrs Serrocold to the study. Mrs Strete was on the left of the fireplace – close to the door out of the Hall to the lobby, and it's a very dark corner. She *could* have gone and come back. Yes, it's possible.'

Curry grinned suddenly.

'And I could go.' He slipped off the music stool and sidled along the wall and out through the door. 'The only person who might notice I wasn't still at the piano would be Gina Hudd. And you remember what Gina said: "Stephen was at the piano to begin with. *I don't know where he was later.*"'

'So you think it's Stephen?'

'I don't know who it is,' said Curry. 'It wasn't Edgar Lawson or Lewis Serrocold or Mrs Serrocold or Miss Jane Marple. But for the rest – ' He sighed. 'It's probably the American. Those fused lights were a bit too convenient – a coincidence. And yet, you know, I rather like the chap. Still, that isn't evidence.'

He peered thoughtfully at some music on the side of the piano. 'Hindemith? Who's he? Never heard of him. Shostakovitch! What names these people have.' He got up and then looked down at the old-fashioned music stool. He lifted the top of it.

'Here's the old-fashioned stuff. Handel's Largo, Czerny's Exercises. Dates back to old Gulbrandsen, most of this. "I know a lovely Garden" – Vicar's wife used to sing that when I was a boy – '

He stopped – the yellow pages of the song in his hand. Beneath them, reposing on Chopin's Preludes, was a small automatic pistol.

'Stephen Restarick,' exclaimed Sergeant Lake joyfully.

'Now don't jump to conclusions,' Inspector Curry warned him. 'Ten to one that's what we're meant to think.'

CHAPTER FIFTEEN

Miss Marple climbed the stairs and tapped on the door of Mrs Serrocold's bedroom.

'May I come in, Carrie Louise?'

'Of course, Jane dear.'

Carrie Louise was sitting in front of the dressing table, brushing her silvery hair. She turned her head over her shoulder.

'Is it the police? I'll be ready in a few minutes.'

'Are you all right?'

'Yes, of course. Jolly insisted on my having my breakfast in bed. And Gina came into the room with it on tiptoe as though I might be at death's door! I don't think people realize that tragedies like

Christian's death are much less of a shock to someone old. Because one knows by then how anything may happen – and how little anything really matters that happens in this world.'

'Ye – es,' said Miss Marple dubiously.

'Don't you feel the same, Jane? I should have thought you would.'

Miss Marple said slowly:

'Christian was murdered.'

'Yes . . . I see what you mean. You think that *does* matter?'

'Don't you?'

'Not to Christian,' said Carrie Louise simply. 'It matters, of course, to whoever murdered him.'

'Have you any idea who murdered him?'

Mrs Serrocold shook her head in a bewildered fashion.

'No, I've absolutely no idea. I can't even think of a reason. It must have been something to do with his being here before – just over a month ago. Because otherwise I don't think he would have come here suddenly again for no particular reason. Whatever it was must have started off then. I've thought and I've thought, but I can't remember anything unusual.'

'Oh! The same people who are here now – yes, Alex was down from London about then. And – oh yes, Ruth was here.'

'Ruth?'

'Her usual flying visit.'

'Ruth,' said Miss Marple again. Her mind was active. Christian Gulbrandsen and Ruth? Ruth had come away worried and apprehensive, but had not known why. Something was wrong was all that Ruth could say. Christian Gulbrandsen had known or suspected something that Ruth did not. He had known or suspected that someone was trying to poison Carrie Louise. How had Christian Gulbrandsen come to entertain those suspicions? What had he seen or heard? Was it something that Ruth also had seen or heard but which she had failed to appreciate at its rightful significance? Miss Marple wished that she knew what it could possibly have been. Her own vague hunch that it (whatever it was) had to do with Edgar Lawson seemed unlikely since Ruth had not mentioned him.

She sighed.

'You're all keeping something from me, aren't you?' asked Carrie Louise.

Miss Marple jumped a little as the quiet voice spoke.

'Why do you say that?'

616

'Because you are. Not Jolly. But everyone else. Even Lewis. He came in while I was having my breakfast, and he acted very oddly. He drank some of my coffee and even had a bit of toast and marmalade. That's so unlike him, because he always has tea and he doesn't like marmalade, so he must have been thinking of something else – and I suppose he must have forgotten to have his own breakfast. He does forget things like meals, and he looked so concerned and preoccupied.'

'Murder – ' began Miss Marple.

Carrie Louise said quickly:

'Oh I know. It's a terrible thing. I've never been mixed up in it before. You have, haven't you, Jane?'

'Well – yes – actually I have,' Miss Marple admitted.

'So Ruth told me.'

'Did she tell you that last time she was down here?' asked Miss Marple curiously.

'No, I don't think it was then. I can't really remember.'

Carrie Louise spoke vaguely, almost absent-mindedly.

'What are you thinking about, Carrie Louise?'

Mrs Serrocold smiled and seemed to come back from a long way away.

'I was thinking of Gina,' she said. 'And of what you said about Stephen Restarick. Gina's a dear girl, you know, and she does really love Wally. I'm sure she does.'

Miss Marple said nothing.

'Girls like Gina like to kick up their heels a bit.' Mrs Serrocold spoke in an almost pleading voice. 'They're young and they like to feel their power. It's natural, really. I know Wally Hudd isn't the sort of man we imagined Gina marrying. Normally she'd never have met him. But she did meet him, and fell in love with him – and presumably she knows her own business best.'

'Probably she does,' said Miss Marple.

'But it's so very important that Gina should be happy.'

Miss Marple looked curiously at her friend.

'It's important, I suppose, that everyone should be happy.'

'Oh yes. But Gina's a very special case. When we took her mother – when we took Pippa – we felt that it was an experiment that had simply got to succeed. You see, Pippa's mother – '

Carrie Louise paused.

Miss Marple said:

'Who was Pippa's mother?'

617

Carrie Louise said: 'Eric and I agreed that we should never tell anybody that. She never knew herself.'

'I'd like to know,' said Miss Marple.

Mrs Serrocold looked at her doubtfully.

'It isn't just curiosity,' said Miss Marple. 'I really – well – *need* to know. I can hold my tongue, you know.'

'You could always keep a secret, Jane,' said Carrie Louise with a reminiscent smile. 'Dr Galbraith – he's the Bishop of Cromer now – he knows. But no one else. Pippa's mother was Katherine Elsworth.'

'Elsworth? Wasn't that the woman who administered arsenic to her husband? Rather a celebrated case.'

'Yes.'

'She was hanged?'

'Yes. But you know it's not at all sure that she did it. The husband was an arsenic eater – they didn't understand so much about those things then.'

'She soaked flypapers.'

'The maid's evidence, we always thought, was definitely malicious.'

'And Pippa was her daughter?'

'Yes. Eric and I determined to give the child a fresh start in life – with love and care and all the things a child needs. We succeeded. Pippa was – herself. The sweetest, happiest creature imaginable.'

Miss Marple was silent a long time.

Carrie Louise turned away from the dressing table.

'I'm ready now. Perhaps you'll ask the Inspector or whatever he is to come up to my sitting-room. He won't mind, I'm sure.'

II

Inspector Curry did not mind. In fact he rather welcomed the chance of seeing Mrs Serrocold on her own territory.

As he stood there waiting for her, he looked round him curiously. It was not his idea of what he termed to himself 'a rich woman's boudoir.'

It had an old-fashioned couch and some rather uncomfortable looking Victorian chairs with twisted woodwork backs. The chintzes were old and faded but of an attractive pattern displaying the Crystal

Palace. It was one of the smaller rooms, though even then it was larger than the drawing-room of most modern houses. But it had a cosy rather crowded appearance with its little tables, its bric-à-brac, and its photographs. Curry looked at an old snapshot of two little girls, one dark and lively, the other plain and staring out sulkily on the world from under a heavy fringe. He had seen that same expression that morning. 'Pippa and Mildred' was written on the photograph. There was a photograph of Eric Gulbrandsen hanging on the wall, with a gold mount and a heavy ebony frame. Curry had just found a photograph of a good-looking man with eyes crinkling with laughter who he presumed was John Restarick when the door opened and Mrs Serrocold came in.

She wore black, a floating and diaphanous black. Her little pink and white face looked unusually small under its crown of silvery hair, and there was a frailness about her that caught sharply at Inspector Curry's heart. He understood at that moment a good deal that had perplexed him earlier in the morning. He understood why people were so anxious to spare Caroline Louise Serrocold everything that could be spared her.

And yet, he thought, she isn't the kind that would ever make a fuss . . .

She greeted him, asked him to sit down, and took a chair near him. It was less he who put her at her ease than she who put him at his. He started to ask his questions and she answered them readily and without hesitation. The failure of the lights, the quarrel between Edgar Lawson and her husband, the shot they had heard . . .

'It did not seem to you that the shot was in the house?'

'No, I thought it came from outside. I thought it might have been the backfire of a car.'

'During the quarrel between your husband and this young fellow Lawson in the study, did you notice anybody leaving the Hall?'

'Wally had already gone to see about the lights. Miss Bellever went out shortly afterwards – to get something, but I can't remember what.'

'Who else left the Hall?'

'Nobody, so far as I know.'

'Would you know, Mrs Serrocold?'

She reflected a moment.

'No, I don't think I should.'

'You were completely absorbed in what you could hear going on in the study?'

'Yes.'

'And you were apprehensive as to what might happen there?'

'No – no, I wouldn't say that. I didn't think anything would really happen.'

'But Lawson had a revolver?'

'Yes.'

'And was threatening your husband with it?'

'Yes. But he didn't mean it.'

Inspector Curry felt his usual slight exasperation at this statement. So she was another of them!

'You can't possibly have been sure of that, Mrs Serrocold.'

'Well, but I was sure. In my own mind, I mean. What is it the young people say – putting on an act? That's what I felt it was. Edgar's only a boy. He was being melodramatic and silly and fancying himself as a bold desperate character. Seeing himself as the wronged hero in a romantic story. I was quite sure he would never fire that revolver.'

'But he did fire it, Mrs Serrocold.'

Carrie Louise smiled.

'I expect it went off by accident.'

Again exasperation mounted in Inspector Curry.

'It was not an accident. Lawson fired that revolver twice – and fired it at your husband. The bullets only just missed him.'

Carrie Louise looked startled and then grave.

'I can't really believe that. Oh yes' – she hurried on to forestall the Inspector's protest – 'of course I have to believe it if you tell me so. But I still feel there must be a simple explanation. Perhaps Dr Maverick can explain it to me.'

'Oh yes, Dr Maverick will explain it all right,' said Curry grimly. 'Dr Maverick can explain anything. I'm sure of that.'

Unexpectedly Mrs Serrocold said:

'I know that a lot of what we do here seems to you foolish and pointless, and psychiatrists can be very irritating sometimes. But we *do* achieve results, you know. We have our failures, but we have successes too. And what we try to do is *worth* doing. And though you probably won't believe it, Edgar is really devoted to my husband. He started this silly business about Lewis's being his father because he wants so much to have a father like Lewis. But what I can't understand is why he should suddenly get *violent*. He had been so very much better – really practically normal. Indeed he has always seemed normal to me.'

The Inspector did not argue the point.

He said: 'The revolver that Edgar Lawson had was one belonging to your granddaughter's husband. Presumably Lawson took it from Walter Hudd's room. Now tell me, have you ever seen *this* weapon before?'

On the palm of his hand he held out the small black automatic.

Carrie Louise looked at it.

'No, I don't think so.'

'I found it in the piano stool. It has recently been fired. We haven't had time to check on it fully yet, but I should say that it is almost certainly the weapon with which Mr Gulbrandsen was shot.'

She frowned.

'And you found it in the piano stool?'

'Under some very old music. Music that I should say had not been played for years.'

'Hidden, then?'

'Yes. You remember who was at the piano last night?'

'Stephen Restarick.'

'He was playing?'

'Yes. Just softly. A funny melancholy little tune.'

'When did he stop playing, Mrs Serrocold?'

'When did he stop? I don't know.'

'But he did stop? He didn't go on playing all through the quarrel.'

'No. The music just died down.'

'Did he get up from the piano stool?'

'I don't know. I've no idea what he did until he came over to the study door to try and fit a key to it.'

'Can you think of any reason why Stephen Restarick should shoot Mr Gulbrandsen?'

'None whatever.' She added thoughtfully, 'I don't believe he did.'

'Gulbrandsen might have found out something discreditable about him.'

'That seems to me very unlikely.'

Inspector Curry had a wild wish to reply:

'Pigs may fly but they're very unlikely birds.' It had been a saying of his grandmother's. Miss Marple, he thought, was sure to know it.

Carrie Louise came down the broad stairway and three people converged upon her from different directions, Gina from the long corridor, Miss Marple from the library, and Juliet Bellever from the Great Hall.

Gina spoke first.

'Darling!' she exclaimed passionately. 'Are you all right? They haven't bullied you or given you third degree or anything?'

'Of course not, Gina. What odd ideas you have! Inspector Curry was charming and most considerate.'

'So he ought to be,' said Miss Bellever. 'Now, Carrie, I've got all your letters here and a parcel. I was going to bring them up to you.'

'Bring them into the library,' said Carrie Louise.

All four of them went into the library.

Carrie Louise sat down and began opening her letters. There were about twenty or thirty of them.

As she opened them, she handed them to Miss Bellever, who sorted them into heaps, explaining to Miss Marple as she did so:

'Three main categories. One – from relations of the boys. Those I hand over to Dr Maverick. Begging letters I deal with myself. And the rest are personal – and Cara gives me notes on how to deal with them.'

The correspondence once disposed of, Mrs Serrocold turned her attention to the parcel, cutting the string with scissors.

Out of the neat wrappings there appeared an attractive box of chocolates tied up with gold ribbon.

'Someone must think it's my birthday,' said Mrs Serrocold with a smile.

She slipped off the ribbon and opened the box. Inside was a visiting card. Carrie Louise looked at it with slight surprise.

'*With love from Alex,*' she said. 'How odd of him to send me a box of chocolates by post on the same day he was coming down here.'

Uneasiness stirred in Miss Marple's mind.

She said quickly:

'Wait a minute, Carrie Louise. Don't eat one yet.'

Mrs Serrocold looked faintly surprised.

'I was going to hand them round.'

'Well, don't. Wait while I ask – Is Alex about the house, do you know, Gina?'

Gina said quickly: 'Alex was in the Hall just now, I think.'

She went across, opened the door, and called him.

Alex Restarick appeared in the doorway a moment later.

'Madonna darling! So you're up. None the worse?'

He came across to Mrs Serrocold and kissed her gently on both cheeks.

Miss Marple said:

'Carrie Louise wants to thank you for the chocolates.'

Alex looked surprised.

'What chocolates?'

'These chocolates,' said Carrie Louise.

'But I never sent you any chocolates, darling.'

'The box has got your card in,' said Miss Bellever.

Alex peered down.

'So it has. How odd. How very odd . . . I certainly didn't send them.'

'What a very extraordinary thing,' said Miss Bellever.

'They look absolutely scrumptious,' said Gina, peering into the box. 'Look, Grandam, there are your favourite Kirsch ones in the middle.'

Miss Marple gently but firmly took the box away from her. Without a word she took it out of the room and went to find Lewis Serrocold. It took her some time because he had gone over to the College – she found him in Dr Maverick's room there. She put the box on the table in front of him. He listened to her brief account of the circumstances. His face grew suddenly stern and hard.

Carefully, he and the doctor lifted out chocolate after chocolate and examined them.

'I think,' said Dr Maverick, 'that these ones I have put aside have almost certainly been tampered with. You see the unevenness of the chocolate coating underneath? The next thing to do is to get them analysed.'

'But it seems incredible,' said Miss Marple. 'Why, everyone in the house might have been poisoned!'

Lewis nodded. His face was still white and hard.

'Yes. There is a ruthlessness – a disregard – ' he broke off. 'Actually I think all these particular chocolates are Kirsch flavouring. That is Caroline's favourite. So, you see, there is knowledge behind this.'

Miss Marple said quietly:

'If it is as you suspect – if there is – *poison* – in these chocolates,

623

then I'm afraid Carrie Louise will have to know what is going on. She must be put upon her guard.'

Lewis Serrocold said heavily:

'Yes. She will have to know that someone wants to kill her. I think that she will find it almost impossible to believe.'

CHAPTER SIXTEEN

''Ere, Miss. Is it true as there's an 'ideous poisoner at work?'

Gina pushed the hair back from her forehead and jumped as the hoarse whisper reached her. There was paint on her cheek and paint on her slacks. She and her selected helpers had been busy on the backcloth of the Nile at Sunset for their next theatrical production.

It was one of these helpers who was now asking the question. Ernie, the boy who had given her such valuable lessons in the manipulation of locks. Ernie's fingers were equally dexterous at stage carpentry, and he was one of the most enthusiastic theatrical assistants.

His eyes now were bright and beady with pleasurable anticipation.

Ernie shut one eye.

'It's all round the dorms,' he said. 'But look 'ere, Miss, it wasn't one of *us*. Not a thing like that. And nobody wouldn't do a thing to Mrs Serrocold. Even Jenkins wouldn't cosh *her*. 'Tisn't as though it was the old bitch. Wouldn't 'alf like to poison 'er, I wouldn't.'

'Don't talk like that about Miss Bellever.'

'Sorry, Miss. It slipped out. What poison was it, Miss? Strickline, was it? Makes you arch your back and die in agonies, that does. Or was it Prussian acid?'

'I don't know what you're talking about, Ernie.'

Ernie winked again.

'Not 'alf you don't! Mr Alex it was done it, so they say. Brought them chocs down from London. But that's a lie. Mr Alex wouldn't do a thing like that, would he, Miss?'

624

'Of course he wouldn't,' said Gina.

'Much more likely to be Mr Baumgarten. When he's giving us P.T. he makes the most awful faces, and Don and I think as he's batty.'

'Just move that turpentine out of the way.'

Ernie obeyed, murmuring to himself:

'Don't 'arf see life 'ere! Old Gulbrandsen done in yesterday and now a secret poisoner. D'you think it's the same person doing both? What 'ud you say, Miss, if I told you as I know oo it was done 'im in?'

'You can't possibly know anything about it.'

'Coo, carn't I neither? Supposin' I was outside last night and saw something.'

'How could you have been out? The College is locked up after roll call at seven.'

'Roll call . . . I can get out whenever I likes, Miss. Locks don't mean nothing to me. Get out and walk around the grounds just for the fun of it, I do.'

Gina said:

'I wish you'd stop telling lies, Ernie.'

'Who's telling lies?'

'You are. You tell lies and you boast about things that you've never done at all.'

'That's what you say, Miss. You wait till the coppers come round and arsk me all about what I saw last night.'

'Well, what did you see?'

'Ah,' said Ernie, 'wouldn't you like to know?'

Gina made a rush at him and he beat a strategic retreat. Stephen came over from the other side of the theatre and joined Gina. They discussed various technical matters and then, side by side, they walked back towards the house.

'They all seem to know about Grandam and the chocs,' said Gina. 'The boys, I mean. How do they get to know?'

'Local grapevine of some kind.'

'And they knew about Alex's card. Stephen, surely it was very stupid to put Alex's card in the box when he was actually coming down here.'

'Yes, but who knew he was coming down here? He decided to come on the spur of the moment and sent a telegram. Probably the box was posted by then. And if he hadn't come down, putting his card in would have been quite a good idea. Because he does send Caroline chocolates sometimes.'

625

He went on slowly:

'What I simply can't understand is – '

'Is why anyone should want to poison, Grandam,' Gina cut in. 'I know. It's *inconceivable*! She's so adorable – and absolutely everyone *does* adore her.'

Stephen did not answer. Gina looked at him sharply.

'I know what you're thinking, Steve!'

'I wonder.'

'You're thinking that Wally – doesn't adore her. But Wally would never poison anyone. The idea's laughable.'

'The loyal wife!'

'Don't say that in that sneering tone of voice.'

'I didn't mean to sneer. I think you *are* loyal. I admire you for it. But darling Gina, you can't keep it up, you know.'

'What do you mean, Steve?'

'You know quite well what I mean. You and Wally don't belong together. It's just one of those things that doesn't work. He knows it too. The split is going to come any day now. And you'll both be much happier when it has come.'

Gina said:

'Don't be idiotic.'

Stephen laughed.

'Come now, you can't pretend that you're suited to each other or that Wally's happy here.'

'Oh, I don't know what's the matter with him,' cried Gina. 'He sulks the whole time. He hardly speaks. I – I don't know what to do about him. Why can't he enjoy himself here? We had such fun together once – everything was fun – and now he might be a different person. Why do people have to change so?'

'Do I change?'

'No, Steve darling. You're always Steve. Do you remember how I used to tag round after you in the holidays?'

'And what a nuisance I used to think you – that miserable little kid Gina. Well, the tables are turned now. You've got me where you want me, haven't you, Gina?'

Gina said quickly:

'Idiot.' She went on hurriedly, 'Do you think Ernie was lying? He was pretending he was roaming about in the fog last night, and hinting that he could tell things about the murder. Do you think that might be true?'

626

'True? Of course not. You know how he boasts. Anything to make himself important.'

'Oh, I know. I only wondered – '

They walked along side by side without speaking.

II

The setting sun illumined the west façade of the house. Inspector Curry looked towards it.

'Is this about the place where you stopped your car last night?' he asked.

Alex Restarick stood back a little as though considering.

'Near enough,' he said. 'It's difficult to tell exactly because of the fog. Yes, I should say this was the place.'

Inspector Curry stood looking round with an appraising eye.

The gravelled sweep of drive swept round in a slow curve, and at this point, emerging from a screen of rhododendrons, the west façade of the house came suddenly into view with its terrace and yew hedges and steps leading down to the lawns. Thereafter the drive continued in its curving progress, sweeping through a belt of trees and round between the lake and the house until it ended in the big gravel sweep at the east side of the house.

'Dodgett,' said Inspector Curry.

Police Constable Dodgett, who had been holding himself at the ready, started spasmodically into motion. He hurled himself across the intervening space of lawn in a diagonal line towards the house, reached the terrace, went in by the side door. A few moments later the curtains of one of the windows were violently agitated. Then Constable Dodgett reappeared out of the garden door, and ran back to rejoin them, breathing like a steam engine.

'Two minutes and forty-two seconds,' said Inspector Curry, clicking the stop watch with which he had been timing him. 'They don't take long, these things, do they?'

His tone was pleasantly conversational.

'I don't run as fast as your constable,' said Alex. 'I presume it *is* my supposed movements you have been timing?'

'I'm just pointing out that you had the opportunity to do murder. That's all, Mr Restarick. I'm not making any accusations – as yet.'

Alex Restarick said kindly to Constable Dodgett, who was still panting:

627

'I can't run as fast as you can, but I believe I'm in better training.'

'It's since 'aving the bronchitis last winter,' said Dodgett.

Alex turned back to the Inspector.

'Seriously, though, in spite of trying to make me uncomfortable and observing my reactions – and you must remember that we artistic folk are oh! so sensitive, such tender plants!' – his voice took on a mocking note – 'you can't really believe I had anything to do with all this? I'd hardly send a box of poisoned chocolates to Mrs Serrocold and put my card inside, would I?'

'That might be what we are meant to think. There's such a thing as a double bluff, Mr Restarick.'

'Oh, I see. How ingenious you are. By the way, those chocolates *were* poisoned?'

'The six chocolates containing Kirsch flavouring in the top layer were poisoned, yes. They contained aconitine.'

'Not one of my favourite poisons, Inspector. Personally, I have a weakness for curare.'

'Curare has to be introduced into the bloodstream, Mr Restarick, not into the stomach.'

'How wonderfully knowledgeable the police force are,' said Alex admiringly.

Inspector Curry cast a quiet sideways glance at the young man. He noted the slightly pointed ears, the un-English Mongolian type of face. The eyes that danced with mischievous mockery. It would have been hard at any time to know what Alex Restarick was thinking. A satyr – or did he mean a faun? An overfed faun, Inspector Curry thought suddenly, and somehow there was an unpleasantness about that idea.

A twister with brains – that's how he would sum up Alex Restarick. Cleverer than his brother. Mother had been a Russian or so he had heard. 'Russians' to Inspector Curry were what 'Bony' had been in the early days of the nineteenth century, and what 'the Huns' had been in the early twentieth century. Anything to do with Russia was bad in Inspector Curry's opinion, and if Alex Restarick had murdered Gulbrandsen he would be a very satisfactory criminal. But unfortunately Curry was by no means convinced that he had.

Constable Dodgett, having recovered his breath, now spoke.

'I moved the curtains as you told me, sir,' he said. 'And counted thirty. I noticed that the curtains have a hook torn off at the top.

628

Means that there's a gap. You'd see the light in the room from outside.'

Inspector Curry said to Alex:

'Did you notice light streaming out from that window last night?'

'I couldn't see the house at all because of the fog. I told you so.'

'Fog's patchy, though. Sometimes it clears for a minute here and there.'

'It never cleared so that I could see the house – the main part, that is. The gymnasium building close at hand loomed up out of the mist in a deliciously unsubstantial way. It gave a perfect illusion of dock warehouses. As I told you, I am putting on a Limehouse Ballet and – '

'You told me,' agreed Inspector Curry.

'One gets in the habit, you know, of looking at things from the point of view of a stage set, rather than from the point of view of reality.'

'I daresay. And yet a stage set's real enough, isn't it, Mr Restarick?'

'I don't see exactly what you mean, Inspector.'

'Well, it's made of real materials – canvas and wood and paint and cardboard. The illusion is in the eye of the beholder, not in the set itself. That, as I say, is real enough, as real behind the scenes as it is in front.'

Alex stared at him.

'Now that, you know, is a *very* penetrating remark, Inspector. It's given me an idea.'

'For another ballet?'

'No, not for another ballet . . . Dear me, I wonder if we've all been rather stupid?'

III

The Inspector and Dodgett went back to the house across the lawn. (Looking for footprints, Alex said to himself. But here he was wrong. They had looked for footprints very early that morning and had been unsuccessful because it had rained heavily at 2 a.m.) Alex walked slowly up the drive, turning over in his mind the possibilities of his new idea.

He was diverted from this, however, by the sight of Gina walking on the path by the lake. The house was on a slight eminence, and

629

the ground sloped gently down from the front sweeps of gravel to the lake, which was bordered by rhododendrons and other shrubs. Alex ran down the gravel and found Gina.

'If you could black out that absurd Victorian monstrosity,' he said, screwing up his eyes, 'this would make a very good Swan Lake, with you, Gina, as the Swan Maiden. You are more like the Snow Queen though, when I come to think of it. Ruthless, determined to have your own way, quite without pity or kindliness or the rudiments of compassion. You are very, *very* feminine, Gina dear.'

'How malicious you are, Alex dear!'

'Because I refuse to be taken in by you? You're very pleased with yourself, aren't you, Gina? You've got us all where you want us. Myself, Stephen, and that large simple husband of yours.'

'You're talking nonsense.'

'Oh no, I'm not. Stephen's in love with you. I'm in love with you, and Wally's desperately miserable. What more could a woman want?'

Gina looked at him and laughed.

Alex nodded his head vigorously.

'You have the rudiments of honesty, I'm glad to see. That's the Latin in you. You don't go to the trouble of pretending that you're not attractive to men – and that you're terribly sorry about it if they are attracted to you. You like having men in love with you, don't you, cruel Gina? Even miserable little Edgar Lawson!'

Gina looked at him steadily.

She said in a quiet serious tone:

'It doesn't last very long, you know. Women have a much worse time of it in the world than men do. They're more vulnerable. They have children, and they mind – terribly – about their children. As soon as they lose their looks, the men they love don't love them any more. They're betrayed and deserted and pushed aside. I don't blame men. I'd be the same myself. I don't like people who are old or ugly or ill or who whine about their troubles or who are ridiculous like Edgar, struting about and pretending he's important and worthwhile. You say I'm cruel? It's a cruel world! Sooner or later it will be cruel to *me*! But now I'm young and I'm nice looking and people find me attractive.' Her teeth flashed out in her peculiar warm sunny smile. 'Yes, I enjoy it, Alex. Why shouldn't I?'

'Why indeed?' said Alex. 'What I want to know is what are you going to do about it. Are you going to marry Stephen or are you going to marry me?'

630

'I'm married to Wally.'

'Temporarily. Every woman should make one mistake matrimonially – but there's no need to dwell on it. Having tried out the show in the provinces, the time has come to bring it to the West End.'

'And you're the West End?'

'Indubitably.'

'Do you really want to marry me? I can't imagine you married.'

'I insist on marriage. *Affaires*, I always think, are so very old-fashioned. Difficulties with passports and hotels and all that. I shall *never* have a mistress unless I can't get her any other way!'

Gina's laugh rang out fresh and clear.

'You do amuse me, Alex.'

'It is my principal asset. Stephen is much better looking than I am. He's extremely handsome and very intense which, of course, women adore. But intensity is fatiguing in the home. With me, Gina, you will find life entertaining.'

'Aren't you going to say you love me madly?'

'However true that may be, I shall certainly not say it. It would be one up to you and one down to me if I did. No, all I am prepared to do is to make you a businesslike offer of marriage.'

'I shall have to think about it,' said Gina smiling.

'Naturally. Besides, you've got to put Wally out of his misery first. I've a lot of sympathy with Wally. It must be absolute hell for him to be married to you and trailed along at your chariot wheels into this heavy family atmosphere of philanthropy.'

'What a beast you are, Alex!'

'A perceptive beast.'

'Sometimes,' said Gina, 'I don't think Wally cares for me one little bit. He just doesn't notice me any more.'

'You've stirred him up with a stick and he doesn't respond? Most annoying.'

Like a flash Gina swung her palm and delivered a ringing slap on Alex's smooth cheek.

'Touché!' cried Alex.

With a quick deft movement he gathered her into his arms and before she could resist, his lips fastened on hers in a long ardent kiss. She struggled a moment and then relaxed . . .

'Gina!'

They sprang apart. Mildred Strete, her face red, her lips quivering, glared at them balefully. For a moment the eagerness of her words choked their utterance.

'Disgusting . . . disgusting . . . you abandoned beastly girl . . . you're just like your mother . . . You're a bad lot . . . I always knew you were a bad lot . . . utterly depraved . . . and you're not only an adulteress – you're a murderess too. Oh yes, you are. I know what I know!'

'And what do you know? Don't be ridiculous, Aunt Mildred.'

'I'm no aunt of yours, thank goodness. No blood relation to you. Why, you don't even know who your mother was or where she came from! But you know well enough what my father was like and my mother. What sort of a child do you think they would adopt? A criminal's child or prostitute's probably! That's the sort of people they were. They ought to have remembered that bad blood will tell. Though I daresay that it's the Italian in you that makes you turn to *poison*.'

'How dare you say that?'

'I shall say what I like. You can't deny now, can you, that somebody tried to poison mother? And who's the most likely person to do that? Who comes into an enormous fortune if mother dies? You do, Gina, and you may be sure that the police have not overlooked that fact.'

Still trembling, Mildred moved rapidly away.

'Pathological,' said Alex. 'Definitely pathological. Really *most* interesting. It makes one wonder about the late Canon Strete . . . religious scruples, perhaps? . . . Or would you say impotent?'

'Don't be disgusting, Alex. Oh I hate her, I hate her, I hate her.'

Gina clenched her hands and shook with fury.

'Lucky you hadn't got a knife in your stocking,' said Alex. 'If you had, dear Mrs Strete might have known something about murder from the point of view of the victim. Calm down, Gina. Don't look so melodramatic and like Italian Opera.'

'How dare she say I tried to poison Grandam?'

'Well, darling, *somebody* tried to poison her. And from the point of view of motive you're well in the picture, aren't you?'

'Alex!' Gina stared at him, dismayed. 'Do the police think so?'

'It's extremely difficult to know what the police think. . . . They keep their own counsel remarkably well. They're by no means fools, you know. That reminds me – '

'Where are you going?'

'To work out an idea of mine.'

632

CHAPTER SEVENTEEN

'You say somebody has been trying to *poison* me?'

Carrie Louise's voice held bewilderment and disbelief.

'You know,' she said, 'I can't really believe it . . .'

She waited a few moments, her eyes half closed.

Lewis said gently, 'I wish I could have spared you this, dearest.'

Almost absently she stretched out a hand to him and he took it.

Miss Marple, sitting close by, shook her head sympathetically.

Carrie Louise opened her eyes.

'Is it really true, Jane?' she asked.

'I'm afraid so, my dear.'

'Then everything – ' Carrie Louise broke off.

She went on:

'I've always thought I knew what was real and what wasn't . . . *This* doesn't seem real – but it is . . . So I may be wrong everywhere . . . But who could want to do such a thing to me? Nobody in this house could want to – *kill* me?'

Her voice still held incredulity.

'That's what I would have thought,' said Lewis. 'I was wrong.'

'And Christian knew about it? That explains it.'

'Explains what?' asked Lewis.

'His manner,' said Carrie Louise. 'It was very odd, you know. Not at all his usual self. He seemed – upset about me – as though he was wanting to say something to me – and then not saying it. And he asked me if my heart was strong? And if I'd been well lately? Trying to hint to me, perhaps. But why not say something straight out? It's so much simpler just to say it straight out.'

'He didn't want to – cause you pain, Caroline.'

'Pain? But why – Oh I see . . .' Her eyes widened. 'So *that's* what you believe. But you're wrong, Lewis, quite wrong. I can assure you of that.'

Her husband avoided her eyes.

'I'm sorry,' said Mrs Serrocold after a moment or two. 'But I can't believe anything of what has happened lately is true. Edgar shooting at you. Gina and Stephen. That ridiculous box of chocolates. It just isn't *true*.'

Nobody spoke.

Caroline Louise Serrocold sighed.

'I suppose,' she said, 'that I must have lived outside reality for a long time . . . Please, both of you, I think I would like to be alone . . . I've got to try and understand . . .'

II

Miss Marple came down the stairs and into the Great Hall to find Alex Restarick standing near the large arched entrance door with his hand flung out in a somewhat flamboyant gesture.

'Come in, come in,' said Alex happily and as though he were the owner of the Great Hall. 'I'm just thinking about last night.'

Lewis Serrocold, who had followed Miss Marple down from Carrie Louise's sitting-room, crossed the Great Hall to his study and went in and shut the door.

'Are you trying to reconstruct the crime?' asked Miss Marple with subdued eagerness.

'Eh?' Alex looked at her with a frown. Then his brow cleared.

'Oh *that*,' he said. 'No, not exactly. I was looking at the whole thing from an entirely different point of view. I was thinking of this place in the terms of the theatre. Not reality, but artificiality! Just come over here. Think of it in the terms of a stage set. Lighting, entrances, exits. Dramatis Personae. Noises off. All very interesting. Not all my own idea. The Inspector gave it to me. I think he's rather a cruel man. He did his best to frighten me this morning.'

'And did he frighten you?'

'I'm not sure.'

Alex described the Inspector's experiment and the timing of the performance of the puffing Constable Dodgett.

'Time,' he said, 'is so very misleading. One thinks things take such a long time, but really, of course, they don't.'

'No,' said Miss Marple.

Representing the audience, she moved to a different position. The stage set now consisted of a vast tapestry covered wall going up to dimness, with a grand piano up L. and a window and window seat up R. Very near the window seat was the door into the library. The piano stool was only about eight feet from the door into the square lobby which led to the corridor. Two very convenient exits! The audience, of course, had an excellent view of both of them . . .

But last night, there had been no audience. Nobody, that is to say, had been facing the stage set that Miss Marple was now facing. The audience, last night, had been sitting with their backs to that particular stage.

How long, Miss Marple wondered, would it have taken to slip out of the room, run along the corridor, shoot Gulbrandsen and come back? Not nearly so long as one would think. Measured in minutes and seconds a very short time indeed . . .

What had Carrie Louise meant when she had said to her husband: 'So *that*'s what you believe – but you're wrong, Lewis!'

'I must say that that was a very penetrating remark of the Inspector's,' Alex's voice cut in on her meditations. 'About a stage set being real. Made of wood and cardboard and stuck together with glue and as real on the unpainted as on the painted side. "The illusion," he pointed out, "is in the eyes of the audience."'

'Like conjurers,' Miss Marple murmured vaguely. '*They do it with mirrors* is, I believe, the slang phrase.'

Stephen Restarick came in, slightly out of breath.

'Hallo, Alex,' he said. 'That little rat, Ernie Gregg – I don't know if you remember him?'

'The one who played Feste when you did Twelfth Night? Quite a bit of talent there, I thought.'

'Yes, he's got talent of a sort. Very good with his hands too. Does a lot of our carpentry. However, that's neither here nor there. He's been boasting to Gina that he gets out at night and wanders about the grounds. Says he was wandering round last night and boasts he saw something.'

Alex spun round.

'Saw what?'

'Says he's not going to tell. Actually I'm pretty certain he's only trying to show off and get into the limelight. He's an awful liar, but I thought perhaps he ought to be questioned.'

Alex said sharply: 'I should leave him for a bit. Don't let him think we're too interested.'

'Perhaps – yes, I think you may be right there. This evening, perhaps.'

Stephen went on into the library.

Miss Marple, moving gently round the Hall in her character of mobile audience, collided with Alex Restarick as he stepped back suddenly.

Miss Marple said, 'I'm so sorry.'

Alex frowned at her, said in an absent sort of way:

'I beg your pardon,' and then added in a surprised voice: 'Oh, it's *you*.'

It seemed to Miss Marple an odd remark for someone with whom she had been conversing for some considerable time.

'I was thinking of something else,' said Alex Restarick. 'That boy Ernie – ' He made vague motions with both hands.

Then, with a sudden change of manner, he crossed the Hall and went through the library door, shutting it behind him.

The murmur of voices came from behind the closed door, but Miss Marple hardly noticed them. She was uninterested in the versatile Ernie and what he had seen or pretended to see. She had a shrewd suspicion that Ernie had seen nothing at all. She did not believe for a moment that on a cold raw foggy night like last night, Ernie would have troubled to use his lockpicking activities and wander about in the Park. In all probability he never had got out at night. Boasting, that was all it had been.

'Like Johnnie Backhouse,' thought Miss Marple, who always had a good storehouse of parallels to draw upon selected from inhabitants of St Mary Mead.

'I seen you last night,' had been Johnnie Backhouse's unpleasant taunt to all he thought it might affect.

It had been a surprisingly successful remark. So many people, Miss Marple reflected, have been in places where they are anxious not to be seen!

She dismissed Johnnie from her mind and concentrated on a vague something which Alex's account of Inspector Curry's remarks had stirred to life. Those remarks had given Alex an idea. She was not sure that they had not given her an idea, too. The same idea? Or a different one?

She stood where Alex Restarick had stood. She thought to herself, 'This is not a real Hall. This is only cardboard and canvas and wood. This is a stage scene . . .' Scrappy phrases flashed across her mind. 'Illusion – ' 'In the eyes of the audience.' 'They do it with mirrors . . .' Bowls of goldfish . . . yards of coloured ribbon . . . vanishing ladies . . . all the panoply and misdirection of the conjurer's art . . .

Something stirred in her consciousness – a picture – something that Alex had said . . . something that he had described to her . . .

636

Constable Dodgett puffing and panting . . . Panting . . . Something shifted in her mind – came into sudden focus . . .

'Why of *course*!' said Miss Marple. 'That must be it . . .'

CHAPTER EIGHTEEN

'Oh, Wally, how you startled me!'

Gina, emerging from the shadows by the theatre, jumped back a little, as the figure of Wally Hudd materialized out of the gloom. It was not yet quite dark, but had that eerie half light when objects lose their reality and take on the fantastic shapes of nightmare.

'What are you doing down here? You never come near the theatre as a rule.'

'Maybe I was looking for you, Gina. It's usually the best place to find you, isn't it?'

Wally's soft, faintly drawling voice held no special insinuation, and yet Gina flinched a little.

'It's a job and I'm keen on it. I like the atmosphere of paint and canvas, and back stage generally.'

'Yes. It means a lot to you. I've seen that. Tell me, Gina, how long do you think it will be before this business is all cleared up?'

'The inquest's tomorrow. It will just be adjourned for a fortnight or something like that. At least, that's what Inspector Curry gave us to understand.'

'A fortnight,' said Wally thoughtfully. 'I see. Say three weeks, perhaps. And after that – we're free. I'm going back to the States then.'

'Oh! but I can't rush off like that,' cried Gina. 'I couldn't leave Grandam. And we've got these two new productions we're working on – '

'I didn't say "*we*." I said *I* was going.'

Gina stopped and looked up at her husband. Something in the effect of the shadows made him seem very big. A big, quiet figure – and in some way, or so it seemed to her, faintly menacing . . . Standing over her. Threatening – what?

637

'Do you mean' – she hesitated – 'you don't want me to come?'

'Why, no – I didn't say that.'

'You don't care if I come or not? Is that it?'

She was suddenly angry.

'See here, Gina. This is where we've got to have a showdown. We didn't know much about each other when we got married – not much about each other's backgrounds, not much about the other one's folks. We thought it didn't matter. We thought nothing mattered except having a swell time together. Well, stage one is over. Your folks didn't – and don't – think much of me. Maybe they're right. I'm not their kind. But if you think I'm staying on here, kicking my heels, and doing odd jobs in what I consider is just a crazy set-up – well, think again! I want to live in my own country, doing the kind of job I want to do, and can do. My idea of a wife is the kind of wife who used to go along with the old pioneers, ready for anything, hardship, unfamiliar country, danger, strange surroundings . . . Perhaps that's too much to ask of you, but it's that or nothing! Maybe I hustled you into marriage. If so, you'd better get free of me and start again. It's up to you. If you prefer one of these arty boys – it's your life and you've got to choose. But I'm going home.'

'I think you're an absolute *pig*,' said Gina. 'I'm enjoying myself here.'

'Is that so? Well, I'm not. You even enjoy murder, I suppose?'

Gina drew in her breath sharply.

'That's a cruel wicked thing to say. I was very fond of Uncle Christian. And don't you realize that someone has been quietly poisoning Grandam for months? It's horrible!'

'I told you I didn't like it here. I don't like the kind of things that go on. I'm quitting.'

'If you're allowed to! Don't you realize you'll probably be arrested for Uncle Christian's murder? I hate the way Inspector Curry looks at you. He's just like a cat watching a mouse with a nasty sharp-clawed paw all ready to pounce. Just because you were out of the Hall fixing those lights, and because you're not English, I'm sure they'll go fastening it on you.'

'They'll need some evidence first.'

Gina wailed:

'I'm frightened for you, Wally. I've been frightened all along.'

'No good being scared. I tell you they've got nothing on me!'

They walked in silence towards the house.

Gina said:

'I don't believe you really want me to come back to America with you . . .'

Walter Hudd did not answer.

Gina Hudd turned on him and stamped her foot.

'I hate you. I hate you. You are horrible – a beast – a cruel unfeeling beast. After all I've tried to do for you! You want to be rid of me. You don't care if you never see me again. Well, I don't care if *I* never see *you* again! I was a stupid little fool ever to marry you, and I shall get a divorce as soon as possible, and I shall marry Stephen or Alexis and be much happier than I ever could be with you. And I hope you go back to the States and marry some horrible girl who makes you really miserable!'

'Fine!' said Wally. 'Now we know where we are!'

II

Miss Marple saw Gina and Wally go into the house together.

She was standing at the spot where Inspector Curry had made his experiment with Constable Dodgett earlier in the afternoon.

Miss Bellever's voice behind her made her jump.

'You'll get a chill, Miss Marple, standing about like that after the sun's gone down.'

Miss Marple fell meekly into step with her and they walked briskly through the house.

'I was thinking about conjuring tricks,' said Miss Marple. 'So difficult when you're watching them to see how they're done, and yet, once they are explained, so absurdly simple. (Although, even now, I can't imagine how conjurers produce bowls of goldfish!) Did you ever see the Lady who is Sawn in Half – *such* a thrilling trick. It fascinated me when I was eleven years old, I remember. And I never *could* think how it was done. But the other day there was an article in some paper giving the whole thing away. I don't think a newspaper should do that, do you? It seems it's not one girl – but *two*. The head of one and the feet of the other. You think it's one girl and it's really two – and the other way round would work equally well, wouldn't it?'

Miss Bellever looked at her with faint surprise.

Miss Marple was not often so fluffy and incoherent as this. 'It's all been too much for the old lady,' she thought.

'When you only look at one side of a thing, you only see one side,' continued Miss Marple. 'But everything fits in perfectly well if you can only make up your mind what is reality and what is illusion.' She added abruptly, 'Is Carrie Louise – all right?'

'Yes,' said Miss Bellever. 'She's all right, but it must have been a shock, you know – finding out that someone wanted to kill her. I mean particularly a shock to her, because she doesn't understand violence.'

'Carrie Louise understands some things that we don't,' said Miss Marple thoughtfully. 'She always has.'

'I know what you mean – but she doesn't live in the real world.'

'Doesn't she?'

Miss Bellever looked at her in surprise.

'There never was a more unworldly person than Cara – '

'You don't think that perhaps – ' Miss Marple broke off, as Edgar Lawson passed them, swinging along at a great pace. He gave a kind of shamefaced nod, but averted his face as he passed.

'I've remembered now who he reminds me of,' said Miss Marple. 'It came to me suddenly just a few moments ago. He reminds me of a young man called Leonard Wylie. His father was a dentist, but he got old and blind and his hand used to shake, and so people preferred to go to the son. But the old man was very miserable about it, and moped, said he was no good for anything any more, and Leonard who was very soft-hearted and rather foolish, began to pretend he drank more than he should. He always smelt of whisky and he used to sham being rather fuddled when his patients came. His idea was that they'd go back to the father again and say the younger man was no good.'

'And did they?'

'Of course not,' said Miss Marple. 'What happened was what anybody with any sense could have told him would happen! The patients went to Mr Reilly, the rival dentist. So many people with good hearts have no sense. Besides, Leonard Wylie was so unconvincing . . . His idea of drunkenness wasn't in the least like real drunkenness, and he overdid the whisky – spilling it on his clothes, you know, to a perfectly impossible extent.'

They went into the house by the side door.

CHAPTER NINETEEN

Inside the house, they found the family assembled in the library. Lewis was walking up and down, and there was an air of general tension in the atmosphere.

'Is anything the matter?' asked Miss Bellever.

Lewis said shortly: 'Ernie Gregg is missing from roll call tonight.'

'Has he run away?'

'We don't know. Maverick and some of the staff are searching the grounds. If we cannot find him we must communicate with the police.'

'Grandam!' Gina ran over to Carrie Louise, startled by the whiteness of her face. 'You look ill.'

'I am unhappy. The poor boy . . .'

Lewis said: 'I was going to question him this evening as to whether he had seen anything noteworthy last night. I have the offer of a good post for him and I thought that after discussing that, I would bring up the other topic. Now – ' he broke off.

Miss Marple murmured softly:

'Foolish boy . . . Poor foolish boy . . .'

She shook her head, and Mrs Serrocold said gently:

'So *you* think so too, Jane . . .?'

Stephen Restarick came in. He said, 'I missed you at the theatre, Gina. I thought you said you would – Hallo, what's up?'

Lewis repeated his information, and as he finished speaking, Dr Maverick came in with a fair-haired boy with pink cheeks and a suspiciously angelic expression. Miss Marple remembered his being at dinner on the night she had arrived at Stonygates.

'I've brought Arthur Jenkins along,' said Dr Maverick. 'He seems to have been the last person to talk to Ernie.'

'Now, Arthur,' said Lewis Serrocold, 'please help us if you can. Where has Ernie gone? Is this just a prank?'

'I dunno, sir. Straight, I don't. Didn't say nothing to me, he didn't. All full of the play at the theatre he was, that's all. Said as how he'd had a smashing idea for the scenery, what Mrs Hudd and Mr Stephen thought was first class.'

'There's another thing, Arthur. Ernie claims he was prowling about the grounds after lock-up last night. Was that true?'

''Course it ain't. Just boasting, that's all. Perishing liar, Ernie. *He* never got out at night. Used to boast he could, but he wasn't that good with locks! He couldn't do anything with a lock as was a lock. Anyway 'e was in larst night, that I do know.'

'You're not saying that just to satisfy us, Arthur?'

'Cross my heart,' said Arthur virtuously.

Lewis did not look quite satisfied.

'Listen,' said Dr Maverick. 'What's that?'

A murmur of voices was approaching. The door was flung open and looking very pale and ill, the spectacled Mr Baumgarten staggered in.

He gasped out: 'We've found him – them. It's horrible . . .'

He sank down on a chair and mopped his forehead.

Mildred Strete said sharply:

'What do you mean – found *them*?'

Baumgarten was shaking all over.

'Down at the theatre,' he said. 'Their heads crushed in – the big counterweight must have fallen on them. Alexis Restarick and that boy Ernie Gregg. They're both dead . . .'

CHAPTER TWENTY

'I've brought you a cup of strong soup, Carrie Louise,' said Miss Marple. 'Now please drink it.'

Mrs Serrocold sat up in the big carved oak four-poster bed. She looked very small and childlike. Her cheeks had lost their pink flush, and her eyes had a curiously absent look.

She took the soup obediently from Miss Marple. As she sipped it, Miss Marple sat down in a chair beside the bed.

'First, Christian,' said Carrie Louise, 'and now Alex – and poor, sharp, silly little Ernie. Did he really – know anything?'

'I don't think so,' said Miss Marple. 'He was just telling lies – making himself important by hinting that he had seen or knew something. The tragedy is that somebody believed his lies . . .'

Carrie Louise shivered. Her eyes went back to their far away look.

'We meant to do so much for these boys . . . We did do something. Some of them have done wonderfully well. Several of them are in really responsible positions. A few slid back – that can't be helped. Modern civilized conditions are so complex – too complex for some simple and undeveloped natures. You know Lewis's great scheme? He always felt that transportation was a thing that had saved many a potential criminal in the past. They were shipped overseas – and they made new lives in simpler surroundings. He wants to start a modern scheme on that basis. To buy up a great tract of territory – or a group of islands. Finance it for some years, make it a co-operative self supporting community – with everyone taking a stake in it. But cut off so that the early temptation to go back to cities and the bad old days can be neutralized. It's his dream. But it will take a lot of money, of course, and there aren't many philanthropists with vision now. We want another Eric. Eric would have been enthusiastic.'

Miss Marple picked up a little pair of scissors and looked at them curiously.

'What an odd pair of scissors,' she said. 'They've got two fingers holes on one side and one on the other.'

Carrie Louise's eyes came back from that frightening far distance.

'Alex gave them to me this morning,' she said. 'They're supposed to make it easier to cut your right hand nails. Dear boy, he was so enthusiastic. He made me try them then and there.'

'And I suppose he gathered up the nail clippings and took them tidily away,' said Miss Marple.

'Yes,' said Carrie Louise. 'He – ' She broke off. 'Why did you say that?'

'I was thinking about Alex. He had brains. Yes, he had brains.'

'You mean – that's why he died?'

'I think so – yes.'

'He and Ernie – it doesn't bear thinking about. When do they think it happened?'

'Late this evening. Between six and seven o'clock probably . . .'

'After they'd knocked off work for the day?'

'Yes.'

Gina had been down there that evening – and Wally Hudd. Stephen, too, said he had been down to look for Gina . . .

But as far as that went, anybody could have –

Miss Marple's train of thought was interrupted.

Carrie Louise said quietly and unexpectedly:

'How much do you know, Jane?'

Miss Marple looked up sharply. The eyes of the two women met.

Miss Marple said slowly: 'If I was quite sure . . .'

'I think you are sure, Jane.'

Jane Marple said slowly, 'What do you want me to do?'

Carrie leaned back against her pillows.

'It is in your hands, Jane – You'll do what you think right.'

She closed her eyes.

'Tomorrow' – Miss Marple hesitated – 'I shall have to try and talk to Inspector Curry – if he'll listen . . .'

CHAPTER TWENTY-ONE

Inspector Curry said rather impatiently:

'Yes, Miss Marple?'

'Could we, do you think, go into the Great Hall.'

Inspector Curry looked faintly surprised.

'Is that your idea of privacy? Surely in here – '

He looked round the study.

'It's not privacy I'm thinking of so much. It's something I want to show you. Something Alex Restarick made me see.'

Inspector Curry, stifling a sigh, got up and followed Miss Marple.

'Somebody has been talking to you?' he suggested hopefully.

'No,' said Miss Marple. 'It's not a question of what people have said. It's really a question of conjuring tricks. They do it with mirrors, you know – that sort of thing – if you understand me.'

Inspector Curry did not understand. He stared and wondered if Miss Marple was quite right in the head.

Miss Marple took up her stand and beckoned the Inspector to stand beside her.

'I want you to think of this place as a stage set, Inspector. As it was on the night Christian Gulbrandsen was killed. You're here in the audience looking at the people on the stage. Mrs Serrocold and myself and Mrs Strete, and Gina and Stephen – and just like on the stage there are entrances and exits and the characters go out to different places. Only you don't think when you're in the audience where they are really going to. They go out "to the front door" or "to the kitchen" and when the door opens you see a little bit of painted backcloth. But *really* of course they go out to the wings – or the back of the stage with carpenters and electricians, and other characters waiting to come on – they go out – to a different world.'

'I don't quite see, Miss Marple – '

'Oh, I know – I daresay it sounds very silly – but if you think of this as a play and the scene is "the Great Hall at Stonygates" – what exactly is *behind* the scene? – I mean – what is back stage? The *terrace* – isn't it? – the terrace *and a lot of windows opening on to it.*

'And that, you see, is how the conjuring trick was done. It was the trick of the Lady Sawn in Half that made me think of it.'

'The Lady Sawn in Half?' Inspector Curry was now quite sure that Miss Marple was a mental case.

'A most thrilling conjuring trick. You must have seen it – only not really one girl but two girls. The head of one and the feet of the other. It looks like one person and is really two. And so I thought it could just as well be *the other way about. Two* people could be really one person.'

'Two people really one?' Inspector Curry looked desperate.

'Yes. Not for long. How long did your constable take in the Park to run to this house and back? Two minutes and forty-five seconds, wasn't it? This would be less than that. Well under two minutes.'

'What was under two minutes?'

'The conjuring trick. The trick when it wasn't two people but one person. In there – in the study. We're only looking at the visible part of the stage. Behind the scenes there is the terrace and a *row of windows*. So easy when there are two people in the study to open the study window, get out, run along the terrace (those footsteps Alex heard), in at the side door, shoot Christian Gulbrandsen and run back, and during that time, the other person in the study does

645

both voices so that we're all quite sure there are *two* people in there. And so there were most of the time, but not for that little period of under two minutes.'

Inspector Curry found his breath and his voice.

'Do you mean that it was *Edgar Lawson* who ran along the terrace and shot Gulbrandsen? Edgar Lawson who poisoned Mrs Serrocold?'

'But you see, Inspector, *no one has been poisoning Mrs Serrocold at all*. That's where the misdirection comes in. Someone very cleverly used the fact that Mrs Serrocold's sufferings from arthritis were not unlike the symptoms of arsenical poisoning. It's the old conjurer's trick of forcing a card on you. Quite easy to add arsenic to a bottle of tonic – quite easy to add a few lines to a typewritten letter. But the *real* reason for Mr Gulbrandsen's coming here was the most likely reason – something to do with the Gulbrandsen Trust. Money, in fact. Suppose that there had been embezzlement – embezzlement on a very big scale – you see where that points? To just one person – '

Inspector Curry gasped: 'Lewis Serrocold?' he murmured incredulously.

'*Lewis Serrocold* . . .' said Miss Marple.

CHAPTER TWENTY-TWO

Part of letter from Gina Hudd to her aunt Mrs Van Rydock:

  – and so you see, darling Aunt Ruth, the whole thing has been just like a nightmare – especially the end of it. I've told you all about this funny man Edgar Lawson. He always was a complete rabbit – and when the Inspector began questioning him and breaking him down, he lost his nerve completely and scuttled like a rabbit. Just lost his nerve and ran – literally ran. Jumped out of the window and round the house and down the drive and then there was a policeman coming to head him off, and he swerved and ran full tilt for the lake. He leaped into a rotten old punt that's mouldered there for years and pushed off. Quite a mad senseless thing to do, of course, but as I say he was just a panic-stricken rabbit. And then Lewis gave a great shout and said 'That punt's rotten,' and raced off to the lake too. The punt went down

and there was Edgar struggling in the water. He couldn't swim. Lewis jumped in and swam out to him. He got to him but they were both in difficulty because they'd got among the reeds. One of the Inspector's men went in with a rope round him but he got entangled too and they had to pull him in. Aunt Mildred said 'They'll drown – they'll drown – they'll both drown . . .' in a silly sort of way, and Grandam just said 'Yes.' I can't describe to you just how she made that one word sound. Just 'YES' and it went through you like – like a sword.

Am I being just silly and melodramatic? I suppose I am. But it did sound like that . . .

And then – when it was all over, and they'd got them out and tried artificial respiration (but it was no good), the Inspector came to us and said to Grandam: 'I'm afraid, Mrs Serrocold, there's no hope.'

Grandam said very quietly:

'Thank you, Inspector.'

Then she looked at us all. Me longing to help but not knowing how, and Jolly, looking grim and tender and ready to minister us usual, and Stephen stretching out his hands, and funny old Miss Marple looking so sad, and tired, and even Wally looking upset. All so fond of her and wanting to do SOMETHING.

But Grandam just said 'Mildred.' And Aunt Mildred said 'Mother.' And they went away together into the house, Grandam looking so small and frail and leaning on Aunt Mildred. I never realized, until then, how fond of each other they were. It didn't show much, you know, but it was there all the time.

Gina paused and sucked the end of her fountain pen. She resumed:

About me and Wally – we're coming back to the States as soon as we can . . .

CHAPTER TWENTY-THREE

'What made you guess, Jane?'

Miss Marple took her time about replying. She looked thoughtfully at the other two – Carrie Louise thinner and frailer and yet curiously untouched – and the old man with the sweet smile and the thick white hair. Dr Galbraith, Bishop of Cromer.

The Bishop took Carrie Louise's hand in his.

'This has been a great sorrow to you, my poor child, and a great shock.'

'A sorrow, yes, but not really a shock.'

'No,' said Miss Marple. 'That's what I discovered, you know. Everyone kept saying how Carrie Louise lived in another world from this and was out of touch with reality. But actually, Carrie Louise, it was reality you were in touch with, and not the illusion. You are never deceived by illusion like most of us are. When I suddenly realized that, I saw that I must go by what *you* thought and felt. You were quite sure that no one would try to poison you, you couldn't believe it – and you were quite right *not* to believe it, because it wasn't so! You never believed that Edgar would harm Lewis – and again you were right. He never *would* have harmed Lewis. You were sure that Gina did not love anyone but her husband – and that again was quite true.

'So therefore, if I was to go by you, all the things that *seemed* to be true were only illusions. Illusions created for a definite purpose – in the same way that conjurers create illusions, to deceive an audience. We were the audience.

'Alex Restarick got an inkling of the truth first because he had the chance of seeing things from a different angle – from the outside angle. He was with the Inspector in the drive, and he looked at the house and realized the possibilities of the windows – and he remembered the sound of running feet he had heard that night, and then the timing of the constable showed him what a very short time things take to what we should imagine they would take. The constable panted a lot, and later, thinking of a puffing constable, I remembered that Lewis Serrocold was out of breath that night when he opened the study door. He'd just been running hard, you see . . .

'But it was Edgar Lawson that was the pivot of it all to me. There was always something wrong to me about Edgar Lawson. All the things he said and did were exactly right for what he was supposed to be, but he himself wasn't right. Because he was actually a normal young man playing the part of a schizophrenic – and he was always, as it were, a little larger than life. He was always theatrical.

'It must have all been very carefully planned and thought out. Lewis must have realized on the occasion of Christian's last visit

648

that something had aroused his suspicions. And he knew Christian well enough to know that if he suspected he would not rest until he had satisfied himself that his suspicions were either justified or unfounded.'

Carrie Louise stirred.

'Yes,' she said. 'Christian was like that. Slow and painstaking, but actually very shrewd. I don't know what it was aroused his suspicions but he started investigating – and he found out the truth.'

The Bishop said: 'I blame myself for not having been a more conscientious trustee.'

'It was never expected of you to understand finance,' said Carrie Louise. 'That was originally Mr Gilfoy's province. Then, when he died, Lewis's great experience put him in what amounted to complete control. And that, of course, was what went to his head.'

The pink colour came up in her cheeks.

'Lewis was a great man,' she said. 'A man of great vision, and a passionate believer in what could be accomplished – with money. He didn't want it for himself – or at least not in the greedy vulgar sense – he did want the power of it – he wanted the power to do great good with it – '

'He wanted,' said the Bishop, 'to be God.' His voice was suddenly stern. 'He forgot that man is only the humble instrument of God's will.'

'And so he embezzled the Trust funds?' said Miss Marple.

Dr Galbraith hesitated.

'It wasn't only that . . .'

'Tell her,' said Carrie Louise. 'She is my oldest friend.'

The Bishop said:

'Lewis Serrocold was what one might call a financial wizard. In his years of highly technical accountancy, he had amused himself by working out various methods of swindling which were practically foolproof. This had been merely an academic study, but when he once began to envisage the possibilities that a vast sum of money could encompass, he put these methods into practice. You see, he had at his disposal some first-class material. Amongst the boys who passed through here, he chose out a small select band. They were boys whose bent was naturally criminal, who loved excitement and who had a very high order of intelligence. We've not got nearly to the bottom of it all, but it seems clear that this esoteric circle was secret and specially trained and were later placed in key positions, where, by carrying out Lewis's directions, books were falsified in such a way that large sums of money were converted without any suspicion being aroused. I gather that the operations and the ramifications are so complicated that it will be months before the auditors can unravel it all. But the net result seems to be that under various names and banking accounts and companies Lewis Serrocold would have been able to dispose of a colossal sum with which he intended to establish an overseas colony for a cooperative experiment in which juvenile delinquents should eventually own this territory and administer it. It may have been a fantastic dream – '

'It was a dream that might have come true,' said Carrie Louise.

'Yes, it might have come true. But the means Lewis Serrocold adopted were dishonest means, and Christian Gulbrandsen discovered that. He was very upset, particularly by the realization of what the discovery and the probable prosecution of Lewis would mean to you, Carrie Louise.'

'That's why he asked me if my heart was strong, and seemed so worried about my health,' said Carrie Louise. 'I couldn't understand it.'

'Then Lewis Serrocold arrived back from the North and Christian met him outside the house and told him that he knew what was going on. Lewis took it calmly, I think. Both men agreed they must do all they could to spare you. Christian said he would write to me and ask me to come here, as a co-trustee, to discuss the position.'

'But of course,' said Miss Marple, 'Lewis Serrocold had already prepared for this emergency. It was all planned. He had brought the young man who was to play the part of Edgar Lawson to the house. There was a real Edgar Lawson – of course – in case the police looked up his record. This false Edgar knew exactly what he had to do – act the part of a schizophrenic victim of persecution – and give Lewis Serrocold an alibi for a few vital minutes.

'The next step had been thought out too. Lewis's story that you, Carrie Louise, were being slowly poisoned – when one actually came to think of it there was only Lewis's story of what Christian had told *him* – that, and a few lines added on the typewriter whilst he was waiting for the police. It was easy to add arsenic to the tonic. No danger for you there – since he was on the spot to prevent you drinking it. The chocolates were just an added touch – and of course the original chocolates weren't poisoned – only those he substituted before turning them over to Inspector Curry.'

'And Alex guessed,' said Carrie Louise.

'Yes – that's why he collected your nail parings. They would show if arsenic actually had been administered over a long period.'

'Poor Alex – poor Ernie.'

There was a moment's silence as the other two thought of Christian Gulbrandsen, of Alexis Restarick, and of the boy Ernie – and of how quickly the act of murder could distort and deform.

'But surely,' said the Bishop, 'Lewis was taking a big risk in persuading Edgar to be his accomplice – even if he had some hold over him – '

Carrie shook her head.

'It wasn't exactly a hold over him. Edgar was devoted to Lewis.'

'Yes,' said Miss Marple. 'Like Leonard Wylie and his father. I wonder perhaps if – '

She paused delicately.

'You saw the likeness, I suppose?' said Carrie Louise.

'So you knew that all along?'

'I guessed. I knew Lewis had once had a short infatuation for an actress, before he met me. He told me about it. It wasn't serious, she was a gold-digging type of woman and she didn't care for him, but I've no doubt at all that Edgar was actually Lewis's son . . .'

'Yes,' said Miss Marple. 'That explains everything . . .'

'And he gave his life for him in the end,' said Carrie Louise. She looked pleadingly at the Bishop. 'He did, you know.'

There was a silence and then Carrie Louise said:

'I'm glad it ended that way . . . with his life given in the hope of saving the boy . . . People who can be very good can be very bad, too. I always knew that was true about Lewis . . . But – he loved me very much – and I loved him.'

'Did you – ever suspect him?' asked Miss Marple.

'No,' said Carrie Louise. 'Because I was puzzled by the poisoning. I knew Lewis would never poison me and yet that letter of Christian's said definitely that someone *was* poisoning me – so I thought that everything I thought I knew about people must be wrong . . .'

Miss Marple said: 'But when Alex and Ernie were found killed. You suspected then?'

'Yes,' said Carrie Louise. 'Because I didn't think anyone else but Lewis would have dared. And I began to be afraid of what he might do next . . .'

She shivered slightly.

'I admired Lewis. I admired his – what shall I call it – his goodness? But I do see that if you're – good, you have to be humble as well.'

Dr Galbraith said gently:

'That, Carrie Louise, is what I have always admired in you – your humility.'

The lovely blue eyes opened wide in surprise.

'But *I'm* not clever – and not particularly good. I can only admire goodness in other people.'

'Dear Carrie Louise,' said Miss Marple.

EPILOGUE

'I think Grandam will be quite all right with Aunt Mildred,' said Gina. 'Aunt Mildred seems much nicer now – not so peculiar, if you know what I mean?'

'I know what you mean,' said Miss Marple.

'So Wally and I will go back to the States in a fortnight's time.'

Gina cast a look sideways at her husband.

'I shall forget all about Stonygates and Italy and all my girlish past and become a hundred per cent American. Our son will be always addressed as Junior. I can't say fairer than that, can I, Wally?'

'You certainly cannot, Kate,' said Miss Marple.

Wally, smiling indulgently at an old lady who got names wrong, corrected her gently:

'Gina, not Kate.'

But Gina laughed.

'She knows what she's saying! You see – she'll call *you* Petruchio in a moment!'

'I just think,' said Miss Marple to Walter, 'that you have acted very wisely, my dear boy.'

'She thinks you're just the right husband for me,' said Gina.

Miss Marple looked from one to the other. It was very nice, she thought, to see two young people so much in love, and Walter Hudd was completely transformed from the sulky young man she had first encountered into a good-humoured smiling giant . . .

'You two remind me,' she said, 'of – '

Gina rushed forward and placed a hand firmly over Miss Marple's mouth.

'No, darling,' she exclaimed. 'Don't say it. I'm suspicious of these village parallels. They've always got a sting in the tail. You really are a wicked old woman, you know.'

Her eyes went misty.

'When I think of you, and Aunt Ruth and Grandam all being

653

young together . . . How I wonder what you were all like! I can't imagine it somehow . . .'

'I don't suppose you can,' said Miss Marple. 'It was all a long time ago . . .'